Houghton
Mifflin
Harcourt

READING

W9-BON-072

Welcome, Reader!

In this magazine, you will explore places from the Milky Way to Death Valley, from the Alaska Range to the African savannah. You'll investigate animals as big as a colossal squid and as small as a honeybee.

You'll read poems and articles about wild storms and outer space, and you'll interact with nature through lots of fun activities.

Your adventure begins as soon as you turn the page!

"Moon" from *Space Songs* by Myra Cohn Livingston. Text copyright © 1988 by Myra Cohn Livingston. Reprinted by permission of the author c/o Marian Reiner, Literary Agent. "Satellites" from *Space Songs* by Myra Cohn Livingston. Text copyright © 1988 by Myra Cohn Livingston. Reprinted by permission of the author c/o Marian Reiner, Literary Agent. "Twelve Below" from *Letters from Maine* by May Sarton. Copyright © 1984 by May Sarton. Reprinted by permission of W. W. Norton & Co. "Desert Day" from *Central Heating: Poems About Fire and Warmth* by Marilyn Singer. Text copyright © 2005 by Marilyn Singer. Reprinted by permission of Alfred A. Knopf, an imprint of Random House Children's Books, a division of Random House, Inc. "Straight Talk" by Nikki Grimes. Copyright © by Nikki Grimes. Reprinted by permission of Curtis Brown Ltd. "An evenly balanced word W H A L E..." from *Words with Wrinkled Knees: Animal Poems* by Barbara Juster Esbensen. Text copyright © 1986 by Barbara Juster Esbensen. Reprinted by permission of Wordsong, a division of Boyds Mills Press, Inc. "Snow" from *A Pocketful of Poems* by Nikki Grimes. Text copyright © 2001 by Nikki Grimes. Reprinted by permission of Houghton Mifflin Harcourt Publishing Company. "The Elephant" by Hilaire Belloc. Reprinted by permission of PFD. "The Wind" from *Mummy Took Cooking Lessons and Other Poems* by John Ciardi. Text copyright © 1990 by Judith C. Ciardi. Reprinted by permission of Houghton Mifflin Harcourt Publishing Company.

2014 Edition
Copyright © by Houghton Mifflin Harcourt Publishing Company

Printed in the U.S.A.

ISBN: 978-0-547-88880-4

14 15-0877-21 20 19 18 17 16 15

4500518345   B C D E F G

Lesson 26

1

SPACE

Oxygen pack. *Check*. Tether cord. *Check*. Cameras. *Check*. Thermal gloves. *Check*. Astronaut Ed White was ready.

Boosting himself out of the *Gemini 4* hatch, White began America's first space walk. It was 1965. White beamed as he floated at the end of his twenty-five-foot tether, shooting photographs. Too soon, the spectacular walk ended. White made his way slowly back to the spacecraft. But before he handed his gear to his fellow astronaut, he dropped a spare glove! That glove joined an assortment of odds and ends we call space trash.

Over the years, the trash circling around our globe has grown. Space shuttle *Atlantis* astronauts lost a couple of bolts in space. *Discovery* astronauts lost a spatula while repairing their shuttle with special putty. A camera, bits of broken equipment, and even garbage bags tossed out by the Mir space station have added to the debris in space. At least 10,000 pieces of junk measuring four inches or larger are orbiting our planet. The United States space program tracks this trash because even though the debris is way up in space, it could cause us big problems here on earth if it hits something.

TRASH

It Started with the Satellites

For fifty years now, people have been sending objects into space. Some of those things have been brought safely down to earth, but others have been left in space to drift.

It all began in 1957, when the Soviet Union launched *Sputnik 1*, the world's first artificial satellite. A satellite is anything that revolves around a planet and is held in orbit by the gravitational pull of the planet. Our moon, for instance, is a natural satellite. Artificial satellites are objects that people make and send into space.

To launch satellites out of Earth's atmosphere and into space, rockets must travel at least 18,000 miles per hour and fly more than 120 miles into the sky. Such rockets have several powerful engines, a large supply of fuel, and a *payload*. The payload is the object being sent into the sky, like a satellite. When the rocket fires its engines one after another, the used-up parts of the rocket fall away and become part of space trash.

Sputnik 1 circled Earth every 96 minutes. The United States launched its first satellite, *Explorer 1*, the next year. Scientists used *Explorer 1* to measure how much radiation Earth had in its atmosphere. Today, about 850 satellites orbit our planet.

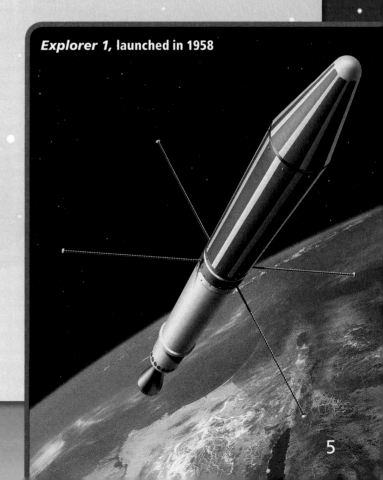

Explorer 1, launched in 1958

5

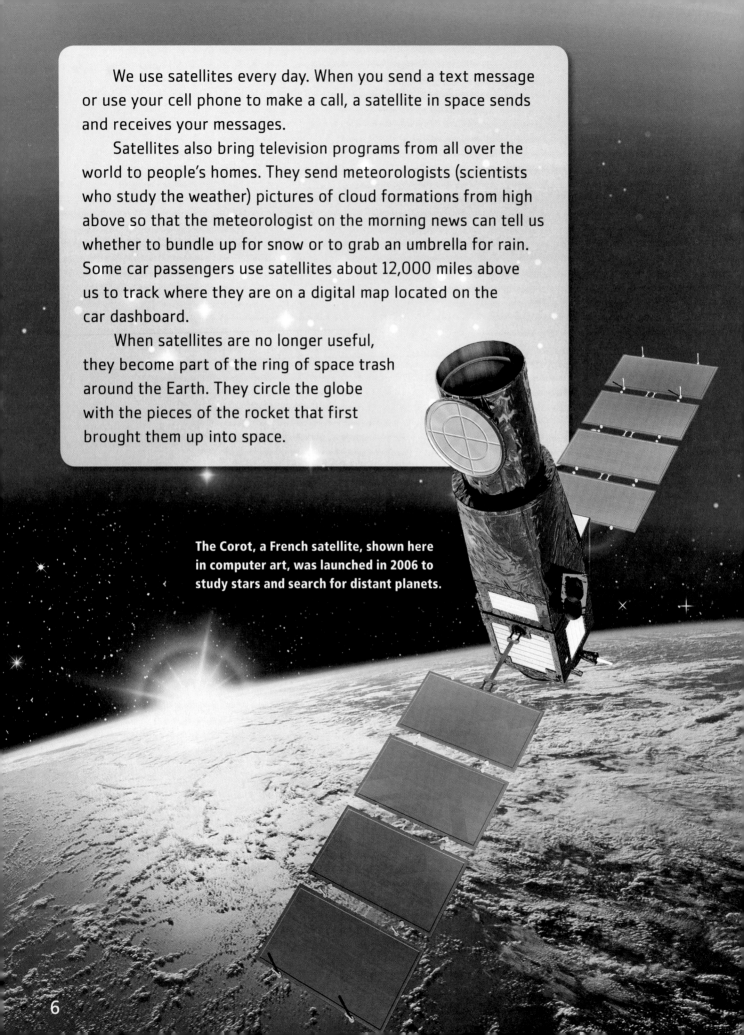

We use satellites every day. When you send a text message or use your cell phone to make a call, a satellite in space sends and receives your messages.

Satellites also bring television programs from all over the world to people's homes. They send meteorologists (scientists who study the weather) pictures of cloud formations from high above so that the meteorologist on the morning news can tell us whether to bundle up for snow or to grab an umbrella for rain. Some car passengers use satellites about 12,000 miles above us to track where they are on a digital map located on the car dashboard.

When satellites are no longer useful, they become part of the ring of space trash around the Earth. They circle the globe with the pieces of the rocket that first brought them up into space.

The Corot, a French satellite, shown here in computer art, was launched in 2006 to study stars and search for distant planets.

In and Out of Orbit

Around our planet lies a sixty-mile-thick blanket of air called our atmosphere. The farther from Earth, the thinner the air becomes. Gravity also becomes weaker. Satellites and space trash orbit outside Earth's atmosphere and remain in orbit because of their speed, or velocity. Earth's gravity holds such objects just enough to keep them from flying off into outer space.

After many, many orbits, a satellite begins to lose velocity. Gravity wins the battle and pulls the object downward. It then drops to Earth at an extremely fast speed. This speed creates intense heat that makes the object burn. Spacecraft also heat up when they enter the atmosphere on a trip back to earth.

Russian space experts think *Sputnik I* and the *Sputnik* satellites that followed burned up this way. But the people of Manitowoc, Wisconsin, see things differently. They believe that *Sputnik IV* landed in their town in 1962, right in the middle of Eighth Street. A big chunk of metal lay embedded into the middle of the street, while two police officers puzzled over it. Finally, the townspeople sent the 20-pound lump of metal to Washington, D.C. From there, it was returned to the Soviet Union. Today, a brass ring marks the spot on the street in Manitowoc where the chunk landed.

The incident in Wisconsin wasn't the only time space trash has fallen into an area where people live. In 1997, a 500-pound rocket fuel tank landed in a field close to a Texas farmhouse. In 2000, people in South Africa found a large, battered metal tank in a dusty field. Though it looked like a giant ostrich egg, it was a piece of space trash that had fallen to earth.

This chunk of space metal smashed the roof of a house in Oberhausen, Germany in 1999.

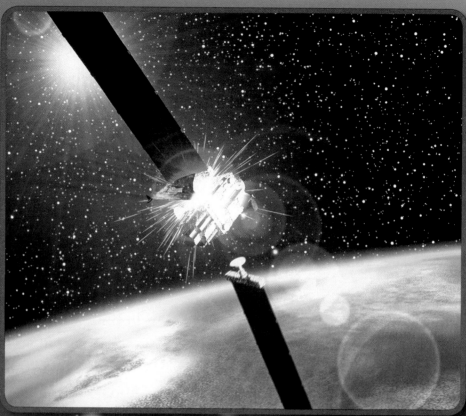

In this artist's simulation, a sliver of metal collides with a satellite's solar panel.

WHY WORRY?

While most objects that reenter the Earth's atmosphere burn up, scientists agree that some space trash can survive the fall to earth. Most of this junk they expect to fall into areas with few or no people, such as the world's vast ocean, desert, or tundra areas.

Even though it's extremely unlikely that falling space trash will harm anyone, there's a good reason to worry about space trash. This junk can hit other spacecraft.

An object must travel 17,000 miles per hour to stay in orbit. An object the size of a tennis ball traveling at that speed could seriously damage weather satellites, space telescopes, and other instruments used for gathering information.

Even things as small as chips of paint could damage other objects at such high speeds. A chip of paint made a nick in a window of the space shuttle *Challenger*. Scientists believe the dangers of this whirling junk belt around our planet will continue to grow, as objects continue colliding and creating more debris.

CLEAN UP TIME!

More than 400 people have traveled in space. Right now, astronauts live on the International Space Station. Scientists are working hard to find ways to keep these astronauts safe from speeding space trash. The National Aeronautics and Space Administration (NASA) even has a special office to deal with the problem.

Scientists have considered ways to get rid of used rockets and payloads in space. One way would be to just shoot used satellites far into outer space. Another way would be to create a special space ship that would travel around snatching and destroying these objects. Still another way would be to zap the trash with powerful lasers.

Just as with garbage on Earth, space junk needs to be managed. And in space, as on Earth, it may be that prevention is the best cure.

In 2001, a titanium motor casing from a rocket landed in the Saudi Arabian desert.

How the Milky Way

Long ago, when time began, there were only a few stars in the sky. When people looked up at night, the sky was almost completely black.

At that time people depended on corn for their food. They would dry some of the corn and grind it into cornmeal. They stored the cornmeal outside in large baskets. During the cold winters, people would use cornmeal to make delicious corn bread and mush.

One morning when an elderly couple went to fetch some cornmeal, they found their basket overturned. Cornmeal was scattered all over the ground. The couple was upset. Stealing was unheard of in Cherokee villages. Who could have done such a thing?

As they looked more closely at the ground, they noticed what looked like a dog's paw prints. But these paw prints were huge. No dog they had ever seen was that size.

The couple went quickly to tell the other villagers about what had happened. After hearing the story, the people decided the dog must have been a spirit dog. They didn't want the dog coming back to their village, so they made a plan.

Came to Be:
A Cherokee Tale

When the dog returned, they would frighten it away. That night, people collected all their drums and rattles and hid behind the cornmeal basket, waiting.

Suddenly they heard what sounded like a flock of birds with their wings all flapping at once. A doglike shape came down from the sky. It landed near the cornmeal basket. The dog stuck its nose inside and began to eat the cornmeal.

Jumping out from behind the basket, the villagers banged their drums and shook their rattles. They made the biggest racket they could. The frightened dog ran from the village with the people chasing it. It ran to the top of a hill and leaped into the sky, the cornmeal falling from its mouth.

The dog ran across the black sky until it was out of sight. The cornmeal that had fallen from its mouth made a pattern of stars. The Cherokee call this pattern of stars *Gil'liutsun stanun' yi,* which means "the place where the dog ran."

And that's the story of how the Milky Way came to be.

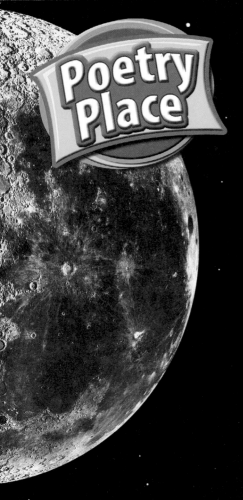

MOON

By Myra Cohn Livingston

Moon remembers.

Marooned in shadowed night,

white powder plastered
on her pockmarked face,
scarred with craters,
filled with waterless seas,
she thinks back
to the Eagle,
to the flight
of men from Earth,
of rocks sent back in space,
and one
faint
footprint
in the Sea of Tranquility.

Monitors of space,
these space detectives seek
clues to the beginning of our galaxy.
Informers of the energy of stars, of gamma rays;
weighted with sensors,
They listen, watch, and speak
of radiation, solar flares,
atmospheric density.

Stalking magnetic fields,

they serve out their days.

SATELLITES

By Myra Cohn Livingston

SPACE!

Imagine you are a board game manufacturer. Working with a partner, or in a small group, create a game in which the goal is to clean up the debris floating around in space. Write a set of rules and instructions that make it clear how the game is played and how it's won. Include a set of "chance" cards to make the game more interesting. After you've created the instructions, design the board. Once your game is complete, swap with other groups and play.

Some say sun,

Some say star.

Sunshine Sunshine Sunshine Sunshine Sunshine Sunshine

Either way,

it shines from afar.

Look Up! Shape Poems

You've
just read two
poems that take the shape
of their subject. Now try writing
your own shape poem. All you need is
a pencil and some paper. First pick something that would appear in the sky—a star,
the sun, a planet, a rocket, or a comet, for
example. Next, write a short poem about that
object, not worrying yet about the shape.
Once you've written the poem the way
you want it, draw the shape of the
poem on a piece of paper. Then
write the words into the
shape.

Catch That Trash!

In "Space Trash," you learned about the thousands of pieces of space debris and the dangers they pose. How do we get rid of this trash? Design a device to clean up space trash. Imagine that you're applying for a patent for your invention. Draw a picture of the trash picker, label its parts, and write a statement explaining how it works.

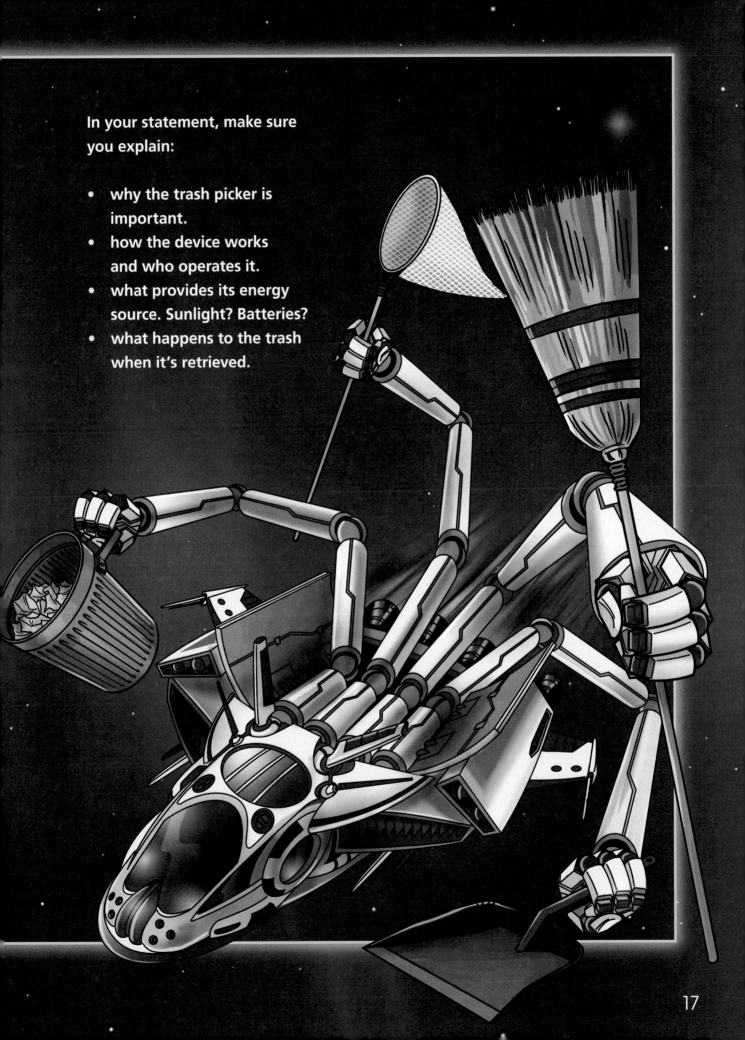

In your statement, make sure you explain:

- why the trash picker is important.
- how the device works and who operates it.
- what provides its energy source. Sunlight? Batteries?
- what happens to the trash when it's retrieved.

Denali Dog Sled Journal

Sled dogs, also known as Alaskan huskies, are strong runners. They have two layers of thick fur to keep them warm, and they follow orders well.

Saturday, December 8:

Today is Saturday, but we Denali National Park rangers have to patrol our part of the park's six million acres every day, so I climbed onto the sled runners and my dog team took off.

We have a week-long patrol ahead of us. The dogs looked as excited as I feel when I start on patrol. The dog team patrols started in the 1920s, soon after Denali became Alaska's first park. We can't take cars or snowmobiles into the park, so the dogs pulling the sleds are our transportation. The dogs allow us to take care of visitors, haul supplies, and watch to be sure all is well. We glide over the snow-covered ground. The ground under the snow is called permafrost. It stays frozen throughout the year.

Dog team at Wonder Lake

We were lucky today because there had been no snowstorm. The trail was clear. We easily traveled the thirty miles to the first patrol cabin. I was glad to get a fire going and heat up soup. My traveling companions were tail-wagging happy to see full dog food bowls!

Sunday, December 9:

A snowstorm kicked up during the night. All day today I walked ahead of the team to clear the trail. As I shoveled snow out of the way, I uncovered a small bush. I marvel at the plants that manage to survive these frigid temperatures.

While there are only eight types of trees in Denali National Park, there are many types of shrubs, like alders. Alders thrive in ground that has been disturbed by rockslides. Hundreds of other plants survive the winters, including wild-flowers such as fireweed.

As I cleared the trail, a wolf howled in the distance, and the dogs howled back.

Fireweed in the snow

19

Thirty-nine types of mammals in the park also manage to survive the cold. Mice tunnel under the snow where they can stay warmer. Moose, caribou, and sheep search for food all winter. Grizzly bears hibernate. A long snooze sounds good to me, too!

Dinosaurs once roamed the Denali National Park area. In 2005, dinosaur footprints were found in the park.

Monday, December 10:

When I radioed in my report to park headquarters, I learned there was an earthquake early this morning. As with most of our earthquakes, I never even noticed it. The quakes are the result of the Denali Fault which cuts through the park.

The Denali is North America's largest fault. On either side of this deep crack, the plates of Earth's crust move a tiny bit all the time. Over millions of years, the plates shaped the 400-mile sweep of mountains called the Alaska Range.

Today in the patrol cabin, I had a chess partner! No, I haven't taught one of the dogs the game. My partner was Dr. Chang, a scientist who is studying the park's winter wildlife. The dogs and I bring him supplies. In return, he feeds us stew and popcorn, and we share his cozy fire.

Avalanche from a Denali quake

Mount McKinley

Tuesday, December 11:

As I left Dr. Chang's cabin today, I received a radio call. Two snowshoers, Andy and Marla Perez, had not checked in at the Wilderness Access Center. I passed Wonder Lake, where visitors often go for the view of Mount McKinley. At 20,320 feet it is North America's tallest mountain. Native Americans called it *Denali*, which means "the high one."

People have climbed Mount McKinley since 1910. Every year, between May and the first week in July, more than one thousand people try to reach the top of the mountain. About one of every two climbers reaches the top.

There was no sign of the Perezes, so the dogs and I moved on toward the patrol cabin. I saw moose tracks, but no snow-shoe tracks. At the cabin, I talked to headquarters. There had been no word from Andy and Marla Perez. Tonight we are all worried about them. Where are they? Are they okay?

Wednesday, December 12:

This morning I traveled to Muldrow Glacier, searching for the Perezes. I only hoped the Perezes hadn't hiked on a glacier. Glaciers have cracks called crevasses that can be big enough to swallow an entire dog sled. Crevasses are hard to see under snow, so they are very dangerous.

Suddenly the dogs yipped and growled. We were face to face with a moose! He didn't look glad to see us—in fact, he looked angry. I quickly turned the dogs around. We zoomed off across a frozen river. I could see a small cabin on the far shore. I headed toward it.

As we approached the cabin, I was surprised to see a kerosene lamp glowing through the window. Even better were the two sets of snowshoes next to the door. The Perezes were as excited to see me as I was to see them! They had gotten lost and weren't able to make their way back to the Wilderness Access Center. They were lucky to find the cabin.

A glacier is made when snow falls over many years and turns into ice. A glacier flows very slowly, like a river in slow motion.

Muldrow Glacier

Bull moose on a ridge

It was a treat to share our stories. It gets lonely out on patrol. Andy and Marla gladly agreed to my offer of a ride in my dog sled for the next two days. They were tired from all that snowshoeing. As I write this, they're playing with the dogs, who enjoy company as much as I do.

Thursday, December 13:

Marla and Andy and I talked about how little Denali National Park has changed over the years. Traveling through it by dog sled feels the way it must have felt in the old days, complete with the dangers and pleasures. Dog sled travel maintains a tradition important to the park.

The Perezes were amazed when I told them the south side of the park is completely different from the north. It's a panorama of lofty, sharp mountain peaks and dark, thick forests. I told them they should fly over it. Flying is the best way to see the area, which is too densely wooded to travel by foot.

The park kennels

Friday, December 14:

Marla and Andy are on their way home, but they say they will be back to visit.

I spent the morning doing paperwork. In the afternoon, I gave my report to the ranger who will cover my area next. Before I headed home, I visited the dogs' kennels. I patted each of the dogs I'd just spent a week with, thanking them for taking such good care of me.

I have a few days off now. All the better to rest up for my next adventures on dog sled patrol!

Native Athabaskans have lived in the Denali area for about eleven thousand years. They lived off the land, eating game, berries, and fish. When winter came, they sheltered in low valleys.

Today, many Athabaskans still depend on the land's bounty. They grow gardens and pick berries, hunt and fish, and harvest wood for fuel and building material.

Denali National Park

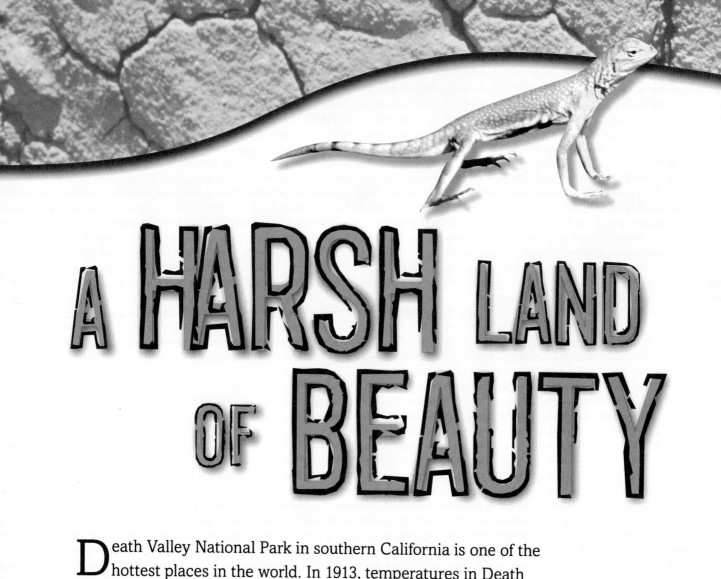

A HARSH LAND OF BEAUTY

Death Valley National Park in southern California is one of the hottest places in the world. In 1913, temperatures in Death Valley reached a record 134 degrees Fahrenheit. Today, summer temperatures are often above 120 degrees Fahrenheit.

The shape of the valley contributes to its hot, dry weather. High mountains surround the valley and act like walls to hold in the heat. The heat evaporates water quickly, making the air and soil very dry. The valley once held a lake, but the water evaporated over time, leaving behind a thick crust of salt. Within this salty area is the lowest point in North America.

Plants and animals have different adaptations for surviving in this harsh environment. Some plants have long roots that reach down more than ten times the height of a person to search for water. Other plants have shallow roots that reach in many directions to gather water quickly after winter rains. Most plants have thick stems and leaves that prevent water from evaporating. Many animals survive the heat by being active at night and hiding under rocks and in burrows during the day.

In 1849, a group of pioneers barely survived their journey across what is now Death Valley. The pioneers thought the valley was a shortcut to California, where they hoped to make their fortunes panning for gold. They faced water shortages and great hardship as they traveled. Afterwards, the region was named Death Valley.

TWELVE BELOW

By May Sarton

A bitter gale
Over frozen snow
Burns the skin like hail.
It is twelve below.

Too cold to live
Too cold to die
Warm animals wait
And make no cry.

Their feathers puff
Their eyes are bright
Their fur expands.
Warm animals wait.

They make no sign
They waste no breath
In this cold country
Between life and death.

DESERT DAY

By Marilyn Singer

Denizens of the desert
   understand under, inside,
   between, below.
Each rattlesnake, wren,
   rabbit, fox, or spider
lays claim to every scrubby tree and cactus,
   arroyo, burrow, boulder, branch
to sleep, or sit out the sun.
And when moving is a must,
   they wheel, flap, sidewind, scuttle,
   run across the blistering sand.
Denizens of the desert
   learn to balance
   the stillness and the scramble.
Few amble.

Activity Central

eXtreme Museum

Hottest and coldest. Wettest and driest. Highest and lowest. These are examples of extremes.

You've just been hired as a member of a team in charge of a new museum called the Extreme Museum. You must decide on what extremes to exhibit. Working in small groups or pairs, follow the steps below to get your museum ready for its grand opening.

1. **Plan your museum.** Make a list of as many extremes as you can think of. Each member of your team should then choose one set of extremes to put on display.

2. **Find your objects.** Cut up old magazines or print out pictures from a computer. For example, if your extremes are most furry and least furry, you might look for pictures of a sheepdog and a hairless cat.

3. **Display your collection.** Glue your pictures to a piece of cardboard. Write a sentence explaining the pairs. Prop up or hang your extremes around your classroom.

most furry

least furry

Letter Play

An anagram is a word or phrase formed by rearranging the letters of another word or phrase. Rearrange the following anagrams to find some words that you read in "Denali Dog Sled Journal." Use the clue below the anagram if you need help with the answer.

Example

county milkmen
Clue: highest mountain in North America
answer: Mount McKinley

Anagrams

1. **ace girl**
   Clue: slow-moving river of ice

2. **lasagna rake**
   Clue: 400 miles of mountains in Denali

3. **nailed**
   Clue: "the high one" in Athabaskan

4. **whose sons**
   Clue: used to walk on snow without sinking

5. **farmer spot**
   Clue: layer of soil and ice that is always frozen

6. **a snake hauls ski**
   Clue: another term for *sled dogs*

7. **a keen world**
   Clue: body of water with a wonderful view

8. **log paddles rot**
   Clue: team of huskies on the job

Answers
1. glacier • 2. Alaska Range • 3. Denali • 4. snowshoes • 5. permafrost • 6. Alaskan huskies • 7. Wonder Lake • 8. sled dog patrol

Stay

What does it take to survive the frozen tundra or a hot desert? Animals and plants have special adaptations that allow them to survive in harsh environments. But how do people deal with extreme cold or heat? Working with a partner or in small groups, imagine you've been chosen to write a survival guide for a research team going to a very hot or a very cold place for a month. Your guide will help the team survive—whether in the Sahara or Antarctica.

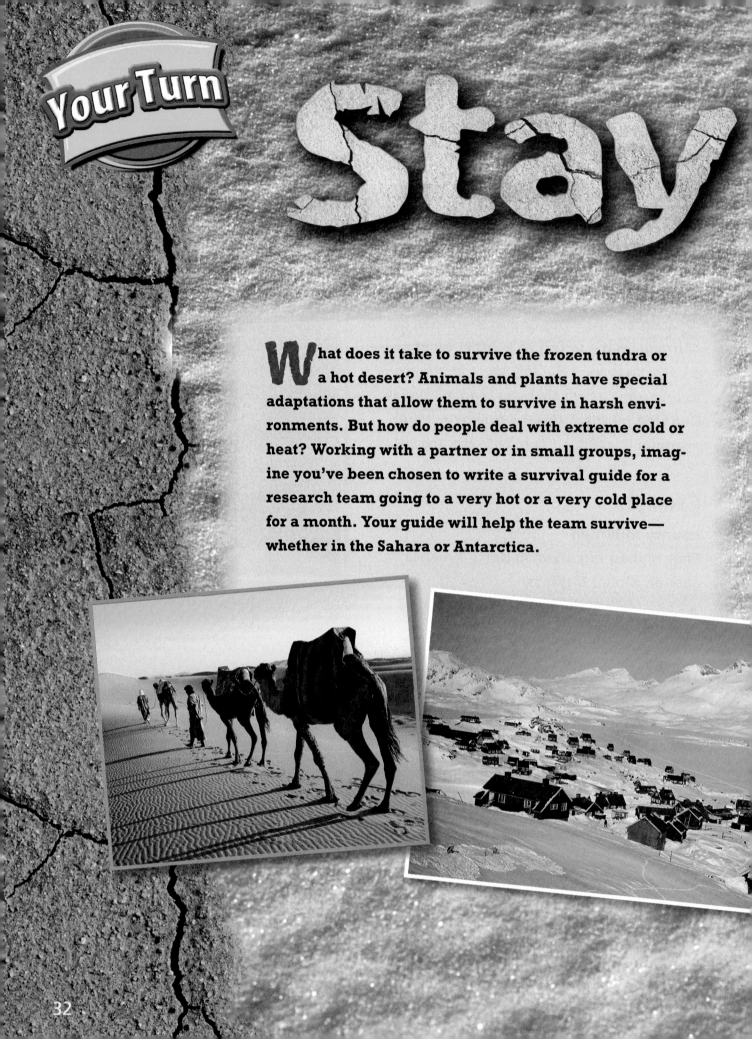

Alive!

First, research your destination. Gather information on its climate, vegetation, and animal life. Next, create a section in your guide for each of these areas. Be sure to note what kind of clothing is necessary, where to find food, and the dangers that nature may pose. Finally, summarize the most important points for survival.

Vanishing Act

Thousands more like this one

are missing in action.

It's a mystery. Call me.

The morning the dead bee arrived in the mail, my mind was already buzzing with ideas. Unfortunately, none of them were about my science project. The letter addressed to me had grabbed my attention.

"A note from my cousin Justin," I thought at first. I nearly tossed the envelope aside, but Justin's handwriting was usually close to impossible to read.

This was unusually careful and clear. I opened the envelope and unfolded the piece of blue paper inside. A bee carcass fell on my desk.

At least I thought it was a bee. I always have a hard time telling apart flying, stinging insects—such as wasps, hornets, and bees—when they're alive. A dead one was even trickier to identify. The note said:

"Thousands more like this one are missing in action. It's a mystery. Call me."

No signature on the note. But it was from Justin. I was sure of it.

I found a magnifying glass and studied the dead bug my cousin had sent. I compared it to images in the encyclopedia. I learned that wasps always have yellow and black stripes, whereas honeybees are often a golden brown. Since bees in cartoons are almost always yellow-and-black striped and cute, you can understand my initial confusion. But the dead insect was definitely a honeybee. I picked up the phone to call Justin.

"Hey, stop sending dead stuff to me," I said when he picked up.

"It got your attention, didn't it?" he replied.

"What's going on?" I asked.

"I'm at Grandpa Ray's farm. When we got here on Friday night, he was having a fit because the hives he rented were empty," Justin said.

"Wait a second. Your grandpa rents hives?" I asked. Justin's Grandpa Ray wasn't my grandpa but I'd been to his farm dozens of times. I'd learned a lot about farming from the visits, but I had no idea what Justin was talking about. "Empty hives?"

"Yeah, lots of farmers rent beehives," Justin said, clearly impatient with me. "Grandpa has beekeepers bring hives here every February for the almond harvest. All the farmers do it. Grandpa said they need millions of bees to pollinate the crops. And that's just for the almond orchards."

Raising bees was a much bigger business than I'd imagined. Our class went on a field trip to visit beekeepers when we were in fourth grade. We learned all about pollination from a beekeeper who wore what looked like a white space suit that completely covered her.

The insect carcass fell out of the envelope. On close inspection, I determined it was, indeed, a dead honeybee.

35

I was mostly interested in the beeswax candles and jars of honey that they sold in the gift shop, so I kind of forgot that bees have a bigger job in the scheme of things. If honeybees don't pollinate plants, those plants won't reproduce and make seeds for new plants. Farmers could get desperate for bees.

"I need you to come out here and take a look. I need you to be my eyes," Justin said.

"What *I* need to do is to come up with an idea for a science project. And it can't be just one of my regular kind of brilliant ideas. This has to be *especially* brilliant because the whole town will see it at the science fair. If I don't have something by dinner, Mom will ground me and I'll never get to see you again," I said.

"Tia," Justin said with a long, dramatic sigh. "Don't you get it? This *is* your science project. That's why I wrote to you."

"What about my keen observational skills?" I asked.

"That too."

Justin was a year ahead of me in school and he knew all about the required sixth-grade independent science project. He was right. An investigation into the missing honeybees *did* sound like a good science project.

I'd seen a beekeeper in full protective gear.

When Mom got back from the store, we decided to take a trip to the farm. I called Justin and arranged to meet him there in the afternoon.

When we arrived at the farm, Mom went into the house to visit Grandma Ray. Grandpa Ray took Justin and me out to the orchards, narrating our walk as if we were being filmed for a TV nature program. "Bees pollinate more than 90 crops in the U.S. We bring them in every spring for the almonds. We use them for avocadoes, cherries, and kiwis, too. But look what we have here." He stopped at a hive, poking it with a stick. "Go ahead and look. Believe me, nothing will hurt you."

I peered inside.

"It's empty," I said, taking a photograph.

"Exactly," Grandpa Ray said.

"Would someone steal them and then sell them or rent them to another farmer?" I asked.

"Seems like they'd need to take the whole hive in order to make any money," Justin commented.

"I'm afraid some young yahoo is trying to cause trouble. Probably doesn't realize that without bees there won't be as much food," Grandpa Ray said. "So much of what we eat wouldn't be possible without honeybees. In California, the almond crops alone are worth about two billion dollars."

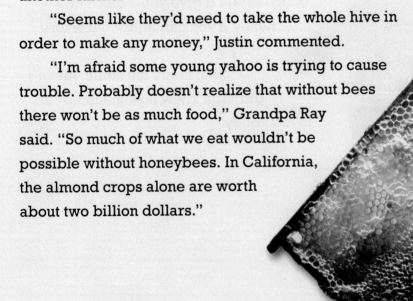

Justin was right: There were no bees at home in this hive.

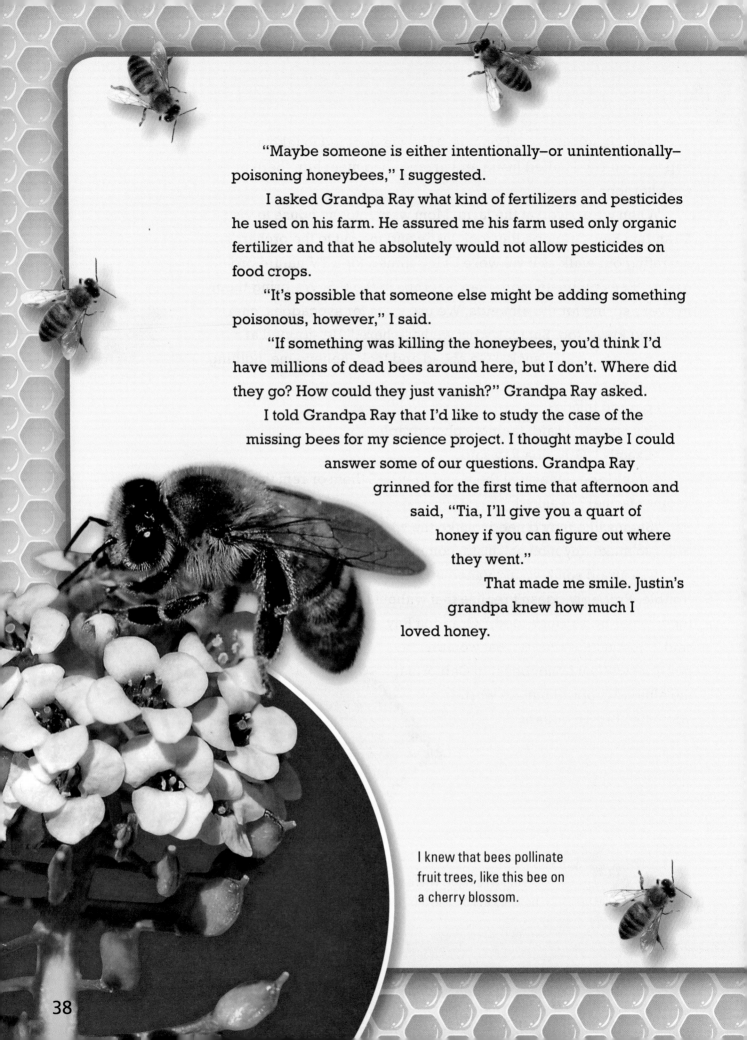

"Maybe someone is either intentionally–or unintentionally–poisoning honeybees," I suggested.

I asked Grandpa Ray what kind of fertilizers and pesticides he used on his farm. He assured me his farm used only organic fertilizer and that he absolutely would not allow pesticides on food crops.

"It's possible that someone else might be adding something poisonous, however," I said.

"If something was killing the honeybees, you'd think I'd have millions of dead bees around here, but I don't. Where did they go? How could they just vanish?" Grandpa Ray asked.

I told Grandpa Ray that I'd like to study the case of the missing bees for my science project. I thought maybe I could answer some of our questions. Grandpa Ray grinned for the first time that afternoon and said, "Tia, I'll give you a quart of honey if you can figure out where they went."

That made me smile. Justin's grandpa knew how much I loved honey.

I knew that bees pollinate fruit trees, like this bee on a cherry blossom.

I started on my project right away and began by taking several dozen photographs around the farm as well as the surrounding landscape.

Was it crazy to think someone would intentionally steal or kill honeybees?

When we got back to the farmhouse, I hooked my camera up to Justin's laptop so I could look at the photos I'd taken.

"Tell me what you see there," Justin said, moving his head so he could see from the corner of his eye. Justin's legally blind, but that doesn't mean he's totally blind. He has peripheral vision, which means he can see things off to the side. It takes people a while to get used to how he moves so that he can see their faces. He uses a computer all the time, but it would be next to impossible for him to see any details that would be in the photographs that I just took. I zoomed in on one photo.

"What do you see?" Justin asked, leaning in.

"It's what I don't see," I said. "It looks like a large electricity transmitter, but there aren't any wires going into it or coming out of it."

"Sounds like a cell site," Justin said.

"A sell sight?" I asked. "What's that?"

"For cell phones. They pick up cell phone signals." Justin launched into a long description of how my cell phone worked. My mind was elsewhere.

Could this be a clue?

Justin knew it was a cell site in my photo. Could cell phone signals interfere with honeybees?

Almond orchards in California produce a harvest worth two billion dollars each year.

When we got home, I told Mom I was off to research the disappearance of the honeybees. In just a couple of hours of online research I learned that our county wasn't the only one with missing honeybees. Since the fall of 2006, about half of the states reported dramatic declines in the number of honeybees. Estimates were that some commercial beekeepers had lost between thirty and ninety percent of their honeybee colonies. That's a huge range, but even losing thirty percent of these hard-working pollinators could be destructive for farms and, later, for people. Reports were also coming in from Germany, Spain, Greece, and other countries that beekeepers were losing hives.

The buzz about honeybees was that the bees were dying.

This case sounded more serious all the time. I started thinking about what the disappearance of the bees might mean. I wondered if there would be any more honey for sale. I wondered how people would be affected by a big decrease in the number of fruits and nuts available. It seemed like those foods would definitely get more expensive. It also seemed that I might not get honey for my morning toast even if I figured out what happened to the bees. What if they were just gone forever?

I spent the next several months researching why the bees had disappeared. I also decided to title my science project "Vanishing Act: The Mystery of the Disappearing Honeybees." My title was a little more interesting than "Colony Collapse Disorder" (CCD), which is what scientists had officially dubbed the phenomenon. Cell phone towers, certain pesticides, and drought were at first possible culprits for CCD. Eventually all were ruled out.

By the time I presented my science project at the end of the school year, the best theory available was that a virus had caused bees to weaken and, eventually, die. Some bees may have left the hive and then became too weak to pollinate or to return.

I scored a 98 percent on my presentation of "Vanishing Act." The score wasn't perfect, but it was pretty good.

I really scored on the honey, though. Grandpa Ray dropped off some of the best honey I've ever tasted after he saw my presentation. I don't know where he got it, but that's a mystery I won't worry about solving just yet.

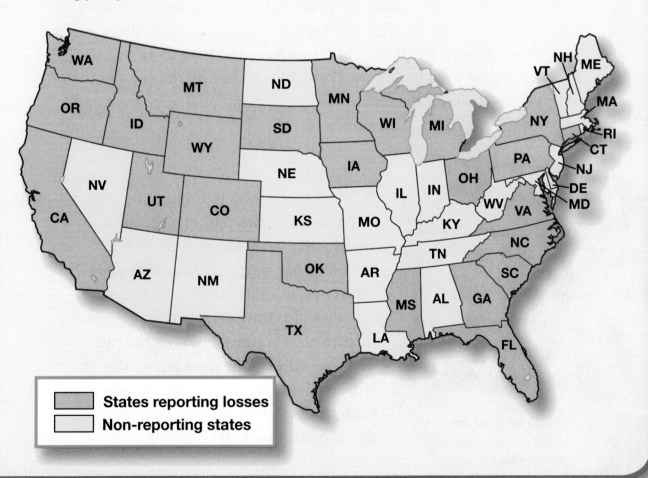

States reporting losses
Non-reporting states

The Smart Swarm

Have you ever seen hundreds of ants moving in an orderly line along a sidewalk? How do so many ants find their way to a spill of soda? They have no sergeants, yet they march like trained soldiers, all focused on a single task. Scientists call this ability to work effectively in large groups *swarm intelligence.*

Think about a good sports team. When team members work well as a group, the team has more success than a team that does not work together. Certain animals also have more success when they work in groups. These animals rely on the work of the group to carry out a number of tasks, including finding food and avoiding predators.

Weaver or tailor ants make an ant bridge to get to their feeding grounds.

Trail Building

When an ant goes to forage, or find food, it leaves a faint trail of a chemical called a *pheromone* along its path. The pheromone has a scent or taste that other ants recognize. When other ants follow the path, they also leave a scented trail. Then the path most traveled becomes the path that is paved with the most pheromone. It is the trail that is easiest to follow and it tends to be the best route to the best food, thanks to the work of the group.

Evasive Moves

When a flock of birds or a school of fish darts away from a predator, it is using the skills of the group to keep it safe. If an individual separates from the group, it would be easy prey. But if the group sticks together, the predator has difficulty focusing on an individual to attack. Swarm intelligence works when one member sees a predator and changes direction. Others in the group immediately react and move together to avoid the predator. The action of the group keeps the animals safe.

A school of blue-striped grunt

Learning from Animals

Scientists are looking at ways to apply swarm intelligence to fleets of robots that can choose the best route through a crowded or dangerous area. Business leaders are using swarm intelligence to determine the best delivery routes. Their truck drivers don't leave a trail of chemicals along the road, but they do share the information about the routes with other drivers, and together they choose the best route. The next time you find yourself in a moving crowd, watch how the group chooses the best route. You might find that people are a bit more like ants than you realized.

Flocks of the red-billed quelea, an African bird, often number in the hundreds of thousands.

Bee, I'm Expecting You

By Emily Dickinson

Bee, I'm expecting you!
Was saying yesterday
To somebody you know
That you were due.

The frogs got home last week,
Are settled and at work,
Birds mostly back,
The clover warm and thick.

You'll get my letter by
The seventeenth; reply,
Or better, be with me.

Yours,
  Fly.

Straight Talk

By Nikki Grimes

Look, Bee
Fair is fair.
I don't burst into
Your honeycomb
Willy-nilly
Or interrupt you
While you feed on
Rose and Lily
So leave me alone, drone
Show yourself the door
And don't come
Buzzing round here
Anymore

45

The Shape of Nature

The natural world is filled with patterns. One of these patterns is called a *tessellation*. A tessellation is the repeated pattern of a shape. The sides of the repeated shapes fit together like tiles on a floor.

We can see tessellations in the honeycombs of bees. The repeated shape in the honeycomb is a hexagon, a six-sided figure.

Choose a simple geometric shape and create a tessellation pattern with the shape. Then color each shape and create a mosaic with your tessellation.

Swarming Shapes

Tessellations can also be made with more complex figures. Artists have sometimes used complex tessellation patterns that resemble swarming birds, insects, or fish.

To create your own tessellation pattern of a swarming animal, follow these steps:

1. Cut out a 3-inch by 3-inch square of paper.

2. Draw a line inside the square on one side to represent the head of the animal.

3. Cut along this line, creating two new pieces of paper. Tape the straight edges of these back pieces to the straight edge of the front piece.

4. Draw a line inside the figure on the bottom of the animal to represent a wing or fin.

5. Cut along this line, creating another piece of paper. Tape the straight edge of this wing or fin to the straight edge of the top back piece. Your figure is complete and it should fit with another figure of the same shape.

6. Use this shape to trace a tessellation pattern on a large sheet of paper. Color the shapes similarly so that they resemble a swarm of birds, insects, or fish.

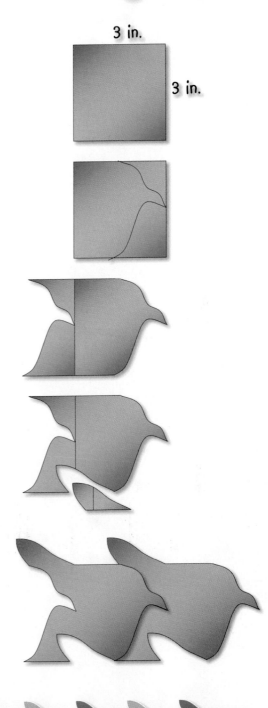

3 in.

3 in.

A Mystery

In "Vanishing Act," Tia tries to solve the mystery of the missing honeybees. She talks to people, gathers information, and considers reasons why the bees are missing. In the end, she doesn't find the bees, but she learns why they may have vanished.

Nature is full of mysteries. Many we have solved, but they still seem mysterious. Why do birds and butterflies migrate? Why do leaves change color? What causes a rainbow? Why are no two snow-flakes alike?

# of Nature

Write a mystery story about something interesting in nature. Think about the weather, animals, plants, or rocks. Even if it's something you know the answer to, have a detective try to solve the mystery by gathering information the way Tia did. Make a story map. Here's an example to help you write your story.

Story Map

Characters: Jo (detective), Dan (friend), Sal (TV meteorologist)	**Setting:** Jo's town

Problem: Why do leaves change color in the fall?

Solution: Less sun causes trees to stop making chlorophyll.

Events:

1. Jo collects leaves for a project.

2. Dan tells her that Jack Frost makes them change color.

3. Jo calls Sal at the TV station.

4. He shows her leaf cells under a microscope.

ELEPHANTS ON THE SAVANNAH

CAST OF CHARACTERS:
* Narrator
* Judith: Kenyan ranger/guide
* Maya
* Antonio
* Jordan

Narrator: In Kenya, East Africa, it's just before dawn in Amboseli National Park. This famous park is a great place to watch African elephants. Maya, Antonio, and Jordan have traveled here from the United States. Now they are ready for their first day on the savannah.

Judith: Good morning! How was your first night in Amboseli?

Jordan: I'm still tired!

Judith: Don't worry. You'll have a chance to rest after our morning drive. Does everyone have sunscreen and a water bottle?

Maya: It's hard to remember sunscreen when it's still dark out.

Judith: Ready to see African elephants?

Antonio: Definitely! I've got my binoculars.

Judith: This time of day the elephants are usually heading towards the swamps. So we'll go in that direction too.

Narrator: Jordan, Maya, and Antonio follow Judith to her jeep and climb in. It gets lighter as they go.

Maya: Wow, there's Mount Kilimanjaro! That is one big mountain.

Antonio: Hey, I see elephants!

Narrator: Eleven elephants are slowly walking near the road. The herd includes two babies. One elephant trumpets loudly.

Jordan: Okay! I'm awake!

Antonio: Wow. That first elephant is one big dude! He must be ten feet tall. And look at those tusks.

Judith: Actually, that "dude" is a female. Herds are family groups led by the oldest female. She is called the matriarch.

Maya: I like that!

Judith: And by the way, African elephants have tusks whether they are male or female.

Jordan: Do the herds always stay together?

Judith: The females and young elephants do. All the females in a herd help teach and protect the calves. They're like "extra moms."

Antonio: Which ones are the dads?

Judith: No dads here. Grown-up males are called bulls. They can weigh six tons or more. Bulls leave their herds when they are about fourteen. After that they live mostly alone.

Antonio: The elephants have stopped walking. It seems like they're listening to something.

Jordan: Want to hear a cool thing I read about elephants?

Maya: I'm all ears.

Jordan: Elephants listen through their feet. Right, Judith?

Judith: Their feet have special vibration sensors. Elephants detect rumbles through the ground. That way they can communicate with other elephants miles away. Elephants make all sorts of other noises. They can scream, grunt, or trumpet. Each sound means something different.

Maya: Antonio, what are you looking at?

Antonio: Check it out. There's another family group way down in the valley. Maybe this herd is talking to that one.

Maya: And now these elephants are walking in that direction. Can we go that way too?

Narrator: The four get in the jeep and head toward the swamp, across open savannah. They park near the elephants.

Maya: Yikes. Aren't we close enough? These are big guys. I mean, big *gals*.

Judith: Don't worry. The females are usually pretty gentle. The ones here in Amboseli are used to jeeps. Let's watch for a while.

Jordan: They sure flap their ears a lot.

Maya: I read about that. The ears have lots of blood veins in them. Flapping cools the blood off in hot weather.

Jordan: Now they're wading in the swamp.

Antonio: Looks like bath time. Look at them spray their own backs with their trunks.

Maya: Those elephants are smart. It's getting hot out here!

Judith: Hey gang, it's almost 9:30. Let's head back to camp. We'll have breakfast. Then later, we can cool off in the camp pool.

Jordan: Yes!

Maya: Sort of like the elephants.

Antonio: Won't we miss some action?

Judith: Not really. During the hottest part of the day, elephants mostly rest in the shade. I want to show you something on the way back.

Narrator: They drive for a few minutes. Judith parks near a pile of big bones.

Jordan: Wow. Did an elephant die here?

Judith: Yes. About two years ago one of the matriarchs died.

Maya: Why are all the bones scattered?

Judith: Elephants mourn their dead. They still stop by here to gently pick up the bones with their trunks. That's why the bones are spread around.

Antonio: I guess they must remember the matriarch.

Judith: They seem to. They also remember people. For example, they will sometimes approach familiar humans, such as researchers they've seen before.

Narrator: The group heads back to camp. Soon, all four are in the pool. The African heat is intense. But by late afternoon it begins to cool off. Shadows become longer as evening approaches.

Judith: Okay, it's four o'clock. Everyone ready to continue our safari?

Maya: Let's go! Do you think we'll get to see elephants eating?

Antonio: I've heard they need at least three hundred pounds of food a day.

Narrator: The four climb back in the jeep. They drive for a few minutes. Then they park in the shade of an acacia tree.

Jordan: There they are. Are those the same elephants we saw before?

Judith: Yes. See the two calves? They are hiding between their mother's legs.

Maya: Did you see that? That elephant picked up a single blade of grass with her trunk! How could she do that?

Judith: There are at least 40,000 muscles in an elephant's trunk. All those muscles mean they can move their trunks very precisely.

Jordan: Those trunks can really multi-task.

Judith: They sure can. Elephants use their trunks to express emotion, eat, smell, drink, touch, make noise, and move things.

Antonio: Check it out. That big elephant is trying to tear out that tree with her trunk. Wow. She did it! She knocked over the whole tree.

Maya: Now she's eating the leaves off the top. So is that calf. How cute.

Jordan: I hear buzzing. Do elephants buzz, too?

Narrator: Suddenly the matriarch begins to run away. The other elephants follow in a hurry.

Judith: Oh no! The trunk of that tree contained a bees' nest! See the bees swarming into that one elephant's eyes?

Antonio: I had no idea elephants could run that fast.

Judith: They can run twenty-four miles per hour. We don't want to get stung either. Let's follow the elephants' lead and get out of here.

Narrator: Everyone piles into the jeep and they zoom away fast.

Maya: Whew. That was close. I'm glad no one was stung.

Jordan: Why is such a big animal afraid of bees?

Antonio: Yeah, isn't their skin too thick to sting through?

Judith: Bees can sting the tender skin behind their ears. Bees can even go up an elephant's trunk.

Jordan: Ouch!

Judith: Let's head back to camp. We'll see more elephants tomorrow. How did you like your first day on the savannah?

Maya: It was fantastic.

Antonio: It sure was! Thank you, Judith.

Jordan: I can't wait to get up tomorrow morning!

A Colossal Catch

Imagine being in a fishing boat when an enormous creature begins to rise from beneath the water! How would you feel? In February 2007, the crew of a New Zealand fishing boat was fishing in the Ross Sea near Antarctica when one of the giants of the deep came to the surface. It was the rarely seen colossal squid.

A hooked fish in its mouth, the squid was almost dead. Still, it took nine people two hours to haul the huge creature onto the boat.

The crew had caught something special. It was the largest colossal squid ever found. From tentacle tip to fin, the squid measured thirty-three feet long and weighed 1,091 pounds. This was an exciting moment for scientists. It was a rare chance to learn more about the colossal squid, believed to be the largest squid in the world.

MYSTERIOUS AND FRIGHTENING

People have long found large squid frightening. For years, sailors told terrifying tales of sea monsters with tangles of arms attacking ships. In Jules Verne's *Twenty Thousand Leagues Under the Sea*, first published in 1870, a ferocious large squid strikes Captain Nemo's submarine. Could these stories have any truth in them? People knew so little about large squid that they weren't sure.

Scientists first identified the colossal squid in 1925 from two arms found in a sperm whale's stomach. Since then, colossal squid have been seen only a few times, and no one has ever studied one in its habitat. These squid live in the icy waters around Antarctica at a depth of more than 3,280 feet. The waters are so dark that it is difficult for scientists to explore.

For years scientists were unable to verify any facts about the colossal squid because there was so little information about it. Most scientists now believe the colossal squid reaches lengths of up to forty-six feet. That's as long as a city bus!

Squid have large eyes for the size of their bodies. The eyes of the colossal squid, as big as dinner plates, are believed to be the largest eyes of any animal. Can you imagine looking into the eye of a colossal squid? Its large eyes help it see prey in the dark ocean depths.

Part of a twenty-foot squid tentacle found off the coast of Japan

A twenty-four foot giant squid, nearly as large as its colossal cousin, attacks a bait squid south of Tokyo, Japan.

The colossal squid is one of the most frightening predators in the ocean. Like other squid, it has eight arms and two longer tentacles. Two rows of sharp, swiveling hooks line the ends of the tentacles. The squid uses these hooks to snag prey.

Awaiting Answers

Today, the colossal squid caught in 2007 is at the Museum of New Zealand in Wellington. It is frozen, but it will be thawed and studied. Scientists want to know many things. How large do colossal squid get? How long do they live? How do they reproduce? Perhaps these and other questions will soon be answered.

The Elephant

By Hilaire Belloc

When people call this beast to mind,
They marvel more and more
At such a little tail behind,
So *large* a trunk before.

By Barbara Juster Esbensen

An evenly balanced
word **WHALE**
it floats
lazily on the page
or dives straight down
to the bottom and beyond
all breath held   held
held   then whoooosh!
The   A   blows its top
into the sun! **WHALE**
serene
sings to us   wet
green sounds from the deepest
part of the alphabet

Activity Central

Comic Creativity

Writers of comic strips and graphic novels use both pictures and words to tell a story. The pictures help show the setting, action, and emotions of the characters.

This week you read stories about two enormous animals—the elephant and the colossal squid. Create a comic strip that features these animals, or two other animals of your choice. Use both pictures and words to tell a story in four to eight panels.

As you create your comic strip, remember these tips:

1. Keep your story simple.

2. Give your story a beginning, middle, and end.

3. Use exact details.

4. Exaggerate the characteristics of your characters to make them humorous.

True or False?

Read the four bizarre animal stories below. Pick the story that just happens to be false. The other three are strange but true.

1 Scientists were thrilled to discover a plump, **purple frog** in western India. The colorful amphibian gives them clues about a frog ancestor that lived 130 million years ago. One scientist called the purple frog "a once-in-a-century find." **TRUE OR FALSE?**

2 A creature called a **sea squirt** is famous for eating its own brain. It uses its simple brain only to find a place to settle for life. Once the sea squirt has found a home, it no longer needs its brain, so it eats it! **TRUE OR FALSE?**

3 A young amphibian called a **walking stick** can stroll on land before it grows legs, as long as it has a willing partner. The two amphibians twist together right below their heads. Then they use their snake-shaped bodies as legs to walk along sandy shores. **TRUE OR FALSE?**

4 An **African elephant** has been found imitating traffic noises. A scientist in Kenya noticed a young, orphaned elephant making odd sounds after sunset. It turns out the elephant was imitating the sounds of trucks going down the highway. **TRUE OR FALSE?**

Answer key: 1. true; 2. true; 3. false; 4. true

SPEAKING UP
FOR THE ANIMALS

In "Elephants on the Savannah" and "A Colossal Catch" you read about two of Earth's amazing creatures. Harmful human activities have endangered many others.

Think about an animal that you would like to see protected. It can be as big as a blue whale or as small as a monarch butterfly. It can be as exotic as a Siberian tiger or as American as a bald eagle. It can be a mammal or bird; reptile or amphibian; fish or insect. It should be an animal you like and feel strongly about.

Got your animal? Now write a persuasive speech to convince others to protect this animal and its habitat.

SPEECH POINTERS

1. Start your speech by telling why the animal you chose is special. Use interesting facts or tell a personal story about it.

2. Describe problems that this animal faces, such as loss of habitat or the danger of hunters.

3. Explain why you think it is important to protect this animal.

4. Suggest solutions to the problems this animal faces.

5. State how you want listeners to help.

Storm Chasers

Outside, a long siren sounds. On the radio, an announcer says: *"The National Weather Service reports a tornado moving east of Johnstown at 40 mph."*

If we heard a warning like this, most of us would do what we're supposed to do. We would head for shelter indoors. We would retreat to the basement, or to an interior hallway or room such as a closet, staying away from windows. We would use blankets or pillows to cover our bodies and wait for the storm to pass.

But a small group of scientists and researchers would head in the opposite direction—right toward the storm. These people, known as *storm chasers*, pursue tornadoes in specially equipped cars, vans, and trucks. They hope to arrive in time for the worst of the weather, so that they can collect as much information about the storm as possible.

Other storm trackers stay closer to home. These trained volunteers, known as *storm spotters*, keep a close watch on the weather in their own community. They pass along storm information to local weather agencies. Sometimes even sophisticated radar devices don't pick up storms, and the trained eye of the storm spotters can help to save lives. Listen closely to weather reports on your local TV stations and you may hear the forecasters talk about reports they receive from storm spotters.

Tornadoes can strike at any time of year in the United States, but they are generally most common from late winter through mid-summer.

Tornadoes, like this one near Gruver, Texas, usually form in a large area of the U.S. called Tornado Alley, located between the Rocky Mountains and the Appalachian Mountains.

▲ A hurricane seen from space.

A Hercules weather airplane gets ready. ▶

Both the U.S. Air Force and the National Oceanic and Atmospheric Administration (NOAA) fly missions into storms over the ocean waters.

Hurricane Hunters

Storm chasers don't just follow tornadoes. *Hurricane hunters* take special training to fly planes right into the center of hurricanes and other severe tropical storms.

Outside, heavy rain and high winds batter the aircraft. Inside, the noise is deafening. Despite the roar and the roller coaster ride, the crew carefully collects information on temperature, air pressure, wind speed, and wind direction. This information will be used to help predict the size, strength, and path of the storm.

After flying through the solid ring of thunderstorms that make up the wall of the hurricane, the plane enters a place of near-silence— the eye of the hurricane. Sometimes in this calm center, the hurricane hunters see blue sky, sun, and even stars. But the plane still has to go back through the menacing storm before returning home. In fact, most hurricane hunters make at least four trips through the storm before returning to land!

The hurricane season runs from about June through November in the Pacific and Atlantic oceans.

Pioneers of Storm Chasing

Roger Jensen, a North Dakotan, is believed to have been the first storm chaser. "I was born loving storms," he once said. Jensen began chasing storms in 1953 and continued to do so for the next forty years. During his lifetime he took thousands of pictures of storms.

A scientist named Howard Bluestein had an early introduction to storms. In 1954, when Bluestein was five, a hurricane blew the shingles off the roof of his family's house. When he grew up he decided to make storm study his life's work. Today, Bluestein studies storms as a researcher and professor of meteorology at the University of Oklahoma. The movie *Twister* was inspired in part by Bluestein's work.

Hurricane hunting began in World War II, when a U.S. Air Force training aircraft flew into the eye of a hurricane on a dare. To prove his plane's strength, American pilot Colonel Joseph Duckworth told the British that he could fly into the eye of a hurricane. After doing so, Duckworth pioneered the science of hurricane hunting.

Storm Chasers in Kansas

Hail, Lightning, Winds, and . . . Traffic Accidents?

Being in a severe storm is dangerous. Storm chasers can be struck by flying debris or by baseball-sized hail. They can be trapped by flash floods or downed power lines. Fortunately, most professional storm chasers keep a safe distance from the deadly storm center—usually one to two miles. They respect the power of the storm.

Lightning is also a great risk to storm chasers. Lightning strikes injure scores of people each year. The risk rises for storm chasers, who spend more time than the average person in the most extreme weather that Mother Nature serves up.

But the riskiest part of storm chasing is actually driving to the storm. Crashes happen because drivers are hurrying to reach the heart of the storm and are looking at the sky instead of the road ahead of them. Blowing dust, heavy rain and fog, hail, skidding on wet pavement, running out of gas, and getting stuck in mud can also make the chase difficult and dangerous.

Hurricane hunters face a different set of risks because they are flying an airplane through the most powerful part of a storm. Violent winds can shake the plane severely, making it difficult to fly. Equipment inside the plane can get tossed around, causing possible injury. The wind can also damage the aircraft, and a sudden blast can send a plane plunging into the ocean.

Storm spotting and storm chasing should never be done without proper training, experience, and equipment. Hurricane hunting is an activity for experts. For most of us, the best way to experience storm chasing is by watching a TV documentary or movie! As long as there are storm chasers filming the most dramatic weather events, we can sit in the safety of our homes and movie theaters and comfortably experience nature at its wildest.

WHITEOUT!
The Great Blizzard of 1888

A Slow Start

On March 10, the weather up and down the East Coast was clear and unseasonably warm. It was so pleasant that people headed outdoors to enjoy the warm temperatures. Some families even went picnicking. But while spring appeared to be knocking on the door, winter wasn't over.

The blizzard that was later nicknamed "The Great White Hurricane" began as a drizzle on March 11. The rain grew heavier overnight and quickly changed to snow as temperatures fell below zero. A ferocious wind developed.

People in small towns and big cities from Maryland to Maine woke up the next morning to heavy snowfall. Surely they were surprised by the sudden change in the weather, but many went about their lives as usual.

Farmers braved howling winds to tend to their animals. Children trudged to school. Workers sloshed their way to their jobs. Among those who braved the blizzard in New York City was future president Theodore Roosevelt. He slogged through the snow to keep an appointment with a librarian, only to find she had stayed home.

A New York City street during the Blizzard of 1888. Many power lines were brought down by the snow and high winds.

A grocery awning has collapsed under the weight of the snow. Drifts up to fifty feet deep were reported.

Buried Under Snow

By noon on March 12, many areas in the Northeast were already buried under a blanket of snow. In some places, huge snowdrifts covered trees and the tops of houses. Families were trapped in their homes without food or fuel, hungry and cold. Trains were stopped in their tracks. Fire stations couldn't mobilize to fight fires. Communication became impossible when telegraph and telephone lines snapped under the weight of the snow. High winds helped to ground or wreck more than two hundred ships.

But the blizzard wasn't finished. For thirty-six hours, snow continued to fall. When it finally did stop, the blizzard had dumped between forty and fifty inches of snow in Connecticut, Maine, Massachusetts, New York, and New Jersey. It took weeks for people to completely dig out. In all, hundreds died from the storm and the cold. The Great Blizzard of 1888 has taken its place in history as America's most famous snowstorm.

Weather

Whether the weather be fine,
Or whether the weather be not,
Whether the weather be cold,
Or whether the weather be hot,
We'll weather the weather
Whatever the weather
Whether we like it or not.

Anonymous

In the Night

In the night
The rain comes down.
Yonder at the edge of the earth
There is a sound of cracking,
There is a sound of falling.
Down yonder it goes on slowly rumbling,
It goes on shaking.

from *Papago Indians*

Snow

The word begins to melt
inside my pocket. SNOW.
I fling its lacy coldness
in the air, then watch it
floating there.

Nikki Grimes

The Wind

The morning after the night before,
   The wind came in when I opened the door.
It blew the "Welcome" off the mat.
   It blew the fur right off my cat.
It blew my shirttail out of my pants.
   It grabbed the curtains and started to dance
Around and around and around about
   Till I opened a window and kicked it out.

John Ciardi

Weather in a Box

Blizzard Blaster

Create your own blizzard!

Need a day off from school?
Is summer making you sweat?
Open the box!

Winter, spring, summer, or fall—let it snow!

Imagine that you work for a company that makes weather you can carry in a box. Create a poster advertising your product. You can choose any kind of weather–blizzard, fog, rain, sunshine, even a tornado.

Include artwork and give your product a catchy name and slogan. Your poster should include the following information:

❄ Who the target audience is
❄ Why people should buy this product
❄ How people can use it

Capture It with a Caption

Suppose you are a writer and photographer for a newspaper. Your job is to take pictures and to write captions for them—short descriptions that tell about the pictures in one or two sentences.

Study the pictures on this page and read the information about them. Then write captions that capture, or vividly describe, what each picture is about.

- What: Dust Storm
- Where: Stratford, Texas
- When: April 18, 1935

- What: Lightning
- Where: Nanjing, China
- When: August 1, 2006

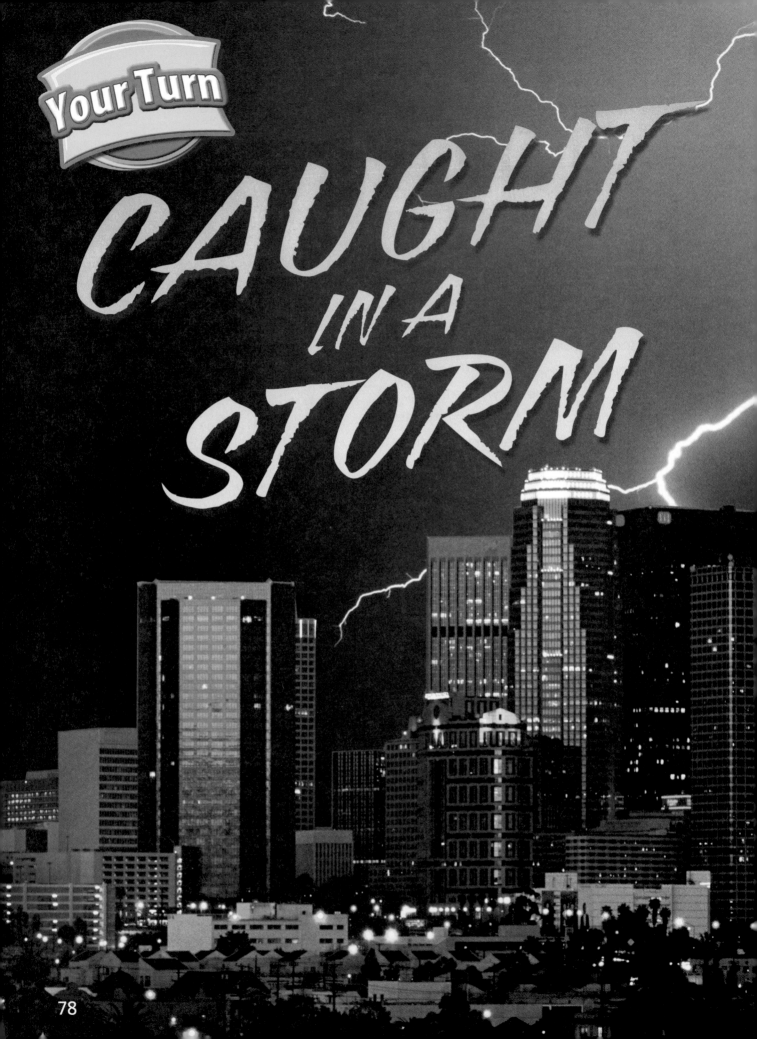

As you read in "Storm Chasers," some people chase tornadoes or fly into hurricanes on purpose. Most of us, though, experience a storm by accident. Do you remember a time when you were caught in a big storm? Or can you imagine what it might be like?

Write a page in your journal that describes a storm vividly, either from memory or from your imagination. Picture a rainstorm, blizzard, tornado, hurricane, hailstorm, windstorm, or ice storm!

Start your journal entry by setting the stage. Where were you? What kind of day was it? When the storm hit, what did you see, hear, and feel? Storms are dramatic, so try to show and not tell. Include sensory details that stand out, like wind rattling the windows, snow swirling, or thunder booming.

Make your readers feel that they're caught in a storm, too!

Credits

Photo Credits

KEY: (t) top, (b) bottom, (l) left, (r) right, (c) center, (bg) background, (fg) foreground, (i) inset

Exploring Business

Exploring Business

Karen Collins

Lehigh University

Pearson Education International

Library of Congress Cataloging-in-Publication Data

Collins, Karen (Karen M.)
 Exploring business Karen Collins.
   p. cm.
 ISBN 978-0-13-236732-5
 1. Business. 2. Economics. 3. Industrial management. I. Title.
 HF1008.C65 2008
 650—dc22

                                             2006039180

Executive Editor: David Parker
Acquisitions Editor: Jon Axelrod
VP/Editorial Director: Jeff Shelstad
Development Editor: Ron Librach
Assistant Editor: Denise Vaughn
Product Development Manager, Media: Nancy Welcher
Marketing Manager: Anne Howard
Marketing Assistant: Susan Osterlitz
Associate Director, Production Editorial: Judy Leale
Permissions Coordinator: Charles Morris
Associate Director, Manufacturing: Vinnie Scelta
Manufacturing Buyer: Arnold Vila
Design Manager: Christy Mahon
Composition Liaison: Suzanne Duda
Art Director: Janet Slowik
Interior Design: Anthony Gemmellaro
Cover Design: Anthony Gemmellaro
Cover Illustration/Photo: Courtesy of Nike
Interior Illustrations: ElectraGraphics, Inc.
Director, Image Resource Center: Melinda Patelli
Manager, Rights and Permissions: Zina Arabia
Manager, Visual Research: Beth Brenzel
Image Permission Coordinator: Debbie Hewitson
Photo Researcher: Melinda Alexander
Composition: GGS Book Services
Printer/Binder: Quebecor World Color/Versailles
Typeface: Palatino 10/12

Credits and acknowledgments borrowed from other sources and reproduced, with
permission, in this textbook appear on the appropriate page within text.

10 9 8 7 6 5 4 3
0-13-140365-6

To the memory of my parents, Bob and Theresa McLaughlin, who provided me with constant encouragement and love.

About the Author

Karen Collins is an associate professor in the College of Business and Economics at Lehigh University. Dr. Collins developed Lehigh's Introduction to Business course with assistance from an Accenture Faculty Fellowship for Excellence in Teaching. She has served as its coordinator and has taught sections of the course since its inception in 1997. Dr. Collins was honored with an Innovation in Teaching Award for the course from the Middle Atlantic Association of Colleges of Business Administration (AACSB regional association of management education deans and program leaders) and also has received a number of teaching awards including the Deming Lewis Faculty Award for having the strongest influence on the ten-year graduating class, the Stabler Award for Excellence in Teaching for demonstrating superior ability in communicating knowledge to others, and the Coopers and Lybrand Excellence in Teaching and Learning Award given to faculty from four universities who demonstrated innovative teaching techniques.

Karen Collins received her Ph.D. from Virginia Tech in accounting with minors in organizational behavior and psychology. She has published in leading accounting and management journals such as *Accounting, Organizations and Society, Accounting Horizons*, and *Journal of Vocational Behavior*. Her research areas include stress, work/home conflict, and upward mobility of women. Dr. Collins is a CPA and practiced in public accounting in the small business area prior to starting her teaching career.

Brief Contents

Contents

CHAPTER 3

Business Ethics and Social Responsibility 44

CHAPTER 5

Recruiting, Motivating, and Keeping Quality Employees 102

CHAPTER 6

Developing and Producing Goods and Services   131

CHAPTER 7

Marketing: Providing Value to Customers   163

CHAPTER 8

Business in a Global Environment 196

CHAPTER 9

The Role of Accounting in Business 224

CHAPTER 10

CHAPTER 11

Exploring Business

An overview of business at an early stage can spark students' interest in future business courses. Using this textbook package, you can create an Introduction to Business course that enables your students to learn about business in an exciting way. As in other Introduction to Business books, this text uses a wide variety of company-specific examples. However, we improve on the traditional approach by adding an integrated case study of a dynamic organization. The company chosen for this purpose is Nike, as you will note from the "swoosh" on the cover. In future editions, other case-study companies will be added.

Nike: An Integrated Case Study

Through an in-depth study of a real company, students can learn not only about the functional areas of business, but how these functional areas fit together. Students learn about Nike by reading a case study online based on extensive research and executive interviews. We've broken the case down into 26 individual case notes, which are linked to the appropriate sections of the text. Each provides a real-world example to help students master a particular business topic.

After reading about the ways companies promote their products, for example, students are directed to a Nike case note that traces the evolution of the company's promotional strategies, including its well-known sports marketing efforts.

 ABOUT NIKE 4.2

After reviewing several leadership styles, take a moment to find out how the top executives of Nike direct and motivate members of the organization.

Go to www.exploringbusinessonline.com

WHAT WOULD NIKE DO?
Whenever this callout appears in the text, the real and exciting world of business is just a click (or two) away. Students can study Nike in 26 integrated installments.

We help students expand their understanding of Nike by providing videos featuring key company executives discussing topics such as Nike's history, corporate-responsibility challenges and initiatives, product-innovation programs, and entrance into the soccer shoe market. Current (and sometimes controversial) topics can be woven into the class through Nike-related memo writing (or debating) assignments accompanying each chapter.

Because Nike case materials are delivered online (at www.exploringbusinessonline. com), we can update them each semester. In this way, students learn what's happening at Nike now, not what happened a few years ago. Studying a dynamic organization on a real-time basis allows students to discover the challenges that it faces and exposes them to critical issues affecting the business, such as globalization, ethics and social responsibility, product innovation, diversity, supply chain management, and e-business.

DON'T TAKE OUR WORD FOR IT
Specially commissioned videos feature Nike executives explaining how one very innovative—and very successful—company goes about its business.

Business Plan Project

We're convinced that having students develop a business plan as a component of an Introduction to Business course has considerable academic value. The project introduces students to the excitement and challenges of starting a business and helps them discover how the functional areas of business interact. Thus this textbook package includes an optional business plan project that's *fully integrated* into the book. We explain the importance of business planning in Chapter 2, which deals with the process of starting a business. At the end of the chapter, we introduce students to the business plan project and provide detailed instructions on preparing the business plan. In each of the subsequent chapters, we help students complete sections of a 10-part business plan.

Because this project is carefully woven into the course, students are able to readily apply what they learn to the preparation of each section of the plan. We also furnish, online, a simple-to-use Excel template to aid students in the preparation of the financial section of the business plan.

Business Plan Project

Group Report: *Marketing Plan*

REPORT

Your team should submit a written report that gives an overview of your marketing plan, including target market, customer needs, product characteristics, pricing, distribution, and promotion. Your report should also describe any proposed uses of the Internet to promote or sell your products. For details on what you should include in the report, go to Appendix A at the back of the book, entitled "Introducing Your Business Plan" (p. XXX), and consult the section headed "Marketing." Also consider two other issues:

a. *Customer Needs and Product Characteristics*
   Identify your customers' needs/wants and link them to the product characteristics   earance, features, quality,   , ease of maintenance) that   ucts and production group

   otion and Sales
   use the Internet to promote   s section should provide   estions:

- Will your company have a Web site? Who will visit the site?
- What will it look like? What information will it supply?
- Will you sell products over the Internet?
- How will you attract customers to your site and entice them to buy from your company?

The report should be about two double-spaced typed pages. The name of your proposed business and the names of all team members should appear on the report.

REASONABLE CONTRIBUTIONS

All members of the team who make a reasonable contribution to the report should sign it. (If any team member does not work on the report, his or her name should *not* appear on it.) If a student who has made a contribution is unable to sign the report (because of sickness or some other valid reason), the team can sign his or her name. To indicate that a name was signed by the team on a member's behalf, be sure to attach a note to the signature.

HOW TO TEND TO YOUR OWN BUSINESS

With this detailed 10-part project, students can plan their own businesses (and work on their teamwork skills while they're at it).

Enhanced Learning

As an epigraph for this book, we've chosen a nugget from the treasure trove of Benjamin Franklin's considerable educational experience:

> *Tell me and I forget. Teach me and I remember. Involve me and I learn.*

We believe that this quote encapsulates an important goal of this textbook package: *to encourage students to be active learners.* Thus we've designed the online component of this package to facilitate the attainment of this goal. To give you a flavor of the purpose of these online materials, let's take a quick tour of the features available for each chapter:

- **eBook**—which looks exactly like the printed text with the same page numbers.
- **Active Figures**—which simulate the process that a faculty member goes through in class when diagramming a concept on the board, one piece at a time.

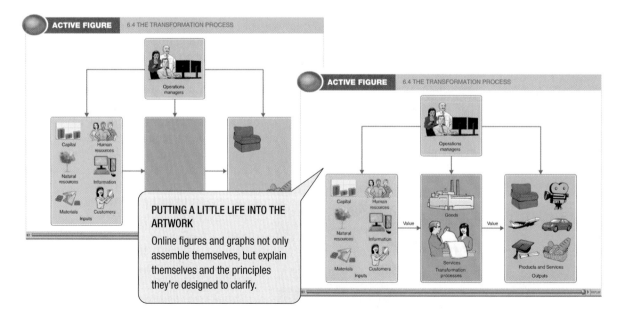

PUTTING A LITTLE LIFE INTO THE ARTWORK

Online figures and graphs not only assemble themselves, but explain themselves and the principles they're designed to clarify.

- **Nike Materials**—case notes, videos, writing assignments, questions.
- **Learning Labs**—which engage students in active learning and help them master key concepts.

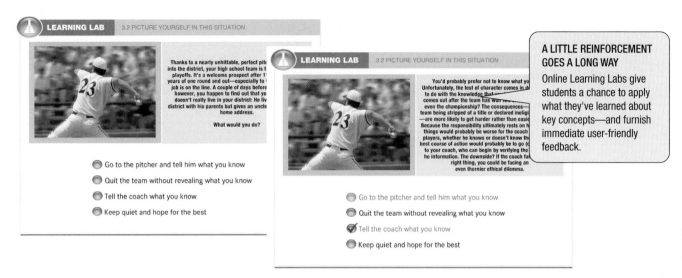

A LITTLE REINFORCEMENT GOES A LONG WAY
Online Learning Labs give students a chance to apply what they've learned about key concepts—and furnish immediate user-friendly feedback.

- Quick Quizzes—which provide students with instant feedback and reinforce learning.

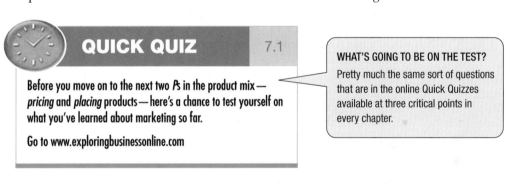

WHAT'S GOING TO BE ON THE TEST?
Pretty much the same sort of questions that are in the online Quick Quizzes available at three critical points in every chapter.

> All of the above materials are available to students online, at www.exploringbusinessonline.com

We also strive to enhance student learning through end-of-chapter questions, problems, and cases that ask students to do more than merely regurgitate information from the text. Most of these exercises require students to assess a situation, think about it critically, and reach a conclusion.

Team-Building Skills AACSB

Taking Stock of Ratios

Your class has been told that each group of three students will receive a share of stock in one of three companies in the same industry. But there's a catch: Each group has to decide which of the companies it wants to own stock in. To reach this decision, your team will use ratio analysis to compare the three companies. Each team member will analyze one of the companies using the ratios presented in this chapter. Then, you'll get together, compare your results, and choose a company. Here are the details of the project:

1. The team selects a group of three companies in the same industry. Here are just a few examples:
   - Auto Manufacturers: Ford, General Motors, Daimler-Chrysler
   - Airlines: Southwest, Continental, American Airlines

2. Every team member gets a copy of one company's most recent annual report (which includes its financial statements) from the company's Web site (investor section).

3. Every member calculates the following ratios for the company for the last two years: gross profit margin, net profit margin, inventory turnover (if applicable), return on assets, current ratio, debt-to-equity, and interest coverage.

4. Get together as a group and compare your results. Decide as a group which company you want to own stock in.

5. Write a report indicating the company that your team selected and explain your choice. Attach the following items to your team report:

WHY 2 (OR 3 OR 4) HEADS ARE BETTER THAN ONE
In every chapter, Team-Building exercises help students understand why, in successful businesses, problem solving is usually a group effort.

Many are based on current business situations involving well-known companies of interest to students. Throughout, we believe, questions are challenging and stimulating, and most are appropriate for in-class discussions.

DO THE RIGHT THING (AND STAY OUT OF JAIL)

Assignments in every chapter give students an opportunity to explore their ethical horizons and make ethical (and legal) judgments.

Ethics Angle AACSB

Sugarcoating the News at Krispy Kreme

According to Krispy Kreme's "Code of Ethics for Chief Executive and Senior Financial Officers," the company's top executives are expected to practice and promote honest and ethical conduct. They're also responsible for the health and overall performance of the company. Recently, however, things have gone wrong in the top echelons of the doughnut-shop chain.

First, a little background: Founded as one small doughnut shop in Winston-Salem, North Carolina, in 1937, the brand became increasingly popular over the next six decades, taking off in the 1980s and 1990s. By 2003, Krispy Kreme (which went public in 2000) was selling more than a billion doughnuts a year. That's when things started to go stale. (For more details on the company's ups and downs, go to www.exploringbusinessonline.com to link to the *Detroit News* Web site and read the article "Krispy Kreme: The Rise, Fall, Rise and Fall of a Southern Icon.")

When sales first started to decline in the fall of 2003, CEO Scott Livengood offered a variety of creative explanations, mostly for the benefit of anxious investors: High gas prices discouraged people from driving to doughnut shops; supermarket sales were down because grocery ~~re losing business to Wal-Mart; people~~

diet. Unfortunately, other (more plausible) explanations were beginning to surface. To complete this exercise, you'll need to find out what they were. Go to www. exploringbusinessonline.com to link to the *Business Week* and *USA Today* Web sites and read these articles: "The Best and Worst Managers of the Year" and "Krispy Kreme Must Restate Earnings by $25.6M." Once you have a good grasp of the company's problems and you've read about the people who are responsible, answer the following questions, being sure to provide explanations for your responses:

1. What factors contributed to the problems at Krispy Kreme? What happened to the company? Who was hurt?

2. Should the firm's problems be attributed to poor management, unethical behavior on the part of the executive team, or both?

3. Judging from the lessons of the Krispy Kreme case, how important do you think it is for a firm to have ~~strong~~

More than 70 percent of our end-of-chapter items help students build skills in areas designated as critical by AACSB, including analysis skills, ethical awareness and reasoning, multicultural understanding and global perspectives, information technology, communications, and teamwork. Each AACSB inspired exercise is identified by an AACSB tag and a note indicating the relevant skill area.

Questions and Problems

1. **AACSB ▸ Analysis**

We use the concepts of absolute and comparative advantage to explain why countries import some products and export others. We can also use them to explain how work can be divided between two people. Two consultants—John and Jennifer—have a client who needs a company report written and a PowerPoint presentation prepared within the next two weeks. Both John and Jennifer have experience writing reports and preparing presentations, but neither has the time to do both jobs. From past experience, they know how much time each of them needs to complete each type of project:

Consultant	Write a report	Prepare a presentation
John	80 hours	40 hours
Jennifer	150 hours	60 hours

Using the information contained in the grid above, answer each of the following questions:

a. Does either John or Jennifer have an absolute advantage in (1) writing reports and/or (2) preparing presentations?

~~ither have a comparative advantage?~~

e. Does Jennifer have a comparative advantage in either task? What should she specialize in?

2. **AACSB ▸ Analysis**

What happens if, during a given year, you spend more money than you take in? What happens if you finance your overspending by running up your credit-card balance to some outrageous limit? Would you have trouble borrowing in the future? Would you have to pay higher interest rates? How would you get out of debt?

Now let's change *you* to *the United States*. The United States has just run up the largest one-year trade deficit in history—nearly $600 billion. Respond to the following items:

a. Define the term *trade deficit* and explain how the United States ended up with such a large one.

b. Is the trade deficit a good or bad thing? Why or why not?

c. Define the term *balance of payments* and explain ~~wha~~ ~~unfa-~~

WHAT TO DO WITH WHAT YOU KNOW

With a little advice from AACSB, end-of-chapter Questions and Problems are designed to help students develop the kinds of skills that they'll need to succeed in the business world.

Author-Prepared *Instructor's Manual*

For the past ten years, I have been developing, coordinating, and teaching an Introduction to Business course in which first-year students are introduced to business through the study of Nike and the preparation of a business plan. During this ten-year period, more than 3,000 students have taken the course. Over the years, sections of the course have been taught by a mix of permanent faculty, graduate students, adjuncts, and even the dean. Each semester, I oversee the course and guide approximately ten instructors as they teach their sections—a task that's been made possible through the development and continuous improvement of extensive teaching materials.

Because I feel strongly that well-structured and easily understood teaching materials are vital to the success of this course, I have personally written the *Instructor's Manual*, including teaching notes and solutions to end-of-chapter problems. In doing this, I relied on the experiences that I've gained in developing these materials for and with my faculty team.

Designing for Flexibility/Power and Simplicity/Support

We have designed this textbook package to be *flexible* and meet the needs of three groups of instructors—those who want to

- teach the course using the textbook alone
- teach the course using the Nike case (or a company of their choice)
- teach the course by incorporating both the company case study and the business plan project

The package is designed to be a *powerful but simple to use teaching tool.* We've included a broad range of features that allow instructors to introduce students to business in an exciting way, but we've also worked to fashion material that's straightforward, current, relevant, and easy to teach from. The text is purposely brief and covers "business essentials" without burdening students or faculty with unnecessary detail. We hope that the user-friendly writing captures students' attention and makes reading the chapters enjoyable.

Finally, we've tried to build a textbook package that's as *supportive* as possible to both students and faculty. We've supplied marginal definitions and detailed end-of-chapter summaries (and a few cartoons) to assist students as they learn from the text.

Our ExploringBusinessOnline web site supports learning through interactive and multimedia content designed to help students not only master topics but assess their learning. An extensive author-prepared instructors' edition and excellent set of PowerPoint slides provide teaching support to instructors. Test Item file developed using assessment techniques supports faculty in evaluating student performance.

My desire in writing this text was to provide faculty with a fully developed teaching package that allows them to enhance student learning and introduce students to business in an exciting way. I hope you enjoy teaching the course as much as I do.

Karen Collins

Karen Collins

Running with NIKE

This is the only Introduction to Business text that introduces students to business using an exciting and integrated case—one which is in fact *updated each semester*. We believe that learning about business through the study of a dynamic organization allows students to be students.

- benefit from real-world examples that underscore business concepts
- learn about the functional areas of business and see how they interact
- experience the opportunities and challenges faced by a real company
- familiarize themselves with many of the critical issues in today's business world, including globalization, ethics and social responsibility, product innovation, diversity, supply chain management, and e-business.

Why Nike?

Because students

- can identify with the company and use its products
- can appreciate its entrepreneurial history and enjoy learning about its co-founders
- are familiar with the industry in which it operates
- understand its focus on product innovation and marketing
- can benefit from studying its global operations
- can comprehend its financial activities
- enjoy debating a few controversial actions

We've found that, by studying Nike, students willingly participate in classroom discussions. Why? Because Nike is on just about everybody's radar screen. Students enjoy discussing the opportunities and challenges faced by Nike and speculating on what the company intends to do about them, now and in the future. Discovering business concepts through the study of one of the best known companies in the world excites them about business and sparks their interest in future business courses.

Integrating Nike Into Your Course

Our experience has shown that faculty can integrate the Nike case study into the course in a number of ways.

About Nike Case Notes* Students learn about Nike by reading a 26-part case study developed through both research and executive interviews. Each case note provides a real-world example to help students master a specific topic. For example, after reading chapter materials on the pros and cons of doing business in a global environment, students can read a Nike case note that examines both the benefits that Nike derives from its international operations and the responsibilities that it has to the countries in which it operates. After reading about the ways companies obtain funds to finance growth, students can read a Nike case note that reveals how Nike almost went out of business because of several financial crises and details the steps that co-founder Phil Knight took to resolve each crisis and establish a financially strong company. Discussion questions solicit feedback from students and enhance classroom debates on the topics covered in the cases.

Nike Videos* We've produced four videos featuring Nike executives discussing specifically chosen topics: the company's history, its corporate responsibility challenges and initiatives, its commitment to product innovation, and its carefully orchestrated entrance into the soccer shoe market. We structured interview questions to elicit information that will be valuable to students in mastering particular topics, and we've selected and organized footage to capture students' attention. Faculty can show the 15-minute videos in class or ask students to watch the videos online at www.exploringbusinessonline.com. Discussion questions, written by the author, aid classroom discussions on the topics covered in the videos.

Nike Memo Writing Assignments (or Debates)*   Current, and often controversial, Nike topics can be woven into the class through Nike memo-writing assignments. These assignments, which are updated each semester, provide students with an opportunity to strengthen their writing skills and form opinions on current issues affecting Nike. One assignment, for example, asks students to deliver an opinion on Nike's efforts to connect with female consumers by writing a memo to employees at the San Francisco NikeTown. Another asks them to explain the benefits and risks of Nike's decision to enter Wal-Mart with its recently acquired Starter brand by writing a memo to a hypothetical investor. Once the memos themselves have been composed, they underpin excellent in-class discussions or debates. In fact, as an alternative to having students write memos, faculty might ask them to research the topic and come to class prepared to debate the pertinent issues.

Nike Questions*   Each chapter contains a multi-part question on one of the Nike case notes covered in the chapter. These questions require students to think about the case and present their opinions on the issues covered.

Teaching Notes   For the past ten years, Karen Collins has been developing, coordinating, and teaching an Introduction to Business course in which students are introduced to business through an integrated study of Nike. Each fall, approximately 300 students take the course, which is taught by a team of about ten instructors. She simplifies the teaching task for her team by preparing teaching notes that integrate Nike materials into basic business related topics. By means of these teaching notes, faculty can introduce a topic and then expand it using Nike as a convenient and relevant example. Karen Collins' teaching notes are available in the author-written *Instructor's Manual Exploring Business*.

> * Nike Case Notes, Videos, Memo Writing Assignments, and Nike Questions
> are available to students at www.exploringbusinessonline.com.

Integrating the Business Plan

We're aware that several other Introduction to Business texts include business plan projects. We've found, however, that most of them tend merely to "bolt on" a review of the business plan without trying to make it an integral part of the book. We've designed this textbook package to incorporate a fully integrated, though optional, business plan *project*.

Karen Collins had the business plan project in mind when she first developed her Introduction to Business course and, as an outgrowth of that experience, this text. During the last ten years, under her guidance and that of her teaching teams, more than 200 student teams have prepared and presented business plans. The continuous improvements in the project are the result of the experience that she's gained in working with both faculty and student teams.

Project Overview

Karen designed her course to expose students to the excitement of starting a business and the importance of creating a business plan. She introduces the project in Chapter 2. If the instructor elects to assign the business plan project, the book presents students with the first of ten business plan assignments, which asks them to review a document describing the business plan project. In each subsequent chapter, they're asked to complete another section of the business plan. By the time they've reached the end of the course, they're shown how to integrate each of these individual sections into a final version of the plan. Because the project is carefully coordinated with the presentation of course materials, students are able to apply what they're learning, as they're learning it, to the practical process of preparing a business plan.

Financial Reports

Because we understand that preparing the financial section of the business plan can be difficult for students, we've developed a process to make the task much easier. In particular, we furnish students, at www.exploringbusinessonline.com with an Excel template that simplifies the process of preparing financial reports for their proposed businesses. They don't even need to be competent in Excel to use it; it's designed to be simple to use, and we provide detailed instructions. The template follows a business-decision approach: As the student team makes decisions about its proposed businesses (decisions about such factors as projected sales in units, cost of goods sold as a percentage of sales, and purchase prices for capital items), the template enters and compiles the information to create a financial report.

Link to Nike

Any instructor who wishes to do so can connect the business plan project to the study of Nike. They can, for example, ask students to prepare a business plan for a fictitious company in the same industry as Nike—say, a competitor, a supplier, a retailer, or a service provider in the athletic footwear, apparel, and equipment industry.

Proven Success

This textbook package provides considerable guidance to students as they prepare their business plans and to instructors as they guide student projects. The outcome is amazing. As Karen Collins has discovered, students who were unfamiliar with business terminology at the beginning of the semester are able to create a business plan that equals many prepared in the business world. More important, students can immediately apply what they're learning in the course to the preparation of their business plans. They become excited about the prospect of starting a business and begin to understand how the functional areas of business interact.

Enhanced Learning

According to AACSB,

> *"The most effective learning takes place when students are involved in their educational experiences. Passive learning is ineffective and of short duration."*

That's why the *Exploring Business* textbook package offers several approaches to help students become active learners and engage them in the learning process.

Dynamic Figures and Graphs

In the printed book, figures and graphs are static. In the online version, however, at www.exploringbusinessonline.com, we've endowed many of them with a pedagogical life of their own: They move and talk, demonstrate their own functions, and grab the reader's attention. They're designed to simulate the process that a teacher goes through when diagramming concepts on the board, one piece at a time. In this case, of course, students can replay figures until they master the topic.

Sample a few **Active Figures** at www.exploringbusinessonline.com.

Learning Labs

Discussions of key business concepts are supplemented by what we call **Learning Labs**—interactive online exercises designed to engage students in active learning and help them test their grasp of business concepts. We've also designed them to satisfy another AACSB recommendation—namely, to provide frequent and timely feedback. According to AACSB, "Learning situations should provide 'practice field' situations where students can take risks and then learn from their successes and failures. Individual faculty members should continuously work to improve their skills at providing feedback in ways that enable and motivate learning."

Try out a couple of **Learning Labs** at www.exploringbusinessonline.com.

Quick Quizzes

To further reinforce learning and provide students with more instant feedback, we've situated mini true/false multiple-choice tests at the end of each major section of every chapter. When a student gets one of these test style questions wrong, he or she is immediately furnished with the correct answer and brief explanation of why it's the right one. When appropriate, moreover, we've built in a link to the section of the chapter where the concept is discussed and where the student can return to review the topic in context.

Check out a couple of **Quick Quizzes** at www.exploringbusinessonline.com.

Thought-Provoking End-of-Chapter Materials

We've tried to ensure that our end-of-chapter questions, problems, and cases—many of which ask students to assess situations, think about them critically, and reach practical conclusions—are thought-provoking (and even fun). Often, we ask them to gather information before answering a question. Many items are based on current business situations involving companies of interest to students, and most are appropriate for in-class discussions. Each chapter presents ten **Questions and Problems** as well as five cases on areas of skill and knowledge endorsed by AACSB: **Learning on the Web, Career Opportunities, The Ethics Angle, Team-Building Skills,** and **The Global View.**

Supplements

Instructor's Manual

The author-written **Instructor's Manual** includes comprehensive teaching notes that integrate material from the chapter, material geared toward Nike, and material dedicated to the business plan project. Easy-to-use notes include teaching tips and ample in-class activities. We've also included author-prepared solutions to end-of-chapter questions and problems and added supplemental teaching materials that Karen Collins has used in teaching her own Introduction to Business course. In addition, the *Instructor's Manual* includes Nike materials.

Instructor's Resource Center on CD

This supplement gives instructors access to the *Instructor's Manual*, Test Item File, and PowerPoints in downloadable format. If you ever need assistance, our dedicated technical-support team is ready to help with the media supplements that accompany this text. Visit http://.247.prenhall.com for answers to frequently asked questions and toll-free user-support phone numbers.

Test Item File

The Test Item File contains approximately 150 questions per chapter. Each question is fully referenced to corresponding learning objectives, AACSB objectives, page references, and difficulty level.

TestGen Test-Generating Software

The computerized test bank contains approximately 150 questions per chapter, including multiple choice, true/false, short-answer, and scenario-based items. We identify suggested answers, learning objectives, AACSB objectives, difficulty levels, and page references for all questions.

Nike Videos

Lively, up-to-date, and relevant, specially produced Nike videos on DVD expand upon company content contained in the Nike case notes. These clips are also available as streaming video on the companion Web site.

VangoNotes in MP3 Format

We give students the opportunity to study on the go with VangoNotes—chapter reviews in downloadable MP3 format that offer brief audio segments for each chapter:

- **Big Ideas**: the vital ideas in each chapter
- **Practice Test**: lets students know if they need to keep studying
- **Key Terms**: audio "flashcards" that review key concepts and terms
- **Rapid Review**: a quick drill session—helpful right before tests

vango notes · In partnership with Audible Education · Hear it. Get It.

Study on the go with VangoNotes.

Just download chapter reviews from your text and listen to them on any mp3 player. Now wherever you are-- whatever you're doing--you can study by listening to the following for each chapter of your textbook:

Big Ideas: Your "need to know" for each chapter

Practice Test: A gut check for the Big Ideas--tells you if you need to keep studying

Key Terms: Audio "flashcards" to help you review key concepts and terms

Rapid Review: A quick drill session--use it right before your test

VangoNotes.com

Acknowledgments

The author would like to thank the following colleagues who have reviewed the text in its many stages and provided comprehensive feedback and insightful comments and suggestions for improving the manuscript:

Ken Anglin, Minnesota State University at Mankato
John R. Anstey, University of Nebraska at Omaha
Debra Arvanites, Villanova University
Kitty Campbell, Southeastern Oklahoma State University
Robert Clark, University of Evansville
Cheryl Davis, Longwood University
Dave Dusseau, University of Oregon
Steve Edwards, University of North Dakota
Brenda Eichelberger, Portland State University
Jim Hess, Ivy Tech Community College
Thomas Kemp, Tarrant County College – NW
Christine Kydd, University of Delaware
J. Ford Laumer, Auburn University
Jimmy Lawrence, Auburn University
Baeyong Lee, Fayetteville State University
Therese Maskulka, Walsh University
Margaret Myers, Northern Kentucky University
Jude Rathburn, University of Wisconsin
Elizabeth Wibker, Louisiana Tech University

This text relies heavily on ancillary material for its full benefit in the classroom. A special thank you goes to the following professionals who have contributed to the supplement package for the text:

Test Item File—David Murphy, Madisonville Community College
PowerPoints—Chuck Bowles, Pikes Peak Community College
Business Plan Excel Template—Joseph Manzo, Lehigh University
Nike Videos—Judy Minot, Wald Productions
Multimedia and Online Content—Rob Spierenburg, All Things Media

I am sincerely grateful to my development editor, Ron Librach, for his extensive contributions to *Exploring Business*. Throughout this project, he has been my writing partner, product champion, and friend. I also want to express my appreciation to a great team of individuals at Prentice Hall who made working on this project an enjoyable and memorable experience. Special thanks to David Parker (Executive Editor), and Jeff Shelstad (Editorial Director) for their confidence in me and in the project, to Judy Leale (Associate Director, Production Editorial) and Janet Slowik (Art Director) for their dedication to quality and their positive attitudes, to Nancy Welcher (Product Development Manager, Media), Anne Howard (Marketing Manager) and Jon Axelrod (Acquisitions Editor) for their enthusiastic support, and to others at Prentice Hall who have played a valuable role in the project: Steve Deitmer (Director of Development), Denise Vaughn (Assistant Editor), Christy Mahon, and Dave Moles.

Thanks also to a number of individuals outside Prentice Hall who made substantial contributions to the textbook project: Judy Minot created the Nike videos, Joseph Manzo developed the Excel template used in the business plan project, Rob Spierenburg provided programming support for the interactive figures and Learning Labs, Chuck Bowles created PowerPoint slides, David Murphy wrote the Test Item File, and Melinda Alexander served as photo researcher. James Schmotter, Sam Weaver, Jim Hall, Dave Dousseau, David Sell, and Fred Fraenkel wrote draft materials on particular topics. Tara Collins and Eleanore Stinner provided assistance on a number of manuscript-preparation tasks.

Several Nike people deserve recognition for the help they provided as we developed the Nike case notes and videos: Nigel Powell, Nelson Farris, Hannah Jones, John Hoke, Trevor Edwards, Alan Marks, Joani Komlos, and Shannon Shoul.

Thanks to the members of the Introduction to Business faculty team at Lehigh University who are a constant source of ideas and advice. Their excitement about the course and dedication to our students create a positive and supportive teaching and learning environment. I enjoy the hours we spend in the BUS 01 "bullpen" sharing teaching tips, brainstorming ways to improve the course, and just having fun. I also thank the Lehigh students who have offered helpful feedback on draft versions of the text.

Finally, I thank my husband, Bill, and my sons, Don and Mark, for their support and encouragement during this project. They're the best of my world.

1 The Foundations of Business

After studying this chapter, you will be able to:

1. Identify the main participants of business, the functions that most businesses perform, and the external forces that influence business activities.

2. Define *economics* and explain how economists answer the three key economics questions.

3. Describe the different forms of competition.

4. Explain how supply and demand interact to set prices in a free market system.

5. Understand the criteria used to assess the status of the U.S. economy.

6. Discuss the government's role in managing the economy.

PM Images/Getty Images Inc.–Stone Allstock

INTRODUCTION

It's an interesting time to study business. The Internet and other improvements in communication now affect the way we do business. Advances in technology are bringing rapid changes in the ways we produce and deliver goods and services. Companies are expanding international operations, and the workforce is more diverse than ever. Corporations are also being held responsible for the behavior of their executives, and more people share the opinion that companies should be good corporate citizens.

As you go through the course with the aid of this text, we'll introduce you to the various activities that businesspeople engage in—accounting, finance, information technology, management, marketing, and operations. We'll help you understand the roles that these activities play in an organization, and we'll show you how they work together. We hope that by exposing you to the things that businesspeople do, we'll help you decide if business is right for you and, if so, what areas of business you'd like to study further.

Nike

We also hope that you'll enjoy learning about business in an exciting and integrative way. One of the aims of this course is to help you develop a perspective on business by studying a real company—Nike. We've developed a wealth of online materials to give you a variety of perspectives on Nike. Throughout the text, you'll be directed (via our Web site www.exploringbusinessonline. com) to information about the company that provides real-world examples to aid you in understanding the business concepts being covered. For example, you'll learn about Nike by reading a multi-section case study based not only on research but on interviews that we've conducted with company executives.

By studying a dynamic organization up close, you'll learn about many of the critical factors in today's business world, including technology, e-business, supply chain management, globalization, ethics and social responsibility, and cultural diversity. You'll find out how Nike designs, develops, produces, and markets products. You'll discover the opportunities and challenges faced by Nike, and you'll find out what the company intends to do about them, now and in the future.

Abercrombie & Fitch sells "casual luxury" clothing through its 350 stores for the purpose of making a profit. It will make a profit if it sells its clothing for more money than it costs to make the clothes and operate its stores. Abercrombie & Fitch clothing has particular appeal to teenagers and college students aged 18 to 24.

INTRODUCTION TO NIKE

At this point, let's make our first visit to Nike. We begin with a report that simply introduces the company. You'll be revisiting many of the issues covered here throughout the course.

 ABOUT NIKE   1.1

Here's a chance to learn about Nike's founding, its founder's vision for it, and the mission that guides its activities.

Go to www.exploringbusinessonline.com

Getting Down to Business

A **businesss** is any activity that provides goods or services to consumers for the purpose of making a profit. When Phil Knight and Bill Bowerman, his running coach at the University of Oregon, created Blue Ribbon Sports (the predecessor of Nike), they started a business. The product was athletic shoes, and the company's founders hoped to sell shoes to runners for more than it cost to make and market them. If they were successful (which they were), they'd make a **profit**.

Before we go on, let's make a couple of important distinctions concerning the terms in our definitions. First, whereas Nike produces and sells *goods* (athletic shoes, apparel, and equipment), many businesses provide *services*. Your bank is a service company, as is your Internet provider. Airlines, law firms, movie theaters, and hospitals are also service companies. Many companies provide both goods and services. For example, your local car dealership sells goods (cars) and also provides a service (automobile repairs).

Second, some organizations are not set up to make profits. Many are established to provide social or educational services. Such **not-for-profit (or nonprofit) organizations** include the U.S. Post Office, museums, almost all colleges and universities, the Sierra Club, and the American Red Cross. Most of these organizations, however, function in much the same way as a business. They establish goals and work to meet them in an effective and efficient manner. Thus, most of the business principles introduced in this course also apply to nonprofits.

BUSINESS PARTICIPANTS AND ACTIVITIES

Let's begin our discussion of business by identifying the main participants of business and the functions that most businesses perform. Then we'll finish this section by discussing the external factors that influence the activities of a business.

Participants

Every business must have one or more *owners* whose primary role is to invest money in the business. When a business is being started, it's generally the owner who polishes the business idea and brings together the resources (money and people) needed to turn the idea into a business. The owner hires *employees* to work for the company and help it reach its goals. Owners and employees depend on a third group of participants—*customers*. Ultimately, the goal of any business is to satisfy the needs of its customers.

Functional Areas of Business

The activities needed to operate a business can be divided into a number of *functional areas*: management, operations, marketing, accounting, and finance. Let's briefly explore each of these functions.

Management Managers are responsible for the work performance of other people. **Management** involves planning for, organizing, staffing, directing, and controlling a company's resources so that it can achieve its goals. Managers *plan* by setting goals and developing strategies for achieving them. They *organize* activities and resources to ensure that company goals are met. They *staff* the organization with qualified employees and *direct* them to accomplish organizational goals. Finally, managers design *controls* for assessing the success of plans and decisions and take corrective action when needed.

Operations All companies must convert resources (labor, materials, money, information, and so forth) into goods or services. Some companies, such as automobile makers, convert resources into *tangible* products— cars. Others, such as hospitals, convert resources into *intangible* products—health care. The person who designs and oversees the transformation of resources into goods or services is called an **operations manager**. This individual is also responsible for ensuring that products are of high quality.

Marketing **Marketing** consists of everything that a company does to identify customers' needs and design products to meet those needs. Marketers develop the benefits and features of products, including price and quality. They also decide on the best method of delivering products and the best means of promoting them to attract and keep customers. They manage relationships with customers and make them aware of the organization's desire and ability to satisfy their needs.

Accounting Managers need accurate, relevant, timely financial information, and accountants provide it. **Accountants** measure, summarize, and communicate financial and managerial information and advise other managers on financial matters. There are two fields of accounting. *Financial accountants* prepare financial statements to help users, both inside and outside the organization, assess the financial strength of the company. *Managerial accountants* prepare information, such as reports on the cost of materials used in the production process, for internal use only.

Finance **Finance** involves planning for, obtaining, and managing a company's funds. Finance managers address such

---

business
Activity that provides goods or services to consumers for the purpose of making a profit.

profit
Difference between the revenue that a company brings in from selling goods and services and the costs of generating this revenue.

not-for-profit (or nonprofit) organization
Organization that has a purpose other than returning profits to owners.

management
Process of planning for, organizing, staffing, directing, and controlling a company's resources so that it can achieve its goals.

operations manager
Person who designs and oversees the process that converts resources into goods or services.

marketing
All of the organizational activities involved in identifying customers' needs and in designing, pricing, promoting and delivering products to meet those needs.

accountant
Financial advisor responsible for measuring, summarizing, and communicating financial and managerial information.

finance
Activities involved in planning for, obtaining, and managing a company's funds.

questions as: How much money does the company need? How and where will it get the necessary money? How and when will it pay the money back? What should it do with its funds? What investments should be made in plant and equipment? How much should be spent on research and development? How should excess funds be invested? Good financial management is particularly important when a company is first formed because new business owners usually need to borrow money in order to get started.

EXTERNAL FORCES THAT INFLUENCE BUSINESS ACTIVITIES

Businesses don't operate in a vacuum: They're influenced by a number of external factors. These include the economy, government, consumer trends, and public pressure to act as good corporate citizens. Figure 1.1 sums up the relationship among the participants in a business, its functional areas, and the external forces that influence its activities. One industry that's clearly affected by all these factors is the fast food industry. A strong *economy* means people have more money to eat out at places where food standards are monitored by a *government* agency, the Food and Drug Administration. Preferences for certain types of foods are influenced by *consumer*

trends (eating fried foods might be okay one year and out the next). Finally, a number of decisions made by the industry result from its *desire to be a good corporate citizen*. For example, several fast food chains have responded to environmental concerns by eliminating Styrofoam containers.[1] As you move through this text, you'll learn more about these external influences on business. (The next section of this chapter will introduce one of these external factors—the economy—in detail.)

QUICK QUIZ 1.1

Before beginning your study of economic concepts, take a few minutes to test your knowledge of the material that you've just read.

Go to www.exploringbusinessonline.com

What Is Economics?

To appreciate how a business functions, we need to know something about the economic environment in which it operates. The following section provides an overview of economic principles. We begin with a discussion of the *free-enterprise system*, the concepts of *supply and demand*, and the nature of *competition*. Then we'll explain the ways in which the health of an economy is measured.

RESOURCES: INPUTS AND OUTPUTS

Economics is the study of how scarce resources are used to produce outputs—goods and services—to be distributed among people. **Resources** are the *inputs* used to produce *outputs*. Resources may include any or all of the following:

- Land and other natural resources
- Labor (physical and mental)
- Capital, including buildings, equipment, and money
- Entrepreneurship

Resources are combined to produce goods and services. Land and natural resources

Figure 1.1

Business and Its Environment

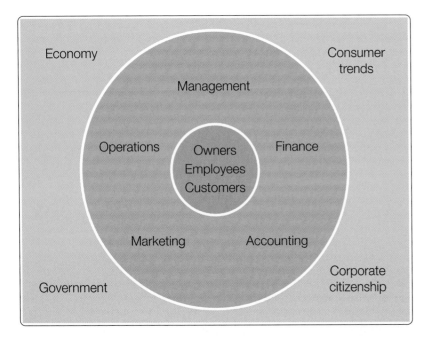

provide the needed raw materials. Labor transforms raw materials into goods and services. Capital (equipment, buildings, vehicles, cash, and so forth) are needed for the production process. Entrepreneurship provides the skill and creativity needed to bring the other resources together in order to capitalize on an idea.

Because a business uses resources to *produce* things, we also call them **factors of production**. The factors of production used to produce a shirt would include:

- The land that the shirt factory sits on, the electricity used to run the plant, and the raw cotton from which the shirts are made.

- The laborers who make the shirts.

- The factory and equipment used in the manufacturing process as well as the money needed to operate the factory.

- The entrepreneurship skill used to coordinate the other resources to initiate the production process.

Input and Output Markets

Many of the factors of production (or resources) are provided to businesses by households. For example, households provide businesses with labor (as workers), land and buildings (as landlords), and capital (as investors). In turn, businesses pay households for these resources by providing them with income, such as wages, rent, and interest. The resources obtained from households are then used by businesses to produce goods and services, which are sold to the same households that provide businesses with revenue. The revenue obtained by businesses is then used to buy additional resources, and the cycle continues. This circular flow is described in Figure 1.2, which illustrates the dual roles of households and businesses:

- Households not only provide factors of production (or resources) but also consume goods and services.

- Businesses not only buy resources but also produce and sell goods and services.

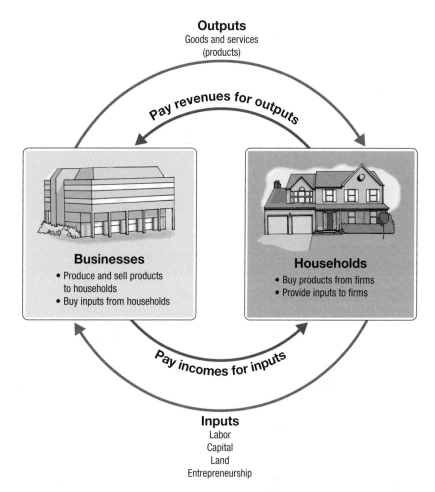

Figure 1.2 ACTIVE

The Circular Flow of Inputs and Outputs

The Questions Economists Ask

Economists study the interactions between households and businesses and look at the ways in which the factors of production are combined to produce the goods and services that people need. Basically, economists try to answer three sets of questions:

1. *What goods and services should be produced to meet consumers' needs?* In what quantity? When should they be produced?

2. *How should goods and services be produced?* Who should produce them and what resources, including technology, should be combined to produce them?

3. *Who should receive the goods and services produced?* How should they be allocated among consumers?

economics
Study of how scarce resources are used to produce outputs—goods and services—that are distributed among people.

resources
Inputs used to produce outputs.

factors of production
Resources consisting of land, labor, capital (money, buildings, equipment), and entrepreneurial skills combined to produce goods and services.

Apple uses a number of inputs, or resources, to make the iPod that this customer is enjoying. It gets these resources (labor, materials, capital) from individuals. It pays individuals for these resources by providing them with income, such as wages or interest. These individuals can then use the money they receive to buy goods and services, including iPods. If this customer buys the iPod he's trying out, Apple can use the revenues it receives from the sale to buy more resources to make more iPods.

ECONOMIC SYSTEMS

The answers to these questions depend on a country's **economic system**—the means by which a society (households, businesses, and government) makes decisions about allocating resources to produce products and about distributing those products. The degree to which individuals and business owners, as opposed to the government, enjoy freedom in making these decisions varies according to the type of economic system. Generally speaking, economic systems can be divided into two systems: *planned systems* and *free market systems*.

Planned Systems

In a planned system, the government exerts control over the allocation and distribution of all or some goods and services. The system with the highest level of government control is **communism**. In theory, a communist economy is one in which the government owns all or most enterprises. Central planning by the government dictates which goods or services are produced, how they are produced, and who will receive them. In practice, pure communism is practically nonexistent today, and only a few countries (notably North

Korea and Cuba) operate under rigid centrally planned economic systems.

Under **socialism**, industries that provide essential services, such as utilities, banking, and health care, may be government owned. Other businesses are owned privately. Central planning allocates the goods and services produced by government-run industries and tries to ensure that the resulting wealth is distributed equally. In contrast, privately owned companies are operated for the purpose of making a profit for their owners. In general, workers in socialist economies work fewer hours, have longer vacations, and receive more health, education, and childcare benefits than do workers in capitalist economies. To offset the high cost of public services, taxes are generally steep. Examples of socialist countries include Sweden and France.

Free Market System

The economic system in which most businesses are owned and operated by individuals is the **free market system**, also known as **capitalism**. As we will see next, in a free market, *competition* dictates how goods and services will be allocated. Business is conducted with only limited government involvement. The economies of the United States and other countries, such as Japan, are based on capitalism.

How Economic Systems Compare

In comparing economic systems, it is helpful to think of a continuum with communism at one end and pure capitalism at the other, as in Figure 1.3. As you move from left to right, the amount of government control over business diminishes. So, too, does the level of social services, such as free health care, childcare services, social security, unemployment benefits.

Mixed Market Economy

Although it's possible to have a pure communist system, or a pure capitalist (free market) system, in reality many economic systems are mixed. A **mixed market economy** relies on both markets and the government to allocate resources. We have already seen that this is what happens in socialist economies in which the government controls selected major industries, such as transportation and health care, while allowing individual ownership of other industries. Even previously communist economies, such as those of Eastern Europe and China, are becoming more mixed as they adopt capitalistic characteristics and convert previously government-owned businesses to private ownership through a process called **privatization**.

The U.S. Economic System

Like most countries, the United States features a mixed market system: Although the U.S. economic system is primarily a free market system, the federal government controls some basic services, such as the postal service and air traffic control. The U.S. economy also has some characteristics of a socialist system, such as providing social security retirement benefits to retired workers.

The free market system was espoused by Adam Smith in his book *The Wealth of Nations*, published in 1776.[2] According to Smith, competition alone would ensure that consumers received the best products at the best prices. In the kind of competition assumed by Smith, a seller who tries to charge more for his product than other sellers won't be able to find any buyers. A job-seeker who asks more than the going wage won't be hired. Because the "invisible hand" of competition will make the market work effectively, there will be no need to regulate prices or wages.

Almost immediately, however, a tension developed among free market theorists between the principle of *laissez-faire*—leaving things alone—and government intervention. Today, it's common for the U.S. government to intervene in the operation of the economic system. For example, government exerts influence on the food and pharmaceutical industries through the Food and Drug Administration, which protects consumers by preventing unsafe or mislabeled products from reaching the market.

To appreciate how businesses operate, we must first get an idea of how prices are set in

Planned systems   Free market systems

| Communism | Socialism | Capitalism |

High degree of government control   Low degree of government control
High level of social services   Low level of social services

Figure 1.3

The Spectrum of Economic Systems

competitive markets. Thus, the next section begins by describing how markets set prices in an environment of *perfect competition*. We then explore other variations on the competitive model.

Types of Competition

Under a mixed economy, such as we have in the United States, businesses make decisions about what goods to produce or services to offer and how they are priced. Because there are many businesses making goods or providing services, customers can choose among a wide array of products. The competition for sales among businesses is a vital part of our economic system. Economists have identified four types of competition—*perfect competition, monopolistic competition, oligopoly*, and *monopoly*—that we will cover in this section.

PERFECT COMPETITION

Perfect competition exists when there are many consumers buying a standardized product from numerous small businesses. Because no seller is big enough or influential enough to affect price, sellers and buyers accept the going price. For example, when a fisherman brings his fish to the local market, he has little control over the price he gets and must accept the going rate.

economic system
Means by which a society makes decisions about allocating resources to produce and distribute products.

communism
Economic system featuring the highest level of government control over allocation and distribution.

socialism
Economic system falling between communism and capitalism in terms of government control over allocation and distribution.

free market system
Economic system in which most businesses are owned and operated by individuals.

capitalism
Economic system featuring the lowest level of government control over allocation and distribution.

mixed market economy
Economic system that relies on both markets and government to allocate resources.

privatization
Process of converting government-owned businesses to private ownership.

perfect competition
Market in which many consumers buy standardized products from numerous small businesses.

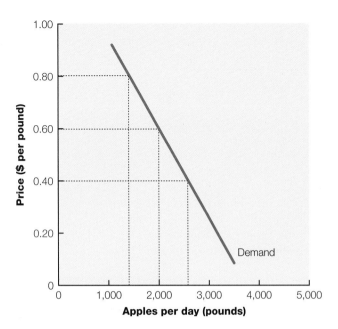

Figure 1.4

The Demand Curve

Finally, we'll see how supply and demand interact to create an *equilibrium price*—the price at which buyers are willing to purchase the amount that sellers are willing to sell.

Demand and the Demand Curve

Demand is the quantity of a product that buyers are willing to purchase at various prices. The quantity of a product that people are willing to buy depends on its price. You are typically willing to buy *less* of a product when prices *rise* and *more* of a product when prices *fall*. Generally speaking, we find products more attractive at lower prices, and we buy more at lower prices because our income goes further.

Using this logic, we can construct a **demand curve** that shows the quantity of a product that will be demanded at different prices. Let's assume that the diagram in Figure 1.4 represents the daily price and quantity of apples sold by farmers at a local market. Note that as the price of apples goes down, buyers' demand goes up. Thus, if a pound of apples sells for $0.80, buyers will be willing to purchase only 1,500 pounds per day. But if apples cost only $0.60 a pound, buyers will be willing to purchase 2,000 pounds. At $0.40 a pound, buyers will be willing to purchase 2,500 pounds.

The Basics of Supply and Demand

To appreciate how perfect competition works, we need to understand how buyers and sellers interact in a market to set prices. In a market characterized by perfect competition, price is determined through the mechanisms of *supply* and *demand*. Prices are influenced both by the supply of products from sellers and by the demand for products by buyers.

To illustrate this concept, let's create a *supply and demand schedule* for one particular good sold at one point in time. Then we'll define *demand* and create a *demand curve* and define *supply* and create a *supply curve*.

Supply and the Supply Curve Supply is the quantity of a product that sellers are willing to sell at various prices. The quantity of a product that a business is willing to sell depends on its price. Businesses are *more* willing to sell a product when the price *rises* and *less* willing to sell it when prices *fall*. Again, this fact makes sense: Businesses are set up to make profits, and there are larger profits to be made when prices are high.

Now we can construct a **supply curve** that shows the quantity of apples that farmers would be willing to sell at different prices, regardless of demand. As you can see in Figure 1.5, the supply curve goes in the opposite direction from the demand curve: As prices rise, the quantity of apples that farmers are willing to sell also goes up. The supply curve shows that farmers are willing to sell only 1,000 pounds of apples when the price is $0.40 a pound, 2,000 pounds when the price is $0.60, and 3,000 pounds when the price is $0.80.

Figure 1.5

The Supply Curve

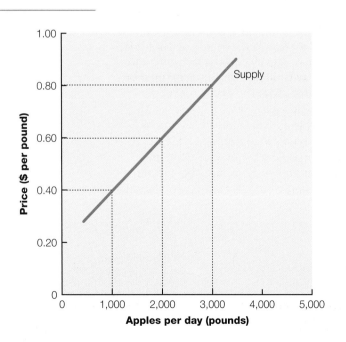

Equilibrium Price We can now see how the market mechanism works under perfect competition. We do this by plotting both the supply curve and the demand curve on one graph, as we've done in Figure 1.6. The point at which the two curves intersect is the **equilibrium price**. At this point, buyers' demand for apples and sellers' supply of apples is in equilibrium.

You can see in Figure 1.6 that the supply and demand curves intersect at the price of $0.60 and quantity of 2,000 pounds. Thus, $0.60 is the equilibrium price: At this price, the quantity of apples demanded by buyers equals the quantity of apples that farmers are willing to supply. If a farmer tries to charge more than $0.60 for a pound of apples, he won't sell very many and his profits will go down. If, on the other hand, a farmer tries to charge less than the equilibrium price of $0.60 a pound, he will sell more apples but his profit per pound will be less than at the equilibrium price.

What have we learned in this discussion? We've learned that without outside influences, markets in an environment of perfect competition will arrive at an equilibrium point at which both buyers and sellers are satisfied. But we must be aware that this is a very simplistic example. Things are much more complex in the real world. For one thing, markets rarely operate without outside influences. Sometimes, sellers supply more of a product than buyers are willing to purchase; in that case, there's a *surplus*. Sometimes, they don't produce enough of a product to satisfy demand; then we have a *shortage*.

Circumstances also have a habit of changing. What would happen, for example, if income rose and buyers were willing to pay more for apples? The demand curve would change, resulting in an increase in equilibrium price. This outcome makes intuitive sense: As demand increases, prices will go up. What would happen if apple crops were larger than expected because of favorable weather conditions? Farmers might be will-

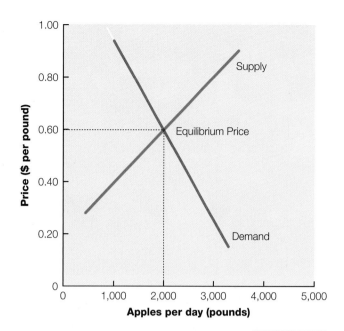

ing to sell apples at lower prices. If so, the supply curve would shift, resulting in another change in equilibrium price: The increase in supply would bring down prices.

MONOPOLISTIC COMPETITION

In **monopolistic competition**, we still have many sellers (as we had under perfect competition). Now, however, they don't sell identical products. Instead, they sell *differentiated* products—products that differ somewhat, or are *perceived* to differ, even though they serve a similar purpose. Products can be differentiated in a number of ways, including quality, style, convenience, location, and brand name. Some people prefer Coke over Pepsi, even though the two products are quite similar. But what if there was a substantial price difference between the two? In that case, buyers could be persuaded to switch from one to the other. Thus, if Coke has a big promotional sale at a supermarket chain, it will get some Pepsi drinkers to switch (at least temporarily).

How is product differentiation accomplished? Sometimes, it's simply geographical; you probably buy gasoline at the station

---

demand
Quantity of a product that buyers are willing to purchase at various prices.

demand curve
Graph showing the quantity of a product that will be bought at certain prices.

supply
Quantity of a product that sellers are willing to sell at various prices.

supply curve
Graph showing the quantity of a product that will be offered for sale at certain prices.

equilibrium price
Price at which buyers are willing to buy exactly the amount that sellers are willing to sell.

monopolistic competition
Market in which many sellers supply differentiated products.

Coca-Cola and Pepsi bottlers operate under monopolistic competition. Even though both sodas serve a similar purpose, their companies try to differentiate them through advertising. Here, we see ads for the products placed side-by-side on billboards in India.

closest to your house regardless of the brand. At other times, perceived differences between products are promoted by advertising designed to convince consumers that one product is different:—and better than—another. Regardless of customer loyalty to a product, however, if its price goes too high, the seller will lose business to a competitor. Under monopolistic competition, therefore,

How would you like to have this car? It looks great but comes with a pretty high price tag. Porsche, like other automobile companies, operates in an oligopolistic market. The number of sellers in the market is limited because it's such an expensive business to get into.

companies have only limited control over price.

OLIGOPOLY

Oligopoly means few sellers. In an oligopolistic market, each seller supplies a large portion of all the products sold in the marketplace. In addition, because the cost of starting a business in an oligopolistic industry is usually high, the number of firms entering it is low.

Companies in oligopolistic industries include such large-scale enterprises as automobile companies and airlines. As large firms supplying a sizeable portion of a market, these companies have some control over the prices they charge. But there's a catch: Because products are fairly similar, when one company lowers prices, others are often forced to follow suit in order to remain competitive. You see this practice all the time in the airline industry: When American Airlines announces a fare decrease, Continental, United Airlines, and others do likewise. When one automaker offers a special deal, its competitors usually come up with similar promotions.

MONOPOLY

In terms of number of sellers and degree of competition, monopolies are at the opposite end of the spectrum from perfect competition. In perfect competition, there are many small companies, none of whom can control prices; they simply accept the market price determined by supply and demand. In a **monopoly**, there is only one seller in the market. The market could be a geographical area, such as a city or a regional area, and does not necessarily have to be an entire country.

There aren't very many monopolies in the United States because the government limits them. Most fall into one of two categories: *natural* and *legal*. **Natural monopolies** include public utilities, such as electricity and gas suppliers. Such enterprises require huge investments, and it would be inefficient to duplicate the products that they provide. They inhibit competition, but they're legal because they're important to society. In exchange for the right to conduct business without competition, they're regulated. For instance, they can't charge whatever prices

Because almost all PCs use Microsoft's Windows as their operating system, Microsoft is almost a monopoly in that area. Bill Gates, chairman and chief software architect of Microsoft (and world's wealthiest person), sits in front of a wall of Windows software packages.

they want, but, must adhere to government-controlled prices. As a rule, they're required to serve all customers, even if doing so isn't cost efficient.

A **legal monopoly** arises when a company receives a patent giving it exclusive use of an invented product or process. Patents are issued for a limited period of time, generally 20 years.[3] During this period, other companies can't use the invented product or process without permission from the patent holder. Patents allow companies a period of time to recover the heavy costs of researching and developing products and technologies. A classic example of a company that enjoyed a patent-based legal monopoly is Polaroid, which for years held exclusive ownership of instant-film technology.[4] Polaroid priced the product high enough to recoup, over time, the high cost of bringing it to market. Without competition, in other words, it enjoyed a monopolistic position in regard to pricing.

QUICK QUIZ   1.2

Before you learn how the government influences the economy, test your understanding of the economic concepts introduced in this section.

Go to www.exploringbusinessonline.com

Measuring the Health of the Economy

Every day, we are bombarded with economic news. We're told that the economy has been in a recession and unemployment is on the rise, or that industrial production has gone up, inflation is flat, housing starts have soared, jobless claims have dropped, and consumer confidence is up. As a student learning about business, you need to understand the nature of the U.S. economy and the terminology that we use to describe it. You need to have some idea of where the

oligopoly
Market in which a few sellers supply a large portion of all the products sold in the marketplace.

monopoly
Market in which there is only one seller supplying products at regulated prices.

natural monopoly
Monopoly, in which, because of the industry's importance to society, one seller is permitted to supply products without competition.

legal monopoly
Monopoly in which one seller supplies a product or technology to which it holds a patent.

economy is heading, and you need to know something about the government's role in influencing its direction.

ECONOMIC GOALS

All the world's economies share three main goals:

1. Growth

2. High employment

3. Price stability

Let's take a closer look at each of these goals, both to find out what they mean and to show how we know whether or not they're being met. Later in the chapter, we'll discuss the government's role in helping the U.S. economy achieve these goals.

Economic Growth

One purpose of an economy is to provide people with goods and services—cars, computers, video games, houses, rock concerts, fast food, amusement parks. One way in which economists measure the performance of an economy is by looking at a widely used measure of total output called **gross domestic product (GDP)**. GDP is defined as the market value of all goods and services produced by the economy in a given year. In the United States, it's calculated by the Department of Commerce. GDP includes only those goods and services produced domestically; goods produced outside the country are excluded. GDP also includes only those goods and services that are produced for the final user; intermediate products are excluded. For example, the chip that goes into a computer (an intermediate product) would not count even though the computer would.

By itself, GDP doesn't necessarily tell us very much about the state of the economy. But *change* in GDP does. If GDP (after adjusting for inflation) goes up, the economy is growing. If it goes down, the economy is contracting.

The Business Cycle The economic ups and downs due to expansion and contraction constitute the **business cycle**. A typical cycle runs from three to five years but could last much longer. Though typically irregular, a cycle can be divided into four general phases: *prosperity*, *recession*, *depression* (which the cycle generally skips), and *recovery*:

- During *prosperity*, the economy expands, unemployment is low, incomes rise, and consumers buy more products. Businesses respond by increasing production and offering new and better products.

- Eventually, however, things slow down. GDP decreases, unemployment goes up, and because people have less money to spend, business revenues decline. This slowdown in economic activity is called a **recession**. Economists often say that we're entering a recession when GDP goes down for two consecutive quarters.

- Generally, a recession is followed by a *recovery* in which the economy starts growing again.

- If, however, a recession lasts a long time (perhaps a decade or so), unemployment remains very high, and production is severely curtailed, the economy could sink into a **depression**. Though not impossible, it's unlikely that the U.S. will experience another severe depression like that of the 1930s. The federal government has a number of economic tools (some of which we'll discuss shortly) with which to fight any threat of a depression.

Full Employment

In order to keep the economy going strong, people must spend money on goods and services. A reduction in personal expenditures for things like food, clothing, appliances, automobiles, housing, and medical care could severely reduce GDP and weaken the economy. Because most people earn their spending money by working, an important goal of all economies is making jobs available to everyone who wants one. In principle, **full employment** occurs when everyone who wants to work has a job. In practice, we say that we have "full employment" when about 95 percent of those wanting to work are employed.

The Unemployment Rate The U.S. Department of Labor tracks unemployment and reports the **unemployment rate**: the percentage of the labor force that's unemployed and actively seeking work. The unemployment rate is an important measure of economic health. It goes up during recessionary periods because companies are reluctant to hire workers when demand for goods and services is low.

Conversely, it goes down when the economy is expanding and there is high demand for products and workers to supply them.

Figure 1.7 traces the U.S. unemployment rate between 1970 and 2005. If you want to know the current unemployment rate, go to the CNNMoney Web site, locate the "Jobs and Economy" section, and click on "Job Growth."

Price Stability

A third major goal of all economies is maintaining **price stability**. Price stability occurs when the average of the prices for goods and services either does not change or changes very little. Rising prices are troublesome for both individuals and businesses. For individuals, rising prices mean you have to pay more for the things you need. For businesses, rising prices mean higher costs, and, at least in the short run, they might have trouble passing on higher costs to consumers. When the overall price level goes up, we have **inflation**. Figure 1.8 shows inflationary trends in the U. S. economy since 1960. When the price level goes down (which rarely happens), we have **deflation**.

The Consumer Price Index The most widely publicized measure of inflation is the **consumer price index (CPI)**, which is reported monthly by the Bureau of Labor Statistics. The CPI measures the rate of inflation by determining price changes of a hypothetical basket of goods, such as food, housing, clothing, medical care, appliances, automobiles, and so forth, bought by a typical household.

The CPI base period is 1982 to 1984, which has been given an average value of 100. Table 1.1 gives CPI values computed for selected years. The CPI value for 1950, for instance, is 24. This means that $1 of typical

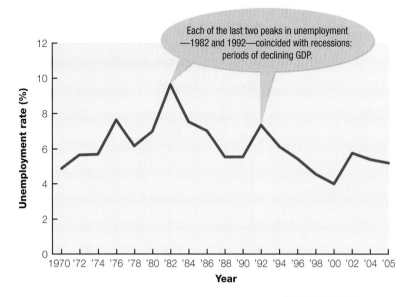

purchases in 1982 through 1984 would have cost $0.24 cents in 1950. Conversely, you would have needed $1.95 to purchase the same $1 worth of typical goods in 2005. The difference registers the effect of inflation. In fact, that's what an *inflation rate* is—*the percentage change in a price index*.

You can find out the current CPI by going to the CNNMoney Web site, locate

Figure 1.7

The U.S. Unemployment Rate, 1970–2005

Figure 1.8

The U.S. Inflation Rate, 1960–2005

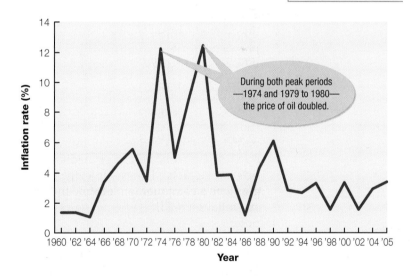

---

gross domestic product (GDP)
Measure of the market value of all goods and services produced by a nation's economy in a given year.

business cycle
Pattern of expansion and contraction in an economy.

recession
Economic slowdown measured by a decline in gross domestic productivity.

depression
Severe, long-lasting recession.

full employment
Condition under which about 95% of those who want to work are employed.

unemployment rate
Percentage of the total labor force that's currently unemployed and actively seeking work.

price stability
Conditions under which the prices for products remain fairly constant.

inflation
Rise in the overall price level.

deflation
Decrease in overall price level.

consumer price index (CPI)
Index that measures inflation by measuring the prices of goods purchased by a typical consumer.

TABLE 1.1

Selected CPI Values, 1950–2005

Year	CPI
1950	24.1
1960	29.1
1970	38.8
1980	82.4
1990	130.7
1991	136.2
1992	140.3
1993	144.5
1994	148.2
1995	152.4
1996	156.9
1997	160.5
1998	163.0
1999	166.6
2000	172.2
2001	177.1
2002	179.9
2003	184.0
2004	188.9
2005	195.3

the "Jobs and Economy" section, and click on "Inflation (CPI)."

ECONOMIC FORECASTING

In the previous section, we introduced several measures that economists use to assess the performance of the economy at a given point in time. By looking at changes in GDP, for instance, we can see whether the economy is growing. The CPI allows us to gauge inflation. These measures help us understand where the economy stands today. But what if we want to get a sense of where it's headed in the future? To a certain extent, we can forecast future economic trends by analyzing some leading economic indicators.

Economic Indicators

An **economic indicator** is a statistic that provides valuable information about the economy. There is no shortage of economic indicators, and trying to follow them all would be an overwhelming task. Thus, economists and businesspeople track only a select few, including those that we will discuss in the next section.

Lagging and Leading Indicators Statistics that report the status of the economy a few months in the past are called **lagging economic indicators**. One such indicator is *average length of unemployment*. If unemployed workers have remained out of work for a long time, we may infer that the economy has been slow. Indicators that predict the status of the economy three to twelve months in the future are called **leading economic indicators**. If a leading indicator rises, the economy is likely to expand in the coming year. If it falls, the economy is likely to contract.

To predict where the economy is headed, we must obviously examine several leading indicators. It's also helpful to look at indicators from different sectors of the economy—labor, manufacturing, and housing. One useful indicator of the outlook for future jobs is the number of new *claims for unemployment insurance*. This measure tells us how many people recently lost their jobs. If it's rising, it signals trouble ahead because unemployed consumers can't buy as many goods and services as they could if they had paychecks.

To gauge the level of goods to be produced in the future (which will translate into future sales), economists look at a statistic called *average weekly manufacturing hours*. This measure tells us the average number of hours worked per week by production workers in manufacturing industries. If it's on the rise, the economy will probably improve. For assessing the strength of the housing market, *building permits* is often a good indicator. An increase in this statistic—which tells us how many new housing units are being built—indicates that the economy is improving. Why? Because increased building brings money into the economy, not only through new home sales but through sales of furniture and appliances to furnish them.

Finally, if you want a measure that combines all of these economic indicators, as well as others, a private research firm called the Conference Board publishes a *U.S. leading index*. To get an idea of what leading economic indicators are telling us about the state of the economy today, go to the "Jobs and Economy" section of the CNNMoney Web site, and click on "Leading Indicators."

Consumer Confidence Index The Conference Board also publishes a **consumer confidence index** based on results of a monthly survey of 5,000 U.S. households. The survey gathers consumers' opinions on the health of the economy and their plans for future purchases. It's often a good indicator of future buying intent on the part of consumers. For information on current consumer confidence, go to the CNNMoney Web site , click on the "Jobs and Economy" section, and then click on "Consumer Confidence."

Government's Role in Managing the Economy

In every country, the government takes steps to help the economy achieve the goals of growth, full employment, and price stability. In the United States, the government influences economic activity through two approaches: monetary policy and fiscal policy. Through **monetary policy**, the government exerts its power to regulate the money supply and level of interest rates. Through **fiscal policy**, it uses its power to tax and to spend.

MONETARY POLICY

Monetary policy is exercised by the Federal Reserve System ("the Fed"), which is empowered to take various actions that decrease or increase the money supply and raise or lower short-term interest rates, making it harder or easier to borrow money. When the Fed believes that inflation is a problem, it will use *contractionary policy* to decrease the money supply and raise interest rates. When rates are higher, borrowers

The unemployment rate is the percentage of the labor force that's unemployed and actively seeking work. Average length of unemployment is a lagging economic indicator: If most of the people at this job service center have been out of work for a long time, we can infer that the economy has been slow. If most of these people have filed new claims for unemployment insurance, they've probably lost their jobs recently. This situation is a leading economic indicator because is signals trouble ahead.

have to pay more for the money they borrow, and banks are more selective in making loans. Because money is "tighter"—more expensive—demand for goods and services will go down, and so will prices. In any case, that's the theory.

To counter a recession, the Fed uses *expansionary policy* to increase the money supply and reduce interest rates. With lower interest rates, it's cheaper to borrow money, and banks are more willing to loan it. We then say that money is "easy." Attractive interest rates encourage businesses to borrow money in order to expand production and encourage consumers to buy more goods and services. In theory, both sets of actions will help the economy escape the recession.

FISCAL POLICY

Fiscal policy relies on the government's powers of spending and taxation. Both taxation and government spending can be used

---

economic indicator
Statistic that provides information about trends in the economy.

lagging economic indicator
Statistical data that measure economic trends after the overall economy has changed.

leading economic indicator
Statistical data that predict the status of the economy three to twelve months in the future.

consumer confidence index
Measure of optimism that consumers express about the economy as they go about their everyday lives.

monetary policy
Efforts exerted by the Federal Reserve System ("the Fed") to regulate the nation's money supply.

fiscal policy
Governmental use of taxation and spending to influence economic conditions.

to reduce or increase the total supply of money in the economy—the total amount, in other words, that businesses and consumers have to spend. When the country is in a recession, the appropriate policy is to increase spending, reduce taxes, or both. Such expansionary actions will put more money in the hands of businesses and consumers, encouraging businesses to expand and consumers to buy more goods and services. When the economy is experiencing inflation, the opposite policy is adopted: The government will decrease spending and/or increase taxes. Because such contractionary measures reduce spending by businesses and consumers, prices come down and inflation eases.

The National Debt

If, in any given year, the government takes in more money (through taxes) than it spends on goods and services (for things such as defense, transportation, and social services), the result is a budget *surplus*. If, on the other hand, the government spends more than it takes in, we have a budget *deficit* (which the government pays off by borrowing through the issuance of Treasury bonds). Historically, deficits have occurred much more often than surpluses; typically, the government spends more than it takes in. Consequently, the U.S. government now has a total **national debt** of more than $7 *trillion*.

As you can see in Figure 1.9, this number has risen dramatically in the last 65 years. The significant jump that starts in the 1980s reflects several factors: a big increase in government spending (especially on defense), a substantial rise in interest payments on the

debt, and lower tax rates. As of this writing, your share is $28,197.30. If you want to see what the national debt is today—and what your current share is—go on the Web to the U.S. National Debt Clock.

MACROECONOMICS AND MICROECONOMICS

In the preceding discussion, we've touched on two main areas in the field of economics: (1) *macroeconomics*—the study of the economy as a whole—and (2) *microeconomics*—the study of the economic choices made by individual consumers or businesses. Macroeconomics examines the economywide effect of inflation, while microeconomics considers such decisions as the price you're willing to pay to go to college. Macroeconomics investigates overall trends in imports and exports, while microeconomics explains the price that teenagers are willing to pay for concert tickets. Although they are often regarded as separate branches of economics, we can gain a richer understanding of the economy by studying issues from both perspectives. As we've seen in this chapter, for instance, you can better understand the overall level of activity in an economy (a macro issue) through an understanding of supply and demand (a micro issue).

QUICK QUIZ   1.3

Test your understanding of criteria for assessing the economy and government's role in influencing its direction.

Go to www.exploringbusinessonline.com

Where We're Headed

In this chapter, we introduced some basic concepts of business and economics. You got an overview of the people and functional activities of business, and the chapters that follow will build on this foundation as you continue your study of the dynamic world of business. In Chapter 2, we'll discuss the challenges and risks involved in starting and managing a new business. You'll also learn about the advantages and disadvantages of business ownership and the importance of planning for your own business.

Figure 1.9

The U.S. National Debt, 1940–2005

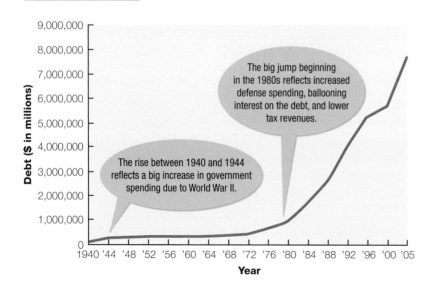

The rise between 1940 and 1944 reflects a big increase in government spending due to World War II.

The big jump beginning in the 1980s reflects increased defense spending, ballooning interest on the debt, and lower tax revenues.

Debt ($ in millions)

Year

Summary of Learning Objectives

1. **Identify the main participants of business, the functions that most businesses perform, and the external forces that influence business activities.**

    The main participants in a business are its owners, employees, and customers. Businesses are influenced by such external factors as the economy, government, consumer trends, and public pressure to act as good corporate citizens. The activities needed to run a business can be divided into five functional areas: (1) **Management** involves planning, organizing, staffing, directing, and controlling resources to achieve organizational goals. (2) **Operations** transforms resources (labor, materials, money, etc.) into products. (3) **Marketing** works to identify and satisfy customers' needs. (4) **Finance** involves planning for, obtaining, and managing company funds. (5) **Accounting** entails measuring, summarizing, and communicating financial and managerial information.

2. **Define *economics* and explain how economists answer the three key economics questions.**

    Economics is the study of how scarce resources (or **factors of production**) are used to produce the goods and services that will be distributed among people. Economists address these three questions: (1) What goods and services should be produced to meet consumer needs? (2) How should they be produced, and who should produce them? (3) Who should receive goods and services? The answers to these questions depend on a country's **economic system**. The primary economic systems that exist today are planned and free market systems. In a planned system, such as **communism** and **socialism**, the government exerts control over the production and distribution of all or some goods and services. In a **free market system**, also known as **capitalism**, business is conducted with only limited government involvement. Competition determines what goods and services are produced, how they are produced, and for whom.

3. **Describe the different forms of competition.**

    In a free market system, there are four types of competition: (1) Under **perfect competition**, many small companies sell identical products. Because no company is large enough to control price, each simply accepts the market price. (2) Under **monopolistic competition**, many sellers offer differentiated products—products that differ slightly (or are perceived to be different) but serve similar purposes. By making consumers aware of product differences, sellers exert some control over price. (3) In an **oligopoly**, a few sellers supply a sizable portion of products in the market. They exert some control over price, but because their products are similar, when one company lowers prices, the others follow. (4) Under a **monopoly**, a single seller is able to control prices.

4. **Explain how supply and demand interact to set prices in a free market system.**

    In a free market system, buyers and sellers interact in a market to set prices. When the market is characterized by **perfect competition**, price is determined by supply and demand. **Supply** is the quantity of a product that sellers are willing to sell at various prices. **Demand** is the quantity of a product that buyers are willing to purchase at various prices. The quantity of a product that people will buy depends on its price: They'll buy more when the price is low and less when it's high. Price also influences the quantity of a product that producers are willing to supply: They'll sell more of a product when prices are high and less when they're low. In a competitive market, the decisions of buyers and sellers interact until the market reaches an **equilibrium price**—the price at which buyers are willing to buy the same amount that sellers are willing to sell.

5. **Understand the criteria used to assess the status of the U.S. economy.**

    All economies share three goals: (1) *Growth*. An economy provides people with goods and services, and economists measure its performance by studying **gross domestic product (GDP)**—the market value of all goods and services produced by the economy in a given year. If GDP goes up, the economy is growing; if it goes down, the economy is contracting. (2) *High employment*. Because most people earn their money by working, a goal of all economies is making jobs available to everyone who wants one. The U.S. government reports an **unemployment rate**—the percentage of the labor force that's unemployed and actively seeking work. This rate goes up during recessionary periods and down

national debt
Total amount of money owed by the federal government.

when the economy is expanding. (3) *Price stability.* **Price stability** occurs when the average prices of products either do not change or change very little. When overall prices go up, we have **inflation**; when they go down, we have **deflation**. The **consumer price index (CPI)** measures inflation by determining the change in prices of a hypothetical basket of goods bought by a typical household. GDP and CPI measure the current status of the economy. To get a sense of where it's headed in the future, we use statistics called **economic indicators**. Indicators which, like *average length of unemployment*, report the status of the economy a few months in the past are **lagging economic indicators**. Those, like *new claims for unemployment insurance*, that predict the status of the economy three to twelve months in the future are **leading economic indicators**.

6. **Discuss the government's role in managing the economy.**

   The U.S. government uses two types of policies to influence economic performance, both of which have the same purpose: to help the economy achieve growth, full employment, and price stability. (1) **Monetary policy** is used to control the money supply and interest rates. It is exercised through an independent government agency called the Federal Reserve System ("the Fed"), which has the power to control the money supply and interest rates. When the Fed believes that inflation is a problem, it will use *contractionary policy* to decrease the money supply and raise interest rates; to counter a recession, it will use *expansionary policy* to increase the money supply and reduce interest rates. (2) **Fiscal policy** uses the government's power to spend and tax. When the country is in a recession, the government will increase spending, reduce taxes, or do both to expand the economy. When we're experiencing inflation, it will decrease spending and/or increase taxes. When the government takes in more money in a given year (through taxes) than it spends, the result is a *surplus*. When the opposite happens—government spends more money than it takes in—we have a *deficit*. The cumulative sum of deficits is the **national debt**—the total amount of money owed by the federal government.

Questions and Problems

1. **AACSB** ▶ **Analysis**

   The Martin family has been making guitars out of its Nazareth, PA, factory for more than 150 years. In 2004, Martin Guitar was proud to produce its millionth instrument. Go to www.exploringbusinessonline.com to link to the Martin Guitar Web site and read about the company's long history. You'll discover that, even though it's a family-run company with a fairly unique product, it operates like any other company. Identify the main activities or functions of Martin Guitar's business and explain how each activity benefits the company.

2. **AACSB** ▶ **Analysis**

   Name four external factors that have an influence on business. Give examples of the ways in which each factor can affect the business performance of two companies: McDonald's and General Motors.

3. If you started a business that made surfboards, what factors of production would you need to make your product? Where would you get them? Where would you get the money you'd need to pay for additional resources?

4. What three key questions do economists try to answer? Will answers to these questions differ depending on whether they're working in the United States or Cuba? Explain your answer.

5. Identify the four types of competition, explain the differences among them, and provide two examples of each. (Use examples that are different from those given in the text.)

6. **AACSB** ▶ **Analysis**

   You just ran across three interesting statistics: (1) the world's current supply of oil is estimated to be 1.3 trillion barrels; (2) the worldwide use of oil is 30 billion barrels a year; and (3) at this rate of consumption, we'll run out of oil in 43 years. Overcoming an initial sense of impending catastrophe, you remember the discussion of supply and demand in this chapter and realize that things aren't as simple as they seem. After all, many factors affect both the supply of oil and the demand for products made from it, such as gasoline. These factors will influence when (and if) the world runs out of oil. Answer the following questions and provide explanations for your answers:

   a. What is the major factor that affects the *supply* of oil? (*Hint:* It's the same major factor affecting the *demand* for oil.)

   b. If producers find additional oil reserves, what will happen to the price of oil?

c. If producers must extract oil from more costly wells, what will happen to the price that you pay to fill up your gas tank?

d. If China's economy continues to expand rapidly, what will happen to the price of oil?

e. If drivers in the United States start favoring fuel-efficient cars over SUVs, will gas be cheaper or more expensive?

f. In your opinion, will oil producers be able to supply enough oil to meet the increasing demand for oil-related products, such as gasoline?

7. AACSB ▶ **Analysis**

Congratulations! You entered a sweepstakes and won a fantastic prize: a trip around the world. There's only one catch: You have to study the economy of each country (from the list below) that you visit and identify the current phase of its business cycle. Be sure to explain your responses.

- *Country 1:* Although the landscape is beautiful and the weather is superb, a lot of people seem unhappy. Business is slow, and production has dropped steadily for the past six months. Revenues are down, companies are laying off workers, and there's less money around to spend.

- *Country 2:* Here, people are happily busy. Almost everyone has a job and makes a good income. They spend freely, and businesses respond by offering a steady outflow of new products.

- *Country 3:* Citizens of this country report that, for a while, life had been tough; lots of people were jobless, and money was tight. But things are getting much better. Workers are being called back to their jobs, production is improving, and people are spending again.

- *Country 4:* This place makes you so depressed that you can't wait to get back home. People seem defeated, mostly because many have been without jobs for a long time. Lots of businesses have closed down, and those that have managed to stay open are operating at reduced capacity.

8. What are the three main economic goals of most economies, including that of the United States? What economic measures do we examine in order to determine whether or how well these goals are being met?

9. Let's say that you're the Fed chairperson and that the country is in a recession. What actions should the Fed take in order to pull the country out of the recession? What would you advise government officials to do to improve the economy? Justify your recommendations.

10. Browsing through your college's catalogue, you notice that all business majors must take two economics courses: macroeconomics and microeconomics. Explain what's covered in each of these courses. In what ways will what you learn in each course help you in the future?

Learning on the Web AACSB

The "Jobs and Economy" section of the CNNMoney Web site provides current information on a number of economic indicators. Go to www.exploringbusinessonline.com to link to this site and find answers to parts 1 and 2 of this exercise.

1. You read in the chapter that an important goal of all economies is to make jobs available to everyone who wants one. Review the CNNMoney discussion on job growth and then answer the following questions:

a. Is the current level of unemployment rising or falling?

b. What do economists expect will happen to unemployment rates in the near future?

c. Is the current level of unemployment a burden or an asset to the economy? In what ways?

2. A number of leading economic indicators are used to forecast future economic trends. Answer the following questions after reviewing the CNNMoney discus-sions of leading economic indicators and consumer confidence:

a. What leading economic indicators were mentioned in the article you read? What did they tell you about the short-term future direction of the economy? Will it get stronger, weaker, or stay the same?

b. Is consumer confidence up or down? What does the answer to this question tell you about the future direction of the economy?

3. Do you remember the first dollar you earned? Maybe you earned it delivering newspapers, shoveling snow, mowing lawns, or babysitting. How much do you think that dollar is worth today? Go to www.prenhall.com/collins to link to the WestEgg Web site and find the answer to this question. After determining the current value of your first dollar, explain how the calculator was created. (*Hint:* Apply what you know about CPI.)

Career Opportunities

Is a Career in Economics for You?

Are you wondering what a career in economics would be like? Go to www.exploringbusinessonline.com to link to the U.S. Department of Labor Web site and review the occupational outlook for economists. Look for answers to the following questions:

1. What issues interest economists?

2. What kinds of jobs do government economists perform? What about those who work in private industry? In education?

3. What educational background and training is needed for these jobs?

4. What is the current job outlook for economists?

5. What is the entry-level salary for an economist with a bachelor's degree? With a master's degree?

Ethics Angle AACSB

How Much Is That CD in the Window?

The early 1990s were a good time to buy CDs, mainly because discounters like Circuit City, Wal-Mart, and Best Buy were accumulating customers by dropping prices from $15 to $10. They were losing money, but they figured that the policy still made good business sense. Why? They reasoned that while customers were in the store to shop for CDs, they'd find other, more profitable products.

The policy was a windfall for CD buyers, but a real problem for traditional music retailers like Musicland Stores and Tower Records. With discounters slashing prices, CD buyers were no longer willing to pay the prices asked by traditional music retailers. Sales plummeted.

Ultimately, the discounters' strategy worked: Stores like Wal-Mart and Best Buy gained customers who once bought CDs at stores like Musicland Stores and Tower Records.

Let's pause at this point to answer the following questions:

1. Does selling a product below cost make business sense?

2. Whom does it hurt? Whom does it help?

3. Is it ethical?

Let's continue and find out how traditional music retailers responded to this situation.

They weren't happy, and neither were the record companies. They worried that traditional retailers would put pressure on them to reduce the price that they charged for CDs so that retailers could lower their prices and compete with discounters. The record companies didn't want to lower prices. They just wanted things to return to "normal"—to the world in which CDs sold for $15 each.

Most of the big record companies and several traditional music retailers got together and made a deal affecting every store that sold CDs. The record companies agreed with retail chains and other CD outlets to charge a minimum advertised price for CDs. Any retailer who broke ranks by advertising below-price CDs would incur substantial financial penalties. Naturally, CD prices went up.

Now, what do you think:

1. Does the deal made between the record companies and traditional retailers make business sense?

2. Whom does it hurt? Whom does it help?

3. Is it ethical?

4. Is it legal?

Team-Building Skills AACSB

Get together in groups of four selected by your instructor and pick any three items from the following list:

- Pint of milk

- Gallon of gas

- Roundtrip airline ticket between Boston and San Francisco

- Large pizza

- Monthly cost of a DSL line

- CD by a particular musician

- Two-day DVD rental

- Particular brand of DVD player

- Quarter-pound burger

Outside of class, each member of the team should check the prices of the three items, using his or her own sources. At the next class meeting, get together and compare the prices found by team members. Based on your findings, answer the following questions as a group:

1. Are the prices of given products similar, or do they vary?

2. Why do the prices of some products vary while those of others are similar?

3. Can any price differences be explained by applying the concepts of supply and demand or types of competition?

The Global View AACSB

Life Is Good in France (If You Have *Le Job*)

A strong economy requires that people have money to spend on goods and services. Because most people earn their money by working, an important goal of all economies is making jobs available to everyone who wants one. A country has "full employment" when 95 percent of those wanting work are employed. With a current unemployment rate just shy of 5 percent, the United States gets a good grade on meeting its goal of full employment. This isn't true for all economies. France, for example, currently has a 10-percent unemployment rate overall and a 20-percent unemployment rate among young people.

Does this mean that France isn't trying as hard as the United States to achieve full employment? A lot of people in France would say yes.

Let's take a quick trip to France to see what's going on economically. The day is March 19, 2006, and more than a million people are marching through the streets to protest a proposed new employment law that would make it easier for companies to lay off workers under the age of 26 during their first two years of employment. Granted, the plan doesn't sound too youth-friendly, but, as usual, economic issues are never as clear-cut as they seem (or as we'd like them to be).

To get some further insight into what's going on in France, go to www.exploringbusinessonline.com to link to the *Business Week* Web site and read the article "Job Security Ignites Debate in France." Then, answer the following questions:

1. Why does the French government support the new law—the so-called "First Employment Contract?" Who's supposed to be helped by the law?

2. Which two groups are most vocal in protesting the law? Why?

3. If you were a long-time worker at a French company, would you support the new law? Why or why not?

4. If you were a young French person who'd just graduated from college and were looking for your first job, would you support the law? Why or why not?

5. What do you think of France's focus on job security? Does the current system help or hurt French workers? Does it help or hurt recent college graduates?

6. Does the French government's focus on job security help or hinder its economy? Should the government be so heavily involved in employment matters?

CHAPTER 2

The Challenges of Starting a Business

After studying this chapter, you will be able to:

1. Define *entrepreneurship* and identify the reasons some individuals become entrepreneurs.

2. Describe the importance of small businesses to the U.S. economy and identify the industries in which small businesses are concentrated.

3. Explain what it takes to start a business and summarize the advantages and disadvantages of business ownership.

4. Evaluate the various small business ownership options— starting a new business, buying an existing business, or obtaining a franchise.

5. Discuss the importance of planning for your business and identify the key sections of a business plan.

6. Discuss ways to succeed in managing a business and explain why some businesses fail.

BUILD A BETTER BABY AND THEY WILL COME

In 1993, Mary and Rick Jurmain were watching a TV program about teenage pregnancy.[1] To simulate the challenge of caring for an infant, teens on the program were carrying around sacks of flour. Rick commented that holding a sack of flour was a poor substitute for taking care of a baby. Mary challenged him to use his engineering expertise to come up with a better baby substitute. Two weeks later, he unveiled the prototype of the "Baby Think It Over" infant simulator— a cloth doll with an internal electronic box for making baby noises. Thus, BTIO Educational Products, Inc., was born.

Mary and Rick were willing to accept the risk of starting and running a company to pursue what they identified as a great business opportunity. They set up a manufacturing shop in the garage and an office in the kitchen, and today, their idea has grown into a comprehensive

Chris Clinton/
Getty Images In
Stone Allstock

parenting-education program that teaches young people about the responsibilities of parenting, with the goal of reducing unwanted teenage pregnancies. Since 1993, more than a million teens have gotten a glimpse of what it's like to spend all their time feeding, burping, changing, and rocking simulated babies.

What Is an Entrepreneur?

Like BTIO, many entrepreneurial ventures are based on innovative ideas. Others are improvements on already existing goods or services. Howard Shultz formed Starbucks to reinvent the coffee experience—to provide customers with quality coffee in a tranquil atmosphere. Michael Dell improved the process of selling computers by eliminating distributors and retail stores and selling directly to the customer.

Do you ever wonder what it would be like to start your own business? Do you ever think that someday you might be an entrepreneur—maybe even an extremely successful entrepreneur like Tom Anderson or Chris DeWolfe, founders of MySpace, the Juice Guys (Nantucket Nectars founders Tom Scott and Tom First), or Pierre Omidyar, who started eBay? Have you thought about the importance of small businesses to the U.S. economy? Would you like some answers to questions like the following: Should I start a business? What are the advantages and disadvantages of starting a business? Should I build a business from scratch, buy an existing business, or invest in a franchise? How do I come up with a business idea? How do I go about planning a business? What steps are involved in developing a business plan? Where would I find help in getting my business started and operating it through the start-up phase? How can I increase the likelihood that I'll succeed?

Answers to these questions can be found in this chapter. Let's start by answering a question that's been implied in just about everything we've said so far: What is an entrepreneur? We'll go with this definition: An **entrepreneur** is someone who identifies a business opportunity and assumes the risk of creating and running a business to take advantage of it.

WHY BECOME AN ENTREPRENEUR?

Why do people start businesses? According to the **Small Business Administration (SBA)**, a government agency that provides assistance to small businesses, the most common reasons for starting a business are as follows:[2]

- To be your own boss
- To achieve financial independence
- To enjoy creative freedom
- To use your skills and knowledge

What are entrepreneurs like? In general, they're creative people who sometimes accomplish extraordinary things because they're passionate about what they're doing. They are risk-taking optimists who commit themselves to working long hours to reach desired goals. They take pride in what they're doing and get satisfaction from doing something they enjoy. They also have the flexibility to adjust to changing situations in order to achieve their goals.

Entrepreneurs usually start small. They begin with limited resources and build their businesses through personal effort. At the end of the day, their success will depend on their ability to manage and grow the organization that they created to implement their vision.

DISTINGUISHING ENTREPRENEURS FROM SMALL BUSINESS OWNERS

Although most entrepreneurial ventures begin as small businesses, not all small business owners are entrepreneurs.

entrepreneur
Individual who identifies a business opportunity and assumes the risk of creating and running a business to take advantage of it.

Small Business Administration (SBA)
Government agency that helps prospective owners set up small businesses, obtain financing, and manage ongoing operations.

While graduate students at Stanford University, Larry Page and Sergey Brin came up with a novel idea for a search engine that ranked Web sites according to the number of hits. They quit graduate school and founded Google in 1998. Their entrepreneurial venture paid off big time—by 2006, both were worth about $13 billion.

Entrepreneurs are innovators who start companies to create new or improved products. They strive to meet a need that's not being met, and their goal is to grow the business and eventually expand into other markets.

In contrast, many people either start or buy small businesses for the sole purpose of providing an income for themselves and their families. They do not intend to be particularly innovative, nor do they plan to expand significantly. This desire to operate is what's sometimes called a "lifestyle business."[3] The neighborhood pizza parlor or beauty shop, the self-employed consultant who works out of the home, even a local printing company—all of these are typically lifestyle businesses. In the next section, we discuss the positive influences that both lifestyle and entrepreneurial businesses have on the U.S. economy.

Importance of Small Business to the U.S. Economy

To assess the value of small businesses to the U.S. economy, we first need to know what constitutes a **small business**. Let's start by looking at the criteria used by the SBA. According to the SBA, a small business is one that is independently owned and operated, exerts little influence in its industry, and (with a few exceptions) has fewer than 500 employees.[4]

There are more than 20 million small businesses in the United States, and these businesses generate about 50 percent of our gross domestic product.[5] Clearly, they're a major force in our economy. The millions of individuals who have started businesses in the United States have shaped the business world as we know it today. Some small business founders like Henry Ford and Thomas Edison have even gained places in history. Others, including Bill Gates (Microsoft), Sam Walton (Wal-Mart), Steve Jobs (Apple Computer), Michael Dell (Dell, Inc.), and Steve Case (AOL), have changed the way business is done today. Still millions of others have collectively contributed to our standard of living.

Small businesses are important to us for a number of reasons. In particular, they create jobs, spark innovation, and provide opportunities for many people, including women and minorities, to achieve financial success and independence.[6] In addition, small businesses complement the economic activity of large organizations by providing them with components, services, and distribution of their products. These contributions are discussed later in the chapter.

JOB CREATION

Small businesses are a major source of employment. More than half of all U.S. adults are either self-employed or work for businesses with fewer than 500 employees. The majority of Americans made their first entrance into the business world by working for a small business.[7] These enterprises are constantly creating jobs and providing opportunities for a vast number of workers. Figure 2.1 shows just how many jobs were created by small (and very small) firms between 1992 and 1996, the last year for which there are data. Note particularly the performance of large companies (those with more than 500 employees) over the same period.

INNOVATION

Given the financial resources available to large businesses, you'd expect them to introduce most of the new products that hit the market. But according to the SBA, 55 percent of all product innovations come from small businesses.[8] For example, the list of important innovations by small high-tech businesses is impressive. It includes the airplane, personal computer, tape recorder, pacemaker, and soft contact lenses.[9]

Owners of small businesses are also responsible for finding new ways of doing old things. In 1994, for example, a young computer-science graduate working on Wall Street came up with the then-novel idea of selling books over the Internet. During the first year of operations, sales at Jeff Bezos's new company—Amazon.com—reached half a million dollars. In less than 10 years, annual sales grew to more than $3 billion. Bezos's innovative approach to online retailing not only made its founder very rich but has become a model for the e-commerce industry.

Why are small businesses so innovative? For one thing, they tend to offer environments that appeal to individuals with the talent to invent new products or improve the way things are being done. They tend to make faster decisions, their research programs tend to be focused, and their compensation structures tend to reward top performers.[10] Supportive environments have enabled small firms to turn out twice as many product innovations per employee as large firms.[11]

The success of small businesses in fostering creativity has not gone unnoticed by big businesses. In fact, many companies, such as General Electric, have responded by downsizing to act more like small companies.[12] Some large organizations now have separate work units whose purpose is to spark innovation. Individuals working on these teams can focus their attention on creating new products that can then be developed by the company.

OPPORTUNITIES FOR WOMEN AND MINORITIES

Small business is the portal through which many people enter the economic mainstream. Business ownership allows individ-

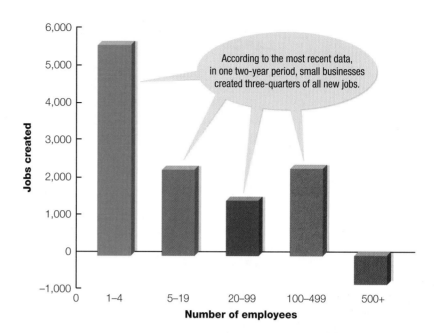

uals, including women and minorities, to achieve financial success as well as pride in their accomplishments. Although the majority of small businesses are still owned by white males, the past two decades have seen a substantial increase in the number of businesses owned by women and minorities. Figure 2.2 gives you an idea of how many American businesses are owned by women and minorities and indicates how much the numbers grew between 1982 and 2002, the last year for which there are reliable data.

Figure 2.1

Net New Jobs by Firm Size

Figure 2.2

Women- and Minority-Owned Businesses

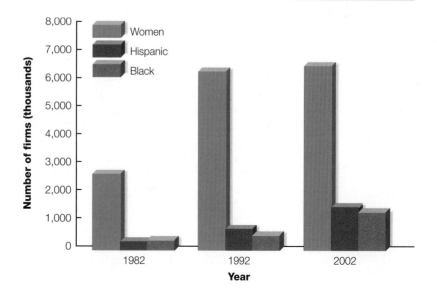

HOW SMALL BUSINESSES HELP LARGE BUSINESSES

Small firms complement large firms in a number of ways. They supply many of the components needed by big companies. For example, a substantial portion of the mind-boggling $90 billion paid annually by General Motors to parts suppliers goes to small businesses. Small firms also provide large ones with such services as accounting, legal, and insurance. Many small firms provide *outsourcing* services to large firms—that is, they hire themselves out to help with special projects or handle certain business functions. A large firm, for example, might hire a small one to handle its billing or collection services or to manage its health care benefits. A large company might contract with a small information technology firm to manage its Web site or oversee software upgrades.

Small companies provide another valuable service to large companies by acting as sales agents for their products. For example, automobile dealerships, which are generally small businesses, sell vehicles for the big car makers. Local sporting goods stores sell athletic shoes made by industry giants, such as Adidas and Nike. Your corner deli sells products made by large companies like Coca-Cola and Frito Lay.

After getting *A*'s in a correspondence course on ice cream making, Ben Cohen and Jerry Greenfield (friends since the seventh grade) decided to enter the goods-producing sector by making ice cream. Ben & Jerry's ice cream factory in Vermont churns out 190,000 pints of ice cream daily (and lets each worker keep three pints), and enthusiastic employees tour the country giving away free scoops of ice cream.

What Industries Are Small Businesses In?

If you wanted to start a new business, there are some types of businesses that you'd probably reject. For example, it's unlikely that you'd decide to set up a new company to make automobiles or aluminum. Such ventures require tremendous investments in property, plant, and equipment, and you'd have no way to raise the needed funds or attract the human capital you'd need. But there are, of course, other types of businesses that require low initial investment. Not surprisingly, these types of companies are attractive as small business opportunities.

INDUSTRIES BY SECTOR

To understand where small businesses are concentrated, we first need to divide businesses into two sectors: the goods-producing sector and the service-producing sector. The **goods-producing sector** includes all businesses that produce tangible goods. Companies in this sector include those involved in manufacturing, construction, and agriculture. The **service-producing sector** includes all businesses that provide a service but do not make tangible goods. These include firms involved in retail and wholesale trade, transportation, communications, finance, insurance, real estate, and such professional services as health care, advertising, accounting, and personal services.

About 80 percent of small businesses in the U.S. are concentrated in the service-producing sector. Of these, about 25 percent are in retailing, 10 percent in wholesaling, and 35 percent in professional and business services. The goods-producing sector is home to only 20 percent of all small businesses. Nearly two-thirds of these are in construction, the other one-third in manufacturing.[13]

The high concentration of small businesses in the service-producing sector reflects the makeup of the overall U.S. economy. Over the past 40 years, the service-producing sector has been growing at an impressive rate. In 1960, the goods-producing sector accounted for 38 percent of gross domestic product, the service-producing sector for 62 percent. By 2000, the goods-producing sector accounted for only 23 percent of GDP, while the service-producing sector had grown to 77 percent.[14]

Goods-Producing Sector

The largest areas of the goods-producing sector are construction and manufacturing. Construction businesses are often started by skilled workers, such as electricians, painters, plumbers, and homebuilders. They tend to be small and generally work on local projects. Although manufacturing is primarily the domain of large businesses, there are exceptions. For example, Jeffrey Berndt started a company called Reveal Entertainment to manufacture and distribute board games. The company began with its award-winning game, Tripoly—a three-dimensional finance and real estate game in which players buy and build cities. The product line now includes dozens of board games.[15]

Service-Producing Sector

Many small businesses in this sector are *retailers*—they buy goods from other firms and sell them to consumers, either in stores, by phone, through direct mailings, or over the Internet. Increasingly, entrepreneurs are starting online ventures. This approach was taken by Tony Roeder, who had a fascination with the red Radio Flyer wagons that many of today's adults had owned as children. In 1998, he started an online store through Yahoo! to sell red wagons from his home. In three years, he turned his online store into a million-dollar business.[16] Internet entrepreneurship was also attractive to Sean Lundgren and Todd Livdahl— two computer engineers who gave up successful careers at Disney to turn their fascination with video games and DVDs into an online business. To their delight, the small start-up venture, which they call Sneetch.com, generated sales of $1.2 million during its first year of operation.[17]

Other small business owners in this sector are wholesalers who sell products to businesses who buy them for resale or for company use. A local bakery is acting as a wholesaler when it sells desserts to a restaurant, which then sells them to its customers. A small business that buys flowers from a local grower (the manufacturer) and sells them to a retail store (the retailer) is another example of a wholesaler.

A high proportion of small businesses in this sector provide professional, business, or personal services. Doctors and dentists are part of the service industry, as are insurance agents, accountants, and lawyers. So are businesses that provide personal services, such as dry cleaning and hairdressing.

David Marcks, for instance, entered the service industry 14 years ago when he learned that his border collie enjoyed chasing geese at the golf course where he worked. Anyone who's been on a golf course recently recognizes the problems created by geese. Although they are lovely to look at, they leave behind an unwelcome litter of droppings. That's why frustrated course managers are happy to hire Marcks' company, Geese Police, to chase the geese away using specially trained dogs. Marcks now has 27 trucks, 32 border collies, and 5 offices. Golf courses are now only about 5 percent of his business, as his dogs now

Taco Bell is part of the service-producing sector. Each year, close to 150,000 Taco Bell employees serve Mexican-inspired fast food to more than two billion consumers. Annually, its 6,000 franchise and company-owned restaurants in the United States use 3.8 billion corn and flour tortillas, 120 million pounds of lettuce, 62 million pounds of pinto beans, 295 million pounds of seasoned ground beef, and 106 million pounds of cheese.

goods-producing sector
All businesses whose primary purpose is to produce tangible goods.

service-producing sector
All businesses whose primary purpose is to provide a service rather than make tangible goods.

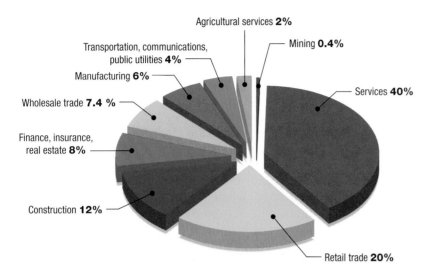

patrol corporate parks and playgrounds as well.[18]

Figure 2.3 provides a more detailed breakdown of small businesses by industry.

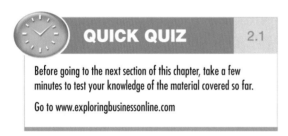

QUICK QUIZ 2.1

Before going to the next section of this chapter, take a few minutes to test your knowledge of the material covered so far.

Go to www.exploringbusinessonline.com

Should You Start a Business?

Do you want to be a business owner someday? Before deciding, you might want to consider the following advantages and disadvantages of business ownership.[19]

ADVANTAGES OF SMALL BUSINESS OWNERSHIP

Being a business owner can be very rewarding. Having the courage to take a risk and start a venture is part of the American dream. Success brings with it many advantages:

- *Independence.* As a business owner, you're your own boss. You can't get fired. More importantly, you have the freedom to make the decisions that are crucial to your own business success.
- *Financial Rewards.* In spite of high financial risk, running your own business gives you a chance to make more money than if you were employed by someone else.
- *Lifestyle.* Owning a small business gives you certain lifestyle advantages. Because you're in charge, you decide when and where you want to work. If you want to spend more time on non-work activities or with your family, you don't have to ask for the time off. If it's important that you be with your family all day, you might decide to run your business from your home. Given today's technology, it's relatively easy to do. Moreover, it eliminates commuting time.
- *Learning Opportunities.* As a business owner, you'll be involved in all aspects of your business. This situation creates numerous opportunities to gain a thorough understanding of the various business functions.
- *Creative Freedom and Personal Satisfaction.* As a business owner, you'll be able to work in a field that you really enjoy. You'll be able to put your skills and knowledge to use, and you'll get personal satisfaction from implementing your ideas, working directly with customers, and watching your business succeed.

DISADVANTAGES OF SMALL BUSINESS OWNERSHIP

As the little boy said when he got off his first roller-coaster ride: "I like the ups but not the downs!" Here are some of the risks you run if you want to start a small business:

- *Financial Risk.* The financial resources needed to start and grow a business can be extensive. You may need to commit most of your savings or even go into debt to get started. If things don't go well, your financial loss can be great. In addition, there's no guaranteed income. There might be times, especially in the first few years, when the business isn't generating enough cash for you to live on.
- *Stress.* As a business owner, you *are* the business. There's a bewildering array of things to worry about—competition, employees, bills, equipment breakdowns, customer problems. As the owner, you're also responsible for the well-being of your employees.

- *Time Commitment.* People often start businesses so that they'll have more time to spend with their families. Unfortunately, running a business is extremely time-consuming. Even though you have the freedom to take time off, you might not be able to get away. In fact, you'll probably have less free time than you'd have working for someone else. For many entrepreneurs and small business owners, a 40-hour workweek is a myth; see Figure 2.4. Vacations will be difficult to take and will often be interrupted. In recent years, the difficulty of getting away from the job has been compounded by cell phones and e-mail, and many small business owners have come to regret that they're always reachable.

- *Undesirable Duties.* When you start up, you'll undoubtedly be responsible for either doing or overseeing just about everything that needs to be done. You can get bogged down in detail work that you don't enjoy. As a business owner, you'll probably have to perform some unpleasant tasks, like firing people.

In spite of these and other disadvantages, most small business owners are pleased with their decision to start a business. A survey conducted by the *Wall Street Journal* and Cicco and Associates indicates that small business owners and top-level corporate executives agree overwhelmingly that small business owners have a more satisfying business experience. The researchers had anticipated that the small business owners would be happy with their positions, but they were surprised at the number of corporate executives who believed that the grass was greener in the world of small business ownership.[20]

Starting a Business

Starting a business takes talent, determination, hard work, and persistence. It also requires a lot of research and planning. Before starting your business, you should

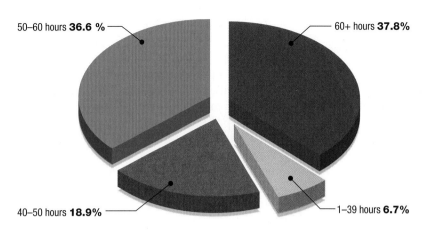

50–60 hours **36.6 %**

60+ hours **37.8%**

40–50 hours **18.9%**

1–39 hours **6.7%**

Figure 2.4

The Entrepreneur's Work Week

appraise your strengths and weaknesses and assess your personal goals to determine if business ownership is for you.[21]

If you're interested in starting a business, you need to make decisions, such as the following:

- What type of business is right for you? Do you want to be a manufacturer, a retailer, or a wholesaler? Do you want to provide professional or personal services? Do you want to start a business that you can operate out of your home?

- Do you want to run a business that's similar to many others, or do you want to innovate—create a new product or approach to doing business?

- What is your business idea? Is it feasible?

- Do you want to start a new business, buy an existing business, or buy a franchise?

- Do you want to start the business by yourself or with others?

- What form of business organization do you want? Do you want to own the business yourself, or do you want to have other owners and operate as a partnership or a corporation?

After making these decisions, you'll need to take the most important step in the process of starting a business. You must describe your future business in the form of a **business plan**, which is a document that

business plan
Formal document describing a proposed business concept, management team, goods or services, competition, product-development process, production methods, and marketing model, and stating financial projections.

identifies the goals of your proposed company and explains how they will be achieved. Think of a business plan as a blueprint for a proposed company: It shows how the business will be built and how you intend to make sure that it's sturdy. Your final step before actually starting the business will be to get financing—the money from individuals, banks, or both that you'll need to get started. If you have the necessary funds to finance the business, you can skip this last step.

THE BUSINESS IDEA

For some, coming up with a great business idea is a gratifying adventure. For most, however, it's a daunting task. The key to coming up with a business idea is giving customers something they want—or, more importantly, filling an unmet need. The purpose of starting a business is to satisfy customers—the ultimate users of your goods or services. In coming up with a business idea, do not ask "What do we want to sell?" but rather "What does the customer want to buy?"[22]

To come up with an innovative business idea, you need to be creative. The idea itself

Dean Kamen has no trouble coming up with great business ideas. While an undergraduate, he invented the first wearable infusion pump to deliver precise dosages of medications. He is well-known for two of his people-moving inventions. One, called the Independence iBOT Mobility System, is a stair-climbing wheelchair. The other, the Segway Human Transporter, is a self-balancing personal transportation machine.

can come from various sources. Prior experience accounts for the bulk of new business ideas. Many people generate ideas for industries they're already working in. Past experience in an industry also increases your chances of success. Take Sam Walton, the late founder of Wal-Mart. He began his retailing career at J.C. Penney and then became a successful franchiser of a Ben Franklin five-and-dime store. In 1962, he came up with the idea of opening large stores with low costs and heavy discounts in rural areas. He founded his first Wal-Mart store in 1962, and when he died 30 years later, his family's net worth was $25 billion.[23]

Industry experience also gave Howard Schultz his breakthrough idea. In 1981, Schultz, a New York executive for a housewares company, noticed that a small customer in Seattle, Starbucks Coffee, Tea and Spice, ordered more coffeemaker cone filters than Macy's and a lot of other large customers. So he flew across the country to find out why. His meeting with the owner-operators of the original Starbucks Coffee Co., which resulted in his becoming part owner of the company, changed his life and the life of coffee lovers forever. Schultz' vision for the company far surpassed that of its other owners. While they wanted Starbucks to remain small and local, Schultz saw potential for a national business that not only sold world-class quality coffee beans, but offered customers a European coffee-bar experience. After trying unsuccessfully to convince his partners to try his experiment, Schultz left Starbucks and started his own chain of coffee bars, which he called *Il Giornale* (after an Italian newspaper). Two years later, he bought out the original owners and reclaimed the name "Starbucks."[24]

Other people come up with business ideas because of hobbies or personal interests. This was the case with Nike founder Phil Knight, who was an avid runner. He was convinced that it was possible to make high-quality track shoes that cost less than the European shoes then dominating the market. His track experience, coupled with his knowledge of business (Knight holds an MBA from Stanford and worked as an accountant), inspired him to start Nike. From a young age, Michael Dell was obsessed with taking computers apart and putting them back together again, and it was this personal interest that led to his great business idea. At college, instead of attending classes, he spent his time assembling computers and, eventually, founded Dell Computers.

ABOUT NIKE   2.1

Before you begin your study of small business options and the preparation of a business plan, here's a chance to read about how Nike was started and how it survived during its early years.

Go to www.exploringbusinessonline.com

OWNERSHIP OPTIONS

As we have already seen, you can become a small business owner in one of three ways: by starting a new business, buying an existing business, or obtaining a franchise. Each has its advantages and disadvantages.

Starting from Scratch

The most common—and the riskiest—option is starting from scratch. This approach lets you start with a clean slate and allows you to build the business the way you want. You select the goods or services to be offered, the location, and all your employees, and it's up to you to develop a customer base and build a reputation.

Buying an Existing Business

If you decide to buy an existing business, some things will be easier. You will already have a proven product, customers, suppliers, a known location, and trained employees. It will also be much easier to predict the future success of the business. But this route, of course, comes with its own disadvantages. First, it's hard to determine how much you should pay for a business. You can easily determine how much things like buildings and equipment are worth, but how much should you pay for the fact that the business has steady customers?

In addition, a business, like a used car, might have problems of which you are not aware. Perhaps the current owners have disappointed customers; maybe the location isn't as good as it used to be. You

might inherit employees that you wouldn't have hired yourself. Finally, what if the previous owners set up a competing business that draws away their former—and your current—customers?

Getting a Franchise

Lastly, you can buy a **franchise**. Under this set up, a *franchiser* (the company that sells the franchise) grants the *franchisee* (the buyer) the right to use a brand name and to sell its goods or services. Franchises are used to market products in a variety of industries, including food, retail, hotels, travel, real estate, business services, cleaning services, and even weight-loss centers and wedding services. There are thousands of franchises, many of which are quite familiar—SUBWAY®, McDonald's, 7-Eleven, Holiday Inn, Budget Rent-A-Car, Radio Shack, and Jiffy Lube.

As you can see from Figure 2.5, franchising has become an extremely popular way to do business. A new franchise outlet opens once every 8 minutes in the United States, where 1 of 12 businesses is now a franchise. Franchises employ 8 million people and account for 40 percent of all retail sales in this country.[25]

In addition to the right to use a company's brand name and sell its products, the franchisee gets help in picking a location, starting and operating the business, and

Figure 2.5

The Growth of Franchising, 1980–2004

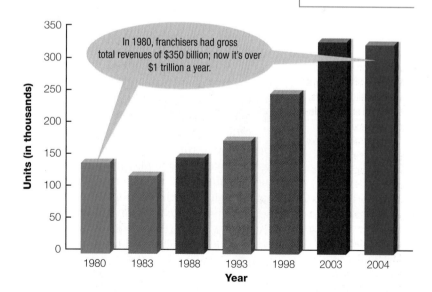

In 1980, franchisers had gross total revenues of $350 billion; now it's over $1 trillion a year.

Units (in thousands)

Year

franchise
Form of business ownership in which a *franchiser* (a seller) grants a *franchisee* (a buyer) the right to use a brand name and to sell its products or services.

advertising. In effect, you've bought a prepackaged, ready-to-go business that's proven successful elsewhere. You also get ongoing support from the franchiser, which has a vested interest in your success.

All these advantages don't come cheaply. Franchises can be very expensive, usually depending on the amount of business that a location is expected to do. For example, some McDonald's franchises require an initial investment of $500,000 to $1.6 million. This fee includes the cost of the property, equipment, training, start-up costs, and the *franchise fee*—a one-time charge for the right to operate as a McDonald's. A KFC outlet is in the same price range. Subways are more affordable, with expected initial investments ranging from $70,000 to $220,000. If you don't want to deal in food, you might want to buy a dating service. The Right One franchises go for an initial investment of $100,000 to $250,000, depending on location.[26]

In addition to your initial investment, you'll have to pay two other fees on a monthly basis—a *royalty fee* (typically from 3 to 12 percent of sales) for continued support from the franchiser and the right to keep using the company's trade name and an *advertising fee* to cover your share of national and regional advertising. You'll also be expected to buy your products from the franchiser.[27]

Why do would-be business owners like franchises? For one thing, buying a franchise lets you start up in a fairly safe environment, with a proven model for running a company and an ongoing support team. You can profit from name recognition without having to develop your own image in the marketplace, and you can be your own boss (as long as you comply with the standards set by the franchiser).

But there are disadvantages. The cost of obtaining and running a franchise can be high, and you have to play by the franchiser's rules, even when you disagree with them. Finally, franchisers don't always keep their promises. What do you do if promised advertising doesn't materialize? As with any business venture, you need to do your homework before investing in a franchise.

The Business Plan

If you're starting a business, it's essential that you prepare a business plan. It should tell the story of your business concept, spec-

ify the qualifications of your management team, describe your legal form of business ownership, explain the goods or services that you intend to sell, identify your customers and competitors, describe your product development and production methods and marketing activities, and state your projected profit and borrowing needs.

The business plan is a blueprint for the company, and it's an indispensable tool in attracting investors and/or obtaining loans. Remember: The value of your business plan is not limited to the planning stages of your business and the process of finding start-up money. Once you've acquired start-up capital, don't just stuff your plan in a drawer. Treat it as an ongoing guide to your business and a yardstick by which you can measure your performance. Keep it handy, update it periodically, and use it to assess your progress.

Preparing a business plan takes a lot of time, but it's time well spent. A business plan forces you to think critically about your proposed business and reduces your risk of failure. It forces you to analyze your business concept and the industry in which you'll be operating, and it helps you determine how you can gain a percentage of sales in that industry. In developing and writing a business plan, you have to make strategic decisions in the areas of management, staffing, production, marketing, and finance—in all the functional areas of business that we described in Chapter 1.

The most common use of a business plan is persuading investors and/or lenders to provide financing. These two groups look for different things. Investors are particularly interested in the quality of the business concept and the ability of management to make the venture successful. Bankers are primarily concerned with the company's ability to generate cash to repay loans. To persuade investors and lenders to support your business, you need a professional, well-written business plan that paints a clear picture of your proposed business.

SECTIONS OF THE BUSINESS PLAN

Although formats can vary, a business plan generally includes the following sections: executive summary, description of proposed business, industry analysis, mission statement, management plan, goods and/or services, development and production, marketing, global issues, and financial plan. Let's explore each of these sections in turn.

Executive Summary

The **executive summary** is a one- to three-page overview of the business plan. It's actually the most important part of the business plan: It's what the reader looks at first, and if it doesn't capture the reader's attention, it might be the only thing that he or she looks at. It should therefore emphasize the key points of the plan and get the reader excited about the prospects of the business.

Even though the executive summary is the first thing read, it's written *after* the other sections of the plan are completed. An effective approach in writing the executive summary is to paraphrase key sentences from each section of the business plan. This process will ensure that the key information of each section is included in the executive summary.

Description of Proposed Business

Here, you present a *brief* description of the company and answer the following questions:

- What will your proposed company do? Will it be a manufacturer, a retailer, or a service provider?
- What goods or services will it provide?
- Why are your goods or services unique?
- Who will be your main customers?
- How will your goods or services be sold?
- Where will your business be located?

Because later parts of the plan will provide more detailed discussions of many of these issues, this section needs to provide only an overview of these topics.

Industry Analysis

This section provides a brief introduction to the industry in which you propose to operate. It describes both the current situation in the industry as well as future possibilities and addresses such questions as the following:

- Who are the players in the industry?
- What is the outlook for the industry?

- What are the total projected sales for the industry? Is it growing or shrinking?
- What factors will influence future expansion or contraction?
- How will predicted future economic conditions affect the industry?

Mission Statement and Core Values

This portion of the business plan states the company's *mission statement* and *core values*. The **mission statement** describes the purpose or *mission* of your organization—its reason for existence. It tells the reader what the organization is committed to doing. The mission statement can be concise, like the one from Merck Pharmaceutical: "To preserve and improve human life." Or, it can be more detailed, like the one from Southwest Airlines: "The mission of Southwest Airlines is dedication to the highest quality of customer service delivered with a sense of warmth, friendliness, individual pride, and company spirit."

Core values are fundamental beliefs about what is and is not appropriate and what is important in conducting company activities. Core values are not about profits but rather about ideals. They will help guide the behavior of individuals in the organization. For example, Coca-Cola reports that its core values—honesty, integrity, diversity, quality, respect, responsibility, and accountability—help employees know what behaviors are acceptable.

Management Plan

It isn't enough just to have a good business idea: You need a talented management team that can turn your concept into a profitable venture. The management plan section provides information about the qualifications of each member of the management team. Its purpose is to convince the reader that the company will be run by well-qualified, experienced managers. It describes each individual's education, experience, and expertise, as well as each person's responsibilities. This section also specifies the proposed legal

---

executive summary
Overview emphasizing the key points of a business plan in order to get the reader excited about the prospects of the business.

mission statement
Statement describing an organization's purpose or *mission*—its reason for existence—and telling stakeholders what the organization is committed to doing.

core values
Statement of fundamental beliefs describing what is appropriate and important in conducting organizational activities and providing a guide for the behavior of organization members.

form of the organization: sole proprietorship (personal ownership), partnership (ownership shared with one or more partners), or corporation (ownership through shares of stock).

Goods and/or Services

To succeed in attracting investors and lenders, you must be able to describe your goods or services clearly (and enthusiastically). Here, you describe all the goods and services that you will provide the marketplace. This section explains why your proposed offerings are better than those of competitors and indicates what market needs will be met by your goods or services. It addresses a key question: What *competitive advantage* will the company have over similar goods or services now on the market?

Development and Production

This section indicates how you plan to obtain or make your products. Naturally, the write-up will vary depending on whether you're proposing a service company, a retailer, or a manufacturer. If it's a service company, describe the process of providing services. If it's a retail company, tell the reader where you will purchase products for resale.

If you're going to be a manufacturer, you must furnish information on product design, development, and production process. You must address questions like the following:

- How will products be designed?
- What technology will be needed to design and manufacture products?
- Will the company run its own production facilities, or will its products be manufactured by someone else?
- Where will production facilities be located?
- What type of equipment will be used?
- What are the design and layout of the facilities?
- How many workers will be employed in the production process?
- How many units will be produced?
- How will the company ensure that products are of high quality?

Marketing

This critical section focuses on four marketing-related areas—target market, pricing, distribution, and promotion:

1. *Target Market.* Describe future customers and provide a profile of them based on age, gender, income, interests, and so forth. If your company will sell to other companies, describe your typical business customer.

2. *Pricing.* State the proposed price for each product. Compare your pricing strategy to that of competitors.

3. *Distribution.* Explain how your goods or services will be distributed to customers. Indicate whether they will be sold directly to customers or through retail outlets.

4. *Promotion.* Identify a promotion strategy, indicating what types of advertising you'll be using.

Global Issues

Indicate whether you'll be involved in international markets, either by buying or selling in other countries. If you're going to operate across borders, identify the challenges you'll face in your global environment and explain how you'll overcome them. If you don't plan initially to be involved in international markets, state what strategies, if any, you'll use to move into international markets at a later date.

Financial Plan

In preparing the financial section of your business plan, specify the company's cash needs and explain how you'll be able to repay debt. This information is vital in obtaining financing. It presents financial projections, including expected sales, costs, and profits (or losses). It refers to a set of financial statements included in an appendix to the business plan. It reports the amount of cash needed by the company for start-up and initial operations and provides an overview of proposed funding sources.

Appendices

Here you furnish supplemental information that may be of interest to the reader. For example, you might attach the résumés of your management team and a set of financial statements.

QUICK QUIZ 2.2

Before reading the next section on how to succeed in managing a business, take a moment to test your understanding of how to start a business and write a business plan.

Go to www.exploringbusinessonline.com

How to Succeed in Managing a Business

Being successful as a business owner requires more than coming up with a brilliant idea and working hard. You need to learn how to manage and grow your business. As an owner, you'll face numerous challenges, a number of which have been identified through focus groups of business owners.[28] Your ability to meet challenges like those discussed next will be a major factor in your success (or failure) as a business owner.

- *Know Your Business.* It seems obvious, but it's worth stating: Successful businesspeople know what they're doing. They're knowledgeable about the industry in which they operate (both as it stands today and where it's headed in the future), and they know who their competitors are. They know how to attract customers and who the best suppliers and distributors are, and they understand the impact of technology on their business.

- *Know the Basics of Business Management.* You might be able to *start* a business on the basis of a great idea, but to *manage* it, you need to understand the functional areas of business—accounting, finance, management, marketing, production. You need to be a salesperson as well as a decision maker and planner.

- *Have the Proper Attitude.* When you own a business, you *are* the business. If you're going to devote the time and energy needed to transform an idea into a successful business, you need to have a passion for your work. You should believe in what you're doing

and make a strong personal commitment to your business.

- *Get Adequate Funding.* It takes a lot of money to start a business and guide it through the start-up phase (which can last for over a year). You can have the most brilliant idea in the world, the best marketing approach, and a talented management team, but if you run out of cash, your career as a business owner could be very brief. Plan for the long term and work with lenders and investors to ensure that you'll have sufficient funds to get open, stay open during the start-up phase, and, ultimately, expand.

- *Manage Your Money Effectively.* As a business owner, you'll be under constant pressure to come up with the money to meet payroll and pay your other bills. That's why you need to pay attention to *cash flow*—money coming in and money going out. You need to control costs and to collect money that's owed you, and generally, you need to know how to gather the financial information that you need to run your business.

- *Manage Your Time Efficiently.* A new business owner can expect to work 60 hours a week. If you want to grow a business and have some type of non-work life at the same time, you'll need to give up some control—to let others take over some of the work. Thus, you must develop time-management skills and learn how to delegate responsibility.

- *Know How to Manage People.* Hiring, keeping, and managing good people are crucial to business success. As your business grows, you'll depend more on your employees. You need to develop a positive working relationship with them, train them properly, and motivate them to provide quality goods or services.

- *Satisfy Your Customers.* You might attract customers through impressive advertising campaigns, but you'll keep them only by providing quality goods or services. Commit yourself to satisfying—or even exceeding—customer needs.

- *Know How to Compete.* Find your niche in the marketplace, keep an eye on your competitors, and be prepared to react to changes in the marketplace. The history of business (and much of life) can be summed up in three words: "Adapt or perish."

ABOUT NIKE 2.2

Take a few minutes to learn about some of the most notable successes in the history of Nike, as well as some of the crucial challenges that it faced in a period of sustained growth. We'll explore both the successes and the challenges in more detail in subsequent chapters.

Go to www.exploringbusinessonline.com

HELP FROM THE SBA

Small business owners can get a wealth of assistance from the Small Business Administration (SBA). The SBA bills itself as "America's Small Business Resource"[29] because it offers an array of programs to help small business owners and prospective business owners. Services include assistance in developing a business plan, starting a business, obtaining financing, and managing an organization.

Through various programs, for example, the SBA is responsible for seeing that small business owners get more than $60 billion a year in financing from lenders and investors. Each year, the SBA *7(a) loan guarantee program* helps some 43,000 small businesspeople get loans from private lenders, and as you can see from Figure 2.6, the amount of

money guaranteed by the program has risen considerably in the last 30 years.[30]

The SBA also offers management and technical-services training. This assistance is available through a number of channels, including the SBA's extensive Web site, online courses, and training programs. A full array of individualized services is also available through SBA programs. The **Small Business Development Center (SBDC)**[31] assists current and prospective small business owners with business problems and provides free training and technical information on all aspects of small business management. These services are available at approximately 1,000 locations around the country, many housed at colleges and universities.

If you need individualized advice from experienced executives, you can get it through the **Service Corps of Retired Executives (SCORE)**.[32] Under the SCORE program, a businessperson needing advice is matched with a team of retired executives who work on a volunteer basis. Together, the SBDC and SCORE help more than 900,000 small businesspersons every year.

WHY DO BUSINESSES FAIL?

By definition, starting a business is risky. Although many businesses succeed, a large proportion fail. For example, one-third of small businesses that have employees go out of business within the first two years. By the four-year mark, 55 percent have gone out of business.[33]

If you've paid any attention to the occupancy of shopping malls over a few years, time, you've noticed that some retailers close and new ones open up constantly. The same thing happens with restaurants—indeed, with all kinds of small businesses.

There are many and varied reasons why businesses fail, but many experts agree that the vast majority of failures results from some combination of the following problems:

- *Bad Business Idea.* If you got the idea of selling snowblowers in Hawaii, you wouldn't have much competition, but you'd still be doomed to failure.

- *Cash Problems.* Too many new businesses are underfunded. The owner borrows enough money to set up the business but doesn't have enough extra cash to operate during the start-up phase,

Figure 2.6

SBA Loan Guarantees, 1976–2004

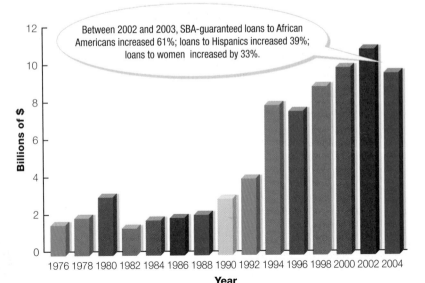

when very little money is coming in but a lot is being spent.

- *Managerial Inexperience or Incompetence.* Many new business owners have no experience in running a business; many have limited management skills. Maybe an owner knows how to make or market a product but doesn't know how to manage people. Maybe an owner can't attract and keep talented employees. Maybe an owner has poor leadership skills and isn't willing to plan ahead.

- *Lack of Customer Focus.* A major advantage of a small business is the ability to provide special attention to customers. But some small businesses fail to seize this advantage. Maybe the owner doesn't anticipate customers' needs or keep up with changing markets or keep an eye on the customer-focused practices of competitors.

- *Inability to Handle Growth.* You'd think that a sales increase would be a good thing. Often it is, but sometimes it can be a major problem. When a company grows, the owner's role changes. The owner needs to delegate work to others and build a business structure that can handle the increase in volume. Some owners don't make the shift and find themselves overwhelmed. Things don't get done, customers become unhappy, and expansion actually damages the company.

This couple has been running a candy store for three years. Because they now want to add two full-time employees, they need to know more about calculating payroll deductions and filing payroll records. Where can they go to get free advice? They could contact the Small Business Development Center (SBDC), which provides free training on all aspects of small business management. If they log on to the SBDC Web site, they could learn about a video-based course called *By the Numbers*, which helps businesspeople with the basic mathematical issues that they face every day.

QUICK QUIZ   2.3

Before you leave this chapter, take a moment to test your understanding of the last few sections by giving yourself a final "Quick Quiz."

Go to www.exploringbusinessonline.com

Where We're Headed

This chapter introduced you to the challenges of starting and growing a business. You gained an understanding of the importance of small businesses to the U.S. economy. You explored issues related to starting and managing a company. Perhaps most importantly, you learned about the value of developing a business plan. You found that a business plan is not only an indispensable tool in planning a business, but is necessary to obtain financing for your venture. The remaining chapters of the text will provide you with the knowledge needed to prepare a business plan.

Small Business Development Center (SBDC)
SBA program in which centers housed at colleges and other locations provide free training and technical information to current and prospective small business owners.

Service Corps of Retired Executives (SCORE)
SBA program in which a businessperson needing advice is matched with a team of retired executives working on a volunteer basis.

Summary of Learning Objectives

1. Define *entrepreneurship* and identify the reasons some individuals become entrepreneurs.

An **entrepreneur** is someone who identifies a business opportunity and assumes the risk of creating and running a business to take advantage of it. Commonly cited reasons for becoming an entrepreneur are being your own boss, achieving financial independence, enjoying creative freedom, and using your skills and knowledge.

2. Describe the importance of small businesses to the U. S. economy and identify the industries in which small businesses are concentrated.

The **Small Business Administration (SBA)**, a government agency that offers an array of programs to help prospective business owners, defines a **small business** as one that is independently owned and operated, exerts little influence in its industry, and has fewer than 500 employees. Small businesses are essential to the U.S. economy because they create jobs, spark innovation, and provide opportunities for many people, including women and minorities, to achieve financial independence. Small businesses also complement the economic activity of large organizations by providing them with components and services and distributing their products.

About 80 percent of small businesses in the U.S. are in the **service-producing sector**. Within this sector, the heaviest concentration of small businesses are in retail and professional and business services. The **goods-producing sector** is home to only about 20 percent of all small businesses, nearly two-thirds in construction.

3. Explain what it takes to start a business and summarize the advantages and disadvantages of business ownership.

Starting a business takes talent, determination, hard work, and persistence. It also requires a lot of research and planning. Small business ownership brings with it a number of advantages, including independence, the potential for financial rewards, the possibility of an improved lifestyle, learning opportunities, creative freedom, and personal satisfaction. Small business ownership also comes with some disadvantages, including financial risk, increased stress, substantial time commitment, and the necessity of performing some unpleasant tasks, like firing people. It also entails the risk of failure.

4. Evaluate the various small business ownership options—starting a new business, buying an existing business, or obtaining a franchise.

Each of these common options for starting a small business has advantages and disadvantages. The riskiest (though most common) choice is starting from scratch. Although this approach lets you build the business the way you want, you have to do everything yourself—come up with a product, location, customer base, and employees—and it's up to you to build a reputation. Buying an existing business is somewhat easier: You already have a proven product, a known location, customers, and trained employees. On the downside, it's hard to determine an appropriate price to pay for an existing business. You might also inherit problems that you don't want or didn't count on, such as disappointed customers, employees that you wouldn't have hired yourself, and competition from the previous owner (who might set up a similar business at a new location).

The third option, buying a **franchise**, also has advantages and disadvantages. When you buy a franchise, you obtain the right to use a brand name and to sell the franchiser's goods or services. You can choose from products in a variety of industries, including food, retail, travel, and real estate, and you're getting a prepackaged, ready-to-go business that's proven successful elsewhere. You get help from the *franchiser* (the company that sells the franchise) in picking a location, starting and operating the business, and advertising. As a *franchisee*, you profit from the franchiser's name recognition without having to develop your image in the marketplace. But all this help does not come cheaply. Both initial investment costs and operating costs are high, and you have to play by the franchiser's rules even if you disagree with them. Even though you run your own business, you're not entirely your own boss.

5. Discuss the importance of planning for your business and identify the key sections of a business plan.

If you're interested in starting a business, you need to make a lot of decisions: What type of business is best for you? What is your business idea? Do you want to create a new product or approach to doing business or start a business that is similar to others? Do you want to start a new business, buy an existing business, or buy a franchise? What form of business organization do you want? Do you want to own the business yourself or share ownership with others?

After making these decisions, you'll need to take the most important step in the process of starting a business: planning for it. You should describe your future business in the form of a **business plan**, which is a formal document describing the company that you want to start. The business plan is a blueprint for your company, and it's an essential tool in attracting investors and/or obtaining loans. It's also valuable as an ongoing guide to your business and a yardstick by which you can measure your performance. Preparing a business plan takes a lot of time, but it's worth the effort. It forces you to think critically about your proposed business and reduces your risk of failure.

Although formats vary, a business plan generally includes the following sections: an **executive summary**, which describes the proposed business and analyzes the industry in which it's going to compete; a **mission statement** and statement of **core values**; a management plan; a description of goods and/or services; a description of development and production processes; and marketing and financial plans.

6. **Discuss ways to succeed in managing a business and explain why some businesses fail.**

As a business owner, you'll need to be able to manage and grow your business. It's a difficult under-taking, but you increase the likelihood of success if you understand the basics of business management and know your business and its industry; have a positive attitude and believe in what you're doing; get adequate funding to start and continue operating your business; manage your money effectively; make efficient use of your time; understand how to motivate people and develop positive working relationships with your employees; satisfy your customers; and know how to compete in the marketplace.

You can get help in starting and growing a business from the SBA. The SBA also helps small business owners obtain financing, and it offers training and management assistance through a number of programs. The **Small Business Development Center (SBDC)** provides free training and technical information on all aspects of small business management at over 1,000 locations throughout the country. For individualized advice from experienced executives, business owners can call on the **Service Corps of Retired Executives (SCORE)**, which matches business owners with retired executives who volunteer their services.

Despite all the available assistance, the failure rate for small businesses is high. Some of the reasons for small business failure include bad business ideas, managerial inexperience or incompetence, lack of customer focus, and inability to handle growth.

Questions and Problems

1. **AACSB ▶ Analysis**
Do you have what it takes to be an entrepreneur? To find out, review the attributes mentioned in the text that can be used to characterize entrepreneurs. Next, use the following three-point scale to indicate the extent to which each of the attributes characterizes you: (1) doesn't sound like me, (2) sounds like me to a certain extent, or (3) sounds a lot like me. Based on your responses, do you think that you have the attributes of an entrepreneur? Do you think you could be a successful entrepreneur? Why or why not?

2. **AACSB ▶ Analysis**
Because you're convinced that the best way to get rich is to work for yourself, you're thinking about starting your own business. You have an idea and $100,000 that you just inherited from a great aunt. You even have a location: Palo Alto, California, which (according to a May 2004 *Forbes* magazine article by Betsy Schiffman) is the best place in the United States to get rich. But, there's a downside: To move to California and start your own business, you'll have to drop out of college.

What financial risks should you consider in making your decision? What are your chances of succeeding with your plan? Are you willing to take the financial risk needed to start a business? Why or why not? Are you likely to make more money running your own business than working for someone else?

3. How "small" is a small business? If a substantial portion of small businesses in the United States suddenly closed, what would be the impact on the U.S. economy? How would all these closings affect workers, consumers, and other businesses?

4. Why are most small businesses found in the service-producing sector? Identify five small service-producing businesses that you patronize frequently. What kinds of small businesses are found in the goods-producing sector? What small goods-producing firms do you do business with regularly?

5. **AACSB ▶ Analysis**
First, identify five advantages of small-business ownership. Next, rank these advantages according to their

importance to you. Why did you rank them as you did? What factors discourage individuals from small-business ownership? Indicate which of these factors might discourage you from starting a business. Explain why.

6. AACSB ▶ Analysis

It's the same old story: You want to start a small business but don't have much money. Go to www.prenhall.com/collins to link to the About.com Web site and read the article, "Business on a Budget." Identify some businesses that you can start for $20 or less (that's right—$20 or less). Select one of these opportunities that interests you. Why did you select this business? Why does the idea interest you? What would you do to ensure the business was a success? If you needed assistance starting up or operating your business, where could you find help, and what type of assistance would be available?

7. AACSB ▶ Analysis

If business ownership interests you, you can start a new business, buy an existing business, or obtain a franchise. Evaluate the advantages and disadvantages of each option. Which option do you find most appealing and why? Describe the business you would probably start.

8. Why do some businesses succeed while others fail? Identify three factors that you believe to be the most critical to business success. Why did you select these factors? Identify three factors that you believe to be primarily responsible for business failures, and indicate why you selected these factors.

9. AACSB ▶ Analysis

Let's start with three givens: (1) college students love chocolate chip cookies, (2) you have a special talent for baking cookies, and (3) you're always broke. Given these three conditions, you've come up with the idea of starting an on-campus business—selling chocolate chip cookies to fellow students. As a business major, you want to start out right by preparing a business plan. To get started, you identified a number of specifics about your proposed business. Now, you need to put these various pieces of information into the relevant section of your business plan. Using the business plan format described in this chapter, indicate the section of the business plan into which you'd put each of the following pieces of information:

a. You'll bake the cookies in the kitchen of a friend's apartment.

b. You'll charge $1 each or $10 a dozen.

c. Your purpose is to make the best cookies on campus and deliver them fresh. You value integrity, consideration of others, and quality.

d. Each cookie will have 10 chocolate chips and will be superior to those sold in nearby bakeries and other stores.

e. You expect sales of $6,000 for the first year.

f. Chocolate chip cookies are irresistible to college students. There's a lot of competition from local bakeries, but your cookies will be superior and popular with college students. You'll make them close to campus using only fresh ingredients and sell them for $1 each. Your management team is excellent. You'll market your product by placing ads in the school paper. You expect first-year sales of $6,000 and net income of $1,500. You estimate start-up costs at $600.

g. You'll place ads for your product in the college newspaper.

h. You'll hire a vice president at a salary of $100 a week.

i. You can ship cookies anywhere in the United States and in Canada.

j. You need $600 in cash to start the business.

k. There are six bakeries within walking distance of the college.

l. You'll bake nothing but cookies and sell them to college students. You'll make them in an apartment near campus and deliver them fresh.

10. AACSB ▶ Analysis

How would you like to spend your summer collecting trash in a used pickup? Doesn't sound very appealing, does it? Would you quit college to do it full time? Probably not. But that's exactly what Brian Scudamore did. And he got very rich doing it. His summer job turned into the company known as 1-800-GOT-JUNK, one of the fastest-growing franchises in the United States and Canada. Go to www.exploringbusinessonline.com to link to the 1-800-GOT-JUNK Web site and learn more about the company. After looking at the site, answer the following questions:

a. What is the company's business model? What does it do? Where does it do it?

b. Are you the kind of person the company wants to attract as a franchise partner?

c. How much would it cost you to buy a franchise? How much total capital would you need?

d. What kinds of support and services would you receive from the company?

e. Assuming that you had enough money, would you buy a franchise? Why or why not?

As a reward for working hard, take a break and click on the Junk Genie icon on the Web site's home page. Can you figure out the trick? Pass it along to your friends.

Learning on the Web AACSB

Would You Like to Own a Sub Shop?

How would you like to own your own sandwich shop? You could start one on your own or buy one that's already in business, but an easier way might be buying a franchise from Subway, the largest fast food franchise in the world (even bigger than McDonald's). Subway began in 1965 when 17-year-old Fred DeLuca opened a tiny sandwich shop in Bridgeport, Connecticut, hoping to put himself through college. As it turns out, his venture did much more than that. By 1974, DeLuca was franchising his business concept, and today, there are more than 15,000 Subway franchisees in more than 75 countries.

Go to www.exploringbusinessonline.com to link to the Subway Web site and learn more about franchise opportu-nities with the company. After reviewing the information provided on the company's Web site, answer the following questions:

1. What do you have to do to get a Subway franchise?

2. How much would it cost to open a Subway shop?

3. What training and support would you receive from Subway?

4. What advantages do you see in buying a Subway fran-chise rather than starting a business from scratch? What disadvantages do you see?

Career Opportunities

Do You Want to Be an Entrepreneur?

Want to learn what it's like to be an entrepreneur? To help you decide if life as an entrepreneur might be for you, go to www.exploringbusinessonline.com to link to the WetFeet Web site and review the entrepreneur profiles. Select *two* entrepre-neurs who interest you and for each, do the following:

1. Describe the company that he or she founded.

2. Explain the reasons why he or she became an entrepreneur.

3. Explain what qualities and/or background prepared the individual to start a business.

After reading the interviews with these two entrepre-neurs, answer the following questions:

1. What aspects of being an entrepreneur are particu-larly rewarding?

2. What's the downside of being an entrepreneur?

3. What challenges do entrepreneurs face?

4. Is entrepreneurship for you? Why or why not?

Ethics Angle AACSB

Term Papers for Sale

You and some fellow classmates are sitting around over pizza one night when someone comes up with an idea for a busi-ness. All of you have old term papers and essays lying around, and a couple of you know how to set up a Web page. What if you combine these two assets and start a business selling term papers over the Internet? Over time, you could collect or buy additional inventory from other students, and since some of you are good at research and others are good writers, you could even offer "clients" the option of customized papers researched and written just for them. You figure that you can charge $15 for an "off-the-rack" paper, and for customized jobs, $10 per double-spaced page seems reasonable.

You all agree that the idea is promising, and you and a partner volunteer to put together a business plan. You have no difficulty with the section describing your proposed busi-ness: You know what your business will do, what products it will offer, who your customers will be, how your products will be sold, and where you'll be located. So far, so good.

Let's pause at this point to consider the following questions:

1. Does selling term papers over the Internet make busi-ness sense? Is it a good business idea?

2. Could the venture be profitable?

Let's continue and find out how the business plan proceeds.

Now, you're ready for your section on industry analy-sis. The first question you need to answer is: Who are the players in the industry? To get some answers, you go online, log on to Google, and enter the search term "term papers for sale." Much to your surprise, up pop dozens of links to companies that have beaten you to market. The first company you investigate claims that it has 250,000 papers in stock, plus a team of graduate students on hand to write papers for anyone needing specialized work.

There's also a statement that says, "Our term papers and essays are designed only to help students prepare their own work. Students using our term papers and essays are responsible for writing their own papers, and our work should be cited by these students."

But back to your business plan. You realize that you're facing not only stiff competition but an issue which, so far, you and your partners have preferred to ignore: Is this an ethical business that you have in mind? It occurs to you that you could probably find the answer to this question in at least 1 of the 8,484 term papers on ethics available on your competitor's Web site, but you decide that it would be more efficient to give the question some thoughts of your own.

Let's pause again to state the question that you're going to ask yourself:

1. Is the sole purpose of running a business to make a profit, or do you need to be concerned about what your products will be used for? Explain your reasoning.

2. Do you need to consider the ethics of what other people do with your product? Explain your reasoning.

When you report on the problem that you've uncovered, your would-be partners are pretty discouraged, some by the prospect of competition and some by the nagging ethical issue. Just as you're about to dissolve the partnership, one person speaks up: "How about selling software that lets faculty search to see if students have plagiarized material on the Web?"

"Sorry," says someone else. "It's already out there. Two students at Berkeley have software that compares papers to a hundred million Web pages."

Team-Building Skills AACSB

Knowing how to be an effective team member is a vital lifetime skill. It will help you in your academic career, in the business world, and in non-work activities. It takes time and effort to learn how to work in a team. Part of the challenge is learning how to adjust your behavior to the needs of the group. Another part is learning how to motivate members of a group. A well-functioning team allows members to combine knowledge and skills, and this reliance on diverse backgrounds and strengths often results in team decisions that are superior to those made by individuals working alone.

1. **Are You a Team Player?**
   As a first step, you should do a self-assessment to evaluate whether you possess characteristics that will help you be a successful team member. You can do this by taking a "Team Player" quiz available at the career Web site on

Monster.com. Go to www.exploringbusinessonline.com to link to this site. You'll get feedback that helps you identify the characteristics you need to work on if you want to improve your teamwork skills.

2. **Working Together as a Team**
   The best approach to specifying appropriate behavior for team members is to have the team come up with some ground rules. Get together with three other students selected by your instructor and establish working guidelines for your team. Prepare a team report in which you identify the following:

   a. Five things that team members can do to increase the likelihood of group success.

   b. Five things that team members can do to jeopardize group success.

The Global View AACSB

Global Versions of MySpace.com

When Chris DeWolfe and Tom Anderson founded MySpace.com in July 2003, they had no idea that they were headed for an overnight success. Well, almost overnight. Two and one-half years after their entrepreneurial venture had been launched, MySpace.com had nearly 50 million users in the United States, where 1 out of every 10 ads viewed on the Internet was seen on the site. Its popularity caught the attention of news and entertainment mogul Rupert Murdoch, whose News Corporation dished out $580 million for MySpace.com while allowing its founders to stay on as CEO and president.

What's ahead for MySpace.com? Can its business model be exported outside the United States? Murdoch thinks so; he immediately launched a British version of the site. If you were in charge of global expansion for MySpace.com, what country would you enter next? What country would you avoid? To identify promis-

ing and not-so-promising foreign markets, go to www.exploringbusinessonline.com to link to the Country Profiles Web site maintained by BBC News. Study the economic and political profiles of possible candidates and answer the following questions:

1. Why do you think MySpace.com has been so successful in the United States? Cite some examples of the challenges that it faces.

2. If you were in charge of global expansion at MySpace.com, which country would you enter next? Why do you think the MySpace.com business concept will succeed in this country? What challenges will the company face?

3. What country would you avoid? Why is it incompatible with the MySpace.com business concept?

Business Plan Project

Group Report: *Your Great Business Idea*

INITIAL REPORT

The selection of a business idea is the most important choice that your team will make in this course. Give it some thought, and make your choice carefully. If you need some further advice or guidance on coming up with a great business idea (and most students do), go to Appendix A at the back of this book, entitled "Introducing Your Business Plan," and consult the section headed "Type of Company." The team should submit a written report identifying its great business idea and explaining its choice. The report should be about two double-spaced typed pages. The name of your proposed business and the names of all team members should appear on the report.

REASONABLE CONTRIBUTIONS

All members of the team who make **a reasonable contribution to the report** should sign it. If any team member does not work on the report, his or her name should *not* appear on it. If a student who has made a contribution is unable to sign the report (because of sickness or some other valid reason), the team can sign his/her name. To indicate that a name was signed by the team on a member's behalf, be sure to attach a note to the signature.

CHAPTER 3

Business Ethics and Social Responsibility

After studying this chapter you will be able to:

1. Define *business ethics* and explain what it means to act ethically in business.

2. Specify the steps that you'd take to solve an ethical dilemma and make an ethical decision.

3. Identify ethical issues that you might face in business and analyze rationalizations for unethical behavior.

4. Specify actions that managers can take to create and sustain ethical organizations.

5. Define *corporate social responsibility* and explain how organizations are responsible to their stakeholders.

6. Identify threats to the natural environment and explain how businesses are addressing them.

Philip Condit II/Getty Images, Inc.

"MOMMY, WHY DO YOU HAVE TO GO TO JAIL?"

"Mommy, why do you have to go to jail?" That's the one question Betty Vinson would prefer to avoid.[1] Vinson graduated with an accounting degree from Mississippi State and married her college sweetheart. After a series of jobs at small banks, she landed a mid-level accounting job at WorldCom, at the time still a small long-distance provider. Sparked by the telecom boom, however, WorldCom soon became a darling of Wall Street, and its stock price soared. Now working for a wildly successful company, Vinson rounded out her life by reading legal thrillers and watching her 12-year-old daughter play soccer.

Her moment of truth came in mid-2000, when company executives learned that profits had plummeted. They asked Vinson to make some accounting adjustments to boost income by $828 million. She knew that the scheme was unethical (at the very least) but gave in and made the

Former WorldCom accountant Betty Vinson enters Manhattan federal court in New York. She was sentenced to five months in jail and five months house arrest for her guilty plea in the company's $11 billion accounting fraud.

adjustments. Almost immediately, she felt guilty and told her boss that she was quitting. When news of her decision came to the attention of CEO Bernard Ebbers and CFO Scott Sullivan, they hastened to assure Vinson that she'd never be asked to cook any more books. Sullivan explained it this way: "We have planes in the air. Let's get the planes landed. Once they've landed, if you still want to leave, then leave. But not while the planes are in the air."[2] Besides, she'd done nothing illegal, and if anyone asked, he'd take full responsibility. So Vinson decided to stay. After all, Sullivan was one of the top CFOs in the country; at age 37, he was already making $19 million a year.[3] Who was she to question his judgment?[4]

Six months later, Ebbers and Sullivan needed another adjustment—this time for $771 million. This scheme was even more unethical than the first: It entailed forging dates to hide the adjustment. Pretty soon, Vinson was making adjustments on a quarterly basis—first for $560 million, then for $743 million, and yet again, for $941 million. Eventually, Vinson had juggled almost $4 billion, and before long, the stress started to get to her: She had trouble sleeping, lost weight, looked terrible, and withdrew from people at work. But when she got a promotion and a $30,000 raise, she decided to hang in.

By the spring of 2002, however, it was obvious that adjusting the books was business as usual at WorldCom. Vinson finally decided that it was time to move on, but, unfortunately, an internal auditor had already put two and two together and blown the whistle. The Securities and Exchange Commission charged WorldCom with fraud amounting to $11 billion—the largest in U.S. history. Seeing herself as a valuable witness, Vinson was eager to tell what she knew. The government, however, regarded her as more than a mere witness. When she was named a co-conspirator, she agreed to cooperate fully and pleaded guilty to criminal conspiracy and securities fraud. And that's why Betty Vinson will spend five months in jail. But she won't be the only one doing time: Scott Sullivan—who claims he's innocent—will be in jail for 5 years, and Bernie Ebbers—who swears he's innocent also—will be locked up for 25 years.[5]

So where did Betty Vinson, mild-mannered mid-level executive and mother, go wrong? How did she manage to get involved in a scheme that not only bilked investors billions but cost 17,000 people their jobs?[6] Ultimately, of course, we can only guess. Maybe she couldn't say no to her bosses; maybe she believed that they'd take full responsibility for her accounting "adjustments." Maybe she was afraid of losing her job. Perhaps she didn't fully understand the ramifications of what she was doing. What we do know is that she disgraced herself and headed for jail.[7]

Misgoverning Corporations: An Overview

The WorldCom situation is not an isolated incident. The boom years of the 1990s were followed by revelations of massive corporate corruption, including criminal schemes at companies such as Enron, Adelphia, and Tyco. In fall 2001, executives at Enron, an energy supplier, admitted to accounting practices concocted to overstate the company's income over a period of four years. In the wake of the company's collapse, stock prices plummeted from $90 to $1 a share, inflicting massive financial losses on the investment community. Thousands of employees lost not only their jobs but their retirement funds.[8] Before the Enron story was off the front pages, officials at Adelphia, the nation's sixth-largest cable company, disclosed that founder and CEO John Rigas had treated the publicly owned firm as a personal piggy bank, siphoning off billions of dollars to support his family's extravagant lifestyle and bankrupting the company in the process.[9] Likewise, CEO Dennis Koslowzki of conglomerate Tyco International was apparently confused about what was his and what belonged to the company. Besides treating himself to a $30 million estate in Florida and a $7 million Park Avenue apartment, Koslowzki indulged a taste for expensive office accessories—such as a $15,000 umbrella stand, a $17,000 traveling toilette box, and a $2,200 wastebasket—that eventually drained $600 million from company coffers.[10] Are these cases just aberrations?

A *Time* /CNN poll conducted in the midst of all these revelations found that 72 percent of those surveyed don't think so. They think that breach of investor and employee trust represents an ongoing and long-standing pattern of deceptive behavior by officials at a large number of companies.[11] If they're right, then a lot of questions need to be answered. Why do such incidents happen (and with such apparent regularity)? Who are the usual suspects? How long until the new bankruptcy record is set? What action can be taken—by individuals, organizations, and the government—to discourage such behavior?

THE IDEA OF BUSINESS ETHICS

Believe it or not, it's in the best interests of a company to operate ethically. Trustworthy companies are better at attracting and keeping customers, talented employees, and capital. Those tainted by questionable ethics suffer from dwindling customer bases, employee turnover, and investor mistrust.

Let's begin this section by addressing one of the questions that we posed previously: What can individuals, organizations, and government agencies do to foster an environment of ethical and socially responsible behavior in business? First, of course, we need to define two terms: *business ethics* and *social responsibility*. They're often used interchangeably, but they don't mean the same thing.

What Is *Ethics*?

You probably already know what it means to be **ethical**: to know right from wrong and to know when you're practicing one instead of the other. At the risk of oversimplifying, then, we can say that **business ethics** is the application of ethical behavior in a business context. Acting ethically in business means more than just obeying applicable laws and regulations: It also means being honest, doing no harm to others, competing fairly, and declining to put your own interests above those of your company, its owners, and its workers. You obviously need a strong sense of what's right and what's wrong (not always an easy task). You need the personal conviction to *do* what's right, even if it means doing something that's difficult or disadvantageous personally.

What Is *Social Responsibility*?

Corporate social responsibility deals with actions that affect a variety of parties in a company's environment. A socially responsible company shows concern for its **stakeholders**—anyone who, like owners, employees, customers, and the communities in which it does business, has a "stake" or interest in it. We'll discuss corporate responsibility in the second part of the chapter. At this point, we'll focus on ethics.

How Can You Recognize an Ethical Organization?

One goal of anyone engaged in business should be to foster ethical behavior in the organizational environment. How do we know when an organization is behaving ethically? Most lists of ethical organizational activities include the following criteria:

- Treating employees, customers, investors, and the public fairly.

- Making fairness a top priority.

- Holding every member personally accountable for his or her actions.

- Communicating core values and principles to all members.

- Demanding and rewarding integrity from all members in all situations.[12]

If you work for a business (or for a nonprofit organization), you probably have a sense of whether your employer is ethical or unethical. Employees at companies that consistently make *Business Ethics* magazine's list of the "100 Best Corporate Citizens" regard the items on the above list as business as usual in the workplace. Companies that routinely win good-citizenship awards include Procter & Gamble, Intel, Avon Products, Herman Miller, Timberland, Cisco Systems, Southwest Airlines, AT&T, Starbucks Coffee, Merck, and Medtronic.[13] (Interestingly, their employees not only see these firms as ethical, but also tend to enjoy working for them.)

On the other hand, employees with the following attitudes tend to suspect that their employers aren't as ethical as they should be:

- They consistently feel uneasy about the work they do.

- They object to the way they're treated.

- They're uncomfortable about the way coworkers are treated.

- They question the appropriateness of management directives and policies.[14]

In the early 1990s, many workers in Sears automotive service centers shared suspicions about certain policies, including the ways in which they were supposed to deal with customers. In particular, they felt uncomfortable with a new compensation plan that rewarded them for selling alignments, brake jobs, shock absorbers, and other parts and services. Those who met quotas got bonuses; those who didn't were often fired. The results shouldn't be surprising: In their zeal to meet quotas and keep their jobs, some employees misled customers into believing they needed unnecessary parts and services. Before long, Sears was flooded with complaints from customers—as were law-enforcement officials—in more than 40 states. Sears denied any intent to deceive customers but was forced not only to eliminate sales commissions, but to pay out $60 million in refunds.

WHY STUDY ETHICS?

Ideally, prison terms, heavy fines, and civil suits should put a damper on corporate misconduct, but, unfortunately, many experts suspect that this assumption may be a bit optimistic. Whatever the condition of the ethical environment in the near future, one thing seems clear: The next generation entering business—which includes most of you—will find a world much different than the one waiting for the previous generation. Recent history tells us in no uncertain terms that today's business students—including tomorrow's business leaders—need a much sharper understanding of the difference between what is and isn't ethically acceptable. As a business student, one of your key tasks is learning how to recognize and deal with the ethical challenges that will confront you.

Moreover, knowing right from wrong will make you more marketable as a job candidate. Asked what he looked for in a new hire, Warren Buffet, the world's most successful investor, replied: "I look for three things. The first is personal integrity, the second is intelligence, and the third is a high energy level." He paused and then added: "But if you don't have the first, the second two don't matter."[15]

---

ethics
Ability and willingness to distinguish right from wrong and when you're practicing one or the other.

business ethics
Application of ethical behavior in a business context.

corporate social responsibility
Approach that an organization takes in balancing its responsibilities toward different stakeholders when making legal, economic, ethical, and social decisions.

stakeholders
Parties who are interested in the activities of a business because they're affected by them.

The Individual Approach to Ethics

Betty Vinson didn't start out at WorldCom with the intention of going to jail. She undoubtedly knew what the right behavior was, but the bottom line is that she didn't *do* it. How can you make sure that you *do* the right thing in the business world? How should you respond to the kinds of challenges that you'll be facing? Because your actions in the business world will be strongly influenced by your moral character, let's begin by assessing your current moral condition. Which of the following best applies to you (select one)?

1. I'm always ethical

2. I'm mostly ethical

3. I'm somewhat ethical

4. I'm seldom ethical

5. I'm never ethical

Now that you've placed yourself in one of these categories, here are some general observations. Very few people put themselves below the second category. Most of us are ethical most of the time, and most people assign themselves to category number two—"I'm *mostly* ethical." Why don't more people claim that they're *always* ethical? Apparently, most people realize that being ethical all of the time takes a great deal of moral energy. If you placed yourself in category number two, ask yourself this question: How can I change my behavior so that I can move up a notch? The answer to this question may be very simple. Just ask yourself an easier question: How would I like to be treated in a given situation?[16]

Unfortunately, practicing this philosophy might be easier in your personal life than in the business world. Ethical challenges arise in business because business organizations (especially large ones) have multiple stakeholders and because stakeholders make conflicting demands. Making decisions that affect multiple stakeholders isn't easy even for seasoned managers; and for new entrants to the business world, the task can be extremely daunting. Many managers need years of experience in an organization before they feel comfortable making decisions that affect various stakeholders. You can, however, get a head start in learning how to make ethical decisions by looking at two types of challenges that you'll encounter in the business world: *ethical dilemmas* and *ethical decisions*.

ADDRESSING ETHICAL DILEMMAS

An **ethical dilemma** is a morally problematic situation: You have to pick between two or more acceptable but often opposing alternatives that are important to different groups. Experts often frame this type of situation as a "right-versus-right" decision. It's the sort of decision that Johnson & Johnson (J&J) CEO James Burke had to make in 1982.[17] On September 30, 12-year-old Mary Kellerman of Chicago died after her parents gave her Extra-Strength Tylenol. That same morning, 27-year-old Adam Janus, also of Chicago, died after taking Tylenol for minor chest pain. That night, when family members came to console his parents, Adam's brother and his wife took Tylenol from the same bottle and died within 48 hours. Over the next two weeks, 4 more people in Chicago died after taking Tylenol. The actual connection between Tylenol and the series of deaths wasn't made until an off-duty fireman realized from news reports that every victim had taken Tylenol. As consumers panicked, J&J pulled Tylenol off of Chicago-area retail shelves. Researchers discovered Tylenol capsules containing large amounts of deadly cyanide. Because the poisoned bottles came from batches originating at different J&J plants, investigators determined that the tampering had occurred after the product had been shipped.

So J&J wasn't at fault. But CEO Burke was still faced with a very serious dilemma: Was it possible to respond to the tampering cases without destroying the reputation of an extremely profitable brand? Burke had two options:

- He could recall only the lots of Extra-Strength Tylenol that were found to be tainted with cyanide. This was the path followed by Perrier executives in 1991 when they discovered that cases of bottled water had been poisoned with benzine. This option favored the company financially but possibly put more people at risk.

• He could order a nationwide recall—of all bottles of Extra-Strength Tylenol. This option would reverse the priority of the stakeholders, putting the safety of the public above the financial interests of stockholders.

Burke opted to recall all 31 million bottles of Extra-Strength Tylenol on the market. The cost to J&J was $100 million, but public reaction was quite positive. Less than six weeks after the crisis began, Tylenol capsules were reintroduced in new tamper-resistant bottles, and by responding quickly and appropriately, J&J was eventually able to restore the Tylenol brand to its previous market position. When Burke was applauded for moral courage, he replied that he'd simply adhered to the long-standing J&J credo that put the interests of customers above those of other stakeholders. His only regret was that the tamperer was never caught.[18]

If you're wondering what your thought process should be if you're confronted with an ethical dilemma, you could do worse than remember the mental steps listed in Figure 3.1—which happen to be the steps that James Burke took in addressing the Tylenol crisis.

MAKING ETHICAL DECISIONS

In contrast to the "right-versus-right" problem posed by an ethical dilemma, an **ethical decision** entails a "right-versus-wrong" decision—one in which there is a right (ethical) choice and a wrong (unethical or illegal) choice. When you make a decision that's unmistakably unethical or illegal, you've committed an **ethical lapse**. Betty Vinson, for example, had an ethical lapse when she caved in to her bosses' pressure to cook the WorldCom books. If you're presented with what appears to be this type of choice, asking yourself the questions in Figure 3.2 (on p. 50) will increase your odds of making an ethical decision.

To test the validity of this approach, let's take a point-by-point look at Betty Vinson's decisions:

1. Her actions were clearly illegal.

2. They were unfair to the workers who lost their jobs and to the investors who suf-

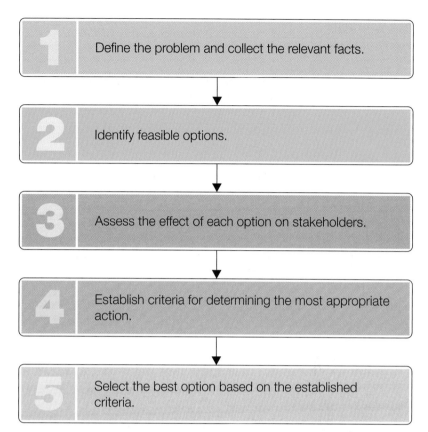

1. Define the problem and collect the relevant facts.

2. Identify feasible options.

3. Assess the effect of each option on stakeholders.

4. Establish criteria for determining the most appropriate action.

5. Select the best option based on the established criteria.

Figure 3.1

How to Face an Ethical Dilemma

fered financial losses (and to her family, who shared her public embarrassment).

3. She definitely felt badly about what she'd done.

4. She was embarrassed to tell other people what she'd done.

5. Reports of her actions appeared in her local newspaper (and just about every other newspaper in the country).

So Vinson could have answered our five test questions with five yeses. To simplify matters, remember the following rule of thumb: If you answer yes to *any one of these five questions*, odds are that you're about to do something you shouldn't.

What to Do When the Light Turns Yellow

Like our five questions, some ethical problems are pretty straightforward. Others, unfortunately, are more complicated, but it will help to think of our five-question test as a set of signals which will warn you that

---

ethical dilemma
Morally problematic situation.

ethical decision
Decision in which there is a right (ethical) choice and a wrong (unethical or illegal) choice.

ethical lapse
Situation in which an individual makes a decision that's unmistakably unethical or illegal.

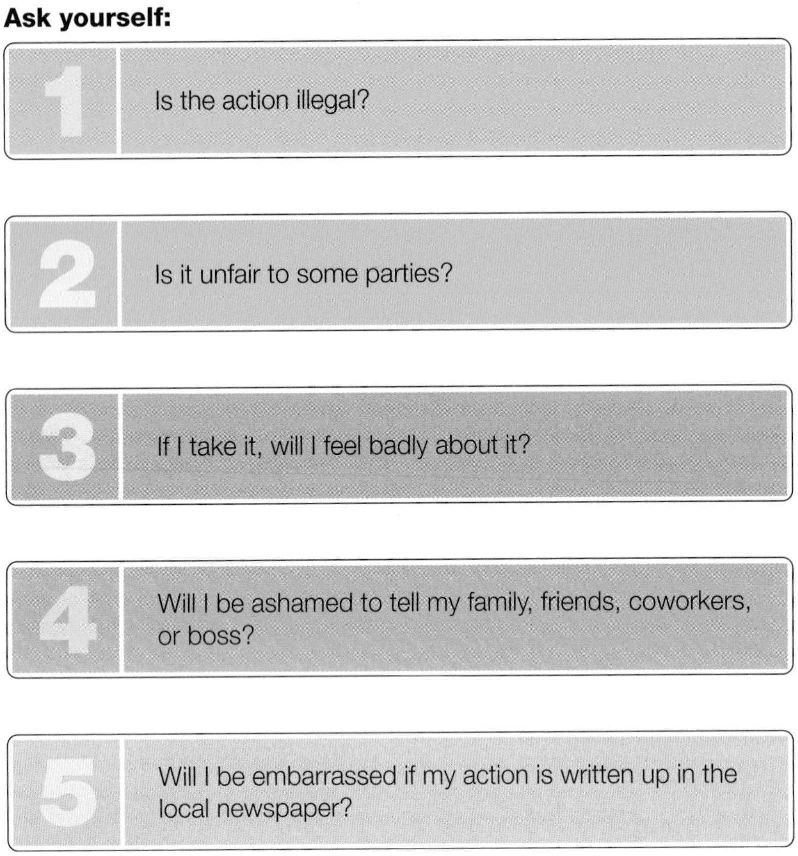

Ask yourself:

1   Is the action illegal?

2   Is it unfair to some parties?

3   If I take it, will I feel badly about it?

4   Will I be ashamed to tell my family, friends, coworkers, or boss?

5   Will I be embarrassed if my action is written up in the local newspaper?

Figure 3.2

How to Avoid an Ethical Lapse

you're facing a particularly tough decision—that you should think carefully about it and, perhaps, consult someone else. The situation is like approaching a traffic light. Red and green lights are easy; you know what they mean and exactly what to do. Yellow lights are trickier. Before you decide which pedal to hit, try posing our five questions. If you get a single yes, you'll be much better off hitting the brake.[19]

QUICK QUIZ   3.1

Before going on to find out more about specific ethical issues, take a few minutes to test what you've learned about the principles of ethics, ethical dilemmas, and ethical decision making.

Go to www.exploringbusinessonline.com

IDENTIFYING ETHICAL ISSUES

Make no mistake about it: When you enter the business world, you'll find yourself in situations in which you'll have to choose the appropriate behavior. How, for example, would you answer questions like the following?

- Is it okay to accept a pair of sports tickets from a supplier?
- Can I buy office supplies from my brother-in-law?
- Is it appropriate to donate company funds to my local community center?
- If I find out that a friend is about to be fired, can I warn her?
- Will I have to lie about the quality of the goods I'm selling?
- Can I take personal e-mails and phone calls at work?
- What do I do if I discover that a coworker is committing fraud?

Obviously, the types of situations are numerous. Fortunately, we can break them down into a few basic categories: *bribes, conflicts of interest, conflicts of loyalty, issues of honesty and integrity,* and *whistle-blowing.* Let's look a little more closely at each of these categories.

Bribes versus Gifts

It's not uncommon in business to give and receive small gifts of appreciation. But when is a gift unacceptable? When is it really a bribe? If it's okay to give a bottle of wine to a corporate client during the holidays, is it okay to make it a case? If your company is trying to get a big contract, is it appropriate to send a gift to the key decision maker? If it's all right to invite a business acquaintance to dinner or to a ballgame, is it also all right to offer the same person a fully paid weekend getaway?

There's often a fine line between a gift and a bribe. The questions that we've just asked, however, may help in drawing it because they raise key issues in determining how a gesture should be interpreted: the cost of the item, the timing of the gift, the type of gift, and the connection between the giver and the receiver. If you're on the receiving end, it's a good idea to refuse any item that's overly generous or given for the purpose of influencing a decision. But because accepting even small gifts may violate company rules, the best advice is to check on company policy.

J.C. Penney's "Statement of Business Ethics," for instance, states that employees cannot accept any cash gifts or any non-cash gifts except those which have a value below $50 and which are generally used by the giver for promotional purposes. They can attend paid-for business functions, but other forms of entertainment, such as sports events and golf outings, can be accepted only if it's practical for the Penney's employee to reciprocate. Trips of several days cannot be accepted under any circumstances.[20]

Conflicts of Interest

Conflicts of interest occur when individuals must choose between taking actions that promote their personal interests over the interests of others. A conflict can exist, for example, when an employee's own interests interfere with, or have the potential to interfere with, the best interests of the company's stakeholders (management, customers, owners). Let's say that you work for a company with a contract to cater events at your college and that your uncle owns a local bakery. Obviously, this situation could create a conflict of interest (or at least give the appearance of one—which, by the way, is a problem in itself). When you're called upon to furnish desserts for a luncheon, you might be tempted to throw some business your uncle's way even if it's not in the best interest of the catering company that you work for.

What should you do? You should probably disclose the connection to your boss, who can then arrange things so that your personal interests don't conflict with the company's. You may, for example, agree that if you're assigned to order products like those that your uncle makes, you're obligated to find another supplier. Or your boss may make sure that someone else orders bakery products.

The same principle holds that an employee shouldn't use private information about an employer for personal financial benefit. Say, for example, that you learn from a coworker at your pharmaceutical company that one of its most profitable drugs will be pulled off the market because of dangerous side effects. The recall will severely hurt the company's financial performance and cause its stock price to plummet. Before the news becomes public, you sell all the stock you own in the company. What you've done isn't merely unethical: It's called **insider trading**, it's illegal, and you could go to jail.

Conflicts of Loyalty

Sometimes you find yourself in a bind between being loyal to either your employer or to a friend or family member. Perhaps you just learned that a coworker and friend is about to be downsized out of his job. You also happen to know that he and his wife are getting ready to make a deposit on a house near the company headquarters. From a work standpoint, you know that you shouldn't divulge the information. From a friendship standpoint, however, you feel it's your duty to tell your friend. Wouldn't he tell you if the situation were reversed? What do you do? As tempting as it is to be loyal to your friend, you shouldn't. As an employee, your primary responsibility is to your employer. You might be able to soften your dilemma by convincing a manager with the appropriate authority to tell your friend the bad news before he puts down his deposit.

Issues of Honesty and Integrity

Master investor Warren Buffet once told a group of business students:

> I cannot tell you that honesty is the best policy. I can't tell you that if you behave with perfect honesty and integrity somebody somewhere won't behave the other way and make more money. But honesty is a good policy. You'll do fine, you'll sleep well at night and you'll feel good about the example you are setting for your coworkers and the other people who care about you.[21]

If you work for a company that settles for its employees merely obeying the law and a few internal regulations, you might think about moving on. If you're being asked to deceive customers about the quality or value of your product, you're in an ethically unhealthy environment.

---

conflict of interest
Situation in which an individual must choose between the promotion of personal interests and the interests of others.

insider trading
Practice of illegally buying or selling of securities using important information about the company before it's made public.

Think about this story:

A chef put two frogs in a pot of warm soup water. The first frog smelled the onions, recognized the danger, and immediately jumped out. The second frog hesitated: The water felt good, and he decided to stay and relax for a minute. After all, he could always jump out when things got too hot (so to speak). As the water got hotter, however, the frog adapted to it, hardly noticing the change. Before long, of course, he was the main ingredient in frog-leg soup.[22]

So, what's the moral of the story? Don't sit around in an ethically toxic environment and lose your integrity a little at a time; get out before the water gets too hot, and your options have evaporated.

Fortunately, there are a few rules of thumb. We've summed them up in Figure 3.3.

Whistle-Blowing

As we've seen, the misdeeds of Betty Vinson and her accomplices at WorldCom didn't go undetected. They caught the eye of Cynthia Cooper, the director of internal auditing.

Figure 3.3

How to Maintain Honesty and Integrity

Follow your own code of personal conduct; act according to your own convictions rather than doing what's convenient (or profitable) at the time.

While at work, focus on your job, not on nonwork-related activities, such as e-mails and personal phone calls.

Don't appropriate office supplies or products or other company resources for your own use.

Be honest with customers, management, coworkers, competitors, and the public.

Remember that it's the small, seemingly trivial, day-to-day activities and gestures that build your character.

Cooper, of course, could have looked the other way, but instead, she summoned up the courage to be a **whistle-blower**—an individual who exposes illegal or unethical behavior in an organization. Like Vinson, Cooper had majored in accounting at Mississippi State and was a hard-working, dedicated employee. Unlike Vinson, however, she refused to be bullied by her boss, CFO Scott Sullivan. In fact, she had tried to tell not only Sullivan but auditors from Arthur Andersen that there was a problem with WorldCom's books. The auditors dismissed her warnings, and when Sullivan angrily told her to drop the matter, she started cleaning out her office. But she didn't relent. She and her team worked late each night, conducting an extensive, secret investigation. Two months later, Cooper had evidence to take to Sullivan, who told her once again to back off. Again, however, she stood up to him, and although she regretted the consequences for her WorldCom coworkers, she reported the scheme to the company's board of directors. Within days, Sullivan was fired and the largest accounting fraud in history became public.

As a result of Cooper's actions, executives came clean about the company's financial situation. The conspiracy of fraud was brought to an end, and although public disclosure of WorldCom's problems resulted in massive stock-price declines and employee layoffs, investor and employee losses would have been greater without Cooper's intervention.

Even though Cooper did the right thing the experience wasn't exactly gratifying. A lot of people applauded her action, but many coworkers shunned her; some even blamed *her* for the company's troubles. She's never been thanked by any senior executive at WorldCom. Five months after the fraud went public, new CEO Michael Capellas assembled what was left of the demoralized workforce to give them a pep talk on the company's future. The senior management team mounted the stage and led the audience in a rousing rendition of "If you're happy and you know it, clap your hands!" Cynthia Cooper wasn't invited.[23]

Whistle-blowing often means career suicide. A survey of 200 whistle-blowers conducted by the National Whistleblower Center found that half of them had been fired for blowing the whistle.[24] Even those who get to keep their jobs experience painful repercussions. As long as they stay, some people will treat them (as one whistle-blower puts it) "like skunks at a picnic"; if they leave, they're frequently blackballed in the industry.[25] On a positive note, there's the 2002 Sarbanes-Oxley Act, which protects whistle-blowers under federal law.

For her own part, Cynthia Cooper doesn't regret what she did. As she told a group of students at Mississippi State: "Strive to be persons of honor and integrity. Do not allow yourself to be pressured. Do what you know is right even if there may be a price to be paid."[26] If your company tells employees to do whatever it takes, push the envelope, look the other way, and be sure that we make our numbers, you have three choices: go along with the policy, try to change things, or leave. If your personal integrity is part of the equation, you're probably down to the last two choices.[27]

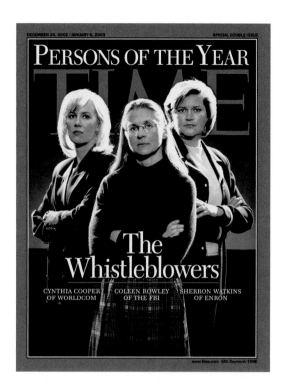

Cynthia Cooper, who blew the whistle on the WorldCom fraud, shares *Time* magazine's 2002 "Persons of the Year" award with two other whistle-blowers: Sherron Watkins of Enron and Coleen Rowley of the FBI.

REFUSING TO RATIONALIZE

Despite all the good arguments in favor of doing the right thing, why do many reasonable people act unethically (at least at times)? Why do good people make bad choices? According to one study, there are four common rationalizations for justifying misconduct:[28]

1. *My behavior isn't really illegal or immoral.* Rationalizers try to convince themselves that an action is okay if it isn't downright illegal or blatantly immoral. They tend to operate in a gray area where there's no clear evidence that the action is wrong.

2. *My action is in everyone's best interests.* Some rationalizers tell themselves: "I know I lied to make the deal, but it'll bring in a lot of business and pay a lot of bills." They convince themselves that they're expected to act in a certain way, forgetting the classic parental parable about jumping off a cliff just because your friends are.[29]

3. *No one will find out what I've done.* Here, the self-questioning comes down to: "If I didn't get caught, did I really do it?" The answer is yes. There's a sim-

ple way to avoid succumbing to this rationalization: Always act as if you're being watched.

4. *The company will condone my action and protect me.* This justification rests on a fallacy. Betty Vinson may honestly have believed that her actions were for the good of the company and that her boss would, therefore, accept full responsibility (as he promised). When she goes to jail, however, she'll go on her own.

Here's another rule of thumb: If you find yourself having to rationalize a decision, it's probably a bad one. Over time, you'll develop and hone your ethical decision-making skills.

The Organizational Approach to Ethics

Ethics is more than a matter of individual behavior; it's also about organizational behavior. Employees' actions aren't based solely on personal values alone: They're influenced by other members of the

whistle-blower
Individual who exposes illegal or unethical behavior in an organization.

organization, from top managers and supervisors to coworkers and subordinates. So how can ethical companies be created and sustained? In this section, we'll examine some of the most reasonable answers to this question.

Ethical Leadership

Organizations have unique *cultures*—ways of doing things that evolve through shared values and beliefs. An organization's culture is strongly influenced by senior executives, who tell members of the organization what's considered acceptable behavior and what happens if it's violated. In theory, the tone set at the top of the organization promotes ethical behavior, but sometimes (as at Enron) it doesn't.

Prior to its sudden demise, Enron fostered a growth-at-any-cost culture that was defined by the company's top executives. Said one employee: "It was all about taking profits now and worrying about the details later. The Enron system was just ripe for corruption." Coupled with the relentless pressure to generate revenue—or at least to look as if you were—was a climate that discouraged employees from questioning the means by which they were supposed to do it. There may have been chances for people to speak up, but no one did. "I don't think anyone started out with a plan to defraud the company," reflects another ex-employee. "Everything at Enron seemed to start out right, but somewhere something slipped. People's mentality switched from focusing on the future good of the company to 'let's just do it today.'"[30]

Exercising Ethical Leadership

Leaders should keep in constant touch with subordinates about ethical policies and expectations. They should be available to help employees identify and solve ethical problems and should encourage them to come forward with concerns. They are responsible for minimizing opportunities for wrongdoing and for exerting the controls needed to enforce company policies. They should also think of themselves as role models. Subordinates look to their supervisors to communicate policies and practices regarding ethical behavior, and as a rule, actions speak more loudly than words: If managers behave ethically, subordinates will probably do the same.

This is exactly the message that senior management at Martin Marietta (now a part of Lockheed Martin) sent to members of their organization. A leading producer of construction components, the company at the time was engaged in a tough competitive battle over a major contract. Because both Martin Marietta and its main competitor were qualified to do the work, the job would go to the lower bid. A few days before bids were due, a package arrived at Martin Marietta containing a copy of the competitor's bid sheet (probably from a disgruntled employee trying to sabotage his or her employer's efforts). The bid price was lower than Martin Marietta's. In a display of ethical backbone, executives immediately turned the envelope over to the government and informed the competitor. No, they didn't change their own bid in the meantime, and, no, they didn't get the job. All they got was an opportunity to send a very clear message to the entire organization.[31]

By the same token, leaders must be willing to hold subordinates accountable for their conduct and to take appropriate action. The response to unethical behavior should be prompt and decisive. One CEO of a large company discovered that some of his employees were "dumpster-diving" in the trash outside a competitor's offices (which is to say, they were sifting around for information that would give them a competitive advantage). The manager running the espionage operation was a personal friend of the CEO's, but he was immediately fired, as were his "operatives." The CEO then informed his competitor about the venture and returned all the materials that had been gathered. Like the top managers at Martin Marietta, this executive sent a clear message to people in his organization: namely, that deviations from accepted behavior would not be tolerated.[32]

It's always possible to send the wrong message. In August 2004, newspapers around the country carried a wire-service story entitled "Convicted CEO Getting $2.5 Million Salary While He Serves Time." Interested readers found that the board of directors of Fog Cutter Capital Group had agreed to pay CEO Andrew Wiederhorn (and give him a bonus) while he served an 18-month federal-prison term for bribery, filing false tax returns, and financially ruining his previous employer (from whom he'd also borrowed $160 million). According to the board, they couldn't afford to lose a man of Wiederhorn's ability. The whole episode ended up on TheStreet.com's list of "The Five Dumbest Things on Wall Street This Week."[33]

TIGHTENING THE RULES

In response to the recent barrage of corporate scandals, more large companies have taken additional steps to encourage employees to behave according to specific standards and to report wrongdoing. Even companies with excellent reputations for integrity have stepped up their efforts.

Codes of Conduct

Like many firms, Hershey Foods now has a formal **code of conduct**: a document describing the principles and guidelines that all employees must follow in the course of all job-related activities. It's available on the company intranet and in printed form, and to be sure that everyone understands it, the company offers a training program. The Hershey code covers such topics as the use of corporate funds and resources, conflict of interest, and the protection of proprietary information. It explains how the code will be enforced, emphasizing that violations won't be tolerated. It encourages employees to report wrongdoing and provides instructions on reporting violations (which are displayed on posters and printed on wallet-size cards). Reports can be made though a Concern Line, by e-mail, or by regular mail; they can be anonymous, and retaliation is also a serious violation of company policy.[34]

ABOUT NIKE   3.1

Now that you know something about what it means to act ethically in business, take a moment to read about the standards of conduct that Nike expects of its employees.

Go to www.exploringbusinessonline.com

QUICK QUIZ   3.2

Before going on to study corporate social responsibility, give yourself a quick quiz on what you learned in the previous section about ethical issues and ethical leadership in the business world.

Go to www.exploringbusinessonline.com

Corporate Social Responsibility

Corporate social responsibility refers to the approach that an organization takes in balancing its responsibilities toward different stakeholders when making legal, economic, ethical, and social decisions. What motivates companies to be "socially responsible" to their various stakeholders? We hope it's because they want to do the right thing, and for many companies, "doing the right thing" is a key motivator. The fact is, it's often hard to figure out what the "right thing" is: What's "right" for one group of stakeholders isn't necessarily just as "right" for another. One thing, however, is certain: Companies today are held to higher standards than ever before. Consumers and other groups consider not only the quality and price of a company's products, but its character as well. If too many groups see a company as a poor corporate citizen, it will have a harder time attracting qualified employees, finding investors, and selling its products. Good corporate citizens, on the other hand, are more successful in all of these areas.

Figure 3.4 (page 56) presents a model of corporate responsibility based on a company's relationships with its *stakeholders*. In this model, the focus is on managers—not owners—as the principals involved in all these relationships. Here, owners are the stakeholders who invest risk capital in the firm in expectation of a financial return. Other stakeholders include employees, suppliers, and the communities in which the firm does business. Proponents of this

---

code of conduct
Statement that defines the principles and guidelines employees must follow in the course of all job-related activities.

corporate social responsibility
Approach that an organization takes in balancing its responsibilities toward different stakeholders when making legal, economic, ethical, and social decisions.

model hold that customers, who provide the firm with revenue, have a special claim to managers' attention. The arrows indicate the two-way nature of corporation-stakeholder relationships: All stakeholders have some claim on the firm's resources and returns, and it's management's job to make decisions that balance these claims.[35]

Let's look at some of the ways in which companies can be "socially responsible" in considering the claims of various stakeholders.

OWNERS

Figure 3.4 **ACTIVE**
The Corporate Citizen

Owners invest money in companies. In return, the people who run a company have a responsibility to increase the value of owners' investments through profitable

operations. Managers also have a responsibility to provide owners (as well as other stakeholders with financial interests, such as creditors and suppliers) with accurate and reliable information about the performance of the business. Clearly, this is one of the areas in which WorldCom managers fell down on the job. Upper-level management purposely deceived shareholders by presenting them with fraudulent financial statements.

Fiduciary Responsibilities

Finally, managers have a **fiduciary responsibility** to owners: They're responsible for safeguarding the company's assets and handling its funds in a trustworthy manner. This is a responsibility that was ignored by top executives at Adelphia and Tyco, whose

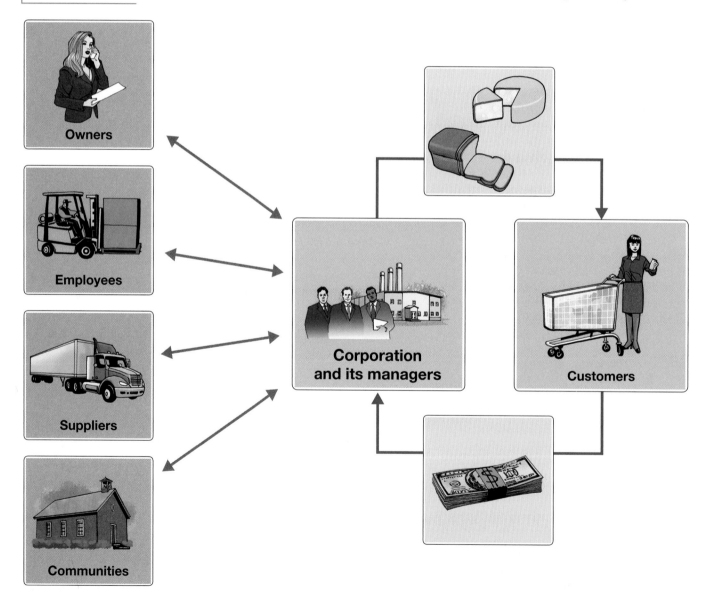

Owners

Employees

Suppliers

Communities

Corporation and its managers

Customers

associates and family virtually looted company assets. To enforce managers' fiduciary responsibilities for a firm's financial statements and accounting records, the Sarbanes-Oxley Act of 2002 requires CEOs and CFOs to attest to their accuracy. The law also imposes penalties on corporate officers, auditors, board members, and others who commit fraud.

EMPLOYEES

Companies are responsible for providing employees with safe and healthy places to work—as well as environments that are free from sexual harassment and all types of discrimination. They should also offer appropriate wages and benefits. In the following sections, we'll take a closer look at each of these areas of responsibility.

Safety and Health

Although it seems obvious that companies should guard workers' safety and health, a lot of them simply don't. For over 40 years, for example, executives at Johns Manville suppressed evidence that one of its products, asbestos, was responsible for the deadly lung disease developed by many of its workers.[36] The company concealed chest X-rays from stricken workers, and executives decided that it was simply cheaper to pay workers' compensation claims (or let workers die) than to create a safer work environment. A New Jersey court was quite blunt in its judgment: Johns Manville, it held, had made a deliberate, cold-blooded decision to do nothing to protect at-risk workers, in blatant disregard of their rights.[37]

About 4 out of every 100,000 U.S. workers die in workplace incidents each year. The Department of Labor categorizes deaths caused by conditions like those at Johns Manville as "exposure to harmful substances or environments." How prevalent is this condition as a cause of workplace deaths? See Figure 3.5(a), which breaks down workplace fatalities by cause. Some jobs are more dangerous than others.

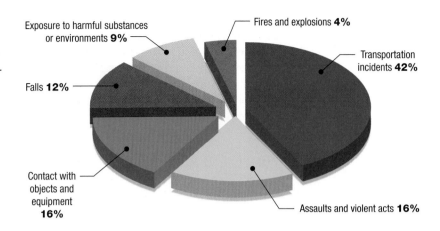

For a comparative overview based on workplace deaths by occupation, see Figure 3.5(b).

For most people, fortunately, things are better than they were at Johns Manville. Procter & Gamble (P&G), for example, considers the safety and health of its employees paramount and promotes the attitude that "Nothing we do is worth getting hurt for." With nearly 100,000 employees worldwide, P&G uses a measure of worker safety called "total incident rate per employee," which records injuries resulting in loss of consciousness, time lost from work, medical transfer to another job, motion restriction, or medical treatment beyond first aid. The company attributes the low rate of such incidents—less than 1 incident per 100 employees—to a variety of programs to promote workplace safety.[38]

Figure 3.5a

Workplace Deaths by Event or Exposure, 1998–2003

Figure 3.5b

Workplace Deaths by Occupation, 2003

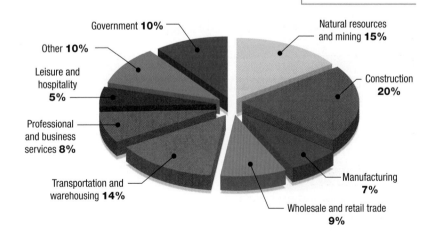

fiduciary responsibility
Duty of management to safeguard a company's assets and handle its funds in a trustworthy manner.

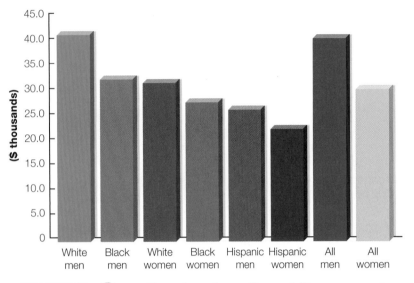

Figure 3.6a ● ACTIVE

Median Annual
Earnings by Gender
and Race

Figure 3.6b

Median Annual
Earnings by Gender,
Age, and Degree Level

Freedom from Sexual Harassment

What is *sexual harassment*? The law is
pretty precise:

- It's sexual harassment when an
  employee makes "unwelcome sexual
  advances, requests for sexual favors,
  and other verbal or physical conduct of
  a sexual nature" to another employee
  who doesn't welcome the advances.

- It's also sexual harassment when "submission to or rejection of this conduct
  explicitly or implicitly affects an individual's employment, unreasonably inter-

feres with an individual's work performance or creates an intimidating, hostile
or offensive work environment."[39]

To prevent—or at least minimize the likelihood of—sexual harassment, a company
should adopt a formal antiharassment policy describing prohibited conduct, asserting
its objections to the behavior, and detailing
penalties for violating the policy.[40] Employers also have an obligation to investigate
harassment complaints. Failure to enforce
antiharassment policies can be very costly.
In 1998, for example, Mitsubishi paid $34
million to more than 350 female employees
of its Normal, Illinois, plant to settle a sexual
harassment case supported by the Equal
Employment Opportunity Commission
(EEOC). The EEOC reprimanded the company for permitting an atmosphere of verbal
and physical abuse against women, charging that female workers had been subjected
to various forms of harassment, ranging
from exposure to obscene graffiti and vulgar
jokes to fondling, and groping.[41]

Equal Opportunity and Diversity

People must be hired, evaluated, promoted,
and rewarded on the basis of merit, not personal characteristics. This, too, is the law
(namely, Title VII of the 1964 Civil Rights
Act). Like most companies, P&G has a formal
policy on hiring and promotion that forbids
discrimination based on race, color, religion,
gender, age, national origin, citizenship, sexual orientation, or disability. P&G expects all
employees to support its commitment to
equal employment opportunity and warns
that those who violate P&G's company policies will face strict disciplinary action, including termination of employment.[42]

Equal Pay and the Wage Gap The
Equal Pay Act of 1963 requires equal pay for
both men and women in jobs that entail
equal skill, equal effort, equal responsibility,
or similar working conditions. What's been
the effect of the law after 40 years? In 1963,
women earned, on average, $0.589 for every
$1 earned by men. Today, that difference—
which we call the *wage gap* has been closed
to $0.755 to $1, or approximately 75 percent.
Figure 3.6(a) provides some interesting
numbers on the differences in annual earnings based not only on gender but on race as
well. Figure 3.6(b) throws further light on
the gender wage gap when age and education are taken into consideration.

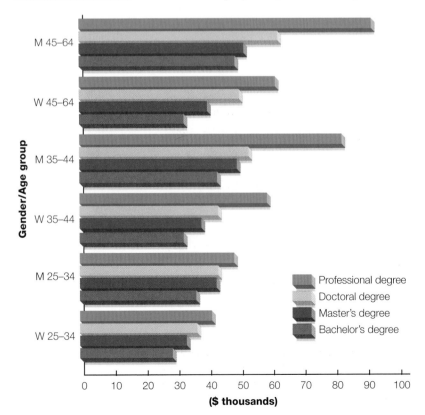

What accounts for the difference despite the mandate of federal law? For one thing, the jobs typically held by women tend to pay less than those typically held by men. In addition, men often have better job opportunities. For example, a man newly hired at the same time as a woman will often get a higher-paying, entry-level assignment. Coupled with the fact that the same sort of discrimination applies when it comes to training and promotions, women are usually relegated to a lifetime of lower earnings.

Building Diverse Workforces In addition to complying with equal employment opportunity laws, many companies make special efforts to recruit employees who are underrepresented in the workforce according to sex, race, or some other characteristic. In helping to build more diverse workforces, such initiatives contribute to competitive advantage for two reasons: (1) People from diverse backgrounds bring new talents and fresh perspectives to an organization, typically enhancing creativity in the development of new products. (2) By reflecting more accurately the changing demographics of the marketplace, a diverse workforce improves a company's ability to serve an ethnically diverse population.

Wages and Benefits

At the very least, employers must obey laws governing minimum wage and overtime pay. A minimum wage is set by the federal government, although states can set their own rates. The current federal rate, for example, is $5.15, while the rate in the state of Washington is $7.16. When there's a difference, the higher rate applies.[43] By law, employers must also provide certain benefits—social security (which provides retirement benefits), unemployment insurance (which protects against loss of income in case of job loss), and workers' compensation (which covers lost wages and medical costs in case of on-the-job injury). Most large companies pay most workers more than minimum wage and offer considerably broader benefits, including medical, dental, and vision care as well as pension benefits.

CUSTOMERS

The purpose of any business is to satisfy customers, who reward businesses by buying their products. Sellers are also responsible—both ethically and legally—for treating customers fairly. The rights of consumers were first articulated by President John F. Kennedy in 1962 when he submitted to Congress a presidential message devoted to consumer issues.[44] Kennedy identified four consumer rights:

1. *The right to safe products.* A company should sell no product that it suspects of being unsafe for buyers. Thus, producers have an obligation to safety-test products before releasing them for public consumption. The automobile industry, for example, conducts extensive safety testing before introducing new models (although recalls remain common).

2. *The right to be informed about a product.* Sellers should furnish consumers with the product information that they need to make an informed purchase decision. That's why pillows have labels identifying the materials used to make them.

3. *The right to choose what to buy.* Consumers have a right to decide which products to purchase, and sellers should let them know what their options are. Pharmacists, for example, should tell patients if a prescription can be filled with a cheaper brand-name or generic drug. Telephone companies should explain alternative calling plans.

4. *The right to be heard.* Companies must tell customers how to contact them with complaints or concerns. They should also listen and respond.

Companies share the responsibility for the legal and ethical treatment of consumers with several government agencies: the Federal Trade Commission (FTC); which enforces consumer-protection laws, the Food and Drug Administration (FDA), which oversees the labeling of food products; and the Consumer Product Safety Commission, which enforces laws protecting consumers from the risk of product-related injury.

COMMUNITIES

For obvious reasons, most communities see getting a new business as an asset and losing one—especially a large employer—as a detriment. After all, the economic impact of business activities on local communities is substantial: They provide jobs, pay taxes, and support local education, health, and recreation programs. Both big and small businesses donate funds to community projects, encourage employees to volunteer their time, and donate equipment and products for a variety of activities. Larger companies can make greater financial contributions. Let's start by taking a quick look at the philanthropic activities of a few U.S. corporations.

Financial Contributions

Many large corporations donate a percentage of sales or profits to worthwhile causes. Retailer Target, for example, donates 5 percent of its profits—about $2 million per week—to schools, neighborhoods, and local projects across the country. Store-based grants underwrite programs in early childhood education, the arts, and family-violence prevention.[45] Actor Paul Newman donates 100 percent of the profits from "Newman's Own" foods (salad dressing, pasta sauce, popcorn, and other products sold in eight countries). The profits go to thousands of organizations, including the Hole in the Wall Gang camps for seriously ill children.[46]

Volunteerism

Many companies support employee efforts to help local communities. Fannie Mae, for example, allows employees to spend 10 hours of paid time per month doing volun-

teer work.[47] Patagonia (a maker of outdoor gear and clothing) lets employees leave their jobs and work full-time for any environmental group for two months—with full salary and benefits. So far, more than 350 employees have taken advantage of the program.

Supporting Social Causes

Companies and executives often take active roles in initiatives to improve health and social welfare in the United States and elsewhere. Microsoft CEO Bill Gates intends to distribute more than $3 billion through the Bill and Melinda Gates Foundation, which funds global health initiatives, particularly vaccine research aimed at preventing infectious diseases in undeveloped countries.[48] Noting that children from low-income families have twice as many cavities and often miss school because of dental-related diseases, P&G invests $1 million a year to set up "cavity-free zones" for 3.3 million economically disadvantaged children at Boys and Girls Clubs nationwide. In addition to giving away toothbrushes and toothpaste, P&G provides educational programs on dental hygiene. At some locations, the company maintains clinics providing affordable oral care to poor children and their families.[49]

Environmentalism

Today, virtually everyone agrees that companies must figure out how to produce products without compromising the right of future generations to meet their needs. Clearly, protecting natural resources is the right thing to do, but it's also become a business necessity: Their customers demand that companies respect the environment. Let's identify some key environmental issues and highlight the ways in which the business community has addressed them.

Land Pollution The land we live on has been polluted by the dumping of waste and increasing reliance on agricultural chemicals. It's pockmarked by landfills stuffed with the excess of a throwaway society. It's been strip-mined and deforested, and urban sprawl on every continent has squeezed out wetlands and farmlands and destroyed wildlife habitats.

Protecting the land from further damage, then, means disposing of waste in responsible ways (or, better yet, reducing the amount

Bono and Bill and Melinda Gates were named as *Time* magazine's 2006 "Persons of the Year" for their efforts to reduce poverty and disease worldwide. Bono, an Irish rock musician from the band U2, was one of the organizers of the Live 8 concerts held in cities around the world that propelled leaders of the wealthiest countries to forgive $40 billion in debt owed by the poorest nations. The Bill and Melinda Gates Foundation committed $750 million to immunize children in poor countries.

DECEMBER 26, 2005 / JANUARY 2, 2006   www.time.com AOL Keyword: TIME

PERSONS OF THE YEAR

TIME

THE GOOD SAMARITANS
BILL GATES
BONO
MELINDA GATES

of waste). At both national and global levels, we must resolve the conflicts of interest between those who benefit economically from logging and mining and those who argue that protecting the environment is an urgent matter. Probably municipalities must step in to save open spaces and wetlands.

Patagonia has for years been in the forefront of efforts to protect the land. Each year, the company pledges either 1 percent of sales revenue or 10 percent of profits (whichever is larger) to protect and restore the natural environment. According to its "Statement of Purpose," "Patagonia exists as a business to inspire and implement solutions to the environmental crisis." Instead of traditional materials for making clothes (such as regular cotton and fleece), Patagonia relies on organically grown cotton, which is more expensive, because it doesn't requires harmful chemicals. Fleece products are made with *post-consumer recycled* (PCR) fleece, which is actually made with recycled plastic bottles. So far, the company's efforts to build a more sustainable system has saved 86 million plastic bottles from ending up in landfills.[50]

Air Pollution It's amazing what we can do to something as large as the atmosphere. Over time, however, we've managed to pollute the air with emissions of toxic gases and particles from factories, power plants, office buildings, cars, trucks, and even farms. In addition, our preferred method of deforestation is burning, which is a major source of air pollution. In some places, polluted air causes respiratory problems, particularly for the young and elderly. Factory emissions, including sulfur and other gases, mix with air and rain to produce *acid rain*, which returns to the earth to pollute forests, lakes, and streams. Perhaps most importantly, many experts—scientists, government officials, and businesspeople—are convinced that the heavy emission of carbon dioxide is altering the earth's climate. Predictions of the effect of unchecked global warming include extreme weather conditions, flooding, oceanic disruptions, shifting storm patterns, reduced farm output, animal extinctions, and droughts.[51]

Curbing global warming will require international cooperation. More than 120 nations (though not the United States) have stated their support for this initiative by endorsing the Kyoto Protocol, an agreement

In the 1960s, Yvon Chouinard visited the coastal region of Patagonia, Argentina. He was so enthralled by its beauty that he named his small clothing company after the region. Years later, he was able to give back to the area by helping a nonprofit group transform the wild places of Patagonia into Argentina's first coastal national park so its beauty and wildlife could be preserved. Here a group of Patagonia employees assist in that effort by removing fences that prevent wild native animals from traveling uninhibited through the region.

to slow global warming by reducing worldwide carbon-dioxide emissions.

What can business do? Businesses can reduce greenhouse emissions by making vehicles, factories, and other facilities more energy efficient. In response to a government ban on chlorofluorocarbons that damage the ozone layer, DuPont has cut greenhouse emissions by 65 percent over the last 15 years through improvements in manufacturing processes and a commitment to increased energy efficiency.[52] Toyota now markets hybrid gas-electric cars, and General Motors is working on hydrogen-powered vehicles. General Electric is designing more energy-efficient appliances and investing heavily to research wind power.[53]

Water Pollution Water makes up more than 70 percent of the earth's surface, and it's no secret that without it we wouldn't be here. Unfortunately, that doesn't stop us from polluting our oceans, rivers, and lakes and generally making our water unfit for use. Massive pollution occurs when such substances as oil and chemicals are dumped into bodies of water. The damage to the water, to the marine ecosystem, and to coastal wildlife from the accidental spilling of oil from supertankers and offshore drilling operations can be disastrous, and the cleanup can cost billions. Most contaminants, however, come from the agricultural fertilizers, pesticides, wastewater, raw sewage, and silt that make their way into water systems over time.[54] In some parts of the world—including some areas in this country—water supplies are dwindling, partly because of diminishing rainfall and partly because of increased consumption.

The Environmental Protection Agency has been a major force in cleaning up U.S. waters. Companies are now held to stricter standards in the discharge of wastes into water systems. In some places, particularly where water supplies are dangerously low, such as the Southwest, local governments have instituted conservation programs. In Arizona (which suffers a severe shortage), Home Depot works with governmental and nongovernmental agencies on a $1.8 million water-conservation campaign. From its 40 stores, the company runs weekend workshops to educate consumers on conservation basics, including drought-resistant gardening techniques.[55]

ABOUT NIKE   3.2

Now that you've learned about ways in which organizations are responsible to their stakeholders, take a few minutes to explore the corporate social-responsibility initiatives undertaken by Nike.

Go to www.exploringbusinessonline.com

STAGES OF CORPORATE RESPONSIBILITY

We expect companies to recognize issues of social importance and to address them responsibly. The ones that do earn reputations as good corporate citizens and enjoy certain benefits: the ability to keep satisfied customers, attract capital, and attract and retain talented employees. But companies don't become good corporate citizens overnight. Learning to identify and develop the capacity to address social concerns takes time and requires commitment. The task is hard because so many different issues are important to so many different members of the public, ranging from the environment, to worker well-being (both at home and abroad), to fairness to customers, to respect for the community in which a company operates.

The Five Faces of Corporate Responsibility

Faced with public criticism of a particular practice, how does a company respond? What actions does it take to demonstrate a higher level of corporate responsibility? According to Harvard University's Simon Zadek, exercising greater corporate responsibility generally means going through the series of five different stances summarized in Figure 3.7.[56]

1. *Defensive.* When they're first criticized over some problem or issue, companies tend to take a defensive, often legalistic stance. They reject allegations of wrongdoing and refuse to take responsibility, arguing that fixing the problem or addressing the issue isn't their job.

2. *Compliant.* During this stage, companies adopt policies that acknowledge the wishes of the public. As a rule, however, they do only what they have to do to satisfy their critics, and little more. They're acting mainly to protect brands or reputations and to reduce the risk of litigation.

3. *Managerial.* When it becomes clear that the problem won't go away, companies admit that they need to take responsibility and action and look for practical long-term solutions.

4. *Strategic.* At this point, they may start to reap the benefits of acting responsibly. They often find that responding to public needs gives them a competitive edge and enhances long-term success.

5. *Civil.* Ultimately, many companies recognize the importance of getting other companies to follow their lead. They may promote participation by other firms in their industries, endorsing the principle that the public is best served through collective action.

Here's Your Salad—How About Fries?

About five years ago, McDonald's found itself in a public relations nightmare. The fast-food giant faced massive public criticism for serving unhealthy food that contributed to a national epidemic of obesity. Let's look at McDonald's responses to these criticisms and assess how far along the five-stage process the company has progressed.

The Defensive Stage As the documentary *SuperSize Me* demonstrated, a steady diet of McDonald's burgers and fries will cause you to gain weight. It was certainly inevitable that one day the public would make a connection between the rising level of obesity in the United States and a diet heavy in fat-laden fast foods. McDonald's fast food/obesity link got a lot of attention in 2002 when obese adults and teenagers filed suits against the company claiming it was responsible for their excess pounds. McDonald's reaction to the public outcry against the company's menu items was defensive. For example, an owner of seven McDonald's in midtown Manhattan said, "We offer healthy choices. It is up to individuals to set limits and to be informed . . . . McDonald's discloses nutritional information about its foods in its restaurants."[57]

The Compliant Stage In early 2004, the public's attention was drawn to McDonald's "super-size" options. Despite the fact that a super-sized meal delivered more than 1,500 calories, 1 out of 10 customers went for the upgrade. McDonald's faced daily criticisms on its super-sizing campaign from nutritionists, doctors, advocacy groups, and lawyers who held it up as a "grossly overweight" poster child for U.S. obesity concerns. And the company feared public criticism would escalate when the movie *SuperSize Me* hit the theaters. The documentary tells the story of a young man who gained 24 pounds and wrecked his health by eating only McDonald's food for a month. Even worse, one scene shows him getting sick in his car after trying to wolf down a super-size meal. So McDonald's immediately moved from the defensive stage to the complaint stage and announced that it was eliminating its super-size option by the end of 2004. The move, although small, was in the right direction. It was touted by the company as a "menu simplification" process, but a spokesman did state that, "It certainly is consistent with and on a parallel path with our ongoing commitment to a balanced lifestyle."[58]

The Managerial Stage Criticisms of McDonald's continued customers stayed away and its profits plummeted. The company searched for ways to win back customers and keep them long-term. To do

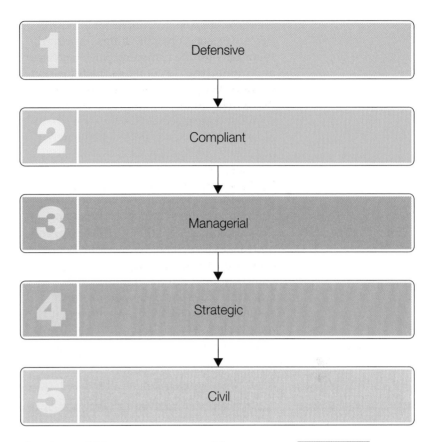

Figure 3.7

Stages of Corporate Responsibility

this, it would have to come up with a healthier menu. Although McDonald's had served salads for years, they weren't very good. The company got serious about salads and introduced new and improved "premium salads" complete with Newman's Own salad dressing (a nice public relations touch, as all profits on the salad dressings are donated to charities). The company improved the Happy Meal by letting kids substitute fries and soda for apple slices and low-fat milk. Oprah Winfrey's personal trainer was brought in to promote an adult version of the Happy Meal called the GoActive meal, which includes a salad, a bottle of water, a book on nutrition, and a clip-on pedometer that measures the number of steps you take. The fat calories in Chicken McNuggets were lowered by coming out with all-white-meat McNuggets. And to appease those between-meal munchies, it added a fruit and walnut salad to its menu. McDonald's goal was to convince customers that it had turned a corner and would forever more offer adults and children healthy choices.

The Strategic Stage The new focus on healthy choices worked and customers started returning. McDonald's salads were well received and accounted for about 10 percent of sales. Overall, things improved financially for the company: Sales increased and profits rose. To complete the transition to a healthier image, McDonald's came up with a new theme: helping adults and children live a balanced, active lifestyle. To go along with the theme, it launched a new active-life public-awareness campaign: "It's what I eat and what I do. . . I'm lovin' it." McDonald's demonstrated its concern for the health of its customers through permanent menu changes and an emphasis on the value of physical fitness. Even Ronald McDonald helped out by shooting hoops with NBA basketball star Yao Ming. The company launched a program called GoActive to help people find fun ways to build physical activity and fitness into their daily lives.

The Civil Stage McDonald's hasn't advanced to the final stage yet; it hasn't enlisted the cooperation of other fast-food companies in encouraging children and adults to eat healthier foods. It's difficult to predict whether it will assume this role in the future, or even whether the company will stick with its healthier lifestyle theme. It's hard to reconcile McDonald's commitment to helping people eat healthier and a recent promotion in the Chicago area that gave a free 42-ounce "super-size" soda to anyone buying a Big Mac and fries. Given that a Big Mac and medium fries delivers 910 calories, it's hard to justify encouraging customers to pile on an additional 410 calo-

ries for a big drink (at least it's hard to justify this if you're promoting yourself as a company helping people eat better).[59]

ABOUT NIKE   3.3

Now that you can identify the stages of corporate responsibility, take a moment to review the history of corporate responsibility at Nike.

Go to www.exploringbusinessonline.com

Where We're Headed

In this chapter, we stressed the importance of ethics in the behavior of both individuals and organizations. We introduced a process for solving ethical dilemmas and making ethical decisions. We explored the socially responsible ways in which companies can act toward their stakeholders (owners, employees, customers, communities). In the next chapter, we'll examine the functions of management and describe the various forms of business organization.

QUICK QUIZ   3.3

Before finishing the chapter, take a few minutes to test your understanding of corporate social responsibility.

Go to www.exploringbusinessonline.com

Summary of Learning Objectives

1. **Define *business ethics* and explain what it means to act ethically in business.**

   Business ethics is the application of ethical behavior in a business context. Acting ethically in business means more than just obeying laws and regulations. It also means being honest, doing no harm to others, competing fairly, and declining to put your own interests above those of your employer and coworkers. To act ethically in business situations, you need a good idea of what's right and wrong (not always an easy task). You also need the personal conviction

   to do what's right even if it means doing something that's difficult or personally disadvantageous.

2. **Specify the steps you'd take to solve an ethical dilemma and make an ethical decision.**

   Businesspeople face two types of ethical challenges. An **ethical dilemma** is a morally problematic situation in which you must choose between two or more alternatives that aren't equally acceptable to different groups. Such a dilemma is often characterized as a "right-versus-right" decision and is usually solved in a series of five steps: (1) define the problem and collect the relevant facts; (2) identify feasible options; (3) assess the effect of each option on **stakeholders** (owners, employees, customers, communities); (4) establish criteria for determining the most appropriate option; and (5) select the best option based on the established criteria.

An **ethical decision** entails a "right-versus-wrong" decision—one in which there's a right (ethical) choice and a wrong (unethical or downright illegal) choice. When you make a decision that's unmistakably unethical or illegal, you've committed an **ethical lapse**. If you're presented with what appears to be an ethical decision, asking yourself the following questions will improve your odds of making an ethical choice: (1) Is the action illegal? (2) Is it unfair to some parties? (3) If I take it, will I feel badly about it? (4) Will I be ashamed to tell my family, friends, coworkers, or boss about my action? (5) Would I want my decision written up in the local newspaper? If you answer yes to *any* one of these five questions, you're probably about to do something that you shouldn't.

3. Identify ethical issues that you might face in business and analyze rationalizations for unethical behavior.

When you enter the business world, you'll find yourself in situations in which you'll have to choose the appropriate behavior. You'll need to know how to tell a bribe from an acceptable gift. You'll encounter situations that give rise to a **conflict of interest**—situations in which you'll have to choose between taking action that promotes your personal interests and action that favors the interest of others. Sometimes you'll be required to choose between loyalty to your employer and loyalty to a friend or family member. In business, as in all aspects of your life, you should act with honesty and integrity. At some point in your career, you might become aware of wrongdoing on the part of others and will have to decide whether or not to report the incident and become a **whistle-blower**—an individual who exposes illegal or unethical behavior in an organization.

Despite all the good arguments in favor of doing the right thing, some businesspeople still act unethically (at least at times). Sometimes they use one of the following rationalizations to justify their conduct: (1) the behavior isn't really illegal or immoral; (2) the action is in everyone's best interests; (3) no one will find out what I've done; (4) the company will condone my action and protect me.

4. Specify actions that managers can take to create and sustain ethical organizations.

Ethics is more than a matter of individual behavior; it's also about organizational behavior. Employees' actions aren't based solely on personal values; they're also influenced by other members of the organization. Organizations have unique *cultures*—ways of doing things that evolve through shared values and beliefs. An organization's culture is strongly influenced by top managers, who are responsible for letting members of the organization know what's considered acceptable behavior and what happens if it's violated. Subordinates look to their supervisors as role models of ethical behavior: If managers act ethically, subordinates will probably do the same. Those in positions of leadership should hold subordinates accountable for their conduct and take appropriate action. Many organizations have a formal **code of conduct** that describes the principles and guidelines that all members must follow in the course of job-related activities.

5. Define *corporate social responsibility* and explain how organizations are responsible to their stakeholders.

Corporate social responsibility refers to the approach that an organization takes in balancing its responsibilities toward different stakeholders when making legal, economic, ethical, and social decisions. Companies are socially responsible to their various stakeholders—owners, employees, customers, and the communities in which they conduct business. Owners invest money in companies. In return, the people who manage it have a responsibility to increase the value of owners' investments through profitable operations. Managers have a responsibility to provide owners and other stakeholders with accurate and reliable financial information. They also have a **fiduciary responsibility** to safeguard the company's assets and handle its funds in a trustworthy manner.

Companies have a responsibility to guard workers' safety and health and to provide them with a work environment that's free from sexual harassment. Businesses should pay appropriate wages and benefits, treat all workers fairly, and provide equal opportunities for all employees. Many have discovered the benefits of valuing diversity.

The purpose of any business is to satisfy the customers who will reward it by buying its products. Sellers are also responsible—both ethically and legally—for treating customers fairly. Consumers have certain rights: to safe products, to be informed about products, to choose what to buy, and to be heard. Companies also have a responsibility to the communities in which they produce and sell their products. The economic impact of businesses on local communities is substantial: They provide jobs, pay taxes, and support local education, health, and recreation activities. They donate funds to community projects, encourage employees to volunteer their time, and donate equipment and products for a variety of activities.

6. Identify threats to the natural environment and explain how businesses are addressing them.

Companies have a responsibility to produce products without compromising the right of future generations to meet their needs. Customers demand that companies respect the environment. Our land, air, and water all face environmental threats. Land is polluted by the dumping of waste and an increasing reliance on agricultural chemicals. It's pock-marked by landfills, shredded by strip mining, and laid bare by deforestation. Urban sprawl has squeezed out wetlands and farmlands and destroyed wildlife habitats. To protect the land from further damage, we must dispose of waste in responsible ways, control strip mining and logging, and save open spaces and wetlands.

Emissions of toxic gases and particles from factories, power plants, office buildings, cars, trucks, and even farms pollute the air, which is also harmed by the burning associated with deforestation. Many experts believe that the heavy emission of carbon dioxide by factories and vehicles is altering the earth's climate: Carbon dioxide and other gases, they argue, act as a "greenhouse" over the earth, producing global warming—a heating of the earth which could have dire consequences. Many companies have taken actions to reduce air pollution.

Water is polluted by such substances as oil and chemicals. Most of the contaminants come from agricultural fertilizers, pesticides, wastewater, raw sewage, and silt. Also of concern is the dwindling supply of water in some parts of the world brought about by diminishing rainfall and increased consumption. The Environmental Protection Agency has been a major force in cleaning up U.S. waters. Many companies have joined with governmental and nongovernmental agencies in efforts to help people protect and conserve water.

Questions and Problems

1. AACSB ▸ Analysis

Although the terms *business ethics* and *corporate responsibility* are often used interchangeably, they don't mean the same thing. Define each term and explain how the following events could have transpired: Fannie Mae, the largest buyer of U.S. home mortgages, has been named one of the "100 Best Corporate Citizens" by *Business Ethics* magazine five years in a row, making it to the top spot in 2004. Shortly after the announcement of the award, news of a massive accounting scandal involving several Fannie Mae executives hit the news. How can a company be recognized as a good corporate citizen and still experience serious ethical failure?

2.

Explain the difference between an ethical dilemma and an ethical decision and provide an example of each. Describe an ethical lapse and provide an example.

3. AACSB ▸ Analysis

You're the CEO of a company that sells golf equipment, including clubs, bags, and balls. When your company was started and had only a handful of employees, you were personally able to oversee the conduct of your employees. But with your current workforce of nearly 50, it's time to prepare a formal code of conduct in which you lay down some rules that employees must follow in performing job-related activities. As a model for your own code, you've decided to use Johnson & Johnson's *Policy on Business Conduct*. Go to www.exploringbusinessonline.com to link to the Johnson & Johnson (J&J) Web site to view the company's posted code of conduct. Your document won't be as thorough as J&J's, but it will cover the following areas: (1) conflicts of interest; (2) acceptance of gifts, services, or entertainment; and (3) use of company funds or assets for personal purposes. Draw up a code of conduct for your company.

4. AACSB ▸ Analysis

Each December, *Time* magazine devotes its cover to the person who has made the biggest impact on the world that year. *Time*'s 2002 pick was not one person, but three: Cynthia Cooper (WorldCom), Coleen Rowley (FBI) and Sherron Watkins (Enron). All three were whistle-blowers. We detailed Cynthia Cooper's courage in exposing fraud at WorldCom in this chapter, but the stories of the other two whistle-blowers are equally worthwhile. Go to www.exploringbusinessonline.com to link to the Time.com and CNN.com Web sites and read a posted story about *either* Rowley or Watkins. Then answer the following questions:

- What wrongdoing did the whistle-blower expose?

- What happened to her when she blew the whistle? Did she experience retaliation?

- Did she do the right thing? Would you have blown the whistle? Why or why not?

5. **AACSB** ▸ Reflective Skills

   Think of someone whom you regard as an ethical leader. It can be anyone connected with you—a businessperson, educator, coach, politician, family member. Explain why you believe the individual is ethical in his or her leadership.

6. Nonprofit organizations (such as your college or university) have social responsibilities to their stakeholders. Identify your school's stakeholders. For each category of stakeholder, indicate the ways your school is socially responsible to that group.

7. **AACSB** ▸ Analysis

   You own a tax-preparation company with 10 employees who prepare tax returns. In walking around the office, you notice that several of your employees spend a lot of time making personal use of their computers, checking personal e-mails, or shopping online. After doing an Internet search on employer computer monitoring, respond to these questions: Is it unethical for your employees to use their work computers for personal activities? Is it ethical for you to monitor computer usage? Do you have a legal right to do it? If you decide to monitor computer usage in the future, what rules would you make, and how would you enforce them?

8. **AACSB** ▸ Analysis

   In many ways, Eastman Kodak (a multinational manufacturer and distributor of photographic equipment and supplies) is a model corporate citizen. *Fortune* magazine has ranked it as one of the country's most admired companies, applauding it in particular for its treatment of minorities and women. Its community-affairs programs and contributions have also received praise, but Eastman Kodak remains weak in one important aspect of corporate responsibility: It has consistently received low scores on environmental practices. Recently, for example, the watchdog group Scorecard rated Eastman Kodak's Rochester, New York, facility as the third-worst emitter of airborne carcinogens in the United States. Other reports have criticized the company for dumping cancer-causing chemicals into the nation's waters.

   Go to www.exploringbusinessonline.com to link to the Eastman Kodak Web site and read its own assessment of its environmental practices. Then answer the following questions:

   - Based on the information provided on its Web site, how favorable do you feel about Eastman Kodak's environmental practices?

   - In what ways is the company responding to criticisms of its environmental practices and improving them?

   - Do the statements on the Web site mesh with the criticism that the company has received? If not, what accounts for the differences?

9. **AACSB** ▸ Communication

   Pfizer is one of the largest pharmaceutical companies in the United States. It's in the business of discovering, developing, manufacturing, and marketing prescription drugs. Although it's headquartered in New York, it sells products worldwide, and its corporate responsibility initiatives also are global. Go to www.exploringbusinessonline.com to link to the Pfizer Web site and read about the firm's global corporate-citizenship initiatives. Write a brief report describing the focus of Pfizer's efforts and identifying a few key programs. In your opinion, why should U.S. companies direct corporate-responsibility efforts at people in countries outside of the United States?

10. This chapter discusses a five-stage process that companies go through in responding to public criticism. Consider the situation in which McDonald's found itself when it faced massive public criticism for serving unhealthy food that contributed to a national epidemic of obesity. Given what you know about the firm's reaction, identify the steps that it took in response to this criticism. In particular, show how its responses do or don't reflect the five stages of corporate responsibility outlined in the chapter. In your opinion, how far along the five-stage process has McDonald's progressed?

Learning on the Web AACSB

Lessons in Community Living

Executives consider it an honor to have their company named one of *Business Ethics* magazine's "100 Best Corporate Citizens." Companies are chosen from a group of 1,000 according to how well they serve their stakeholders—owners, employees, customers, and the communities with which they share the social and natural environment. Being in the top 100 for five years in a row is cause for celebration. Two of the twenty-nine companies that enjoy this distinction are Timberland and the New York Times Company.

The two companies are in very different industries. Timberland designs and manufactures boots and other footwear, apparel, and accessories; the New York Times Company is a media giant, with 19 newspapers (including the *New York Times* and the *Boston Globe*), 8 television stations, and more than 40 Web sites. Go to www. exploringbusinessonline.com to link to the Timberland and New York Times Company Web sites to learn how each, in its own way, supports the communities with which it shares the social and natural environment. Look specifically for information that will help you answer the following questions:

1. How does each company assist its community? To what organizations does each donate money? How do employees volunteer their time? What social causes does each support?

2. How does each company work to protect the natural environment?

3. Are the community-support efforts of the two companies similar or dissimilar? In what ways do these activities reflect the purposes of each organization?

4. In your opinion, why do these companies support their communities? What benefits do they derive from being good corporate citizens?

Career Opportunities

Is "WorldCom Ethics Officer" an Oxymoron?

As you found out in this chapter, WorldCom's massive accounting scandal cost investors billions and threw the company into bankruptcy. More than 100 employees who either participated in the fraud or passively looked the other way were indicted or fired, including accountant Betty Vinson, CFO Scott Sullivan, and CEO Bernard Ebbers. With the name "WorldCom" indelibly tarnished, the company reclaimed its previous name, "MCI." It was put on court-imposed probation and ordered to follow the directives of the court. One of those directives called for setting up an ethics office. Nancy Higgins, a corporate attorney and onetime vice president for ethics at Lockheed Martin, was brought in with the title of chief ethics officer.

Higgins' primary responsibility is to ensure that MCI lives up to new CEO Michael Capellas's assertion that the company is dedicated to integrity and its employees committed to high ethical standards. Her tasks are the same as those of most people with the same job, but she's under more pressure because MCI can't afford any more ethical lapses. She oversees the company's ethics initiatives, including training programs and an ethics hotline. She spends a lot of her time with employees, listening to their concerns and promoting company values.

Higgins is a member of the senior executive team and reports to the CEO and board of directors. She attends all board meetings and provides members with periodic updates on the company's newly instituted ethics program (including information gleaned from the new ethics hotline).

Answer the following questions:

1. Would you be comfortable in Higgins' job? Does the job of ethics officer appeal to you? Why or why not?

2. Would you find it worthwhile to work in an ethics office for a few years at some point in your career? Why or why not?

3. What qualities would you look for if you were hiring an ethics officer?

4. What factors will help (or hinder) Higgins' ability to carry out her mandate to bolster integrity and foster ethical standards?

5. Would the accounting scandals have occurred at WorldCom if Higgins had been on the job back when Vinson, Sullivan, and Ebbers were still there? Explain your opinion.

Ethics Angle AACSB

Is Honesty Academic?

Just as businesses have codes of conduct for directing employee behavior in job-related activities, colleges and universities have codes of conduct to guide students' academic behavior. They're called various things—*honor codes, academic integrity policies, policies on academic honesty, student codes of conduct*—but they all have the same purpose: to promote academic integrity and to create a fair and ethical environment for all students.

At most schools, information on academic integrity is available from one of the following sources:

- The school Web site (probably under the "Dean of Students" or "Student Life")

- The student handbook

- Printed materials available through the Dean of Students' office

ASSIGNMENT

Locate information on your school's academic-integrity policies and answer the following questions:

1. What behavior violates academic integrity?

2. What happens if you're accused of academic dishonesty?

3. What should you do if you witness an incident of academic dishonesty?

Team-Building Skills AACSB

What Are the Stakes When You Play with Wal-Mart?

In resolving an ethical dilemma, you have to choose between two or more opposing alternatives which, though both acceptable, are important to different groups. Both alternatives may be ethically legitimate, but you can act in the interest of only one group.

This project is designed to help you learn how to analyze and resolve ethical dilemmas in a business context. You'll work in teams to address three ethical dilemmas involving Wal-Mart, the world's largest company. Before meeting as a group, every team member should go to www.exploringbusinessonline.com to link to the *BusinessWeek* Web site and read, "Is Wal-Mart Too Powerful?" The article discusses Wal-Mart's industry dominance and advances arguments for why Wal-Mart is both admired and criticized.

Your team should then get together to analyze the three dilemmas that follow. Start by reading the overview of the dilemma and any assigned material. Then debate the issues, working to reach a resolution through the five-step process summarized in Figure 3.1 (page 49).

1. Define the problem and collect the relevant facts.

2. Identify feasible options.

3. Assess the effect of each option on stakeholders.

4. Establish criteria for determining the most appropriate action.

5. Select the best option based on the established criteria.

Finally, prepare a report on your deliberations over each dilemma, making sure that each report contains all the following items:

- The team's recommendation for resolving the dilemma
- An explanation of the team's recommendation
- A summary of the information collected for and the decisions made at each step of the dilemma-resolution process

THREE ETHICAL DILEMMAS

Ethical Dilemma 1

Should Wal-Mart Close a Store Because It Unionizes?

Scenario: In February 2005, Wal-Mart closed a store in Quebec, Canada, after its workers voted to form a union.

The decision has ramifications for various stakeholders, including employees, customers, and stockholders. In analyzing and arriving at a resolution to this dilemma, assume that you're the CEO of Wal-Mart but *ignore the decision already made by the real CEO*. Arrive at your own recommendation, which may or may not be the same as that reached by your real-life counterpart.

Prior to analyzing this dilemma, go to www.exploring businessonline.com to link to the *Washington Post* Web site and read the article: "Wal-Mart Chief Defends Closing Unionized Store."

Ethical Dilemma 2

Should Levi Strauss Go into Business with Wal-Mart?

Scenario: For years, the words *jeans* and *Levi's* were synonymous. Levi Strauss, the founder of the company that carries his name, invented blue jeans in 1850 for sale to prospectors in the gold fields of California. Sales peaked at $7 billion in 1996 but then plummeted to $4 billion by 2003. Management has admitted that the company must reverse this downward trend if it hopes to retain the support of its 12,000 employees, operate its remaining U.S. factories, and continue its tradition of corporate-responsibility initiatives. At this point, Wal-Mart made an attractive offer: Levi Strauss could develop a low-cost brand of jeans for sale at Wal-Mart. The decision, however, isn't as simple as it may seem: Wal-Mart's relentless pressure to offer "everyday low prices" can have wide-ranging ramifications for its suppliers' stakeholders—in this case, Levi Strauss's shareholders, employees, and customers as well as the beneficiaries of its various social-responsibility programs. Assume that, as the CEO of Levi Strauss, you have to decide whether to accept Wal-Mart's offer. Again, ignore any decision already made by your real-life counterpart and work toward an independent recommendation.

Prior to analyzing this dilemma, go to www. exploringbusinessonline.com to link to the *Fast Company* Web site and read the article: "The Wal-Mart You Don't Know."

Ethical Dilemma 3

Should You Welcome Wal-Mart into Your Neighborhood?

Scenario: In 2002, Wal-Mart announced plans to build 40 "supercenters" in California—a section of the country that's traditionally resisted Wal-Mart's attempts to dot the landscape with big-box stores. Skirmishes soon broke out in California communities between those in favor of welcoming

Wal-Mart and those determined to fend off mammoth retail outlets.

You're a member of the local council of a California city, and you'll be voting next week on whether to allow Wal-Mart to build in your community. The council's decision will affect Wal-Mart as well as many local stakeholders, including residents, small business owners, and employees of local supermarkets and other retail establishments. As usual, ignore any decisions already made by your real-life counterparts.

Prior to working on this dilemma, go to www.exploringbusinessonline.com to link to the *USA Today* Web site and read the article "California Tries to Slam Lid on Big-Boxed Wal-Mart."

The Global View AACSB

What to Do When the "False" Alarm Goes Off

If someone tried to sell you a "Rolex" watch for $20, you'd probably suspect that it's a fake. But what about a pair of New Balance athletic shoes? How do you know they're authentic? How can you tell? Often you can't. Counterfeiters are getting so good at copying products that even experts have trouble telling a fake from the real thing. What if the counterfeit product in question was a prescription drug? Even worse, what if it had been counterfeited with unsterile equipment?

How likely is it that you'll buy a counterfeit product in the next year? Unfortunately, it's very likely. To learn a little more about the global counterfeiting business, go to www.exploringbusinessonline.com to link to the *BusinessWeek* and *Washington Post* Web sites. Read the articles "Fakes!" and "Counterfeit Goods That Trigger the 'False' Alarm." After you read these articles, answer the following questions:

1. How has the practice of counterfeiting changed over time? What factors have allowed it to escalate?

2. What types of products are commonly counterfeited, and why might they be unsafe? What counterfeit products are particularly dangerous?

3. How do the counterfeiters get goods onto the market? How can you reduce your chances of buying fake goods?

4. Why is counterfeiting so profitable? How can counterfeiters compete on price with those making the authentic goods? How do counterfeiters harm U.S. businesses?

5. What efforts are international companies and governments (including China) making to stop counterfeiters?

6. If you know that a product is fake, is it ethical to buy it?

Business Plan Project

Group Report: *Industry Analysis*

REPORT

The team should submit a written report that provides an overall assessment of the industry in which your proposed company will compete. To find out what information belongs in this report, go to Appendix A at the back of this book, entitled "Introducing Your Business Plan" (p. 307), and consult the section headed "Industry Analysis." The report should be about two double-spaced typed pages. The name of your proposed business and the names of all team members should appear on the report.

REASONABLE CONTRIBUTIONS

All members of the team who make **a reasonable contribution to the report** should sign it. (If any team member does not work on the report, his or her name should *not* appear on it.) If a student who has made a contribution is unable to sign the report (because of sickness or some other valid reason), the team can sign his or her name. To indicate that a name was signed by the team on a member's behalf, be sure to attach a note to the signature.

CHAPTER 4

Managing for Business Success

After studying this chapter, you will be able to:

1 Identify the four interrelated functions of management: planning, organizing, directing, and controlling.

2 Understand the process by which a company develops and implements a strategic plan.

3 Discuss different options for organizing a business and create an organization chart.

4 Explain how managers direct others and motivate them to achieve company goals.

5 Describe the process by which a manager monitors operations and assesses performance.

6 Discuss three organizational forms of business: sole proprietorship, partnership, and corporation.

NOTEWORTHY MANAGEMENT

Consider this scenario. You're about halfway through the semester and ready for your first round of midterms. You open up your class notes and declare them "pathetic." You regret scribbling everything so carelessly (and skipping class so many times). You wish you had better notes. That's when it hits you: What if there was a note-taking service on campus? When you were ready to study for a big test, you could buy complete (and completely legible) class notes. You've heard that there are class-notes services at some larger schools, but there's no such thing on your campus. So you ask yourself: Why don't *I* start a note-taking business? This upcoming set of exams may not be salvageable, but after that, I'd always have great notes. And while I was at it, I could learn how to manage a business (isn't that what majoring in business is all about?).

So you sit down to work on your great business idea. First, you'll hire a bunch of students to take class notes and type them out. Then the note takers will e-mail the notes to

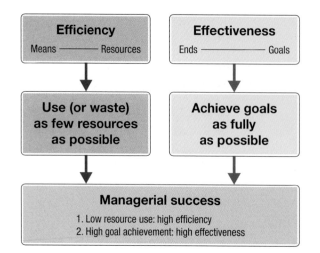

Figure 4.1

Managerial Efficiency and Effectiveness

your assistant, who'll get them copied (on a special type of blue paper that can't be duplicated). The last step will be assembling packages of notes and, of course, selling them. You decide to name your company "Notes-4-You."

It sounds like a great idea, but you're troubled by one question: Why does this business need *you*? Do the note takers need a boss? Couldn't they just sell the notes themselves? This process *could* work, but it would probably work a lot *better* if there was someone to oversee the operations: a manager—someone like you—to make sure that the operations involved in preparing and selling notes were performed in both an effective and efficient manner. You'd make the process *effective* by ensuring that the right things got done and that they all contributed to the success of the enterprise. You'd make the process *efficient* by ensuring that activities were performed in the right way and used the fewest possible resources. As you can see from Figure 4.1, that's the job that you perform as a **manager**: making a group of people more *effective* and *efficient* with you than they would be without you.

What Do Managers Do?

You'll accomplish this task through **management**: the process of planning, organizing, directing, and controlling resources to achieve specific goals. A *plan* allows you to take your business concept beyond the idea stage. It does not, however, get the work *done*. You have to *organize* things if you want your plan to become a reality. You have to put people and other resources in place in order to make things happen. And because your note-taking venture is supposed to be better off with you in charge, you need to be a *leader* who can motivate your people to do well. Finally, in order to know if things are in fact going well, you'll have to *control* your operations—that is, measure the results and compare them with the results that you laid out in your plan. Figure 4.2 gives you a good idea of the interrelationship between planning and the other functions that managers perform.

Figure 4.2 **ACTIVE**

The Role of Planning

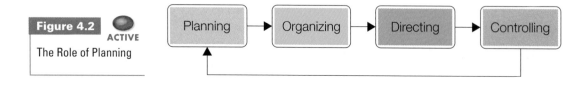

Functions of Management

If you visit any small or large company, not-for-profit organization, or government agency, you'll find managers doing the same things you'd be doing to run your note-taking business—*planning, organizing, directing*, and *controlling*. Let's look at these four interrelated functions in more detail.

PLANNING

Without a plan, it's hard to succeed at anything. The reason is simple: If you don't know where you're going, you can't really move forward. Successful managers decide where they want to be and then figure out how to get there. In **planning**, managers set goals and determine the best way to achieve them. As a result of the planning process, everyone in the organization knows what should be done, who should do it, and how it should be done.

Developing a Strategic Plan

Coming up with an idea—say, starting a note-taking business—is a good start, but it's only a start. Planning for it is a step forward. Planning begins at the highest level and works its way down through the organization. Step one is usually called **strategic planning**, which is the process of establishing an overall course of action. To begin this process, you should ask yourself a couple of very basic questions: Why, for example, does the organization exist? What value does it create? Sam Walton posed these questions in the process of founding Wal-Mart: His new chain of stores would exist in order to offer customers the lowest prices with the best possible service.[1]

After you've identified the purpose of your company, you're ready to take the remaining steps in the strategic-planning process:

- Write a mission statement that tells customers, employees, and others why your organization exists.

- Identify core values or beliefs that will guide the behavior of members of the organization.

- Assess the company's strengths, weaknesses, opportunities, and threats.

- Establish goals and objectives, or performance targets, to direct all the activities that you'll perform in order to achieve your mission.

- Develop and implement tactical and operational plans to achieve goals and objectives.

In the next few sections, we'll examine these components of the strategic-planning process.

Mission Statement As we saw in Chapter 2, the *mission statement* describes the purpose of your organization—the reason for its existence. It tells the reader what the organization is committed to doing. It can be

manager
Individual in an organization who is responsible for making a group of people more effective and efficient.

management
Process of planning for, organizing, directing, and controlling a company's resources so that it can achieve its goals.

planning
Process of setting goals and determining the best way to achieve them.

strategic planning
Process of establishing an overall plan or course of action for an organization.

very concise, like the one from Merck Pharmaceutical: "To preserve and improve human life." Or it can be as detailed as the one from Southwest Airlines: "The mission of Southwest Airlines is dedication to the highest quality of customer service delivered with a sense of warmth, friendliness, individual pride, and company spirit."

What about Notes-4-You? A simple, concise mission statement for your enterprise could be: "To provide high-quality class notes to college students." On the other hand, you could prepare a more detailed statement that explains what the company is committed to doing, who its customers are, what its focus is, what goods or services it provides, and how it serves its customers. In that case, your mission statement might be:

> *Notes-4-You is committed to earning the loyalty of college students through its focus on customer service. It provides high-quality, dependable, competitively priced class notes that help college students master complex academic subjects.*

Core Values Having defined your mission, your next step is to ask: What does this organization stand for? What values will define it? What principles should guide our actions as we build and operate the business? In Chapter 2, we explained that the small set of guiding principles that you identify as crucial to your company are known as *core values*—fundamental beliefs about what's important and what is and isn't appropriate in conducting company activities. Core values affect the overall planning processes and operations. At Volvo, for example, three core values— safety, quality, and environmental care— define the firm's "approach to product development, design and production."[2] Core values should also guide the behavior of every individual in the organization. Coca-Cola, for example, reports that its stated core values—honesty, integrity, diversity, quality, respect, responsibility, and accountability—tell employees exactly what behaviors are acceptable. How do companies communicate core values to employees and hold them accountable for putting those values into practice? They link core values to performance evaluations and compensation.[3]

In choosing core values for Notes-4-You, you're determined not to fall back on some list of the world's most popular core values: ethics/integrity, accountability, respect for others, and open communication.[4] You want yours to be unique to Notes-4-You. After some thought, you settle on *teamwork, trust,* and *dependability*. Why these three? As you plan your business, you realize that it will need a workforce that functions as a team, trusts each other, and can be depended on to satisfy customers. In building your workforce, you'll seek employees who'll embrace these values.

ABOUT NIKE 4.1

Here's a chance to see how the mission and core values of Nike have evolved over time.

Go to www.exploringbusinessonline.com

Conduct a SWOT Analysis

The next step in the strategic-planning process is to assess your company's fit with its environment. A common approach to *environmental analysis* is matching the strengths of your business with the opportunities available to it. It's called **SWOT analysis** because it calls for analyzing an organization's **S**trengths, **W**eaknesses, **O**pportunities, and **T**hreats. It begins with an examination of *external* factors that could influence the company in either a positive or negative way. These could include economic conditions, competition, emerging technologies, laws and regulations, and customers' expectations.

One purpose of assessing the external environment is to identify both *opportunities* that could benefit the company and *threats* to its success. For example, a company that manufactures children's bicycle helmets would view a change in federal law requiring all children to wear helmets as an opportunity. The news that two large sports-equipment companies were coming out with bicycle helmets would be a threat.

The next step is to evaluate the company's strengths and weaknesses. *Strengths* might include a motivated workforce, state-of-the-art technology, impressive managerial talent, or a desirable location. The opposite of any of these strengths (poor workforce, obsolete technology, incompetent management, or poor location) could signal a potential *weakness*. Armed with a good idea of external opportunities and threats and internal strengths and weaknesses, managers want to capitalize on opportunities by taking advantage of organizational strengths. Likewise, they want to protect the organization from both external threats and internal weaknesses.

Let's start with our strengths. Now that we know what they are, how do we match them with our available opportunities (while also protecting ourselves from our threats and overcoming our weaknesses)? Here's a possibility: By providing excellent service and price while we're still small (with few customers and low costs), we can solidify our position on campus. When the market grows (as it will because of the increase in the number of classes—especially those at 8:00 A.M.—and increases in student enrollment), we'll have built a strong reputation and will put ourselves in a position to grow. So even if a competitor comes to campus (a threat), we'll be the preferred supplier of class notes. This strategy will work only if we make sure that our note takers are dependable and that we don't alienate the faculty or administration.

Set Goals and Objectives

Your mission statement affirms what your organization is *generally* committed to doing, but it doesn't tell you *how* to do it. So the next step in the strategic-planning process is establishing goals and objectives. **Goals** are major accomplishments that the company wants to achieve over a long period of time (say, five years). **Objectives** are shorter-term performance targets that direct the activities of the organization toward the attainment of a goal. They should be clearly stated, attainable, and measurable: They should give target dates for the completion of tasks and stipulate who's responsible for taking necessary actions.[5]

An organization will have a number of goals and related objectives. Some will focus on financial measures, such as profit maximization and sales growth. Others will target operational efficiency or quality control. Still others will govern the company's relationships with its employees, its community, its environment, or all three.

Finally, goals and objectives change over time. As a firm reassesses its place in its business environment, it rethinks not only its mission but also its approach to fulfilling it. The reality of change was a major theme when the late McDonald's CEO Jim Cantalupo explained his goal to revitalize the company:

> *The world has changed. Our customers have changed. We have to change too. Growth comes from being better, not just expanding to have more restaurants. The new McDonald's is focused on building sales at existing restaurants rather than on adding new restaurants. We are introducing a new level of discipline and efficiency to all aspects of the business and are setting a new bar for performance.*[6]

This change in focus was accompanied by specific performance objectives—annual sales growth of 3 to 5 percent and income growth of 6 to 7 percent at existing restaurants, and a five-point improvement (based on customer surveys) in speed of service, friendliness, and food quality.

In setting strategic goals and performance objectives for Notes-4-You, you should keep things simple. Because you know you need to make money to stay in business, you could include a financial goal (and related objectives). Your mission statement promises "high-quality, dependable, competitively priced class notes," so you could focus on the quality of the class notes that you'll be taking and distributing. Finally, because your mission is to serve students, one goal could be customer oriented. When all's said and done, your list of goals and objectives might look like this:

- **Goal 1:** Achieve a 10-percent return on profits in your first five years. *Objective:* Sales of $20,000 and profit of $2,000 for the first 12 months of operations.

- **Goal 2:** Produce a high-quality product. *Objective:* First-year satisfaction scores of 90 percent or higher on quality of notes

---

SWOT analysis
Approach used to assess a company's fit with its environment by analyzing its strengths, weaknesses, opportunities, and threats.

goals
Major accomplishments that a company wants to achieve over a long period of time.

objectives
Intermediate-term performance targets that direct the activities of an organization toward the attainment of a goal.

(based on survey responses to three measures—understandability, readability, and completeness).

- **Goal 3:** Attain 98-percent customer satisfaction by the end of your fifth year. *Objective:* Making notes available within two days after class 95 percent of the time.

Develop Tactical and Operational Plans

The planning process begins at the top of the organization, where upper-level managers create a strategic plan, but it doesn't end there. The *execution* of the strategic plan involves managers at all levels.

Tactical Plans The overall plan is broken down into more manageable, shorter-term components called **tactical plans**. These plans specify the activities and allocation of resources (people, equipment, money) needed to implement the overall strategic plan over a given time period. Often, a long-range strategic plan is divided into several tactical plans; a five-year strategic plan, for instance, might be implemented as five one-year tactical plans.

Operational Plans The tactical plan is then broken down into various **operational plans** that provide detailed action steps to be taken by individuals or groups in order to implement the tactical plan and, consequently, the strategic plan. Operational plans cover only a brief period of time—say, a week or a month. At Notes-4-You, for example, note takers might be instructed to turn in typed class notes five hours earlier than normal on the last day of the semester (an operational guideline). The goal is to improve the customer-satisfaction score on dependability (a *tactical goal*) and, as a result, to earn the loyalty of students through attention to customer service (a *strategic goal*).

Plan for Contingencies and Crises

Even with great planning, things don't always turn out the way they're supposed to. Perhaps your plans were flawed or maybe you had great plans but something in the environment shifted unexpectedly. Successful managers anticipate and plan for the unexpected. Dealing with uncertainty requires *contingency planning* and *crisis management*.

Contingency Planning With **contingency planning**, managers identify those aspects of the business that are most likely to be adversely affected by change. Then, they develop alternative courses of action in case an anticipated change does occur. You probably do your own contingency planning: For example, if you're planning to take in a sure-fire hit movie on its release date, you may decide on an alternative movie in case you can't get tickets to your first choice.

Crisis Management Organizations also face the risk of encountering crises that require immediate attention. Rather than wait until such a crisis occurs and then scrambling to figure out what to do, many firms practice **crisis management**. Some, for instance, set up teams trained to deal with emergencies. Members gather information quickly and respond to the crisis while everyone else carries out his or her normal duties. The team also keeps the public, employees, the press, and government officials informed about the situation and the company's response to it.[7]

An example of how to handle crisis management involves Wendy's. After learning that a woman claimed she found a fingertip in a bowl of chili she bought at a Wendy's restaurant in San Jose, California, the company's public relations team responded quickly. Within a few days, the company announced that the finger didn't come from an employee or a supplier. Soon after, the police arrested the woman and charged her with attempted grand larceny for lying about how the finger got in her bowl of chili and trying to extort $2.5 million from the company. But the crisis was not over for Wendy's. The incident was plastered all over the news as the grossed-out public sought an answer to the question: "Whose finger is (or was) it?" A $100,000 reward was offered by Wendy's to anyone with information that would help the police answer this question. The challenge Wendy's faced was how to entice customers to return to its 50 San Francisco-area restaurants (where sales had plummeted) while keeping a low profile nationally. It accomplished this by giving out free milkshakes and discount coupons to customers in the affected regions and to avoid attention to the missing finger, making no changes in its national advertising. The crisis-management strategy worked and the story died down (although it flared up temporarily when the police arrested the woman's husband, who allegedly bought the finger from a co-worker who had severed it in an accident months earlier).[8]

Even with crisis-management plans in place, however, it's unlikely that most companies will emerge from a damaging or potentially damaging episode as unscathed as Wendy's did. For one thing, the culprits in the Wendy's case were caught and the public is willing to forgive an organization it views as a victim. Given the current public distrust of corporate behavior, companies whose reputations have suffered due to questionable corporate judgment do not fare as well. These companies include Firestone and Ford (who were responsible for faulty tire treads), Exxon (one of whose oil tankers ran aground and polluted Alaska's Prince William Sound), and ValuJet (which wasn't particularly forthcoming after a plane crash in the Everglades). Then, there are the companies at which executives have crossed the line between the unethical to the downright illegal—Arthur Andersen, Enron, Adelphia, ImClone, to name just a few. It should come as no surprise that contemporary managers spend more time anticipating crises and practicing their crisis-management responses.

Organizing

Now that you've developed a strategic plan for Notes-4-You, you need to organize your company so that it can implement your plan. A manager engaged in **organizing** allocates *resources* (people, equipment, and money) to achieve a company's plans. Successful managers make sure that all of the activities identified in the planning process are assigned to some person, department, or team and that everyone has the resources needed to perform assigned activities.

LEVELS OF MANAGEMENT: HOW MANAGERS ARE ORGANIZED

In a typical organization, there are several layers of management. Think of these layers as forming a pyramid like the one in Figure 4.3, with top managers occupying the narrow space at the peak, first-line managers the broad base, and middle-managers the levels in between. As you move up the pyramid, management positions get more demanding, but they carry more authority and responsibility (along with more power, prestige, and

Figure 4.3

Levels of Management

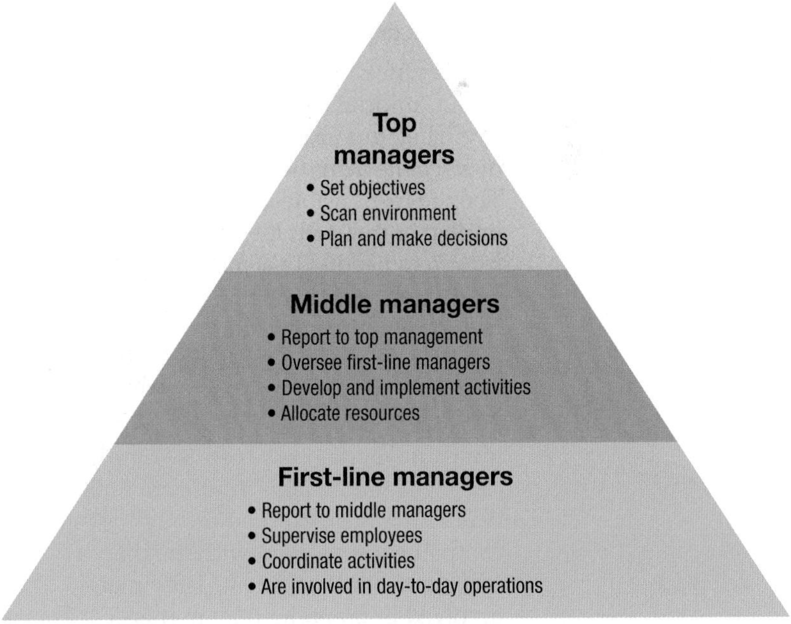

Top managers
- Set objectives
- Scan environment
- Plan and make decisions

Middle managers
- Report to top management
- Oversee first-line managers
- Develop and implement activities
- Allocate resources

First-line managers
- Report to middle managers
- Supervise employees
- Coordinate activities
- Are involved in day-to-day operations

QUICK QUIZ   4.1

Before you study the organizing and directing functions of managers, take a few minutes to test your knowledge of the planning function.

Go to www.exploringbusinessonline.com

---

tactical plans
Short-term plans that specify the activities and resources needed to implement a company's strategic plan.

operational plans
Detailed action steps to be taken by individuals or groups to implement tactical plans.

contingency planning
Process of identifying courses of action to be taken in the event a business is adversely affected by a change.

crisis management
Action plans that outline steps to be taken by a company in case of a crisis.

organizing
Management process of allocating resources to achieve a company's plans.

pay). Top managers spend most of their time in planning and decision making, while first-line managers focus on day-to-day operations. For obvious reasons, there are far more people with positions at the base of the pyramid than there are with jobs at the other two levels (as you get to the top, there are only a few positions). Let's look at each management level in more detail.

Top Managers

Top managers are responsible for the health and performance of the organization. They set the objectives, or performance targets, designed to direct all the activities that must be performed if the company is going to fulfill its mission. Top-level executives routinely scan the external environment for opportunities and threats and redirect company efforts when needed. They spend a considerable portion of their time planning and making major decisions. They represent the company in important dealings with other businesses and government agencies, and they promote it to the public. Job titles at this level typically include *chief executive officer (CEO)*, *chief financial officer (CFO)*, *chief operating officer (COO)*, *president*, and *vice president*.

Middle Managers

As the name implies, **middle managers** are in the "middle" of the management hierarchy: They report to top management and oversee the activities of first-line managers. They're responsible for developing and implementing activities and allocating the resources needed to achieve the objectives set by top management. Common job titles include *operations manager*, *division manager*, *plant manager*, and *branch manager*.

First-Line Managers

First-line managers supervise employees and coordinate their activities to make sure that the work performed throughout the company is consistent with the plans of top and middle management. They're less involved in planning than higher-level managers and more involved in day-to-day operations. It's at this level that most people get their first managerial experience. The job titles vary considerably but include such designations as *department head*, *group leader*, *office manager*, *foreman*, and *supervisor*.

Let's take a quick survey of the management hierarchy at Notes-4-You. As president, you are, of course, a member of *top management*, and you're responsible for the overall performance of your company. You spend much of your time setting objectives, or performance targets, to ensure that the company meets the goals you've set for it—increased sales, higher-quality notes, and timely distribution.

Several *middle managers* report to you, including your operations manager. As a middle manager, this individual focuses on implementing two of your objectives: producing high-quality notes and distributing them to customers in a timely manner. To accomplish this task, the operations manager oversees the work of two *first-line managers*—the note-taking supervisor and the copying supervisor. Each first-line manager supervises several nonmanagerial employees to make sure that their work is consistent with the plans devised by top and middle management.

ORGANIZATIONAL STRUCTURE: HOW COMPANIES GET THE JOB DONE

The organizing process raises some important questions: What jobs need to be done? Who does what? Who reports to whom? What are the formal relationships among people in the organization? You provide answers to these questions by developing an **organizational structure**: an arrangement of positions that's most appropriate for your company at a specific point in time. Remember: Given the rapidly changing environment in which businesses operate, a structure that works today might be outdated tomorrow. That's why you hear so often about companies **restructuring**—altering existing organizational structures to become more competitive under conditions that have changed. In building an organizational structure, you engage in two activities: *job specialization* (dividing tasks into jobs) and *departmentalization* (grouping jobs into units). We'll now see how these two processes are accomplished.

Specialization

The first step in designing an organizational structure is twofold:

1. Identifying the activities that need to be performed in order to achieve organizational goals.

2. Breaking down these activities into tasks that can be performed by individuals or groups of employees.

This twofold process of organizing activities into clusters of related tasks that can be handled by certain individuals or groups is called **specialization**. Its purpose is to improve efficiency.

Would specialization make Notes-4-You more efficient? You could have each employee perform all tasks entailed by taking and selling notes. Each employee could take notes in an assigned class, type them up, get them copied, and sell them outside the classroom at the start of the next class meeting. The same person would keep track of all sales and copying costs and give any profit—sales minus copying costs minus compensation—to you. The process seems simple, but is it really *efficient*? Will you earn the maximum amount of profit? Probably not. Even a company as small as Notes-4-You can benefit from specialization. It would function more efficiently if some employees specialized in taking notes, others in copying and packaging them, and still others in selling them. Higher-level employees could focus on advertising, accounting, finance, and human resources.

Obviously, specialization has advantages. In addition to increasing efficiency, for example, it results in jobs that are easier to learn. But it has disadvantages, too. Doing the same thing over and over bores people and will eventually leave employees dissatisfied with their jobs. Before long, you'll notice decreased performance and increased absenteeism and turnover.

Departmentalization

The next step in designing an organizational structure is **departmentalization**—grouping specialized jobs into meaningful units. Depending on the organization and the size of the work units, they may be called *divisions*, *departments*, or just plain *groups*. Traditional groupings of jobs result in different organizational structures, and for the sake of simplicity, we'll focus on two types—*functional* and *divisional organizations*.

Functional Organization A functional **organization** groups together people who have comparable skills and perform similar tasks. This form of organization is fairly typical for small to medium-size companies, which group their people by business functions: accountants are grouped together, as are people in finance, marketing and sales, human resources, production, and research and development. Each unit is headed by an individual with expertise in the unit's particular function. The head of the accounting department, for example, will be a senior accountant; the head of a hospital nursing unit will obviously be an experienced nurse. This structure is also appropriate for nonprofits. Think about your school, for instance: mathematics teachers are in the math department, history teachers are in the history department, those who run athletic programs are in the athletic department, and librarians work at the library.

If Notes-4-You adopted a functional approach to departmentalization, jobs might be grouped into four clusters:

- Human resources (hiring, training, and evaluating employees)
- Operations (overseeing note takers and copiers)
- Marketing (arranging for advertising, sales, and distribution)
- Accounting (handling cash collection and disbursement)

There are a number of advantages to the functional approach. The structure is simple to understand and allows the staff to specialize in particular areas; everyone in the marketing group would probably have similar interests and expertise. But homogeneity also has drawbacks: It can hinder communication and decision making between units

---

top managers
Those at the top of the management hierarchy who are responsible for the health and performance of the organization.

middle managers
Those in the "middle" of the management hierarchy who report to top management and oversee the activities of first-line managers.

first-line managers
Those at the bottom of the management hierarchy who supervise employees and coordinate their activities.

organizational structure
Organizational arrangement of jobs in an organization that's most appropriate for the company at a specific point in time.

restructuring
Process of altering an existing organizational structure to become more competitive under changing conditions.

specialization
Process of organizing activities into clusters of related tasks that can be handled by specific individuals or groups.

departmentalization
Process of grouping specialized jobs into meaningful units.

functional organization
Form of business organization that groups together people who have comparable skills and perform similar tasks.

and even promote interdepartmental conflict. The marketing department, for example, might butt heads with the accounting department because marketers want to spend as much as possible on advertising while accountants want to control costs. Marketers might feel that accountants are too tight with funds, and accountants might regard marketers as spendthrifts.

Divisional Organization Large companies often find it unruly to operate as one large unit under a functional organizational structure. Sheer size makes it difficult for managers to oversee operations and serve customers. To rectify this problem, most large companies are structured as **divisional organizations** made up of several smaller, self-contained units, or divisions, which are accountable for their own performance. Each division functions autonomously because it contains all the functional expertise (production, marketing, accounting, finance, human resources) needed to meet its objectives. The challenge is to find the most appropriate way of structuring operations to achieve overall company goals. Toward this end, divisions can be formed according to *products, customers, processes,* or *geography.*

Product Division **Product division** means that a company is structured according to its product lines. Sara Lee Corp., for example, has four product-based divisions: Sara Lee Bakery (baked goods), Sara Lee Foods (packaged meats), Sara Lee/DE (beverages, household and body-care products), and Sara Lee Branded Apparel (knitwear and other clothing).[9]

Customer Division Some companies prefer a **customer division** structure because it allows them to better serve their various categories of customers. Thus, Johnson & Johnson's 200 operating companies are grouped into three customer-based business

segments: consumer business (personal-care and hygiene products sold to the general public), pharmaceuticals (prescription drugs sold to pharmacists), and professional business (medical devices and diagnostics products used by physicians, optometrists, hospitals, laboratories, and clinics).[10]

Process Division If goods move through several steps during production, a company might opt for a **process division** structure. This form works well at Bowater Thunder Bay, a Canadian company that harvests trees and processes wood into newsprint and pulp. The first step in the production process is harvesting and stripping trees. Then, large logs are sold to lumber mills and smaller logs chopped up and sent to Bowater's mills. At the mill, wood chips are chemically converted into pulp. About 90 percent is sold to other manufacturers (as raw material for home and office products), and the remaining 10 percent is further processed into newspaper print. Bowater, then, has three divisions: tree cutting, chemical processing, and finishing (which makes newsprint).[11]

Geographical Division **Geographical division** allows companies that operate in several locations to be responsive to customers at a local level. McDonald's, for example, is organized according to the regions of the world in which it operates. In the United States, the national unit is further subdivided into five geographic operating divisions: the Northeast, Southeast, Great Lakes, Midwest, and West.[12] (This approach might be appealing to Notes-4-You if it expands to serve schools around the country.)

There are pluses and minuses associated with divisional organization. On the one hand, divisional structure usually enhances the ability to respond to changes in a firm's environment. If, on the other hand, services must be duplicated across units, costs will

be higher. In addition, some companies have found that units tend to focus on their own needs and goals at the expense of the organization as a whole.

THE ORGANIZATION CHART

Once an organization has set its structure, it can represent that structure in an **organization chart**: a diagram delineating the interrelationships of positions within the organization. Having decided that Notes-4-You will adopt a functional structure, you might create the organization chart shown in Figure 4.4.

Begin by putting yourself at the top of the chart, as the company's president. Then fill in the level directly below your name with the names and positions of the people who work directly *for you*—your accounting, marketing, operations, and human resources managers. The next level identifies the people who work for these managers. Because you've started out small, neither your accounting manager nor your human resources manager will be managing anyone directly. Your marketing manager, however, will oversee one person in advertising and a sales supervisor (who in turn oversees the sales staff). Your operations manager will oversee two individuals—one to supervise note takers and one to supervise the people responsible for making copies.

Reporting Relationships

With these relationships in mind, you can now draw lines to denote **reporting relationships**, or patterns of formal communication. Because four managers report to you, you'll be connected to four positions; that is, you'll have four direct "reports." Your marketing and operations managers will each be connected to two positions and their supervisors to one position each. The organization chart shows that if a member of the sales staff has a problem, he or she will report it to

the sales supervisor. If the sales supervisor believes that the problem should be addressed at a higher level, then he or she will report it to the marketing manager.

Theoretically, you will communicate only with your four direct reports, but this isn't the way things normally work. Behind every formal communication network there lies a network of informal communications—unofficial relationships among members of an organization. You might find that over time, you receive communications directly from members of the sales staff; in fact, you might encourage this line of communication.

Now let's look at the chart of an organization that relies on a divisional structure based on goods or services produced—say, a theme park. The top layers of this company's organization chart might look like the one in Figure 4.5(a) (page 82). We see that the president has two direct reports—a vice president in charge of rides and a vice president in charge of concessions. What about a bank that's structured according to its customer base? The bank's organization chart would begin like the one in Figure 4.5(b) (page 82). Once again, the company's top manager has two direct reports, in this

Figure 4.4

Organization Chart for Notes-4-You

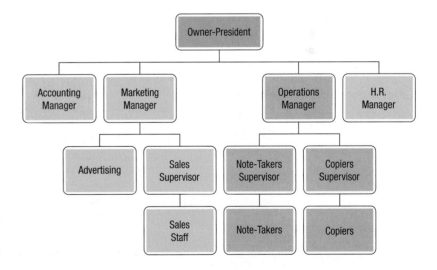

---

divisional organization
Form of organization that groups people into several smaller, self-contained units, or divisions, which are accountable for their own performance.

product division
Organizational structure made up of divisions based on product lines.

customer division
Organizational structure that groups employees into customer-based business segments.

process division
Organizational structure that groups people into operating units based on various stages in the production process.

geographical division
Organizational structure that groups people into divisions based on location.

organization chart
Diagram representing the interrelationships of positions within an organization.

reporting relationships
Patterns of formal communication among members of an organization.

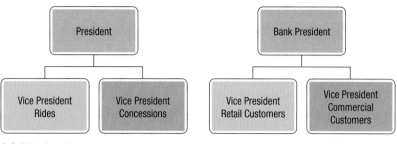

(a) Divisional structure by product

(b) Divisional structure by customer base

Figure 4.5

Organization Charts for Divisional Structures

case a VP of retail-customer accounts and a VP of commercial-customer accounts

Over time, companies revise their organizational structures to accommodate growth and changes in the external environment. It's not uncommon, for example, for a firm to adopt a functional structure in its early years. Then, as it becomes bigger and more complex, it might move to a divisional structure—perhaps to accommodate new products or to become more responsive to certain customers or geographical areas. Some companies might ultimately rely on a combination of functional and divisional structures. This could be a good approach for a credit card company that issues cards in both the United States and Europe. A skeleton of this firm's organization chart might look like the one in Figure 4.6.

Lines of Authority

Figure 4.6 **ACTIVE**

Organization Chart: Combination Divisional and Functional Structures

You can learn a lot about a firm's reporting and authority relationships by looking at its organization chart. To whom does a particular person report? Does each person report to one or more supervisors? How many peo-

ple does a manager supervise? How many layers are there, for example, between the top managerial position and the lowest managerial level?

Chain of Command The vertical connecting lines in the organization chart show the firm's **chain of command**: the authority relationships among people working at different levels of the organization. That is to say, they show *who reports to whom*. When you're examining an organization chart, you'll probably want to know whether each person reports to one or more supervisors: To what extent, in other words, is there *unity of command*? To understand why unity of command is an important organizational feature, think about it from a personal standpoint. Would you want to report to more than one boss? What happens if you get conflicting directions? Whose directions would you follow?

There are, however, conditions under which an organization and its employees can benefit by violating the unity-of-command principle. Under a **matrix structure**, for example, employees from various functional areas (accounting, marketing, operations, and so forth) form teams to combine their skills in working on a specific project. Nike sometimes uses this type of arrangement. To design new products, the company may create product teams made up of designers, marketers, and other specialists with expertise in particular sports categories—say, running shoes or basketball shoes. Each team member would be evaluated by both the team manager

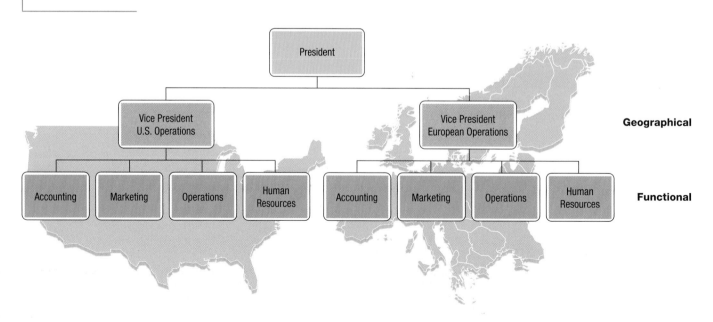

and the head of his or her functional department.

Span of Control Another thing to notice about a firm's chain of command is the number of layers between the top managerial position and the lowest managerial level. As a rule, new organizations (such as Notes-4-You) have only a few layers of management—an organizational structure that's often called *flat*. Let's say, for instance, that a member of the Notes-4-You sales staff wanted to express concern about slow sales among a certain group of students. That person's message would have to filter upward through only two management layers—the sales supervisor and marketing manager—before reaching the president.

As a company grows, however, it tends to add more layers between the top and the bottom; that is, it gets *taller*. Added layers of management can slow down communication and decision making, causing the organization to become less efficient and productive. That's one reason why many of today's organizations are restructuring in order to become flatter.

There are tradeoffs between the advantages and disadvantages of flat and tall organizations. Companies determine what tradeoffs to make according to a principle called **span of control**, which measures the number of people reporting to a particular manager. If, for example, you remove layers of management to make your organization flatter, you end up increasing the number of positions reporting to a particular supervisor. If you refer back to the organization chart in Figure 4.4 (page 81), you'll recall that, under your present structure, four managers report to you as the president of Notes-4-You: the heads of accounting, marketing, operations, and human resources. In turn, two of these managers have positions reporting to them: The advertising manager and sales supervisor report to the marketing manager, while the note-taker's supervisor and the copier's supervisor report to the operations manager. Let's say that you remove a layer of management by getting rid of the marketing and operations managers. Your organization would be flatter, but what would happen to your workload? As president, you'd now have six direct reports rather than four: accounting manager, advertising manager, sales manager, note-taker supervisor, copier supervisor, and human resources manager.

What's better—a *narrow* span of control (with few direct reports) or a *wide* span of control (with many direct reports)? The answer to this question depends on a number of factors, including frequency and type of interaction, proximity of subordinates, competence of both supervisor and subordinates, and the nature of the work being supervised. For example, you'd expect a much wider span of control at a nonprofit call center than in a hospital emergency room.

Delegating Authority

Given the tendency toward flatter organizations and wider spans of control, how do managers handle increased workloads? They must learn how to handle **delegation**—the process of entrusting work to subordinates. Unfortunately, many managers are reluctant to delegate. As a result, they not only overburden themselves with tasks that could be handled by others, but deny subordinates the opportunity to learn and develop new skills.

Responsibility and Authority As owner of Notes-4-You, you'll probably want to control every aspect of your business, especially during the start-up stage. But as the organization grows, you'll have to assign responsibility for performing certain tasks to other people. You'll also have to accept the fact that *responsibility* alone—the duty to perform a task—won't be enough to get the job done. You'll have to grant subordinates the *authority* they need to complete a task—that is, the power to make the necessary decisions. (And they'll also need sufficient resources.) Ultimately, you'll also hold your subordinates accountable for their performance.

Centralization and Decentralization

If and when your company expands (say, by offering note-taking services at other schools), you'll have to decide whether most

---

chain of command
Authority and reporting relationships among people working at different levels of an organization.

matrix structure
Structure in which employees from various functional areas form teams to combine their skills in working on a specific project.

span of control
Number of people reporting to a particular manager.

delegation
Process of entrusting work to subordinates.

decisions should still be made by individuals at the top or delegated to lower-level employees. The first option, in which most decision making is concentrated at the top, is called **centralization**. The second option, which spreads decision making throughout the organization, is called **decentralization**.

Let's say that you favor decentralizing Notes-4-You four or five years down the road, when the company has expanded. Naturally, there are some decisions—such as strategic planning—that you won't delegate to lower-level employees, but you could certainly delegate the management of copy-center operations. In fact, putting someone in charge of this function would probably improve customer satisfaction because copy-center customers would be dealing directly with the manager. It would also give the manager valuable decision-making experience, and while he or she is busy making daily decisions about the copy center, you'll have more time to work on higher-level tasks. The more you think about the possibility of decentralizing your company, the more you like the idea. First, you have to see it through its difficult start-up years.

Directing

The third management function is **directing**—providing focus and direction to others and motivating them to achieve organizational goals. As owner and president of Notes-4-You, you might think of yourself as an orchestra leader. You have given your musicians (employees) their sheet music (plans). You've placed them in sections (departments) and arranged the sections (organizational structure) so the music will sound as good as possible. Now your job is to tap your baton and lead the orchestra so that its members make beautiful music together.[13]

LEADERSHIP STYLES

Actually, it's fairly easy to pick up a baton, cue each section, and strike up the band. But it doesn't follow that the music will sound good. What if your cues are ignored or misinterpreted or ambiguous? Maybe your musicians don't like your approach to making music and will just walk away. On top of everything else, you don't simply want to make music: You want to inspire your musi-

cians to make *great* music. How do you accomplish this goal? How do you become an effective leader? What style, or approach, should you use to motivate others to achieve organizational goals?

Unfortunately, there are no definitive answers to questions like these. Over time, every manager refines his or her own **leadership style**, or way of interacting with and influencing others. Despite a vast range of personal differences, leadership styles tend to reflect one of the following approaches to directing and motivating people: the *autocratic, democratic,* or *laissez-faire.* Let's see how managerial styles reflect each of them in a work situation.

- *Autocratic Style.* Managers who've developed an **autocratic leadership style** tend to make decisions without soliciting input from subordinates. They exercise authority and expect subordinates to take responsibility for performing the required tasks without undue explanation.

- *Democratic Style.* Managers who favor a **democratic leadership style** generally seek input from subordinates while retaining the authority to make the final decisions. They're also more likely to keeps subordinates informed about things that affect their work.

- *Laissez-Faire Style.* In practicing a **laissez-faire leadership style**, managers adopt a "hands-off" approach and provide relatively little direction to subordinates. They may advise employees but usually give them considerable freedom to solve problems and make decisions on their own.

At first glance, you'd probably not want to work for an autocratic leader. After all, you certainly don't want to be told what to do without having any input. You probably like the idea of working for a democratic leader; it's flattering to be asked for your input. Although working in a laissez-faire environment might seem a little unsettling at first, the opportunity to make your own decisions is appealing.

In general, your assessments of the three leadership styles would be accurate. Employees generally dislike working for autocratic leaders; they like working for democratic leaders, and they find working for laissez-faire leaders rewarding (as long as they feel they can handle the job). But there are situations when these generalities don't hold.

To learn what these situations are, let's turn things around and pretend you're the leader. To make it applicable to your current life, we'll say that you're leading a group of fellow students in a team project for your class. Are there times when it would be best for you to use an autocratic leadership style? What if your team was newly formed, unfamiliar with what needs to be done, under a very tight deadline, and looking to you for direction? In this situation, you might find it appropriate to follow an autocratic leadership style (on a temporary basis) and assign tasks to each member of the group.

Now let's look at the leadership style you probably prefer—the democratic leadership style. Can you think of a situation where this style would *not* work for your team? What if the members of your team are unmotivated, do not seem interested in providing input, and are not getting along? It might make sense to move away from a democratic style of leadership (temporarily) and delegate specific tasks to each member of the group that they can do on their own.

How about laissez-faire leadership? Will this always work with your group? Not always. It will work if your team members are willing and able to work independently and welcome the chance to make decisions. Otherwise, it could cause the team to miss deadlines or do poorly on the project.

The point being made here is that no one leadership style is effective all the time for all people. While the democratic style, and to a lesser extent the laissez-faire style, are viewed as the most appropriate, there are times when following an autocratic style is better. Good leaders learn how to adjust their styles to fit the situation as well as the individuals being directed.

Transformational Leadership

Theories on what constitutes effective leadership evolve over time. One theory that's received a lot of attention in the last decade contrasts two leadership styles: *transactional* and *transformational*. So-called **transactional leaders** exercise authority based on their rank in the organization. They let subordinates know what's expected of them and what they will receive if they meet stated objectives. They focus their attention on identifying mistakes and disciplining employees for poor performance. By contrast, **transformational leaders** mentor and develop subordinates, providing them with challenging opportunities, working one-on-one to help them meet their professional and

---

centralization
Decision-making process in which most decision making is concentrated at the top.

decentralization
Decision-making process in which most decision making is spread throughout the organization.

directing
Management process that provides focus and direction to others and motivates them to achieve organizational goals.

leadership style
Particular approach used by a manager to interact with and influence others.

autocratic leadership style
Management style identified with managers who tend to make decisions without soliciting input from subordinates.

democratic leadership style
Management style used by managers who generally seek input from subordinates while retaining the authority to make the final decision.

laissez-faire leadership style
Management style used by those who follow a "hands-off" approach and provide relatively little direction to subordinates.

transactional leaders
Managers who exercise authority based on their rank in the organization and focus their attention on identifying mistakes.

transformational leaders
Managers who mentor and develop subordinates and stimulate them to look beyond personal interests to those of the group.

personal needs, and encouraging people to approach problems from new perspectives. They stimulate employees to look beyond personal interests to those of the group.

So which leadership style is more effective? You probably won't be surprised by the opinion of most experts. In today's organizations, in which team building and information sharing are important and projects are often collaborative in nature, transformational leadership has proven to be more effective. Modern organizations look for managers who can develop positive relationships with subordinates and motivate employees to focus on the interests of the organization.[14]

ABOUT NIKE 4.2

After reviewing several leadership styles, take a moment to find out how the top executives of Nike direct and motivate members of the organization.

Go to www.exploringbusinessonline.com

Controlling

Let's pause for a minute and reflect on the management functions that we've discussed so far—planning, organizing, and directing. As founder of Notes-4-You, you began by establishing plans for your new company. You defined its mission and set objectives, or performance targets, which you needed to meet in order to achieve your mission. Then, you organized your company by allocating the people and resources needed to carry out your plans. Finally, you provided focus and direction to your employees and motivated them to

achieve organizational objectives. Is your job finished? Can you take a well-earned vacation? Unfortunately, the answer is no: Your work has just begun. Now that things are rolling along, you need to monitor your operations in order to see if everything is going according to plan. If it's not, you'll need to take corrective action. This process of comparing actual to planned performance and taking necessary corrective action is called **controlling**.

A Five-Step Control Process

You can think of the control function as the five-step process outlined in Figure 4.7.

Let's see how this process might work at Notes-4-You. Let's assume that, after evaluating class enrollments, you estimate that you can sell 100 notes packages per month to students taking the sophomore-level geology course popularly known as "Rocks for Jocks." So you set your standard at 100 packages. At the end of the month, however, you look over your records and find that you sold only 80 packages. Comparing your actual performance with your planned performance, you realize that you came up 20 packages short. In talking with your salespeople, you learn why: It turns out that the copy machine broke down so often that packages frequently weren't ready on time. You immediately take corrective action by increasing maintenance on the copy machine.

Now, let's try a slightly different scenario. Let's say that you still have the same standard (100 packages) and that actual sales are still 80 packages. In investigating the reason for the shortfall, you find that you overestimated the number of students taking "Rocks for Jocks." Calculating a more accurate number of students, you see that your original standard—estimated sales—was too high by 20 packages. In this case, you should adjust your standards to reflect expected sales of 80 packages.

In both situations, your control process has been helpful. In the first instance, you were alerted to a problem that cut into your sales. Correcting this problem would undoubtedly increase sales and, therefore, profits. In the second case, you encountered a defect in your planning and learned a good managerial lesson: Plan more carefully.

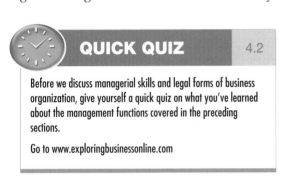

QUICK QUIZ 4.2

Before we discuss managerial skills and legal forms of business organization, give yourself a quick quiz on what you've learned about the management functions covered in the preceding sections.

Go to www.exploringbusinessonline.com

Managerial Skills

To be a successful manager, you'll have to master a number of skills. To get an entry-level position, you'll have to be technically competent at the tasks you're asked to perform. To advance, you'll need to develop strong interpersonal and conceptual skills. The relative importance of different skills varies from job to job and organization to organization, but to some extent, you'll need them all to forge a managerial career. Throughout your career, you'll also be expected to communicate ideas clearly, use your time efficiently, and reach sound decisions.

TECHNICAL SKILLS

You'll probably be hired for your first job based on your **technical skills**—the ones you need to perform specific tasks—and you'll use them extensively during your early career. If your college major is accounting, you'll use what you've learned to prepare financial statements. If you have

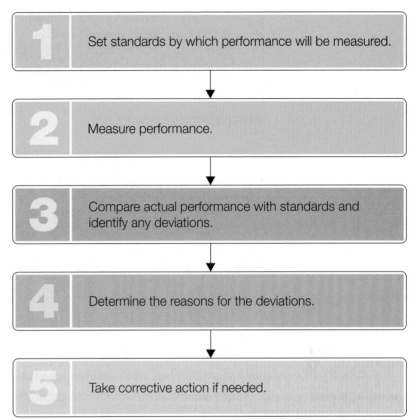

1. Set standards by which performance will be measured.

2. Measure performance.

3. Compare actual performance with standards and identify any deviations.

4. Determine the reasons for the deviations.

5. Take corrective action if needed.

Figure 4.7

A Five-Step Control Process

a marketing degree and you join an ad agency, you'll use what you know about promotion to prepare ad campaigns. Technical skills will come in handy when you move up to a first-line managerial job and oversee the task performance of subordinates. Technical skills, though developed through job training and work experience, are generally acquired during the course of your formal education.

INTERPERSONAL SKILLS

As you move up the corporate ladder, you'll find that you can't do everything yourself: You'll have to rely on other people to help you achieve the goals for which you're responsible. That's why **interpersonal skills**—the ability to get along with and motivate other people—are critical for managers in mid-level positions. These managers play a pivotal role because they report to top-level managers while overseeing the activities of first-line managers. Thus, they need

controlling
Management process of comparing actual to planned performance and taking corrective actions when necessary.

technical skills
Skills needed to perform specific tasks.

interpersonal skills
Skills used to get along with and motivate other people.

strong working relationships with individuals at all levels and in all areas. More than most other managers, they must use "people skills" to foster teamwork, build trust, manage conflict, and encourage improvement.[15]

CONCEPTUAL SKILLS

Managers at the top, who are responsible for deciding what's good for the organization from the broadest perspective, rely on **conceptual skills**—the ability to reason abstractly and analyze complex situations. Senior executives are often called on to "think outside the box"—to arrive at creative solutions to complex, sometimes ambiguous problems. They need both strong analytical abilities and strong creative talents.

COMMUNICATION SKILLS

Effective communication skills are crucial to just about everyone. At all levels of an organization, you'll often be judged on your ability to communicate, both orally and in writing. Whether you're talking informally or making a formal presentation, you must express yourself clearly and concisely. Talking too loudly, rambling, and using poor grammar reduces your ability to influence others, as does poor written communication. Confusing and error-riddled documents (including e-mails) don't do your message any good, and they will reflect badly on you.[16]

TIME-MANAGEMENT SKILLS

Managers face multiple demands on their time, and their days are usually filled with interruptions. Ironically, some technologies that were supposed to save time, such as voicemail and e-mail, have actually increased workloads. Unless you develop certain **time-management skills**, you risk reaching the end of the day feeling that you've worked a lot but accomplished little. What can managers do to ease the burden? Here are a few common-sense suggestions:

- Prioritize tasks, focusing on the most important things first.

- Set aside a certain time each day to return phone calls and answer e-mail.

- Delegate routine tasks.

- Don't procrastinate.

- Insist that meetings start and end on time and stick to an agenda.

- Eliminate unnecessary paperwork.[17]

DECISION-MAKING SKILLS

Every manager is expected to make decisions, whether alone or as part of a team. Drawing on your **decision-making skills** is often a process in which you must define a problem, analyze possible solutions, and select the best outcome. As luck would have it, because the same process is good for making personal decision we'll use a personal example to demonstrate the process approach to decision making. Consider the following scenario: You're upset because your midterm grades are much lower than you'd hoped. To make matters worse, not only are you in trouble academically, but the other members of your business-project team are annoyed because you're not pulling your weight. Your lacrosse coach is very upset because you've missed too many practices, and members of the mountain-biking club that you're supposed to be president of are talking about impeaching you if you don't show up at the next meeting. And your girlfriend says you're ignoring her. (You can substitute boyfriend here, of course; we're just trying to keep our exposition as simple as possible.)

A Six-Step Approach to Problem Solving

Assuming that your top priority is salvaging your GPA, let's tackle your problem by using a six-step approach to solving problems that don't have simple solutions. We've summarized this model in Figure 4.8:[18]

1. *Identify the problem you want to work on.* Step one is getting to know your problem, which you can formulate by asking yourself a basic question: "How can I improve my grades?"

2. *Gather relevant data.* Step two is gathering information that will shed light on the problem. Let's rehash some of the relevant information that you've already identified: (a) You did poorly on your finals because you didn't spend enough time studying. (b) You didn't study because you went to see

your girlfriend (who lives about three hours from campus) over the weekend before your exams (and on most other weekends, as a matter of fact). (c) What little studying you got in came at the expense of your team project and lacrosse practice. (d) While you were away for the weekend, you forgot to tell members of the mountain-biking club that you had to cancel the planned meeting.

3. *Clarify the problem.* Once you review all of the above facts, you should see your problem is bigger than just getting your grades up; your life is pretty much out of control. You can't handle everything to which you've committed yourself. Something has to give. You clarify the problem by summing it up with another basic question: "What can I do to get my life back in order?"

4. *Generate possible solutions.* If you thought defining the problem was tough, wait until you've moved on to this stage. Let's say that you've come up with the following possible solutions to your problem: (a) Quit the lacrosse team. (b) Step down as president of the mountain-biking club. (c) Let team members do your share of work on the business project. (d) Stop visiting your girlfriend so frequently. The solution to your problem—how to get your life back in order—will probably require multiple actions.

5. *Select the best option.* This is clearly the toughest part of the process. Working your way through your various options, you arrive at the following conclusions: (a) You can't quit the lacrosse team because you'd lose your scholarship. (b) You can resign your post in the mountain-biking club, but that won't free up much time. (c) You can't let your business-project team down (and besides, you'd just get a low grade). (d) She wouldn't like the idea, but you could visit your girl-

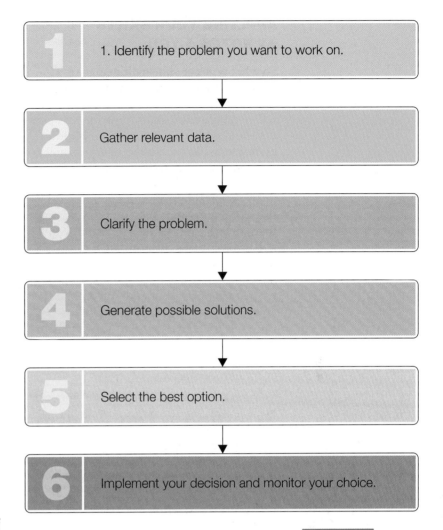

1. Identify the problem you want to work on.

2. Gather relevant data.

3. Clarify the problem.

4. Generate possible solutions.

5. Select the best option.

6. Implement your decision and monitor your choice.

Figure 4.8

How to Solve a Problem

friend, say, once a month rather than once a week.

So what's the most feasible (if not necessarily perfect) solution? Probably visiting your girlfriend once a month and giving up the presidency of the mountain-biking club.

6. *Implement your decision and monitor your choice.* When you call your girlfriend, you're pleasantly surprised to find that she understands. The vice president is happy to take over the mountain-biking club. After the first week, you're able to attend lacrosse practice, get caught up on your team business project, and catch up in all your other classes. The real test of your solution will be the results of the semester's finals.

conceptual skills
Skills used to reason abstractly and analyze complex situations.

time-management skills
Skills used to manage time effectively.

decision-making skills
Skills used in defining a problem, analyzing possible solutions, and selecting the best outcome.

APPLYING YOUR SKILLS AT NOTES-4-YOU

So what types of skills will managers at Notes-4-You need? To oversee note-taking and copying operations, first-line managers will need technical skills, probably in operations and perhaps in accounting. Middle managers will need strong interpersonal skills to maintain positive working relationships with subordinates and to motivate them. As president, because you have to solve problems and come up with creative ways to keep the business growing, you'll need conceptual skills. And everyone will have to communicate effectively: After all, inasmuch as you're in the business of selling written notes, it would look pretty bad if your employees wrote poorly. Finally, everyone will have to use time efficiently and call on problem-solving skills to handle the day-to-day crises that seem to plague every new company.

Selecting a Legal Form of Business

If you're starting a new business, you have to decide which legal form of ownership is best for you and your business. Do you want to own the business yourself and operate as a sole proprietorship? Or, do you want to share ownership, operating as a partnership or a corporation? Before we discuss the pros and cons of these three types of ownership—sole proprietorship, partnership, and corporation—let's address some of the questions that you'd probably ask yourself in choosing the appropriate legal form for your business.

1. *How much control do you want?* Do you want to own the company yourself, or do you want to share ownership with other people? Are you willing to share responsibility for running the business? Do you have the talent and skills to run the business yourself, or would the business benefit from a diverse group of owners? Are you likely to get along with co-owners over an extended period of time?

2. *Do you want to share profits with others?* Do you want to be the sole benefactor of your efforts or are you willing to share profits with other people? Do

you want to be in charge of deciding how much of its profits will be retained in the business?

3. *How much liability exposure are you willing to accept?* Are you willing to risk your personal assets—your bank account, your car, maybe even your home—for your business? Are you prepared to pay business debts out of your personal funds? Do you feel uneasy about accepting personal liability for the actions of fellow owners?

4. *What are your financing needs?* How do you plan to finance your company? Will you need a lot of money to start, operate, and grow your business? Can you furnish the money yourself, or will you need some investment from other people? Will you need bank loans? If so, will you have difficulty getting them yourself?

5. *What are you willing to do to set up and operate your business?* Do you want to minimize the costs of getting started? Do you hope to avoid complex government regulations and reporting requirements?

6. *Should it be possible for the business to continue without you?* Is it important to you that the business survive you? Do you want to know that other owners can take over if you die or become disabled? Do you want to make it easy for ownership to change hands?

No single form of ownership will give you everything you want. You'll have to make some tradeoffs. Because each option has advantages and disadvantages, your job is to decide which one offers the features that are most important to you. Let's compare the three options on the six dimensions that we identified previously: control, profit sharing, liability exposure, ability to obtain financing, setup costs and government regulations, and continuity.

SOLE PROPRIETORSHIPS

A **sole proprietorship** is a business owned by only one person. The most common form of ownership, it accounts for about 75 percent of all U.S. businesses.[19] It's the easiest and cheapest type of business to form: If you're using your own name as the name of your business, you just need a license to get started, and once you're in business, you're subject to few government regulations.

As sole owner, you have complete control over your business. You make all important decisions, and you're generally responsible for all day-to-day activities. In exchange for assuming all of this responsibility, you get all of the income earned by the business.

For many people, however, the sole proprietorship is not suitable. The flip side of enjoying complete control, for example, is having to supply all the different talents that may be necessary to make the business a success. And if you die, the business dissolves.

Unlimited Liability and the Sole Proprietorship

You also have to rely on your own resources for financing: In effect, you *are* the business, and any money borrowed by the business is loaned to *you personally*. Even more important, the sole proprietor bears **unlimited liability** for any losses incurred by the business. As you can see from Figure 4.9, the principle of unlimited personal liability means that if the *company* incurs a debt or suffers a catastrophe (say, getting sued for causing an injury to someone), the *owner* is personally liable. As a sole proprietor, you put your personal assets (your bank account, your car, maybe even your home) at risk for the sake of your business. You can lessen your risk with insurance, but your liability exposure can still be substantial.

PARTNERSHIPS

A **partnership** (or, more precisely, a **general partnership**) is a business owned jointly by two or more people. About 6 percent of U.S. businesses are partnerships, and although the vast majority are small, some are quite large. For example, the big four public accounting firms are partnerships. Setting up a partnership is more complex than setting up a sole proprietorship, but it's still relatively easy and inexpensive. The cost varies according to size and complexity. It's possible to form a simple partnership without the help of a lawyer or an accountant, but it's usually a good idea to get professional advice. Professionals can help you identify and resolve issues that may later create disputes among partners.

The Partnership Agreement

The impact of disputes can be lessened if the partners have executed a well-planned *partnership agreement* that specifies everyone's rights and responsibilities. The agreement might provide such details as:

- Amount of cash and other contributions to be made by each partner.
- Division of partnership income (or loss).
- Partner responsibilities—who does what.
- Conditions under which a partner can sell an interest in the company.
- Conditions for dissolving the partnership.
- Conditions for settling disputes.

Unlimited Liability and the Partnership

Figure 4.10 (page 92) shows that a major problem with partnerships, as with sole proprietorships, is unlimited liability: Each partner is personally liable not only for his or her own actions but *for the actions of all the partners*. In a partnership, it may work

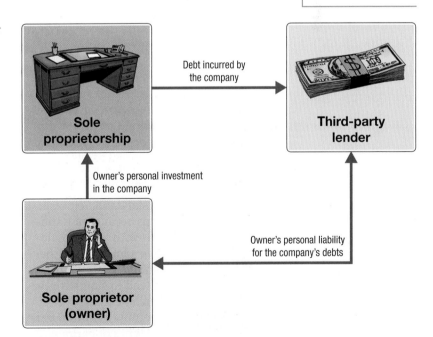

Figure 4.9   ACTIVE

Sole Proprietorship and Unlimited Liability

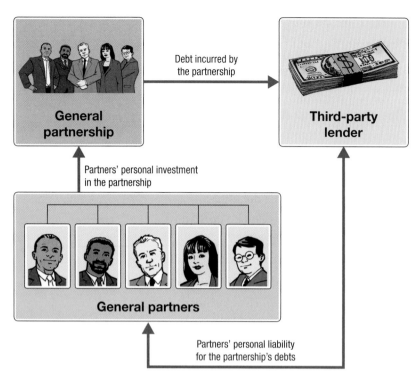

Figure 4.10   ACTIVE
General Partnership and Unlimited Liability

according to the following scenario. Say that you're a partner in a dry cleaning business. One day, you return from lunch to find your establishment on fire. You're intercepted by your partner, who tells you that the fire started because he fell asleep while smoking. As you watch your livelihood go up in flames, your partner tells you something else: Because he forgot to pay the bill, your fire insurance was canceled. When it's all over, you estimate the loss to the building and everything inside at $1,200,000. And here's the really bad news: If the business doesn't have the cash or other assets to cover losses, *you can be personally sued for the amount*. In other words, any party who suffered a loss because of the fire can go after your personal assets.

Limited Partnerships

Many people are understandably reluctant to enter into partnerships because of unlimited liability. Individuals with substantial assets, for example, have a lot to lose if they get sued for a partnership obligation (and when people sue, they tend to start with the richest partner). To overcome this defect of partnerships, the law permits a **limited partnership**, which has two types of partners: a single *general partner* who runs the business and is responsible for its liabilities and any number of *limited partners* who have limited

involvement in the business and whose losses are limited to the amount of their investment.

Advantages and Disadvantages of Partnerships

The partnership has several advantages over the sole proprietorship. First, it brings together a diverse group of talented individuals who share responsibility for running the business. Second, it makes financing easier: The business can draw on the financial resources of a number of individuals. The partners not only contribute funds to the business, but can use personal resources to secure bank loans. Finally, continuity needn't be an issue because partners can agree legally to allow the partnership to survive if one or more partners die.

But there are some negatives. Being a partner means that you have to share decision making, and many people aren't comfortable with that situation. Not surprisingly, partners often have differences of opinion on how to run a business, and disagreements can escalate to the point of actual conflict; in fact, they can even jeopardize the continuance of the business. In addition to sharing ideas, partners also share profits. This arrangement can work as long as all partners feel that they're being rewarded according to their efforts and accomplishments, but that isn't always the case.

CORPORATIONS

A **corporation** differs from a sole proprietorship and a partnership because it is a legal entity that is entirely separate from the parties who own it. It can enter into binding contracts, buy and sell property, sue and be sued, be held responsible for its actions, and be taxed. As Figure 4.11 shows, corporations account for 19 percent of all U.S. businesses but generate almost 90 percent of the revenues. Most large well-known businesses are corporations, but so are many of the smaller firms with which you do business.

Ownership and Stock

Corporations are owned by **shareholders** who invest money in the business by buying shares of **stock**. The portion of the corporation they own depends on the percentage of stock they hold. For example, if a corporation has issued 100 shares of stock, and you own 30 shares, you own 30 percent of the company. The shareholders elect a **board of directors**, a group of people (primarily from outside the corporation) who are legally responsible for governing the corporation. The board oversees the major policies and decisions made by the corporation, sets goals and holds management accountable for achieving them, and hires and evaluates the top executive, generally called the CEO (chief executive officer). The board also approves the distribution of income to shareholders in the form of cash payments called **dividends**.

Benefits of Incorporation

The corporate form of organization offers several advantages, including limited liability for shareholders, greater access to financial resources, and continuity.

Limited Liability The most important benefit of incorporation is the **limited liability** to which shareholders are exposed: They are not responsible for the obligations of the corporation, and they can lose *no more than the amount that they have personally invested in the company*. Clearly, limited liability would have been a big plus for the unfortunate individual whose business partner burned down their cleaning establishment. Had they been incorporated, the *corporation* would have been liable for the debts incurred by the fire. If the corporation didn't have enough money to pay the debt, the individual shareholders would not have been obligated to pay anything. They would have lost all the money that they'd invested in the business, but no more.

Financial Resources Incorporation also makes it possible for businesses to raise funds by selling stock. This is a big advantage as a company grows and needs more

funds to operate and compete. Depending on its size and financial strength, the corporation also has an advantage over other forms of business in getting bank loans. An established corporation can borrow its own funds, but when a small business needs a loan, the bank usually requires that it be guaranteed by its owners.

Continuity Another advantage of incorporation is continuity. Because the corporation has a legal life separate from the lives of its owners, it can (at least in theory) exist forever. Transferring ownership of a corporation is easy: Shareholders simply sell their stock to others. Some founders, however, want to restrict the transferability of their

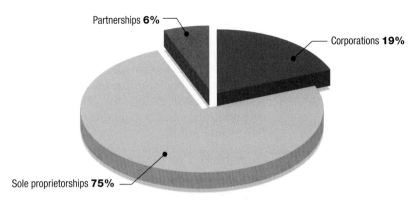

Partnerships **6%**
Corporations **19%**
Sole proprietorships **75%**

Number of businesses

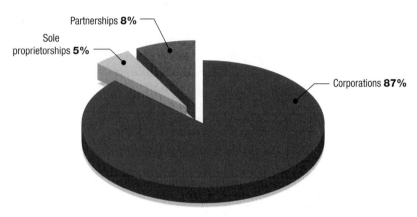

Partnerships **8%**
Sole proprietorships **5%**
Corporations **87%**

Sales revenue

Figure 4.11

Types of U.S. Business

stock and so choose to operate as a **private (or closely held) corporation**. The stock in these corporations is held by only a few individuals who are not allowed to sell it to the general public. Companies with no such restrictions on stock sales are called **public corporations**; stock is available for sale to the general public.

Drawbacks to Incorporation

Like sole proprietorships and partnerships, corporations have both positive and negative properties. In sole proprietorships and partnerships, for instance, the individuals who own and manage a business are the same people. Corporate managers, however, don't necessarily own stock, and shareholders don't necessarily work for the company. This situation can be troublesome if the goals of the two groups differ significantly. Managers, for example, might be more interested in career advancement than the overall profitability of the company. Stockholders might care about profits without regard for the well-being of employees.

Another drawback to incorporation—one that often discourages small businesses from incorporating—is the fact that corporations are costly to set up. Finally, they're all subject to levels of regulation and governmental oversight that can place a burden on small businesses.

After weighing the pros and cons of the three forms of ownership, which form would you choose for Notes-4-You? At this early stage of your enterprise, there's no one whom you'd want to involve as an owner. Thus, you'll probably decide to start up as a sole proprietorship, which is fairly easy to do. You're a little concerned about the personal liability to which you're exposing yourself, but you don't think that this risk is worth the added cost of incorporating, at least not right now.

Down the road, you might consider adding partners (assuming that you can find people with whom you'd feel comfortable working). You'll go the partnership route if the business does well and you need other people to help you grow the company: Partners could not only help you manage the business but could bring needed funds into the venture. You'd still face that disturbing liability problem, which would be even worse with partners:

Not only would you have to worry about your own bad decisions, but you'd have to worry about what your partners were doing.

These concerns could cause you to consider incorporation despite the expense. In the long run, incorporation is probably best for you: It would eliminate your liability problem and allow you to attract additional investors and the money you need to expand.

ABOUT NIKE   4.3

Now that you know about the three organizational forms of business, take a few minutes to review the evolution of organizational forms at Nike.

Go to www.exploringbusinessonline.com

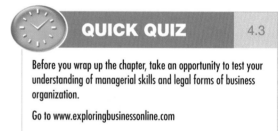

QUICK QUIZ   4.3

Before you wrap up the chapter, take an opportunity to test your understanding of managerial skills and legal forms of business organization.

Go to www.exploringbusinessonline.com

Where We're Headed

In this chapter, we introduced the four functions of management: planning, organizing, directing, and controlling. You learned how a strategic plan is developed and how a business can be structured to best achieve its goals. You explored contrasting leadership styles and learned how a manager monitors operations. Finally, you investigated the advantages and disadvantages of various forms of business ownership. In Chapter 5, we'll build on the management concepts discussed in this chapter as we introduce you to the basics of human resource management—the process of attracting, developing, motivating, evaluating, and retaining quality employees.

Summary of Learning Objectives

1. **Identify the four interrelated functions of management: planning, organizing, directing, and controlling.**

   Managers plan, organize, direct, and control resources to achieve specific goals. In **planning**, they set goals and determine the best way to achieve them. **Organizing** means allocating resources (people, equipment, and money) to carry out the company's plans. **Directing** is the process of providing focus for employees and motivating them to achieve organizational goals. **Controlling** involves comparing actual to expected performance and taking corrective action when necessary.

2. **Understand the process by which a company develops and implements a strategic plan.**

   Successful managers decide where they want the organization to go and then determine how to get there. **Planning** for a business starts at the top and works its way down. It begins with **strategic planning**—the process of establishing an overall course of action. Step one is identifying the purpose of the organization. Then, management is ready to take the remaining steps in the strategic planning process: (1) Prepare a *mission statement* that describes the purpose of the organization and tells customers, employees, and others what it's committed to doing. (2) Select the *core values* that will guide the behavior of members of the organization by letting them know what is and isn't appropriate and important in conducting company activities. (3) Use **SWOT analysis** to assess the company's strengths and weaknesses and its fit with the external environment. (4) Set **goals** and **objectives**, or performance targets, to direct all the activities needed to achieve the organization's mission. (5) Develop **tactical plans** and **operational plans** to implement objectives.

3. **Discuss different options for organizing a business and create an organization chart.**

   Managers coordinate the activities identified in the planning process among individuals, departments, or other units and allocate the resources needed to perform them. Typically, there are three levels of management: **top managers**, who are responsible for overall performance; **middle managers**, who report to top managers and oversee lower-level managers; and **first-line managers**, who supervise employees to make sure that work is performed correctly and on time. The skills needed by managers vary according to level. Top managers need strong **conceptual skills**, while those at mid levels need good interpersonal skills and those at lower levels need **technical skills**. All managers need strong **communication**, **decision-making**, and **time-management skills**.

   Management must develop an **organizational structure**, or arrangement of people within the organization, that will best achieve company goals. The process begins with **specialization**—dividing necessary tasks into jobs; the principle of grouping jobs into units is called **departmentalization**. Units are then grouped into an appropriate organizational structure. **Functional organization** groups people with comparable skills and tasks; **divisional organization** creates a structure composed of self-contained units based on **product**, **customer**, **process**, or **geographical division**. Forms of organizational division are often combined.

   An organization's structure is represented in an **organization chart**—a diagram showing the interrelationships of its positions. This chart highlights the **chain of command**, or authority relationships among people working at different levels. It also shows the number of layers between the top and lowest managerial levels. An organization with few layers has a wide **span of control**, with each manager overseeing a large number of subordinates; with a narrow span of control, only a limited number of subordinates reports to each manager.

4. **Explain how managers direct others and motive them to achieve company goals.**

   A manager's **leadership style** varies depending on the manager, the situation, and the people being directed. There are three common styles. Using an **autocratic style**, a manager tends to

---

private (or closely held) corporation
Corporation that restricts the transferability of its stock.

public corporation
Corporation whose stock is available to the general public.

make decisions without soliciting input and expects subordinates to follow instruction without undue explanation. Managers who prefer a **democratic style** seek input into decisions. Exercising a **laissez-faire style**, the manager provides no more guidance than necessary and lets subordinates make decisions and solve problems. One current leadership theory focuses on two contrasting leadership styles. Managers adopting a **transactional style** exercise authority according to their rank in the organization, let subordinates know what's expected of them, and step in when mistakes are made. Practicing a **transformational style**, managers mentor and develop subordinates and motivate them to achieve organizational rather than merely personal goals. Transformational leadership is effective in organizations that value team building and information sharing.

5. **Describe the process by which a manager monitors operations and assesses performance.**

The process of comparing actual to planned performance and taking corrective action is called **controlling**. The control function can be viewed as a five-step process: (1) establish standards; (2) measure performance; (3) compare actual performance with standards and identify any deviations; (4) determine the reason for deviations; and (5) take corrective action if needed.

6. **Discuss three organizational forms of business: sole proprietorship, partnership, and corporation.**

A **sole proprietorship** is a business owned by one person. A sole proprietor has complete control—a situation that benefits the owner but can limit his or her ability to attract the varied talents needed to make the business a success. The business dissolves when the owner dies. A **partnership** is owned jointly by two or more people. It has several advantages over the sole proprietorship: (1) It brings a diverse group of people together to share managerial responsibility. (2) It makes financing easier. (3) Partners can agree legally to allow the partnership to survive if one or more partners die. But there are drawbacks: (1) Shared decision making can result in disagreements. (2) Profits must be shared. (3) Each partner is personally liable not only for his or her own actions but for those of all partners—a principle called **unlimited liability**.

A **corporation** is a legal entity which is separate from the parties who own it. Corporations are owned by **shareholders** who invest money in them by buying shares of **stock**. They elect a **board of directors** that's legally responsible for governing the corporation. An important advantage of incorporation is **limited liability**: Owners are not responsible for the obligations of the corporation and can lose no more than the amount that they have personally invested in the company. Incorporation also makes it easier to access financing, and because the corporation is a separate legal entity, it exists beyond the lives of its owners.

Questions and Problems

1. **AACSB** ▸ **Analysis**
Consider the things that the principal of your old high school had to do to ensure that the school met the needs of its students. Identify these activities and group them by the four functions of management: planning, organizing, directing, and controlling. What skills are needed to perform these activities?

2. **AACSB** ▸ **Reflective Skills**
Without a plan, it's hard to succeed. Successful managers set goals and determine the best ways to reach them. Successful students do the same thing. Develop a strategic plan for succeeding in this course that includes the following steps:

1. Assess your strengths, weaknesses, opportunities, and threats as they relate to this course.

2. Establish goals and objectives, or performance targets, to direct all the activities that you'll perform in order to earn a high grade in this course.

3. Describe tactical and operational plans for achieving your stated goals and objectives.

3. **AACSB** ▸ **Analysis**
If you were the CEO of a large organization, what core values would you want to guide the behavior of your employees? First, assume that you oversee a large company that manufacturers and sells medical

devices, such as pacemakers, defibrillators, and insulin pumps. Your company was a pioneer in bringing these products to the market. Identify six core values that you would want to guide the behavior of your employees. For these core values, be sure to:

- Indicate why it's important to the functioning of the organization.

- Explain how you'll communicate it to your employees and encourage them to embrace it.

- Outline the approaches that you'll take in holding employees accountable for embracing it.

Now, repeat the process. This time, however, assume that you're the CEO of a company that rents videos, DVDs, and video games at more than 8,000 outlets across the country.

4. AACSB ▶ Analysis

How can you help your college or university assess its fit with its environment? For one thing, you could apply SWOT analysis. Here's how:

- Identify internal factors, either positive or negative, that are unique to your school. Based on your analysis, list at least five factors that are *strengths* and five that are *weaknesses*.

- Identify external factors that could influence your school in either a positive or negative way. Based on your analysis, list at least five *opportunities* that could benefit your school and five *threats* to its success.

- Suggest several ways in which your school can take advantage of opportunities by making the most of its strengths.

- Suggest several ways in which your school can protect itself from threats and overcome its weaknesses.

5. AACSB ▶ Analysis

How would you like to work at the "Sweetest Place on Earth"? Then consider a career at Hershey Foods, the chocolate and candy maker. Your career path at Hershey Foods might follow a typical trajectory: When you finish college, you may enter the business world as a first-line manager. After about 10 years, you will probably have advanced to the middle-management level. Perhaps you'll keep moving up and eventually find yourself in a top-level management position with a big salary. Examining job opportunities may be an opportunity to start identifying the kinds of positions that interest you. Go to www.exploringbusinessonline.com to link to the Hershey Foods Web site and check out available positions. Then, take the following steps:

- Find an interesting entry-level management position. Describe the duties of the job and explain why you'd classify it as a first-line management position.

- Pick a middle-level position to which you might advance after 10 years with the company. Describe the duties of the job and explain why you'd classify it as a middle-level management position.

- Finally, identify a top-level management position that you'd like to attain later in your career.

To find these positions, you'll have to click on "Investors," "Corporate Governance," and "Management Team." Because Hershey Foods doesn't describe its management-team positions, you'll have to fill in a few blanks. Start by listing what you imagine to be the duties of a given position; then, explain why these duties qualify it as a top-level management position.

6. AACSB ▶ Communication

If you were to ask a job recruiter what skills he or she looks for in a candidate, one of the first things you'll hear is "communication skills." Strong communication skills will not only help you get a good job, but they'll also help you move up the ladder. How can you strengthen your written and oral communication skills while you're still a college student? Here are a few steps you can take:

- Look for courses (or course components) designed to strengthen communication skills, such as writing (or composition) or speech classes.

- Find out if your college has a writing program.

- Check into nonacademic programs designed to strengthen communication skills, such as courses on interview techniques offered by the career services office.

- Find out how you can do some writing for the school newspaper or, if you're a little more outgoing, how you can appear in theatrical productions.

By following these suggestions, you should get a very good idea of what your college can do to help you develop both written and oral communication skills. Write a brief report detailing your findings.

7. AACSB ▶ Reflective Skills

Do you ever reach the end of the day and wonder what you've accomplished? To succeed in management, you need to learn how to manage your time. The Internet is an interesting place to start. For many college students, it takes up a lot of time that could be put to better use. How much time do you spend online, instant-messaging, shopping, playing games, blogging, or indulging in some other enjoyable but time-consuming activity? One approach to solving the problem of wasted online time is to apply the six-step, problem-solving procedure that we outlined in the chapter. Write a brief report detailing each of the steps that you take to solve the problem and implement a solution.

8. Define *organizational structure* and identify five different forms that it can take. For each form, identify a type of company that might use it and explain why it would be appropriate for the company. Use examples other than those mentioned in the chapter.

9. Describe a *partnership* and a *corporation* and list the advantages and disadvantages of each. Now ask yourself this question: If you and three friends were starting a business today to sell sporting-goods equipment, what form of organization would you choose? Why?

10. Compare and contrast three forms of leadership—democratic, autocratic, and laissez-faire. Which style would you prefer to use yourself? Which would you prefer your boss to use? Explain your answers in both cases. Next, compare and contrast the transactional-leadership style with the transformational-leadership style? Which style would you adopt as a manager? Why?

Learning on the Web AACSB

Mission "Improvisable"

A mission statement tells customers, employees, and stakeholders why the organization exists—its purpose. It can be concise, like the one from Mary Kay Cosmetics—"To give unlimited opportunity to women"—or it can be more detailed, such as the following from FedEx:

FedEx is committed to our People-Service-Profit Philosophy. We will produce outstanding financial returns by providing totally reliable, competitively superior, global, air-ground transportation of high-priority goods and documents that require rapid, time-certain delivery.

Mission statements are typically constructed to communicate several pieces of information: what the company strives to accomplish, what it's known for, and how it serves its customers (and perhaps employees and shareholders). Here are a few examples:

America West: *America West will support and grow its market position as a low-cost, full-service nationwide airline. It will be known for its focus on customer service and its high-performance culture. America West is committed to sustaining financial strength and profitability, thereby providing stability for its employees and shareholder value for its owners.*

Saturn: *Our mission is to earn the loyalty of Saturn owners and grow our family by developing and marketing U.S.-manufactured vehicles that are world leaders in quality, cost, and customer enthusiasm through the integration of people, technology, and business systems.*

American Diabetes Association: *The mission of the organization is to prevent and cure diabetes, and to improve the lives of all people affected by diabetes. To fulfill this mission, the American Diabetes Association funds research, publishes scientific findings, provides information and other services to people with diabetes, their families, health care professionals and the public and advocates for scientific research and for the rights of people with diabetes.*

Hershey Foods: *Our mission is to be a focused food company in North America and selected international markets and a leader in every aspect of our business. Our goal is to enhance our #1 position in the North American confectionery market, be the leader in U.S. chocolate-related grocery products, and to build leadership positions in selected international markets.*

ASSIGNMENT

Create hypothetical mission statements for each of these four companies: Outback Steakhouse, Tesoro, Got Junk?, and Staples. To find descriptions of all four, go to www.exploringbusinessonline.com to link to the SBA Success Stories Web site—a Web site maintained by the SBA. For additional information, link to the Web site for each of the companies.

In composing your four mission statements, follow the format suggested previously: Each statement should be about two or three sentences long and should provide several pieces of information—what the company strives to accomplish, what it's known for, and how it serves its customers (and perhaps its employees and shareholders).

One last thing: *Your statements should be originals, not duplicates of the companies' official statements.*

Career Opportunities

To Manage or Not To Manage?

Are you interested in a career that pays well and offers power, prestige, and a feeling of accomplishment? A career in management may be for you, but be forewarned that there's a downside: You have to make tough decisions, other people will be after your job, and it can be lonely at the top. To find out more about the pros and cons of a management career, go to www.exploringbusinessonline.com to link to the About.com Web site and read the article "Is Management for Me?" Then, answer the following questions, being sure to provide an explanation for each of your answers:

- Which of the pros of being a manger are important to you? Which are not?

- Which of the cons might discourage you from pursuing a management career? Which might not?

- Considering balance, does a career in management appeal to you? Why or why not?

Ethics Angle AACSB

Sugarcoating the News at Krispy Kreme

According to Krispy Kreme's "Code of Ethics for Chief Executive and Senior Financial Officers," the company's top executives are expected to practice and promote honest and ethical conduct. They're also responsible for the health and overall performance of the company. Recently, however, things have gone wrong in the top echelons of the doughnut-shop chain.

First, a little background: Founded as one small doughnut shop in Winston-Salem, North Carolina, in 1937, the brand became increasingly popular over the next six decades, taking off in the 1980s and 1990s. By 2003, Krispy Kreme (which went public in 2000) was selling more than a billion doughnuts a year. That's when things started to go stale. (For more details on the company's ups and downs, go to www.exploringbusinessonline.com to link to the *Detroit News* Web site and read the article "Krispy Kreme: The Rise, Fall, Rise and Fall of a Southern Icon.")

When sales first started to decline in the fall of 2003, CEO Scott Livengood offered a variety of creative explanations, mostly for the benefit of anxious investors: High gas prices discouraged people from driving to doughnut shops; supermarket sales were down because grocery stores were losing business to Wal-Mart; people were cutting back on carbohydrates because of the popular Atkins

diet. Unfortunately, other (more plausible) explanations were beginning to surface. To complete this exercise, you'll need to find out what they were. Go to www.exploringbusinessonline.com to link to the *Business Week* and *USA Today* Web sites and read these articles: "The Best and Worst Managers of the Year" and "Krispy Kreme Must Restate Earnings by $25.6M." Once you have a good grasp of the company's problems and you've read about the people who are responsible, answer the following questions, being sure to provide explanations for your responses:

1. What factors contributed to the problems at Krispy Kreme? What happened to the company? Who was hurt?

2. Should the firm's problems be attributed to poor management, unethical behavior on the part of the executive team, or both?

3. Judging from the lessons of the Krispy Kreme case, how important do you think it is for a firm to have strong top-down leadership?

4. If you'd been the CEO of Krispy Kreme, what things would you have done differently?

Team-Building Skills AACSB

Legally Speaking

Here's the scenario: You and your team serve as consultants to business owners who need help in deciding which legal form of ownership is best for them. You're currently working with three clients. For each client, you'll evaluate possible legal forms of organization, debate the alternatives, and make a recommendation. Then, you'll write a report to your client, presenting your recommendation and explaining why you arrived at your conclusion.

In addition to learning the basic facts about each company, you've gathered additional information by asking each client the following questions:

- How much control do you want?

- Do you want to share profits with others?

- How much liability exposure are you willing to accept?

- What are your financing needs?

- What are you willing to do to set up and operate your business?

- Should it be possible for the business to continue without you?

The following is the information that you've collected about each client.

CLIENT 1: RAINFOREST ADVENTURES

Rainforest Adventures offers one-day and multiday tours of several locations in Australia. It works with both tourists and study groups, and its clientele varies from people who want a relaxing experience away from hectic urban life to those who are keenly interested in the exotic environment. The business is dedicated to the preservation of Australia's tropical and wetland reserves. Its guides have many years of experience leading tourists through the rain forests, particularly at night when they come alive.

Rainforest Adventures was started three years ago by Courtney Kennedy, who has 15 years of experience in the ecotourism industry. She runs the business as a sole proprietorship but is considering a partnership. (She doesn't want the cost or hassle of doing business as a corporation.) In questioning her, you found out the following: Kennedy is dedicated to preserving the Australian wetlands and sees her business as a way of encouraging people to support conservation efforts. However, her guides have displayed an "it's just-a-job" attitude, become increasingly undependable, and declined to share her commitment. On the other hand, Kennedy has several trusted friends who not only have years of experience as guides, but who share her enthusiasm for environmental preservation. She's optimistic that they'd be willing to join her in the business. She dreams of expanding her business to offer classes on the ecology of the rain forest but doesn't have enough cash, and she's afraid that a loan application will be turned down by the bank.

Options

Because Kennedy doesn't want to incorporate, she's left with two options: to continue doing business as a sole proprietorship or to find one or more individuals to join her in a partnership. After evaluating these two alternatives, you should recommend the one that you consider most appropriate. You should discuss the pros and cons of both options and explain how each applies to Kennedy's situation. If you recommend forming a partnership, you need to distinguish between a general partnership and a limited partnership as well as explaining what a partnership agreement is, what it covers, and why it's important.

CLIENT 2: SCUFFY THE TUGBOAT

Scuffy the Tugboat is a family-run business that, as the name suggests, makes tugboats. It was formed as a partnership in 1986 by the three McLaughlin bothers—Mick (a naval architect), Jack (an accountant), and Bob (a marine engineer). Their first tugboat is still towing ships in Boston harbor, and over the years, success has allowed them to grow the company by plowing money back into it. Last year's sales were more than $7 million. Now, how-

ever, they want to double production by expanding their factory by 24,000 square feet. They estimate a cost of about $1 million, but a bigger facility would enable them to avoid late-delivery penalties that can run up to $2,000 a day. They're not sure, however, about the best way to raise the needed funds. None of the brothers has $1 million on hand, and because lenders are often hesitant to loan money to shipbuilders, even those with good performance records, local banks haven't been encouraging.

Unlike many partners, the three brothers get along quite well. They are concerned, however, about the risks of taking on personal debts for the business. In particular, they don't like being liable not only for their own actions, but for the actions of all of the partners.

Options

You should recommend that Scuffy the Tugboat either remain a partnership or become a private corporation. State the pros and cons of both forms of organization and explain how they apply to the brothers' situation.

CLIENT 3: DINNER RENDEZVOUS

For three years, owner Peggy Deardon has been operating Dinner Rendezvous, which gives individuals an opportunity to meet others and expand their social networks, in Austin, Texas. Interested clients go to the company's Web site and fill out applications and privacy statements. There's an annual membership fee of $125 and a $10 charge for each dinner attended (plus the cost of dinner and drinks). Deardon sets up all dinners and is onsite at the restaurant to introduce guests and serve complimentary champagne. Although the company has a steady clientele, it's not a big moneymaker. If Deardon didn't have a regular full-time job, she couldn't keep the business running. She stays with it because she enjoys it and believes that she provides a good service for Austin residents. Because it's run out of her home, and because her biggest cost is the champagne, it's a low-risk business with no debts. With a full-time job, she also appreciates the fact that it requires only a few hours of her time each week.

Options

Because your client wants advice on whether or not to incorporate, you should evaluate two options—remaining a sole proprietorship or forming a corporation. In addition to your recommendation, you should state the pros and cons of both forms of organization and explain how they apply to Deardon's situation.

The Global View AACSB

The Art and Science of Organizational Evolution

A company's organizational structure defines the formal relationships among the people in it. It also reflects an arrangement of positions that's most appropriate for the

company at a specific point in time. As the business expands or changes directions, its organizational structure should also change.

With these principles in mind, let's trace the evolution of a hypothetical company called High-Tech Cases, which manufacturers and sells DVD cases made out of a special high-tech material.

STAGE 1

When the company was founded, it operated under a functional organizational structure, with the following key positions and reporting relationships:

Position	Reports to
CEO	No one
VP of Sales and Marketing	CEO
VP of Production	CEO
VP of Finance	CEO
Director of Sales	VP Sales/Marketing
Director of Advertising	VP Sales/Marketing
Director of Operations	VP Production
Director of Engineering	VP Production
Treasurer	VP Finance
Controller	VP Finance

In addition, two salespeople reported to the director of sales. The directors of advertising, operations, and engineering each had two assistants, as did the treasurer and controller.

STAGE 2

About three years after the company's founding, the management team decided to expand sales into Asia. The director of sales retained responsibility for the United States, while a new director was added for Asia. The two salespeople who'd been with the company since its beginning focused on U.S. sales, and two new salespeople were hired to handle Asia. No other position changed, and for the next two years, all personnel worked out of the U.S. headquarters.

STAGE 3

By the beginning of the fifth year of operations, Asian and U.S. sales were about the same. At this point, management decided to set up two separate operations—one in the United States and the other in China. A senior VP was hired to head each operation—senior VP of U.S. operations and senior VP of Asian operations. Both would report to the CEO. Each operational unit would run its own production facilities, arrange its own financing, and be in charge of its sales and marketing activities. As a result, High-Tech Cases almost doubled in size, but management believed that the restructuring was appropriate and would increase profits in the long run.

ASSIGNMENT

Create three organization charts—one for each stage in High-Tech's development. Ideally, you should make your charts with some type of organization-chart software. To use the tool available on Microsoft Word, go to the *Standard Toolbar* in MS Word, click on "Help," and type in *organization chart*.

Business Plan Project

Group Report: *Management Plan (Mission, Values, Form, and Structure)*

REPORT

The team should submit a written report providing the following management plans for your proposed company:

- Mission statement
- Core values
- Legal form of organization
- Organizational structure

You can find some guidance on developing a mission statement and core values in the "Mission Statement and Core Values" section of Appendix A, "Introducing Your Business Plan." Be sure to report the legal form of business ownership chosen by your company, along with the rationale for your choice. Finally, describe the relationships among individuals within the company, listing the major responsibilities of each member of your management team. Present these relationships graphically by including an **organization chart**, either in the body of the document or as an appendix. Legal forms of *business ownership* and forms of *business organization* are among the topics discussed in this chapter.

REASONABLE CONTRIBUTIONS

All members of the team who make a reasonable contribution to the report should sign it. (If any team member does not work on the report, his or her name should *not* appear on it.) If a student who has made a contribution is unable to sign the report (because of sickness or some other valid reason), the team can sign his or her name. To indicate that a name was signed by the team on a member's behalf, be sure to attach a note to the signature.

CHAPTER 5

Recruiting, Motivating, and Keeping Quality Employees

After studying this chapter, you will be able to:

1 Define *human resource management* and explain how managers develop and implement a human resource plan.

2 Explain how companies train and develop employees and discuss the importance of a diverse workforce.

3 Define *motivation* and describe several theories of motivation.

4 Identify factors that make an organization a good place to work, including competitive compensation and benefit packages.

5 Explain how managers evaluate employee performance and retain qualified employees.

6 Explain why workers unionize and how unions are structured and describe the collective-bargaining process.

THE GROUNDS OF A GREAT WORK ENVIRONMENT

Howard Schultz has vivid memories of his father slumped on the couch with his leg in a cast.[1] The ankle would heal, but his father had lost another job—this time as a driver for a diaper service. It was a crummy job, but it put food on the table, and if his father couldn't work, there wouldn't be any money. Howard was seven, but he understood the gravity of the situation, particularly because his mother was seven months pregnant, and the family had no insurance.

This was just one of the many setbacks that plagued Howard's father throughout his life—an honest, hard-working man frustrated by a system that wasn't designed to cater to the needs of common workers. He'd held a series of blue-collar jobs (cab driver, truck driver, factory worker), sometimes holding two or three at a time. Despite his willingness to work, he never earned enough money to move his family out of Brooklyn's federally subsidized housing projects. Howard Schultz's father died never having found fulfillment in his work life—or even a meaningful job. It was the saddest day of Howard's life.

Stewart Cohen
Getty Images
Inc.–Image Bar

102

As a kid, did Howard ever imagine that one day he'd be the founder and chairman of Starbucks Coffee Company? Of course not. But he did decide that if he was ever in a position to make a difference in the lives of people like his father, he'd do what he could. Remembering his father's struggles and disappointments, Schultz has tried to make Starbucks the kind of company where he wished his father had worked. "Without even a high school diploma," Schultz admits, my father

probably could never have been an executive. But if he had landed a job in one of our stores or roasting plants, he wouldn't have quit in frustration because the company didn't value him. He would have had good health benefits, stock options, and an atmosphere in which his suggestions or complaints would receive a prompt, respectful response.[2]

Schultz is motivated by both personal and business considerations: "When employees have self-esteem and self-respect," he argues, "they can contribute so much more: to their company, to their family, to the world."[3] His commitment to his employees is imbedded in Starbuck's mission statement, whose first objective is to "provide a great work environment and treat each other with respect and dignity."[4]

Human Resource Management

Employees at Starbucks are vital to the company's success. They are its public face, and every dollar of sales passes through their hands.[5] According to Howard Schultz, they can make or break the company. If a customer has a positive interaction with an employee, the customer will come back. If an encounter is negative, the customer is probably gone for good. That's why it's crucial for Starbucks to recruit and hire the right people, train them properly, motivate them to do their best, and encourage them to stay with the company. Thus, the company works to provide satisfying jobs, a positive work environment, appropriate work schedules, and fair compensation and benefits. These activities are part of Starbucks's strategy to deploy human resources in order to gain competitive advantage. The process is called **human resource management (HRM)**, which consists of all actions that an organization takes to attract, develop, and retain quality employees. Each of these activities is complex. Attracting talented employees involves the recruitment of qualified candidates and the selection of those who best fit the organization's needs. Development encompasses both new-employee orientation and the training and development of current workers. Retaining good employees means motivating them to excel, appraising their performance, compensating them appropriately, and doing what's possible to retain them.

HUMAN RESOURCE PLANNING

How does Starbucks make sure that its worldwide retail locations are staffed with just the right number of committed employees? How does Walt Disney World ensure that it has enough qualified cast members to provide visitors with a "magical" experience? How does Norwegian Cruise Lines make certain that when the *Norwegian Dawn* pulls out of New York harbor, it has a complete, fully trained crew on board to feed, entertain, and care for its passengers? Managing these tasks is a matter of **strategic human resource planning**—the process of developing a plan for satisfying an organization's human resources (HR) needs.

A strategic HR plan lays out the steps that an organization will take to ensure that it has the right number of employees with the right skills in the right places at the right times. HR managers begin by analyzing the company's mission, objectives, and

human resource management (HRM)
All actions that an organization takes to attract, develop, and retain quality employees.

strategic human resource planning
Process of developing a plan for satisfying an organization's human resource needs.

strategies. Starbucks' objectives, for example, include the desire to "develop enthusiastically satisfied customers"[6] as well as to foster an environment in which employees treat both customers and each other with respect. Thus, the firm's HR managers look for people who are "adaptable, self-motivated, passionate, creative team members."[7] Likewise, Disney's overall objectives include not only making all visitors feel as if they're special in a special place, but ensuring that employees' appearance reflects a special image (there's a 47-page book on the subject).[8] Disney looks for people who best fulfill these job requirements. The main goal of Norwegian Cruise Lines—to lavish passengers with personal attention—determines not only the type of employee desired (one with exceptionally good customer-relation skills and a strong work ethic) but the number needed (one for every two passengers on the *Norwegian Dawn*).[9]

Job Analysis

To develop an HR plan, HR managers must obviously be knowledgeable about the jobs that the organization needs performed. They organize information about a given job by performing a **job analysis** to identify the tasks, responsibilities, and skills that it entails, as well as the knowledge and abilities needed to perform it. Managers also use the information collected for the job analysis to prepare two documents:

* A **job description**, which lists the duties and responsibilities of a position.
* A **job specification**, which lists the qualifications—skills, knowledge, and abilities—needed to perform the job.

HR Supply and Demand Forecasting

Once they've analyzed the jobs within the organization, HR managers must forecast future hiring (or firing) needs. This is the three-step process summarized in Figure 5.1.

Starbucks, for instance, might find that it needs 300 new employees to work at stores scheduled to open in the next few months. Disney might determine that it needs 2,000 new cast members to handle an anticipated surge in visitors. The *Norwegian Dawn* might be short 25 restaurant workers because of an unexpected increase in reservations.

After calculating the disparity between supply and future demand, HR managers must draw up plans for bringing the two numbers into balance. If the demand for labor is going to outstrip the supply, they may hire more workers, encourage current workers to put in extra hours, subcontract work to other suppliers, or introduce labor-saving initiatives. If the supply is greater than the demand, they may deal with over-staffing by not replacing workers who leave, encouraging early retirements, laying off workers, or (as a last resort) firing workers.

Recruiting Qualified Employees

Armed with information on the number of new employees to be hired and the types of positions to be filled, the HR manager then develops a strategy for recruiting potential employees. **Recruiting** is the process of identifying suitable candidates and encouraging them to apply for openings in the organization.

Before going any further, we should point out that, in recruiting and hiring, managers must comply with antidiscrimination laws; violations can have legal consequences. **Discrimination** occurs when a person is treated unfairly on the basis of a characteristic unrelated to ability. Under federal law, it's illegal to discriminate in recruiting and hiring on the basis of race, color, religion, sex, national origin, age, or disability. (The same rules apply to other employment activities, such as promoting, compensating, and firing.)[10] The **Equal Employment Opportunity Commission (EEOC)** enforces a number of federal employment laws, including the following:

* Title VII of the Civil Rights Act of 1964, which prohibits employment discrimi-

Figure 5.1

How to Forecast Hiring
(and Firing) Needs

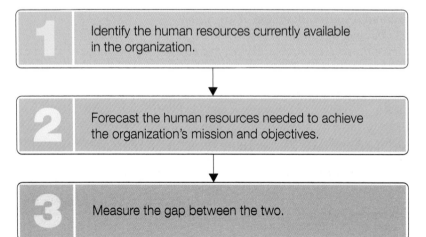

1 Identify the human resources currently available in the organization.

2 Forecast the human resources needed to achieve the organization's mission and objectives.

3 Measure the gap between the two.

nation based on race, color, religion, sex, or national origin. Sexual harassment is also a violation of Title VII.

- Equal Pay Act of 1963, which protects both women and men who do substantially equal work from sex-based pay discrimination.

- Age Discrimination in Employment Act of 1964, which protects individuals who are 40 or older.

- Title I and Title V of the Americans with Disabilities Act of 1990, which prohibits employment discrimination against individuals with disabilities. [11]

WHERE TO FIND CANDIDATES

The first step in recruiting is to find qualified candidates. Where do you look for them, and how do you decide if they're qualified? Let's start with the second part of the question first. A qualified person must be able to perform the duties listed in the job description and must possess the skills, knowledge, and abilities detailed in the job specification. In addition, he or she must be a good "fit" for the company. A Disney recruiter, for example, wants a candidate who fits a certain image—someone who's clean-cut and "wholesome" looking. The same recruiter might also favor candidates with certain qualities—someone who has a "good attitude," who's a "go-getter" and a "team player," and who's smart, responsible, and stable.[12]

Internal Versus External Recruiting

Where do you find people who satisfy so many criteria? Basically, you can look in two places: inside and outside your own organization. Both options have pluses and minuses. Hiring internally sends a positive signal to employees that they can move up in the company—a strong motivation tool and a reward for good performance. In addition, because an internal candidate is a known quantity, it's easier to predict his or her suc-

cess in a new position. Finally, it's cheaper to recruit internally. On the other hand, you'll probably have to fill the promoted employee's position. Going outside gives you an opportunity to bring fresh ideas and skills into the company. In any case, it's often the only alternative, especially if no one inside the company has just the right combination of skills and experiences. Entry-level jobs usually have to be filled from the outside.

HOW TO FIND CANDIDATES

Whether you search inside or outside the organization, you need to publicize the opening. If you're looking internally in a small organization, you can alert employees informally. In larger organizations, HR managers generally post openings on bulletin boards (often online) or announce them in newsletters. They can also seek direct recommendations from various supervisors.

Recruiting people from outside is more complicated. It's a lot like marketing a product to buyers: In effect, you're marketing the virtues of working for your company. Starbucks uses the following outlets to advertise openings:

- Newspaper classified ads

- Local job fairs

- A dedicated section of the corporate Web site ("Job Center," which lists openings, provides information about the Starbucks experience, and facilitates the submission of online applications)

- Announcements on employment Web sites like Monster.com and Vault.com

- In-store recruiting posters

- Informative "business cards" for distribution to customers[13]

- College-campus recruiting (holding on-campus interviews and information sessions and participating in career fairs)

- Internships designed to identify future talent among college students

---

job analysis
Identification of the tasks, responsibilities, and skills of a job, as well as the knowledge and abilities needed to perform it.

job description
Outline of the duties and responsibilities of a position.

job specification
Detailed list of the qualifications needed to perform a job, including required skills, knowledge, and abilities.

recruiting
Process of identifying suitable candidates and encouraging them to apply for openings in the organization.

discrimination
Practice of treating a person unfairly on the basis of a characteristic unrelated to ability.

Equal Employment Opportunity Commission (EEOC)
Federal agency in charge of enforcing federal laws on employment discrimination.

When asked what it takes to attract the best people, Starbucks' senior executive Dave Olsen replied, "Everything matters." Everything Starbucks does as a company bears on its ability to attract talent. Accordingly, everyone is responsible for recruiting, not just HR specialists. In fact, the best source of quality applicants is the company's own labor force.[14]

THE SELECTION PROCESS

Recruiting gets people to apply for positions, but once you've received applications, you still have to select the best candidate—another complicated process. The **selection** process entails gathering information on candidates, evaluating their qualifications, and choosing the right one. At the very least, the process can be time-consuming—particularly when you're filling a high-level position—and often involves several members of an organization.

Let's examine the selection process more closely by describing the steps that you'd take to become a special agent for the Federal Bureau of Investigation (FBI).[15] Most business students don't generally aspire to become FBI agents, but the FBI is quite interested in business graduates—especially if you have a major in accounting or finance. With one of these backgrounds, you'll be given priority in hiring. Why? Unfortunately, there's a lot of white-collar crime that needs to be investigated, and people who know how to follow the money are well suited for the task.

Application

The first step in becoming a gun-toting accountant is, obviously, applying for the job. Don't bother unless you meet the minimum qualifications: You must be a U.S.

citizen, age 23 to 37, physically fit, and have a bachelor's degree. To provide factual information on your education and work background, you'll submit an **application**, which the FBI will use as an initial screening tool.

Employment Tests

Next comes a battery of tests (a lot more than you'd take in applying for an everyday business position). Like most organizations, the FBI tests candidates on the skills and knowledge entailed by the job. Unlike most businesses, however, the FBI will also measure your aptitude, evaluate your personality, and assess your writing ability. You'll have to take a polygraph (lie-detector) test to determine the truthfulness of the information you've provided, uncover the extent of any drug use, and disclose potential security problems.

Interview

If you pass all these tests (with sufficiently high marks), you'll be granted an **interview**. It serves the same purpose as it does for business recruiters: It allows them to learn more about you and gives you a chance to learn more about your prospective employer and your possible future in the organization. The FBI conducts *structured interviews*—a series of standard questions. You're judged both on your answers and your ability to communicate orally.

Physical Exam and Reference Checks

Let's be positive and say you passed the interview. What's next? You still have to pass a rigorous physical examination (including a drug test), as well as background and reference checks. Given its mission, the FBI sets all these hurdles a little higher than the average retail clothing chain. Most businesses will ask you to take a physical exam, but you probably won't have to meet the fitness standards set by the FBI. Likewise, many businesses check references to verify that applicants haven't lied (or exaggerated) about their education and work experience. The FBI goes to great lengths to ensure that candidates are suitable for law-enforcement work.

Final Decision

The last stage in the process is out of your control. Will you be hired or rejected? This decision is made by one or more people who work for the prospective employer. For a business, the decision maker is generally the line manager who oversees the position being filled. At the FBI, the decision is made by a team at FBI headquarters. If you're hired as a special agent, you'll spend 16 weeks of intensive training at the FBI Academy in Quantico, Virginia.

CONTINGENT WORKERS

Although most people hold permanent, full-time positions, there's a growing number of individuals who work at temporary or part-time jobs. Many of these are **contingent workers** hired to supplement a company's permanent workforce. Most of them are independent contractors, consultants, or freelancers who are paid by the firms that hire them. Others are *on-call workers* who work only when needed. Still others are *temporary workers* (or "temps") who are employed and paid by outside agencies or contract firms that charge fees to client companies.

The use of contingent workers provides companies with a number of benefits. Because they can be hired and fired easily, employers can better control labor costs. When things are busy, they can add temps, and when business is slow, they can release unneeded workers. Temps are often cheaper than permanent workers, particularly because they rarely receive costly benefits. Employers can also bring in people with specialized skills and talents to work on special projects without entering into long-term employment relationships. Finally, companies can "try out" temps: If someone does well, the company can offer permanent employment; if the fit is less than perfect, the employer can easily terminate the relationship. There are downsides to the use of contingent workers. Many employers believe that because temps are usually less committed to company goals than permanent workers, productivity suffers.

The Pluses and Minuses of Temp Work

What about you? Does temporary work appeal to you? On the plus side, you can move around to different companies and gain a variety of skills. You can see a company from the inside and decide up front if it's the kind of place you'd like to work at permanently. There are also some attractive lifestyle benefits. You might, for example, work at a job or series of jobs for, say, ten months and head for the beach for the other two. On the other hand, you'll probably get paid less, receive no benefits, and have no job security. For most people, the idea of spending two months a year on the beach isn't *that* appealing.

Developing Employees

Because companies can't survive unless employees do their jobs well, it makes economic sense to train them and develop their skills. This type of support begins when an individual enters the organization and continues as long as he or she stays there.

NEW-EMPLOYEE ORIENTATION

Have you ever started your first day at a new job feeling upbeat and optimistic only to walk out at the end of the day feeling that

selection
Process of gathering information on candidates, evaluating their qualifications, and choosing the right one.

application
Document completed by a job applicant that provides factual information on the person's education and work background.

interview
Formal meeting during which the employer learns more about an applicant and the applicant learns more about the prospective employer.

contingent worker
Temporary or part-time worker hired to supplement a company's permanent workforce.

maybe you've taken the wrong job? If this happens too often, your employer may need to revise its approach to **orientation**—the way it introduces new employees to the organization and their jobs. Starting a new job is a little like beginning college; at the outset, you may be experiencing any of the following sensations:

- Somewhat nervous but enthusiastic

- Anxious to impress but not wanting to attract too much attention

- Interested in learning but fearful of being overwhelmed with information

- Hoping to fit in and worried about looking new or inexperienced[16]

The employer who understands how common such feelings are is not only more likely to help newcomers get over them, but to avoid the pitfalls often associated with new-employee orientation:

- Failing to have a workspace set up for you

- Ignoring you or failing to supervise you

- Neglecting to introduce you to coworkers (or introducing you to so many people that you have no chance of remembering anybody's name)

- Assigning you no work or giving you busy work unrelated to your actual job

- Swamping you with facts about the company[17]

Starbucks' employees are vital to its success. If an employee enthusiastically greets a customer, exchanges a few pleasant words, and then delivers a drink made exactly as ordered, the customer will return another day. Consequently, customer service is a major component of on-the-job training received by every new employee.

A good employer will take things slowly, providing you with information about the company and your job on a need-to-know basis while making you feel as comfortable as possible. You'll get to know the company's history, traditions, policies, and culture over a period of time. You'll learn more about salary and benefits and how your performance will be evaluated. Most importantly, you'll find out how your job fits into overall operations and what's expected of you.

TRAINING AND DEVELOPMENT

It would be nice if employees came preprogrammed with all the skills they need to do their jobs. It would also be nice if job requirements stayed the same: Once you've learned how to do a job (or been preprogrammed), you'd know how to do it forever. In reality, new employees must be trained; moreover, as they grow in their jobs or as their jobs change, they'll need additional training. Unfortunately, training is costly and time-consuming.

How costly? For every $1 in payroll that it spends, the consulting firm Booz Allen Hamilton invests almost $0.08 in employee training and development. At Pfizer, the world's largest pharmaceutical company, the total is $0.14 out of every payroll dollar.[18] What's the payoff? Why are such companies willing to spend so much money on their employees? Pfizer, whose motto is "Succeed through People," regards employee growth and development as its top priority. At Booz Allen Hamilton, consultants specialize in finding innovative solutions to client problems, and their employer makes sure that they're up-to-date on all the new technologies by maintaining a "technology petting zoo" at its training headquarters. It's called a "petting zoo" because employees get to see, touch, and interact with new technologies such as the Segway Human Transporter (which makes a battery-operated vehicle that responds to the rider's movements) even before they hit the market.[19]

At Booz Allen Hamilton's technology "petting zoo," employees are receiving **off-the-job training**. This approach allows them to focus on learning without the distractions that would occur in the office. More common, however, is informal **on-the-job training**, which may be supplemented with formal training programs. This is the method, for example, by which you'd move up from mere coffee maker to a full-fledged "barista" if you worked at Starbucks.[20] You'd begin by reading a large spiral book (entitled *Starbucks University*) on the responsibilities of the barista. After you've passed a series of tests on the reading material, you'll move behind the coffee bar, where a manager or assistant manager will give you hands-on experience in making drinks. According to the rules, you can't advance to a new drink until you've mastered the one you're working on; the process, therefore, may take a few days (or even weeks). Next, you have to learn enough about different types of coffee to be able to describe them to customers. (Because this course involves drinking a lot of coffee, you don't have to worry about staying awake.) Eventually, you'll be declared a coffee connoisseur, but there's still one more set of skills to master: You must complete a customer-service course, which trains you in making eye contact with customers, anticipating their needs, and making them feel welcome.[21]

QUICK QUIZ   5.1

Before you acquaint yourself with the most important theories of employee motivation, take a few minutes to test yourself on what you've learned about HR planning and recruiting and developing employees.

Go to www.exploringbusinessonline.com

Motivating Employees

Motivation refers to an internally generated drive to achieve a goal or follow a particular course of action. Highly motivated employees focus their efforts on achieving specific goals; those who are unmotivated don't. It's the manager's job, therefore, to motivate employees—to get them to try to do the best job they can. But what motivates employees to do well? How does a manager encourage employees to show up for work each day and do a good job? Paying them helps, but many other factors influence a person's desire (or lack of it) to excel in the workplace. What are these factors? Are they the same for everybody? Do they change over time? To address these questions, we'll examine four of the most influential theories of motivation: *hierarchy-of-needs theory, two-factor theory, expectancy theory*, and *equity theory*.

HIERARCHY-OF-NEEDS THEORY

Psychologist Abraham Maslow's **hierarchy-of-needs theory** proposed that we are motivated by the five unmet needs, arranged in the hierarchical order shown in Figure 5.2, which also lists examples of each type of need in both the personal and work spheres of life. Look, for instance, at the list of personal needs in the left-hand column. At the bottom are *physiological* needs (such life-sustaining needs as food and shelter). Working up the hierarchy we experience *safety* needs (financial stability, freedom from physical harm), *social* needs (the need

Figure 5.2

Maslow's Hierarchy-of-Needs Theory

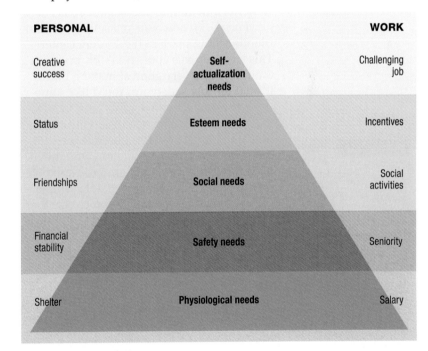

to belong and have friends), *esteem* needs (the need for self-respect and status), and *self-actualization* needs (the need to reach one's full potential or achieve some creative success).

There are two things to remember about Maslow's model:

1. We must satisfy lower-level needs before we seek to satisfy higher-level needs.

2. Once we've satisfied a need, it no longer motivates us; the next higher need takes its place.

Let's say, for example, that you've just returned to college and that for a variety of reasons that aren't your fault, you're broke, hungry, and homeless. Because you'll probably take almost any job that will pay for food and housing (*physiological* needs), you go to work repossessing cars. Fortunately, your student loan finally comes through, and with enough money to feed yourself, you can look for a job that's not so risky (a *safety* need). You find a job as a night janitor in the library, and although you feel secure, you start to feel cut off from your friends, who are active during daylight hours. You want to work among people, not books (a *social* need). So now you join several of your friends selling pizza in the student center. This job improves your social life, but even though you're very good at making pizzas, it's not terribly satisfying. You'd like something that will let you display your intellectual talents (an *esteem* need). So you study hard and land a job as an intern in the governor's office. Upon graduation, you move up through a series of government appointments and eventually run for state senator. As you're sworn into office, you realize that you've reached your full potential (a *self-actualization* need) and comment to yourself, "It doesn't get any better than this."

Needs Theory and the Workplace

What implications does Maslow's theory have for business managers? There are two key points: (1) Not all employees are driven by the same needs, and (2) the needs that motivate individuals can change over time. Managers should consider which needs different employees are trying to satisfy and structure rewards and other forms of recognition accordingly. For example, when you got your first job repossessing cars, you were motivated by the need for money to buy food. If you'd been given a choice between a raise or a plaque recognizing your accomplishments, you'd undoubtedly have opted for the money. As a state senator, on the other hand, you may prefer public recognition of work well done (say, election to higher office) to a pay raise.

TWO-FACTOR THEORY

Another psychologist, Frederick Herzberg, set out to determine which work factors (such as wages, job security, or advancement) made people feel good about their jobs and which factors made them feel bad about their jobs. He surveyed workers, analyzed the results, and concluded that in order to understand employee *satisfaction* (or *dissatisfaction*), he had to divide work factors into two categories:

- *Motivation factors.* Those factors that are strong contributors to job satisfaction.

- *Hygiene factors.* Those factors that are *not* strong contributors to satisfaction but which must be present to meet a worker's expectations and prevent job dissatisfaction.

Figure 5.3 illustrates Herzberg's **two-factor theory**. Note that motivation factors (such as promotion opportunities) relate to *the nature of the work itself and the way the employee performs it.* Hygiene factors (such as physical working conditions) relate to *the environment in which it's performed.* (Note, too, the similarity between Herzberg's motivation factors and Maslow's esteem and self-actualization needs.)

Two-Factor Theory and the Workplace

We'll ask the same question about Herzberg's model as we did about Maslow's: What does it mean for managers? Suppose you're a

Figure 5.3 ● ACTIVE

Herzberg's Two-Factor Theory

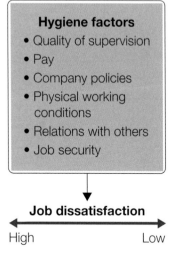

Hygiene factors
- Quality of supervision
- Pay
- Company policies
- Physical working conditions
- Relations with others
- Job security

Job dissatisfaction

High   Low

Low   High

Job satisfaction

Motivation factors
- Promotion opportunities
- Opportunities for personal growth
- Recognition
- Responsibility
- Achievement

senior manager in an accounting firm, where you supervise a team of accountants, each of whom has been with the firm for five years. How would you use Herzberg's model to motivate the employees who report to you? Let's start with hygiene factors. Are salaries reasonable? What about working conditions? Does each accountant have his or her own workspace, or are they crammed into tiny workrooms? Are they being properly supervised or are they left on their own to sink or swim? If hygiene factors like these don't meet employees' expectations, they may be dissatisfied with their jobs.

As you can see in Figure 5.3, fixing problems related to hygiene factors may alleviate job *dissatisfaction*, but it won't necessarily improve anyone's job *satisfaction*. In order to increase satisfaction (and motivate someone to perform better), you must address motivation factors. Is the work itself challenging and stimulating? Do employees receive recognition for jobs well done? Will the work that an accountant has been assigned help him or her to advance in the firm? According to Herzberg, motivation requires a twofold approach: eliminating dissatisfiers and enhancing satisfiers.

EXPECTANCY THEORY

If you were a manager, wouldn't you like to know how your employees decide to work hard or goof off? Wouldn't it be nice to know if a planned rewards program will have the desired effect—namely, motivating them to perform better in their jobs? Wouldn't it be helpful if you could measure the effect of bonuses on employee productivity? These are the issues considered by psychologist Victor Vroom in his **expectancy theory**, which proposes that employees will work hard to earn rewards which they value and which they consider obtainable.

As you can see from Figure 5.4, Vroom argues that an employee will be motivated to exert a high level of effort to obtain a reward under three conditions:

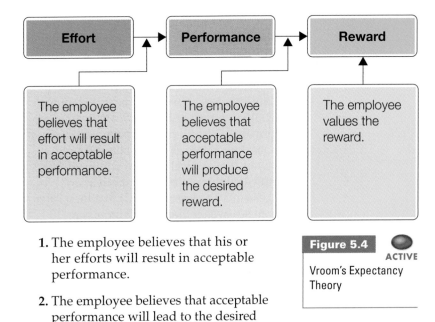

1. The employee believes that his or her efforts will result in acceptable performance.

2. The employee believes that acceptable performance will lead to the desired outcome or reward.

3. The employee values the reward.

Figure 5.4 ACTIVE
Vroom's Expectancy Theory

Expectancy Theory and the Workplace

To apply expectancy theory to a real-world situation, let's analyze an automobile-insurance company with 100 agents who work from a call center. Assume that the firm pays a base salary of $2,000 a month, plus a $200 commission on each policy sold above 10 policies a month. In terms of expectancy theory, under what conditions would an agent be motivated to sell more than 10 policies a month?

1. The agent would have to believe that his or her efforts would result in policy sales (that, in other words, there's a positive link between effort and performance).

2. The agent would have to be confident that if he or she sold more than 10 policies in a given month, there would indeed be a bonus (a positive link between performance and reward).

3. The bonus per policy—$200—would have to be of value to the agent.

two-factor theory
Theory which holds that motivation involves both motivation factors (which contribute to job satisfaction) and hygiene factors (which help to prevent job dissatisfaction).

expectancy theory
Theory of motivation which proposes that employees will work hard to earn rewards they value and consider obtainable.

Now let's alter the scenario slightly. Say that the company raises prices, thus making it harder to sell the policies. How will agents' motivation be affected? According to expectancy theory, motivation will suffer. Why? Because agents may be less confident that their efforts will lead to satisfactory performance. What if the company introduces a policy whereby agents get bonuses only if buyers don't cancel policies within 90 days? How will this policy affect motivation? Now agents may be less confident that they'll get bonuses even if they do sell more than 10 policies. Motivation will decrease because the link between performance and reward has been weakened. Finally, what will happen if bonuses are cut from $200 to $25? Obviously, the reward would be of less value to agents, and, again, motivation will suffer. The message of expectancy theory, then, is fairly clear: Managers should offer rewards that employees value, set performance levels that they can reach, and ensure a strong link between performance and reward.

EQUITY THEORY

What if you spent 30 hours working on a class report, did everything you were supposed to do, and (in your opinion) handed in an excellent assignment. Your roommate, on the other hand, spent about 5 hours and put everything together at the last minute. You know, moreover, that he ignored half the requirements and never even ran his assignment through a spell-checker. A week later, your teacher returns the reports. You get a *C* and your roommate gets a *B+*. In all likelihood, you'll feel that you've been treated unfairly relative to your roommate.

Your reaction makes sense according to the **equity theory** of motivation, which focuses on our perceptions of how fairly we're treated *relative to others*. Applied to the work environment, this theory proposes that employees analyze their contributions or job inputs (hours worked, education, experience, work performance) and their rewards or job outcomes (salary, benefits, recognition). Then they create a contributions/rewards ratio and compare it to those of other people. The basis of comparison can be any one of the following:

- Someone in a similar *position*
- Someone holding a different position in the same *organization*

- Someone with a similar *occupation*
- Someone who shares certain *characteristics* (such as age, education, or level of experience)
- Oneself at another point in time

When individuals perceive that the ratio of their contributions to rewards is comparable to that of others, they perceive that they're being treated equitably; when they perceive that the ratio is out of balance, they perceive inequity. Occasionally, people will perceive that they're being treated better than others. More often, however, they conclude that others are being treated better (and that they themselves are being treated worse). This is what you concluded when you saw your grade. You've calculated your ratio of contributions (hours worked, research and writing skills) to rewards (project grade), compared it to your roommate's ratio, and concluded that the two ratios are out of balance.

What will an employee do if he or she perceives an inequity? The individual might try to bring the ratio into balance, either by decreasing inputs (working fewer hours, refusing to take on additional tasks) or by increasing outputs (asking for a raise). If this strategy fails, an employee might complain to a supervisor, transfer to another job, leave the organization, or rationalize the situation (perhaps deciding that the situation isn't so bad after all). Equity theory advises managers to focus on treating workers fairly, especially in determining compensation, which is, naturally, a common basis of comparison.

What Makes a Great Place to Work?

Every year, the Great Places to Work Institute analyzes comments from thousands of employees and compiles a list of "The 100 Best Companies to Work for in America," which is published in *Fortune* magazine. Having compiled its list for more than 20 years, the Institute concludes that the defining characteristic of a great company to work for is trust between managers and employees. Employees overwhelmingly say that they want to work at a place where employees "trust the people they work for, have pride in what they do, and enjoy the people they work with."[22] They report that they're motivated to perform well because they're challenged, respected, treated fairly, and appreciated. They take pride in what they do, are made to feel that they make a difference, and are given opportunities for advancement.[23] The most effective motivators, it would seem, are closely aligned with Maslow's higher-level needs and Hertzberg's motivating factors.

JOB REDESIGN

The average employee spends more than 2,000 hours a year at work. If the job is tedious, unpleasant, or otherwise unfulfilling, the employee probably won't be motivated to perform at a very high level. Many companies practice a policy of **job redesign** to make jobs more interesting and challenging. Common strategies include *job rotation*, *job enlargement*, and *job enrichment*.

Job Rotation

Specialization promotes efficiency because workers get very good at doing particular tasks. The drawback is the tedium of repeating the same task day in and day out. The practice of **job rotation** allows employees to rotate from one job to another on a systematic basis, eventually cycling back to their original tasks. A computer maker, for example, might rotate a technician into the sales department to increase the employee's awareness of customer needs and to give the employee a broader understanding of the company's goals and operations. A hotel might rotate an accounting clerk to the check-in desk for a few hours each day to add variety to the daily workload. Rotated employees develop new skills and gain experience that increases their value to the company, which benefits management because cross-trained employees can fill in for absentees, thus providing greater flexibility in scheduling.

Job Enlargement

Instead of a job in which you performed just one or two tasks, wouldn't you prefer a job that gave you many different tasks? In theory, you'd be less bored and more highly

The on-site fitness center is just one reason why software maker SAS Institute is a regular on *Fortune* magazine's annual list of "The 100 Best Companies to Work For." The fitness center features volleyball courts, soccer fields, and a ten-lane pool. There are three tennis courts (where racquet restringing is free), and employees also enjoy massages, laundry, and day-care service. The principle behind the company's employee-oriented culture is simple—happy employees create happy customers—and SAS Institute's turnover rate of 4 percent is well below the industry average.

motivated if you had a chance at **job enlargement**—the policy of enhancing a job by adding tasks at similar skill levels (see Figure 5.5). The job of sales clerk, for example, might be expanded to include gift-wrapping and packaging items for shipment. The additional duties would add variety without entailing higher skill levels.

Job Enrichment

As you can see from Figure 5.5, merely expanding a job by adding similar tasks won't necessarily "enrich" it by making it more challenging and rewarding. **Job enrichment** is the practice of adding tasks that increase both responsibility and opportunity for growth. It provides the kinds of benefits which, according to Maslow and Herzberg, contribute to job satisfaction: stimulating work, sense of personal achievement, self-esteem, recognition, and a chance to reach your potential.

---

equity theory
Theory of motivation which focuses on our perceptions of how fairly we're treated relative to others.

job redesign
Management strategy used to increase job satisfaction by making jobs more interesting and challenging.

job rotation
Job redesign strategy which allows employees to rotate from one job to another on a systematic basis.

job enlargement
Job redesign strategy in which management enhances a job by adding tasks at similar skill levels.

job enrichment
Job redesign strategy in which management enriches a job by adding tasks that increase both responsibility and opportunity for growth.

Figure 5.5

Job Enlargement Versus Job Enrichment

Consider, for example, the evolving role of support staff in the contemporary office. Today, employees who used to be called "secretaries" assume many duties previously in the domain of management, such as project coordination and public relations. Information technology has enriched their jobs because they can now apply such skills as word processing, desktop publishing, creating spreadsheets, and managing databases. That's why we now hear such terms as *administrative assistant* instead of *secretary*.[24]

WORK/LIFE QUALITY

Building a career requires a substantial commitment in time and energy, and most people find that they aren't left with much time for nonwork activities. Fortunately, many organizations recognize the need to help employees strike a balance between their work and home lives.[25] By helping employees combine satisfying careers and fulfilling personal lives, companies tend to end up with a happier, less-stressed, and more productive workforce. The financial benefits include lower absenteeism, turnover, and health-care costs.

Alternative Work Arrangements

The accounting firm KPMG, which has made the list of the "100 Best Companies for Working Mothers" for seven years running, is committed to promoting a balance between its employees' work and personal lives. KPMG offers a variety of work arrangements designed to accommodate different employee needs and provide scheduling flexibility.[26]

Flextime Employers who provide for **flextime** set guidelines that allow employees to designate starting and quitting times. Guidelines, for example, might specify that all employees must work 8 hours a day (with an hour for lunch) and that 4 of those hours must be between 10 A.M. and 3 P.M. Thus, you could come in at 7 A.M and leave at 4 P.M while coworkers arrive at 10 A.M and leave at 7 P.M. With permission you could even choose to work from 8 a.m to 2 p.m., take 2 hours for lunch, and then work from 4 p.m to 6 p.m.

Compressed Workweeks Rather than work 8 hours a day for five days a week, you might elect to earn a three-day weekend by working 10 hours a day for four days a week.

Part-Time Work If you're willing to have your pay and benefits adjusted accordingly you can work fewer than 40 hours a week.

Job Sharing Under **job sharing**, two people share one full-time position, splitting the salary and benefits of the position as each handles half the job. Often they arrange their schedules to include at least an hour of shared time during which they can communicate about the job.

Telecommuting Telecommuting means that you work from home (or from some other nonwork location) on a regular basis. You're connected to the office by computer, fax, and phone. You save on commuting time, enjoy more flexible work hours, and have more opportunity to spend time with your family. A study of 5,500 IBM employees (one-fifth of whom telecommute) found that those who worked at home not only had a better balance between work and home life, but were more highly motivated and were less likely to leave the organization.[27]

Although it's hard to count telecommuters accurately, some estimates put the number at more than 30 million.[28] Telecommuting isn't for everyone. Working at home means that you have to discipline yourself to avoid distractions, such as TV, and some people feel isolated from social interaction in the workplace.

Family-Friendly Programs

In addition to alternative work arrangements, many employers, including KPMG, offer programs and benefits designed to help employees meet family and home obligations while maintaining busy careers. KPMG offers each of the following benefits.

Dependent Care Caring for dependents—young children and elderly parents—is of utmost importance to some employees, but combining dependent-care responsibilities with a busy job can be particularly difficult. KPMG provides on-site child care during tax season (when employees are especially busy) and offers emergency back-up dependent care all year-round, either at a provider's facility or in the employee's home. To get referrals or information, employees can call KPMG's LifeWorks Resource and Referral Service. KPMG is by no means unique in this respect: More than 8,000 companies maintain on-site day care,[29] and 18 percent of all U.S. companies offer child-care resources or referral services.[30]

Paid Parental Leave Any employee (male or female) who becomes a parent can take two weeks of paid leave. New mothers also get time off through short-term disability benefits.

Caring for Yourself Like many companies, KPMG allows employees to aggregate all paid days off and use them in any way they want. In other words, instead of getting, say, 10 sick days, 5 personal days, and 15 vacation days, you get a total of 30 days to use for anything. If you're having personal problems, you can contact the Employee Assistance Program. If staying fit makes you happier and more productive, you can take out a discount membership at one of more than 9,000 health clubs.

Unmarried Without Children

You've undoubtedly noticed by now that many programs for balancing work and personal lives target married people, particularly those with children. Single individuals also have trouble striking a satisfactory balance between work and nonwork activities, but many single workers feel that they aren't getting equal consideration from employers.[31] They report that they're often expected to work longer hours, travel more, and take on difficult assignments to compensate for married employees with family commitments.

Needless to say, requiring singles to take on additional responsibilities can make it harder for them to balance their work and personal lives. It's harder to plan and keep personal commitments while meeting heavy work responsibilities, and establishing and maintaining social relations is difficult if work schedules are unpredictable or too demanding. Frustration can lead to increased stress and job dissatisfaction. In several studies of stress in the accounting profession, unmarried workers reported higher levels of stress than any other group, including married people with children.[32]

With singles, as with married people, companies can reap substantial benefits from programs that help employees balance their work and nonwork lives: They can increase job satisfaction and employee productivity and reduce turnover. PepsiCo, for example, offers a "concierge service," which maintains a dry cleaner, travel agency, convenience store, and fitness center on the premises of its national office in Somers, New York. Single employees seem to find these services helpful, but what they value most of all is control over their time. In particular, they want predictable schedules that allow them to plan social and personal activities. They don't want employers assuming that being single means that they can change plans at the last minute. It's often more

---

flextime
Alternative work arrangement that allows employees to designate starting and quitting times.

job sharing
Work arrangement in which two people share one full-time position.

telecommuting
Work arrangement in which the employee works from home on a regular basis.

difficult for singles to deal with last-minute changes because, unlike married coworkers, they don't have the at-home support structure to handle such tasks as caring for pets or tending to elderly parents.

QUICK QUIZ 5.2

The following sections include discussions of performance appraisal, compensation, and labor relations. First, however, give yourself a brief test on your knowledge of employee motivation and employee-friendly workplaces.

Go to www.exploringbusinessonline.com

Performance Appraisal

Employees generally want their managers to tell them three things: what they should be doing, how well they're doing it, and how they can improve their performance. Good managers address these issues on an ongoing basis. On a semiannual or annual basis, they also conduct formal **performance appraisals** to discuss and evaluate employees' work performance.

Figure 5.6

How to do a Performance Appraisal.

> **1** Set goals and performance expectations and specify the criteria that will be used to measure performance.

> **2** Complete a written evaluation that rates performance according to the stipulated criteria.

> **3** Meet with the employee to discuss the evaluation and suggest means of improving performance.

THE BASIC THREE-STEP PROCESS

Appraisal systems vary both by organization and by the level of the employee being evaluated, but as you can see in Figure 5.6, it's generally a three-step process:

1. Before managers can measure performance, they must set goals and performance expectations and specify the criteria (such as quality of work, quantity of work, dependability, initiative) that they'll use to measure performance.

2. At the end of a specified time period, managers complete written evaluations that rate employee performance according to the predetermined criteria.

3. Managers then meet with each employee to discuss the evaluation. Jointly, they suggest ways in which the employee can improve performance, which might include further training and development.

It sounds pretty simple, but why do so many managers report that, except for firing people, giving performance appraisals is their least favorite task?[33] To get some perspective on this question, we'll look at performance appraisals from both sides, explaining the benefits and identifying potential problems with some of the most common practices.

Among other benefits, formal appraisals provide:

- An opportunity for managers and employees to discuss an employee's performance and to set future goals and performance expectations

- A chance to identify and discuss appropriate training and career-development opportunities for an employee

- Formal documentation of the evaluation that can be used for salary, promotion, demotion, or dismissal purposes[34]

As for disadvantages, most stem from the fact that appraisals are often used to determine salaries for the upcoming year. Consequently, meetings to discuss performance tend to take on an entirely different dimension: The manager appears judgmental (rather than supportive), and the employee gets defensive. It's the adversarial atmosphere that makes many managers not only uncomfortable with the task but unlikely to give honest feedback. (They tend to give higher marks in order to avoid delving into critical evaluations.) HR professionals disagree about whether performance appraisals should be linked to pay increases. Some experts argue that the connection eliminates the manager's opportunity to use the appraisal to improve an employee's performance. Others maintain that it increases employee satisfaction with the process and distributes raises on the basis of effort and results.[35]

360-DEGREE AND UPWARD FEEDBACK

Instead of being evaluated by one person, how would you like to be evaluated by several people—not only those above you in the organization, but those below and beside you? The approach is called *360-degree feedback*, and the purpose is to ensure that employees (mostly managers) get feedback from all directions— from supervisors, reporting subordinates, coworkers, and even customers. If it's conducted correctly, this technique furnishes managers with a range of insights into their performance in a number of roles.

Some experts, however, regard the 360-degree approach as too cumbersome. An alternative technique, called *upward feedback*, requires only the manager's subordinates to provide feedback. Computer maker Dell uses this approach as part of its manager-development plan. Every six months, 40,000 Dell employees complete a survey in which

they rate their supervisors on a number of dimensions, such as practicing ethical business principles and providing support in balancing work and personal life. Like most companies using this technique, Dell uses survey results for development purposes only, not as direct input into decisions on pay increases or promotions.[36]

Retaining Valuable Employees

When a valued employee quits, the loss to the employer can be serious. Not only will the firm incur substantial costs to recruit and train a replacement, but it may suffer temporary declines in productivity and lower morale among remaining employees who have to take on heavier workloads. Given the negative impact of **turnover**—the permanent separation of an employee from a company—most organizations do whatever they can to retain qualified employees. Compensation plays a key role in this effort: Companies that don't offer competitive compensation packages (including benefits) tend to lose employees. But other factors come into play, some of which we discussed earlier, such as training and development and helping employees achieve a satisfying work/nonwork balance. In the following sections, we'll look at a few other strategies not only for reducing turnover but for increasing productivity as well.[37]

Creating a Positive Work Environment

Employees who are happy at work are more productive, provide better customer service, and are more likely to stay with the company. A study conducted by Sears, for instance, found a positive relationship between customer satisfaction and employee attitudes on 10 different issues: A 5-percent improvement in employee attitudes results in a 1.3-percent increase in customer satisfaction and a 0.5-percent increase in revenue.[38]

performance appraisals

Formal process in which a manager evaluates an employee's work performance.

turnover

Permanent separation of an employee from a company.

The Employee-Friendly Workplace

What sort of things improve employee attitudes? The 10,000 employees of software maker SAS Institute fall into the category of "happy workers." They choose the furniture and equipment in their own (private) offices, eat subsidized meals at one of three on-site restaurants, enjoy free soft drinks, fresh fruit on Mondays, M&M's on Wednesdays, and a healthy breakfast snack on Fridays in convenient break rooms, and swim and work out at a 77,000-square-foot fitness center. They set their own work hours, and they're encouraged to stay home with sick children. They also have job security: No one's been laid off in 26 years. The employee-friendly work environment helps SAS employees focus on their jobs and contribute to the attainment of company goals.[39] Not surprisingly, it also results in very low turnover.

Recognizing Employee Contributions

Thanking people for work done well is a powerful motivator. People who feel appreciated are more likely to stay with a company than those who don't.[40] Although personal thank-yous are always helpful, many companies also have formal programs for identifying and rewarding good performers. The Container Store, a national storage and container retailer, rewards employee accomplishments in a variety of ways. Recently, for example, 12 employees chosen by coworkers were rewarded with a Colorado vacation with the company's owners; the seven winners of a sales contest got a trip to visit an important supplier—in Sweden.[41] The company is known for its supportive environment and has frequently been selected as one of the top U.S. companies to work for.

Involving Employees in Decision Making

Companies have found that involving employees in decisions saves money, makes workers feel better about their jobs, and reduces turnover. Some have found that it pays to take their advice. When General Motors asked workers for ideas on improving manufacturing operations, management was deluged with more than 44,000 suggestions during one quarter. Implementing a few of them cut production time on certain vehicles by 15 percent and resulted in sizable savings.[42]

Similarly, in 2001, Edward Jones, a personal investment company, faced a difficult situation during the stock-market downturn. Costs had to be cut, and laying off employees was one option. Instead, however, the company turned to its workforce for solutions. As a group, employees identified cost savings of more than $38 million. At the same time, Jones convinced experienced employees to stay with the company by assuring them that they'd have a role in managing it.

WHY PEOPLE QUIT

As important as such initiatives can be, one bad boss can spoil everything. The way a person is treated by his or her boss may be the primary factor in determining whether an employee stays or goes. People who've quit their jobs cite the following behavior by superiors:

- Making unreasonable work demands
- Refusing to value their opinions
- Failing to be clear about what's expected of subordinates
- Rejecting work unnecessarily
- Showing favoritism in compensation, rewards, promotions[43]

Holding managers accountable for excessive turnover can help alleviate the "bad-boss" problem, at least in the long run. In any case, whenever an employee quits, it's a good idea for someone—someone other than the individual's immediate supervisor—to conduct an exit interview to find out why. Knowing why people are quitting gives an organization the opportunity to correct problems that are causing high turnover rates.

INVOLUNTARY TERMINATION

Before we leave this section, we should say a word or two about *termination*—getting fired. Although turnover—voluntary separations—can create problems for employers, they're not nearly as devastating as the effects of involuntary termination on employees. Losing your job is what psychologists call a "significant life change," and it's high on the list of "stressful life events" regardless of the circumstances. Sometimes, employers lay off workers because revenues are down and they must resort to **downsizing**—to cutting costs by eliminating jobs. Sometimes, a particular job is being phased out, and sometimes, an employee has simply failed to meet performance requirements.

Employment-at-Will

Is it possible for you to get fired even if you're doing a good job and there's no economic justification for your being laid off? In some cases, yes—especially if you're not working under a contract. Without a formal contract, you're considered to be *employed at will*, which means that both you and your employer have the right to terminate the employment relationship at anytime. *You* can quit whenever you want (which is good for you), but your *employer* can fire you whenever it wants (which is obviously bad for you).

Fortunately (for you), over the past several decades, the courts have undercut employers' rights under the **employment-at-will** doctrine.[44] By and large, management can no longer fire employees at will: Usually, employers must show just cause for termination, and in some cases, they must furnish written documentation to substantiate the reasons for terminating an employee. If it's a case of poor performance, the employee is generally warned in advance that his or her current level of performance could result in termination. As a rule, managers give employees who've been warned a reasonable opportunity to improve performance. When termination is unavoidable, it should be handled in a private conversation, with the manager explaining precisely why the action is being taken.

Compensation and Benefits

Although paychecks and benefits packages aren't the only reasons why people work, they do matter. Competitive pay and benefits also help organizations attract and retain qualified employees. Companies that pay their employees more than their competitors generally have lower turnover. Consider, for example, The Container Store, which regularly appears on *Fortune* magazine's list of "The 100 Best Companies to Work For."[45] The retail chain staffs its stores with fewer employees than its competitors but pays them more—in some cases, three times the industry average for retail workers. This strategy allows the company to attract extremely talented workers who, moreover, aren't likely to leave the company. Low turnover is particularly valuable in the retail industry because it depends on service-oriented personnel to generate repeat business.

In addition to salary and wages, compensation packages often include other financial incentives, such as bonuses and profit-sharing plans, as well as benefits, such as medical insurance, vacation time, sick leave, and retirement accounts.

WAGES AND SALARIES

The largest, and most important, component of a compensation package is the payment of wages or salary. If you're paid according to the number of hours you work, you're earning **wages**. Counter personnel at McDonald's, for instance, get wages, which are determined by multiplying an employee's hourly-wage rate by the number of hours worked during the pay period. On the other hand, if you're paid for fulfilling the responsibilities of a position—regardless of the number of hours required to do it—you're earning a **salary**. The McDonald's manager gets a salary for overseeing the operations of the restaurant. He or she is expected to work as long as it takes to get the job done without any adjustment in compensation.

Piecework and Commissions

Sometimes it makes more sense to pay workers according to the quantity of product that they produce or sell. Byrd's Seafood, a crab-processing plant in

downsizing
Practice of eliminating jobs to cut costs.

employment-at-will
Legal doctrine that allows an employer to fire an employee at will.

wages
Compensation paid to employees based on the number of hours worked.

salary
Compensation paid for fulfilling the responsibilities of a position regardless of the number of hours required to do it.

Crisfield, Maryland, pays workers on **piecework**: Workers' pay is based on the amount of crabmeat that's picked from recently cooked crabs. (A good picker can produce 15 pounds of crabmeat an hour and earn about $100 a day.)[46] If you're working on **commission**, you're probably getting paid for quantity of sales. If you were a sales representative for an insurance company, like The Hartford, you'd get a certain amount of money for each automobile or homeowner policy that you sell.[47]

INCENTIVE PROGRAMS

In addition to regular paychecks, many people receive financial rewards based on performance, whether their own, their employer's, or both. At computer-chip maker Texas Instruments (TI), for example, employees may be eligible for bonuses, profit sharing, and stock options. All three plans are **incentive programs**: programs designed to reward employees for good performance.[48]

Bonus Plans

TI's year-end **bonuses**—annual income given in addition to salary—are based on company-wide performance. If the company has a profitable year—and if you contributed to that success—you'll get a bonus. If the company doesn't do well, you're out of luck, regardless of what you contributed.

Bonus plans have become quite common, and the range of employees eligible for bonuses has widened in recent years. In the past, bonus plans were usually reserved for managers above a certain level. Today, however, companies have realized the value of extending plans to include employees at virtually every level. The magnitude of bonuses still favors those at the top. High-ranking officers (such as CEOs and CFOs) often get bonuses ranging from 30 percent to 50 percent of their salaries. Upper-level managers may get from 15 percent to 25 percent and middle managers from 10 percent to 15 percent. At lower levels, employees may expect bonuses from 3 percent to 5 percent of their annual compensation.[49]

Profit-Sharing Plans

TI also maintains a **profit-sharing plan**, which relies on a predetermined formula to distribute a share of the company's profits to eligible employees. Today, about 40 percent of all U.S. companies offer some type of profit-sharing program.[50] TI's plan, however, is a little unusual: While most plans don't allow employees to access profit-sharing funds until retirement or termination, TI employees get their shares immediately—in cash.

TI's plan is also pretty generous—as long as the company has a good year. Here's how its works. An employee's profit share depends on the company's operating profit for the year. If profits from operations reach 10 percent of sales, the employee gets a bonus worth 4 percent of his or her salary. If operating profit soars to 20 percent, the employee bonuses go up to 26 percent of salary. If operating profits fall short of a certain threshold, nobody gets anything.[51] (This is what happened in 2001, 2002, and 2003; things turned around in 2004.)

Stock-Option Plans

Like most **stock-option plans**, the TI plan gives employees the right to buy a specific number of shares of company stock at a set price on a specified date. At TI, an employee may buy stock at its selling price at the time when he or she was given the option. So, if the price of the stock goes up, the employee benefits. Say, for example, that the stock was selling for $30 a share when the option was granted in 2003. In 2005, it was selling for $40 a share. Exercising his or her option, the employee could buy TI stock at the 2003 price of $30 a share—a bargain price.[52]

At TI, stock options are used as an incentive to attract and retain top people. Starbucks, on the other hand, isn't nearly as selective in awarding stock options. At Starbucks, all employees can earn "Bean Stock"—the Starbucks employee stock-option plan. Both full- and part-time employees get options to buy Starbucks shares at a set price. If the company does well and its stock goes up, employees make a profit. CEO Howard Schultz believes that Bean Stock pays off: Because employees are rewarded when the company does well, they have a stronger incentive to add value to the company (and so drive up its stock price). Shortly after the program was begun, the phrase "bean-stocking" became workplace lingo for figuring out how to save the company money.

BENEFITS

Another major component of an employee's compensation package is **benefits**—compensation other than salaries, hourly wages, or financial incentives. Types of benefits include the following:

- Legally required benefits (Social Security and Medicare, unemployment insurance, workers' compensation)
- Paid time off (vacations, holidays, sick leave)
- Insurance (health benefits, life insurance, disability insurance)
- Retirement benefits

Unfortunately, the cost of providing benefits is staggering. According to the U.S. Chamber of Commerce, it costs an employer 42 percent of a worker's salary to provide the same worker with benefits. So if you're a manager making $100,000 a year, your employer is also paying out another $42,000 for your benefits. The most money goes for health care (15 percent of salary costs), paid time off (12 percent), and retirement benefits (6 percent).[53]

Some workers receive only benefits required by law, including Social Security, unemployment, and workers' compensation. Low-wage workers generally get only limited benefits and part-timers often nothing at all.[54] Again, Starbucks is generous in offering benefits. The company provides benefits even to the part-timers who make up two-thirds of the company's workforce; anyone working at least 20 hours a week gets medical coverage.

ABOUT NIKE   5.1

Now that you know something about the kinds of benefits that are available at other companies, take a few minutes to read about the benefits offered by Nike.

Go to www.exploringbusinessonline.com

Starbucks' workforce is representative of the general population. The company promotes a diverse, inclusive culture and values each employee's unique talents, experiences, and points of view. It believes that the more its customers see Starbucks' workforce as a reflection of themselves, the more comfortable they'll feel visiting its stores.

Diversity in the Workplace

The makeup of the U.S. workforce has changed dramatically over the past 50 years. In the 1950s, more than 60 percent was composed of white males.[55] Today's workforce, however, reflects the broad range of differences in the population—differences in gender, race, ethnicity, age, physical ability, religion, education, and lifestyle. As you can see in Table 5.1 (page 122), more women and minorities have entered the workforce, and white males now make up only 37 percent of the workforce.[56] Their percentage representation diminished as more women and minorities entered the workforce.

Most companies today strive for diverse workforces. HR managers work hard to recruit, hire, develop, and retain a workforce

---

piecework
Compensation paid to workers according to the quantity of a product that they produce or sell.

commission
Compensation paid to employees based on the dollar amount of sales that they make.

incentive program
Program designed to financially reward employees for good performance.

bonuses
Annual income given to employees (in addition to salary) based on companywide performance.

profit-sharing plan
Incentive program that uses a predetermined formula to distribute a share of company profits to eligible employees.

stock-option plans
Incentive program that allows eligible employees to buy a specific number of shares of company stock at a set price on a specified date.

benefits
Compensation other than salaries, hourly wages, or financial incentives.

TABLE 5.1

Employment by Gender and Ethnic Group			
Group	**Total (%)**	**Males (%)**	**Females (%)**
All employees	100	52	48
White	70	37	33
African- American	14	6	8
Hispanic or Latino	11	6	5
Asian/Pacific Islander/Other	5	3	2

that's representative of the general population. In part, these efforts are motivated by legal concerns: Discrimination in recruiting, hiring, advancement, and firing is illegal under federal law and is prosecuted by the EEOC.[57] Companies that violate antidiscrimination laws are not only subject to severe financial penalties but risk damage to their reputations. In November 2004, for example, the EEOC charged that recruiting policies at Abercrombie & Fitch, a national chain of retail clothing stores, had discriminated against minority and female job applicants between 1999 and 2004. The employer, charged the EEOC, had hired a disproportionate number of white salespeople, placed minorities and women in less visible positions, and promoted a virtually all-white image in its marketing efforts. Six days after the EEOC had filed a lawsuit, the company settled the case at a cost of $50 million, but the negative publicity will hamper both recruitment and sales for some time to come.[58]

There's good reason for building a diverse workforce that goes well beyond mere compliance with legal standards. It even goes beyond commitment to ethical standards. It's good business. People with diverse backgrounds bring fresh points of view that can be invaluable in generating ideas and solving problems. In addition, they can be the key to connecting with an ethnically diverse customer base. If a large percentage of your customers are Hispanic, it might make sense to have a Hispanic marketing manager. In short, capitalizing on the benefits of a diverse workforce means that employers should view differences as assets rather than liabilities.

 **ABOUT NIKE** 5.2

Now that you understand something about the organizational importance of a diverse workforce, take a moment to review the diversity initiatives undertaken by Nike.

Go to www.exploringbusinessonline.com

Labor Unions

As we saw earlier, Maslow believed that individuals are motivated to satisfy five levels of unmet needs (physiological, safety, social, esteem, and self-actualization). From this perspective, employees should expect that full-time work will satisfy at least the two lowest-level needs: They should be paid wages that are sufficient for them to feed, house, and clothe themselves and their families, and they should have safe working conditions and some degree of job security. Organizations also have needs: They need to earn profits that will satisfy their owners. Sometimes, the needs of employees and employers are consistent: The organization can pay decent wages and provide workers with safe working conditions and job security while still making a satisfactory profit. At other times, there is a conflict—real, perceived, or a little bit of both—between the needs of employees and those of employers. In such cases, workers may be motivated to join a **labor union**—an organized group of workers that bargains with employers to improve its members' pay, job security, and working conditions.

Figure 5.7 charts *labor-union density*—union membership as a percentage of payrolls—in the United States from 1930 to 2005. As you can see, there's been a steady decline since the mid-1950s. Only membership among public workers (those employed by federal, state, and local governments, such as teachers, police, and firefighters) has remained steady, and, today, only about 12.5 percent of U.S. workers (about 10 percent in the private sector and 40 percent in the public sector) belong to unions.[59]

Why the decline? Many factors come into play. For one thing, there are more women in the workforce, and they're more likely to work part-time or intermittently. In addition, we've shifted from a manufacturing-based economy characterized by large, historically unionized companies to a service-based economy made up of many small firms that are hard to unionize.[60]

UNION STRUCTURE

Unions have a pyramidal structure much like that of large corporations. At the bottom are *locals* that serve workers in a particular geographical area. Certain members are designated as *shop stewards* to serve as go-betweens in disputes between workers and supervisors. Locals are usually organized into *national unions* that assist with local contract negotiations, organize new locals, negotiate contracts for entire industries, and lobby government bodies on issues of importance to organized labor. In turn, national unions may be linked by a *labor federation*, such as the American Federation of Labor/Congress of Industrial Organizations (AFL/CIO), which provides assistance to member unions and serves as the principal political organ for organized labor.

COLLECTIVE BARGAINING

In a nonunion environment, the employer makes largely unilateral decisions on issues affecting its labor force, such as salary and benefits. Management, for example, may

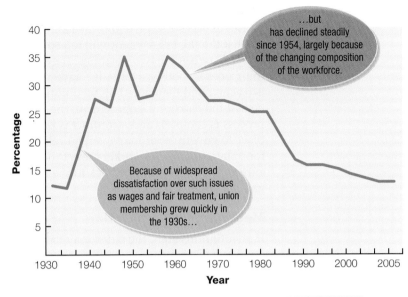

Figure 5.7

Labor Union Density, 1930–2005

simply set an average salary increase of 3 percent and require employees to pay an additional $50 a month for medical insurance. Typically, employees are in no position to bargain for better deals. (At the same time, however, for reasons that we've discussed earlier in this chapter, employers have a vested interest in treating workers fairly. A reputation for treating employees well, for example, is a key factor in attracting talented people.)

The process is a lot different in a union environment. Basically, union representatives determine with members what they want in terms of salary increases, benefits, working conditions, and job security. Union officials then tell the employer what its workers want and ask what they're willing to offer. When there's a discrepancy between what workers want and what management is willing to give—as there usually is—union officials serve as *negotiators* to bring the two sides together. The process of settling differences and establishing mutually agreeable conditions under which employees will work is called **collective bargaining**.

The Negotiation Process

Negotiations start when each side states its position and presents its demands. As in most negotiations, these opening demands

---

labor union
Organized group of workers that bargains with employers to improve its members' pay, job security, and working conditions.

collective bargaining
Process by which management and union-represented workers settle differences.

simply stake out starting positions. Both parties expect some give-and-take and realize that the final agreement will fall somewhere between the two positions. If everything goes smoothly, a tentative agreement is reached and then voted on by union members. If they accept the agreement, the process is complete and a contract is put into place to govern labor-management relations for a stated period. If workers reject the agreement, negotiators go back to the bargaining table.

Mediation and Arbitration

If negotiations stall, the sides may call in outsiders. One option is **mediation**, under which an impartial third party assesses the situation and makes recommendations for reaching an agreement. A mediator's advice can be accepted or rejected. If the two sides are willing to accept the decision of a third party, they may opt instead for **arbitration**, under which the third party studies the situation and arrives at a binding agreement.

Grievance Procedures

Another difference between union and nonunion environments is the handling of **grievances**—worker complaints on contract-related matters. When nonunion workers feel that they've been treated unfairly, they can take up the matter with supervisors, who may or may not satisfy their complaints. When unionized workers have complaints (such as being asked to work more hours than stipulated under their contract), they can call on union representatives to resolve the problem in conjunction with supervisory personnel. If the outcome isn't satisfactory, the union can take the problem to higher-level management. If there's still no resolution, the union may submit the grievance to an arbitrator.

WHEN NEGOTIATIONS BREAK DOWN

There are times when labor and management can't resolve their differences through collective bargaining or formal grievance procedures. When this happens, each side may resort to a variety of tactics to win support for its positions and force the opposition to agree to its demands.

Union Tactics

The tactics available to the union include *striking*, *picketing*, and *boycotting*. When they go on **strike**, workers walk away from their jobs and refuse to return until the issue at hand has been resolved. As undergraduates at Yale discovered when they arrived on campus in the fall of 2003, the effects of a strike can engulf parties other than employers and strikers: With 4,000 dining room workers on strike, they had to scramble to find food at local minimarkets. The strike—the ninth at the school since 1968—lasted 23 days, and in the end, the workers got what they wanted: better pension plans.

Although a strike sends a strong message to management, it also has consequences for workers, who don't get paid when they're on strike. Unions often ease the financial pressure on strikers by providing cash payments. (Some unionized workers, by the way, don't have the right to strike. Strikes by federal employees, such as air-traffic controllers, are illegal because they jeopardize the public interest.)

When you see workers parading with signs outside a factory or an office building (or even a school), they're probably **picketing**. The purpose of picketing is informative—to tell people that a workforce is on strike or to publicize some management practice that's unacceptable to the union. In addition, because other union workers typically won't cross picket lines, marchers can interrupt the daily activities of the targeted organization. How would you like to show up for classes to find faculty picketing outside the classroom building? In April 2001, faculty at the University of Hawaii, unhappy about salaries, went on strike for 13 days. Initially, many students cheerfully headed for the beach to work on their tans, but before long, many more—particularly graduating seniors—began to worry about finishing the semester with the credits they needed to keep their lives on schedule.[61]

The final tactic available to unions is **boycotting**, in which union workers refuse to buy a company's products and try to get other people to follow suit. The tactic is often used by the AFL/CIO, which maintains a national "Don't Buy or Patronize" boycott list. In 2003, for example, at the behest of two affiliates, the Actor's Equity Association and the American Federation of Musicians, it added the road show of the Broadway musical *Miss Saigon* to the list.

Why? The unions objected to the use of nonunion performers who worked for particularly low wages and to the use of a "virtual orchestra," an electronic apparatus that can replace a live orchestra with software-generated orchestral accompaniment.[62]

Management Tactics

Management doesn't sit by passively, especially if the company has a position to defend or a message to get out. One available tactic is the **lockout**—closing the workplace to workers—but it's rarely used because it's legal only when unionized workers pose a credible threat to the employer's financial viability. Another tactic is replacing striking workers with **strikebreakers**—nonunion workers who are willing to cross picket lines to replace strikers. Although the law prohibits companies from permanently replacing striking workers, it's often possible for a company to get a court injunction that allows it to bring in replacement workers.

Lockout tactics were used in the 2004–2005 labor dispute between the National Hockey League (NHL) and the National Hockey League Players Association (NHLPA). When club owners and players failed to reach a salary agreement prior to the 2004 season, the owners imposed a lockout. Neither side would give in: The players wanted to retain a market-based salary system that let them negotiate salaries individually, while owners argued for a salary structure with some type of "salary cap" that would put a limit on total salaries. With the 2004–2005 season defunct, the NHL considered the option of declaring an impasse and bringing in replacement players (strikebreakers) for the 2005–2006 season. Although legally possible (at least in the U.S.), the action would certainly have been unpopular among the consumers of their product (the fans).[63]

THE FUTURE OF UNIONS

As we noted earlier, union membership in the United States is declining. So what's the future of organized labor? Will membership continue to decline and unions lose even more power? The AFL/CIO is optimistic about union membership, pointing out recent gains in membership among women and immigrants, as well as health-care workers, graduate students, and professionals.[64]

But convincing workers to unionize is still more difficult than it used to be and could become even harder in the future. For one thing, employers have developed strategies for dissuading workers from unionizing—in particular, tactics for withholding job security. If unionization threatens higher costs for wages and benefits, they can resort to part-time or contract workers. They can also outsource work, eliminating jobs entirely, and more employers are now investing in technology designed to reduce the amount of human labor needed to produce goods or offer services.

QUICK QUIZ   5.3

Before finishing the chapter, take a minute to test yourself on what you learned in the preceding sections about performance appraisal, compensation and benefits, workforce diversity, and labor relations.

Go to www.exploringbusinessonline.com

Where We're Headed

In this chapter, we explained how managers recruit, select, hire, evaluate, compensate and retain qualified employees. We discussed the importance of training, developing, and motivating workers and introduced several theories of motivation.

mediation
Approach used to resolve a labor-contract dispute by following the recommendation of an impartial third party.
arbitration
Process of resolving a labor-contract dispute by having a third party study the situation and arrive at a *binding* agreement.
grievances
Union worker complaints on contract-related matters.

strike
Union tactic by which workers walk away from their jobs and refuse to return until a labor-management dispute has been resolved.
picketing
Union tactic of parading with signs outside a factory or other facility to publicize a strike.

boycotting
Method used by union members to voice displeasure with certain organizations by refusing to buy the company's products and encouraging others to follow suit.
lockout
Management tactic of closing the workplace to union workers.
strikebreakers
Nonunion workers who are willing to cross picket lines to replace strikers.

We examined some of the actions that companies can take to make themselves more desirable places to work, and we stressed the importance of diversity in the workforce. Finally, we explained why workers join unions and how the collective bargaining process works. In the next chapter, we'll examine the process through which companies develop and produce goods and services.

Summary of Learning Objectives

1. **Define *human resource management* and explain how managers develop and implement a human resource plan.**

    The process of **human resource management** consists of all the actions that an organization takes to attract, develop, and retain quality employees. To ensure that the organization is properly staffed, managers engage in **strategic human resource planning**—the process of developing a plan for satisfying the organization's human resource needs. Managers organize information about a given job by performing a **job analysis**, which they use to prepare two documents: a **job description** listing the duties and responsibilities of a position and a **job specification**, which lists the qualifications—skills, knowledge, and abilities—needed to perform the job.

    After analyzing the jobs that must be performed, the HR manager forecasts future hiring needs and begins the **recruiting** process to identify suitable candidates and encourage them to apply. In recruiting and hiring, managers must comply with antidiscrimination laws enforced by the **Equal Employment Opportunity Commission (EEOC)**. **Discrimination** occurs when a person is treated unfairly on the basis of a characteristic unrelated to ability, such as race, color, religion, sex, national origin, age, or disability. Once a pool of suitable candidates has been identified, managers begin the **selection** process, reviewing information provided by candidates on employment **applications** and administering tests to assess candidates' skills and knowledge. Candidates who pass this stage may be granted an **interview** and, perhaps, offered a job.

2. **Explain how companies train and develop employees and discuss the importance of a diverse workforce.**

    The process of introducing new employees to their jobs and to the company is called **orientation**. An effective approach is to take things slowly, providing new employees with information on a need-to-know basis while making them feel as comfortable as pos-

sible. New employees will need initial training to start their jobs, and they'll need additional training as they grow in or change their jobs. **Off-the-job training** allows them to focus on learning without the distractions that would occur in the office, but **on-the-job training** is more common.

In addition to having well-trained employees, it's important that a workforce reflects the broad range of differences in the population. The efforts of HR managers to build a workforce that's representative of the general population are driven in part by legal concerns: Discrimination is illegal, and companies that violate antidiscrimination laws are subject to prosecution. But ensuring a diverse workforce goes well beyond both legal compliance and ethical commitment. It's good business because a diverse group of employees can bring fresh points of view that can be valuable in generating ideas and solving problems. Additionally, people from varied backgrounds can help an organization connect with an ethnically diverse customer base.

3. **Define *motivation* and describe several theories of motivation.**

    Motivation describes an internally generated drive that propels people to achieve goals or pursue particular courses of action. There are four influential theories of motivation: (1) **Hierarchy-of-needs theory** proposes that we're motivated by five unmet needs—physiological, safety, social, esteem, and self-actualization— and must satisfy lower-level needs before we seek to satisfy higher-level needs. (2) **Two-factor theory** divides work factors into motivation factors (those that are strong contributors to job satisfaction) and hygiene factors (those which, though not strong contributors to satisfaction, must be present to prevent job dissatisfaction). In order to increase satisfaction (and motivate someone to perform better), managers must address motivation factors. (3) **Expectancy theory** proposes that employees work hard to obtain a reward when they value the reward, believe that their efforts will result in acceptable performance, and believe acceptable performance will lead to a desired outcome or reward. (4) **Equity theory** focuses on our perceptions of how fairly we're treated relative to others. This theory proposes that employees create contributions/rewards ratios which they compare to those of others. If they feel that their ratios are comparable to those of others, they'll perceive that they're being treated equitably.

4. **Identify factors that make an organization a good place to work, including competitive compensation and benefit packages.**

Employees report that they're motivated to perform well when they're challenged, respected, treated fairly, and appreciated. Competitive compensation also helps. Workers who are paid by the hour earn **wages**, while those who are paid to fulfill the responsibilities of the job earn **salaries**. Some people receive **commissions** based on sales or are paid for output, based on a **piecework** approach. In addition to pay, many employees can earn financial rewards based on their own and/or their employer's performance. They may receive year-end **bonuses**, participate in **profit-sharing plans** (which use predetermined formulas to distribute a share of company profits among employees), or receive **stock options** (which let them buy shares of company stock at set prices). Another component of many compensation packages is **benefits**—compensation other than salaries, wages, or financial incentives. Benefits may include paid time off, insurance, and retirement benefits.

Other factors may contribute to employee satisfaction. Some companies use **job redesign** to make jobs more interesting and challenging. **Job rotation** allows employees to rotate from one job to another on a systematic basis. **Job enlargement** enhances a job by adding tasks at similar skill levels. **Job enrichment** adds tasks that increase both responsibility and opportunity for growth. Many organizations recognize the need to help employees strike a balance between their work and home lives and offer a variety of work arrangements to accommodate different employee needs. **Flextime** allows employees to designate starting and quitting times, compress workweeks, or perform part-time work. With **job sharing**, two people share one full-time position. **Telecommuting** means working from home. Many employers also offer dependent care, paid leave for new parents, employee-assistance programs, and on-site fitness centers.

5. **Explain how managers evaluate employee performance and retain qualified employees.**

Managers conduct **performance appraisals** to evaluate work performance, usually following a three-step process: (1) setting goals and performance expectations and specifying the criteria for measuring performance; (2) completing written evaluations to rate performance according to predetermined criteria; and (3) meeting with employees to discuss evaluations and ways to improve performance.

Turnover—the permanent separation of an employee from a company—has a negative effect on an organization. In addition to offering competitive compensation, companies may take a variety of steps to retain qualified employees: providing appropriate training and development, helping employees achieve a satisfying work/nonwork balance in their lives, creating a positive work environment, recognizing employee efforts, and involving employees in decision making. On the other hand, employers may have to terminate the employment of (i.e., fire) some workers. They may lay off workers because revenues are down and they have to **downsize**—to cut costs by eliminating jobs. Sometimes a job is phased out, and sometimes an employee simply fails to meet performance requirements. If there's no written employment contract, the employment relationship falls under the principle of **employment-at-will**, by which an employer can end it at any time. Usually, however, the employer must show just cause.

6. **Explain why workers unionize and how unions are structured and describe the collective bargaining process.**

Some workers belong to **labor unions**—organized groups of workers that bargain with employers to improve members' pay, job security, and working conditions. Unions have a pyramidal structure. At the bottom are *locals*, who serve workers in a particular geographical area. Locals are usually organized into *national unions* that assist with local contract negotiations and negotiate industrywide contracts. Nationals may be linked by a *labor federation*, such as the AFL/CIO, which provides assistance to member unions and serves as the principal political organ for organized labor.

When there's a discrepancy between what workers want in terms of salary increases, benefits, working conditions, and job security and what management is willing to give, the two sides engage in a process called **collective bargaining**. If everything goes smoothly, a contract is soon put into place. If negotiations break down, the sides may resort to **mediation** (in which an impartial third party makes recommendations for reaching an agreement) or **arbitration** (in which the third party imposes a binding agreement). When unionized workers feel that they've been treated unfairly, they can file **grievances**—complaints over contract-related matters that are resolved by union representatives and employee supervisors.

If labor differences can't be resolved through collective bargaining or formal grievance procedures, each side may resort to a variety of tactics. The union can call a **strike** (in which workers leave their jobs until the issue is settled), organize **picketing** (in which workers congregate outside the workplace to publicize their position), or arrange for **boycotting** (in which workers and other consumers are urged to refrain from buying an employer's products). Management may resort to a **lockout**—closing the workplace to workers—or call in **strikebreakers** (nonunion workers who are willing to cross picket lines to replace strikers).

Questions and Problems

1. You're the chairperson of the management department at your college. Describe the steps you'd take to ensure that your department has enough qualified faculty to meet its needs.

2. **AACSB ▶ Reflective Skills**

   Think about a full-time or part-time job that you've held. Was your orientation to the job satisfactory? If not, how would you have improved the process? Did you receive any training? Was it useful? What additional training would have helped you do a better job? How would it have benefited the company?

3. **AACSB ▶ Diversity**

   While visiting a mall in Los Angeles, you noticed two stores located side by side selling electronic-entertainment products—CDs, DVDs, and so on. All the employees in one store were white males. The mix of workers in the other store—which happened to be more profitable—was more diverse. Why do you think the store with the diverse workforce did more business? In terms of diversity, what would be your ideal workforce in a store similar to these in Los Angeles?

4. This chapter describes four theories of motivation: hierarchy-of-needs theory, two-factor theory, expectancy theory, and equity theory. Briefly describe each theory. Which one makes the most intuitive sense to you? Why do you find it appealing?

5. **AACSB ▶ Analysis**

   Describe the ideal job that you'd like to have once you've finished college. Be sure to explain the type of work schedule that you'd find most satisfactory and why. Identify family-friendly programs that you'd find desirable and explain why these appeal to you.

6. What steps does a manager take in evaluating an employee's performance? Explain the benefits of performance appraisals and identify some of the potential problems entailed by the performance-evaluation process.

7. As an HR manager, what steps would you take to retain valuable employees? Under what circumstances would you fire an employee? Can you fire someone without giving that person a warning?

8. Describe a typical compensation package for a sales manager in a large organization. If you could design your own compensation package, what would it include?

9. You've just gotten a job as an autoworker. Would you prefer to work in a unionized or nonunionized plant? Why? If you were hired as a high-level manager in the company, would you want your workers to be unionized? Why or why not? What's your opinion on the future of organized labor? Will union membership grow or decline in the next decade? Why or why not?

10. What happens in a unionized company when negotiations between labor and management break down? Identify and describe the tactics that unions can use against management and those that management can use against unions.

Learning on the Web AACSB

What's Your (Emotional) IQ?

If you were an HR manager, on what criteria would you base a hiring decision—intelligence (IQ), education, technical skills, experience, references, or performance on the interview? All of these can be important determinants of a person's success, but some experts believe that there's an even better predictor of success. It's called *emotional intelligence* (or *EI*), and it gained some currency in the mid-1990s thanks to Daniel Goleman's book *Emotional Intelligence: Why It Can Matter More Than IQ*. EI is the ability to understand both our own emotions and those of others, as well as the ability to use that understanding in managing our behavior, motivating ourselves, and encouraging others to achieve goals.

An attractive aspect of EI is that, unlike IQ, it's not fixed at an early age. Rather, its vital components—self-awareness, self-management, social awareness, and relationship management—can be strengthened over time. To assess your level of EI, go to www.exploringbusinessonline.com to link to the Web site maintained by the Hay Group, a management-consulting firm, and take the 10-item test that's posted there. After completing the test, you'll get your EI score, some instructions for interpreting it, and an answer key.

When you've finished with the test, rank the following items according to the importance that you'd give them in making a hiring decision: intelligence, education, technical skills, experience, references, interview skills, and emotional intelligence. Explain your ranking.

Career Opportunities

Are You a People Person?

You might not like the idea of sitting across the desk from a corporate college recruiter and asking for a job, but what if you were on the other side of the desk? As a recruiter, you'd get to return to campus each year to encourage students to join your company. Or, maybe you'd like to help your company develop a new compensation and benefits program, implement a performance-evaluation system, or create a new training program. All of these activities fall under the umbrella of HR.

To learn more about the field of HR, go to www.exploring businessonline.com to link to the WetFeet Web site and read the page "Human Resources Career Overview." Next, click on "Real People" in the left sidebar and then "Human Resources," and you'll be presented with a list of profession-

als in the HR field. Select three people who look interesting to you. After reading each person's story, answer the following questions:

1. What's the job like?

2. What does the HR professional like about the job? What does he or she dislike?

3. What kind of people do well in the HR field?

4. How would you get this type of job?

Finally, write a paragraph responding to this question: Do you find the HR field interesting? Why or why not?

Ethics Angle AACSB

Misstating the Facts

Life couldn't get much better for George O'Leary when he was named the head football coach at Notre Dame. Unfortunately, he barely had time to celebrate his new job before he was ruled ineligible: After just a week on the job, he was forced to resign, embarrassing himself, his family, his friends, and Notre Dame. Why? Because of a few lies that he'd put on his résumé 20 years earlier. To get the facts behind this story, go to www.exploringbusin-essonline.com to link to the *Sports Illustrated* Web site and read the article "Short Tenure: O'Leary Out at Notre Dame After One Week." Then, answer the following questions:

1. Was O'Leary's punishment appropriate? If you were the athletic director at Notre Dame, would you have meted out the same punishment? Why or why not?

2. False information on his résumé came back to haunt O'Leary after 20 years. Once he'd falsified his résumé, was there any corrective action that he could have taken? If so, what?

3. If O'Leary had told Notre Dame about the falsifications before they came to light, would they have hired him?

4. Would his previous employer take him back?

5. O'Leary was later hired as a head coach by the University of Central Florida. Will the episode involving his résumé undermine his ability to encourage players to act with integrity? Will it affect his ability to recruit players?

6. What's the lesson to be learned from O'Leary's experience? In what ways might a few (theoretical) misstatement on your résumé come back to haunt you?

Team-Building Skills AACSB

Dorm Room Rescue

Any night of the week (at least as of this writing), you can relax in front of the TV and watch a steady stream of shows about how to improve your living space—such as *Trading Spaces*, *While You Were Out*, and *New Spaces*. You like the concept of these programs well enough, but

you're tired of watching them in a tiny, cluttered dorm room that's decorated in early barracks style. Out of these cramped conditions, however, you and a team of friends come up with an idea. Upon graduation, you'll start a business called "Dorm Room Rescue" to provide decorating services to the dorm dwellers who've come after you. You'll help college students pick colors and themes for their rooms and select space-saving furniture, storage materials, area rugs, and wall decorations. Your goal will be to create attractive dorm rooms that provide comfort, functionality, and privacy as well as pleasant spaces in which students can relax and even entertain.

The team decides to develop a plan for the HR needs of your future company. You'll need to address the following issues:

1. HR plan
   - Number of employees
   - Job descriptions: duties and responsibilities for each type of employee
   - Job specifications: needed skills, knowledge, and abilities

2. Recruitment of qualified employees
   - Recruitment plan: how and where to find candidates
   - Selection process: steps taken to select employees

3. Developing employees
   - New-employee orientation
   - Training and development

4. Compensation and benefits
   - Wages, salaries, and incentive programs
   - Benefits

5. Work/Life quality
   - Work schedules and alternative work arrangements
   - Family-friendly programs

6. Performance appraisal
   - Appraisal process
   - Retaining valuable employees

You might want to divide up the initial work, but you'll need to regroup as a team to make your final decisions on these issues and to create a team-prepared report.

The Global View AACSB

Sending Ed to China

You're the HR manager for a large environmental consulting firm that just started doing business in China. You've asked your top engineer, Ed Deardon, to relocate to Shanghai for a year. Although China will be new to Deardon, working overseas won't be; he's already completed assignments in the Philippines and Thailand; as before, his wife and three children will be going with him.

You've promised Deardon some advice on adapting to living and working conditions in Shanghai, and you intend to focus on the kinds of cultural differences that tend to create problems in international business dealings. Unfortunately, you personally know absolutely nothing about living in China and so must do some online research. Go to www.exploringbusinessonline.com to link to some promising sites.

INSTRUCTIONS

Prepare a written report to Deardon in which you identify and explain five or six cultural differences between business behavior in the United States and China and offer some advice on how to deal with them.

Business Plan Project

Group Report: *Management Qualifications and Compensation*

REPORT

The team should submit a written report describing the qualifications of the management team members. It should indicate the compensation to be earned by each member. To find out what information should be included in this report, go to Appendix A, "Introducing Your Business Plan" (p. 307), and review the "Management Plan" section. Be sure to provide information about the qualifications of your management team members (education, experience, expertise, etc.) and to indicate the estimated annual salary to be paid to each member of the team. (*Note: In describing management qualifications, pretend that all team members graduated from college 10 years ago.*)

The report should be about two double-spaced typed pages. The name of your proposed business and the names of all team members should appear on the report.

REASONABLE CONTRIBUTIONS

All members of the team who make a reasonable contribution to the report should sign it. (If any team member does not work on the report, his or her name should *not* appear on it.) If a student who has made a contribution is unable to sign the report (because of sickness or some other valid reason), the team can sign his or her name. To indicate that a name was signed by the team on a member's behalf, be sure to attach a note to the signature.

6

Developing and Producing Goods and Services

After studying this chapter, you will be able to:

1 Define *product* and explain where product ideas come from.

2 Explain how to research an industry and forecast demand for a product.

3 Describe the process of developing a product that meets customer needs.

4 Define *operations management* and discuss the responsibilities of the operations manager in planning and managing the production process in a manufacturing company.

5 List the characteristics that distinguish service operations from manufacturing operations and explain the nature of operations management for service providers.

6 Explain how both manufacturing and service companies use technology, total quality management, and outsourcing to provide value to customers.

PM Images/Getty Images Inc.–Stone Allstock

RIDING THE CREST OF INNOVATION

Have you ever wanted to go surfing but couldn't find a body of water with decent waves? You no longer have a problem: The newly invented PowerSki Jetboard makes its own waves. This innovative product combines the ease of waterskiing with the excitement of surfing. A high-tech surfboard with a 40-horsepower, 40-pound watercraft engine, the PowerSki Jetboard has the power of a small motorcycle. Experienced surfers use it to get to the top of rising ocean waves, but if you're just a weekend water-sports enthusiast, you can get your adrenaline going by skimming across the surface of a local lake at 40 miles an hour. All you have to do is submerge the tail of the board, slide across on your belly, and stand up (with the help of a flexible pole). To innocent bystanders, you'll look like a very fast water-skier without a boat.

Where do product ideas like the PowerSki Jetboard come from? How do people create products that meet customer needs? How are *ideas* developed and turned into actual *products*? How do you forecast demand for a product? How do you protect your product ideas? These are some of the questions that we'll address in this chapter.

To see the PowerSki Jetboard in action, visit the company's Web site at www.powerski.com. Watch the streaming videos that demonstrate what the Jetboard can do.

What Is a Product?

Basically, a **product** is something that can be marketed to customers because it provides them with a benefit and satisfies a need. It can be a physical *good*, such as the PowerSki Jetboard, or a *service*, such as a haircut or a taxi ride. The distinction between goods and services isn't always clear-cut. Say, for example, that a company hires a professional to provide an in-house executive training program on "netiquette" (e-mail etiquette). Off the top of our heads, most of us would say that the company is buying a service. What if the program is offered online? We'd probably still argue that the product is a service. But what if the company buys training materials that the trainer furnishes on DVD? Is the customer still buying a service? Probably not: We'd have to say that when it buys the DVD, the company is buying a tangible good.

In this case, the product that satisfies the customer's need has both a tangible component (the training materials on DVD) and an intangible component (the educational activities performed by the seller). Not surprisingly, many products have both tangible and intangible components. If, for example, you buy a Dell computer, you get not only the computer (a tangible good) but certain promises to answer any technical questions that you might have and certain guarantees to fix your computer if it breaks within a specified time period (intangible services).

WHERE DO PRODUCT IDEAS COME FROM?

Product ideas can come from almost anywhere. How many times have you looked at a product that just hit the market and said, "I could have thought of that"? Just about anybody can come up with a product *idea*; basically, you just need a little imagination. Success is more likely to result from a truly remarkable product—something that grabs the attention of consumers. Entrepreneur and marketing consultant Seth Godin refers to truly remarkable products as "purple cows."[1] He came up with the term while driving through the countryside one day. As he drove along, his interest was attracted by the hundreds of cows dotting the countryside. After a while, however, he started to ignore the cows because looking at them had become tedious. For one thing, they were all brown, and it occurred to him that a glimpse of a *purple* cow would be worth writing home about. People would tend to remember a purple cow; in fact, they might even want one.

Who thinks up "purple cow" ideas? Where do the truly remarkable business ideas come from? As we pointed out in Chapter 2, entrepreneurs and small business owners are a rich source of new product ideas (according to the Small Business Administration, 55 percent of all product innovations come from small businesses). Take Dean Kamen, inventor of the Segway Human Transporter, a battery-operated vehicle that responds to the rider's movements: Lean forward and you can go straight ahead at 12.5 miles per hour; to stop, just tilt backward. This revolutionary product is only one of Kamen's many remarkable business ideas. He invented his first product—a wearable infusion pump for administering chemotherapy and other drugs—while he was still a college undergraduate.[2] Jacob Dunnack is also getting an early entrepreneurial start. At *age six*, Jacob became frustrated one day when he brought his baseball bat to his grandmother's house but forgot to bring any baseballs with him. His solution? A hollow baseball bat that holds baseballs. Dunnack's invention, now called the JD Batball, was quickly developed and now sells in stores such as Toys "R" Us.[3]

Why do so many entrepreneurs and small businesspeople come up with so many purple cows? For one thing, entrepreneurs are often creative people; moreover, they're often willing to take risks. This is certainly true of Bob Montgomery, inventor of the PowerSki Jetboard (which undoubtedly qualifies as a purple cow). With more than 20 years' experience in the watersports industry and considerable knowledge of the personal-watercraft market, Montgomery finally decided to follow his long-cherished dream of creating an entirely new and conceptually different product—one that would offer users ease of operations, high performance, speed, and quality. His creative efforts have earned him the prestigious *Popular Science* "Best of What's New" award.[4]

To remain competitive, medium and large organizations must also identify product development opportunities. Many companies actively solicit product ideas from people inside the organization, including marketing, sales, research, and manufacturing personnel, and some even establish internal "entrepreneurial" units. Others seek product ideas from outside the organization by talking to customers and paying attention to what the competition is doing. In addition to looking out for new product ideas, most companies constantly look for ways to make incremental improvements in existing products by adding features that will broaden their consumer appeal. As you can see from Figure 6.1, the market leaders in most industries are the firms who are most successful at developing new products.

A novel approach to generating new-to-the-world product ideas is hiring "creativity" consultants. One of the best is Doug Hall, who's been called "America's Number 1 Idea Guru." At a Cincinnati idea factory called Eureka!Ranch, Hall and other members of his consulting firm specialize in helping corporate executives get their creative juices flowing.[5] Hall's job is getting people to invent products that make a real difference to consumers, and his strategies are designed to help corporate clients become more innovative—to jump-start their brains. As Hall puts it, "You have to swing to hit home runs."[6] Eureka!Ranch's client list includes Disney, Kellogg, Johnson & Johnson, and P&G as well as a number of budding entrepreneurs. Hall boasts that the average home uses 18 goods or services that the Ranch helped shape, and if he's right, you've probably benefited from one of the company's idea-generating sessions.[7]

IDENTIFY BUSINESS OPPORTUNITIES

Generating product ideas is essential to business success, but needless to say, not all ideas generate business opportunities. An idea turns into a business opportunity when it has commercial potential—when you can make money by selling the product.

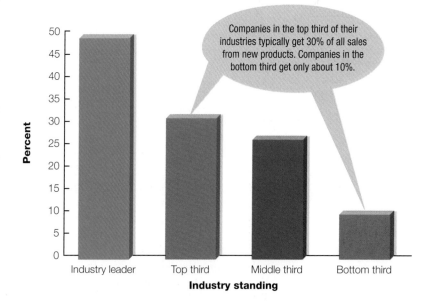

Figure 6.1

Sales from New Products

Companies in the top third of their industries typically get 30% of all sales from new products. Companies in the bottom third get only about 10%.

product
Something that can be marketed to customers because it provides a benefit and satisfies a need.

Remember: Being in business is not about you—it's about the customer. Successful businesspeople don't ask themselves, "What do I want to sell?" but rather, "What does the customer want to buy?"

Customers buy products to fill unmet needs and because they expect to derive some value or benefit from them. People don't buy Alka-Seltzer because they like the taste or even because the price is right: They buy it because it makes their indigestion go away. They don't shop at Amazon.com because the Web site is entertaining: They shop there because they want their purchases delivered quickly. The realization that this kind of service would meet customer needs made Amazon.com a genuine business opportunity.

How can you decide whether an idea has the potential to become a business opportunity? You should start by asking yourself the questions in Figure 6.2: If you can't come up with good answers to these questions, you probably don't have a very promising product. On the other hand, if you conclude that you have a potential product for which people would pay money, you're ready to take the next step: Analyze the market to see if you should go forward with the development of the product.

Understand Your Industry

Before you invest a lot of time and money to develop a new product, you need to understand the industry in which it's going to be sold. As inventor of the PowerSki Jetboard, Bob Montgomery had the advantage of being quite familiar with the industry that he proposed to enter. With more than 20 years' experience in the water-sports and personal-watercraft industry, he was at home in this business environment. He knew who his potential customers were, and he knew who his competitors were. He had experience in marketing similar products, and he was familiar with industry regulations.

Most people don't have the same head start as Bob Montgomery. How does the average would-be businessperson learn about an industry? What should you want to know about it? Let's tackle the first question first.

Evaluating Your Industry Before you can study an industry, you need to know what industry to study. An **industry** is a group of related businesses: They do similar things and they compete with each other. In the footwear industry, for example, firms make and/or sell footwear. Players in the industry include Nike and Adidas, both of whom specialize in athletic footwear; but the industry is also sprinkled with companies like Candies (which sells young women's fashion footwear) and Florsheim (quality men's dress shoes).

Let's say that you want to know something about the footwear industry because your potential purple cow is a line of jogging shoes designed specifically for older people (those over 65) who live in the Southeast. You'd certainly need a broad understanding of the footwear industry, but would general knowledge be enough? Wouldn't you feel more comfortable about pursuing your idea if you could focus on a smaller segment of the industry—namely, the segment that specializes in products similar to the one you plan to sell? Here's a method that will help you narrow your focus.[8]

Segmenting Your Market Begin with the overall industry—in this case, the footwear industry. Within this industry, there are several groups of customers, each of which is a **market**. You're interested in the *consumer market*—retail customers. But this, too, is a fairly broad market; it includes everybody who buys shoes at retail. Your next step, then, is to subdivide this market into smaller **market segments**—groups of potential customers with common characteristics that influence their buying decisions. You can use a variety of standard characteristics, including *demographics* (age, sex, income), *geography* (region, climate, city size), and *psychographics* (lifestyle, activities, interests). The segment you're interested in consists of older people (a demographic vari-

Figure 6.2

When Is an Idea a Business Opportunity?

Ask yourself:

1 Who would my customers be?

2 Why will customers buy the product from me?

3 How will customers benefit from my product?

able) living in the Southeast (a geographic variable) who jog (a psychographic variable). Within this market segment, you might want to subdivide further and find a **niche**—an unmet need. Your niche might be providing high-quality jogging shoes to active adults living in retirement communities in Florida.

The goal of this process is to identify progressively narrower sectors of a given industry. You need to become familiar with the whole industry—not only with the footwear industry, but with the retail market for jogging shoes designed for older people. You also need to understand your niche market, which consists of older people who live active lives in Florida.

Now that we know something about the process of focusing in on an industry, let's look at another example. Suppose that your product idea is offering dedicated cruises for college students. You'd begin by looking at the recreational-activities *industry*. Your *market* would be people who travel for leisure, and within that market, you'd focus on the *market segment* consisting of people who take cruises. Your *niche* would be college students who want to take cruises.

Assessing Your Competition Now that you've identified your industry and its various sectors, you're ready to consider such questions as the following:[9]

- Is the industry growing or contracting? Are sales revenues increasing?

- Who are your major competitors? How does your product differ from those of your competitors?

- What opportunities exist in the industry? What threats?

- Has the industry undergone recent changes? Where is it headed?

- How important is technology to the industry? Has it brought about changes?

- Is the industry mature or are new companies successfully entering it?

- Do companies in the industry make reasonable profits?

Where do you find answers to questions such as these? A good place to start is by studying your competitors: Who are their customers? What products do they sell? How do they price their products? How do they market them? How do they treat their customers? Do they seem to be operating successfully? Observe their operations and buy their goods and services. For example, there's a great deal of information about companies on the Internet, particularly in company Web sites. The Internet is also a good source of industry information. Look for the site posted by the industry trade association. Find out if it publishes a magazine or other materials. Talk with people in the industry—business owners, managers, suppliers; these people are usually experts. And talk with customers. What do they like or dislike about the products that are currently available? What benefits are they looking for? What benefits are they getting?

Understand Customer Needs

It goes without saying, but we'll say it anyway: Without enough customers, your business will go nowhere. So, before you delve into the complex and expensive world of developing and marketing a new product, ask yourself questions like those in Figure 6.3. When Bob Montgomery asked himself these questions, he concluded that he had

Figure 6.3

When to Develop and Market a New Product

Ask yourself:

1. Who are my primary customers?

2. Will I sell to individuals, businesses, or both?

3. If I sell to other businesses, who will be the actual end users, or ultimate consumers, of my product?

---

industry
Group of businesses that compete with one another to market products that are the same or similar.

market
Group of buyers or potential buyers who share a common need that can be met by a certain product.

market segment
Group of potential customers with common characteristics that influence their buying decisions.

niche
Narrowly defined group of potential customers with a fairly specific set of needs.

two groups of customers for the PowerSki Jetboard: (1) the dealerships that would sell the product and (2) the water-sports enthusiasts who would buy and use it. His job, therefore, was to design a product that dealers would want to sell and enthusiasts would buy. When he was confident that he could satisfy these criteria, he moved forward with his plans to develop the PowerSki Jetboard.

After you've identified a group of potential customers, your next step is finding out as much as you can about what they think of your product idea. Remember: Because your ultimate goal is to roll out a product that satisfies customer needs, you need to know ahead of time what your potential customers want. Precisely what are their unmet needs? Ask them questions such as these:[10]

- What do you like about this product idea? What don't you like?
- What improvements would you make?
- What benefits would you get from it?
- Would you buy it? Why or why not?
- What would it take for you to buy it?

Forecast Demand

Before making a substantial investment in the development of a product, you need to ask yourself yet another question: Are there enough customers willing to buy my product at a price that will allow me to make a profit? Answering this question means performing one of the hardest tasks in business: forecasting demand for your proposed product. There are several possible approaches to this task that can be used alone or in combination.

Published Industry Data To get some idea of the total market for products like the one you want to launch, you might begin by examining pertinent industry research. For example, to estimate demand for jogging shoes among consumers 65 and older, you could look at data published on the industry association's Web site, USA Track and Field. Here you'd find that 34 million jogging/running shoes were sold in the United States in 2002 at an average price of $51. The Web site also reports that the number of athletes who are at least 40 and who participate in road events has increased by more than 50 percent over the last 10 years.[11] To find more specific information—say, the number of joggers older than 65—you could call or e-mail USA Track and Field. You might find this

information in an 87-page statistical study of retail sporting-goods sales published by the National Sporting Goods Association.[12] If you still don't get a useful answer, try contacting organizations that sell industry data. American Sports Data, for instance, provides demographic information on 28 fitness activities, including jogging.[13] You'd want to ask them for data on the number of joggers older than 65 living in Florida. There's a lot of valuable and available industry-related information that you can use to estimate demand for your product.

Now, let's say that your research turns up the fact that there are 3 million joggers older than 65 and that 600,000 of them live in Florida, which attracts 20 percent of all people who move when they retire.[14] How do you use this information to estimate the number of jogging shoes that you'll be able to sell during your first year of business? First, you have to estimate your **market share**: your portion of total sales in the older-than-65 jogging shoe market in Florida. Being realistic (but having faith in an excellent product), you estimate that you'll capture 5 percent of the market during your first year. So you do the math: 600,000 pairs of jogging shoes sold in Florida × .05 (5-percent share of the market) = 30,000—the estimated first-year demand for your proposed product.

Granted, this is just an estimate. But at least it's an educated guess rather than a wild one. You'll still want to talk with people in the industry as well as potential customers to get their views on the demand for your product. Only then would you use your sales estimate to make financial projections and decide whether your proposed business is financially feasible. We'll discuss this process in a later chapter.

People in Similar Businesses

Although some businesspeople are reluctant to share proprietary information, such as sales volume, others are willing to help out individuals starting new businesses or launching new products. Talking to people in your prospective industry (or one that's similar) can be especially helpful if your proposed product is a service. Say, for example, that you plan to open a pizza parlor with a soap opera theme: Customers will be able to eat pizza while watching reruns of their favorite soap operas on personal TV/DVD sets. If you visited a few local restaurants and asked owners how many customers they served every day, you'd probably learn enough to estimate the number of pizzas that you'd serve during your first year. If the owners weren't cooperative, you could just hang out and make an informal count of the customers.

Potential Customers You can also learn a lot by talking with potential customers. Ask them how often they buy products similar to the one you want to launch. Where do they buy them and in what quantity? What factors affect demand for them? If you were contemplating a frozen yogurt store in Michigan, it wouldn't hurt to ask customers coming out of an ice cream shop if they'd buy frozen yogurt in the winter.

ABOUT NIKE 6.1

Now that you know why companies analyze the industries in which they operate, it's time to familiarize yourself with the industry in which Nike competes.

Go to www.exploringbusinessonline.com

QUICK QUIZ 6.1

Before we discuss operations management, take a few minutes to test your understanding of the material on product ideas and business opportunities.

Go to www.exploringbusinessonline.com

Operations Management

Like PowerSki, every organization—whether it produces goods or provides services—sees Job 1 as furnishing customers with quality products. Thus, to compete with other organizations, a company must convert resources (materials, labor, money, information) into goods or services as efficiently as possible. The upper-level manager who directs this transformation process is called an *operations manager*. The job of

operations management (OM), then, consists of all the activities involved in transforming a product idea into a finished product, as well as those involved in planning and controlling the systems that produce goods and services. In other words, operations managers manage the process that transforms inputs into outputs. Figure 6.4 (page 138) illustrates this traditional function of operations management.

Operations and Utility

The process of transforming inputs into goods and services offers *value* to customers by providing them with *utility*—that is, by satisfying particular customer needs. There are four types of utility:

1. *Time utility.* A concessionaire selling bottled water at a summer concert is making liquid refreshment available when it's needed.

2. *Place utility.* A street vendor selling hotdogs outside an office building is making fast food available where it's needed.

3. *Ownership utility.* A real estate agent helping a young couple buy a home is transferring ownership from someone who doesn't need it to someone who does.

4. *Form utility.* A company that makes apparel is turning raw material (fabric) into a form (clothing) that people need.

In the rest of this chapter, we'll discuss the major activities of operations managers and the ways in which products are developed to provide utility for consumers. We'll start by describing the process followed to develop a new product. Next, we'll investigate the role played by operations managers in the different processes designed to produce goods and services. First, we'll look at the production of goods in manufacturing firms; then, we'll describe operations management activities in companies that provide services. We'll wrap up the chapter by explaining the role of operations management in such processes as quality control and outsourcing.

---

market share
Company's portion of the market that it has targeted.

operations management (OM)
Management of the process that transforms resources into products.

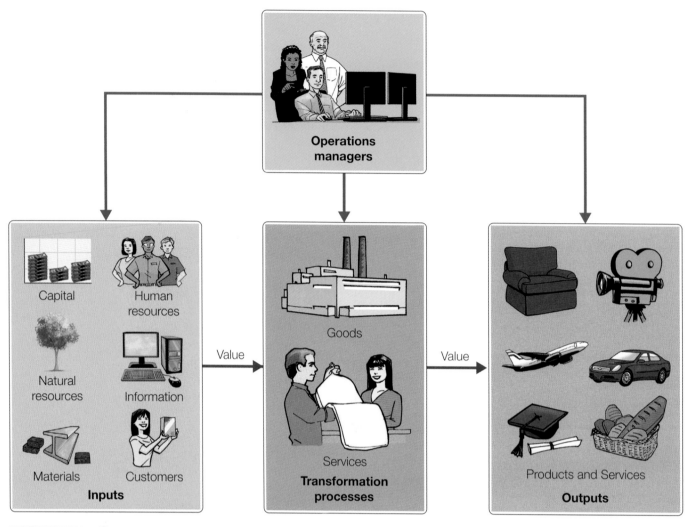

Operations managers

Capital   Human resources

Natural resources   Information

Materials   Customers

Inputs

Value →

Goods

Services

Transformation processes

Value →

Products and Services

Outputs

 Figure 6.4

ACTIVE

The Transformation Process

PRODUCT DEVELOPMENT

The success of a business depends on its ability to identify the unmet needs of consumers and to develop products that meet those needs at a low cost.[15] In other words, effective product development results in goods and services that can be sold at a profit. In addition, it results in high-quality products, which not only satisfy consumer needs but which can be developed in a timely and cost-efficient manner. Accomplishing these goals entails a collaborative effort by individuals from all areas of an organization: operations management (including representatives from engineering, design, and manufacturing), marketing, accounting, and finance. In fact, companies increasingly assign representatives from different functional areas who work together as **a project team** throughout the product development processes. This approach allows individuals with varied backgrounds and experience to provide input as the product is being developed.

Not surprisingly, developing profitable products is difficult, and the success rate is low. On average, for every successful product, a company has 12 failures. At this rate, the firms on the *Fortune* 1000 list waste over $60 billion a year in research and development.[16] There are several reasons why product development is such a risky proposition:

- *Trade-offs.* You might, for instance, be able to make your jogging shoes lighter than your competitors', but if you do, they probably won't wear as well. They could be of higher quality, but that will make them more costly (they might price themselves out of the market).

- *Time pressure.* Developing a product can require hundreds of decisions that must be made quickly and with imperfect information.

- *Economics.* Because developing a product requires a lot of time and money, there's always pressure to make sure that the project not only results in a successful product but gets it to market at the most opportune time. Failure to be first to market with an otherwise desirable new product can cost a company a great deal of money.

Even so, organizations continue to dedicate immense resources to developing new products. Your supermarket, for example, can choose from about 100,000 items to carry on its shelves—including 20,000 *new* products every year. Unfortunately, the typical supermarket can stock only 30,000 products.[17]

The Product Development Process

The **product development process** is a series of activities by which a product idea is transformed into a final product. It can be broken down into the seven steps summarized in Figure 6.5.

Evaluate Opportunities and Select the Best Product Idea

If you're starting your first business, you might have only one product idea. But existing organizations often have several ideas for new products as well as improvements to existing products. Where do they come from? They can come from individuals within the organization or from outside sources, such as customers. Typically, various ideas are reviewed and evaluated by a team of individuals, who identify the most promising ideas for development. They may rely on a variety of criteria: Does the proposed product fill an unmet customer need? Will enough people buy it to make it commercially successful? Do we have the resources and expertise to make it?

Get Feedback to Refine the Product Concept

From the selected product idea, the team generates an initial **product concept** that describes what the product might look like and how it might work. Members talk both with other people in the organization and potential buyers in order to identify customer needs and the benefits that consumers will get from the product. They study the industry in which the product will be sold and investigate competing products. They brainstorm different *product designs*—that is, the specifications for how the product is to be made, what it's to look like, and what performance standards it's to meet.

Based on information gathered through this process, the team will revise the product concept, probably pinpointing several alternative models. Then they'll go back to potential customers and get their feedback on both the basic concept and the various alternatives. Based on this feedback, the team will decide what the product will look like, how it will work, and what features it will have.

Figure 6.5 **ACTIVE**

The Product Development Process

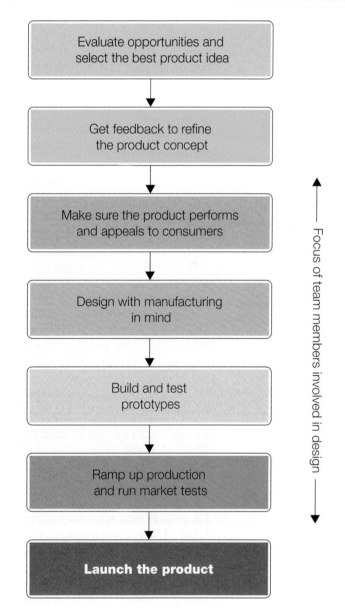

Evaluate opportunities and select the best product idea

↓

Get feedback to refine the product concept

↓

Make sure the product performs and appeals to consumers

↓

Design with manufacturing in mind

↓

Build and test prototypes

↓

Ramp up production and run market tests

↓

Launch the product

Focus of team members involved in design

Make Sure the Product Performs and Appeals to Consumers The team then decides how the product will be made, what components it will require, and how it will be assembled. It will decide if the product should be made in-house or outsourced to other companies. For products to be made in-house, the team determines where parts will be obtained. During this phase, team members are involved in design work to ensure that the product will be appealing, safe, and easy to use and maintain.

Design with Manufacturing in Mind As a rule, there's more than one way to make any product, and some methods are more expensive than others. During the next phase, therefore, the team focuses its attention on making a high-quality product at the lowest possible cost, working to minimize the number of parts and simplify the components. The goal is to build both quality and efficiency into the manufacturing process.

Build and Test Prototypes A prototype is a physical model of the product. In the next phase, prototypes are produced and tested in order to make sure that the product meets the customer needs that it's supposed to. The team usually begins with a preliminary prototype from which, based on feedback from potential customers, a more sophisticated model will then be developed. The process of building and testing prototypes will continue until the team feels comfortable that it's fashioned the best possible product. The final prototype will be extensively tested by customers in order to identify any changes that need to be made before the finished product is introduced.

Ramp Up Production and Run Market Tests During the production **ramp-up stage**, employees are trained in

manufacturing and assembly processes. Products turned out during this phase are carefully inspected for residual flaws. Samples are often demonstrated or given to potential customers for testing and feedback.

Launch the Product In the final stage, the firm starts ongoing production and makes the product available for widespread distribution.

Protecting Your Idea

Let's assume that you just came up with a fantastic product idea—say, a remote-controlled backpack that comes to you when you beep it. So now you don't have to go looking for your stuff every time you need to go to class. In fact, you don't even have to carry it—it will follow you to class like an electronic puppy dog. Naturally, you're enthusiastic about developing your product and eventually selling it to college students all over the world. But you're also afraid (justifiably so) that someone might steal your idea. What can you do?

Getting a Patent You can protect your rights to your idea with a **patent** from the U.S. Patent and Trademark Office, which grants you "the right to exclude others from making, using, offering for sale, or selling" the invention in the United States for 20 years.[18]

What do you need to know about applying for a patent? For one thing, document your idea as soon as you think of it. Simply fill out a form stating the purpose of your invention and the current date. Then sign it and get someone to witness it. The procedure sounds pretty informal, but you may need this document to strengthen your claim that you came up with the idea before someone else who also claims it. Later, you'll apply

formally for a patent by filling out an application (generally with the help of a lawyer), sending it to the U.S. Patent and Trademark Office, and waiting. Nothing moves very quickly through the U.S. Patent and Trademark Office, and it takes a long time for any application to get through the process.

Will your application get through at all? There's a good chance if your invention meets all of the following criteria:

- *It's new.* No one else can have known about it, used it, or written about it before you filed your patent application (so keep it to yourself until you've filed).

- *It's not obvious.* It has to be sufficiently different from everything that's been used for the purpose in the past (you can't patent a new color for a cell phone).

- *It has utility.* It can't be useless; it must have some value.

Applying for a U.S. patent is just the first step. If you plan to export your product outside the United States, you'll need patent protection in each country in which you plan to do business, and as you've no doubt guessed, getting a foreign patent isn't any easier than getting a U.S. patent. The process keeps lawyers busy: During a three-year period, PowerSki International had to take out more than 80 patents on the PowerSki Jetboard. It still has a long way to go to match the number of patents issued to some extremely large corporations. IBM, the world's patent leader, received more than 3,000 patents in 2002.[19]

Clearly, the patent business is booming. Worldwide, there are more than 4 million patents in force, and 700,000 applications are filed annually.[20] The U.S. Patent and Trademark Office issues about 90,000 patents a year—about 1 for every 33,000 residents.[21] One reason for the recent proliferation of patents is the high-tech boom: Over the last 10 years, the number of patents granted has more than doubled.

Applications keep pouring into the U.S. Patent and Trademark Office, creating a current backlog of more than 450,000 applica-

tions. The overworked office has been criticized not only for acting too slowly but for approving such useless inventions as diapers for pet birds. Despite its shortcomings, however, the U.S. patent system succeeds in performing its primary twofold task: encouraging innovation and providing inventors with temporary monopolies on their work.[22]

ABOUT NIKE   6.2

Now that you know something about the process of developing new products, take a moment to read about the product-development practices of Nike.

Go to www.exploringbusinessonline.com

OPERATIONS MANAGEMENT IN MANUFACTURING

Not surprisingly, the product development process can be complex and lengthy, often spanning many years. Developing the PowerSki Jetboard, for example, took 16 years and involved thousands of design changes. Moreover, having a product was just the beginning for PowerSki. The next step was developing a system that would produce high-quality Jetboards at reasonable prices. Before putting this system in place, PowerSki managers had to address several questions:

- What kind of production process should they use to make the Jetboards?

- How large should their production facilities be, and where should they be located?

- How should the plant be laid out?

- Should every component be made in-house, or should some be furnished by subcontractors?

- Where should they buy the materials they needed to build Jetboards?

- What systems would they need to ensure that production was as efficient as possible and that quality standards were maintained?

---

prototype
Physical model of a new product.

ramp-up stage
Stage in the product development process during which employees are trained in necessary production processes and new products are tested.

patent
Grant of the exclusive right to produce or sell a product, process, or invention.

Answering these questions helped PowerSki set up a manufacturing system through which it could accomplish the most important task that it had set for itself: producing quality Jetboards in an efficient manner.

Like PowerSki, all manufacturers set out to perform the same basic function: *to transform resources into finished goods*. To perform this function in today's business environment, manufacturers must continually strive to improve operational efficiency. They must fine-tune their production processes in order to focus on quality, to hold down the costs of materials and labor, and to eliminate all costs that don't add any value to the finished product. Making the decisions involved in the effort to attain these goals is the job of the operations manager. The responsibilities of the operations manager can be grouped as follows:

- *Production planning.* During production planning, managers determine how goods will be produced, where production will take place, and how manufacturing facilities will be laid out.

- *Production control.* Once the production process is under way, managers must continually schedule and monitor the activities that make up that process. They must solicit and respond to feedback and make adjustments where needed. At this stage, they also oversee the purchasing of raw materials and the handling of inventories.

- *Quality control.* Finally, the operations manager is directly involved in efforts to ensure that goods are produced according to specifications and that quality standards are maintained.

Let's take a closer look at each of these responsibilities.

Planning the Production Process

The decisions made in the planning stage have long-range implications and are crucial to a firm's success. Before making decisions about the operations process, managers must consider the goals set by marketing managers. Does the company intend to be a low-cost producer and to compete on the basis of price? Or does it plan to focus on quality and go after the high end of the market? Perhaps it wants to build a reputation for reliability. What if it intends to offer a wide range of products? To make things even more complicated, all of these deci-

sions involve trade-offs. Upholding a reputation for reliability isn't necessarily compatible with offering a wide range of products. Low cost doesn't normally go hand in hand with high quality.

With these factors in mind, let's look at the specific types of decisions that have to be made in the production planning process. We've divided these decisions into those dealing with production methods, site selection, facility layout, and components and materials management.

Production-Method Decisions The first step in production planning is deciding which type of production process is best for making the goods that your company intends to manufacture. In reaching this decision, you should answer such questions as the following:

- How much input do I receive from a particular customer prior to producing my goods?

- Am I making a one-of-a-kind good based solely on customer specifications, or am I producing high-volume standardized goods to be sold later?

- Do I offer customers the option of "customizing" an otherwise standardized good to meet their specific needs?

One way to appreciate the nature of this decision is by comparing three basic types of processes or methods: *make-to-order, mass production*, and *mass customization*. The task of the operations manager is to work with other managers, particularly marketers, to select the process that best serves the needs of the company's customers.

Make-to-Order At one time, most consumer goods, such as furniture and clothing, were made by individuals practicing various crafts. By their very nature, products were *customized* to meet the needs of the buyers who ordered them. This process, which is called a **make-to-order strategy**, is still commonly used by such businesses as print or sign shops that produce low-volume, high-variety goods according to customer specifications.

Mass Production By the early twentieth century, however, a new concept of producing goods had been introduced: **Mass production (or make-to-stock strategy)** is the practice of producing high volumes of identical goods at a cost low enough to price them for large numbers of customers. Goods are made in anticipation of future demand (based on forecasts) and kept in inventory for later sale. This approach is particularly appropriate for standardized goods ranging from processed foods to electronic appliances.

Mass Customization But there's a disadvantage to mass production: Customers, as one contemporary advertising slogan puts it, can't "have it their way": They have to accept standardized products as they come off assembly lines. Increasingly, however, customers are looking for products that are designed to accommodate individual tastes or needs but can still be bought at reasonable prices. To meet the demands of these consumers, many companies have turned to an approach called **mass customization**, which (as the term suggests) combines the advantages of customized products with those of mass production.

This approach requires that a company interact with the customer to find out exactly what the customer wants and then manufacture the good using efficient production methods to hold down costs. One efficient method is to mass-produce a product up to a certain cut-off point and then to customize it to satisfy different customers.

The list of companies devoting at least a portion of their operations to mass customization is growing steadily. Perhaps the best known mass customizer is Dell, which has achieved phenomenal success by allowing customers to configure their own personal computers. The Web has a lot to do with the growth of mass customization. Nike, for instance, now lets customers design their own athletic shoes on the firm's Web site. P&G offers made-to-order, personal-care products, such as shampoos and fragrances, and Mars, Inc. can make M&M's in any color the customer wants (say, school colors).

Naturally, mass customization doesn't work for all types of goods. Most people don't care about customized detergents or paper products. Many of us like the idea of customized clothes from Levi's or Lands' End but aren't willing to pay the higher prices they command.

Facilities Decisions After selecting the best production process, operations managers must then decide where the goods will be manufactured, how large the manufacturing facilities will be, and how those facilities will be laid out.

Site Selection In choosing a location, managers must consider several factors:

- In order to minimize shipping costs, both for raw materials coming into the plant and for finished goods going out, they often want to locate plants close to suppliers, customers, or both.
- They generally want to locate in areas with ample supplies of skilled workers.
- They naturally prefer locations where they and their families will enjoy living.
- They want locations where costs for resources and other expenses—land, labor, construction, utilities, and taxes—are low.

Do you want a computer made just for you according to your specifications? Dell can do this because the company uses mass customization. Your order is written up and sent to a component specialist (shown in the picture), who gathers the parts needed to make your computer and puts them in a plastic bin. The bin is sent to the assembly line where your computer is put together and gets its software. After testing to be sure it works perfectly, the computer designed just for you is packaged and shipped to you.

---

make-to-order strategy
Production method in which products are made to customer specification.

mass production (or make-to-stock strategy)
Production method in which high volumes of products are made at low cost and held in inventory in anticipation of future demand.

mass customization
Production method in which fairly high volumes of customized products are made at fairly low prices.

• They look for locations with a favorable business climate—one in which, for example, local governments might offer financial incentives (such as tax breaks) to entice them to do business in their locales.

They rarely find locations that meet all of these criteria. As a rule, they identify the most important criteria and aim at satisfying them. In deciding to locate in San Clemente, California, for instance, PowerSki was able to satisfy three important criteria: (1) proximity to the firm's suppliers, (2) availability of skilled engineers and technicians, and (3) favorable living conditions. These factors were more important than operating in a low-cost region or getting financial incentives from local government. Because PowerSki distributes its products throughout the world, proximity to customers was also unimportant.

Capacity Planning Now that you know *where* you're going to locate, you have to decide on the quantity of products that you'll produce. You begin by *forecasting* demand for your product. As we saw earlier in this chapter, forecasting isn't easy. In order to estimate the number of units that you're likely to sell over a given period of time, you have to understand the industry that you're in and estimate your likely share of the market by reviewing industry data and conducting other forms of research that we described earlier.

Once you've forecasted the demand for your product, you can calculate the **capacity** requirements of your production facility—the maximum number of goods that it can produce over a given period of time under normal working conditions. In turn, having calculated your capacity requirements, you're ready to determine how much investment in plant and equipment you'll have to make, as well as the number of labor hours required for the plant to produce at capacity.

Like forecasting, capacity planning is difficult. Unfortunately, failing to balance capacity and projected demand can be seriously detrimental to your bottom line. If you set capacity too low (and so produce less than you should), you won't be able to meet demand, and you'll lose sales and customers. If you set capacity too high (and turn out more units than you should), you'll waste resources and inflate operating costs.

Layout Planning The next step in production planning is deciding on plant **layout**—how equipment, machinery, and people will be arranged to make the production process as efficient as possible. In this section, we'll examine four common types of facility layouts: *process, product, cellular,* and *fixed position.*

The **process layout** groups together workers or departments which perform similar tasks. *Goods in process* (goods not yet finished) move from one workstation to another. At each position, workers use specialized equipment to perform a particular step in the production process. To better understand how this layout works, we'll look at the production process at the Vermont Teddy Bear Company. Let's say that you just placed an order for a personalized teddy bear—a "hiker bear" with khaki shorts, a white t-shirt with your name embroidered on it, faux-leather hiking boots, and a nylon backpack with sleeping bag. Your bear begins at the fur-cutting workstation, where its honey-brown "fur" coat is cut. It then moves to the stuffing and sewing workstation to get its insides and have its sides stitched together. Next, it moves to the dressing station, where it's outfitted with all the cool clothes and gear that you ordered. Finally, it winds up in the shipping station and starts its journey to your house. For a more colorful "Online Mini-Tour" of this process, log on to the Vermont Teddy Bear Web site (or see Figure 6.6).

Figure 6.6 ● **ACTIVE**

Process Layout at Vermont Teddy Bear Company

| **Fur-cutting** | **Stuffing and sewing** | **Dressing** | **Shipping** |

In a **product layout**, high-volume goods are produced efficiently by people, equipment, or departments arranged in an *assembly line*—that is, a series of workstations at which already made parts are *assembled*. Just Born, a candy maker located in Bethlehem, Pennsylvania, makes a product called Marshmallow Peeps on an assembly line. First, the ingredients are combined and whipped in huge kettles. Then, sugar is added for color. At the next workstation, the mixture—colored warm marshmallow—is poured into baby-chick–shaped molds carried on conveyor belts. The conveyor-belt parade of candy pieces then moves forward to stations where workers add eyes or other details. When the finished candy reaches the packaging area, it's wrapped for shipment to stores around the world. To take an online tour of the marshmallow peeps production process, log on to the Just Born Web site (or see Figure 6.7).

Both product and process layouts arrange work by *function*. At the Vermont Teddy Bear Company, for example, the cutting function is performed in one place, the stuffing-and-sewing function in another place, and the dressing function in a third place. If you're a cutter, you cut all day; if you're a sewer, you sew all day: That's your function. The same is true for the production of marshmallow peeps at Just Born: If your function is to decorate peeps, you stand on an assembly-line and decorate all day; if your function is packing, you pack all day.

Arranging work by function, however, isn't always efficient. Production lines can back up, inventories can build up, workers can get bored with repetitive jobs, and time can be wasted in transporting goods from one workstation to another. In order to counter some of these problems, many manufacturers have adopted a **cellular layout**, in which small teams of workers handle all aspects of building a component, a "family" of components, or even a finished product. Each team works in a small area equipped with everything that it needs to function as a self-contained unit. Machines are sometimes configured in a *U*-shape, with people working inside the *U*. Because team members often share duties, they're trained to perform several different jobs. Teams monitor both the quantity and quality of their own output. This arrangement often results in faster completion time, lower inventory levels, improved quality, and better employee morale. Cellular manufacturing is used by large manufacturers, such as Boeing, Raytheon, and Pratt & Whitney, as well as by small companies, such as Little Enterprise, which makes components for robots.[23] Figure 6.8 (page 146) illustrates a typical cellular layout.

It's easy to move teddy bears and marshmallow candies around the factory while you're making them, but what about airplanes or ships? In producing large items, manufacturers use **fixed-position layouts** in which the product stays in one place and the workers (and equipment) go to the product.

Figure 6.7   ACTIVE

Product Layout at Just Born, Inc.

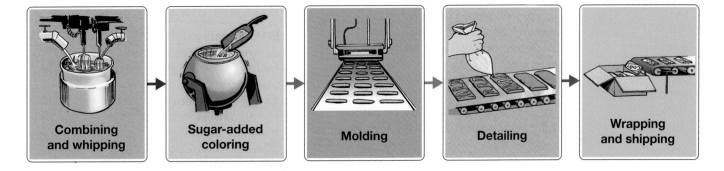

| **Combining and whipping** | **Sugar-added coloring** | **Molding** | **Detailing** | **Wrapping and shipping** |

---

capacity
Maximum number of products that a facility can produce over a given period of time under normal working conditions.

layout
Arrangement in a facility of equipment, machinery, and people to make a production process as efficient as possible.

process layout
Layout that groups together workers or departments who perform similar tasks.

product layout
Layout in which products are produced by people, equipment, or departments arranged in an assembly line.

cellular layout
Layout in which teams of workers perform all the tasks involved in building a component, group of related components, or finished product.

fixed-position layout
Layout in which workers are moved to the product, which stays in one place.

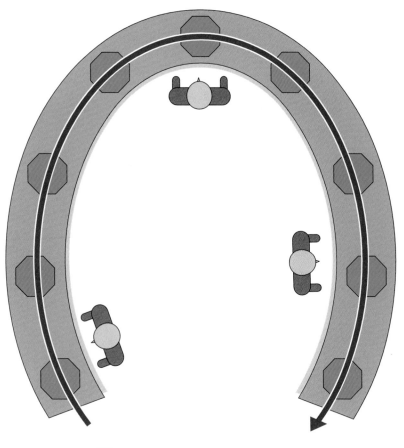

 Task in the manufacturing process

 Employee

 Work flow

Figure 6.8 ACTIVE

Cellular Layout

This is the arrangement used by General Housing Corporation in constructing modular homes. Each house is constructed at the company's factory in Bay City, Michigan, according to the customer's design. Because carpenters, electricians, plumbers, and others work on each building inside the climate-controlled factory, the process can't be hindered by weather. Once it's done, the house is transported in modules to the owner's building site and set up in one day. For a closer view of General Housing Corporation's production process, go to the General Housing Web site.

QUICK QUIZ   6.2

Before going on to the next sections of this chapter—which cover managing production processes and technology, operations planning, and quality management—give yourself a quick quiz on what you've learned about the principles of operations management.

Go to www.exploringbusinessonline.com

Managing the Production Process

Once the production process is in place, the attention of the operations manager shifts to the daily activities of **materials management**, which encompass the following activities: *purchasing, inventory control*, and *work scheduling*.

Purchasing and Supplier Selection

The process of acquiring the materials and services to be used in production is called **purchasing** (or *procurement*). For many products, the costs of materials make up about 50 percent of total manufacturing costs. Not surprisingly, then, materials acquisition gets a good deal of the operations manager's time and attention.

As a rule, there's no shortage of vendors willing to supply parts and other materials, but the trick is finding the *best* suppliers. In selecting a supplier, operations managers must consider such questions as the following:

- Can the vendor supply the needed quantity of materials at a reasonable price?
- Is the quality good?
- Is the vendor reliable (will materials be delivered on time)?
- Does the vendor have a favorable reputation?
- Is the company easy to work with?

Getting the answers to these questions and making the right choices—a process known as *supplier selection*—is a key responsibility of operations management.

E-Purchasing Technology is changing the way businesses buy things. Through *e-purchasing* (or *e-procurement*), companies use the Internet to interact with suppliers. The process is similar to the one you'd use to find a consumer good—say, a 42-inch plasma high-definition TV—over the Internet. You might start by browsing the Web sites of TV manufacturers, such as Sony or Toshiba, or electronics retailers, such as Circuit City or Best Buy. To gather comparative prices, you might go to a comparison-shopping Web site, such as MySimon.com, which displays information on hundreds of brands and models. You might even consider placing a bid on eBay, an online marketplace where sellers and buyers come together to do business through auctions. Once you've decided where to buy your TV, you'd complete your transaction online, even paying for it electronically.

If you were a purchasing manager using the Internet to buy parts and supplies, you'd follow basically the same process. You'd identify potential suppliers by going directly to private Web sites maintained by individual suppliers or to public Web sites that collect information on numerous suppliers. You could do your shopping through online catalogs or you might participate in an online marketplace by indicating the type and quantity of materials you need and letting suppliers bid on prices. (Some of these online marketplaces are quite large. Covisint, for example, which was started by automakers to coordinate online transactions in the auto industry, is used by nearly 100,000 suppliers.) Finally, just as you paid for your TV electronically, you could use a system called **electronic data interchange (EDI)** to process your transactions and transmit all your purchasing documents.

The Internet provides an additional benefit to purchasing managers by helping them communicate with suppliers and potential suppliers. They can use the Internet to give suppliers specifications for parts and supplies, encourage them to bid on future materials needs, alert them to changes in requirements, and give them instructions on doing business with their employers. Using the Internet for business purchasing cuts the costs of purchased products and saves administrative costs related to transactions. And it's faster for procurement and fosters better communications.

Inventory Control If a manufacturer runs out of the materials it needs for production, production stops. In the past, many companies guarded against this possibility by keeping large inventories of materials on hand. It seemed like the thing to do at the time, but it often introduced a

new problem—wasting money. Companies were paying for parts and other materials that they wouldn't use for weeks or even months, and in the meantime, they were running up substantial storage and insurance costs.

Most manufacturers have since learned that to remain competitive, they need to manage inventories more efficiently. This task requires that they strike a balance between two threats to productivity: losing production time because they've run out of materials and wasting money because they're carrying too much inventory. The process of striking this balance is called **inventory control**, and companies now regularly rely on a variety of inventory-control methods.

Just-in-Time Production One method is called **just-in-time (JIT) production**: The manufacturer arranges for materials to arrive at production facilities *just in time* to enter the manufacturing process. Parts and materials don't go unused for long periods of time, and the costs of "holding" inventory are significantly cut. JIT requires considerable communication and cooperation between the manufacturer and the supplier. The manufacturer has to know what it needs and when. The supplier has to commit to supplying the right materials, of the right quality, at exactly the right time.

Material Requirements Planning
Another method, called **material requirements planning (MRP)**, relies on a computerized program to calculate the quantity of materials needed for production and to determine when they should be ordered or made. Let's say, for example, that you and several classmates are planning a fund-raising dinner for the local animal shelter. First, you estimate how many people will attend—say, 50. Next, you plan the menu—lasagna, garlic bread, salad, and cookies. Then, you determine what ingredients you'll need to make the food.

materials management
All decisions pertaining to the purchase of inputs, the inventory of components and finished products, and the scheduling of production processes.

purchasing
Process of acquiring materials and services to be used in production.

electronic data interchange (EDI)
Computerized exchange of business transaction documents.

inventory control
Management of inventory to ensure that a company has enough inventory to keep operations flowing smoothly but not so much that money is being wasted in holding it.

just-in-time production
System for reducing inventories and costs by requiring suppliers to deliver materials *just in time* to go into the production process.

material requirements planning (MRP)
Technique of using a computerized program to calculate the quantity of materials needed for production and to reschedule inventory ordering.

Next, you have to decide when you'll need your ingredients. You don't want to make everything on the afternoon of the dinner; some things—like the lasagna and cookies—can be made ahead of time. Nor do you want to buy all your ingredients at the same time; in particular, the salad ingredients would go bad if purchased too far in advance. Once you've made all these calculations and decisions, you work out a schedule for the production of your dinner that indicates the order and timing of every activity involved. With your schedule in hand, you can determine when to buy each ingredient. Finally, you do your shopping.

Although the production process at most manufacturing companies is a lot more complex than planning a dinner (even for 50 people), an MRP system is designed to handle similar problems. The program generates a production schedule based on estimated output (your food-preparation timetable for 50 guests), prepares a list of needed materials (your shopping list), and orders the materials (goes shopping).

The basic MRP focuses on material planning, but there's a more sophisticated system—called **manufacturing resource planning (MRP II)**—that goes beyond material planning to help monitor resources in all areas of the company. Such a program can, for instance, coordinate the production schedule with HR managers' forecasts for needed labor.

Work Scheduling As we've seen, manufacturers make profits by transforming inputs (materials and other resources) into outputs (finished goods). We know, too, that production activities, like all business activities, have to be *controlled*: They have to be monitored to ensure that actual performance satisfies planned performance. In production, the control process starts when operations managers decide not only *which* goods and *how many* will be produced, but *when*. This detailed information goes into a **master production schedule (MPS)**. In order to draw up an MPS, managers need to know where materials are located and headed at every step in the production process. For this purpose, they determine the *routing* of all materials—that is, the work flow of each item based on the sequence of operations in which it will be used.

Because they also need to control the timing of all operations, managers set up *schedules*: They select jobs to be performed during the production process, assign tasks to work groups, set timetables for the completion of tasks, and make sure that resources will be available when and where they're needed. There are a number of scheduling techniques. We'll focus on two of the most common—*Gantt* and *PERT charts*.

Gantt Charts A **Gantt chart** is an easy-to-use graphical tool that helps operations managers determine the status of projects. Let's say that you're in charge of making the "hiking bear" that we ordered earlier from the Vermont Teddy Bear Company. Figure 6.9 is a Gantt chart for the production of 100 of these bears. As you can see, it shows that several activities must be completed before the bears are dressed: The fur has to be cut, stuffed, and sewn, and the clothes and accessories must be made. Our Gantt chart tells us that by day 6, all accessories and clothing have been made. The stuffing and sewing, however (which must be finished before the bears are dressed), is not scheduled for completion until the end of day 8. As operations manager, you'll have to pay close attention to the progress of the stuffing and sewing operations in order to assure that finished products are ready for shipment by their scheduled date.

PERT Charts Gantt charts are useful when the production process is fairly simple and the activities are not interrelated. For more

Figure 6.9

Gantt Chart for Vermont Teddy Bear

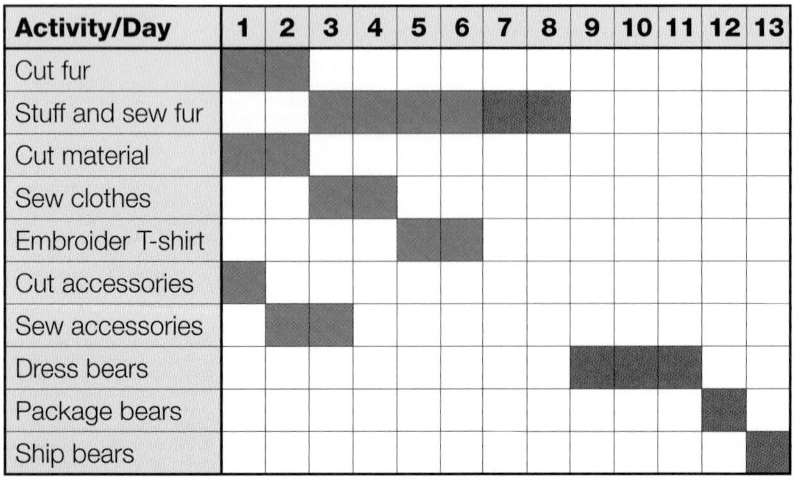

Activity/Day	1	2	3	4	5	6	7	8	9	10	11	12	13
Cut fur	■	■											
Stuff and sew fur			■	■	■	■	■	■					
Cut material	■												
Sew clothes			■	■									
Embroider T-shirt					■								
Cut accessories	■												
Sew accessories		■	■										
Dress bears									■	■	■		
Package bears												■	
Ship bears													■

Lot size: 100 bears

All activities are scheduled to begin at their earliest start time.

■ Completed work

■ Work to be completed

complex schedules, operations managers may use **PERT charts**. PERT (which stands for *Program Evaluation and Review Technique*) is designed to diagram the activities required to produce a good, specify the time required to perform each activity in the process, and organize activities in the most efficient sequence. It also identifies a *critical path*: The sequence of activities that will entail the greatest amount of time. Figure 6.10 is a PERT diagram showing the same process for producing one "hiker" bear at Vermont Teddy Bear.

Our PERT chart shows how the activities involved in making a single bear are related. It indicates that the production process begins at the cutting station. Next, the fur that's been cut for this particular bear moves first to the stuffing and sewing station and then to the dressing station. At the same time that its fur is moving through this sequence of steps, the bear's clothes are being cut and sewn and its t-shirt embroidered. Its backpack and tent accessories are

also being made at the same time. Note that fur, clothes, and accessories all meet at the dressing station, where the bear is dressed and outfitted with its backpack. Finally, the finished bear is packaged and shipped to the customer's house.

What was the critical path in this process? The path that took the longest amount of time was the sequence that included cutting, stuffing, dressing, packaging, and shipping—a sequence of steps taking 65 minutes. If you wanted to produce a bear more quickly, you'd have to save time on this path. Even if you saved the time on any of the other paths—say, the sequence of steps involved in cutting, sewing, and embroidering the bear's clothes—you still wouldn't finish the whole job any sooner: The finished clothes would just have to wait for the fur to be stuffed and sewn and moved to the dressing station. In other words, we can gain efficiency only by improving our performance on one or more of the activities along the critical path.

Figure 6.10   ACTIVE

PERT Chart for Vermont Teddy Bear

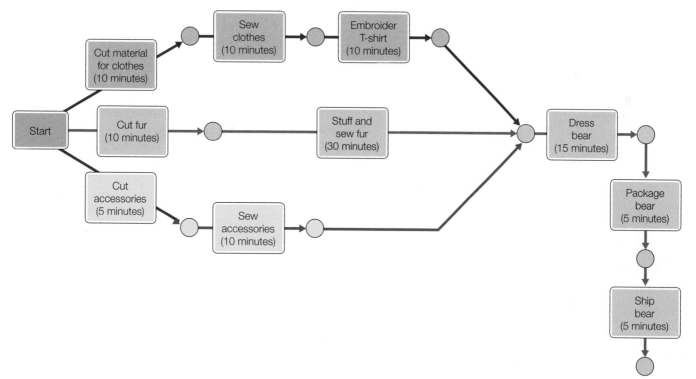

manufacturing resource planning (MRP II)
System for coordinating a firm's material requirements planning activities with the activities of its other functional areas.

master production schedule (MPS)
Timetable that specifies which and how many products will be produced and when.

Gantt chart
Graphical tool for determining the status of projects.

PERT chart
Tool for diagramming the activities required to produce a product, specifying the time required to perform each activity in the process, and organizing activities in the most efficient sequence.

The Technology of Goods Production

PowerSki founder and CEO Bob Montgomery spent 16 years designing the Jetboard and bringing it to production. At one point, in his efforts to get the design just right, he'd constructed 30 different prototypes. Needless to say, this process took a very long time, but even so, Montgomery thought that he could handle the designing of the engine without the aid of a computer. Before long, however, he realized that it was impossible to keep track of all the changes.

Computer-Aided Design That's when Montgomery turned to computer technology for help and began using a **computer-aided design (CAD)** software package to design not only the engine but the board itself and many of its components. The CAD program also allowed Montgomery and his team of engineers to test the product digitally and work out design problems before moving to the prototype stage.

The sophisticated CAD software allowed Montgomery and his team to put their design paper in a drawer and to start building both the board and engine on a computer screen. By rotating the image on the screen, they could even view the design from every angle. Having used their CAD program to make more than 400 design changes, they were ready to test the Jetboard in the water. During the tests, onboard sensors transmitted data to portable computers, allowing the team to make adjustments from the shore while the prototype was still in the water. Nowadays, PowerSki uses *collaboration software* to transmit design changes to the suppliers of the 340 components that make up the Jetboard.

Computer-Aided Manufacturing For many companies, the next step is to link CAD to the manufacturing process. A **computer-aided manufacturing (CAM)** software system determines the steps needed to produce the component and instructs the machines that do the work. Because CAD and CAM programs can talk with each other, companies can build components that satisfy exactly the requirements set by the computer-generated model. CAD/CAM systems permit companies to design and manufacture goods faster, more efficiently, and at a lower cost, and they are also effective in helping firms monitor and improve quality. CAD/CAM technology is used in many industries, including the auto industry, electronics, and clothing.

Computer-Integrated Manufacturing By automating and integrating all aspects of a company's operations, **computer-integrated manufacturing (CIM)** systems have taken the integration of computer-aided design and manufacturing to a higher level—and are in fact revolutionizing the production process. CIM systems expand the capabilities of CAD/CAM. In addition to design and production applications, they handle such functions as order entry, inventory control, warehousing, and shipping. In the manufacturing plant, the CIM system controls the functions of **industrial robots**—computer-controlled machines used to perform repetitive tasks that are also hard or dangerous for human workers.

Flexible Manufacturing Systems Finally, a CIM system is a common element in **flexible manufacturing systems (FMS)**, in which computer-controlled equipment can easily be adapted to produce a variety of goods. An FMS has immense advantages over traditional production lines in which machines are set up to produce only one type of good. When the firm needs to switch a production line to manufacture a new product, substantial time and money are often spent in modifying equipment. An FMS makes it possible to change equipment setups by reprogramming computer-controlled machines. Such flexibility is particularly valuable to companies that produce customized products.

OPERATIONS MANAGEMENT FOR SERVICE PROVIDERS

As the U.S. economy has changed from a goods producer to a service provider, the predominance of the manufacturing sector has declined substantially over the last 50 years. Today, only about 12 percent of U.S. workers are employed in manufacturing.[24] Most of us now hold jobs in the service sector, which accounts for 77 percent of U.S. gross domestic product.[25] Wal-Mart is now America's largest employer, followed by McDonalds and United Parcel Service (UPS). Not until we drop down to the fourth-largest employer—General Motors—do we find a manufacturing company.

Although the primary function of both manufacturers and service providers is to satisfy customer needs, there are several important differences between the two types of operations. Let's focus on three of them:

- *Intangibility.* Manufacturers produce tangible products—things that can be touched or handled, such as automobiles and appliances. Service companies provide intangible products, such as banking, entertainment, or education.

- *Customization.* Manufactured goods are generally standardized; one 12-ounce bottle of Pepsi is the same as any other 12-ounce bottle of Pepsi. Services, on the other hand, are often customized to satisfy the specific needs of a customer. When you go to the barber or the hairdresser, you ask for a haircut that looks good on you because of the shape of your face and the texture of your hair. When you go to the dentist, you ask him or her to fill or pull the tooth that's bothering you.

- *Customer Contact.* You could spend your whole working life assembling cars in Detroit and never meet a customer who bought a car that you helped to make. But if you were a waitress, you'd interact with customers every day. In fact, their satisfaction with your product would be determined in part by the service that you provided. Unlike manufactured goods, many services are bought and consumed at the same time.

Not surprisingly, operational efficiency is just as important in service industries as it is in manufacturing. To get a better idea of the role of operations management in the service sector, we'll look closely at Burger King (BK), home of the Whopper and the world's second-largest restaurant chain. BK has grown substantially since selling the first

Whopper (for $0.37) almost 50 years ago. The instant success of the fire-grilled burger encouraged the Miami founders of the company to expand by selling franchises. Today, there are 11,200 BK restaurants in 58 countries, and they employ 350,000 people. Almost 8 million customers visit BK each day, generating annual worldwide revenues of $11 billion.

Operations Planning

When starting or expanding operations, businesses in the service sector must make a number of decisions quite similar to those made by manufacturers:

- What services (and perhaps what goods) should they offer?

- How will they provide these services?

- Where will they locate their business, and what will their facilities look like?

- How will they forecast demand for their services?

Let's see how service firms like BK answer questions such as these.[26]

Operations Processes Service organizations succeed by providing services that satisfy customers' needs. Companies that provide transportation, such as airlines, have to get customers to their destinations as quickly and safely as possible. Companies that deliver packages, such as FedEx, must pick up, sort, and deliver packages in a timely manner. Colleges must provide quality educations. Companies that provide both services and goods, such as Domino's Pizza, have a dual challenge: They have to produce a quality good and deliver it satisfactorily.

Service providers who produce goods can, like manufacturers, adopt either a *make-to-order* or *make-to-stock* approach to manufacturing them. BK, which encourages patrons to customize burgers and other menu items, uses a make-to-order approach. BK can customize products because it builds

---

computer-aided design (CAD)
System using computer technology to create models representing the design of a product.

computer-aided manufacturing (CAM)
System using computer technology to control production processes and equipment.

computer-integrated manufacturing (CIM)
System in which the capabilities of a CAD/CAM system are integrated with other computer-based functions.

industrial robot
Computer-controlled machine used to perform repetitive tasks that are also hard or dangerous for human workers.

flexible manufacturing system (FMS)
System in which computer-controlled equipment is programmed to handle materials used in manufacturing.

Burger King's famous ad slogan, "Have it your way," encourages customers to order burgers exactly as they want them. Because Burger King's burgers are made from scratch using a make-to-order approach, special requests can be filled quickly.

sandwiches one at a time rather than batch-process them. Meat patties, for example, go from the grill to a steamer for holding until an order comes in. Then the patty is pulled from the steamer and requested condiments added. Finally, the completed sandwich chutes to a counter worker, who gives it to the customer. In contrast, many of BK's competitors, including McDonald's, rely on a make-to-stock approach in which a number of sandwiches are made at the same time with the same condiments. If a customer wants, say, a hamburger without onions, he or she has to wait for a new batch of patties to be grilled. The procedure could take up to five minutes, whereas BK can process a special order in 30 seconds.

Like manufacturers, service providers must continuously look for ways to improve operational efficiency. Throughout its 50-year history, BK has introduced a number of innovations that have helped make the company (as well as the fast-food industry) more efficient. BK, for example, was the first to offer drive-through service (which now accounts for 58 percent of its sales).

It was also a BK vice president, David Sell, who came up with the idea of moving the drink station from behind the counter so that customers could take over the time-consuming task of filling cups with ice and beverages. BK was able to cut back one employee per day at every one of its 11,000 restaurants. Material costs also went down because customers usually fill cups with more ice, which is cheaper than a beverage. Moreover, there were savings on supply costs because most customers don't bother with lids, and many don't use straws. On top of everything else, most customers liked the system (for one thing, it allowed them to customize their own drinks by mixing beverages), and as a result, customer satisfaction went up as well. Overall, the new process was a major success and quickly became the industry standard.

Facilities When starting or expanding a service business, owners and managers must invest a lot of time in selecting a location, determining its size and layout, and forecasting demand. A poor location or badly designed facility can cost customers, and inaccurate estimates of demand for products can result in poor service, excessive costs, or both.

Site Selection People in the real estate industry often say that the three most important factors to consider when you're buying a home are location, location, location. The same principle applies when you're trying to locate a service business. To be successful in a service industry, you need to be accessible to your customers. Some service businesses, such as cable-TV providers, package-delivery services, and e-retailers go to their customers. Many others, however—hotels, restaurants, stores, hospitals, and airports—have to attract customers to their facilities. These businesses must locate where there's a high volume of available customers. Let's see how BK decides where to place a restaurant.

"Through the light and to the right." This is a favorite catch phrase among BK planners who are looking for a promising spot for a new restaurant (at least in the United States). In picking a location, BK planners perform a detailed analysis of demographics and traffic patterns, but the most important factor is usually *traffic count*—the number of cars or people that pass by a specific location in the course of a day. In the United States, where we travel almost everywhere by car, BK looks for busy intersections, interstate interchanges with easy off and on ramps, or such "primary destinations" as shopping malls, tourist attractions, downtown business areas, or movie theaters. In Europe, where public transportation is much more common, planners focus on subway, train, bus, and trolley stops.

Once they've found a site with an acceptable traffic count, they apply other criteria. It must, for example, be easy for vehicles to enter and exit the site, which must also provide enough parking to handle projected business. Local zoning must permit standard signage, especially along interstate highways. Finally, expected business must be high enough to justify the cost of the land and building.

Size and Layout Because manufacturers do business out of plants rarely visited by customers, the size and layout of their facilities are based solely on production needs. In the service sector, however, most businesses must design their facilities with the customer in mind: They must accommodate the needs of their customers while keeping costs as low as possible. Performing this twofold task isn't easy. Let's see how BK has met the challenge.

For its first 30 years, almost all BK restaurants were pretty much the same. They all sat on one acre of land (located through the light and to the right), had about 4,000 square feet of space, and held seating for 70 customers. All kitchens were roughly the same size. As long as land was cheap and sites were readily available, this system worked well enough. By the early 1990s, however, most of the prime sites had been taken, if not by BK itself, then by one of its fast-food competitors or other business needing a choice spot, including gas stations and video stores. With everyone bidding on the same sites, the cost of a prime acre of land had increased from $100,000 to over $1,000,000 in just a few short years.

In order to continue growing, BK needed to change the way it found and developed its locations. Planners decided that they had to find ways to reduce the size of a typical BK restaurant. For one thing, they could reduce the number of seats because the business at a typical outlet had shifted over time from 90 percent inside dining and 10 percent drive-through to a fifty-fifty split. BK customers tended to be in a hurry, and more customers preferred the convenience of drive-through "dining."

David Sell (the same executive who had recommended letting customers fill their own drink cups) proposed to save space by wrapping Whoppers in paper instead of serving them in the cardboard boxes that took up too much space in the back room of every restaurant. So BK switched to a single paper wrapper with the label "Whopper" on one side and "Cheese Whopper" on the other. To show which product was inside, employees just folded the wrapper in the right direction. Ultimately, BK replaced pallets piled high with boxes with a few boxes full of wrappers.

Ideas like these helped BK trim the size of a restaurant from 4,000 square feet to as little as 1,000 square feet. In turn, smaller facilities enabled the company to enter markets that were once cost prohibitive. Now BK could locate profitably in airports, food courts, strip malls, center-city areas, and even schools. The company even designed 10-foot-by-10-foot kiosks that could be transported to special events, stadiums, and concerts.

Capacity Planning Estimating capacity needs for a service business isn't the same thing as estimating those of a manufacturer. A manufacturer can predict overall demand, produce the product, store it in inventory, and ship it to a customer when it's ordered. Service providers, however, can't store their products for later use: Hairdressers can't "inventory" haircuts, hospitals can't "inventory" operations, and amusement parks can't "inventory" roller-coaster rides. Service firms have to build sufficient capacity to satisfy customers' needs on an "as-demanded" basis. Like manufacturers, service providers have to consider many variables when estimating demand and capacity:

- How many customers will I have?

- When will they want my services (which days of the week, which times of day)?

- How long will it take to serve each customer?

- How will external factors, such as weather or holidays, affect the demand for my services?

Forecasting demand is easier for companies like BK, which has a long history of planning facilities, than for brand-new service businesses. BK can predict sales for a new restaurant by combining its knowledge of customer-service patterns at existing restaurants with information collected about each new location, including the number of cars or people passing the proposed site and the effect of nearby competition.

Managing Operations

Overseeing a service organization puts special demands on managers, especially those running firms, such as hotels, retail stores, and restaurants, that have a high degree of contact with customers. Service firms provide customers with personal attention and must satisfy their needs in a timely manner. This task is complicated by the fact that demand can vary greatly over the course of any given day. Managers, therefore, must pay particular attention to employee work schedules and (in some cases) inventory management. Let's see how BK deals with these problems.

Scheduling In manufacturing, managers focus on scheduling the *activities* needed to transform raw materials into finished goods. In service organizations, they focus on scheduling *workers* so that they're available to handle fluctuating customer demand. Each week, therefore, every BK store manager schedules employees to cover not only the peak periods of breakfast, lunch, and dinner, but also the slower periods in between. If he or she staffs too many people, labor cost per sales dollar will be too high. If there aren't enough employees, customers have to wait in lines. Some get discouraged, and even leave, and many may never come back.

Scheduling is made easier by information provided by a point-of-sale device built into every BK cash register. The register keeps track of every sandwich, beverage, and side order sold by the hour, every hour of the day, every day of the week. Thus, to determine how many people will be needed for next Thursday's lunch hour, the manager reviews last Thursday's data, using sales revenue and a specific BK formula to determine the appropriate staffing level. Each manager can adjust this forecast to account for other factors, such as current marketing promotions or a local sporting event that will increase customer traffic.

Inventory Control Businesses that provide both goods and services, such as retail stores, and auto-repair shops, have the same inventory-control problems as manufacturers:

Keeping levels too high costs money, while running out of inventory costs sales. Technology, such as the point-of-sale registers used at BK, makes the job easier. BK's system tracks everything sold during a given period of time and lets each store manager know how much of everything should be kept in inventory. It also makes it possible to count the number of burgers and buns, bags and racks of fries, and boxes of beverage mixes at the beginning or end of each shift. Because there are fixed numbers of supplies—say, beef patties or bags of fries—in each box, employees simply count boxes and multiply. In just a few minutes, the manager knows whether the inventory is correct (and should be able to see if any theft has occurred on the shift).

PRODUCING FOR QUALITY

What do you do if you get it home and your brand-new DVD player doesn't work? What if you were late for class because it took you 20 minutes to get a burger and order of fries at the drive-through window of a fast-food restaurant? Like most people, you'd probably be more or less disgruntled. As a customer, you're constantly assured that when products make it to market, they're of the highest possible quality, and you tend to avoid brands that have failed to live up to your expectations or to producers' claims. You're told that workers in such businesses as restaurants are there to serve you, and you probably don't go back to establishments where you've received poor-quality service.

But what is *quality*? According to the American Society for Quality, **quality** refers to "the totality of features and characteristics of a product or service that bear on its ability to satisfy stated or implied needs." When you buy a DVD player, you expect it to play DVDs. When it doesn't, you question its quality. When you go to a drive-through window, you expect to be served in a reasonable amount of time. If you're forced to sit and wait, you conclude that you're the victim of poor-quality service.

Quality Management

To compete today, companies must deliver quality goods and services that satisfy customers' needs. This is the objective of quality management. **Total quality management (TQM)**, or **quality assurance**, includes all the steps that a company takes to ensure that its goods or services are of sufficiently high quality to meet customers' needs. Generally speaking, a company adheres to TQM principles by focusing on three tasks:

1. Customer satisfaction
2. Employee involvement
3. Continuous improvement

Let's take a closer look at these three principles.

Customer Satisfaction Companies that are committed to TQM understand that the purpose of a business is to generate a profit by satisfying customer needs. Thus, they let their customers define *quality* by identifying and offering those product features that satisfy customer needs. They encourage customers to tell them how to make the right products, both goods and services, that work the right way.

Armed with this knowledge, they take steps to make sure that providing quality is a factor in every facet of their operations—from design, to product planning and control, to sales and service. To get feedback on how well they're doing, many companies routinely use surveys and other methods to monitor customer satisfaction. By tracking the results of feedback over time, they can see where they need to improve.

Employee Involvement Successful TQM requires that everyone in the organization, not just upper-level management, commits to satisfying the customer. When customers wait too long at a drive-through window, it's the responsibility of a number of employees, not just the manager. A defective DVD isn't solely the responsibility of the manufacturer's quality control department; it's the responsibility of every employee involved in its design, production, and even shipping. To get everyone involved in the drive for quality assurance, managers must communicate the importance of quality to subordinates and motivate them to focus on

customer satisfaction. Employees have to be properly trained not only to do their jobs, but to detect and correct quality problems.

In many companies, employees who perform similar jobs work as teams, sometimes called **quality circles**, to identify quality, efficiency, and other work-related problems, to propose solutions, and to work with management in implementing their recommendations.

Continuous Improvement An integral part of TQM is **continuous improvement**: the commitment to making constant improvements in the design, production, and delivery of goods and services. Improvements can almost always be made to increase efficiency, reduce costs, and improve customer service and satisfaction. Everyone in the organization is constantly on the lookout for ways to do things better.

Statistical Process Control Companies can use a variety of tools to identify areas for improvement. A common approach in manufacturing is called **statistical process control (SPC)**. This technique monitors production quality by testing a sample of output to see if goods in process are being made according to predetermined specifications.

Assume for a moment that you work for Kellogg's, the maker of Raisin Bran cereal. You know that it's the company's goal to pack two scoops of raisins in every box of cereal. How can you test to determine whether this goal is being met? You could use an SPC method called a *sampling distribution*. On a periodic basis, you would take a box of cereal off the production line and measure the amount of raisins in the box. Then you'd record that amount on a *control chart* designed to compare actual quantities of raisins with the desired quantity (two scoops). If your chart shows that several samples in a row are low on raisins, you'd shut down the production line and take corrective action.

Benchmarking Sometimes it also helps to look outside the organization for ideas on how to improve operations and to learn how

---

quality
Ability of a product to satisfy customer needs.

total quality management (TQM) (or quality assurance)
All the steps taken by a company to ensure that its products satisfy customer needs.

quality circle
Employees who perform similar jobs and work as teams to identify quality, efficiency, and other work-related problems, to propose solutions, and to work with management in implementing their recommendations.

continuous improvement
Company's commitment to making constant improvements in the design, production, and delivery of its products.

statistical process control (SPC)
Technique for monitoring production quality by testing sample outputs to ensure that they meet specifications.

your company compares with others. Companies routinely use **benchmarking** to compare their performance on a number of dimensions with the performance of other companies who excel in particular areas. Frequent benchmark targets include L.L. Bean, for its superior performance in filling orders, 3M for its record of introducing innovative products, Motorola for its success in maintaining consistent quality standards, and Mary Kay Cosmetics for its skills in inventory control.[27]

International Quality Standards

As a consumer, wouldn't you like to know which companies ensure that their products meet quality specifications? Some of us would like to know which companies take steps to protect the environment. Some consumers want to know which companies continuously improve their performance in both of these areas—that is, practice quality and environmental management. By the same token, if you were a company doing a good job in these areas, wouldn't you want potential customers to know? It might be worth your while to find out if your suppliers were being conscientious in these areas—and even your suppliers' suppliers.

ISO 9000 and ISO 14000 Through the International Organization for Standardization, a nongovernmental agency based in

Switzerland, it's possible to find this kind of information. The resources of this organization will allow you to identify those organizations that have people and processes in place for delivering products that satisfy customers' quality requirements. You can also find out which organizations work to reduce the negative impact of their activities on the environment. Working with representatives from various countries, the organization has established the **ISO 9000** family of international standards for quality management and the **ISO 14000** family of international standards for environmental management.

ISO standards focus on the way a company does its work, not on its output (although there's certainly a strong relationship between the way in which a business functions and the quality of its products). Compliance with ISO standards is voluntary, and the certification process is time consuming and complex. Even so, 610,000 organizations in 160 countries are ISO 9000 and ISO 14000 certified.[28] ISO certification has become an internationally recognized symbol of quality management and is almost essential to be competitive in the global marketplace.

OUTSOURCING

The company's Web site states that "Power-Ski International has been founded to bring a new watercraft, the PowerSki Jetboard, and the engine technology behind it, to market." That goal was reached in May 2003, when the firm emerged from a lengthy design period. Having already garnered praise for its innovative product, PowerSki was ready to begin mass-producing Jetboards. At this juncture, the management team made a strategic decision that's not uncommon in manufacturing today. Rather than producing Jetboards in-house, they opted for **outsourcing**: having outside vendors manufacture the actual product. This decision doesn't mean that the company relinquished control over quality: Every component that goes into the PowerSki Jetboard is manufactured to exact specifications set by PowerSki.

Outsourcing in the Manufacturing Sector
One advantage of outsourcing its production function is that the management team can devote its attention to refining its

PowerSki Jetboards are assembled at the company's San Clemente, California, facilities using subcontracted components. Outsourcing its engines to a Korean engine manufacturer and its hulls to a fiberglass manufacturer with a factory in Mexico enables PowerSki to reduce the cost of producing each Jetboard through manufacturing efficiencies and lower labor costs. All components that go into the Jetboard are made to PowerSki's specifications and are inspected upon arrival to ensure that they meet the company's high-quality standards.

current product design and designing future products. (In fact, the team plans to focus on a product that's currently on the drawing boards—a Jetboard powered by a Lithium-ion electric motor with zero emissions.) Outsourcing also provides PowerSki with a cost-effective means of increasing capacity. Rather than expand its own facilities—a move that would use capital resources badly needed for growth—PowerSki produces fiberglass hulls at an existing plant that's already set up to handle high production levels. In addition, the costs of production, including labor, utilities, and taxes, will be lower at the supplier's Mexican plant than at PowerSki's California facilities.

Understandably, outsourcing is becoming an increasingly popular option among manufacturers. For one thing, few companies have either the expertise or inclination to produce everything needed to make a product. Today, more firms, like PowerSki, want to specialize in the processes that they perform best and outsource the rest. Like PowerSki, they also want to take advantage of outsourcing by linking up with suppliers located in regions with lower labor costs.

Outsourcing in the Service Sector

Outsourcing is by no means limited to the manufacturing sector. Service companies also outsource many of their non-core functions. Your school, for instance, probably outsources such functions as food services, maintenance, book store sales, printing, grounds keeping, security, information-technology support, and even residence operations.

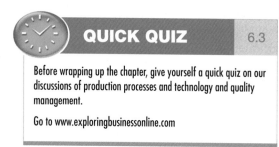

QUICK QUIZ 6.3

Before wrapping up the chapter, give yourself a quick quiz on our discussions of production processes and technology and quality management.

Go to www.exploringbusinessonline.com

Where We're Headed

In this chapter, you learned how product ideas are generated. You found out how to research an industry and forecast demand for a new product. You saw the steps you'd take to transform a product idea into a marketable good or service. You got an overview of operations management and discovered the crucial role played by operations managers in the manufacturing and service sectors. You found out how companies use technology, total quality management, and outsourcing to provide value to customers. In Chapter 7, we'll introduce the principles of marketing and find out how goods and services are priced, promoted, and distributed.

Summary of Learning Objectives

1. Define a *product* and explain where product ideas come from.

A **product** is something that can be marketed to customers because it provides them with a benefit and satisfies a need. Products can be goods or services or a combination of both. The majority of product ideas come from entrepreneurs and small business owners, although medium and large organizations must also identify product-development opportunities in order to remain competitive. Firms seek product ideas from people inside the organization, including those in marketing, sales, research, and manufacturing, as well as from customers and others outside the organization.

2. Explain how to research an industry and forecast demand for a product.

Before developing a new product, you need to understand the industry in which it will be sold. An **industry** is a group of related businesses that

---

benchmarking
Practice of comparing a company's own performance with that of a company that excels in the same activity.

ISO 9000
Set of international quality standards established by the International Organization for Standardization.

ISO 14000
Set of international standards for environmental management established by the International Organization for Standardization.

outsourcing
Practice of using outside vendors to manufacture all or part of a company's actual products.

do similar things and compete with each other. To research an industry, you begin by studying the overall industry and then progressively narrow your search by looking at smaller sectors of the industry, including **markets** (or groups of customers) and **market segments** (smaller groups of customers with common characteristics that influence their buying decisions). Within a market segment, you might want to subdivide further in order to isolate a **niche**, or unmet need. After studying the industry, you need to forecast demand for your proposed product. You might begin by examining published industry data in order to estimate the total market for products like yours and estimate your **market share**, or portion of the targeted market. You can also obtain helpful information about product demand by talking with people in similar businesses and potential customers.

3. **Describe the process of developing a product that meets customer needs.**

The success of a business depends on its ability to identify the unmet needs of consumers and to develop products that meet those needs at a reasonable cost. Accomplishing these goals requires a collaborative effort by individuals from all areas of the organization: operations management (including representatives from engineering, design, and manufacturing), marketing, accounting, and finance. Representatives from these various functional areas often work together as **project teams** throughout the **product development process**, which consists of a series of activities that transform a product idea into a final product. This process can be broken down into seven steps: (1) evaluate opportunities and select the best product mix; (2) get feedback to refine the **product concept** that describes what the product might look like and how it might work; (3) make sure that the product performs and appeals to consumers; (4) design with manufacturing in mind in order to build both quality and efficiency into the manufacturing process; (5) build and test **prototypes**, or physical models of the product; (6) run market tests and enter the **ramp-up stage** during which employees are trained in the production process; and (7) launch the product. If applicable, protect your product idea by applying for a **patent** from the U.S. Patent and Trademark Office.

4. **Define *operations management* and discuss the responsibilities of the operations manager in planning and managing the production process in a manufacturing company.**

The job of **operations management** is to oversee the process of transforming resources into goods and services. The role of operations managers in the manufacturing sector includes production planning, production control, and quality control. During production planning, managers determine how goods will be produced, where production will take place, and how manufacturing facilities will be laid out. In selecting the appropriate production process, managers compare three basic methods: **make-to-order strategy** (goods are made to customer specifications), **mass production** or **make-to-stock strategy** (high volumes of goods are made and held in inventory for later sale), and **mass customization** (high volumes of customized goods are made).

Managers also have several production **layout** choices: **process layout**, in which workers are grouped by task; **product layout**, in which goods are produced in assembly-line fashion; **cellular layout**, which uses teams of workers to produce the product; and **fixed-position layouts**, which are used to make large items (such as ships or buildings) that stay in one place while workers and equipment go to the product.

Once the production process is under way, the attention of the operations manager shifts to the daily activities of **materials management**, which encompasses materials **purchasing**, **inventory control**, and work scheduling. Because material costs often make up about 50 percent of total manufacturing costs, vendor selection and material acquisition gets a good deal of the operations manager's time and attention. In recent years, the purchasing function has been simplified through technology advances, including e-purchasing and **electronic data interchange (EDI)**, which process transactions and transmit purchasing documents. Commonly used inventory control methods include **just-in-time (JIT) production**, by which materials arrive just in time to enter the manufacturing process, and **material requirement planning (MRP)**, which uses computer programming to determine material needs. To schedule jobs, managers create a **master production schedule (MPS)**. They also use graphical tools, such as **Gantt** and **PERT charts**, to diagram the activities involved in producing goods.

5. **List the characteristics that distinguish service operations from manufacturing operations and explain the nature of operations management for service providers.**

Although the primary function of both manufacturers and service providers is to satisfy customer needs, there are several important differences between the two types of operations. While manufacturers produce tangible, generally standardized products, service firms provide intangible products that are often customized to satisfy specific needs. Unlike manufactured goods, many services are bought and consumed at the same time. Operational efficiency is just as important in service industries as it is in manufacturing. Operations managers in the service sector make many decisions that are similar to those made by manufacturers: They decide what services to offer, how to provide these services, where to locate their businesses, what their facilities will look like, and what the demand will be for their services.

Estimating **capacity** needs for a service business is more difficult than for a manufacturer. Service providers can't store their services for later use: Services must be delivered on an as-needed basis. Overseeing a service organization puts special demands on managers, especially services requiring a high degree of contact with customers. Given the importance of personalized service, scheduling workers is more complex in the service industry than in manufacturing. In manufacturing, operations managers focus on scheduling the *activities* needed to produce goods; in service organizations, they focus on scheduling *workers* to ensure that enough people are available to handle fluctuating customer demand.

6. Explain how both manufacturing and service companies use technology, total quality management, and outsourcing to provide value to customers.

Today, companies that compete in both the manufacturing and service sectors must deliver **quality** goods and services that satisfy customers' needs.

Many companies achieve this goal by adhering to principles of **total quality management (TQM)**. Companies using a TQM approach focus on customer satisfaction, engage all members of the organization in quality efforts, and strive for **continuous improvement** in the design, production, and delivery of goods and services. They also **benchmark** other companies to find ways to improve their own performance. To identify areas for improvement, companies can use a technique called **statistical process control (SPC)**, which monitors quality by testing to see if a sample of output is being made to predetermined specifications.

In addition to creating high-quality products, companies must produce and deliver goods and services in an efficient and cost-effective manner. Sophisticated software systems, including **computer-aided design (CAD)**, **computer-aided manufacturing (CAM)**, **computer-integrated manufacturing (CIM)**, and **flexible manufacturing systems (FMS)**, are becoming increasingly important in this area.

Another cost-saving approach is **outsourcing**—having outside vendors manufacture components or even entire products or provide services, such as information-technology support or service center operations. Outsourcing is an appealing option for companies without the expertise in producing everything needed to make a product or those that want to take advantage of low labor costs in developing countries.

Questions and Problems

1. Use your imagination to come up with a hypothetical product idea. Now, identify the steps you'd take to design, develop, and bring your product to market. How would you protect your product idea?

2. In order to introduce a successful new service, you should understand the industry in which you'll be offering it. Select a service business that you'd like to run and explain what information you'd collect on its industry. How would you find it? How would you forecast demand for your service?

3. AACSB ▶ Analysis

Two former surfers invented a material for surfboards that's lighter and stronger than anything manufacturers now use. They've received funding to set up a production facility, and they want you to help them select a location. In addition to your recommendation, identify the factors that you considered in reaching your decision.

4. AACSB ▶ Analysis

As purchasing manager for a company that flies corporate executives around the world, you're responsible for buying everything from airplanes to onboard snacks. You plan to visit all the plants that make the things you buy: airplanes, passenger seats, TV/DVDs that go in the back of the seats, and the specially designed uniforms (with embroidered company logos) worn by the flight attendants. What type of layout should you expect to find at each facility—process, product, or fixed-position? What will each layout look like? Why is it appropriate for the company's production process? Could any of these plants switch to a cellular layout? What would this type of layout look like? What would be its advantages?

5. What is e-purchasing (or e-procurement)? How does it work? What advantages does it give a purchasing manager? How does it benefit a company? How does it change the relationship between purchasing managers and vendors?

6. Compare and contrast three common types of production processes: make-to-order, make-to-stock, and mass customization. What are the advantages and disadvantages of each? Why are more companies devoting at least a portion of their operations to mass customization? Identify three goods that could probably be adapted to mass customization and three that probably couldn't.

7. AACSB ▸ Analysis

Earning a college degree requires not only a lot of hard work but a lot of planning. You must, for example, complete a specified number of credits and take many required courses, particularly in your major. Deciding which courses to take and when to take them can be complicated when some of them have prerequisites. A PERT chart—which diagrams the activities required to complete a goal—might help you determine the order in which you should take courses for your major. Pick a major that interests you and find out what courses you'd need to complete it. Then prepare a PERT chart showing all the courses you'd plan to take each semester to complete your major. (For example, if you select the accounting major, include only accounting courses; do not include your other business courses or your elective courses.) Identify the critical path laid out in your chart. What happens if you fail to take one of your critical-path courses on time?

8. AACSB ▸ Analysis

Ever wonder how Coca-Cola is made? Go to www.exploringbusinessonline.com to link to Coca-Cola's Web site to learn how the soda drink is made (and get to play a few games). After gaining an understanding of the production process to make the soda, pretend that you have just been hired by Coca-Cola as operations manager for a new bottling plant. Your first assignment is to set up a plant somewhere in the United States. Next, identify the planning decisions you'd make and indicate what you would decide. Now, fast-forward two years to the point where the plant is up and running. What responsibilities do you have at this point? What technologies do you use to make your job easier? Finally, quality control is vital to Coca-Cola. What activities are you responsible for that ensure the soda made at your plant meets Coca-Cola's strict quality standards?

9. AACSB ▸ Analysis

You know that organizations adhering to the principles of TQM focus on three tasks: customer satisfaction, employee involvement, and continuous improvement. Think about the course-registration process at your school. Does the process appear to be managed according to TQM principles? Is it designed to satisfy the customer (you)? Do employees in the registrar's office, as well as others involved in the process, focus on customer satisfaction? Does anyone seem to be on the lookout for ways to do things better?

10. The design and production of both goods and services can be facilitated by various high-tech tools, including CAD, CAM, CIM, and FMS. What does CAD software do, and how does it improve a design process? What is CAM, and why is it beneficial to integrate CAD and CAM programs? How do CIM systems expand the capabilities of CAD/CAM? What is an FMS, and what are its advantages over traditional manufacturing systems?

Learning on the Web AACSB

How to Build a BMW

How'd you like to own a BMW? How about a Z4 two-seat roadster for touring town and country? Or maybe an X5 SAV—a sports activity vehicle with the body of a high-performance car and the soul of a sports car? We can't help you finance a BMW, but we can show you how they're made. Go to www.exploringbusinessonline.com to link to the BMW Web site for a virtual tour of the company's South Carolina plant.

Start by clicking on the car of your choice—the X5 SAV or the Z4 Roadster—and then on the blocks on the "Timeline," where you can see each step in the production of your car. Before going any further, answer the following questions:

1. What are the steps in the production of the car?

2. What type of production process is used to make it?

Once you've answered these questions, continue your tour by going to the "Main Navigation" button in the upper-left corner of the screen. Click on the third block to learn about BMW's operational efficiencies and on the fourth block to learn about its quality-control procedures. Now, answer these two questions:

3. What technology does BMW use in the design and production of its vehicles?

4. What procedures does the company follow in order to ensure the production of high-quality vehicles?

Career Opportunities

Wanted: Problem Solvers and Creative Thinkers

If you had a time machine and a craving for a great hamburger, you could return to the early 1950s and swing by Dick and Mac McDonald's burger stand in San Bernardino, California. Take a break from eating and watch the people in the kitchen. You'll see an early application of operations management in the burger industry. Dick and Mac, in an effort to sell more burgers in less time, redesigned their kitchen to use assembly-line procedures. As the number of happy customers grew, word spread about their speedy system and their business thrived. Curiously, it was not Dick and Mac who made McDonald's what it is today, but a traveling milkshake-mixer salesman named Ray Kroc. He visited the hamburger stand to learn how they could sell 20,000 shakes a year. When he saw their operations and the lines of people walking away with bags filled with burgers, fries, and shakes, he knew he had a winner. In cooperation with the McDonald brothers, he started selling franchises around the country, and the rest is history.

So what does this story have to do with a career in operations management? If you're a problem solver like Dick and Mac (who discovered a way to make burgers faster and cheaper) or a creative thinker like Ray Kroc (who recognized the value in an assembly-line burger production system), then a career in operations management might be for you. The field is broad and offers a variety of opportunities. To get a flavor of the choices available, go to www.exploringbusinessonline.com to link to the WetFeet Web site and review the dozen or so operations management positions listed. Provide a brief description of each position. Indicate how interesting you find each position by rating it using a five-point scale (with 1 being uninteresting and 5 being very interesting). Based on your assessment, pick the position you find most interesting and the one you find least interesting. Explain why you made your selections.

Ethics Angle AACSB

Who's Getting Fat from Fast Food?

Product liability laws cover the responsibility of manufacturers, sellers, and others for injuries caused by defective products. Under product liability laws, a toy manufacturer can be held liable if a child is harmed by a toy that's been marketed with a design flaw. The manufacturer can also be held liable for defects in marketing the toy, such as giving improper instructions on its use or failing to warn consumers about potential dangers. But what if the product is not a toy, but rather a fast-food kid's meal? And what if the harm isn't immediately obvious but emerges over time?

These questions are being debated in the legal and health professions (and the media). Some people believe that fast-food restaurants should be held responsible (at least in part) for childhood obesity. They argue that fast-food products—such as kid's meals made up of high-calorie burgers, chicken fingers, fries, and soft drinks—are helping to make U.S. children overweight. They point out that while restaurant chains spend billions each year to advertise fast food to children, they don't do nearly enough to warn parents of the dangers posed by such foods. On the other side of the debate are restaurant owners, who argue that they're not the culprits. They say that their food can be a part of a child's diet—if it's eaten in moderation.

There's no disputing that 15 percent of American children are obese and that fast-food consumption by children has increased by 500 percent since 1970. Most observers also accept the data furnished by the Surgeon General: That obesity in the United States claims some 300,000 lives a year and costs $117 billion in health care. The controversy centers on the following questions:

1. Who really is to blame for the increase in obesity among U.S. children?

2. Under current consumer-protection laws, is fast-food marketing aimed at children misleading?

3. Should fast-food restaurants be held legally liable for the health problems associated with their products?

What's your opinion? If you owned a fast-food restaurant, what action (if any) would you take in response to the charges leveled by critics of your industry?

Team-Building Skills AACSB

Growing Accustomed to Your Fit

Instead of going to the store to try on several pairs of jeans that may or may not fit, wouldn't it be easier to go online and order a pair of perfect-fitting jeans? Lands' End has made this kind of shopping possible through mass-customization techniques and some sophisticated technology.

To get some firsthand experience at shopping for mass-customized goods, have each member of your team go to www.exploringbusinessonline.com to link to the Lands' End Web site. Each team member should go through the process of customizing a pair of jeans but stop just before placing an order (unless you're actually in the market for a pair of mass-customized jeans). After everyone has gone through the process, get together and write a report in which the team explains exactly what's entailed by online mass customization and details the process at Lands' End. Be sure to say which things impressed you and which did not. Explain why Lands' End developed this means of marketing products and, finally, offer some suggestions on how the process could be improved.

The Global View AACSB

What's the State of Homeland Job Security?

Over the past several decades, more U.S. manufacturers began outsourcing production to such low-wage countries as Mexico and China. The number of U.S. manufacturing jobs dwindled, and the United States became more of a service economy. People who were directly affected were understandably unhappy about this turn of events, but most people in this country didn't feel threatened. At least not until service jobs started going to countries which, like India, have large populations of well-educated, English-speaking professionals. Today, more technology-oriented jobs, including those in programming and Internet communications, are being outsourced to countries with lower wage rates. And tech workers aren't alone: the jobs of accountants, analysts, bankers, medical technicians, paralegals, insurance adjusters, and even customer-service representatives have become candidates for overseas outsourcing.

Many U.S. workers are concerned about job security (although the likelihood of a particular individual losing a job to an overseas worker is still fairly low). The issues are more complex than just deciding where U.S. employers should be mailing paychecks, and politicians, economists, business executives, and the general public differ about the causes and consequences of foreign outsourcing. Some people think it's a threat to American quality of life, while others actually think that it's a good thing.

Spend some time researching trends in outsourcing. Formulate some opinions and then answer the following questions:

1. About what percentage of U.S. jobs have left the country in the last five years? What percentage will probably leave in the next five years?

2. What kinds of jobs are being outsourced, and where are they going? What kinds of jobs can't be outsourced?

3. How does global outsourcing help U.S. businesses? How does it hinder them?

4. How has the trend in outsourcing manufacturing and service operations to foreign countries helped average Americans? How has it harmed them?

5. Does overseas outsourcing help or hurt the U.S. economy? In what ways?

Business Plan Project

Group Report: *Products and Production*

REPORT

The team should submit a written report that provides a description of all goods and services to be provided, indicates the advantages that they have over those offered by competitors, and explains how the team intends to obtain or produce the products that it's going to sell. The information in your report will vary depending on whether you've established a service company, a retailer, or a manufacturer. For details on the information required, go to Appendix A at the back of the book, entitled "Introducing Your Business Plan" (p. 307), and consult the section headed "Goods and/or Services." The report should be about two double-spaced typed pages. The name of your proposed business and the names of all team members should appear on the report.

REASONABLE CONTRIBUTIONS

All members of the team who make a reasonable contribution to the report should sign it. (If any team member does not work on the report, his or her name should *not* appear on it.) If a student who has made a contribution is unable to sign the report (because of sickness or some other valid reason), the team can sign his or her name. To indicate that a name was signed by the team on a member's behalf, be sure to attach a note to the signature.

CHAPTER 7

Marketing: Providing Value to Customers

After studying this chapter you will be able to:

1 Define the terms *marketing* and *marketing strategy* and outline the tasks involved in selecting a target market and researching a marketing concept.

2 Discuss various branding approaches and explain the benefits of packaging and labeling.

3 Identify pricing strategies that are appropriate for new and existing products.

4 Explore various product-distribution strategies and explain how companies create value through effective supply chain management.

5 Describe the elements of the promotion mix and explain how companies manage customer relationships.

6 Discuss the factors that influence buyer behavior and describe the external marketing environment in which businesses operate.

A ROBOT WITH ATTITUDE

Mark Tilden used to build robots for NASA to trash on Mars, but after seven years of watching the results of his work meet violent ends 46,000 miles from home, he decided to specialize in robots for earthlings. He left the space world for the toy world and teamed up with Wow Wee Toys Ltd. to create "Robosapien," an intelligent robot with an attitude.[1] The 14-inch-tall robot, which is operated by remote control, has great moves: In addition to the required maneuvers (walking forward and backward and turning), he dances, raps, and gives karate chops. He can pick up (fairly small) stuff and even fling it across the room, and he does everything while grunting, belching, and emitting other bodily sounds.

Gregory Costanzo/
Getty Images–
Digital Images

What does Robosapien have to do with marketing? The answer is fairly simple: Although Mark Tilden is an accomplished inventor who's created a clever product, Robosapien wouldn't be going anywhere without the marketing expertise of Wow Wee (certainly not forward). In this chapter, we'll look at the ways in which marketing converts product ideas like Robosapien into commercial successes.

163

To meet Robosapien's big brother, Robosapien VI (who is twice as big as Robosapien), his dinosaur friend, Roboraptor; and his pet dog, Robopet Robot Dog, go to Wow Wee's Web site at www.wowwee.com.

What Is Marketing?

When you consider the functional areas of business—accounting, finance, management, marketing, and operations—marketing is the one you probably know the most about. After all, as a consumer and target of all sorts of advertising messages, you've been on the receiving end of marketing initiatives for most of your life. What you probably don't appreciate, however, is the extent to which marketing focuses on providing value to the customer. According to the American Marketing Association, **marketing** is a set of processes for creating, communicating, and delivering value to customers and for improving customer relationships.[2]

In other words, marketing isn't just advertising and selling. It includes everything that organizations do to satisfy customer needs:

- Coming up with a product and defining its features and benefits
- Setting its price
- Identifying its target market
- Making potential customers aware of it
- Getting people to buy it
- Delivering it to people who buy it
- Managing relationships with customers after it's been delivered

Not surprisingly, marketing is a team effort involving everyone in the organization. Think about a typical business—a local movie theatre, for example. It's easy to see how the person who decides what movies to show is involved in marketing: He or she selects the product to be sold. It's even easier to see how the person who put ads in the newspaper works in marketing: He or she is in charge of advertising—making people aware of the product and getting them to buy it. But what about the ticket seller and the person behind the counter who gets the popcorn and soda? What about the projectionist? Are they marketing the business? Absolutely: The purpose of every job in the theater is satisfying customer needs, and as we've seen, identifying and satisfying customer needs is what marketing is all about.

If everyone is responsible for marketing, can the average organization do without an official marketing department? Not necessarily: Most organizations have marketing departments in which individuals are actively involved in some marketing-related activity—product design and development, pricing, promotion, sales, and distribution. As specialists in identifying and satisfying customer needs, members of the marketing department manage—plan, organize, direct, and control—the organization's overall marketing efforts.

| 1 Find out what customers need | 2 Develop products to meet those needs | 3 Engage the whole company in efforts to satisfy customers | 4 Achieve company goals (make a profit) |

THE MARKETING CONCEPT

Figure 7.1 is designed to remind you that, in order to achieve business success, you need to do three things:

1. Find out what customers or potential customers need.

2. Develop products to meet those needs.

3. Engage the whole organization in efforts to satisfy customers.

At the same time, you need to achieve organizational goals, such as profitability and growth. This basic philosophy—satisfying customer needs while meeting organizational goals—is called the **marketing concept**, and when it's effectively applied, it guides all of an organization's marketing activities.

The marketing concept puts the customer first: As your most important goal, satisfying the customer must be the goal of everyone in the organization. But this doesn't mean that you ignore the bottom line; if you want to survive and grow, you need to make some profit. What you're looking for is the proper balance between the commitments to customer satisfaction and company survival. Consider the case of Medtronic, a manufacturer of medical devices, such as pacemakers and defibrillators. The company boasts more than 50 percent of the market in cardiac devices and is considered the industry standard setter. Everyone in the organization understands that defects are intolerable in products that are designed to keep people alive. Thus, committing employees to the goal of zero defects is vital to both Medtronic's customer base and its bottom line. "A single quality issue," explains CEO Arthur D. Collins Jr., "can deep-six a business."[3]

Marketing Strategy

Declaring that you intend to develop products that satisfy customers and that everyone in your organization will focus on customers is easy. The challenge is doing it. As you can see in Figure 7.2 (page 166), in order to put the marketing concept into practice, you need a **marketing strategy**—a plan for performing two tasks:

1. Selecting a target market

2. Developing your *marketing mix*—implementing strategies for creating, pricing, promoting, and distributing products that satisfy customers.

We'll use Figure 7.2 as a blueprint for our discussion of target-market selection and analyze the concept of the marketing mix in more detail in the next major section of the chapter.

SELECTING A TARGET MARKET

As we saw back in Chapter 1, businesses earn profits by selling goods or providing services. It would be nice if everybody in the marketplace was interested in your product, but if you tried to sell it to everybody, you'd spread your resources too thin. You need to identify a specific group of consumers who should be particularly interested in your product, who would have access to it, and who have the means to buy it. This group is

---

marketing
Set of processes for creating, communicating, and delivering value to customers and for improving customer relationships.

marketing concept
Basic philosophy of satisfying customer needs while meeting organizational goals.

marketing strategy
Plan for selecting a target market and creating, pricing, promoting, and distributing products that satisfy customers.

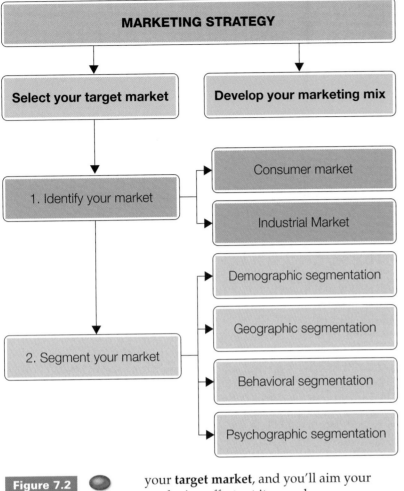

istics that influence their buying decisions. You can use a number of characteristics to narrow a market. Let's look at some of the most useful categories in detail.

Demographic Segmentation

Demographic segmentation divides the market into groups based on such variables, as age, marital status, gender, ethnic background, income, occupation, and education. Age, for example, will be of interest to marketers who develop products for children, retailers who cater to teenagers, colleges who recruit students, and assisted-living facilities that promote services among the elderly. The wedding industry, which markets goods and services to singles who will probably get married in the near future, is interested in trends in marital status. Gender and ethnic background are important to TV networks in targeting different audiences. Lifetime Television for Women targets female viewers; Spike TV targets men, while Telemundo networks target Hispanic viewers. If you're selling yachts, you'll want to find people with lots of money; so income is an important variable. If you're the publisher of *Nurses* magazine, you want to reach people in the nursing profession. When Hyundai offers recent (and upcoming) college graduates the opportunity to buy a new car with no money down, the company's marketers have segmented the market according to education level.[4]

Geographic Segmentation

Geographic segmentation—dividing a market according to such variables as climate, region, and population density (urban, suburban, small-town, or rural)—is also quite common. Climate is crucial for many products—try selling snow shovels in Hawaii or aboveground pools in Alaska. Consumer tastes also vary by region. That's why McDonald's caters to regional preferences, offering a breakfast of Spam and rice in Hawaii, tacos in Arizona, and lobster rolls in Massachusetts.[5] Outside the United States, menus diverge even more widely (you can get seaweed burgers in Japan).[6]

Likewise, differences between urban and suburban life can influence product selection. As exhilarating as urban life can be, for example, it's a hassle to parallel park on crowded city streets. Thus, Toyota engineers have developed a product especially for city dwellers (at least in Japan). The Japanese version of the Prius, Toyota's hybrid gas-

your **target market**, and you'll aim your marketing efforts at its members.

Identifying Your Market

How do marketers identify target markets? First, they usually identify the overall market for their product—the individuals or organizations that need a product and are able to buy it. As Figure 7.2 shows then, this market can include either or both of two groups:

1. A **consumer market**—buyers who want the product for personal use

2. An **industrial market**—buyers who want the product for use in making other products

You might focus on only one market or both. A farmer, for example, might sell blueberries to individuals on the consumer market and, on the industrial market, to bakeries that will use them to make muffins and pies.

Segmenting the Market

The next step in identifying a target market is to divide the entire market into smaller portions, or **market segments**—groups of potential customers with common character-

electric car, can automatically parallel park itself. Using computer software and a rear-mounted camera, the parking system measures the spot, turns the steering wheel, and swings the car into the space (making the driver—who just sits there—look like a master of urban survival skills).[7]

Behavioral Segmentation Dividing consumers by such variables as attitude toward the product, user status, or usage rate, is called **behavioral segmentation**. Companies selling technology-based products might segment the market according to different levels of receptiveness to technology. They could rely on a segmentation scale developed by Forrester Research that divides consumers into two camps: *technology optimists*, who embrace new technology, and *technology pessimists*, who are indifferent, anxious, or downright hostile when it comes to technology.[8]

Some companies segment consumers according to *user status*, distinguishing among nonusers, potential users, first-time users, and regular users of a product. Depending on the product, they can then target specific groups, such as first-time users. Credit-card companies use this approach when they offer promotional gifts to college students in order to induce them to get their first card. Once they start using it, they'll probably be segmented according to usage. "Heavy users" who pay their bills on time will probably get increased credit lines.

Psychographic Segmentation
Psychographic segmentation classifies consumers on the basis of individual lifestyles as they're reflected in people's interests, activities, attitudes, and values. If a marketer profiled you according to your lifestyle, what would the result be? Do you live an active life and love the outdoors? If so, you may be a potential buyer of athletic equipment and apparel. Maybe you'd be interested in an eco-tour offered by a travel agency. If you prefer to sit on your couch and watch TV, you might show up on the radar screen of a

Gap Inc. practices demographic segmentation that focuses on such factors as age and family life cycle. That's why, in addition to the standard Gap store, which features trendy casual clothes for men, women, and children, there are GapKids, BabyGap, and MaternityGap stores. They're often located side by side in the same mall because the mall, too, practices demographic segmentation: Most malls target families by bringing together businesses that offer something of interest to everyone in the family.

TiVo provider. If you're compulsive or a risk taker, you might catch the attention of a gambling casino. If you're thrifty and uncomfortable with debt, Citibank might want to issue you a debit card.

Clustering Segments Typically, marketers determine target markets by combining, or "clustering," segmenting criteria. What characteristics does General Motors look for in marketing the Hummer? Two demographic variables come to mind: sex and age. Buyers are likely to be males ranging in age from about 30 to 55. Because the Hummer can go off-road and performs well on rugged terrain, geography could also be a factor. Income—a socioeconomic factor—is clearly important: Hummers are expensive to buy, maintain, and run. As for psychographics, potential Hummer owners could be people who value prestige and the material rewards of success. (Given the vehicle's

---

target market
Specific group of customers who should be interested in your product, have access to it, and have the means to buy it.

consumer market
Buyers who want a product for personal use.

industrial market
Buyers who want a product for use in making other products.

market segment
Group of potential customers with common characteristics that influence their buying decisions.

demographic segmentation
Process of dividing the market into groups based on such variables as age and income.

geographic segmentation
Process of dividing a market according to such variables as climate, region, and population density.

behavioral segmentation
Process of dividing consumers by behavioral variables, such as attitude toward the product, user status, or usage rate.

psychographic segmentation
Process of classifying consumers on the basis of individual lifestyles as reflected in people's interests, activities, attitudes, and values.

low gas mileage, we'd have to assume that most of them aren't particularly concerned about the environment.) Finally, it would help to know what other vehicles they own; Ferrari owners might be worth targeting.

The Marketing Mix

After identifying a target market, your next step is developing and implementing a marketing program designed to reach it. As Figure 7.3 shows, this program involves a combination of tools called the **marketing mix**, often referred to as the "four *P*s" of marketing:

1. Developing a *product* that meets the needs of the target market

2. Setting a *price* for the product

3. Distributing the product—getting it to a *place* where customers can buy it

4. *Promoting* the product—informing potential buyers about it

The goal is to develop and implement a marketing strategy that combines these four elements. To see how this process works, let's look at Wow Wee Toys' marketing program for Robosapien.[9]

DEVELOPING A PRODUCT

The development of Robosapien was a bit unusual for a company that was already active in its market. Generally, product ideas come from people within the company who understand its customers' needs. Internal engineers are then challenged to design the product. In the case of Robosapien, however, the creator, Mark Tilden, had conceived and designed the product before joining

Wow Wee Toys. The company gave him the opportunity to develop the product for commercial purposes, and Tilden was brought on board to oversee the development of Robosapien into a product that satisfied Wow Wee's commercial needs.

Robosapien is not a "kid's toy," although kids certainly love its playful personality. It's a home-entertainment product that appeals to a broad audience—children, young adults, older adults, and even the elderly. It's a big gift item, and it's developed a following of techies and hackers who take it apart, tinker with it, and even retrofit it with such features as cameras and ice skates. In fact, Tilden wanted the robot to be customizable; that's why he insisted that its internal parts be screwed together rather than soldered.

Conducting Marketing Research

Before settling on a strategy for Robosapien, the marketers at Wow Wee did some homework. First, in order to zero in on their target market, they had to find out what various people thought of the product. More precisely, they needed answers to questions like the following:

- Who are our potential customers? What are they like?
- Do people like Robosapien? What gets them excited about it? What don't they like? What would they change?
- How much are they willing to pay for Robosapien?
- Where will they probably go to buy the product?
- How should it be promoted? How can we distinguish it from competing products?
- Will enough people buy Robosapien to return a reasonable profit?
- Should we go ahead and launch the product?

The last question would be left up to Wow Wee management, but given the size of the investment needed to bring Robosapien to market, Wow Wee couldn't afford to make the wrong decision. Ultimately, the company was able to make an informed decision because its marketing team provided answers to all the other questions. They got these answers through **marketing research**—the process of collecting and analyzing the data that's relevant to a specific marketing situation.

Figure 7.3

The Marketing Mix

This data had to be collected in a systematic way. Market research seeks two types of data:

1. Marketers generally begin by looking at **secondary data**—information already collected, whether by the company or by others, that pertains to the target market.

2. Then, with secondary data in hand, they're prepared to collect **primary data**—newly collected information that addresses specific questions.

You can get secondary data from inside or outside the organization. Internally available data includes sales reports and other information on customers. External data can come from a number of sources. The U.S. Census Bureau, for example, posts demographic information on American households (such as age, income, education, and number of members), both for the country as a whole and for specific geographic areas. You can also find out if an area is growing or declining.

Population data helped Wow Wee estimate the size of its potential U.S. target market. Other secondary data helped the firm assess the size of foreign markets in regions around the world, such as Europe, the Middle East, Latin America, Asia, and the Pacific Rim. This data positioned the company to sell Robosapien in 85 countries including Canada, England, France, Germany, South Africa, Australia, New Zealand, Hong Kong, and Japan.

Using secondary data that's already available (and free) is a lot easier than collecting your own information. Unfortunately, however, secondary data didn't answer all of the questions that Wow Wee was asking in this particular situation. To get these answers, the marketing team had to conduct primary research: They had to work directly with members of their target market. It's a challenging process. First, they had to decide exactly *what* they wanted to know. Then they had to determine *who* to ask. Finally, they had to pick the best *methods* for gathering information.

We know what they wanted to know—we've already listed the questions they asked themselves. As for who to talk to, they randomly selected representatives from their target market. Now, they could have used a variety of tools for collecting information from these people, each of which has its advantages and disadvantages. To understand the marketing-research process fully, we need to describe the most common of these tools:

- *Surveys.* Sometimes marketers mail questionnaires to members of the target market. In Wow Wee's case, the questionnaire could have included photos of Robosapien. It's an effective way to reach people, but the process is time consuming and the response rate is generally low. Phoning people also takes a lot of time, but a good percentage of people tend to respond. Unfortunately, you can't show them the product. Online surveys are easier to answer and get better response rates, and the site can link to pictures or even videos of Robosapien.

- *Personal interviews.* Although time consuming, personal interviews not only let you talk with real people but let you demonstrate Robosapien. You can also clarify answers and ask open-ended questions.

- *Focus groups.* With a **focus group**, you can bring together a group of individuals (perhaps 6 or 10) and ask them questions. A trained moderator can explain the purpose of the group and lead the discussion. If sessions are run effectively, you can come away with valuable information about customer responses to both your product and your marketing strategy.

Wow Wee used focus groups and personal interviews because both approaches had the advantage of allowing people to interact with Robosapien. In particular, focus-group sessions provided valuable opinions about the product, proposed pricing, distribution methods, and promotion strategies. Management was pleased with

---

marketing mix
Combination of product, price, place, and promotion (often called the four Ps) used to market products.

marketing research
Process of collecting and analyzing data that's relevant to a specific marketing situation.

secondary data
Information used in marketing decisions that has already been collected for other purposes.

primary data
Newly collected marketing information that addresses specific questions about the target market.

focus group
Group of individuals brought together for the purpose of asking them questions about a product or marketing strategy.

the feedback and confident that the product would succeed.

Researching your target market is necessary before you launch a new product. But the benefits of marketing research don't extend merely to brand-new products. Companies also use it when they're deciding whether or not to refine an existing product or develop a new marketing strategy for an existing product. Kellogg's, for example, conducted online surveys to get responses to a variation on its Pop-Tarts brand—namely, Pop-Tarts filled with a mixture of traditional fruit filling and yogurt. Marketers had picked out four possible names for the product and wanted to know which one kids and mothers liked best. They also wanted to know what they thought of the product and its packaging. Both mothers and kids liked the new Pop-Tarts (though for different reasons) and its packaging, and the winning name was "Pop-Tarts Yogurt Blasts." The online survey of 175 mothers and their children was conducted in one weekend by an outside marketing research group.[10]

ABOUT NIKE   7.1

Now that you know how a company identifies a target market and develops a product for it, take a moment to review strategies used by Nike to meet the needs of a particular customer group.

Go to www.exploringbusinessonline.com

Branding

Armed with positive feedback from their research efforts, the Wow Wee team was ready for the next step: informing buyers—both consumers and retailers—about their product. They needed a **brand**—some word, letter, sound, or symbol that would differentiate their product from similar products on the market. They chose the brand name *Robosapien*, hoping that people would get the connection between *homo sapiens* (the human species) and *Robosapien* (the company's coinage for its new robot "species"). To prevent other companies from coming out with their own "Robosapiens," they took out a **trademark** by registering the name with the U.S. Patent and Trademark Office.

Although this approach—giving a unique brand name to a particular product—is a bit unusual, it isn't unprecedented. Mattel, for example, established a separate brand for Barbie, and Anheuser-Busch sells beer under the brand name *Budweiser*. Note, however, that the more common approach, which is taken by such companies as Microsoft, Dell, and Apple, calls for marketing all the products made by a company under the company's brand name.[11]

Branding Strategies Companies can adopt one of three major strategies for branding a product:

1. With **private branding** (or *private labeling*), a company makes a product and sells it to a retailer who in turn resells it under its own name. A soft-drink maker, for example, might make cola for Wal-Mart to sell as its Sam's Choice Cola house brand.

2. With **generic branding**, the maker attaches no branding information to a product except a description of its contents. Customers are often given a choice between a brand-name prescription drug or a cheaper generic drug with a similar chemical makeup.

3. With **manufacturer branding**, a company sells one or more products under its own brand names. Adopting a *multiproduct-branding* approach, it sells all its products under one brand name (generally the company name). Using a *multibranding* approach, it will assign different brand names to different products. Campbell's Soup, which markets all of its soups under the company's name, uses the multiproduct-branding approach. Automakers generally use multibranding. Ford, for example, markets to a wide range of potential customers by offering cars under various brand names (Ford, Lincoln, Mercury, Mazda, Volvo, Jaguar, Land Rover, and Aston Martin).

Building Brand Equity Wow Wee went with the multibranding approach, deciding to market Robosapien under the robot's own brand name. Was this a good choice? The answer depends, at least in part, on how the product sells. If customers don't like Robosapien, its failure won't reflect badly on Wow Wee's other products. On the other hand, people might like Robosapien but have no reason to associate it with other Wow Wee products. In this case, Wow Wee wouldn't gain much from its **brand equity**—any added value generated by favorable consumer experiences with Robosapien. To get a better idea of how valuable brand equity is, think for a moment about the effect of the name *Dell* on a product. When you have a positive experience with a Dell product—say, a desktop PC or a laptop—you come away with a positive opinion of the whole Dell product *line* and will probably buy more Dell products. Over time, you may even develop **brand loyalty**: You may prefer—or even insist upon—Dell products. Not surprisingly, brand loyalty can be extremely valuable to a company. Because of customer loyalty, the value of the Coca-Cola brand (whose brand equity has survived such fiascos as New Coke) is estimated at more than $67 billion.[12]

Packaging and Labeling

Packaging—the container that holds your product—can influence a consumer's decision to buy a product or pass it up. Packaging gives customers a glimpse of the product, and it should be designed to attract their attention. **Labeling**—what you say about the product on your packaging—not only identifies the product but provides information on the package contents—who made it and where, what risks are associated with it (such as being unsuitable for small children).

How has Wow Wee handled the packaging and labeling of Robosapien? The robot, as we know, is 14 inches tall, and it's almost as wide. It's also pretty heavy (about 7 pounds), and because it's made out of plastic and has movable parts, it's breakable. The easiest, and least expensive, way of packaging it would be to put it in a square box of heavy cardboard and pad it with Styrofoam. This arrangement would not only protect the product from damage dur-

Worldwide, McDonald's spends about $1.8 billion on advertising, much of it to promote an extremely strong brand image. In London, as elsewhere, the set of associations that make up the McDonald's brand image revolve around the company's familiar golden arches logo, which the firm wants Londoners to associate with convenience, cleanliness, product predictability, and kid-friendliness. In Britain, however, the golden arches are also more closely associated with animal-rights violations and anti-unionism than they are in the United States.

ing shipping but would make the package easy to store. Unfortunately, it would also eliminate any customer contact with the product inside the box (such as seeing what it looks like and what it's made of). Wow Wee, therefore, packages Robosapien in a container that's curved to his shape and has a clear plastic front that allows people to see the whole robot. It's protected during shipping because it's wired to the box. Why did Wow Wee go to this much trouble and expense? Like so many makers of so many products, it has to market the product while it's still in the box. Because he's in a custom-shaped see-through package, you tend to notice Robosapien (who seems to be looking at you) while you're walking down the aisle of the store.

---

brand
Word, letter, sound, or symbol that differentiates a product from similar products on the market.

trademark
Word, symbol, or other mark used to identify and legally protect a product from being copied.

private branding
Product made by a manufacturer and sold to a retailer who in turn resells it under its own name.

generic branding
Product with no branding information attached to it except a description of its contents.

manufacturer branding
Branding strategy in which a manufacturer sells one or more products under its own brand names.

brand equity
Value of a brand generated by a favorable consumer experience with a product.

brand loyalty
Consumer preference for a particular brand that develops over time based on satisfaction with a company's products.

packaging
Container that holds a product and can influence a consumer's decision to buy or pass it up.

labeling
Information on the package of a product that identifies the product and provides details of the package contents.

Meanwhile, the labeling on the package details some of the robot's attributes. The name is highlighted in big letters above the descriptive tagline "A fusion of technology and personality." On the sides and back of the package are pictures of the robot in action with such captions as "Dynamic Robotics with Attitude" and "Awesome Sounds, Robo-Speech & Lights." These colorful descriptions are conceived to entice the consumer to make a purchase because its product features will satisfy some need or want.

Packaging can serve many purposes. The purpose of the Robosapien package is to attract your attention to the product's features. For other products, packaging serves a more functional purpose. Nabisco, for example, packages some of its tastiest snacks—Oreos, Chips Ahoy, and Cheese Nips—in "100 Calorie Packs" that deliver exactly 100 calories per package.[13] Thus, the packaging itself makes life simpler for people who are keeping track of calories (and reminds them of how many cookies they can eat without exceeding 100 calories).

QUICK QUIZ   7.1

Before you move on to the next two *P*s in the product mix — *pricing* and *placing* products — here's a chance to test yourself on what you've learned about marketing so far.

Go to www.exploringbusinessonline.com

PRICING A PRODUCT

The second of the four *P*s in the marketing mix is price. Pricing a product involves a certain amount of trial and error because there are so many factors to consider. If you price too high, a lot of people simply won't buy your product. Or you might find yourself facing competition from some other supplier who feels that it can beat your price. On the other hand, if you price too low, you might not make enough profit to stay in business. So how do you decide on a price? Let's look at several pricing options that were available to the marketers at Wow Wee who were responsible for pricing Robosapien. We'll begin by discussing two strategies that are particularly applicable to products that are being newly introduced.

New Product Pricing Strategies

Right now, Robosapien has little direct competition in its product category. True, there are some "toy" robots available, but they're not nearly as sophisticated. Sony makes a pet dog robot called Aibo, but its price tag of $1,800 is pretty high. Even higher up the price-point scale is the $3,600 iRobi robot made by the Korean company Yujin Robotics to entertain kids and even teach them foreign languages. Parents can also monitor kids' interactions with the robot through its own video-camera eyes; in fact, they can even use the robot itself to relay video messages telling kids to shut it off and go to sleep.[14]

Skimming and Penetration Pricing

Because Wow Wee is introducing an innovative product in an emerging market with few direct competitors, it might consider one of two pricing strategies:

1. With **skimming pricing**, Wow Wee would start off with the highest price that keenly interested customers would pay. This approach would generate early profits, but when competition enters—and it will, because healthy profits can be made in the market— Wow Wee would have to lower its price.

2. Using **penetration pricing**, Wow Wee would initially charge a low price, both to discourage competition and to grab a sizeable share of the market. This strategy might give the company some competitive breathing room (potential competitors won't be attracted to low prices and modest profits). Over time, as its growing market discourages competition, Wow Wee can push up its prices.

Other Pricing Strategies

In their search for the best price level, Wow Wee's marketing managers could consider a variety of other approaches, such as *cost-based pricing*, *demand-based pricing*, *target costing*, *odd-even pricing*, and *prestige pricing*. Any of these methods could be used not only to set an initial price but to establish long-term pricing levels.

Before we examine these strategies, let's pause for a moment to think about the pricing decisions that you have to make if you're selling goods for resale by retailers. Most of us think of price as the amount that we—consumers—pay for a product. But when a manufacturer (such as Wow Wee) sells goods to retailers, the price it gets is not what we the consumers will pay for the product. In fact, it's a lot less.

Here's an example. Say you buy a shirt at a store in the mall for $40. The shirt was probably sold to the retailer by the manufacturer for $20. The retailer then marks up the shirt by 100 percent, or $20, to cover its costs and to make a profit. The $20 paid to the manufacturer plus the $20 markup results in a $40 sales price to the consumer.

Cost-Based Pricing Using **cost-based pricing**, Wow Wee's accountants would figure out how much it costs to make Robosapien and then set a price by adding a profit to the cost. If, for example, it cost $40 to make the robot, Wow Wee could add on $10 for profit and charge retailers $50.

Demand-Based Pricing Let's say that Wow Wee learns through market research how much people are willing to pay for Robosapien. Following a **demand-based pricing** approach, it will use this information to set the price that it charges retailers. If consumers are willing to pay $120 retail, Wow Wee will charge retailers a price that will allow retailers to sell the product for $120. What would that price be? Here's how we would arrive at it: $120 consumer selling price minus a $60 markup by retailers means that Wow Wee can charge retailers $60.

Target Costing With **target costing**, you work backwards. You figure out (again using research findings) how much consumers are willing to pay for a product. From this price—the selling price—you subtract an amount to cover your profit. This process should tell you how much you can spend to make the product. For example, Wow Wee determines that it can sell Robosapien to retailers for $70. The

company decides that it wants to make $15 profit on each robot. Thus, Wow Wee can spend $55 on the product ($70 selling price to the retailer minus $15 profit means that the company can spend $55 to make each robot).

Prestige Pricing Some people associate a high price with high quality—and, in fact, there generally is a correlation. Thus, some companies adopt a **prestige pricing** approach—setting prices artificially high to foster the impression that they're offering a high-quality product. Competitors are reluctant to lower their prices because it would suggest that they're lower-quality products. Let's say that Wow Wee finds some amazing production method that allows it to produce Robosapien at a fraction of its current cost. It could pass the savings on by cutting the price, but it might be reluctant to do so: What if consumers equate low cost with poor quality?

Odd-Even Pricing Do you think $9.99 sounds cheaper than $10? If you do, you're part of the reason that companies sometimes use **odd-even pricing**—pricing products a few cents (or dollars) under an even number. Retailers, for example, might price Robosapien at $99 (or even $99.99) if they thought consumers would perceive it as less than $100.

PLACING A PRODUCT

The next element in the marketing mix is *place*, which refers to strategies for *distribution*. **Distribution** entails all activities involved in getting the right quantity of your product to your customers at the right time and at a reasonable cost. Thus, distribution involves selecting the most appropriate *distribution channels* and handling the *physical distribution* of products.

skimming pricing
Pricing strategy in which a seller generates early profits by starting off charging the highest price that customers will pay.

penetration pricing
Pricing strategy in which the seller charges a low price on a new product to discourage competition and gain market share.

cost-based pricing
Pricing strategy that bases the selling price of a product on its cost plus a reasonable profit.

demand-based pricing
Practice strategy that bases the price of a product on how much people are willing to pay for it.

target costing
Practice strategy that determines how much to invest in a product by figuring out how much customers will pay and subtracting an amount for profit.

prestige pricing
Practice of setting a price artificially high to foster the impression that it is a product is of high-quality.

odd-even pricing
Practice of pricing products a few cents (or dollars) under an even number.

distribution
All activities involved in getting the right quantity of a product to the right customer at the right time and at a reasonable cost.

Distribution Channels

Companies must decide how they will distribute their products. Will they sell directly to customers (perhaps over the Internet)? Or will they sell through an **intermediary**— a wholesaler or retailer who helps move products from their original source to the end user? As you can see from Figure 7.4, various marketing channels are available to companies.

Selling Directly to Customers

Many businesses, especially small ones and those just starting up, sell directly to customers. Michael Dell, for example, started out selling computers from his dorm room. Tom First and Tom Story began operations at Nantucket Nectars by peddling home-brewed fruit drinks to boaters in Nantucket Harbor. Most service companies sell directly to their customers; it's impossible to give a haircut, fit contact lenses, mow a lawn, or repair a car through an intermediary. Many business-to-business sales take place through direct contact between producer and buyer. DaimlerChrysler, for instance, buys components directly from suppliers.

The Internet has greatly expanded the number of companies using direct distribution, either as their only distribution channel or as an additional means of selling. Dell sells only online, while Adidas and Apple Computer sell both on Web sites and in stores. eBay has become the channel of choice for countless small businesses. The advantage of this approach is a certain degree of control over prices and selling activities: You don't have to depend on or pay an intermediary. On the other hand, you must commit your own resources to the sell-

ing process, and that strategy isn't appropriate for all businesses. It would hardly be practical for Wow Wee to sell directly to individual consumers scattered around the world.

Selling Through Retailers

Retailers buy goods from producers and sell them to consumers, whether in stores, by phone, through direct mailings, or over the Internet. Best Buy, for example, buys Robosapiens from Wow Wee and sells them to customers in its stores. Moreover, it promotes Robosapiens to its customers and furnishes technical information and assistance. Each Best Buy outlet features a special display at which customers can examine Robosapien and even try it out. On the other hand, selling through retailers means giving up some control over pricing and promotion, and the wholesale price you get from a retailer, who has to have room to mark up a retail price, is substantially lower than you'd get if you sold directly to consumers.

Selling Through Wholesalers

Selling through retailers works fine if you're dealing with only a few stores (or chains). But what if you produce a product—bandages—that you need to sell through thousands of stores, including pharmacies, food stores, and discount stores). You'll also want to sell to hospitals, day-care centers, and even college health centers. In this case, you'd be committing an immense portion of your resources to the selling process. Besides, buyers like the ones you need don't want to deal directly with you. Imagine a chain like CVS Pharmacy negotiating sales transactions with the maker of every single product that it carries in its stores. CVS deals with **wholesalers** (sometimes called *distributors*): Intermediaries who buy goods from suppliers and sell them to businesses who will either resell or use them. Likewise, you'd sell your bandages to a wholesaler of health care products, who would, in turn, sell them both to businesses like CVS, Kmart, and Giant Supermarkets and to institutions, such as hospitals and college health care centers.

The wholesaler doesn't provide this service for free. Here's how it works. Let's say that CVS is willing to pay $2.00 a box for your bandages. If you go through a wholesaler, you'll probably get only $1.50 a box. In other words, you'd make $0.50 less on each box sold. Your **profit margin**—the amount you earn on each box—would, therefore, be less.

Figure 7.4

Distribution Channels

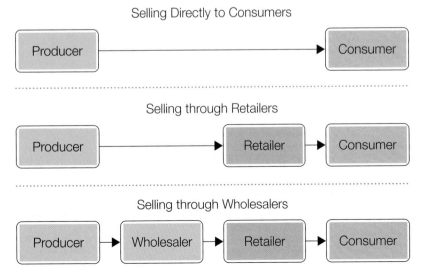

Selling Directly to Consumers

Producer → Consumer

Selling through Retailers

Producer → Retailer → Consumer

Selling through Wholesalers

Producer → Wholesaler → Retailer → Consumer

Although selling through wholesalers will cut into your profit margins, the practice has several advantages. For one thing, wholesalers make it their business to find the best outlets for the goods in which they specialize. They're often equipped to warehouse goods for suppliers and to transport them from the supplier's plant to the point of final sale. These advantages would appeal to Wow Wee. If it sold Robosapiens to just a few retailers, it wouldn't need to go through a distributor. However, the company needs wholesalers to supply an expanding base of retailers who want to carry the product.

Finally, intermediaries, such as wholesalers, can make the distribution channel more cost-effective. Look, for example, at Figure 7.5 (page 176). Because every contact between a producer and a consumer incurs costs, the more contacts in the process (panel *a*), the higher the overall costs to consumers. The presence of an intermediary substantially reduces the total number of contacts (panel *b*).

Physical Distribution

Buyers from the stores that sell Robosapiens don't go to the Wow Wee factory (which happens to be in China) to pick up their orders. The responsibility for getting its products to customers, called **physical distribution**, belongs to Wow Wee. To keep its customers satisfied, Wow Wee must deliver robots on time, in good shape, and in the quantity ordered. To accomplish this, Wow Wee must manage several interrelated activities: *warehousing, materials handling,* and *transportation*.

Warehousing After the robots have been packaged, they're ready for sale. It would be convenient if they've already been sold and just needed to be shipped to customers, but business-to-business (B2B) transactions don't always work out this way. More often, there's a time lag between manufacture and delivery. During this period, the robots must

be stored somewhere. If Wow Wee has to store a large volume over an extended period (perhaps a month or two just prior to the holiday season), it will keep unsold robots in a **storage warehouse**. On the other hand, if Wow Wee has to hold them only temporarily while they're en route to their final destinations, they'll be kept in a **distribution center**.

Wal-Mart, for example, maintains more than 100 distribution centers at which it receives goods purchased from suppliers, sorts them, and distributes them to 3,500 stores, superstores, and SAM's Clubs around the country. Its efficiency in moving goods to its stores is a major factor in Wal-Mart's ability to satisfy customer needs. How major? "The misconception," says one senior executive, "is that we're in the retail business, but in reality, we're in the distribution business."[15]

Materials Handling Making, storing, and distributing Robosapien entails a good deal of **materials handling**—the process of physically moving or carrying goods during production, warehousing, and distribution. Someone (or some machine) needs to move both the parts that go into Robosapien and the partially finished robot through the production process. In addition, the finished robot must be moved into storage facilities and, after that, out of storage and onto a truck, plane, train, or ship. At the end of this leg of the trip, it must be moved into the store from which it will be sold.

Automation All these activities draw on company resources, particularly labor, and there's always the risk of losing money because the robot's been damaged during the process. To sell goods at competitive prices, companies must handle materials as efficiently and inexpensively as possible. One way is by automating the process. For example, parts that go into the production of BMWs are stored and retrieved through

---

intermediary
Wholesaler or retailer who helps move products from their original source to the end user.

retailers
Intermediaries who buy goods from producers and sell them to consumers.

wholesalers (distributors)
Intermediaries who buy goods from suppliers and sell them to businesses who will either resell or use them.

profit margin
Amount that a company earns on each unit sold.

physical distribution
Activities needed to get a product from where it was manufactured to the customer.

storage warehouse
Building used for the temporary storage of goods.

distribution center
Location where products are received from multiple suppliers, stored temporarily, and then shipped to their final destinations.

materials handling
Process of physically moving or carrying goods during production, warehousing, and distribution.

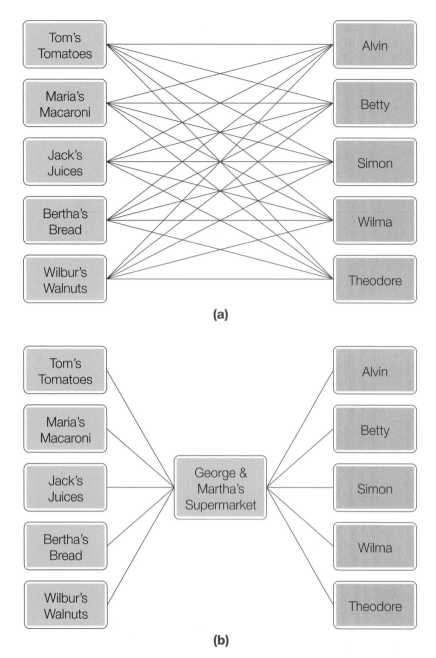

(a)

(b)

Figure 7.5 ACTIVE

What an Intermediary Can Do

the production process. This practice cuts the time and cost entailed by moving raw materials into and out of storage.

Transportation   There are several ways to transport goods from manufacturing facilities to resellers or customers—trucks, trains, planes, ships, and pipelines. Companies select the best mode (or combination of modes) by considering several factors, including cost, speed, match of transport mode to type of good, dependability, and accessibility. The choice usually involves trade-offs. Planes, for example, are generally faster but cost more than other modes. Sending goods by cargo ship or barge is inexpensive but very slow (and out of the question if you want to send something from Massachusetts to Chicago). Railroads are moderately priced, generally accessible, and faster than ships but slower than planes. They're particularly appropriate for some types of goods, such as coal, grain, and bulky items (such as heavy equipment and cars). Pipelines are fine if your product happens to be petroleum or natural gas. Trucks, though fairly expensive, work for most goods and can go just about anywhere in a reasonable amount of time.

According to the U.S. Department of Transportation,[18] trucks are the transportation of choice for most goods, accounting for 65 percent of U.S. transportation expenditures. Trucks also play an important role in the second highest category—multimodal combinations, which account for 11 percent of expenditures. *Multimodal combinations* include rail and truck and water and truck. New cars, for example, might travel from Michigan to California by rail and then be moved to tractor trailers to complete their journey to dealerships. Water accounts for 9 percent of expenditures, air for 8 percent. When used alone, rail accounts for only 4 percent but is commonly combined with other modes. Pipelines account for 3 percent of expenditures. Crowded highways notwithstanding, the economy would come to a standstill without the more than 115,000 (generally small) businesses that make up the U.S. trucking industry.[19]

Creating an Effective Distribution Network: The Supply Chain

Before we go on to the final component in the marketing mix—*promotion*—let's review the elements that we've discussed so far: product, price, and place. As we've seen, to be compet-

automated sequencing centers.[16] Cars are built on moving assembly lines made of skillets large enough to hold workers who move along with the car while it's being assembled. Special assistors are used to help workers handle heavy parts. For hard-to-reach areas under the car, equipment rotates the car 90 degrees and sets the undercarriage at waist level. Records on each car's progress are updated by means of a barcode that's scanned at each stage of production.[17]

Just-in-Time Production   Another means of reducing materials-handling costs is called **just-in-time production**. Typically, companies require suppliers to deliver materials to their facilities *just in time* to go into

itive, companies must produce quality products, sell them at reasonable prices, and make them available to customers at the right place at the right time. To accomplish these three tasks, they must work with a network of other firms, both those that supply them with materials and services and those that deliver and sell their products. To better understand the links that must be forged to create an effective network, let's look at the steps that the candy maker Just Born takes in order to produce and deliver more than one billion Marshmallow Peeps each year to customers throughout the world. On a daily basis, the company engages in the following process:

- Purchasing managers buy raw materials from suppliers (sugar and other ingredients used to make marshmallow, food coloring, and so forth).

- Other operations managers transform these raw materials, or ingredients, into 4.2 million Marshmallow Peeps each day.

- Operations managers in shipping send completed packages to a warehouse where they're stored for later distribution.

- Operations managers at the warehouse forward packaged Marshmallow Peeps to dealers around the world.

- Retail dealers sell the Marshmallow Peeps to customers.

This process requires considerable cooperation, not only among individuals in the organization but between Just Born and its suppliers and dealers. Raw-materials suppliers, for instance, must work closely with Just Born purchasing managers, who must, in turn, work with operations managers in manufacturing at Just Born itself. People in manufacturing have to work with operations managers in the warehouse, who have to work with retail dealers, who have to work with their customers.

If all of the people involved in each of these steps worked independently, the process of turning raw materials into finished Marshmallow Peeps and selling them to customers would be inefficient (to say the least). However, when everyone works in a coordinated manner, all parties benefit. Just Born can make a higher-quality product at a lower cost because it knows that it's going to get cooperation from suppliers whose livelihood, after all, depends on the success of customers like Just Born: Suppliers can operate more efficiently because they can predict the demand for their products (such as sugar and food coloring). At the other end of the chain, dealers can operate efficiently because they can depend on Just Born to deliver a quality product on time. The real beneficiary is ultimately the end user, or customer: Because the process that delivers the product is efficient, its costs are minimized and its quality optimized. The customer, in other words, gets a higher-quality product at a lower price.

Supply Chain Management As you can see in Figure 7.6, the flow that begins with the purchase of raw materials and culminates in the sale of the Marshmallow Peeps to end users is called the **supply chain**. The process of integrating all the activities in the supply chain is called **supply chain management (SCM)**. As you can see from our discussion so far, SCM requires a high level of cooperation among the members of the chain. All parties must be willing to share information and work together to maximize the final customer's satisfaction.[20]

> **Figure 7.6** ACTIVE
>
> A Simplified Supply Chain

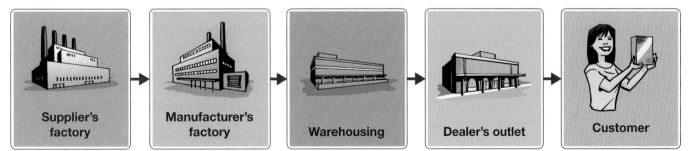

| Supplier's factory | Manufacturer's factory | Warehousing | Dealer's outlet | Customer |

---

just-in-time production
System for reducing inventories and costs by requiring suppliers to deliver materials *just in time* to go into the production process.

supply chain
Flow that begins with the purchase of raw materials and ends in the sale of a finished product to an end user.

supply chain management (SCM)
Process of integrating all the activities in the supply chain.

Managing your supply chain can be difficult, particularly if your company has large seasonal fluctuations.[21] This is certainly true at Just Born. Even though it has a Marshmallow Peep for every season (heart Peeps for Valentine's Day, spooky Peeps for Halloween, patriotic Peeps for July Fourth, and so on), the biggest problem rests with the standard yellow Marshmallow Peep that provides a major spike in sales each spring. Without careful supply chain management, there would be either too many or two few yellow Marshmallow Peeps—both big problems. To reduce the likelihood of both situations, the manager of the company's supply chain works to ensure that all members of the chain work together throughout the busy production season, which begins each fall. Suppliers promise to deliver large quantities of ingredients, workers recognize that they will be busy through February, and dealers get their orders in early. Each member of the chain depends on the others in order to meet a mutually shared goal: getting the right quantity of yellow Marshmallow Peeps to customers at the right time.

But what if a company has multiple sales spikes (and lulls)? What effect does this pattern have on its supply chain? Consider Domino's Pizza. Have you ever thought about what it takes to ensure that a piping-hot pizza will arrive at your door on Super Bowl Sunday (Domino's busiest day of the year)? What about on the average weekend? How about when the weather's bad and you just don't want to go out? Clearly, Domino needs a finely tuned supply chain to stay on top of demand. Each year, the company sells about 400 million pizzas (more than one pizza for every man, woman, and child in the United States). Its suppliers help to make this volume possible by providing the company with about 150 million pounds of cheese and toppings. Drivers do their part by logging 9 million miles a week (the equivalent of 37.5 round trips to the moon every week).

How are these activities managed? Dominos relies on a software system that uses historical data to forecast demand by store; determines, orders, and adjusts supplies; fills staffing needs according to expected sales levels; and facilitates the smooth flow of accurate information among members of the chain. All of this coordination is directed at a single goal—satisfying the largest possible number of end users.[22]

ABOUT NIKE   7.2

Now that you know something about supply chain management, take a moment to learn how Nike gets the right products to the right people at the right time.

Go to www.exploringbusinessonline.com

The Value Chain Supply chain management helps companies to produce better products at lower costs and to distribute them more effectively. Remember, however, that effective supply chain management doesn't necessarily guarantee success. A company must also persuade consumers to buy its products, rather than those of its competitors, and the key to achieving this goal is delivering the most value.

The Customer Value Triad Today's consumer can choose from a huge array of products offered at a range of prices through a variety of suppliers. So how do they decide which product to buy? Most people buy the product that gives them the highest value, and they usually determine value by considering the three factors that many marketers call the **customer value triad**: *quality*, *service*, and *price*.[23] In short, consumers tend to select the product that provides the best combination of these factors.

To deliver high customer value, a company must monitor and improve its **value chain**—the entire range of activities involved in delivering value to customers.[24] Some of these activities arise in the process of supply chain management—obtaining raw materials, manufacturing products, getting finished goods to customers. Others take place outside the supply chain, particularly those associated with marketing and selling products and providing customer support. In addition, companies need to find ways of creating value by improving the internal operations—procurement, research and development, human resource management, and financial management—that support their primary value-chain activities.

The idea is fairly simple: By focusing on the interrelated links in its value chain, a company can increase product quality, provide better service, and cut prices. In other words, it can improve its quality-service-price mix, thereby making its products more competitive.

QUICK QUIZ   7.2

Next we'll talk about product promotion, the product life cycle, the marketing environment, and consumer behavior. Before we do, however, you may want to test yourself on the material that we covered in the preceding sections.

Go to www.exploringbusinessonline.com

PROMOTING A PRODUCT

Your **promotion mix**—the means by which you communicate with customers—may include advertising, personal selling, sales promotion, and publicity. These are all tools for telling people about your product and persuading potential customers, whether consumers or organizational users, to buy it. Before deciding on an appropriate promotional strategy, you should consider a few questions:

- What's the main purpose of the promotion? Am I simply trying to make people aware of my product, or am I trying to get people to buy it right now? Am I trying to develop long-term customers? Am I trying to promote my company's image?

- What's my target market? What's the best way to reach it?

- What product features (quality, price, service, availability, innovativeness) should I emphasize? How does my product differ from those of competitors?

- How much can I afford to invest in a promotion campaign?

- How do my competitors promote their products? Should I take a similar approach?

To promote a product, you need to imprint a clear image of it in the minds of your target audience. What do you think of, for instance, when you hear "Ritz-Carlton"? What about "Motel 6"? They're both hotel chains, but the names certainly conjure up different images. Both have been quite successful in the hospitality industry, but they project very different images to appeal to different clienteles. The differences are evident in their promotions. The Ritz-Carlton Web site describes "luxury hotels" and promises that they provide "the finest personal service and facilities throughout the world." Motel 6, on the other hand, characterizes its facilities as "discount hotels" and assures you that you'll pay "discount hotel rates."

Promotional Tools

We'll now examine each of the elements that can go into the promotion mix—*advertising, personal selling, sales promotion*, and *publicity*. Then we'll see how Wow Wee has incorporated them into a promotion mix to create a demand for Robosapien.

Advertising Advertising is paid, nonpersonal communication designed to create an awareness of a product or company. Ads are everywhere—in print media (such as newspapers, magazines, the *Yellow Pages*), on billboards, in broadcast media (radio and TV), and on the Internet. It's hard to escape the constant barrage of advertising messages; indeed, it's estimated that the average consumer is confronted by about 3,000 each day.[25] For this very reason, ironically, ads aren't as effective as they used to be. Because we've learned to tune them out, companies now have to come up with innovative ways to get through. Campbell Soup, for example, puts ads on parking meters.[26] Even so, advertising is still the most prevalent form of promotion.

Your choice of advertising media depends on your product, your target audience, and your budget. A travel agency selling spring-break getaways to college students might post flyers on campus bulletin boards or run ads in college newspapers. A pharmaceutical com-

---

customer value triad
Three factors that customers consider in determining the value of a product: quality, service, and price.

value chain
Entire range of activities involved in delivering value to customers.

promotion mix
Various ways to communicate with customers, including advertising, personal selling, sales promotion, and publicity.

advertising
Paid, nonpersonal communication designed to create an awareness of a product or company.

pany trying to develop a market for a new allergy drug might focus on TV ads that reach a broad audience of allergy sufferers. A small sandwich shop will probably spend its limited advertising budget on ads in the *Yellow Pages* and local newspapers. The cofounders of Nantucket Nectars found radio ads particularly effective. Rather than pay professionals, they produced their own ads themselves. (Actually, they just got on the radio and started rambling about their product or their lives or anything else that seemed interesting at the time.)[27] As unprofessional as they sounded, the ads worked, and the business grew.

Personal Selling **Personal selling** refers to one-on-one communication with customers or potential customers. This type of interaction is necessary in selling large-ticket items, such as homes, and it's also effective in situations in which personal attention helps to close a sale, such as sales of cars and insurance policies.

Many retail stores depend on the expertise and enthusiasm of their salespeople to persuade customers to buy. Home Depot has grown into a home-goods giant in large part because it fosters one-on-one interactions between salespeople and customers. The real difference between Home Depot and everyone else, says one of its cofounders, isn't the merchandise; it's the friendly, easy-to-understand advice that salespeople give to novice homeowners. Customers who never thought they could fix anything suddenly feel empowered to install a carpet or hang wallpaper.[28]

Sales Promotions "Congratulations! You just won a month's free membership in the health club, and we've entered your name in our million-dollar sweepstakes! All you have to do is sign up for one of our [high-interest, high-late–fee] credit cards." This tactic is a form of **sales promotion** in which a company provides an incentive for a potential customer to buy something. Most sales promotions are more straightforward than our health-club/credit-card offer. Promotional giveaways might feature free samples or money-off coupons. Promotions can involve in-store demonstrations or trade-show displays. They can be cheaper than advertising and can encourage customers to buy something quickly.

Apple Computer promotes the iTunes experience by giving away millions of free music downloads, and it's also joined forces with Pepsi to promote digital music on bottle caps and labels. The joint promotion, which has so far given away 100 million downloads, benefits both companies: While Apple plugged its iTunes download on 300 million Pepsi bottles, Pepsi sold a lot of soda and fostered a connection between Pepsi and music.[29]

Publicity and Public Relations Free **publicity**—say, getting your company or your product mentioned in a newspaper or on TV—can often generate more customer interest than a costly ad. You may remember the buying frenzy surrounding a fuzzy red doll named "Tickle Me Elmo" during the 1996 holiday season. The big break for this product came when the marketing team sent a doll to the one-year-old son of talk-show host Rosie O'Donnell. Two months before Christmas, O'Donnell started tossing dolls into the audience every time a guest said the word *wall*. The product took off, and the campaign didn't cost marketers anything except a few hundred dolls.[30]

Consumer perception of a company is often important to a company's success. Many companies, therefore, manage their **public relations** in an effort to garner favorable publicity for themselves and their products. When the company does something noteworthy, such as sponsoring a fundraising event, the public relations department may issue a press release to promote the event. When the company does something negative, such as selling a prescription drug that has unexpected side effects, the public relations department will work to control the damage to the company. Each year, the accounting firm of PricewaterhouseCoopers and the *Financial Times* jointly survey more than 1,000 CEOs in 20 countries to identify companies that have exhibited exceptional integrity or commitment to corporate governance and social responsibility. Among the companies circulating positive public relations as a result of a recent survey were General Electric, Microsoft, and Toyota.[31]

MARKETING ROBOSAPIEN

Now let's look more closely at the strategy that Wow Wee pursued in marketing Robosapien in the United States. The company's goal was ambitious: to promote Robosapien as a must-have item for kids of all ages. As we know, Wow Wee intended to position Robosapien as a home-entertainment product, not as a toy. In the spring of 2004, therefore, the company rolled out the product at Best Buy, which sells consumer electronics, computers, entertainment software, and appliances. As marketers had hoped, the robot caught the attention of consumers shopping for TV sets, DVD players, home and car audio equipment, music, movies, and games. Its $99 price tag was also consistent with Best Buy's storewide pricing. Indeed, the retail price was a little lower than the prices of other merchandise, and that fact was an important asset: Shoppers were willing to treat Robosapien as an *impulse item*—something extra to pick up as a gift or as a special present for children—as long as the price wasn't too high.

Meanwhile, Robosapien was also getting lots of free publicity. Stories appeared in newspapers and magazines around the world, including the *New York Times*, the *Times of London*, *Time* magazine, and *National Parenting* magazine. Commentators on *The Today Show*, *The Early Show*, CNN, ABC News, and FOX News remarked on it; it was the talk of the prestigious New York Toys Fair. It garnered numerous awards, and experts predicted that it would be a hot item for the holidays.

At Wow Wee, Marketing Director Amy Weltman (who'd already had a big hit with the Rubik's Cube) developed a gala New York event to showcase the product. From mid- to late August, actors dressed in six-foot robot costumes roamed the streets of Manhattan, while the 14-inch version of Robosapien performed in venues ranging from Grand Central Station to city bars. Everything was recorded, and film clips were sent to TV stations.

Then the stage was set for expansion into other stores. Macy's ran special promotions, floating a 24-foot cold-air robot balloon from its rooftop and lining its windows with armies of Robosapiens. Wow Wee trained salespeople to operate the product so that they could help customers during in-store demonstrations. Other retailers, including

The Sharper Image, Spencer's, Linens 'N Things, and Toys "R" Us, carried Robosapien, as did e-retailers, such as Amazon.com. The product was also rolled out (with the same marketing panache) in Europe and Asia.

When national advertising hit in September, all the pieces of the marketing campaign came together—publicity, sales promotion, personal selling, and advertising. Wow Wee ramped up production to meet anticipated fourth-quarter demand and waited to see if Robosapien lived up to commercial expectations.

ABOUT NIKE   7.3

Now that you've explored some of the methods by which companies promote products, take a few minutes to learn about the promotional strategies preferred by Nike.

Go to www.exploringbusinessonline.com

CUSTOMER-RELATIONSHIP MANAGEMENT

Customers are the most important asset that any business has. Without enough good customers, no company can survive, and to survive, a firm must not only attract new customers, but, perhaps more importantly, hold on to its current customers. Why? Because repeat customers are more profitable. It's estimated that it costs as much as six times more to attract and sell to a new customer than to an existing customer.[32] Repeat customers also tend to spend more, and they're much more likely to recommend you to other people.

Retaining customers is the purpose of **customer-relationship management**—a marketing strategy that focuses on using information about current customers to nurture and maintain strong relationships with them. The underlying theory is fairly basic: To keep customers happy, you treat them well, give them what they want, listen to them, reward them

personal selling
One-on-one communication with customers or potential customers.

sales promotion
Sales approach in which a company provides an incentive for potential customers to buy something.

publicity
Form of promotion that focuses on getting a company or product mentioned in a newspaper, on TV, or in some other news media.

public relations
Communication activities undertaken by companies to garner favorable publicity for themselves and their products.

customer-relationship management
Strategy for retaining customers by gathering information about them, understanding them, and treating them well.

with discounts and other loyalty incentives, and deal effectively with their complaints.

Take Harrah's, which operates 40 casinos in 3 countries. Each year, it sponsors the World Series of Poker with a top prize of $5 million. Harrah's gains some brand recognition when the 22-hour event is televised on ESPN, but the real benefit derives from the information cards filled out by the 13,000 entrants who put up $50 to $10,000 for a chance to walk away with $5 million. Data from these cards is fed into Harrah's database, and almost immediately every entrant starts getting special attention, including party invitations, free entertainment tickets, and room discounts. The program is all part of Harrah's strategy for targeting serious gamers and recognizing them as its best customers.[33]

Sheraton Hotels uses a softer approach to entice return customers. Sensing that its resorts needed both a new look and a new strategy for attracting repeat customers, Sheraton launched its "Year of the Bed" campaign: In addition to replacing all of its old beds with luxurious new mattresses and coverings, it issued a "service promise guarantee"—a policy that any guest who's dissatisfied with his or her Sheraton stay will be compensated. The program also calls for a customer-satisfaction survey and discount offers, both designed to keep the hotel chain in touch with customers.

Another advantage of keeping in touch with customers is the opportunity to offer them additional products. Amazon.com is a master at this strategy. When you make your first purchase at Amazon.com, you're also making a lifelong friend—one who will suggest (based on what you've bought before) other things that you might like to buy. Because Amazon.com continually updates its data on your preferences, the company gets better at making suggestions. Now that the Internet firm has expanded past books, Amazon.com can draw on its huge database to promote a vast range of products, and shopping for a variety of products at Amazon.com appeals to people who value time above all else.

Permission Versus Interruption Marketing

Underlying Amazon.com's success in communicating with customers is the fact that customers have given the company permission to contact them. Companies that ask for customers' cooperation engage in *permission marketing*.[34] The big advantage is focusing on an audience of people who've already shown an interest in what they have to offer. Compare this approach with *mass marketing*—the practice of sending out messages to a vast audience of anonymous people. If you advertise on TV, you're hoping that people will listen even though you're interrupting them; that's why some marketers call such standard approaches *interruption marketing*.[35] Remember, however, that permission marketing isn't free. Because winning and keeping customers means giving them incentives, Amazon.com offers its returning customers free shipping and Harrah's lets high rollers sleep and eat free (or at a deep discount). Customer-relations management and permission marketing have actually been around for a long time. But recent advances in technology, especially the Internet, now allow companies to practice these approaches in more cost-effective ways.

The Product Life Cycle

Did you play with LEGO blocks when you were a kid? Almost everyone did. They were a big deal. Store shelves were stacked with boxes of plastic bricks, wheels, and windows, plus packages containing just the pieces you needed to make something special, like a LEGO helicopter. McDonald's put LEGO sets in Happy Meals. If you walk down a toy-store aisle today, you'll still find LEGOs. Now, however, they're shelved alongside Game Boys, Xboxes, Pokémon characters, and other playthings that appeal to contemporary kids. Like these products, they're more sophisticated. They're often tied in with state-of-the-art products—movies like *Star Wars, Spider-Man*, and *Harry Potter*. Nowadays, even the instructions are complicated because the product has changed: LEGOs are no longer marketed as a toy that encourages free-form play. Sadly, LEGO sales are declining drastically. Laments the company's annual report, "2003 was a very disappointing year for LEGO Company." Net sales fell by 26 percent, resulting in a loss in earnings for the year and significant decline in market share. LEGO now plans to drop many of its recent initiatives and focus on its classic LEGO brick products.[36]

The LEGO brand is moving through stages of development and decline.[37]

Marketers call this process the **product life cycle**, which is illustrated in Figure 7.7. In theory, it's a lot like the life cycle that people go through. Once it's developed, a new product is *introduced* to the market. With any success at all, it begins to *grow*, attracting more buyers. At some point, the market stabilizes, and the product becomes *mature*. Eventually, however, its appeal diminishes, and it's overtaken by competing brands or substitute products. Sales *decline*, and it's ultimately taken off the market.

This is a simplified version of the cycle. There are lots of exceptions to the product–life-cycle rules. For one thing, most products never make it past the introduction stage; they die an early death. Second, some products (like some people) avoid premature demise by reinventing themselves. LEGO has been reinventing itself for the last 10 years, launching new products in an effort to recover its customer base and overcome a series of financial crises. Unfortunately, this strategy has been unsuccessful. The introduction of new products and the resulting costs "have not produced the desired results. In some cases," admits the company, "new products have even cannibalized on the sales of LEGO Company's core products and thus eroded earnings."[38]

LIFE CYCLE AND THE CHANGING MARKETING MIX

As a product or brand moves through its life cycle, the company that markets it will shift its marketing-mix strategies. Let's see how the mix might be changed at each stage.

Introduction

At this stage, most companies invest in advertising to make consumers aware of a product. If it faces only limited competition, it might use a skimming-pricing approach. Typically, because it will sell only a relatively small quantity of the product, it will distribute through just a few channels. Because sales are low and advertising and other costs are high, the company tends to lose money during this stage.

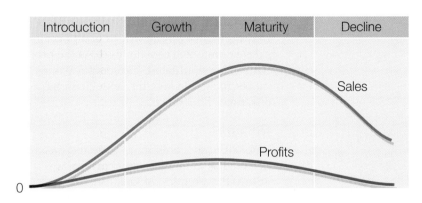

Growth

As the company focuses on building sales, which are increasing rapidly at this stage, its advertising costs will go up. If competition appears, it may respond by lowering prices and distributing through multiple distribution channels. With sales going up and costs going down, the product becomes more profitable.

Maturity

If a product survives the growth stage, it will probably remain in the maturity stage for a long time. Sales still grow, though at a decreasing rate, and will eventually stabilize. Advertising will be used to differentiate

Figure 7.7

The Product Life Cycle

This model of the U.S. Capitol made out of LEGOs, with a LEGO marching band in front, is in LEGOland, Carlsbad, California. It's built to 1:20 scale. The park, one of four LEGO theme parks around the world, has more than 5,000 LEGO creations along with 50 rides, shows, and attractions.

product life cycle
Four stages that a product goes through over its life: introduction, growth, maturity, and decline.

the product from competition. Price wars may occur, but profits will be good because sales volume will remain high. As the product becomes outdated, the company may make changes in keeping with changing consumer preferences.

Decline

LEGO is now in this stage: Demand has declined as more innovative products absorb the attention of kids. Price competition has become more intense, and profits are harder to come by; in fact, they've turned into losses. As we've seen, LEGO has tried to revitalize the product, but ultimately the company may have to give up and pull the product from the market.

The Marketing Environment

By and large, managers can control the four *P*s of the marketing mix: They can decide what products to offer, what prices to charge for them, how to distribute them, and how to reach target audiences. Unfortunately, there are other forces at work in the marketing world—forces over which marketers have much less control. These forces make up a company's **external marketing environment**, which, as you can see in Figure 7.8, we can divide into five sets of factors:

1. regulatory and political
2. economic
3. competitive
4. technological
5. social and cultural

These factors—and changes in them—present both threats and opportunities that require shifts in marketing plans. To spot trends and other signals that conditions may be in flux, marketers must continually monitor the environment in which their companies operate. In order to get a better idea of how they affect a firm's marketing activities, let's look at each of the five areas of the external environment.

THE POLITICAL AND REGULATORY ENVIRONMENT

Federal, state, and local bodies can set rules or restrictions on the conduct of businesses. The purpose of regulation is to protect both consumers and businesses. Businesses favor some regulations (such as patent laws) while chafing under others (such as restrictions on advertising). The tobacco industry, for example, has had to learn to live with a federal ban on TV and radio advertising. More recently, many companies in the food industry have expressed unhappiness over regulations requiring the labeling of trans-fat content. The broadcasting industry is increasingly concerned about fines being imposed by the Federal Communications Commission for offenses against "standards of decency." The loudest outcry probably came from telemarketers in response to the establishment of "do-not-call" registries.

All of these actions occasioned changes in the marketing strategies of affected companies. Tobacco companies rerouted advertising dollars from TV to print media. Food companies reduced trans-fat levels and began targeting health-conscious consumers. Talent coordinators posted red flags next to the names of Janet Jackson (of the now-famous malfunctioning costume) and other performers. The telemarketing industry fired workers and scrambled to reinvent its whole business model.

Figure 7.8

The Marketing Environment

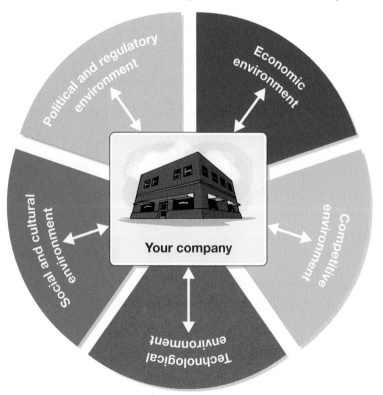

THE ECONOMIC ENVIRONMENT

Marketing managers face a barrage of economic news on a daily basis. They must digest it, assess its impact, and alter marketing plans accordingly. Sometimes, the news is cause for optimism—the economy's improving, unemployment's declining, consumer confidence is up. At other times, the news makes them nervous—we're going into a recession, industrial production is down, jobless claims are rising. Naturally, business thrives when the economy is growing, employment is full, and prices are stable. Marketing products is easier because consumers are willing to buy. On the other hand, when the economy is slowing and unemployment is rising, people have less money to spend and the marketer's job is harder.

Then there's inflation, which pushes interest rates upward. If you're trying to sell cars, you know that people facing higher interest rates aren't so anxious to take out car loans. Sales will slip, and to counteract the anticipated slowdown, you might have to add generous rebates to your promotional plans.

Moreover, if you operate in foreign markets, you can't focus on solely domestic economic conditions: You have to monitor the economy in every region where you do business. For example, if you're the marketing director for a U.S. company whose goods are manufactured in Asia and sold in South America, you'll need to know as much as you can about the economies on three continents. For one thing, you'll have to pay particular attention to fluctuations in exchange rates because changes will affect both your sales and profits.

THE COMPETITIVE ENVIRONMENT

Imagine playing tennis without watching what your opponent was doing. Marketers who don't pay attention to their competitors are playing a losing game. In particular, they need to monitor the activities of two groups of competitors: the makers of competing brands and substitute products. Coke and Pepsi, for instance, are brand competitors who've engaged in the so-called "cola wars" for decades. Each tries to capture market share by convincing people that its soft drinks are better. Because neither wants to lose share to the other, they tend to resort to similar tactics. In the summer of 2004, both companies came out with nearly identical new colas boasting half the sugar, half the calories, and half the carbohydrates of regular colas. Coke called its product Coke C2 and Pepsi named its competing brand PepsiEdge. Both companies targeted cola drinkers who want the flavor of a regular soda but fewer calories.

Meanwhile, both have to watch Nantucket Nectars, whose fruit drinks are substitute products. What if Nantucket Nectars managed to get its drinks into the soda machines at more fast-food restaurants? How would Coke and Pepsi respond? What if Nantucket Nectars, which markets an ice tea with caffeine, introduced an ice tea drink with mega amounts of caffeine? Would marketers at Coke and Pepsi take action? What if Nantucket Nectars launched a marketing campaign promoting the health benefits of fruit drinks over soda? Would Coke and Pepsi reply with campaigns of their own? Would they respond by introducing new non-cola products?

THE TECHNOLOGICAL ENVIRONMENT

When's the last time you went to Blockbuster to get a VHS tape of a new movie? If you had trouble finding it, that's because DVDs are in and videotapes are out. Videotape makers who were monitoring technological trends in the industry would probably have taken steps to keep up (go into DVDs) or otherwise protect themselves from losses (maybe even getting out of the market). In addition to making old products obsolete, technological advances create new products. Where would we be without the cell phone, digital cameras, instant messaging, personal digital assistants, LASIK surgery, and global positioning systems?

external marketing environment
Factors external to the firm that present threats and opportunities and require shifts in marketing plans.

New technologies also transform the marketing mix in another important way: They alter the way companies market their products. Consider the revolutionary changes brought about by the Internet, which offers marketers a new medium for promoting and selling a vast range of goods and services. Marketers must keep abreast of technological advances and adapt their strategies, both to take advantage of the opportunities and to ward off threats.

THE SOCIAL AND CULTURAL ENVIRONMENT

Marketers also have to stay tuned to social and cultural factors that can impact sales. The values and attitudes of American consumers are in a state of almost constant flux; what's cool one year is out of style the next. Think about the clothes you wore five years ago: Would you wear them today? A lot of people wouldn't—they're the wrong style, the wrong fit, the wrong material, the wrong color, or just plain wrong. Now put yourself in the place of a marketer for a clothing company that targets teenagers and young adults. You wouldn't survive if you tried to sell the same styles every year. As we said at the outset of this chapter, the key to successful marketing is meeting the needs of customers. This means knowing what they want right now, not last year.

Here's another illustration. The last few decades have witnessed monumental shifts in the makeup of the American workforce. The number of women at all levels has increased significantly, the workforce has become more diverse, and telecommuting is more common. More people place more importance on balancing their work lives with the rest of their lives, and fewer people are willing to sacrifice their health to the demands of hectic work schedules. With these changes have come new marketing opportunities. As women spend more time at work, the traditional duties of the "homemaker" have shifted to day-care centers, nannies, house-cleaning services, and (for those who can afford them) child chauffeurs, birthday-party coordinators, and even family-photo assemblers.[39] The number of gyms has mushroomed, the selection of home office furniture has expanded, and McDonald's has bowed to the wishes of the health-conscious by eliminating its "super size" option.

Generation Gaps

Clothiers who target teens and young adults (such as Gap and Abercrombie & Fitch) must estimate the size of both current and future audiences. So must companies that specialize in products aimed at customers in other age brackets—say, young children or retirees. Marketers pay particular attention to population shifts because they can have dramatic effects on a consumer base, either increasing or decreasing the number of potential customers.

Marketers tend to assign most Americans born in the last 60 years to one of three groups: the *baby-boom generation* (those born between 1946 and 1964), *Generation X* (1965 to 1975), and *Generation Y*—also known as "echo baby boomers" or "millenniums" (1976 to 2001).[40] In addition to age, members of each group tend to share common experiences, values, and attitudes that stay with them as they mature. These values and attitudes have a profound effect on both the products they want and the marketing efforts designed to sell products to them. Let's look a little more closely at some of the defining characteristics of each group.

Baby Boomers The huge wave of baby boomers began arriving in 1946, following World War II, and marketers have been catering to them ever since. What are they like? Sociologists have attributed to them such characteristics as "individuality, tolerance, and self-absorption."[41] There are 70 million of them,[42] and as they marched through life over the course of five decades, marketers crowded the roadside to supply them with toys, clothes, cars, homes, and appliances—whatever they needed at the time. They're still a major marketing force, but their needs have changed: They're now the target market for Botox, pharmaceutical products, knee surgery, financial investments, cruises, vacation homes, and retirement communities.

Generation X Because birth rates had declined by the time the "Gen X" babies first arrived in 1965, this group had just one decade to grow its numbers. Thus, it's considerably smaller (17 million[43]) than the baby-boomer group, and it's also borne the brunt of rising divorce rates and the arrival of AIDS. Experts say, however, that they're diverse, savvy, and pragmatic[44] and point out that even though they were once thought of as "slackers," they actually tend to be self-reliant and successful. At this point in their lives, most are at their peak earning power and affluent enough to make marketers stand up and take notice.

Generation Y When they became parents, baby boomers delivered a group to rival their own. Born between 1976 and 2001, their 60 million[45] children are sometimes called "echo boomers" (because their population boom is a reverberation of the baby boom). They're still evolving, but they've already been assigned some attributes: They're committed to integrity and honesty, family oriented and close to parents, ethnically diverse and accepting of differences, upbeat and optimistic about the future, education focused, independent, and goal oriented.[46] They also seem to be coping fairly well: Among today's teens, arrests, drug use, drunk driving, and school dropout rates are all down.[47]

Generation Ys are being courted by carmakers: Toyota, Ford, Honda, Nissan, Subaru, and Pontiac have all launched new cars designed to project an image that appeals to the young and the successful.[48] Advertisers are also busy trying to find innovative ways to reach this group, but they're finding that it's not easy. Generation Ys grew up with computers and other modes of high technology, and they're used to doing several things at once—simultaneously watching TV, chatting on the phone, and playing computing games on the computer. As a result, they're quite adept at tuning out ads. Try to reach them through TV ads and they'll channel-surf right past them or hit their TiVo remotes.[49] You can't get to them over the Internet because they know all about pop-up blockers. In one desperate attempt to get their attention, an advertiser paid college students $0.50 to view 30-second ads on their computers.[50] Advertisers keep trying because Generation Y is big enough to wreck a brand by giving it a cold shoulder.

Consumer Behavior

Why did you buy an Apple computer when your friend bought a Dell? What information did you collect before making the deci-

Not a bad way to spend an afternoon. How many things is this Generation Y-er doing at once?

sion? What factors did you consider when evaluating alternatives? How did you make your final choice? Were you happy with your decision? In order to design effective strategies, marketers need to find the answers that consumers give to questions such as these. In other words, they try to improve their understanding of **consumer behavior**—the decision process that individuals go through when purchasing or using products. In the next section, we'll look at the process that buyers go through in choosing one product over another. Then, we'll explore some of the factors that influence consumers' behavior.

THE BUYING PROCESS

Generally speaking, buyers go through a series of steps in deciding whether to purchase a particular product. Some purchases are made without much thought. You probably don't think much, for example, about the brand of gasoline you put in your car; you just stop at the most convenient place. Other purchases, however, require considerable thought. For example, you probably spent a lot of time deciding which college to attend. Let's revisit that decision as a means of examining the five steps which are involved

consumer behavior
Decision process that individuals go through when purchasing or using products.

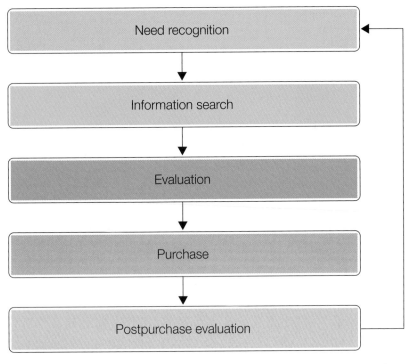

Figure 7.9

The Buying Process

in the consumer buying process and which are summarized in Figure 7.9: *need recognition, information search, evaluation, purchase,* and *postpurchase evaluation.*

1. *Need recognition.* The process began when you recognized a need to go to college. Perhaps you wanted to prepare for a particular career, to become better educated, or to postpone going to work full time. Maybe your parents insisted.

2. *Information search.* Once you recognized the need to go to college, you probably started gathering information about colleges. You may have gone online and studied the Web sites posted by a few schools. Perhaps you attended college fairs or spoke with your high school guidance counselor. You probably talked with friends about your options. Once you let colleges know that you were interested, admissions departments probably sent you tons of information.

3. *Evaluation.* At this point, you studied the information you'd gathered. First, you probably decided what you wanted from a college. Perhaps price was your number-one criterion, or maybe distance from home. Maybe size was important, or reputation or available majors. Maybe it was the quality of the football team or the male-to-female ratio.

4. *Purchase.* Ultimately you made a "purchase" decision. In so doing, you focused on what was most important to you. Naturally, you could choose only among schools that had accepted you.

5. *Postpurchase evaluation.* The buying process didn't end when you selected a school. It continues today, while you're using the product you purchased. How many times have you rethought your decision? Are you happy with it? Would you make the same choice again?

Understanding the buying process of potential students is crucial to college administrators in developing marketing strategies to attract qualified "buyers." They'd certainly like to know what information you found useful, what factors most influenced your decision, and how you made your final choice. They'll also want to know if you're happy with your choice. This is the kind of information that colleges are seeking when they solicit feedback, both from students who chose their schools and those who didn't.

INFLUENCES ON BUYING BEHAVIOR

Did you ever buy something you knew you shouldn't buy but just couldn't help yourself—something you just wanted? Maybe it was a spring-break trip to the Bahamas that you really couldn't afford. Objectively, you may have made a bad decision, but not all decisions are made on a purely objective basis. *Psychological* and *social influences* come into play. Let's take a closer look at each of these factors.

Psychological Influences

Under this category, we can identify at least five variables:

1. *Motivation.* The internal process that causes you to seek certain goals.

2. *Perception.* The way you select, organize, and interpret information.

3. *Learning.* Knowledge gained through experience and study.

4. *Attitudes.* Your predisposition to respond in particular ways because of learned values and beliefs.

5. *Personality.* The collection of attributes that characterize an individual.

Social Influences

Here, we find four factors:

1. *Family.*

2. *Reference groups.* Friends or other people with whom you identify.

3. *Economic or social status.*

4. *Culture.* Your set of accepted values.

It shouldn't be surprising that marketers are keenly interested in the effect of all these influences on your buying decisions. For instance, suppose the travel agency that sold you your spring-break getaway found that you bought the package because you viewed it as a reward for studying hard and doing well academically. In that case, it might promote student summer-travel programs as rewards for a hard year's work at school.

Careers in Marketing

The field of marketing is extensive, and so are the opportunities for someone graduating with a marketing degree. While one person may seek out the excitement of an advertising agency that serves multiple clients, another might prefer to focus on brand management at a single organization. For someone else, working as a buyer for a retail chain is appealing. A few people might want to get into marketing research. Others might have an aptitude for supply chain management or *logistics management*, the aspect of supply chain management that focuses on the flow of products between suppliers and customers. A lot of people are attracted to sales positions because of the potential financial rewards. Let's look more closely at a few of your options.

ADVERTISING

If you're interested in advertising, you'll probably start out at an **advertising agency**—a marketing consulting firm that develops and executes promotional campaigns for clients. Professionals work on either the "creative" side (developing ads and other campaign materials) or the busi-ness side (acting as liaisons between the firm and its clients). If you're new, you'll probably begin as an assistant and work your way up. You might, for example, start as an assistant copywriter, helping to develop advertising messages. Or you could assist an account coordinator, helping in the management of accounts, including the planning and implementation of marketing campaigns.

BRAND AND PRODUCT MANAGEMENT

Brand and product managers are responsible for all aspects of the development and marketing of assigned products. They oversee the marketing program, including marketing research, pricing, distribution, and promotion. They track and analyze sales, gather feedback from customers, and assess the competition. You'd probably join the company as a brand assistant assigned to a more senior-level manager. After a few years, you may be promoted to assistant brand manager and, eventually, to brand manager. At this point, you'd be given responsibility for your own brand or product.

MARKETING RESEARCH

Marketing researchers meet with company managers to determine their information needs. Then they gather and analyze relevant data, write reports, and present their findings and recommendations. If you want to get into this field, you'll need to acquire some skills in disciplines outside marketing, including statistics, research methods, and psychology. You'll start out as an assistant, but you may advance comparatively quickly.

SUPPLY CHAIN AND LOGISTICS MANAGEMENT

Effective supply chain management is vital to success in today's business environment. Those who start their careers in supply chain management typically work in one of the following areas: purchasing and supply management, transportation and logistics,

advertising agency
Marketing consulting firm that develops and executes promotional campaigns for clients.

operations management, or inventory management and control. If this field appeals to you, you'll need to take courses in several disciplines: management, marketing, operations management, and accounting. If you want to specialize in logistics management, you'll be happy to know that many organizations—manufacturers, wholesalers, retailers, service providers, and transportation carriers—are looking for people interested in physical distribution. If you want to go into this field, you'll need strong quantitative skills in addition to a background in business with a specialization in marketing.

RETAILING

Retailing offers all sorts of options, such as merchandise buying and store management. As a buyer, you'd select and buy merchandise for a department, a store, or maybe even a whole chain. Store managers display merchandise, supervise personnel, and handle day-to-day operations. Graduates looking for jobs in both areas generally start as trainees and work their way up.

SALES

Many marketing graduates begin their careers in sales positions, often for service organizations, such as insurance, real estate, and financial-services companies. Others are employed in the wholesale and retail trades or enter the manufacturing sector, selling

anything from industrial goods to pharmaceuticals. To succeed in sales, you need a thorough understanding of customers' needs and an extensive knowledge of your product. You should also be able to communicate well, and you'll need strong interpersonal skills. Bear in mind that experience in sales is excellent preparation for almost any position in business.

QUICK QUIZ   7.3

Before you wrap up this chapter, here's an opportunity to test your understanding of the topics discussed in the preceding sections.

Go to www.exploringbusinessonline.com

Where We're Headed

In this chapter, you were introduced to the field of marketing. You learned how marketers come up with ideas for a product, identify its target market, set its price, promote it, persuade people to buy it, deliver it, and manage relations with customers who buy it. In the next chapter, you'll learn how globalization affects you in the present and how it will influence your future business career. You'll explore opportunities in international trade and find out what steps you can take now, as a student, to prepare yourself to enter a global business world.

Summary of Learning Objectives

1. **Define the terms** *marketing* **and** *marketing strategy* **and outline the tasks involved in selecting a target market and researching a marketing concept.**

   Marketing is a set of processes for creating, communicating, and delivering value to customers and for improving customer relationships. It includes everything that organizations do to satisfy customers' needs. The philosophy of satisfying customers' needs while meeting organizational profit goals is called the **marketing concept** and guides all

   of an organization's marketing activities. To apply this approach, marketers need a **marketing strategy**—a plan for doing two things: (1) selecting a target market and (2) implementing strategies for creating, pricing, promoting, and distributing products that satisfy customers' needs.

   A **target market** is a specific group of consumers who are particularly interested in a product, would have access to it, and are able to buy it. To identify this group, marketers first identify the overall market for the product (from the consumer market, industrial market, or both). Then, they divide the market into **market segments**—groups of customers with common characteristics that influence their buying decisions. The market can be divided according to any of the following variables: **demographics** (age, gender, income, and so on); **geographics** (region, climate, population density); **behavior** (receptiveness to technology, usage); and **psychographics** or lifestyle variables (interests, activities, attitudes, and values).

Before settling on a marketing strategy, marketers often do **marketing research** to collect and analyze relevant data. First, they look at **secondary data** that's already been collected, and then they collect new data, called **primary data**. Methods for collecting primary data include surveys, personal interviews, and **focus groups**.

2. **Discuss various branding approaches and explain the benefits of packaging and labeling.**

A **brand** is a word, letter, sound, or symbol that differentiates a product from its competitors. To protect a brand name, the company takes out a **trademark** by registering it with the U.S. Patent and Trademark Office. There are three major branding strategies. With **private branding**, the maker sells a product to a retailer who resells it under its own name. Under **generic branding**, a no-brand product contains no identification except for a description of the contents. Using **manufacture branding**, a company sells products under its own brand names. When consumers have a favorable experience with a product, it builds **brand equity**. If consumers are loyal to it over time, it enjoys **brand loyalty**.

Packaging—the container holding the product—can influence consumers' decisions to buy products or not buy products. It offers them a glimpse of the product and should be designed to attract their attention. **Labeling**—the information on the packaging—identifies the product. It provides information on the contents, the manufacturer, the place where it was made, and any risks associated with its use.

3. **Identify pricing strategies that are appropriate for new and existing products.**

With a new product, a company might consider the **skimming approach**—starting off with the highest price that keenly interested customers are willing to pay. This approach yields early profits but invites competition. Using a **penetration approach**, marketers begin by charging a low price, both to keep out competition and to grab as much market share as possible.

Several strategies work for existing as well as new products. With **cost-based pricing**, a company determines the cost of making a product and then sets a price by adding a profit to the cost. With **demand-based pricing**, marketers set the price that they think consumers will pay. Using **target costing**, they figure out how much consumers are willing to pay and then subtract a reasonable profit from this price to determine the amount that can be spent to make the product. Companies use **prestige pricing** to capitalize on the common association of high price and quality, setting an artificially high price to substantiate the impression of high quality. Finally, with **odd-even pricing**, companies set prices at such figures as $9.99 (an odd amount), counting on the common impression that it sounds cheaper than $10 (an even amount).

4. **Explore various product-distribution strategies and explain how companies create value through effective supply chain management.**

Distribution entails all activities involved in getting the right quantity of a product to customers at the right time and at a reasonable cost. Companies can sell directly (from stores or over the Internet) or indirectly, through **intermediaries**—retailers or wholesalers who help move products from producers to end users. **Retailers** buy goods from producers and sell them to consumers, whether in stores, by phone, through direct mailings, or over the Internet. **Wholesalers** (or distributors) buy goods from suppliers and sell them to businesses that will resell or use them. **Physical distribution**—the process of getting products from producers to customers—entails several interrelated activities: *warehousing* in either a **storage warehouse** or a **distribution center**, **materials handling** (physically moving products or components), and *transportation* (shipping goods from manufacturing facilities to resellers or customers).

A firm can produce better-quality products at lower cost and distribute them more effectively by successfully managing its **supply chain**—the entire range of activities involved in producing and distributing products, from purchasing raw materials, transforming raw materials into finished goods, storing finished goods, and distributing them to customers. Effective **supply chain management (SCM)** requires cooperation, not only among individuals within the organization but among the company and its suppliers and dealers. A successful company also provides customers with added value by focusing on and improving its **value chain**—the whole range of its value-creating activities.

5. Describe the elements of the promotion mix and explain how companies manage customer relationships.

The **promotion mix**—the ways in which marketers communicate with customers—includes all the tools for telling people about a product and persuading potential customers to buy it. **Advertising** is paid, nonpersonal communication designed to create awareness of a product or company. **Personal selling** is one-on-one communication with customers and potential customers. **Sales promotions** provide potential customers with direct incentives to buy. **Publicity** involves getting the name of the company or its products mentioned in print or broadcast media. Because customers are vital to a business, successful companies practice **customer-relationship management**—retaining good customers by keeping information on current customers in order to foster and maintain strong ongoing relationships.

6. Discuss the factors that influence buyer behavior and describe the external marketing environment in which businesses operate.

Successful marketing often hinges on understanding **consumer behavior**—the decision process that individuals go through when purchasing or using products. Several psychological and social variables influence buyers' decisions, and they go through a series of steps in reaching the decision to buy a product: *need recognition, information search, evaluation, purchase*, and *postpurchase evaluation*.

A number of forces over which it has little or no control affect a company's marketing activities. Taken together, they make up its **external marketing environment**, which includes regulatory and political activity, economic conditions, competitive forces, changes in technology, and social and cultural influences.

Questions and Problems

1. If you were developing a marketing campaign for the Volkswagen Beetle, what group of consumers would you target? What if you were marketing 50-inch Sony plasma TVs? What about time-shares (vacation-ownership opportunities) in Vail, Colorado? For each of these products, identify at least five segmentation characteristics that you'd use in developing a profile of your customers. Explain the segmentation category into which each characteristic falls—demographic, geographic, behavioral, or psychographic. Where it's appropriate, be sure to include at least one characteristic from each category.

2. AACSB ▶ Analysis
When XM Satellite Radio was launched by American Mobile Radio in 1992, no one completely understood the potential for satellite radio. The company began by offering a multichannel, nationwide audio service. In 1997, it was granted a satellite-radio-service license from the FCC, and in 2001, the company began offering more than 150 digital channels of commercial-free satellite-radio programming for the car and home. Revenues come from monthly user fees. In the decade between 1992 and 2001, the company undertook considerable marketing research to identify its target market and refine its offerings. Answer the following questions as if you were in charge of XM Satellite Radio's marketing research:

* To what questions would you seek answers?

* What secondary data would you look at?

* What primary data would you collect and analyze?

* How would you gather these primary data?

3. AACSB ▶ Communication
Most calculators come with a book of instructions. Unfortunately, if you misplace the book, you're left to your own devices in figuring out how to use the calculator. Wouldn't it be easier if the calculator had a built-in "help" function similar to the one on your computer? You could just punch the "Help" key on your keypad and call up the relevant instructions on your display screen. You just invented a calculator with this feature, and you're ready to roll it out. First, however, you have to make some pricing decisions:

* When you introduce the product, should you use skimming or penetration pricing?

* Which of the following pricing methods should you use in the long term: cost-based pricing, demand-based pricing, target costing, or prestige pricing?

Prepare a report describing both your introductory and long-term alternatives. Then explain and justify your choice of the methods that you'll use.

4. Working in the school chemistry lab, you come up with a fantastic-tasting fruit drink. You're confident that it can be a big seller, and you've found a local company that will manufacture it. Unfortunately, you have to handle the distribution yourself—a complex task because your product is made from natural ingredients and can easily spoil. What distribution channels would you use and why? How would you handle the physical distribution of your product?

5. AACSB ▶ Analysis
Students at Penn State University can take a break from their studies to visit an on-campus ice cream stand called the Creamery. Milk for the ice cream comes from cows that graze on university land as part of a program run by the agriculture school. Other ingredients, including sugar and chocolate syrup, are purchased

from outside vendors, as are paper products and other supplies. Using your personal knowledge of ice cream–stand operations (which probably comes from your experience as a customer), diagram the Creamery's supply chain. How would the supply chain change if the company decided to close its retail outlet and sell directly to supermarkets?

6. **AACSB** ▸ Analysis

Did you ever have a Nintendo Game Boy? Is the product still popular? Like all products, Game Boy has a product life cycle. Your job is to describe that product life cycle. To learn something about the product, go to the Web, log on to your favorite search engine (Google, Yahoo!), and enter the phrase *Game Boy history*. Identify each of the product life stages that Game Boy has gone through and speculate on the marketing actions that Nintendo would have taken during each stage. Where do you think Game Boy is now in its product life cycle? Where do you think it will be in five years? Justify your answers.

7. **AACSB** ▸ Analysis

Companies encourage customers to buy their products by using a variety of promotion tools, including advertising, personal selling, sales promotion, and publicity. Your task is to develop a promotion strategy for two products—the Volkswagen Jetta and Red Bolt soda. For each product, answer the following questions:

- What's the purpose of the promotion?

- What's your target market?

- What is the best way to reach that target market?

- What product features should you emphasize?

- How does your product differ from competitors'?

Then describe the elements that go into your promotion mix, and explain why you chose the promotional tools that you did.

8. **AACSB** ▸ Analysis

If you ran an airline, how would you practice CRM? How would you get permission to market your product to customers? What information would you collect on them? What incentives would you offer them to continue flying with you? What advantages can you gain through effective CRM?

9. Shifts in the external marketing environment often necessitate changes in a company's marketing plans. All companies are affected by external factors, but certain factors can have a stronger influence on particular products. Which of these five types of external factors—political/regulatory, economic, competitive, technological, social/cultural—would have the greatest impact on each of the following products: a Toll Brothers home, P&G Tide laundry detergent, Apple iPod, Pfizer heart medicine, and Gap jeans. In matching products with external factors, apply each factor only once. Be sure to explain exactly how a given factor might impact product sales.

10. Experts have ascribed a number of attributes to Generation Y—people born between 1976 and 2001. On a scale of 1 to 10 (with 10 being the highest), indicate the extent to which each of the following attributes applies to you:

Attribute	To no extent									To a great extent
You're committed to integrity and honesty	1	2	3	4	5	6	7	8	9	10
You're family oriented and close to your parents	1	2	3	4	5	6	7	8	9	10
You're accepting of differences among people	1	2	3	4	5	6	7	8	9	10
You're upbeat and optimistic about the future	1	2	3	4	5	6	7	8	9	10
You're education focused	1	2	3	4	5	6	7	8	9	10
You're independent	1	2	3	4	5	6	7	8	9	10
You're goal oriented	1	2	3	4	5	6	7	8	9	10
You're fairly good at coping	1	2	3	4	5	6	7	8	9	10

Learning on the Web AACSB

The Economics of Online Annoyance

You've just accessed a Web page and begun searching for the information you want to retrieve. Suddenly the page is plastered from top to bottom with *banner ads*. Some pop up, some float across the screen, and in some, animated figures dance and prance to inane music. As a user of the Internet, feel free to be annoyed. As a student of business, however, you should stop and ask yourself a few questions: Where do banner ads come from? Who stands to profit from them?

To get a handle on these questions, go to www.exploringbusinessonline.com to link to the How Stuff Works Web site and read the article "How Web Advertising

Works," by Marshall Brain. When you've finished, answer the following questions *from the viewpoint of a company advertising on the Web*:

1. What are the advantages and disadvantages of banner ads? Why are they less popular with advertisers today than they were about 10 years ago?

2. What alternative forms of Web advertising are more common today? (For each of these alternative forms, describe the type of ad, explain how it's more effective than banner advertising, and list any disadvantages.)

3. Why are there so many ads on the Web? Is it easy to make money selling ads on the Web? Why or why not?

4. Assume that you're in charge of Web advertising for a company that sells cell-phone ring tones. On which sites would you place your ads, and what type of ads would you use? Why?

Career Opportunities

So Many Choices

How would you like to work for an advertising agency? How about promoting a new or top-selling brand? What about working in retail, perhaps as a buyer? Want to try your hand at sales? Or does marketing research or logistics management sound more appealing? With a marketing degree, you can pursue any of these career options—and more. To learn more about these options, go to www.exploringbusinessonline.com to link to the WetFeet Web site. Click on "Real People" and then on "Marketing," "Advertising," or both. Select **two** of the profiled professionals who interest you, and for each, answer the following questions:

1. What does the individual do?

2. How did he or she get the job?

3. What kind of people do well in this job?

4. What does the individual like and dislike about the job?

5. How can someone get into this line of work?

Next, answer the following two questions:

1. Does a career in marketing appeal to you? Why or why not?

2. Which of the following marketing career options do you find most interesting—advertising, brand management, logistics, marketing research, retailing, or sales? Why?

Ethics Angle AACSB

A "Late Fee" by Any Other Name

Why is there always time to get a DVD from Blockbuster and watch it, but never enough time to return it within the specified number of days? Are you fed up with late fees? Maybe you should get your movies through a mail-order service, such as Netflix, which lets you hold onto the DVDs for as long as you want in exchange for a monthly fee. But wait: Blockbuster has solved your dilemma by announcing "the end of late fees." Maybe so and maybe not. The end of late fees isn't *really* the end of late fees. As in so many deals that sound too good to be true, there's some fine print. Here's how it really works: The bad news is that eight days after the return date of your movie, your credit card is charged for the *selling price* of the DVD. The good news is that you can get the "sale" removed from your credit card if you return the DVD within 30 days. The bad news is that you're charged a "restocking fee" to cover the cost to Blockbuster of processing the "temporary" sale. You *did* avoid a "late fee." (By the way, not all Blockbuster outlets offer this value-added service; some still keep it simple by charging the time-honored late fee.)

As a business student, you should be wondering if Blockbuster's end-of-late-fees campaign makes business sense. You should wonder whether it's ethical. You may already know that the New Jersey Attorney General has charged Blockbuster with deceptive advertising and filed suit. But even if you know the opinion of one high-ranking legal official, you should (as always) be prepared to form your own. Answer the following questions (being sure to justify your answers):

1. Did Blockbuster's decision to establish a no-late-fee policy make good business sense?

2. In informing consumers about this program, did Blockbuster engage in deceptive advertising?

3. Were Blockbuster's actions unethical?

Team-Building Skills AACSB

Build a Better iPod and They Will Listen

Right now, Apple is leading the pack of consumer-electronics manufacturers with its extremely successful iPod. But that doesn't mean that Apple's lead in the market can't be

surmounted. Perhaps some enterprising college students will come up with an idea for a better iPod and put together a plan for bringing it to market. After all, Apple founders

Steve Jobs and Stephen Wozniak were college students (actually, college dropouts) who found entrepreneurship more rewarding than scholarship. Here's your team assignment for this exercise:

1. Go to www.exploringbusinessonline.com to link to the *BusinessWeek* Web site and read the article "Could Apple Blow Its iPod Lead?"

2. Create a marketing strategy for your hypothetical iPod competitor. Be sure that you touch on all the following bases:

   - Select a target market for your product.

   - Develop your product so that it offers features that meet the needs of your target market.

   - Describe the industry in which you'll compete.

   - Set a price for your product and explain your pricing strategy.

   - Decide what distribution channels you'll use to get your product to market.

   - Develop a promotion mix to create demand for your product.

3. Write a report that details your marketing strategy.

The Global View AACSB

Made in China—Why Not Sell in China?

If Wow Wee manufactures Robosapien in China, why shouldn't it sell the product in China? In fact, the company has introduced its popular robot to the Chinese market through a Toys "R" Us store in Hong Kong. Expanding into other parts of China, however, will require a well-crafted, well-executed marketing plan. You're director of marketing for Wow Wee, and you've been asked to put together a plan to expand sales in China. To get some background, go to www.exploringbusinessonline.com to link to the AXcess News Web site and read the article "China Could Soon Become Booming Toy Market." Then, draw up a brief marketing plan for increasing sales in China, being sure to include all the following components:

- Profile of your target market (gender, age, income level, geographic location, interests, and so forth)

- Proposed changes to the company's current marketing mix: modifications to product design, pricing, distribution, and promotional strategies.

- Estimated sales in units for each of the next five years, including a list of the factors that you considered in arriving at your projections.

- Discussion of threats and opportunities posed by expansion in the Chinese market.

Business Plan Project

Group Report: *Marketing Plan*

REPORT

Your team should submit a written report that gives an overview of your marketing plan, including target market, customer needs, product characteristics, pricing, distribution, and promotion. Your report should also describe any proposed uses of the Internet to promote or sell your products. For details on what you should include in the report, go to Appendix A at the back of the book, entitled "Introducing Your Business Plan" (p. 307), and consult the section headed "Marketing." Also consider two other issues:

a. *Customer Needs and Product Characteristics*
Identify your customers' needs or wants and link them to the product characteristics (appearance, features, quality, reliability, durability, usability, ease of maintenance) that you described in your products and production group report.

b. *E-Business: Internet Promotion and Sales*
In addition, if you intend to use the Internet to promote or sell your products, this section should provide answers to the following questions:

- Will your company have a Web site? Who will visit the site?

- What will it look like? What information will it supply?

- Will you sell products over the Internet?

- How will you attract customers to your site and entice them to buy from your company?

The report should be about two double-spaced typed pages. The name of your proposed business and the names of all team members should appear on the report.

REASONABLE CONTRIBUTIONS

All members of the team who make a reasonable contribution to the report should sign it. (If any team member does not work on the report, his or her name should *not* appear on it.) If a student who has made a contribution is unable to sign the report (because of sickness or some other valid reason), the team can sign his or her name. To indicate that a name was signed by the team on a member's behalf, be sure to attach a note to the signature.

8

Business in a Global Environment

After studying this chapter, you will be able to:

1 Explain why nations and companies participate in international trade and how trade between nations is measured.

2 Identify the various opportunities presented by international business.

3 Appreciate how cultural, economic, legal, and political differences between countries create challenges to successful business dealings.

4 Describe the ways in which governments and international bodies promote and regulate global trade.

5 Discuss the various initiatives designed to reduce international trade barriers and promote free trade.

6 Understand how to prepare for a career in international business.

IT'S A SMALL WORLD

Do you wear Nike shoes or Timberland boots? Buy groceries at Tops Friendly Markets, Giant Stores, or Stop & Shop? Listen to Jennifer Lopez, Bruce Springsteen, or the Dixie Chicks? If you answered yes to any of these questions, you're a global business customer. Both Nike and Timberland manufacture most of their products overseas. The Dutch firm Royal Ahold owns all three supermarket chains. Sony Music, the label that records J. Lo, the Boss, and the Chicks, belongs to a Japanese company.

Take an imaginary walk down Orchard Road, the most fashionable shopping area in Singapore. You'll pass department stores such as Tokyo-based Takashimaya and London's very British Marks & Spencer, both filled with such well-known international labels as Ralph Lauren Polo, Burberry, Chanel, and Nokia. If you need a break, you can also stop for a latté at Seattle-based Starbucks or books, CDs, and DVDs at Borders Books and Music, which is headquartered in Ann Arbor, Michigan.

Ryan McVay/
Getty Images, In
Photodisc

When you're in the Chinese capital of Beijing, don't miss Tiananmen Square. Parked in front of the Great Hall of the People, the seat of Chinese government, are fleets of black Buicks, cars made by General Motors in Flint, Michigan. If you're adventurous enough to find yourself in Faisalabad, a medium-sized city in Pakistan, you'll see locals riding donkeys, camels pulling carts piled with agricultural produce, and, located in a refurbished hotel, Hamdard University. Step inside the computer labs, and the sensation of being in a very faraway place will probably disappear: on the computer screens, you'll recognize the familiar Microsoft flag—the same one emblazoned on screens in Microsoft's hometown of Seattle and just about everywhere else on the planet.

The Globalization of Business

The globalization of business is bound to affect you. Not only will you buy products manufactured overseas, but it's highly likely that you will meet and work with individuals from various countries and cultures as customers, suppliers, colleagues, employees, or employers. The bottom line is: The globalization of world commerce has an impact on all of us. So, it makes sense to learn more about how globalization works.

Never before has business spanned the globe the way it does today. But why is international business important? Why do companies and nations engage in international trade? What strategies do they use in the global marketplace? What challenges do companies face when they do business overseas? How do governments and international agencies promote and regulate international trade? Is the globalization of business a good thing? What career opportunities are there for you in global business? How should you prepare yourself to take advantage of them? These are the questions that we'll be addressing in this chapter. Let's start by looking at the more specific reasons why companies and nations engage in international trade.

WHY DO NATIONS TRADE?

Why does the U.S. import automobiles, steel, digital phones, and apparel from other countries? Why don't we just make them ourselves? Why do other countries buy wheat, chemicals, machinery, and consulting services from us? Because no national economy can produce all the goods and services that its people need. Countries are *importers* when they buy goods and services from

If you travel outside the United States, you won't have to give up your daily Starbucks latté. In 1996, Starbucks began its international expansion by opening a coffeehouse in Tokyo. Today, you can find Starbucks stores in 37 countries. Japan alone has more than 500 stores—200 of which, like this one, are in Tokyo.

other countries; when they sell products to other nations, they're *exporters*. (We'll discuss importing and exporting in greater detail later in the chapter.) The monetary value of international trade is enormous. In 2004, the total value of worldwide trade in merchandise and commercial services was over $11 *trillion*.[1]

Absolute and Comparative Advantage

To understand why certain countries import or export certain products, you need to realize that every country (or region) can't produce the same products. The cost of labor, the availability of natural resources, and the level of know-how vary greatly around the world. Most economists use the concept of *absolute* and *comparative advantage* to explain why countries import some products and export others.

Absolute Advantage A nation has an **absolute advantage** if (1) it's the only source of a particular product or (2) it can make more of a product using the same amount of or fewer resources than other countries. Because of climate and soil conditions, for example, Brazil has an absolute advantage in coffee beans and France has an absolute advantage in wine production. Unless, however, an absolute advantage is based on some limited natural resource, it seldom lasts. That's why there are few examples of absolute advantage in the world today. Even France's dominance of worldwide wine production, for example, is being challenged by growing wine industries in Italy, Spain, and the United States.

Comparative Advantage How can we predict, for any given country, which products will be made and sold at home, which will be imported, and which will be exported? This question can be answered by looking at the concept of **comparative advantage**, which exists when a country can produce a product at a lower opportunity cost compared to another nation. But what is an *opportunity cost*? Opportunity costs are the products that a country must decline to make in order to produce something else. When a country decides to specialize in a particular product, it must sacrifice the production of another product.

Let's simplify things by imagining a world with only two countries—The Republic of High Tech and The Kingdom of Low Tech. Each country knows how to make two and only two products: wooden boats and telescopes. Each country spends half of its resources (labor and capital) on each good. Figure 8.1 shows the daily output for both countries. (They're not very productive; we've imagined two *very* small countries.)

First, note that High Tech has an *absolute advantage* in both boats and telescopes: It can make more boats (3 versus 2) and more telescopes (9 versus 1) than Low Tech can with the same resources. So, why doesn't High Tech make *all* the boats and *all* the telescopes needed for *both* countries? Because it doesn't have sufficient resources and must, therefore, decide how much of its resources to devote to each of the two goods. Assume, for example, that each country could devote 100 percent of its resources on *either* of the two goods. Start with boats. If both countries spend *all* their resources on boats (and make no telescopes), here's what happens:

- High Tech makes, for example, 3 more boats but gives up the opportunity to make the 9 telescopes; thus the opportunity cost of making *each* boat is 3 telescopes ($9 \div 3 = 3$).

- Low Tech makes, for example, 2 more boats but gives up the opportunity to make 1 telescope; thus the opportunity cost of making *each* boat is 1/2 telescope ($1 \div 2 = 1/2$).

- Low Tech, therefore, enjoys a *lower opportunity cost*: Because it must give up less to make the extra boats, it has a comparative advantage for boats. And because it's better—that is, more efficient—at making boats than at making telescopes, it should specialize in boat making.

Now telescopes. Here's what happens if each country spends all its time making telescopes and makes no boats:

- High Tech makes, for example, 9 more telescopes but gives up the opportunity to make 3 boats; thus, the opportunity cost of making *each* telescope is 1/3 of a boat ($3 \div 9 = 1/3$).

- Low Tech makes, for example, 1 more telescope but gives up the opportunity to make 2 boats; thus, the opportunity cost of making *each* telescope is 2 boats ($2 \div 1 = 2$).

- In this case, High Tech has the *lower opportunity cost*: Because it had to give up less to make the extra telescopes, it enjoys a comparative advantage for telescopes. And because it's better—more efficient—at making telescopes than at making boats, it should specialize in telescope making.

Figure 8.1

Comparative Advantage in the Techs

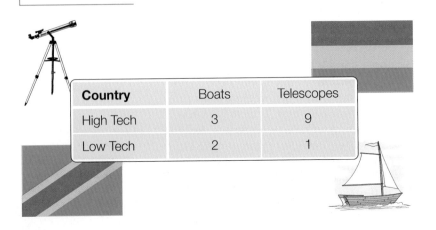

Country	Boats	Telescopes
High Tech	3	9
Low Tech	2	1

Each country will specialize in making the good for which it has a comparative advantage—that is, the good that it can make most efficiently relative to the other country. High Tech will devote its resources to telescopes (which it's good at making), and Low Tech will put its resources into boat making (which it does well). High Tech will export its excess telescopes to Low Tech, which will pay for the telescopes with the money it earns by selling its excess boats to High Tech. Both countries will be better off.

Things are a lot more complex in the real world, but, generally speaking, nations trade in order to exploit their advantages. They benefit from specialization, focusing on what they do best, and trading the output to other countries for what they do best. The United States, for instance, is increasingly an exporter of knowledge-based products, such as software, movies, music, and professional services (management consulting, financial services, and so forth). America's colleges and universities, therefore, are a source of comparative advantage, and students from all over the world come to the United States for the world's best higher-education system.

France and Italy are centers for fashion and luxury goods and are leading exporters of wine, perfume, and designer clothing. Japan's engineering expertise has given it an edge in such fields as automobiles and consumer electronics. With large numbers of highly skilled graduates in technology, India has become the world's leader in low-cost, computer-software engineering.

HOW DO WE MEASURE TRADE BETWEEN NATIONS?

To evaluate the nature and consequences of its international trade, a nation looks at two key indicators. We determine a country's **balance of trade** by subtracting the value of its imports from the value of its exports. If a country sells more products than it buys, it has a favorable balance, called a **trade surplus**. If it buys more than it sells, it has an unfavorable balance, or a **trade deficit**.

For many years, the United States has had a trade deficit: We buy far more goods from the rest of the world than we sell overseas. This fact shouldn't be surprising. With high income levels, we not only consume a sizeable portion of our own domestically produced goods but enthusiastically buy imported goods. Other countries, such as China and Taiwan, which manufacture primarily for export, have large trade surpluses because they sell far more goods overseas than they buy.

Managing the National Credit Card

Are trade deficits a bad thing? Not necessarily. They can be positive if a country's economy is strong enough to keep growing and to generate the jobs and incomes that permit its citizens to buy the best the world has to offer. That was certainly the case in the United States in the 1990s. Some experts, however, are alarmed at our rapidly accelerating trade deficit. Investment guru Warren Buffet, for example, cautions that no country can continuously sustain large and burgeoning trade deficits. Why not? Because creditor nations will eventually stop taking IOUs from debtor nations, and when that happens, the national spending spree will have to cease. "Our national credit card," he warns, "allows us to charge truly breathtaking amounts. But that card's credit line is not limitless."[2]

By the same token, trade surpluses aren't necessarily good for a nation's consumers. Japan's export-fueled economy produced high economic growth in the 1970s and 1980s. But most domestically made consumer goods were priced at artificially high levels inside Japan itself—so high, in fact, that many Japanese traveled overseas to buy the electronics and other high-quality goods on which Japanese trade was dependent. CD players and televisions were significantly cheaper in Honolulu or

absolute advantage
Condition whereby a country is the only source of a product or is able to make more of a product using the same or fewer resources than other countries.

comparative advantage
Condition whereby one nation is able to produce a product at a lower opportunity cost compared to another nation.

balance of trade
Difference between the value of a nation's imports and its exports during a specified period of time.

trade surplus
Condition whereby a country sells more products than it buys, resulting in a favorable trade balance.

trade deficit
Condition whereby a country buys more products than it sells, resulting in an unfavorable trade balance.

Los Angeles than in Tokyo. How did this situation come about? Although Japan manufactures a variety of goods, many of them are made for export. To secure shares in international markets, Japan prices its exported goods competitively. Inside Japan, because competition is limited, producers can put artificially high prices on Japanese-made goods. Due to a number of factors (high demand for a limited supply of imported goods, high shipping and distribution costs, and other costs incurred by importers in a nation that tends to protect its own industries), imported goods are also expensive.[3]

Balance of Payments

The second key measure of the effectiveness of international trade is **balance of payments**: the difference, over a period of time, between the total flow of money coming into a country and the total flow of money going out. As in its balance of trade, the biggest factor in a country's balance of payments is the money that comes in and goes out as a result of imports and exports. But balance of payments includes other cash inflows and outflows, such as cash received from or paid for foreign investment, loans, tourism, military expenditures, and foreign aid. For example, if a U.S. company buys some real estate in a foreign country, that investment counts in the U.S. balance of payments, but not in its balance of trade, which measures only import and export transactions. In the long run, having an unfavorable balance of payments can negatively affect the stability of a country's currency. Some observers are worried about the U.S. dollar, which has undergone an accelerating pattern of unfavorable balances of payments since the 1970s. For one thing, carrying negative balances has forced the United States to cover its debt by borrowing from other countries.[4] Figure 8.2 provides a brief historical overview to illustrate the relationship between the United States' balance of trade and its balance of payments.

Opportunities in International Business

The fact that nations exchange billions of dollars in goods and services each year demonstrates that international trade makes good economic sense. For an American company wishing to expand beyond national borders, there are a variety of ways to get involved in international business. Let's take a closer look at the most popular ones.

IMPORTING AND EXPORTING

Importing (buying products overseas and reselling them in one's own country) and **exporting** (selling domestic products to foreign customers) are the oldest and most prevalent forms of international trade. For many companies, importing is the primary link to the global market. American food and beverage wholesalers, for instance, import the bottled water Evian from its source in the French Alps for resale in U.S. supermarkets.[5] Other companies get into the global arena by identifying an international market for their products and become exporters. The Chinese, for instance, are increasingly fond of fast foods cooked in soybean oil. Because they also have an increasing appetite for meat, they need high-protein soybeans to raise livestock.[6] As a result, American farmers now export over $1 billion worth of soybeans to China every year.

LICENSING AND FRANCHISING

A company that wants to get into an international market quickly while taking only limited financial and legal risks might consider

---

Figure 8.2

U.S. Imports, Exports, and Balance of Trade, 1994–2003

Note: Figures are for "goods" only, not "goods and services."

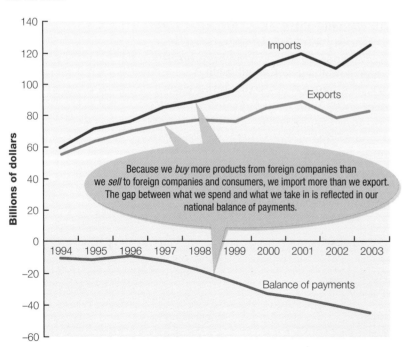

licensing agreements with foreign companies. An **international licensing agreement** allows a foreign company (the *licensee*) to sell the products of a producer (the *licensor*) or to use its intellectual property (patents, trademarks, copyrights) in exchange for royalty fees. Here's how it works: You own a company in the United States that sells coffee-flavored popcorn. You're sure that your product would be a big hit in Japan, but you don't have the resources to set up a factory or sales office in Japan. You can't make the popcorn here and ship it to Japan because it would get stale. So you enter into a licensing agreement with a Japanese company that allows your licensee to manufacture coffee-flavored popcorn using your special process and to sell it in Japan under your brand name. In exchange, the Japanese licensee would pay you a royalty fee.

Another popular way to expand overseas is to sell franchises. Under an **international franchise** agreement, a company (the *franchiser*) grants a foreign company (the *franchisee*) the right to use its brand name and to sell its products or services. The franchisee is responsible for all operations but agrees to operate according to a business model established by the franchiser. In turn, the franchiser usually provides advertising, training, and new product assistance. Franchising is a natural form of global expansion for companies that operate domestically according to a franchise model, including restaurant chains, such as McDonald's and Kentucky Fried Chicken, and hotel chains, such as Holiday Inn and Best Western.

CONTRACT MANUFACTURING AND OUTSOURCING

Because of high domestic labor costs, many U.S. companies manufacture their products in countries where labor costs are lower. This arrangement is called **international contract manufacturing** or **outsourcing**. A U.S. company might contract with a local company in a foreign country to manufacture one of its products. It will, however, retain control of product design and development and put its own label on the finished product. Contract manufacturing is quite common in the U.S. apparel business, with most American brands being made in Asia (China and Malaysia) and Latin America (Mexico and the Dominican Republic).

Thanks to twenty-first–century information technology, nonmanufacturing functions can also be outsourced to nations with lower labor costs. U.S. companies increasingly draw upon a vast supply of relatively inexpensive skilled labor to perform various business services, such as software development, accounting, and claims processing. For years, American insurance companies have processed much of their claims-related paperwork in Ireland. With a large well-educated population, India has become a center for software development and customer-call centers for American companies. In the case of India, as you can see in Table 8.1, (p. 202) the attraction is not only a large pool of knowledge workers, but significantly lower wages as well.

STRATEGIC ALLIANCES AND JOINT VENTURES

What if a company wants to do business in a foreign country but lacks the expertise or resources? Or what if the target nation's government doesn't allow foreign companies to operate within its borders unless it has a local partner? In these cases, a firm might enter into a strategic alliance with a local company or even with the government itself. A **strategic alliance** is an agreement between two companies (or a company and a nation) to pool resources in order to achieve business goals that benefit both partners. For example, Viacom (a leading global media company) has a strategic alliance with Beijing Television

---

balance of payments
Difference between the total flow of money coming into a country and the total flow of money going out.

importing
Practice of buying products overseas and reselling them in one's own country.

exporting
Practice of selling domestic products to foreign customers.

international licensing agreement
Agreement that allows a foreign company to sell a domestic company's products or use its intellectual property in exchange for royalty fees.

international franchise
Agreement in which a domestic company (franchiser) gives a foreign company (franchisee) the right to use its brand and sell its products.

international contract manufacturing (or outsourcing)
Practice by which a company produces goods through an independent contractor in a foreign country.

strategic alliance
Agreement between two companies (or a company and a nation) to pool resources in order to achieve business goals that benefit both partners.

TABLE 8.1

Selected Hourly Wages, United States and India

Occupation	U.S. Wage	Indian Wage
Telephone operator	$12.57	Under $1.00
Health-record technical worker/Medical transcriber	$13.17	$1.50–$2.00
Payroll clerk	$15.17	$1.50–$2.00
Legal assistant/paralegal	$17.86	$6.00–$8.00
Accountant	$23.35	$6.00–$15.00
Financial researcher/analyst	$33.00–$35.00	$6.00–$15.00

Broadcasting in 17 languages, MTV reaches 360 million households in 139 countries. The brand is managed worldwide by MTV Networks International, a division of Viacom International, which uses a variety of arrangements to enter foreign markets. In Russia, for example, it owns shares in a domestic firm called BIZ Enterprises, which operates MTV Russia. MTV Asia and MTV Mandarin are joint ventures with PolyGram, a Dutch-based media giant, and MTV Australia and MTV Japan operate under licensing agreements between MTV Networks International and local media companies.

to produce Chinese-language music and entertainment programming.[7]

An alliance can serve a number of purposes:

- Enhancing marketing efforts
- Building sales and market share
- Improving products
- Reducing production and distribution costs
- Sharing technology

Alliances range in scope from informal cooperative agreements to **joint ventures**—alliances in which the partners fund a separate entity (perhaps a partnership or a corporation) to manage their joint operation. Magazine publisher Hearst, for example, has joint ventures with companies in several countries. So, young women in Israel can read *Cosmo Israel* in Hebrew while Russian women can pick up a Russian version of the same magazine. The U.S. edition serves as a starting point to which nationally appropriate material is added in each different nation. This approach allows Hearst to sell the magazine in more than 50 countries.[8]

FOREIGN DIRECT INVESTMENT AND SUBSIDIARIES

Many of the approaches to global expansion that we've discussed so far allow companies to participate in international markets without investing in foreign plants and facilities. As markets expand, however, a firm might decide to enhance its competitive advantage by making a direct investment in operations conducted in another country. **Foreign direct investment (FDI)** refers to the formal establishment of business operations on foreign soil—the building of factories, sales offices, and distribution networks to serve local markets in a nation other than the company's home country.

FDI is generally the most expensive commitment that a firm can make to an overseas market, and it's typically driven by the size and attractiveness of the target market. For example, German and Japanese automakers, such as BMW, Mercedes, Toyota, and Honda, have made serious commitments to the U.S. market: Most of the cars and trucks that they build in plants in the South and Midwest are destined for sale in the United States.

A common form of FDI is the **foreign subsidiary**: an independent company owned by a foreign firm (called the *parent*). This approach to going international not only gives the parent company full access to local markets, but exempts it from any laws or regulations that may hamper the activities of foreign firms. The parent company has tight control over the operations of a subsidiary, but while senior managers from the parent company often oversee operations, many managers and employees are citizens of the host country. Not surprisingly, most very large firms have foreign subsidiaries. IBM and Coca-Cola, for example, have both had success in the Japanese market through their foreign subsidiaries (IBM-Japan and Coca-Cola-Japan). FDI goes in the other direction, too, and many companies operating in the United States are in fact subsidiaries of foreign firms. Gerber Products, for example, is a subsidiary of the Swiss company Novartis, and Stop & Shop and Giant Food Stores belong to the Dutch company Royal Ahold.

Where does most FDI capital end up? Figure 8.3 provides an overview of amounts, trends, and destinations.

All these strategies have been successful in the arena of global business. But success in international business involves more than

just finding the best way to reach international markets. Doing global business is a complex and risky endeavor. As many companies have learned the hard way, people and organizations don't do things the same way abroad as they do at home. What differences make global business so tricky? That's the question that we'll turn to next.

MULTINATIONAL CORPORATIONS

A company that operates in many countries is called a **multinational corporation (MNC)**. *Fortune* magazine's roster of the top 500 MNCs speaks for the strong global position of U.S. business: Almost 40 percent are headquartered in the United States and these U.S. companies make up half of the top 10: Wal-Mart (1), Exxon Mobil (3), General Motors (5), Ford (8), and General Electric (9).[9] Figure 8.4 (p. 204) lists the 20 largest MNCs in the world, according to revenues.

MNCs often adopt the approach encapsulated in the motto "Think globally, act locally." They often adjust their operations, products, marketing, and distribution to mesh with the environments of the countries in which they operate. Because they understand that a "one-size-fits-all" mentality doesn't make good business sense when

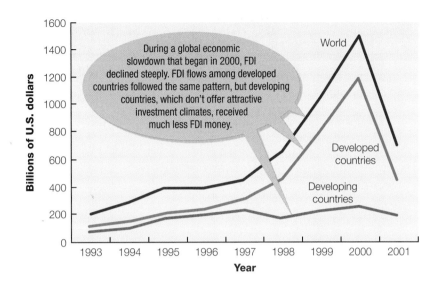

Figure 8.3

Where FDI Goes

---

joint ventures
Alliances in which the partners fund a separate entity (partnership or corporation) to manage their joint operations.

foreign direct investment (FDI)
Formal establishment of business operations (such as the building of factories or sales offices) on foreign soil.

foreign subsidiary
Independent company owned by a foreign firm (called its parent).

multinational corporation (MNC)
Large corporation that operates in many countries.

Rank	MNC (country)	Revenues (in $ millions)
1	Wal-Mart Stores (USA)	$287,989
2	BP (Britain)	285,059
3	Exxon Mobil (USA)	270,772
4	Royal Dutch/Shell Group (Netherlands/Britain)	268,690
5	General Motors (USA)	193,517
6	DaimlerChrysler (Germany)	176,688
7	Toyota Motor (Japan)	172,616
8	Ford Motor (USA)	172,233
9	General Electric (USA)	152,866
10	Total (France)	152,610
11	Chevron Texaco (USA)	147,967
12	ConocoPhillips (USA)	121,663
13	AXA (France)	121,606
14	Allianz (Germany)	118,937
15	Volkswagen (Germany)	110,649
16	Citigroup (USA)	108,276
17	ING Group (Netherlands)	105,886
18	Nippon Telegraph & Telephone (Japan)	100,545
19	American International Group (USA)	97,987
20	IBM (USA)	96,293

Figure 8.4 ACTIVE

The World's 20 Largest MNCs

you're trying to sell products in different markets, they're willing to accommodate cultural and economic differences. Increasingly, MNCs supplement their mainstream product line with products designed for local markets. Coca-Cola, for example, produces coffee and citrus-juice drinks developed specifically for the Japanese market.[10] When such companies as Nokia and Motorola design cell phones, they're often geared to local tastes in color, size, and other features. McDonalds provides a vegetarian menu in India, where religious convictions affect the demand for beef and pork.[11] In Germany, McDonald's caters to local tastes by offering beer in some restaurants.[12]

Likewise, many MNCs have made themselves more sensitive to local market conditions by decentralizing their decision making. While corporate headquarters still maintain a fair amount of control, home-country managers keep a suitable distance by relying on modern telecommunications. Today, fewer managers are dispatched from headquarters; MNCs depend instead on local talent. Not only does decentralized organization speed up and improve decision making, but it allows an MNC to project the image of a local company. IBM, for instance, has been quite successful in the Japanese market because local customers and suppliers perceive it as a Japanese company. Crucial to this perception is the fact that the vast majority of IBM's Tokyo employees, including top leadership, are Japanese nationals.[13]

Criticism of MNC Culture

The global reach of MNCs is a source of criticism as well as praise. Critics argue that they too often destroy the livelihoods of home-country workers by moving jobs to developing countries where workers are willing to labor under poor conditions and for less pay. They also contend that traditional lifestyles and values are being weakened, and even destroyed, as global brands foster a global culture of American movies, fast food, and cheap mass-produced consumer products. Still others claim that the demand of MNCs for constant economic growth and cheaper access to natural resources do irreversible damage to the physical environment. All these negative consequences, critics maintain, stem from the abuses of international trade—from the policy of placing profits above people on a global scale. These views surfaced in violent street demonstrations in Seattle in 1999 and Genoa, Italy, in 2000, and since then, meetings of the International Monetary Fund and World Bank have regularly been assailed by large crowds of protestors who have succeeded in catching the attention of the worldwide media.

In Defense of MNC Culture

Meanwhile, supporters of MNCs respond that huge corporations deliver better, cheaper products for customers everywhere, create jobs, and raise the standard of living in developing countries. They also argue that globalization increases cross-cultural understanding. Says Anne O. Kruger, first deputy managing director of the IMF:

> The impact of the faster growth on living standards has been phenomenal. We have observed the increased well being of a larger percentage of the world's population by a greater increment than ever

before in history. Growing incomes give people the ability to spend on things other than basic food and shelter, in particular on things such as education and health. This ability, combined with the sharing among nations of medical and scientific advances, has transformed life in many parts of the developing world. Infant mortality has declined from 180 per 1,000 births in 1950 to 60 per 1,000 births. Literacy rates have risen from an average of 40 percent in the 1950s to over 70 percent today. World poverty has declined, despite still-high population growth in the developing world."[14]

QUICK QUIZ   8.1

Before you delve into the global business environment, take a few minutes to test your understanding of international trade and opportunities in international business.

Go to www.exploringbusinessonline.com

ABOUT NIKE   8.1

Now that you're aware of the pros and cons of doing business in a global environment, take a few moments to examine both the benefits that Nike derives from its international operations and the responsibilities which it has to the countries in which it operates.

Go to www.exploringbusinessonline.com

The Global Business Environment

In the classic movie *The Wizard of Oz*, a magically misplaced Midwest farm girl takes a moment to survey the bizarre landscape of Oz and then comments to her little dog, "I don't think we're in Kansas anymore, Toto." That sentiment probably echoes the reaction of many businesspeople who find themselves in the midst of international ven-tures for the first time. The differences between the foreign landscape and the one with which they're familiar are often huge and multifaceted. Some are quite obvious, such as differences in language, currency, and everyday habits (say, using chopsticks instead of silverware). But others are subtle, complex, and sometimes even hidden. Success in international business means understanding a wide range of cultural, economic, legal, and political differences between countries. Let's look at some of the most important of these differences.

THE CULTURAL ENVIRONMENT

Even when two people from the same country communicate, there is always a possibility of misunderstanding. When people from different countries get together, that possibility increases substantially. Differences in communication styles reflect differences in **culture**: the system of shared beliefs, values, customs, and behaviors that govern the interactions of members of a society. Cultural differences create challenges to successful international business dealings. We explain a few of these challenges in the following sections.

Language

English is the international language of business. The natives of such European countries as France and Spain certainly take pride in their own languages and cultures, but English is the business language of the European community. Whereas only a few educated Europeans have studied Italian or Norwegian, most have studied English. Similarly, on the South Asian subcontinent, where hundreds of local languages and dialects are spoken, English is the official language. In most corners of the world, English-only speakers—such as most Americans—have no problem finding competent translators and interpreters. So why is language an issue for English speakers doing business in the global marketplace?

In many countries, only members of the educated classes speak English. The larger

---

culture
System of shared beliefs, values, customs, and behaviors that govern the interactions of members of a society.

population—which is usually the market you want to tap—speaks the local tongue. Advertising messages and sales appeals must take this fact into account. More than one English translation of an advertising slogan has resulted in a humorous (and perhaps serious) blunder. Some classics are listed in Table 8.2.

Besides, relying on translators and interpreters puts you at a disadvantage. You're privy only to *interpretations* of the messages that you're getting, and this handicap can result in a real competitive problem. Maybe you'll misread the subtler intentions of the person with whom you're trying to conduct business. The best way to combat this problem is to study foreign languages. Most people appreciate some effort to communicate in their local language, even on the most basic level. Even mistakes resulting from a desire to demonstrate your genuine interest in the language of your counterparts in foreign countries is appreciated. The same principle goes doubly when you're introducing yourself to non-English speakers in the United States. Few things work faster to encourage a friendly atmosphere than a native speaker's willingness to greet a foreign guest in the guest's native language.

Time and Sociability

Americans take for granted many of the cultural aspects of our business practices. Most of our meetings, for instance, focus on business issues, and we tend to start and end our meetings on schedule. These habits stem from a broader cultural preference: We don't like to waste time. (It was an American, Benjamin Franklin, who coined the phrase "Time is Money.") This preference, however, is by no means universal. The expectation that meetings will start on time and adhere to precise agendas is common in parts of Europe (especially the Germanic countries) as well as in the United States, but elsewhere—say, in Latin America and the Middle East—people are often late to meetings.

High- and Low-Context Cultures

Likewise, don't expect businesspeople from these regions—or businesspeople from most of Mediterranean Europe, for that matter—to "get down to business" as soon as a meeting has started. They'll probably ask about your health and that of your family, inquire whether you're enjoying your visit to their country, suggest local foods, and generally appear to be avoiding serious discussion at all costs. For Americans, such

TABLE 8.2

Lost in Translation

- In Belgium, the translation of the slogan of an American auto-body company, "Body by Fisher," came out as "Corpse by Fisher."

- Translated into German, the slogan "Come Alive with Pepsi" became "Come out of the Grave with Pepsi."

- A U.S. computer company in Indonesia translated "software" as "underwear."

- A German chocolate product called "Zit" didn't sell well in the United States.

- An English-speaking car-wash company in Francophone Quebec advertised itself as a "*lavement d'auto*" ("car enema") instead of the correct "*lavage d'auto.*"

- A proposed new soap called "Dainty" in English came out as "aloof" in Flemish (Belgium), "dimwitted" in Farsi (Iran), and "crazy person" in Korea; the product was shelved.

- One false word in a Mexican commercial for an American shirt maker changed "When I used this shirt, I felt good" to "Until I used this shirt, I felt good."

- In the 1970s, GM's Chevy Nova didn't get off the ground in Puerto Rico, in part because *Nova* in Spanish means "It doesn't go."

- A U.S. appliance ad fizzled in the Middle East because it showed a well-stocked refrigerator featuring a large ham, thus offending the sensibilities of Muslim consumers, who don't eat pork.

topics are conducive to nothing but idle chitchat, but in certain cultures, getting started this way is a matter of simple politeness and hospitality.

If you ever find yourself in such a situation, the best advice is to go with the flow and be receptive to cultural nuances. In **high-context cultures**, the numerous interlocking (and often unstated) personal and family connections that hold people together have an effect on almost all interactions. Because people's personal lives overlap with their business lives (and vice versa), it's important to get to know your potential business partners as human beings and individuals.

By contrast, in **low-context cultures**, such as those of the United States, Germany, Switzerland, and the Scandinavian countries, personal and work relationships are more compartmentalized: You don't necessarily need to know much about the personal context of a person's life in order to deal with him or her in the business arena.

comfortable when talking with someone varies by culture. People from the Middle East like to converse from a distance of a foot or less, while Americans prefer more personal space.

Finally, while people in some cultures prefer to deliver direct, clear messages, others use language that's subtler or more indirect. North Americans and most Northern Europeans fall into the former category and many Asians into the latter. But even within these categories, there are differences. Though typically polite, Chinese and Koreans are very direct in expression, while Japanese are indirect. This example brings up two important points. First, avoid lumping loosely related cultures together. We sometimes talk, for example, about "Asian culture," but such broad categories as "Asian" are usually oversimplifications. Japanese culture is different from Korean, which is different from Chinese. Second, never assume that two people from the same culture will always act in a similar

ABOUT NIKE 8.2

Now that you know something about the ways in which cultural differences pose challenges to successful international business dealings, take a few moments to learn how Nike responds to such challenges.

Go to www.exploringbusinessonline.com

Intercultural Communication

Different cultures have different communication *styles*—a fact that can take some getting used to. For example, *degrees of animation in expression* can differ from culture to culture. Southern Europeans and Middle Easterners are quite animated, favoring expressive body language and hand gestures and raised voices. Northern Europeans are far more reserved. The English, for example, are famous for their understated style and the Germans for their formality in most business settings. In addition, the *distance* at which one feels

What's wrong with this picture? The two business people (one from the United States and the other from Japan) are out of sync. Americans greet each other by shaking hands, but the Japanese greet each other by bowing. Before doing business with someone from Japan, you might want to learn something about bows: Bows range from a simple nod of the head to a long, 90-degree bow. The person of lower status is expected to bow deeper and longer. Because most Japanese don't expect people from other countries to know the rules of bowing, a nod of the head works fine (but skip the handshake).

high-context cultures
Cultures in which personal and family connections have an effect on most interactions, including those in business.

low-context cultures
Cultures in which personal and work relationships are compartmentalized.

manner. Not all Latin Americans are casual about meeting times, not all Italians use animated body language, and not all Germans are formal.

In summary, learn about a country's culture and use your knowledge to help improve the quality of your business dealings. Learn to value the subtle differences among cultures, but don't allow cultural stereotypes to dictate how you interact with people from any culture. Treat each person as an individual and spend time getting to know what he or she is about.

THE ECONOMIC ENVIRONMENT

If you plan to do business in a foreign country, you need to know its level of economic development. You also have to be aware of factors influencing the value of its currency and the impact that changes in that value will have on your profits.

Figure 8.5 ⬤ **ACTIVE**

The World's Wealth, 1970 and 2004

Share of GDP, 1970

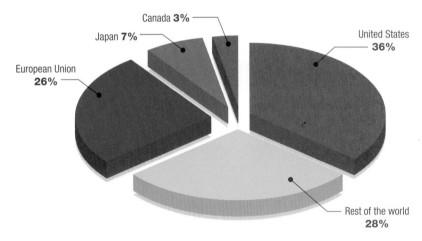

Canada **3%**
Japan **7%**
European Union **26%**
United States **36%**
Rest of the world **28%**

Share of GDP, 2004

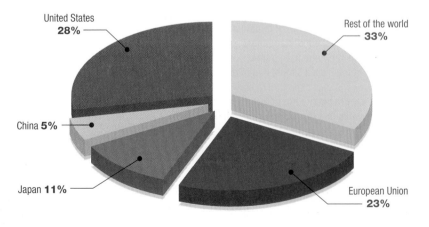

United States **28%**
China **5%**
Japan **11%**
Rest of the world **33%**
European Union **23%**

Economic Development

If you don't understand a nation's level of economic development, you'll have trouble answering some very basic questions. Will consumers in this country be able to afford the product I want to sell? How many units can I expect to sell? Will it be possible to make a reasonable profit?

A country's level of economic development is related to its *standard of living*, which can be evaluated using an economic indicator called **gross national income (GNI) per capita**. To calculate GNI per capita, we divide the value of all goods and services produced in a country (its GNI) by its average population and so arrive at an estimate of *each citizen's share of national income*.

The World Bank, which loans money for improvements in underdeveloped nations, uses per capita GNI to divide countries into four income categories:[15]

- *High income.* $10,066 or higher (United States, Germany, Japan)

- *Upper-middle income.* $3,256 to $10,065 (South Africa, Poland, Mexico)

- *Lower-middle income.* $826 to $3,255 (China, Philippines, Brazil)

- *Low income.* $825 or less (India, Nigeria, Vietnam)

As you can see from Figure 8.5, a large portion of the world's wealth remains concentrated in just a few areas. Remember, however, that even though a country has a low GNI per capita, it can still be an attractive place for doing business. India, for example, is among the poorest countries in the world, but it has a population of a billion, and a segment of that population is well-educated—an appealing feature for many business initiatives.

The long-term goal of many countries is to move up the economic development ladder. Some factors conducive to economic growth include a reliable banking system, a strong stock market, and government policies to encourage investment and competition and discourage corruption. It's also important that a country's *infrastructure*—its systems of communications (telephone, television, newspapers), transportation (roads, railways, airports), energy (gas and electricity, power plants) and social facilities (schools, hospitals)—be strong. These basic systems will help countries attract foreign investors, which can be crucial to economic development.

Currency Valuations and Exchange Rates

If every nation used the same currency, international trade would be a lot easier. Unfortunately, this is not the case. Let's say that your business is importing watches from Switzerland. Because the watchmaker will want to be paid in Swiss francs, you have to figure out how many U.S. dollars you'll need to buy the francs with which to pay the watchmaker. You'd start by finding out the exchange rate between the Swiss franc and the U.S. dollar. The **exchange rate** tells you how much one currency is worth *relative to another currency*. So you need to know the value of the Swiss franc relative to the U.S. dollar.

You could simply look in a newspaper or go to any number of Web sites—say, www.oanda.com. Remember, however, that the exchange rate changes frequently. To keep things simple, let's assume that the exchange rate is 1 Swiss franc = $0.81 (that is, 1 Swiss franc is worth $0.81). Let's also assume that you owe the Swiss watchmaker 1,000 francs. Doing some quick math, you figure that it will take $810 to buy 1,000 francs (1,000 francs × the exchange rate of $0.81 = $810).

Now let's say that you don't have the cash flow to pay the watchmaker for two weeks. When you check the exchange rate two weeks later, you find that it's changed to 1 Swiss franc = $0.85. Are you better off or worse off? It's easy to check: 1,000 francs × the new exchange rate of $0.85 = $850. You've just learned the hard way that when the value of the franc relative to the dollar goes up, it costs you more to buy something from Switzerland. You probably can't help but wonder what would have happened if the value of the franc relative to the dollar had gone down—say, to $0.72 per franc. At this rate, you'd need only $720 to pay the 1,000 francs (1,000 × $0.72). In other words, when the value of the franc relative to the dollar drops, it costs less to buy goods from Switzerland. In sum you've learned that:

- If a foreign currency goes *up* relative to the U.S. dollar, Americans must pay *more* for goods and services purchased from sellers in the country issuing the currency (foreign products are more expensive).
- If a foreign currency goes *down* relative to the U.S. dollar, Americans pay *less* for products from the country issuing the currency (foreign products are cheaper).

In the interest of being thorough, let's look at this phenomenon from the perspective of an American seller and a Swiss buyer. First, we need to know the exchange rate for the U.S. dollar relative to the franc, which happens to be $1 U.S. = 1.23 francs. This means that if I want to sell something—let's say my latest painting—for $1,000 U.S. to an art lover in Switzerland, the Swiss buyer will need 1,230 francs to get the $1,000 needed to pay me. If the exchange rate were $1 U.S. = 1.40 francs, the cost of the painting would be $1,400. So now you also know that:

- If the U.S. dollar goes *up* relative to a foreign currency, foreign buyers must pay *more* for American goods and services (they become more expensive).
- If the U.S. dollar goes *down* relative to a foreign currency, foreign buyers pay *less* for American products (they become cheaper).

THE LEGAL AND REGULATORY ENVIRONMENT

One of the most difficult aspects of doing business globally is dealing with vast differences in legal and regulatory environments. The United States, for example, has an established set of laws and regulations that provide direction to businesses operating within its borders. But because there is no global legal system, key areas of business law—for example, contract provisions and copyright protection—can be treated in different ways in different countries. Companies doing international business

---

gross national income (GNI) per capita
Estimate of each citizen's share of national income.

exchange rate
Value of one currency relative to another.

often face a smorgasbord of inconsistent laws and regulations. To navigate this sea of confusion, American businesspeople must know and follow both U.S. laws and regulations and those of nations in which they operate.

The annals of business history are filled with stories about American companies that have stumbled in trying to comply with foreign laws and regulations. Coca-Cola, for example, ran afoul of Italian law when it printed its ingredients list on the bottle cap rather than on the bottle itself. Italian courts ruled that the labeling was inadequate because most people throw the cap away. In another case, 3M applied to the Japanese government to create a joint venture with the Sumitomo Industrial Group to make and distribute magnetic tape products in Japan. 3M spent four years trying to satisfy Japan's complex regulations, but by the time it got approval, domestic competitors, including Sony, had captured the market. By delaying 3M, Japanese regulators managed, in effect, to stifle foreign competition.[16]

One approach to dealing with local laws and regulations is hiring lawyers from the host country who can provide advice on legal issues. Another is working with local businesspeople who have experience in complying with regulations and overcoming bureaucratic obstacles.

Foreign Corrupt Practices Act One U.S. law that creates unique challenges for American firms operating overseas is the Foreign Corrupt Practices Act (FCPA), which prohibits the distribution of bribes and other favors in the conduct of business. Unfortunately, although they're illegal in this country, such tactics as kickbacks and bribes are business as usual in many nations. According to some experts, American businesspeople are at a competitive disadvantage if they're prohibited from giving bribes or undercover payments to foreign officials or businesspeople who expect them; it's like asking for good service in a restaurant when the waiter knows you won't be giving a tip. In theory, because the FPCA warns foreigners that Americans can't give bribes, they'll eventually stop expecting them.

Where are American businesspeople most likely and least likely to encounter bribe requests and related forms of corruption? Transparency International, an independent German-based organization, annually rates nations according to "perceived corruption," which it defines as "the abuse of public office for private gain." Table 8.3 excerpts the 2004 rankings.

QUICK QUIZ   8.2

The rest of the chapter covers trade controls and agreements. First, however, you can take a brief test to see what you've learned about the different facets of the international business environment.

Go to www.exploringbusinessonline.com

Trade Controls

The debate about the extent to which countries should control the flow of foreign goods and investments across their borders is as old as international trade itself. Governments continue to control trade, and to better understand how and why, let's examine a hypothetical case. Suppose you're in charge of a very small country in which people do two things—grow food and make clothes. Because the quality of both products is high and the prices are reasonable, your consumers are happy to buy locally made food and clothes. But one day, a farmer from a nearby country crosses your border with several wagonloads of wheat to sell. On the same day, a foreign clothes maker arrives with a large shipment of clothes. These two entrepreneurs want to sell food and clothes in your country at prices below those that local consumers now pay for domestically made food and clothes. At first, this seems like a good deal for your consumers: They won't have to pay as much for food and clothes. But then you remember all the people in your country who grow food and make clothes. If no one buys their goods (because the imported goods are cheaper), what will happen to their livelihoods? Will everybody be out of work? And if everyone's unemployed, what will happen to your national economy?

TABLE 8.3

Corruptibility Around the World, 2004

Rank	Country	CPI Score*
1	Finland	9.7
2	New Zealand	9.6
3	Denmark	9.5
	Iceland	9.5
5	Singapore	9.3
6	Sweden	9.2
7	Switzerland	9.1
8	Norway	8.9
9	Austria	8.8
10	Netherlands	8.7
17	Belgium	7.5
	Ireland	7.5
	United States	7.5
133	Congo, Democratic Republic	2.0
	Côte d'Ivoire	2.0
	Georgia	2.0
	Indonesia	2.0
	Tajikistan	2.0
	Turkmenistan	2.0
140	Azerbaijan	1.9
	Paraguay	1.9
142	Chad	1.7
	Myanmar	1.7
144	Nigeria	1.6
145	Bangladesh	1.5
	Haiti	1.5

*A score of 10 means that a country is squeaky clean. Anything under 3 means that corruption is rampant.

That's when you decide to protect your farmers and clothes makers by setting up trade rules. Maybe you'll increase the prices of imported goods by adding a tax to them; you might even make the tax so high that they're more expensive than your homemade goods. Or perhaps you'll help your farmers grow food more cheaply by giving them financial help to defray their costs. The government payments that you give to the farmers to help offset some of their costs of production are called **subsidies**. These subsidies will allow the farmers to lower the price of their goods to a point below that of imported competitor's goods. What's even better is that the lower costs will allow them to export their goods at attractive, competitive prices.

The United States has a long history of subsidizing farmers. Subsidy programs guarantee farmers (including large corporate farms) a certain price for their crops regardless of the market price. This guarantee ensures stable income in the farming community but can have a negative impact on the world economy. How? Critics argue that in allowing American farmers to export crops at artificially low prices, U.S. agricultural subsidies permit them to compete unfairly with farmers in developing countries. A reverse situation occurs in the steel industry, in which a number of countries—China, Japan, Russia, Germany, and Brazil—subsidize domestic producers. U.S. trade unions charge that this practice gives an unfair advantage to foreign producers and hurts the American Steel industry, which can't compete on price with subsidized imports.

Whether they push up the price of imports or push down the price of local goods, such initiatives will help locally produced goods compete more favorably with foreign goods. Both strategies are forms of **trade controls**—policies that restrict free trade. Because they protect domestic industries by reducing foreign competition, the use of such controls is often called **protectionism**. Although there's considerable debate over the pros and cons of protectionism, all countries engage in it to some extent. Before debating the issue, however, let's learn about the most common types of trade restrictions: tariffs, quotas, and, embargoes.

Tariffs

Tariffs are taxes on imports. Because they raise the price of the foreign-made goods, they make them less competitive. The United States, for example, protects domestic makers of synthetic knitted shirts by imposing a tariff of 32.5 percent on imports. Tariffs are also used to raise revenue for a government. Shoe imports are worth $1.63 billion to the federal government.[17]

Quotas

A **quota** imposes limits on the quantity of a good that can be imported over a period of time. Quotas are used to protect specific industries, usually new industries or those facing strong competitive pressure from foreign firms. U.S. import quotas take two forms. An *absolute quota* fixes an upper limit on the amount of a good that can be imported during the given period. A *tariff-rate quota* permits the import of a specified quantity and then adds a high import tax once the limit is reached.

Sometimes quotas protect one group at the expense of another. To protect sugar beet and sugar cane growers, for instance, the United States imposes a tariff-rate quota on the importation of sugar—a policy that has driven up the cost of sugar to five times its actual price.[18] These artificially high prices push up costs for American candy makers, some of whom have moved their operations elsewhere, taking high-paying manufacturing jobs with them. Life Savers, for example, were made in the United States for 90 years but are now produced in Canada, where the company saves $10 million a year on the cost of sugar.[19]

An extreme form of quota is the **embargo**, which, for economic or political reasons, bans the import or export of certain goods to or from a specific country. The United States, for example, bans nearly every commodity originating in Cuba.

Dumping A common political rationale for establishing tariffs and quotas is the need to combat **dumping**: the practice of selling exported goods below the price that producers would normally charge in their home markets (and often below the costs of producing the goods). Usually, nations resort to this practice in order to gain entry and market share in foreign markets, but it can also be used to sell off surplus or obsolete goods. Dumping creates unfair competition for domestic industries, and governments are justifiably concerned when they suspect foreign countries of dumping products on their markets. They often retaliate by imposing punitive tariffs that drive up the price of the imported goods.

THE PROS AND CONS OF TRADE CONTROLS

Opinions on government involvement in international trade vary. Some experts believe that governments should support free trade and refrain from imposing regulations that restrict the free flow of goods and services between nations. Others, however, argue that governments should impose some level of trade regulations on imported goods and services.

Proponents of controls contend that there are a number of legitimate reasons why countries engage in protectionism. Sometimes they restrict trade to protect specific industries and their workers from foreign competition—agriculture, for example, or steel making. At other times, they restrict imports to give new or struggling industries a chance to get established. Finally, some countries use protectionism to shield industries that are vital to their national defense, such as shipbuilding and military hardware.

Despite valid arguments made by supporters of trade controls, most experts believe that such restrictions as tariffs and quotas, as well as practices that don't promote level playing fields, such as subsidies and dumping, are detrimental to the world economy. Without impediments to trade, countries can compete freely. Each nation can focus on what it does best and bring its goods to a fair and open world market. When this happens, the world will prosper. Or so the argument goes. International trade hasn't achieved global prosperity, but it's certainly heading in the direction of unrestricted markets.

REDUCING INTERNATIONAL TRADE BARRIERS

A number of organizations work to ease barriers to trade, and more countries are joining together to promote trade and mutual economic benefits. Let's look at some of these important initiatives.

Trade Agreements and Organizations

Free trade is encouraged by a number of agreements and organizations set up to monitor trade policies. The two most important are the General Agreement on Tariffs and Trade (GATT) and the World Trade Organization (WTO).

General Agreement on Tariffs and Trade (GATT) After the Great Depression and World War II, most countries focused on the protection of home industries, and international trade was hindered by rigid trade restrictions. To rectify this situation, 23 nations joined together in 1947 and signed the **General Agreement on Tariffs and Trade (GATT)**, which encouraged free trade by regulating and reducing tariffs and by providing a forum for resolving trade disputes. The highly successful initiative achieved substantial reductions in tariffs and quotas, and in 1995, its members founded the World Trade Organization to continue the work of GATT in overseeing global trade.

World Trade Organization Based in Geneva, Switzerland, with nearly 150 members, the **World Trade Organization (WTO)** encourages global commerce and lower trade barriers, enforces international rules of trade, and provides a forum for resolving disputes. It is empowered, for instance, to determine whether a member nation's trade policies have violated the organization's rules and can direct "guilty" countries to remove disputed barriers (although it has no legal power to force any country to do anything it doesn't want to do). If the guilty party refuses to comply, the WTO may authorize the plaintiff nation to erect trade barriers of its own, generally in the form of tariffs.

Affected members aren't always happy with WTO actions. In 2002, for example, the Bush administration imposed a three-year tariff on imported steel. In ruling against this tariff, the WTO allowed the aggrieved nations to impose counter-tariffs on some politically sensitive American products,

subsidies
Government payments given to certain industries to help offset some of their costs of production.

trade controls
Government policies that restrict free trade.

protectionism
Use of trade controls to reduce foreign competition in order to protect domestic industries.

tariffs
Government taxes on imports that raise the price of foreign goods and make them less competitive with domestic goods.

quota
Government-imposed restrictions on the quantity of a good that can be imported over a period of time.

embargo
Extreme form of quota which bans the import or export of certain goods to a country for economic or political reasons.

dumping
Practice of selling exported goods below the price that producers would normally charge home markets.

General Agreement on Tariffs and Trade (GATT)
International trade agreement which encourages free trade by regulating and reducing tariffs and provides a forum for resolving trade disputes.

World Trade Organization (WTO)
International organization that monitors trade policies and whose members work together to enforce rules of trade and resolve trade disputes.

such as Florida oranges, Texas grapefruits and computers, and Wisconsin cheese. Reluctantly, the administration lifted its tariff on steel.[20]

Financial Support for Troubled Economies

The key to helping developing countries become active participants in the global marketplace is providing financial assistance. Providing monetary assistance to some of the poorest nations in the world is the shared goal of two organizations: the International Monetary Fund and the World Bank. These organizations, to which most countries belong, were established in 1944 to accomplish different but complementary purposes.

The International Monetary Fund The **International Monetary Fund (IMF)** loans money to countries with troubled economies, such as Mexico in the 1980s and mid-1990s and Russia and Argentina in the late 1990s. There are, however, strings attached to IMF loans: In exchange for relief in times of financial crisis, borrower countries must institute sometimes painful financial and economic reforms. In the 1980s, for example, Mexico received financial relief from the IMF on the condition that it privatize and deregulate certain industries and liberalize trade policies.

The government was also required to cut back expenditures for such services as education, health care, and workers' benefits.[21]

The World Bank The **World Bank** is an important source of economic assistance for poor and developing countries. With backing from wealthy donor countries (such as the United States and Japan), the World Bank provides about $30 billion annually in loans to some of the world's poorest nations. Loans are made to help countries improve the lives of the poor through community-support programs designed to provide health, nutrition, education, and other social services.

Criticism of the IMF and the World Bank In recent years, the IMF and the World Bank have faced mounting criticism, although both have their supporters. Some analysts, for example, think that the IMF is often too harsh in its demands for economic reform; others argue that troubled economies can be turned around only with harsh economic measures. Some observers argue that too many World Bank loans go to environmentally harmful projects, such as the construction of roads through fragile rain forests. Others point to the World Bank's efforts to direct funding away from big construction projects and toward initiatives designed to better the lot of the world's poor—educating children, fighting AIDS, and improving nutrition and health standards.

Trading Blocs

So far, our discussion has suggested that global trade would be strengthened if there were no restrictions on it—if countries didn't put up barriers to trade or perform special favors for domestic industries. The complete absence of barriers is an ideal state of affairs that we haven't yet attained. In the meantime, economists and policy makers tend to focus on a more practical question: Can we achieve the goal of free trade on the *regional* level? To an extent, the answer is yes. In different parts of the world, groups of countries have joined together to allow goods and services to flow without restrictions across their mutual borders. Such groups are called **trading blocs**. Let's examine two of the most powerful trading blocks—NAFTA and the European Union.

North American Free Trade Association (NAFTA) The **North American Free Trade Association (NAFTA)** is an agreement among the governments of the United States, Canada, and Mexico to

These Mexican workers are building GE refrigerators that were once made in Bloomington, Indiana: Because its American workers earned $24 an hour and their Mexican counterparts only $2, GE moved 1,400 of the 3,200 jobs at its Bloomington factory to Mexico. On the other hand, the company invested $100 million to upgrade its American facility and secure the remaining 1,800 jobs. In the first half of the decade after the passage of NAFTA, U.S. companies invested $2.2 billion annually in Mexican manufacturing—a mere 1 percent of the $200 billion invested in the United States every year. Meanwhile, trade with Mexico tripled.

open their borders to unrestricted trade. The effect of this agreement is that three very different economies are combined into one economic zone with almost no trade barriers. From the northern tip of Canada to the southern tip of Mexico, each country benefits from the comparative advantages of its partners: Each nation is free to produce what it does best and to trade its goods and services without restrictions.

When the agreement was ratified in 1994, there was no shortage of skeptics. Many people feared, for example, that without tariffs on Mexican goods, more U.S. manufacturing jobs would be lost to Mexico, where labor is cheaper. A decade later, most such fears have not been realized, and by and large, NAFTA has been an enormous success. Since it went into effect, the value of trade between the United States and Mexico has grown substantially, and Canada and Mexico are now the United States' top trading partners.

The European Union The 40-plus countries of Europe have long shown an interest in integrating their economies. The first organized effort to integrate a segment of Europe's economic entities began in the late 1950s, when six countries joined together to form the *European Economic Community* (*EEC*). Over the next four decades, membership grew, and in the late 1990s, the EEC became the European Union. Today, the **European Union (EU)** is a group of 25 countries that have eliminated trade barriers among themselves (see the map in Figure 8.6).

At first glance, the EU looks similar to NAFTA. Both, for instance, allow unrestricted trade among member nations. But the provisions of the EU go beyond those of NAFTA in several important ways. Most importantly, the EU is more than a trading organization: It also enhances political and social cooperation and binds its members into a single entity with authority to require members to follow common

Original six members (1957)
Later members (1973–1995)
Recent members (2004)

Figure 8.6

The Nations of the European Union

rules and regulations. It is much like a federation of states with a weak central government, not only eliminating internal barriers but enforcing common tariffs on trade from outside the EU. In addition, while NAFTA allows goods and services and capital to pass between borders, the EU also allows *people* to come and go freely: If you have an EU passport, you can work in any EU nation.

The Euro Many EU initiatives have been less successful than those of NAFTA, but it can claim at least one very important exception: the introduction of a common currency. A key step toward unification occurred in 1999, when most (but not all) EU members agreed to abandon their own currencies and adopt a joint currency. The actual conversion occurred in 2002, when a common currency called the *euro* replaced the separate currencies of participating EU countries. The common currency facilitates trade and finance

International Monetary Fund (IMF)
International organization set up to loan money to countries with troubled economies.

World Bank
International financial institution that provides economic assistance to poor and developing countries.

trading blocs
Groups of countries which have joined together to allow goods and services to flow without restrictions across their mutual borders.

North American Free Trade Association (NAFTA)
Agreement among the governments of the U.S., Canada, and Mexico to open their borders to unrestricted trade.

European Union
Association of European countries that joined together to eliminate trade barriers among themselves.

because exchange-rate differences no longer complicate transactions.[22]

Its proponents argue that the EU will not only unite economically and politically distinct countries, but will create an economic power that can compete against the dominant players in the global marketplace. Individually, each European country has limited economic power, but as a group, they could be an economic superpower.

Other Trading Blocs Other countries have also opted for economic integration. Four historical rivals in South America—Argentina, Brazil, Paraguay, and Uruguay—have established MERCOSUR (for *Mercado Commun del Sur*) to eliminate trade barriers. A number of Asian countries, including Indonesia, Malaysia, the Philippines, Singapore, and Thailand, are cooperating to reduce mutual barriers through the Association of Southeast Asian Nations (ASEAN).

Only time will tell whether the trend toward regional trade agreements is good for the world economy. Clearly, they're beneficial to their respective participants; for one thing, they get preferential treatment from other members. But certain questions still need to be answered more fully. Are they, for example, moving the world closer to free trade on a *global* scale—toward a marketplace in which goods and services can be traded anywhere without barriers?

Preparing for a Career in International Business

No matter where your career takes you, you won't be able to avoid the reality and reach of international business. We're all involved in it. Some readers may want to venture more seriously into this exciting arena. The career opportunities are exciting and challenging, but taking the best advantage of them requires some early planning. Here are some hints.

Plan Your Undergraduate Education

Many colleges and universities offer strong majors in international business, and this course of study can be good preparation for a global career. But in planning your education, don't forget the following:

- *Develop real expertise in one of the basic areas of business.* Most companies will hire you as much for your skill and knowledge in accounting, finance, information systems, marketing, or management as for your background in the study of international business. Take courses in both areas.

- *Develop your knowledge of international politics, economics, and culture.* Take liberal arts courses that focus on parts of the world that especially interest you. Courses in history, government, and the social sciences offer a wealth of knowledge about other nations and cultures that's relevant to success in international business.

- *Develop foreign-language skills.* If you studied a language in high school, keep up with it. Improve your reading or conversational skills. Or start a new language in college. Remember: Your competition in the global marketplace is not just other Americans, but individuals from countries, such as Belgium, where everyone's fluent in at least two (and usually three) languages. Lack of foreign-language skills is often a disadvantage for many Americans in international business.

Get Some Direct Experience

Take advantage of study-abroad opportunities, whether offered on your campus or by another college. There are literally hundreds of such opportunities, and your interest in international business will be received much more seriously if you've spent some time abroad. (As a bonus, you'll probably find it an enjoyable, horizon-expanding experience as well.)

Interact with People from Other Cultures

Finally, whenever you can, learn about the habits and traits of other cultures and practice interacting with the people to whom they belong. Go to the trouble to meet international students on your campus and get to know them. Learn about their cultures and values and tell them about yours. You may be uncomfortable or confused in such intercultural exchanges, but you'll find them great learning experiences. By picking up on the details, you'll avoid embarrassing mistakes and even earn the approval of acquaintances from abroad.

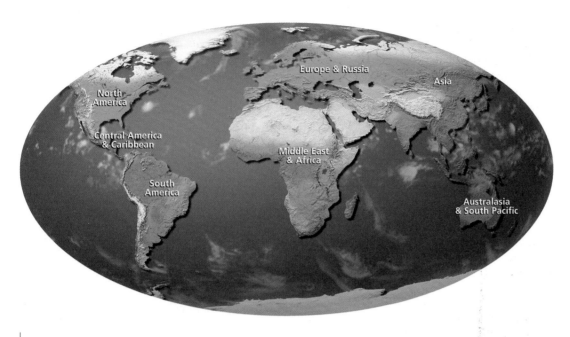

Where do you want to study? While over 60 percent of students who study abroad go to Europe, growing numbers are going to Asia, Central America, and Australia.

Whether you're committed to a career in global business, curious about the international scene, or simply a consumer of worldwide products and services, you can't avoid the effects of globalization. Granted, the experience can be frustrating, maybe even troubling at times. More often, however, it's likely to be stimulating and full of opportunities.

QUICK QUIZ   8.3

Before you finish this chapter, here's an opportunity to test your understanding of the material in the preceding sections on trade controls and agreements.

Go to www.exploringbusinessonline.com

Where We're Headed

In this chapter, we explained why the globalization of business is important to you as both student and consumer and suggested ways in which you can begin preparing for a career in global business. You saw how companies and nations engage in international trade and what strategies they use to compete in the global marketplace. You learned about the challenges that companies face in conducting business outside their countries, and you saw how governments both promote and regulate international trade. In the next chapter, we'll discuss the role of accounting in business and show how accounting information helps managers and other stakeholders make better business decisions.

Summary of Learning Objectives

1. Explain why nations and companies participate in international trade and how trade between nations is measured.

Nations trade because they can't produce all the products that inhabitants need. They import those that they need but don't produce and export those that are needed elsewhere. To understand why cer-

tain countries import or export certain products, you need to realize that not all countries are good at producing or are able to produce the same products. The cost of labor, the availability of natural resources, and the level of know-how vary greatly around the world. To explain how countries decide what products to import and export, economists use the concepts of *absolute* and *comparative advantage*. A nation has an **absolute advantage** if it's the only source of a particular product or can make more of a product with the same amount of or fewer resources than other countries. A **comparative advantage** exists when a country can produce a product at a lower *opportunity cost* than other nations. Nations trade in order to exploit their advantages: They benefit from specialization, focusing on what they do best and trading the output to other countries for what they do best.

To evaluate the impact of its international trade, a nation looks at two key indicators. We determine a country's **balance of trade** by subtracting the value of its imports from the value of its exports. If a country sells more products than it buys, it has a favorable balance, called a **trade surplus**. If it buys more than it sells, it has an unfavorable balance, or a **trade deficit**. The **balance of payments** is the difference, over a period of time, between the total flow coming into a country and the total flow going out. As in its balance of trade, the biggest factor in a country's balance of payments is the money that comes in and goes out as a result of exports and imports. But balance of payments includes other cash inflows and outflows, such as cash received from or paid for foreign investment, loans, tourism, military expenditures, and foreign aid.

2. **Identify the various business opportunities and challenges presented by international business.**

For a company in the United States wishing to expand beyond national borders, there are a variety of ways to get involved in international business. **Importing** involves purchasing products from other countries and reselling them in one's own; **exporting** entails selling products to foreign customers. Under a **franchise agreement**, a company grants a foreign company the right to use its brand name and sell its products. A **licensing agreement** allows a foreign company to sell a company's products or use its intellectual property in exchange for royalty fees. Through **contract manufacturing**, or **outsourcing**, a company has its products manufactured or services provided in other countries. A **strategic alliance** is an agreement between two companies to pool talent and resources to achieve business goals that benefit both partners. A **joint venture** is a specific type of strategic alliance in which a separate entity funded by the participating companies is formed to manage the alliance. **Foreign direct investment (FDI)** refers to the formal establishment of business operations on foreign soil. A common form of FDI is the **subsidiary**, an independent company owned by a foreign firm. A company that operates in many countries is called a **multinational corporation (MNC)**.

3. **Appreciate how cultural, economic, legal, and political differences between countries create challenges to successful business dealings**

Success in international business means understanding an assortment of cultural, economic, and legal differences between countries. Cultural challenges stem from differences in language, concepts of time and sociability, and communication styles. If you do business in a foreign country, you need to know the country's level of economic development. This can be evaluated by using an economic indicator called **gross national income (GNI) per capita**. In dealing with countries whose currency is different from yours, you have to be aware of the impact that fluctuations in **exchange rates** will have on your profits. Finally, in doing business globally, you have to deal with the challenges that come from the vast differences in legal and regulatory environments.

4. **Describe the ways in which governments and international bodies regulate global trade.**

Because they protect domestic industries by reducing foreign competition, the use of controls to restrict free trade is often called **protectionism**. Although there's considerable debate over protectionism, all countries engage in it to some extent. **Tariffs** are taxes on imports. Because they raise the price of the foreign-made goods, they make them less competitive. **Quotas** are restrictions on imports that impose a limit on the quantity of a good that can be imported over a period of time. They're used to protect specific industries, usually new industries or those facing strong competitive pressure from foreign firms. An **embargo** is a quota which, for economic or political reasons, bans the import or export of certain goods to or from a specific country. A common rationale for tariffs and quotas is the need to combat **dumping**—the practice of selling exported goods below the price that producers would normally charge in their home markets (and often below the costs of producing the goods). Some experts believe that governments should support free trade and refrain from imposing regulations that restrict the free flow of products between nations. Others argue that governments should impose some level of trade regulations on imported goods and services.

5. **Discuss the various initiatives designed to reduce international trade barriers and promote free trade.**

Free trade is encouraged by a number of agreements and organizations set up to monitor trade policies. The **General Agreement on Tariffs and Trade (GATT)** encourages free trade by regulating and reducing tariffs and by providing a forum for resolving disputes. The highly successful initiative achieved substantial reductions in tariffs and quotas, and in 1995, its members founded the **World Trade Organization (WTO)**, which encourages global commerce and lower trade barriers, enforces international rules of trade, and provides a forum for resolving disputes.

Providing monetary assistance to some of the poorest nations in the world is the shared goal of two organizations: the **International Monetary Fund (IMF)** and the **World Bank**. Several initiatives have successfully promoted free trade on a regional level. In different parts of the world, groups of countries have joined together to allow goods and services to flow without restrictions across their mutual borders. Such groups are called **trading blocs**. The **North American Free Trade Association (NAFTA)** is an agreement among the governments of the United States, Canada, and Mexico to open their borders to unrestricted trade. The effect of this agreement is that three very different economies are combined into one economic zone with almost no trade barriers. The **European Union (EU)** is a group of 25 countries that have eliminated trade barriers among themselves.

6. Understand how to prepare for a career in international business.

To prepare for a global career, you might want to consider doing some of the following while a student: major in international business; develop your knowledge of international politics, economics, and culture; study a foreign language; take advantage of study-abroad opportunities; and interact with fellow students from other cultures.

Questions and Problems

1. AACSB ▸ Analysis

We use the concepts of absolute and comparative advantage to explain why countries import some products and export others. We can also use them to explain how work can be divided between two people. Two consultants—John and Jennifer—have a client who needs a company report written and a PowerPoint presentation prepared within the next two weeks. Both John and Jennifer have experience writing reports and preparing presentations, but neither has the time to do both jobs. From past experience, they know how much time each of them needs to complete each type of project:

Consultant	Write a report	Prepare a presentation
John	80 hours	40 hours
Jennifer	150 hours	60 hours

Using the information contained in the grid above, answer each of the following questions:

a. Does either John or Jennifer have an absolute advantage in (1) writing reports and/or (2) preparing presentations?

b. Does either have a comparative advantage? (To handle this question, first determine *how many total hours would it take to serve the client if John writes the report and Jennifer prepares the presentation*. Then, determine *how many total hours would be required if, instead, Jennifer writes the report and John prepares the presentation*.)

c. Based on your analysis, how would you recommend that John and Jennifer divide the work?

d. Given your answer to the previous question, would you say that John has a comparative advantage in writing reports, in making presentations, or in both? What should John specialize in?

e. Does Jennifer have a comparative advantage in either task? What should she specialize in?

2. AACSB ▸ Analysis

What happens if, during a given year, you spend more money than you take in? What happens if you finance your overspending by running up your credit-card balance to some outrageous limit? Would you have trouble borrowing in the future? Would you have to pay higher interest rates? How would you get out of debt?

Now let's change *you* to *the United States*. The United States has just run up the largest one-year trade deficit in history—nearly $600 billion. Respond to the following items:

a. Define the term *trade deficit* and explain how the United States ended up with such a large one.

b. Is the trade deficit a good or bad thing? Why or why not?

c. Define the term *balance of payments* and explain whether the United States has a favorable or unfavorable balance of payments.

d. What will be the consequences if the United States repeatedly runs up a negative balance of payments?

3. There are four common ways for a firm to expand its operations into overseas markets—importing, exporting, licensing, and franchising. First, explain what each approach entails. Then, select the one that you'd use if you were the CEO of a large company. Why was this approach particularly appealing?

4. AACSB ▸ Analysis

You own a company, which employs about 200 people in Maine to produce hockey sticks. Why might you decide to outsource your production to Indonesia? Would closing your plant and moving your operations overseas help or hurt the U.S. economy? Who would be hurt? Who would be helped? Now, armed with answers to these questions, ask yourself whether you would indeed move your facilities or continue making hockey sticks in Maine. Explain your decision.

5. AACSB ▶ Ethics

You're the CEO of a multinational corporation and one-fourth of your workforce is infected with AIDS. If you had the means to help your workers and their families, would you do it? This is not strictly a hypothetical question: It's one that's faced by CEOs of multinational corporations with operations in Africa, parts of China, and India. To find out what some of them have decided, go to www.exploringbusinessonline.com to link to the *Business Week* Web site and read the article "Why Business Should Make AIDS Its Business." Then, answer the following questions:

a. Why have some multinationals decided to help control AIDS in their workforces?

b. Why have others failed to help?

c. From a humanitarian perspective, what's the right thing to do? From a business perspective?

d. What would you do if you conducted operations in a nation whose government was unwilling or unable to control the spread of AIDS?

6. AACSB ▶ Communication

After five years at a large sporting-goods company, your boss has asked you to spend six months managing the firm's new office in Rio de Janeiro, Brazil. It's a good opportunity, but, unfortunately, you know absolutely nothing about life or anything else in Brazil. So, to get some advice on how to work and socialize with Brazilian businesspeople, you decide to do some online research. You're particularly interested in understanding cultural differences in communication styles, dress, time, and sociability. Go to www.exploringbusinessonline.com to link to some helpful sites and write a brief report to summarize what you learned about cultural differences between U.S. and Brazilian businesspeople.

7. AACSB ▶ Ethics

You're a partner in a U.S. engineering firm that's interested in bidding on a water-treatment project in China. You know that firms from two other countries—Malaysia and Italy—will submit bids. The U.S. Foreign Corrupt Practices Act forbids you from making any payment to Chinese officials to enlist their help in getting the job. Unfortunately, the governments of Malaysia and Italy don't prohibit local firms from offering bribes. Are you at a disadvantage? Should the Foreign Corrupt Practices Act be repealed? Why or why not?

8. AACSB ▶ Analysis

Because the United States has placed quotas on textile and apparel imports for the last 30 years, certain countries, such as China and India, have been able to export to the United States only as much clothing as their respective quotas permit. One effect of this policy was spreading textile and apparel manufacture around the world and preventing any one nation from dominating the world market. As a result, many developing countries, such as Vietnam, Cambodia, and Honduras, were able to enter the market and provide much-needed jobs for local workers. The rules, however, have changed: As of January 1, 2005, quotas on U.S. textile imports were eliminated, permitting U.S. companies to import textile supplies from any country they choose. In your opinion, what effect will the new U.S. policy have on each of the following groups:

a. U.S. firms that outsource the manufacture of their apparel

b. Textile manufacturers and workers in:
- China
- Indonesia
- Mexico
- United States

c. American consumers

9. What is NAFTA? Why was it formed? What has it accomplished?

10. What is the European Union? Why was it formed? What has it accomplished?

Learning on the Web AACSB

Keeping Current About Currency

On a day-to-day basis, you probably don't think about how much the U.S. dollar (US$) is worth relative to other currencies. But there will probably be times when ups and downs in exchange rates will seem extremely important to you. The following are some hypothetical scenarios that illustrate what these times may be. (*Note:* To respond to the questions raised in each scenario, search Google for a currency converter.)

SCENARIO 1: YOUR SWISS VACATION

Your family came from Switzerland, and you and your parents visited relatives there back in 2002. Now that you're in college, you want to make the trip on your own during spring break. While you're there, you also plan to travel around and see a little more of the country. You remember that in 2002,

US$1 bought 1.64 Swiss Francs (Frs). You estimate that, at this rate, you can finance your trip (excluding airfare) with the $1,000 that you earned this summer. You've heard, however, that the exchange rate has changed. Given the current exchange rate, about how much do you think your trip would cost you? As a U.S. traveler going abroad, how are you helped by a shift in exchange rates? How are you hurt?

SCENARIO 2: YOUR BRITISH FRIENDS

A few years ago, you met some British students who were visiting the United States This year, you're encouraging them to visit again so that you can show them around New York City. When you and your friends first talked about the cost of the trip back in 2002, 1 British pound (£) could be converted into US$1.45. You estimated that each of your British friends would need to save up about £700 to make the trip (again, excluding plane fare). Given today's exchange rate, how much will each person need to make the trip? Have your plans been helped or hindered by the change in exchange rates? Was the shift a plus for the U.S. travel industry? What sort of exchange-rate shift hurts the industry?

SCENARIO 3: YOUR CANADIAN CDS

Because some CDs are just hard to get in the United States, over the years, you've gotten into the habit of buying a lot of music from a company located in Canada. You order CDs by mail and pay in Canadian currency, which you get at your local bank. They cost about $16 in Canadian dollars, and when you bought your first Canadian CD in 2002, US$1 could be converted into $1.60 in Canadian currency. At that conversion rate, you were getting CDs for about US$10. How much would you be paying at the current conversation rate? Would an American company that imports goods from Canada view the current rate more favorably or less favorably than it did back in 2002?

SCENARIO 4: YOUR GERMAN SOCCER BOOTS

Your father rarely throws anything away, and while cleaning out the attic a few years ago, he came across a pair of vintage Adidas soccer boots made in 1955. Realizing that they'd be extremely valuable to collectors in Adidas' home country of Germany, he hoped to sell them for US$5,000 and, to account for the exchange rate at the time, planned to price them at $5,535 in euros. Somehow, he never got around to selling the boots and has asked if you could sell them for him on eBay. If he still wants to end up with US$5,000, what price in euros will you now have to set? Would an American company that exports goods to the European Union view the current rate more favorably or less favorably than it did back in 2002?

Career Opportunities AACSB

Broadening Your Business Horizons

At some point in your life, you'll probably meet and work with people from different countries and cultures. Participating in a college study-abroad program can help you prepare to work in the global business environment, and now is as good a time as any to start exploring this option. Here's one way to go about it:

a. Select a study-abroad program that interests you. To do this, you need to decide what country you want to study in and your academic field of interest. Unless you speak the language of your preferred country, you should pick a program offered in English.

- If your school offers study-abroad programs, pick one that's been approved by your institution.

- If your school doesn't offer study-abroad programs, locate one through a Web search.

b. Describe the program, the school that's offering it, and the country to which it will take you.

c. Indicate why you've selected this particular program, and explain how it will help you prepare for your future business career.

Ethics Angle AACSB

The Right, Wrong, and Wisdom of Dumping and Subsidizing

When companies sell exported goods below the price they'd charge in their home markets (and often below the cost of producing the goods), they're engaging in *dumping*. When governments guarantee farmers certain prices for crops regardless of market prices, the beneficiaries are being *subsidized*. What do you think about these practices? Is dumping an unfair business practice? Why or why not? Does subsidizing farmers make economic sense for the United States? What are the effects of farm subsidies on the world economy? Are the ethical issues raised by the two practices comparable? Why or why not?

Team-Building Skills AACSB

Three Little Words: The China Price

According to business journalists Pete Engardio and Dexter Roberts, the scariest three words that a U.S. manufacturer can hear these days are *the China price*. To understand why, go to www.exploringbusinessonline.com to link to the *Business Week* Web site and read their article "The China Price," which discusses the benefits and costs of China's business expansion for U.S. companies, workers, and consumers. Once you've read the article, each member of the team should be able to explain the paradoxical effect of U.S.–Chinese business relationships—namely, that they can hurt American companies and workers while helping American companies and consumers.

Next, your team should get together and draw up two lists: a list of the top-five positive outcomes and a list of the top-five negative outcomes of recent Chinese business expansion for U.S. businesses, workers, and consumers. Then, the team should debate the pros and cons of China's emergence as a global business competitor and, finally, write a group report that answers the following questions:

1. Considered on balance, has China's business expansion helped or harmed U.S. companies, workers, and consumers? Justify your answers.

2. What will happen to U.S. companies, workers, and consumers in the future if China continues to grow as a global business competitor?

3. How should U.S. companies respond to the threats posed by Chinese competitors in their markets?

4. What can you do as a student to prepare yourself to compete in an ever-changing global business environment?

When you hand in your report, be sure to attach all the following items:

- Members' individually prepared lists of ways in which business relationships with China both hurt and help U.S. businesses, workers, and consumers.

- Your group-prepared list of five positive and negative effects of Chinese business expansion on U.S. businesses, workers, and consumers.

The Global View AACSB

Go East, Young Job Seeker

How brave are you when it comes to employment? Are you brave enough to go halfway around the world to find work? Instead of complaining about U.S. jobs going overseas, you could take the bull by the horns and take one back. It's not that tough to do, and it could be a life-changing experience. U.S. college graduates with business or technical backgrounds are highly sought after by companies that operate in India. If you qualify (and if you're willing to relocate), you could find yourself working in Bangalore or New Delhi for some multinational company like Intel, Citibank, or Glaxo-SmithKline (a pharmaceutical company). In addition, learning how to live and work in a foreign country can build self-confidence and make you more attractive to future employers. To get a glimpse of what it would be like to live and work in India, go to www.exploringbusinessonline.com to link to the *American Way* Magazine, CNN and Money, Web sites. Check out the posted articles: "Passage to India," and "Needs Job, Moves to India." Then, go to the Monster Work Abroad Web site and find a job in India that you'd like to have, either right after graduation or about five years into your career. (When selecting the job, ignore its actual location and proceed as if it's in Bangalore.) After you've pondered the possibility of living and working in India, answer the following questions:

1. What would your job entail?

2. What would living and working in Bangalore be like? What aspects would you enjoy? Which would you dislike?

3. What challenges would you face as an expatriate? What opportunities would you have?

4. How would the experience of working in India help your future career?

5. Would you be willing to take a job in India for a year or two? Why or why not?

Business Plan Project

Group Report: *Global Issues*

REPORT

The team should submit a written report that describes any efforts your company will make to buy, sell, or manufacture goods in other countries. For information on what to include in the report, go to Appendix A at the back of the book, entitled "Introducing Your Business Plan" (p. 307), and consult the section headed "Global Issues." The report should be about two double-spaced typed pages. The name of your proposed business and the names of all team members should appear on the report.

REASONABLE CONTRIBUTIONS

All members of the team who make a reasonable contribution to the report should sign it. (If any team member does not work on the report, his or her name should *not* appear on it.) If a student who has made a contribution is unable to sign the report (because of sickness or some other valid reason), the team can sign his or her name. To indicate that a name was signed by the team on a member's behalf, be sure to attach a note to the signature.

CHAPTER 9

The Role of Accounting in Business

After studying this chapter, you will be able to:

1. Define *accounting* and identify the different uses of accounting information.

2. Understand the functions of the three basic financial statements: income statement, balance sheet, and statement of cash flows.

3. Apply breakeven analysis to determine an appropriate sales level.

4. Understand the difference between cash-basis and accrual accounting.

5. Evaluate a company's performance using financial statements and ratio analysis.

6. Discuss career opportunities in accounting and the future of the profession.

FINANCIALLY SPEAKING

Accounting is often called "the language of business" because it provides much of the information that owners, managers, and investors need to evaluate a company's financial performance. According to the world's most successful investor (and second-richest person), Warren Buffet, the best way to prepare to be an investor is to learn all the accounting you can.[1] Buffet, chairman and CEO of Berkshire Hathaway (a company that invests in other companies), turned an original investment of $10,000 into a net worth of $35 billion in four decades, and he did it, in large part, by relying on financial reports prepared by accountants.[2]

In this chapter, we'll take Warren Buffet's advice. We'll start by explaining what accounting is and by identifying the various uses of accounting information. Then, we'll learn how to prepare a set of financial statements, how to interpret them, and how to analyze a company's performance using a technique called *ratio analysis*. Finally, we'll discuss career opportunities and the future of the accounting profession.

Berkshire Hathaway Chairman Warren Buffett entertains those attending the company's 2005 annual meeting by playing the ukulele as the "Fruit of the Loom Guys" sing in the background. Berkshire Hathaway bought Fruit of the Loom (a clothing manufacturer, specializing mostly in underwear) in 2002. The "Fruit of the Loom Guys"—four actors dressed up as an apple, two grape clusters, and a fig leaf—personify the company's logo.

The Role of Accounting

The purpose of accounting is to help **stakeholders**—parties who are interested in the activities of the business because they're affected by them—make better business decisions by providing them with financial information. **Accounting** consists of measuring and summarizing business activities, interpreting financial information, and communicating the results to management and other decision makers. It's impossible to run an organization or to make sound investment decisions without accurate and timely financial information, and it's the accountant who prepares this information. More importantly, accountants communicate the *meaning* of financial information and work with individuals and organizations to help them use financial information to deal with business problems. Getting numbers is the easy part of accounting, particularly since the introduction of the computer. The hard part is analyzing, interpreting, and communicating information—and doing so clearly while effectively interacting with people from all business disciplines.

FIELDS OF ACCOUNTING

Accounting can be divided into two major fields. **Management accounting** provides information and analysis to decision makers *inside* the organization in order to help them operate the business. **Financial accounting** furnishes information to individuals and groups *both inside and outside* the organization to help them assess the firm's financial performance. In other words, management accounting helps you keep the business running while financial accounting tells you how you're doing in the race.

Let's look a little more closely at each of these two fields.

Management Accounting

Management accounting plays a major role in helping managers carry out their responsibilities. Because the information that it provides is intended for companywide use,

stakeholders
Parties who are interested in the activities of a business because they're affected by them.

accounting
System for measuring and summarizing business activities, interpreting financial information, and communicating the results to management and other decision makers.

management accounting
Branch of accounting that provides information and analysis to decision makers inside the organization in order to help them operate the business.

financial accounting
Branch of accounting that furnishes information to individuals and groups both inside and outside the organization to help them assess the firm's financial performance.

the format for reporting it is flexible. Reports are tailored to the needs of individual managers, and their function is to supply *relevant, accurate, timely information* in a format that will aid managers in making decisions. In preparing, analyzing, and communicating such information, accountants work with individuals from all functional areas of an organization.

Financial Accounting

Accountants prepare the **financial statements**—including the *income statement*, the *balance sheet*, and the *statement of cash flows*—that summarize a company's past performance and evaluate its financial condition. In preparing financial statements, they adhere to a uniform set of rules called **generally accepted accounting principles (GAAP)**: principles for financial reporting that are established by an independent agency called the Financial Accounting Standards Board (FASB). Knowing that financial statements have been prepared according to GAAP assures users that reported information is accurate. They're also confident that they can compare statements from one company to those of another in the same industry. (We'll examine financial statements much more closely later in the chapter.)

WHO USES FINANCIAL ACCOUNTING INFORMATION?

Let's identify some of the users of financial statements and find out what they do with the information that they gather from these statements.

Owners and Managers

In summarizing a company's transactions over a specified period of time, financial statements are report cards for owners and managers. They show whether the company made a profit and furnish other information on the firm's financial condition. They also supply information that managers and owners can use to take corrective action where needed.

Investors and Creditors

Investors and creditors furnish a company with the money it needs to operate. If you loaned money to a friend to start a business, you'd want to know how it was doing.

Investors and creditors feel the same way. They study financial statements to assess a company's performance and to help them make decisions about continued investment. They know that it's impossible to make smart investment and loan decisions without an accurate report on an organization's financial health.

Government Agencies

Businesses are required to provide financial information to a number of government agencies. Publicly owned companies whose shares trade on one of the stock exchanges must provide annual financial reports to the Securities and Exchange Commission (SEC), a federal agency that regulates the trade of stock. Companies must also provide financial information to local, state, and federal taxing agencies, including the Internal Revenue Service.

Other Users

There are a host of other external users with an interest in a company's financial statements. Suppliers, for example, need to know if the company to which they sell their goods is having trouble paying its bills or even at risk of going under. Employees and labor unions are interested because salaries and other forms of compensation are dependent on an employer's performance.

Understanding Financial Statements

If you're in business, you need to understand financial statements. Even high-ranking corporate executives can no longer hold subordinates responsible for a firm's financial statements. They can't plead ignorance or fall back on delegation of authority. In a business environment tainted by fraudulent financial reporting and other misdeeds by corporate officials, top managers are now being held accountable for the financial reports issued by the companies they oversee. Without an understanding of financial statements, an executive would be like an airplane pilot who doesn't understand the instrument readings in the cockpit: He or she might be able keep the plane in the air for a while but wouldn't recognize any signs of impending trouble until it was too late.

THE FUNCTION OF FINANCIAL STATEMENTS

If you were running a company, what type of information would you want to know? Here are just a few pertinent questions to which you'd probably want some answers:

- What are my sales?
- How much are my expenses?
- How much profit have I made?
- What are my total assets?
- How much debt do I have?
- How much have I invested in my company?
- How much cash has the company brought in?
- When cash goes out, where does it go?

Financial statements will give you answers to these questions:

- *Income Statement.* Shows what your sales and expenses are and whether you made a profit.
- *Balance Sheet.* Indicates what assets and liabilities you have and the amount that you've invested in your business.
- *Statement of Cash Flows.* Shows how much cash you have coming in and going out.

Going into Hypothetical Business

Knowing what financial statements will tell you is one thing. But because learning how to prepare them is another matter, we'll go slowly and keep things simple. Let's assume that you need to earn money while you're in college, and you decide to start a small business. Your business—which will sell stuff to other college students—will operate on a "cash" basis: You'll pay for everything with cash, and everyone who buys something from you will pay in cash.

Your first task is to decide what you're going to sell. You notice that with homework, exams, social commitments, and the hectic lifestyle of the average college student, you and most of the people you know

always seem to be under a lot of stress. Sometimes you wish you could go back to the days when all you had to do was play. That's when the idea comes to you: Maybe you could make some money selling a product called the "Stress-Buster Play Pack." Here's your idea: You'll buy small toys and other fun stuff—instant stress relievers—at a local dollar store and pack certain items in a rainbow-colored plastic treasure chest labeled "Stress-Buster." You could also include a list of suggestions on student stress reduction circulated by the dean's office.

You have enough cash to buy a month's worth of plastic treasure chests and toys. After that, you'll use the cash generated from the sale of the Stress-Buster Play Packs to replenish your supply. Each plastic chest will cost $1.00, and you'll fill each one with a selection of five of the following toys, all of which you can buy for $1.00 each:

- Happy face stress ball
- Roomarang (indoor Boomerang)
- High-bounce balls
- Silly putty
- Inflatable beach ball
- Coil "slinky" spring
- Paddle-ball game

You'll experiment with different toy combinations until you get the mix right. You plan to sell each Stress-Buster Play Pack for $10 from a rented table stationed in a sales area outside a major dining hall. The table will cost you $20 a month. Because your own grades aren't what you'd like them to be, you decide to hire fellow students (trustworthy people with better grades) to staff the table at peak traffic periods. They'll be there from noon until 2:00 P.M. each weekday, and you'll pay them $6 an hour. Wages, therefore, will cost you $240 a month (2 hours × 5 days × 4 weeks = 40 hours × $6). Finally, you'll run ads in the college newspaper at a monthly cost of $40. Thus, your total monthly costs will amount to $300 ($20 + $240 + $40).

Stress-Buster Company

Income Statement
Month Ended September 30, 20X1

Sales (100 X $10)		$1,000
Less Cost of goods sold (100 X $6)		600
Gross profit (100 X $4)		400
Less Operating expenses		
Salaries	240	
Advertising	40	
Table rental	20	
	300	
Net income (profit)		$100

Figure 9.1

Income Statement for Stress-Buster Company

THE INCOME STATEMENT

During your first month, you sell 100 play packs. To find out if you made a profit, you prepare an **income statement**, which shows **revenues** (or sales) and **expenses** (cost of doing business). Expenses are divided into two categories. **Cost of goods sold** is the total cost of the *goods being sold*. **Operating expenses** are the costs of *operating the business* except for the costs of things being sold. The difference between sales and cost of goods sold is your **gross profit (or gross margin)**. The difference between gross profit and operating expenses is **net income (or profit)**, which is often called the "bottom line."

Let's prepare an income statement for your proposed company. (Remember that

Figure 9.2

Proposed Income Statement Number One for Stress-Buster Company

Stress-Buster Company

Income Statement
Month Ended September 30, 20X1
[If Cost of goods sold is $5 per unit]

Sales (100 X $10)		$1,000
Less Cost of goods sold (100 X $5)		500
Gross profit (100 X $5)		500
Less Operating expenses		
Salaries	240	
Advertising	40	
Table rental	20	
	300	
Net income (profit)		$200

we've made things simpler by handling everything in cash.) Figure 9.1 is your income statement for the first month.

Your income statement shows that you sold 100 units at $10 each, bringing in *revenues* or *sales* of $1,000. Each unit sold cost you $6 ($1 for the treasure chest plus 5 toys costing $1 each). So your *cost of goods sold* is $600 (100 units × $6 per unit). Your *gross profit* (the amount left after subtracting cost of goods sold from sales) was $400 (100 units × $4 each). After subtracting *operating expenses* of $300 (costs of doing business other than the cost of the products sold), you generated a positive *net income* (or *profit*) of $100.

You were quite relieved to find that you'd made a profit during your first month, but you can't help but wonder what you'll have to do to make even more money next month. You consider three possibilities:

1. Reduce your cost of goods sold (say, put in four toys instead of five)

2. Reduce some of your operating costs (salaries, advertising, table use)

3. Increase the quantity of units sold

To consider these possibilities fully, you need to play a number of "what-if" games to generate new income statements for each option. Because the first possibility (packaging four toys instead of five) is the most appealing, you start there. Your cost of goods sold would go down from $6 to $5 per unit (4 toys @ $1 each + 1 plastic treasure chest @ $1). Figure 9.2 is your hypothetical income statement if you choose this option.

This appears to be a good idea. Under this scenario, your income doubles from $100 to $200 because your per-unit *gross profit* increases by $1 (and you sold 100 stress packs). But there may be a catch: If you cut back on the number of toys, your customers might perceive your product as a lesser value for the money. You remember a conversation with a friend whose father, a restaurant owner, had cut back on the cost of food served by buying less expensive meat. In the short-term, gross profit per meal went up, but customers stopped coming back, and the restaurant nearly went out of business.

So, you decide to consider the second possibility—reducing your operating costs.

In theory, it's a good idea, but in practice—at least in your case—it probably won't work. You can't do without the table, and you need your workers (because your grades haven't improved, you still don't have time to sit at the table yourself). You might cut salaries from $6 to $5 an hour, but you may have a hard time finding people willing to work for you. You could reduce advertising costs by running an ad every two weeks instead of every week. But this tactic would increase your income by only $20 a month and could easily lead to a drop in sales.

You move on to possibility number three—increase sales. The appealing thing about this option is that it has no downside. If you could somehow increase the number of units sold from 100 per month to 150, your income would go up. (You'd stick with your original five-toy product.) Your new what-if income statement is shown in Figure 9.3. As you can see, this is an attractive possibility, even though you haven't yet figured out how you're going to increase sales. (Maybe you could put up some eye-popping posters and play cool music to attract people to your table. Or maybe your workers could attract buyers by demonstrating relaxation and stress-reduction exercises.)

Breakeven Analysis

Playing these what-if games has started you thinking: Is there some way to figure out the level of sales you need to avoid *losing* money—to "break even." Fortunately, as a friend majoring in accounting informs you, there is. Not surprisingly, it's called **breakeven analysis**, and here's how it works: To break even (have no profit or loss), *total sales revenue must exactly equal all your expenses (both variable and fixed)*. For a merchandiser, this balance will occur when gross profit equals all other (fixed) costs.

Stress-Buster Company

Income Statement
Month Ended September 30, 20X1
[If Sales increase to 150 units]

Sales (150 X $10)		$1,500
Less Cost of goods sold (150 X $6)		900
Gross profit (150 X $4)		600
Less Operating expenses		
Salaries	240	
Advertising	40	
Table rental	20	
	300	
Net income (profit)		$300

Figure 9.3

Proposed Income Statement Number Two for Stress-Buster Company

In order to determine the level of sales at which this will occur, you need to do the following:

1. Determine your total **fixed costs**, which are so called because the total cost doesn't change as the quantity of goods sold changes):

   Fixed costs = $240 salaries + $40 advertising + $20 table = $300

2. Identify your **variable costs**. These are costs that vary, in total, as the quantity of goods sold changes but stays constant on a per unit basis. State variable costs on a per-unit basis:

   Variable cost per unit = $6 ($1 for the treasure chest and $5 for the toys)

3. Determine your **contribution margin per unit**: selling price per unit – variable cost per unit:

   Contribution margin per unit = $10 selling price – $6 variable cost per unit = $4

---

income statement
Financial statement summarizing a business's revenues, expenses, and net income.

revenues
Amount of money earned by selling products to customers.

expenses
Costs incurred by selling products to customers.

cost of goods sold
Cost of the products that a business sells to customers.

operating expenses
Costs of selling products to customers, not including costs of goods sold.

gross profit (or **gross margin**)
Positive difference between revenues and cost of goods sold.

net income (or **net profit**)
Positive difference between gross profit and total expenses.

breakeven analysis
Method of determining the level of sales at which the company will break even (have no profit or loss).

fixed costs
Costs that don't change when the amount of goods sold changes.

variable costs
Costs that vary, in total, as the quantity of goods sold changes but stay constant on a per unit basis.

contribution margin per unit
Excess of revenue per unit over variable cost per unit.

Stress-Buster Company

Income Statement
Month Ended September 30, 20X1
[At breakeven level of sales = 75 units]

Sales (75 X $10)		$ 750
Less Cost of goods sold (75 X $6)		450
Gross profit (75 X $4)		300
Less Operating expenses		
Salaries	240	
Advertising	40	
Table rental	20	
	300	
Net income (profit)		$ 0

Figure 9.4

Proposed Income Statement Number Three for Stress-Buster Company

4. Calculate your **breakeven point in units:** fixed costs ÷ contribution margin per unit:

Breakeven in units = $300 fixed costs ÷ $4 contribution margin per unit = 75 units

Your calculation means that if you sell 75 units, you will end up with 0 profit (or loss) and will exactly break even. To test your calculation, you can prepare a what-if income statement for 75 units in sales (which is your breakeven number of sales). The resulting statement is shown in Figure 9.4.

Robots weld car bodies at a DaimlerChrysler plant in St. Louis. American automakers continue to lose market share to foreign competitors, but sales volume—and, thus, revenue from operations—is up. Coupled with such operational efficiencies as this robotic assembly line, which helps hold down operating costs, DaimlerChrysler managed to finish the year somewhat higher than its breakeven point. In other words, net income for the year was slightly above zero.

What if you want to do better than just break even? What if you want to earn a profit of $200 next month? How many Stress-Buster Pack units would you need to sell? You can find out by building on the results of your breakeven analysis. Note that each additional sale will bring in $4 (contribution margin per unit). If you want to make a profit of $200—which is $200 *above your breakeven point*—you must sell an additional 50 units ($200 desired profit divided by $4 contribution margin per unit) above your breakeven point of 75 units. If you sell 125 units (75 breakeven units + the additional 50), you'll make a profit of $200 a month.

As you can see, breakeven analysis is pretty handy. It allows you to determine the level of sales that you must reach to avoid losing money and the level of sales that you have to reach to earn a profit of $200. Such information will help you plan for your business. For example, knowing you must sell 125 Stress-Buster Packs to earn a $200 profit will help you decide how much time and money you need to devote to marketing your product.

THE BALANCE SHEET

The **balance sheet** reports the following information:

- The company's **assets**: the resources from which it expects to gain some future benefit
- Its **liabilities**: the debts that it owes to *outside* individuals or organizations
- Its **owner's equity**: the amount that's been invested by its owners and which owners can claim from its assets

Whereas your income statement tells you how much income you earned *over some period of time*, your balance sheet tells you what you have (and where it came from) *at a specific point in time*.

Most companies prepare financial statements on a 12-month, or **fiscal year** basis that ends on December 31 or some other point in time—for example, June 30 or September 30. A company generally picks a fiscal year-end date that coincides with the end of its peak selling period (a crabmeat processor might end its fiscal year in October, when the crab supply has dwindled). Most companies also produce financial statements on a quarterly or monthly basis. For your hypothetical company, you'd prepare a monthly balance sheet.

The Accounting Equation

The balance sheet is based on the **accounting equation**:

$$\text{Assets} = \text{Liabilities} + \text{Owner's equity}$$

This equation underscores the fact that a company's *assets* came from somewhere: either from borrowing (*liabilities*) or from investments made by owners (*owner's equity*). The asset section of the balance sheet on the one hand and the liability and owner's-equity section on the other must be equal, or *balance*. Hence, the term *balance sheet*.

Let's prepare two balance sheets for your company: one for the first day you started and one for the end of your first month of operations. Let's assume that when you started the business, you borrowed $400 from your parents and put in $200 of your own money. Your first balance sheet is shown in Figure 9.5. It shows clearly that your business has $600 in cash (your *assets*): Of this total, you borrowed $400 (your *liabilities*) and invested $200 of your own money (your *owner's equity*).

Now, let's see how things change at the end of the month. Recall that your business earned $100 (based on sales of 100 units) during the month of September and that you decided to leave these earnings in the business. This $100 profit increases both the *assets* of the company (its cash) and your investment in it (its *owner's equity*). Figure 9.6 shows what your balance sheet will look like on September 30. Once again, your balance sheet "balances." You now have $700 in cash—$400 that you borrowed and $300 that you've invested in the business (your original $200 investment plus the $100 profit from the first month of operations, which you've kept in the business).

Accounting can be helpful for even a very modest company. It tells you whether you made a profit and, if so, how much. It permits you to play what-if games to determine what your profit would be under different assumptions and conditions. It allows you to determine the number of units you need to sell in order to break even or to reach a targeted income level. Finally, it shows you what assets you have and where they came from.

Stress-Buster Company
Balance Sheet
As of September 1, 20X1

Assets

Cash	$600

Liabilities and Owner's equity

Liabilities	400
Owner's equity	200
Total Liabilities and Owner's equity	$600

Figure 9.5

Balance Sheet Number One for Stress-Buster Company

Figure 9.6

Balance Sheet Number Two for Stress-Buster Company

Stress-Buster Company
Balance Sheet
As of September 30, 20X1

Assets

Cash (original $600 plus $100 earned)	$700

Liabilities and Owner's equity

Liabilities	400
Owner's equity ($200 invested by owner plus $100 profits retained)	300
Total Liabilities and Owner's equity	$700

breakeven point in units
Number of sales units at which net income is zero.

balance sheet
Report on a company's assets, liabilities, and owner's equity at a specific point in time.

asset
Resource from which a business expects to gain some future benefit.

liability
Debt owed by a business to an outside individual or organization.

owner's equity
Amount which is invested in a business by its owners and which owners can claim from its assets.

fiscal year
Company's designated business year.

accounting equation
Accounting tool showing the resources of a business (assets) and the claims on those resources (liabilities and owner's equity).

QUICK QUIZ   9.1

Before going on to the next section of this chapter, take a few minutes to test your understanding of the material covered so far.

Go to www.exploringbusinessonline.com

Accrual Accounting

Now, let's go a step further by examining the world of accrual accounting. In our hypothetical example, we've assumed that all your transactions were made in cash. You paid cash for your inputs (plastic treasure chests and toys) and for your other expenses. Customers paid cash when they bought your Stress-Buster Packs. In the real world, things are different. For example:

- Customers don't always pay in cash; they often buy something and pay later. When this happens, the seller is owed money and has an **account receivable** (it will *receive* something later).

- Companies don't generally pay cash for materials and other expenses—they often pay later. If this is the case, a company has an **account payable** (it will *pay* something later).

- Many companies manufacture goods and hold on to them for a while before selling them; others buy goods and hold them for resale. Both practices result in **inventory**.

- Companies buy *long-term assets* (also called *fixed assets*), such as cars, buildings, and equipment, that they plan to use over an extended period of time (as a rule, for more than one year).

In situations such as these, firms use **accrual accounting**: a system in which the accountant records a transaction *when it occurs*, without waiting until cash is paid out or received. Here are a few basic principles of accrual accounting:

- A sale is recognized on the income statement when it takes place, regardless of when cash is collected.

- An expense is recognized on the income statement when it's incurred, regardless of when payment is made.

- An item manufactured for later sale or bought for resale becomes part of inventory and appears on the balance sheet until it's actually sold; at that point, it goes on the income statement under *Cost of goods sold*.

- A long-term asset that will be used for several years—for example, a vehicle, machine, or building—appears on the balance sheet. Its cost is spread over its useful life (the number of years that it will be used). Its annual allocated cost appears on the income statement as a **depreciation expense**.

It's easier to make sense of all this when you see some real numbers. Let's assume that you successfully operated the Stress-Buster Company while you were in college. Now fast-forward to graduation, and rather than work for someone else, you've decided to set up a business—some kind of retail outlet—close to the college. During your four years in school, you noticed that there was no store near campus that met the wide range of students' specific needs. Thus, the purpose of your proposed store: to provide products that satisfy the specific needs of students.

You've decided to call your store "The College Shop." Your product line will range from things needed to outfit a dorm room (linens, towels, small appliances, desks, rugs, dorm refrigerators) to things that are just plain fun and make student life more enjoyable (gift packages, posters, lava lamps, games, inflatable furniture, bean bag chairs, message boards, shower radios, backpacks). And you also plan to sell the original Stress-Buster Fun Pack. You'll advertise to students and parents through the college newspaper and your own Web site.

ACCRUAL-BASIS FINANCIAL STATEMENTS

Now, let's repeat the process we went through with your first business. First, we'll prepare a beginning balance sheet that reflects your new company's assets, liabilities, and owner's equity on your first day of business—January 1, 20X6. Next, we'll prepare an income statement. Finally, we'll create a balance sheet that reflects the company's financial state at the end of your first year of business.

Although the process should now be familiar, the details of our new statements will be more complex because your transactions will be more complicated: You're going to sell and buy stuff on credit, maintain an inventory of goods to be sold, retain assets for use over an extended period of time, borrow money and pay interest on it, and deal with a variety of expenses that you didn't have before (rent, insurance, and so on).

The Beginning Balance Sheet

Your new beginning balance sheet contains the same items as the one you created for your StressBuster Company—cash, loans, and owner's equity. But because you've already performed a broader range of transactions, you'll need some new categories:

- You've bought furniture and equipment that you'll use over the next five years. You'll allocate the cost of these long-term assets by depreciating them. Because you estimate that this furniture and equipment will have a *useful life* of five years, you allocate one-fifth of the cost per year for five years.

- You've purchased an inventory of goods for later resale.

- You've incurred two types of loans: one that's *current* because it's payable in one year and one that's *long-term* because it's due in five years.

You need to prepare a more sophisticated balance sheet than the one you created for your first business. We call this new kind of balance sheet a **classified balance sheet** because it classifies assets and liabilities into separate categories.

Assets On a classified balance sheet, assets are listed in order of **liquidity**—how quickly they can be converted into cash. They're also broken down into two categories:

Here's what your store—The College Shop—looks like. Not bad for your very first store.

1. **Current assets:** assets that you intend to convert into cash within a year.

2. **Long-term assets:** assets that you intend to hold for more than a year.

Your current assets will be cash and inventory, and your long-term assets will be furniture and equipment.

Liabilities Liabilities are grouped in a similar manner:

1. **Current liabilities:** liabilities that you'll pay off within one year.

2. **Long-term liabilities:** liabilities that don't become due for more than one year.

---

account receivable
Record of cash that will be received from a customer to whom a business has sold products on credit.

account payable
Record of cash owed to sellers from whom a business has purchased products on credit.

inventory
Goods that a business has made or bought and expects to sell in the process of normal operations.

accrual accounting
Accounting system that records transactions when they occur, regardless of when cash is paid or received.

depreciation expense
Costs of a long-term or fixed asset spread over its useful life.

classified balance sheet
Balance sheet that totals assets and liabilities in separate categories.

liquidity
Speed with which an asset can be converted into cash.

current asset
Asset that a business intends to convert into cash within a year.

long-term asset (or fixed asset)
Asset that a business intends to hold for more than a year before converting it to cash.

current liability
Liability that a business intends to pay off within a year.

long-term liability
Liability that a business need not pay off within the following year.

The College Shop
Balance Sheet
As of January 1, 20X6

Assets
Current assets

Cash	$ 50,000
Inventory	75,000

Long-term assets

Furniture, displays, and equipment	150,000
Total Assets	**$275,000**

Liabilities and Owner's equity
Current liabilities

Loan payable (due this year)	$ 25,000

Long-term liabilities

Loan payable (due in 5 years)	100,000
Owner's equity	150,000
Total Liabilities and Owner's equity	**$275,000**

Figure 9.7

Balance Sheet for The College Shop

You have two loans: one loan payable in a year, which is considered current, and one long-term loan due in five years.

You're ready to review your beginning balance sheet, which is shown in Figure 9.7. Once again, your balance sheet balances: Total assets of $275,000 equals total liabilities and owner's equity of $275,000. Let's begin our analysis with the liabilities and owner's equity sections. Thanks to a strong business plan, you've convinced a local bank to loan you a total of $125,000—a short-term loan of $25,000 and a long-term loan of $100,000. The bank charges you *interest* (which is the cost of borrowing money); your rate is 8 percent per year. In addition, you personally contributed $150,000 to the business (thanks to a trust fund that paid off when you turned 21).

Now, let's focus on the assets section. What do you have to show for your $275,000 in liabilities and owner's equity? Of this amount, $50,000 is in cash (in your checking, savings, and money market accounts). You used another $75,000 to pay for inventory that you'll sell throughout the year. Finally, you spent $150,000 on several long-term assets, including a sign for the store, furniture, store displays, and computer equipment. You expect to use these assets for five years, at which point you will probably replace them.

The Income Statement

Now, let's look at your income statement, which is shown in Figure 9.8. It's more complex than the one you prepared for your Stress-Buster Company, and the amounts are much larger. In addition, the statement covers a full calendar year.

Note that this statement is designed for a *merchandiser*—a company that makes a profit by selling goods. How can you tell? Businesses that sell services rather than merchandise (such as accounting firms or airlines) don't have a *Cost-of-goods sold* line on their statements.

The format of this income statement highlights the most important financial fact in running a merchandising company: *You must sell goods at a profit (called* gross profit*) that's high enough to cover your operating costs, interest, and taxes.* Your income statement shows that you generated $225,000 in gross profit through the sale of goods. This amount is sufficient to cover your operating costs, interest, and taxes and still produce a net income of $30,000.

A Few Additional Expenses Note that your income statement also lists a few expenses that that your first business didn't incur:

- *Depreciation expense.* Remember that you purchased some long-term assets (store sign, displays, furniture, and equipment) for a total amount of $150,000. In estimating that you would use these assets for five years (your estimate of their useful lives), you spread the cost of $150,000 over five years. For each of these five years, then, your income statement will show $30,000 in *Depreciation* expense ($150,000 ÷ 5 years = $30,000).

- *Interest expense.* When you borrowed money from the bank, you agreed to pay interest at an annual rate of 8 percent. Your *Interest* expense of $10,000 ($125,000 × .08) is a cost of financing your business and appears on your income statement after the subheading *Operating income*.

- *Income taxes.* Your company has to pay income taxes at a rate of 25 percent of net income before taxes. This amount of $10,000 ($40,000 × 25%) appears on your income statement after the subheading *Net income before income taxes*. It's subtracted from *income before income taxes* before you arrive at your "bottom line," or *Net income.*

ABOUT NIKE   9.1

Now that you understand The College Shop's income statement, take a few moments to see how it compares to Nike's income statement.

Go to www.exploringbusinessonline.com

The End-of-the-First-Year Balance Sheet

Let's conclude with your balance sheet for the end of your first year of operations, which is shown in Figure 9.9 (p. 236).

First, your assets. At year's end, you have a cash balance of $70,000 and inventory of $80,000. You also have an accounts receivable of $90,000 because many of your customers have bought goods on credit and will pay later. In addition, the balance sheet now shows two numbers for long-term assets: the original cost of these assets, $150,000, and an accumulated depreciation amount of $30,000. (*Accumulated depreciation* reflects the amount that you've charged as depreciation expense since you purchased the assets.) The net value of the long-term assets is now $120,000 ($150,000 − $30,000), which is the difference between their original cost and the amount that they've been depreciated. The total of your assets is $360,000.

The total of your liabilities of $180,000 and owner's equity of $180,000 also equals $360,000. Your liabilities consist of a long-term loan of $100,000 (that's now due in four years) and accounts payable of $80,000 (money that you'll have to pay out later for purchases that you've made on credit). Your owner's equity (your investment in the business) totals $180,000 (the $150,000 you originally put in and the $30,000 first-year earnings that you retained in the business).

ABOUT NIKE   9.2

Take a few moments to look at Nike's balance sheet. Most of the items on it will now look familiar to you.

Go to www.exploringbusinessonline.com

The College Shop
Income Statement
Year Ended December 31, 20X6

Sales		$500,000
Less Cost of goods sold		275,000
Gross profit		225,000
Less Operating expenses		
Salaries and employee benefits	75,000	
Depreciation ($150,000/5)	30,000	
Rent and utilities	20,000	
Advertising	20,000	
Other (insurance, office expenses, miscellaneous)	30,000	
Total Operating expenses	175,000	
Operating income		50,000
Less Interest expense (8% × loans of $125,000)		10,000
Net income before Income taxes		40,000
Less Income taxes (25% × income before taxes)		10,000
Net income		30,000

Figure 9.8

Income Statement for The College Shop

The Statement of Cash Flows

We now need to examine a type of financial statement that we omitted from our previous discussion. Owners, investors, and creditors can learn a lot from your balance sheet and your income statement. Each tells its own story. The balance sheet tells what assets your company has now and where they came from. The income statement reports earned income on an accrual basis (recognizing revenues when earned and expenses as incurred regardless of when cash is received or paid). But the key to surviving in business is generating cash to keep operating. It's not unusual to hear reports about companies with cash problems. Sometimes they arise because the products in which the firm has invested aren't selling as well as it had forecast. Maybe the company tied up too much money in a plant that's too big for its operations. Maybe it sold products to customers who can't pay. Maybe management just overspent. Whatever the reason, cash problems will hamper any business. Owners and other interested parties need a financial statement that helps them understand a company's cash flow.

The College Shop
Balance Sheet
As of December 31, 20X6

Assets
Current assets

Cash	$ 70,000
Accounts receivable	90,000
Inventory	80,000
Total Current assets	240,000

Long-term assets

Furniture, displays, and equipment	150,000
Less: Accumulated depreciation	(30,000)
Total Long-term assets	120,000
Total Assets	$360,000

Liabilities and Owner's equity
Current liabilities

Accounts payable	$80,000

Long-term liabilities

Loan payable (due in 4 years)	100,000

Owner's equity

(150,000 + 30,000)	180,000
Total Liabilities and Owner's equity	$360,000

Figure 9.9

End-of-the-First-Year Balance Sheet for The College Shop

The **statement of cash flows** tells you where your cash came from and where it went. It furnishes information about three categories of activities that either cause cash to come in (cash inflows) or go out (cash outflows):

1. Cash flows from **operating activities** come from the day-to-day operations of your main line of business.

2. Cash flows from **investing activities** result from buying or selling long-term assets.

Figure 9.10

Statement of Cash Flows for The College Shop

The College Shop
Cash Flow Statement
As of December 31, 20X6

Cash inflows from Operating activities	$45,000
Cash outflows from Financing activities	25,000
Increase in cash during the year	$20,000

3. Cash flows from **financing activities** result from obtaining or paying back funds used to finance your business.

A cash flow statement for The College Shop would look like the one in Figure 9.10. You generated $45,000 in cash from your company's operations (a cash inflow) and used $25,000 of this amount to pay off your short-term loan (a cash outflow). The net result was an increase in cash of $20,000. This $20,000 increase in cash agrees with the change in your cash during the year as it's reported in your balance sheets: You had an end-of-the-year cash balance of $70,000 and a beginning-of-the-year balance of $50,000 (and $70,000 − $50,000 = $20,000). Because you didn't buy or sell any long-term assets during the year, your cash flow statement shows no cash flows from investing activities.

ABOUT NIKE   9.3

Before testing your understanding of the cash flow statement, take a moment to review Nike's cash flow statement. You'll find that it's a bit more complex than the one developed for The College Shop.

Go to www.exploringbusinessonline.com

QUICK QUIZ   9.2

Before going on to the next section of this chapter, take a few minutes to test your understanding of the material covered so far.

Go to www.exploringbusinessonline.com

Financial Statement Analysis

Now that you know how financial statements are prepared, let's see how they're used to help owners, managers, investors, and creditors assess a firm's performance and financial strength. You can glean a wealth of information from financial statements, but first you need to learn a few basic principles for "unlocking" it.

THE COMPARATIVE INCOME STATEMENT

Let's fast-forward again and assume that your business—The College Shop—has just completed its second year of operations.

After creating your second-year income statement, you decide to compare the numbers from this statement with those from your first statement. So you prepare the **comparative income statement** in Figure 9.11, which shows income figures for year 2 and year 1 (accountants generally put numbers for the most recent year in the inside column).

Vertical Percentage Analysis

What does this statement tell us about your second year in business? Some things look good and some do not. Your sales went up from $500,000 to $600,000 (a 20-percent increase—not bad). But your profit was down—from $30,000 to $18,000 (a bad sign). As you stare at the statement, you're asking yourself the question: Why did my profit go down even though my sales went up? Does this result make sense? Is there some way of comparing two income statements that will give me a more helpful view of my company's financial health? One way is called **vertical percentage analysis**. It's useful because it reveals the relationship of each item on the income statement to a specified base—generally sales—by expressing each item as a percentage of that base.

Figure 9.12 (p. 238) shows what comparative income statements look like when you use vertical percentage analysis showing each item as a percentage of sales. Let's see if this helps clarify things. What do you think accounted for the company's drop in income even though The College Shop sales went up?

The percentages help you to analyze changes in the income statement items over time, but it might be easier if you think of the percentages as pennies. In year 1, for example, for every $1.00 of sales, $0.55 went to pay for the goods that you sold, leaving $0.45 to cover your other costs and leave you a profit. Operating expenses (salaries, rent, advertising, and so forth) used up $0.35 of every $1.00 of sales, while interest and taxes took up $0.02 each. After you covered all

your costs, you had $0.06 profit for every $1.00 of sales.

Asking the Right Questions Now, compare these figures to those for year 2. Where is the major discrepancy? It's in *Cost of goods sold*. Instead of using $0.55 of every $1.00 of sales to buy the goods you sold, you used $0.64. As a result, you had $0.09 less ($0.64 – $0.55) to cover other costs. This is the major reason why you weren't as profitable in year 2 as you were in year 1: Your *Gross profit as a percentage of sales* was lower in year 2 than it was in year 1. Although this information doesn't give you all the answers you'd like to have, it does, however, raise some interesting questions. Why was there a change in the relationship between *Sales* and *Cost of goods sold*? Did you have to pay more to buy goods for resale and, if so, were you unable to increase your selling price to cover the additional cost? Did you have to reduce prices to move goods that weren't selling well? (If your costs stay the same but your selling price goes down, you make less on

The College Shop
Comparative Income Statement
Years Ended December 31, 20X7 and 20X6

	12/31/20X7	**12/31/20X6**
Sales	$600,000	$500,000
Less Cost of goods sold	387,000	275,000
Gross profit	213,000	225,000
Less Operating expenses	180,000	175,000
Operating income	33,000	50,000
Less Interest	10,000	10,000
Less Income taxes	5,000	10,000
Net income	$ 18,000	$ 30,000

Figure 9.11

Comparative Income Statement for The College Shop

---

statement of cash flows
Financial statement reporting on cash inflows and outflows resulting from operating, investing, and financing activities.

operating activity
Activity that creates cash inflows or outflows through day-to-day operations.

investing activity
Activity that creates cash inflows or outflows through the selling or buying of long-term assets.

financing activity
Activity that creates cash inflows or outflows through the obtaining or repaying of borrowed or invested funds.

comparative income statement
Financial statement showing income for more than one year.

vertical percentage analysis
Analysis of an income statement treating the relationship of each item as a percentage of a base (usually sales).

The College Shop

Comparative Income Statement
Years Ended December 31, 20X7 and 20X6
[Using vertical percentage analysis showing each item as a % of sales]

	12/31/20X7		12/31/20X6	
	Amount	**Percent**	**Amount**	**Percent**
Sales	$600,000	100	500,000	100
Less Cost of goods sold	387,000	64	275,000	55
Gross profit	213,000	36	225,000	45
Less Operating expenses	180,000	30	175,000	35
Operating income	33,000	6	50,000	10
Less Interest	10,000	2	10,000	2
Less Income taxes	5,000	1	10,000	2
Net income	$ 18,000	3%	$ 30,000	6%

Figure 9.12

Comparative Income Statement Using Vertical Percentage Analysis

each item sold.) Answers to these questions require further analysis, but at least you know what the useful questions are.

RATIO ANALYSIS

Vertical percentage analysis helps you analyze relationships between items on your income statement. But how do you compare your financial results with those of other companies in your industry or to the industry over-all? And what about your balance sheet? Are there relationships on this statement that also warrant an investigation? Should you further examine any relationships between items on your income statement and items on your balance sheet? These issues can be explored by using **ratio analysis**, a technique for evaluating a company's financial performance.

First of all, remember that a *ratio* is just one number divided by another, with the result expressing the relationship between the two numbers. Let's say, for example, that you want to know the relationship between the cost of going to a movie and the cost of renting a DVD movie. You could make the following calculation:

$$\frac{\text{Cost of going to a movie}}{\text{Cost of renting a DVD}} = \frac{\$8}{\$4} = 2 \text{ (or 2 to 1)}$$

Going to a movie costs two times as much as renting a DVD.

Ratio analysis is used to assess a company's performance over time and to compare one company to similar companies or to the overall industry in which it operates. You don't learn much from just one ratio, or even a number of ratios covering the same period of time. The value in ratio analysis lies in looking at the *trend* of ratios over time and in comparing the ratios for several time periods with those of competitors and the industry as a whole. There are a number of different ways to categorize financial ratios. Here's just one set of categories:

- **Profit margin ratios** tell you how much of each sales dollar is left after certain costs are covered.
- **Management efficiency ratios** tell you how efficiently your assets are being managed.
- **Management effectiveness ratios** tell you how effective management is at running the business and measure over-all company performance.
- **Financial condition ratios** help you assess a firm's financial strength.

Using each of these categories, we can find dozens of different ratios, but we'll focus on a few examples.

Profit Margin Ratios

We've already determined the two most common profit margin ratios—*gross profit margin* and *net profit margin*—when we used vertical percentage analysis to determine the relationship to *Sales* of each item on The College Shop's income statement. We were examining gross profit when we found that *Gross profit* for year 1 was 45 percent of *Sales* and that, in year 2, it had declined to 36 percent. We can express the same relationships as ratios:

$$\text{Gross profit margin} = \frac{\text{Gross profit}}{\text{Sales}}$$

$$\text{Year 1: } \frac{\$225,000}{\$500,000} = 45\%$$

$$\text{Year 2: } \frac{\$213,000}{\$600,000} = 36\% \text{ (rounded)}$$

We can see that gross profit margin declined (a situation which, we learned above, probably isn't good). But how can you tell if your gross profit margin for year 2 is appropriate for your company? For one thing, we can use it to compare The College Shop's results to those of its industry. When we make this comparison, we find that the specialized retail industry (in which your company operates) reports an average gross profit margin of 41 percent. For year 1, therefore, we had a higher ratio than the industry; in year 2, although we had a lower ratio, we were still in the proverbial ballpark.

It's worthwhile to track gross profit margin, whether for your company or for companies that you might invest in or lend money to. In particular, you'll gain some insight into *changes* that might be occurring in a business. For instance, what if you discover that a firm's gross profit margin has declined? Is it because it's costing more for the company to buy or make its products, or is it because its competition is forcing it to lower its prices?

Net Profit Margin *Net profit* is the money that a company earns *after paying all of its expenses*, including the costs of buying or making its products, running its operations, and paying interest and taxes. Look again at Figure 9.12. Using vertical percentage analysis, we found that for The College Shop, net profit as a percentage of sales was 6 percent in year 1 but declined to 3 percent in year 2. Expressed as ratios, these relationships would look like this:

$$\text{Net profit margin} = \frac{\text{Net profit}}{\text{Sales}}$$

$$\text{Year 1: } \frac{\$30,000}{\$500,000} = 6\%$$

$$\text{Year 2: } \frac{\$18,000}{\$600,000} = 3\% \text{ (rounded)}$$

You realize that a declining net profit margin is not good, but you wonder how you compare with your industry. A little research informs you that average net profit margin in the industry is 7 percent. You performed nearly as well as the industry in year 1 but fell further from your target in year 2. What does this information tell you? A goal

for year 3 should be trying to increase your net profit margin.

Management Efficiency Ratios

These ratios reveal the way in which assets (shown on the balance sheet) are being used to generate income (shown on the income statement). To compute this group of ratios, therefore, you must look at both statements. In Figure 9.11, we produced a comparative income statement for The College Shop's first two years. Figure 9.13 is a comparative balance sheet for the same period.

Figure 9.13

Comparative Balance Sheet for The College Shop

The College Shop
Comparative Balance Sheet
As of December 31, 20X7 and 20X6

	12/31/20X7	12/31/20X6
Assets		
Current assets		
Cash	$ 76,000	$70,000
Accounts receivable	92,000	90,000
Inventory	110,000	80,000
Total Current assets	278,000	240,000
Long-term assets		
Furniture, equipment net of depreciation	90,000	120,000
Total Assets	368,000	$360,000
Liabilities and Owner's equity		
Current liabilities		
Accounts payable	$ 70,000	80,000
Long-term liabilities		
Loan	100,000	100,000
Total Liabilities	170,000	180,000
Owner's equity	198,000	180,000
Total Liabilities and Owner's equity	$368,000	$360,000

ratio analysis
Technique for financial analysis that shows the relationship between two numbers.

profit margin ratio
Financial ratio showing how much of each sales dollar is left after certain costs are covered.

management efficiency ratio
Financial ratio showing how efficiently a company's assets are being used.

management effectiveness ratio
Financial ratio showing how effectively a firm is being run and measuring its overall performance.

financial condition ratio
Financial ratio that helps to assess a firm's financial strength.

As you can see from Figure 9.13, running even a small business entails a substantial investment in assets. Even if you rent space, for example, you must still buy furniture and equipment. To have products on hand to sell, you need to tie up money in inventory. And once you've sold them, you may have money tied up in accounts receivable while you're waiting for customers to pay you. Thus, investing in assets is a normal part of doing business. Managing your assets efficiently is a basic requirement of business success. Let's look at a representative management efficiency ratio. The **inventory turnover ratio** measures a firm's efficiency in selling its inventory.

You don't make money from unsold inventory. You make money when you sell inventory, and the faster you sell it, the more money you make. To determine how fast your inventory is "turning," you need to examine the relationship between sales and inventory.* Let's see how well The College Shop is doing in moving its inventory:

$$\text{Inventory turnover} = \frac{\text{Sales}}{\text{Inventory}}$$

$$\text{Year 1: } \frac{\$500,000}{\$80,000} = 6.25 \text{ times}$$

$$\text{Year 2: } \frac{\$600,000}{\$110,000} = 5.45 \text{ times}$$

For year 1, The College Shop converted its inventory into sales 6.25 times: On average, your entire inventory was sold and replaced 6.25 times during the year. For year 2, however, inventory was converted into sales only 5.45 times. The industry did better, averaging turnover of 6.58 times. Before we discuss possible reasons for the drop in The College Shop's inventory turnover ratio, let's look at an alternative way of describing this ratio. Simply convert this ratio into the average number of days that you held an item in inventory. In other words, divide 365 days by your turnover ratio:

Year 1: 365 / 6.25 = 58 days
Year 2: 365 / 5.45 = 67 days
Industry: 365 / 6.58 = 55 days

The College Shop was doing fine in year 1 (relative to the industry), but something happened in year 2 to break your stride. Holding onto inventory for an extra 9 days (67 days for year 2 − 58 days for year 1) is costly. What happened? Perhaps inventory levels were too high because you overstocked. It's good to have products available for customers, but stocking too much inventory is costly. Maybe some of your inventory takes a long time to sell because it's not as appealing to customers as you thought. If this is the case, you may have a problem for the next year because you'll have to cut prices (and reduce profitability) in order to sell the same slow-moving inventory.

Optimal inventory turnover varies by industry and even by company. A supermarket, for example, will have a high inventory turnover because many of its products are perishable and because it makes money by selling a high volume of goods (making only pennies on each sale). A company that builds expensive sailboats, on the other hand, will have a low inventory turnover: It sells few boats but makes a hefty profit on each one. Some companies, such as Dell Computer, are known for keeping extremely low inventory levels. Because computers are made to order, Dell maintains only minimal inventory and so enjoys a very high ratio of sales to inventory.

Management Effectiveness Ratios

It takes money to make money. Even the smallest business uses money to grow. Management effectiveness ratios address the question: How well is a company performing with the money that owners and others have invested in it?

These ratios are widely regarded as the best measure of corporate performance. You can give a firm high marks for posting good profit margins or for turning over its inventory quickly, but the final grade depends on how much profit it generates with the money invested by owners and creditors. Or, to put it another way, that grade depends on the answer to the question: Is the company making a sufficiently high return on its assets?

---

*Another way to calculate inventory turnover is to divide *Cost of goods sold* by inventory (rather than dividing *Sales* by inventory). We don't discuss this method here because the available industry data used for comparative purposes reflect *Sales* rather than *Cost of goods sold*.

Like management efficiency ratios, management effectiveness ratios examine the relationship between items on the income statement and items on the balance sheet. From the income statement you always need to know the "bottom line"—net profit. The information that you need from the balance sheet varies according to the ratio that you're trying to calculate, but it's always *some measure of the amount of capital used in the business.* Common measures of capital investment include total equity, total assets, or a combination of equity and long-term debt. Let's see whether The College Shop made the grade. Did it generate a reasonable profit on the assets invested in the company?

$$\text{Return on assets} = \frac{\text{Net Profit}}{\text{Total assets}}$$

$$\text{Year 1: } \frac{\$30,000}{\$360,000} = 8.3\%$$

$$\text{Year 2: } \frac{\$18,000}{\$368,000} = 4.9\%$$

Because the industry average return on assets is 7.9 percent, The College Shop gets an "A" for its first year's performance. It slipped in the second year but is probably still in the "B" range.

Financial Condition Ratios

Financial condition ratios measure the financial strength of a company. They assess its ability to pay its current bills, and to determine whether its debt load is reasonable, they examine the proportion of its debt to its equity.

Current Ratio Let's look first at a company's ability to meet current obligations. The ratio that evaluates this ability is called the **current ratio**, which examines the relationship between a company's current assets and its current liabilities. The balance of The College Shop's current assets and current liabilities appears on the comparative balance sheet in Figure 9.13. By calculating its current ratio, we'll see whether the business

is likely to have trouble paying its current liabilities.

$$\text{Current ratio} = \frac{\text{Current assets}}{\text{Current liabilities}}$$

$$\text{Year 1: } \frac{\$240,000}{\$80,000} = 3 \text{ to } 1$$

$$\text{Year 2: } \frac{\$278,000}{\$70,000} = 4 \text{ to } 1$$

The College Shop's current ratio indicates that, in year 1, the company had $3.00 in current assets for every $1.00 of current liabilities. In the second year, the company had $4.00 of current assets for every $1.00 of current liabilities. The average current ratio for the industry is 2.42. The good news is that The College Shop should have no trouble meeting its current obligations. The bad news is that, ironically, its current ratio might be too high: Companies should have enough liquid assets on hand to meet current obligations, but not too many. Holding excess cash can be costly when there are alternative uses for it, such as paying down loans or buying assets that can generate revenue. Perhaps The College Shop should reduce its current assets by using some of its cash to pay a portion of its debt.

Debt-to-Equity Ratio Now let's look at the way The College Shop is financed. The **debt-to-equity ratio** examines the riskiness of a company's **capital structure**—the relationship between funds acquired from creditors (*debt*) and funds invested by owners (*equity*):

$$\text{Total debt to equity} = \frac{\text{Total liabilities}}{\text{Total equity}}$$

$$\text{Year 1: } \frac{\$180,000}{\$180,000} = 1$$

$$\text{Year 2: } \frac{\$170,000}{\$198,000} = 0.86$$

In year 1, the ratio of 1 indicates that The College Shop has an equal amount of equity

---

inventory turnover ratio
Financial ratio that shows how efficiently a company turns over its inventory.

current ratio
Financial ratio showing the relationship between a company's current assets and current liabilities.

debt-to-equity ratio (or **debt ratio**)
Financial ratio showing the relationship between debt (funds acquired from creditors) and equity (funds invested by owners).

capital structure
Relationship between a company's debt (funds acquired from creditors) and its equity (funds invested by owners).

and debt (for every $1.00 of equity, it has $1.00 of debt). But this proportion changes in year 2, when the company has more equity than debt: For every $1.00 of equity, it now has $0.85 in debt. How does this ratio compare to that of the industry? The College Shop, it seems, is heavy on the debt side: The industry average of 0.49 indicates that, on average, companies in the industry have only $0.49 of debt for every $1.00 of equity. Its high debt-to-equity ratio might make it hard for The College Shop to borrow more money in the future.

How much difference can this problem make to a business when it needs funding? Consider the following example. Say that you have two friends, both of whom want to borrow money from you. You've decided to loan money to only one of them. Both are equally responsible, but you happen to know that one has only $100 in the bank and owes $1,000. The other also has $100 in the bank but owes only $50. To which one would you loan money? The first has a debt-to-equity ratio of 10 ($1,000 debt to $100 equity) and the second a ratio of 0.50 ($50 debt to $100 equity). You—like a banker—will probably loan money to the friend with the better debt-to-equity ratio, even though the other one needs the money more.

It's possible, however, for a company to make its interest payments comfortably even though it has a high debt-to-equity ratio. Thus, it's helpful to compute the ratio called **interest coverage**, which measures the number of times that a firm's operating income can cover its interest expense. We compute this ratio by examining the relationship between interest expense and operating income. A high interest coverage ratio indicates that a company can easily make its interest payments; a low ratio suggests trouble. Here are the interest coverage ratios for The College Shop:

$$\text{Interest coverage} = \frac{\text{Operating income}}{\text{Interest expense}}$$

Year 1: $\dfrac{\$50,000}{\$10,000} = 5$ times

Year 2: $\dfrac{\$33,000}{\$10,000} = 3.3$ times

As the company's income went down, so did its interest coverage (which is not good). But the real problem surfaces when you compare the firm's interest coverage with that of its industry, which is much higher—14.5. This figure means that companies in

the industry have, on average, $14.50 in operating income to cover each $1.00 of interest that it must pay. Unfortunately, The College Shop has only $3.30.

Again, consider an example on a more personal level. Let's say that following graduation, you have a regular interest payment due on some student loans. If you get a fairly low-paying job and your income is only 3 times the amount of your interest payment, you'll have trouble making your payments. If, on the other hand, you land a great job and your income is 15 times the amount of your interest payments, you can cover them much more comfortably.

WHAT HAVE THE RATIOS TOLD US?

So what have we learned about the performance of The College Shop? What do we foresee for the company in the future? To answer this question, let's identify some of the basic things that every businessperson needs to do in order to achieve success:

- Make a good profit on each item you sell.
- Move inventory: The faster you sell inventory, the more money you make.
- Provide yourself and others with a good return on investment: Make investing in your business worthwhile.
- Watch your cash: If you run out of cash and can't pay your bills, you're out of business.

The ratios that we've computed in this section allow us to evaluate The College Shop on each of these dimensions, and here's what we found:

- Profit margin ratios (gross profit margin and net profit margin) indicate that the company makes a reasonable profit on its sales, although profitability is declining.
- One management efficiency ratio (inventory turnover) suggests that inventory is moving quickly, although the rate of turnover is slowing.
- One management effectiveness ratio (return on assets) tells us that the company generated an excellent return on its assets in its first year and a good return in its second year. But again, the trend is downward.
- Financial condition ratios (current ratio, total debt-to-equity, and interest cover-

age) paint a picture of a company heading for financial trouble. Although meeting current bills is not presently a problem, the company has too much debt and isn't earning enough money to make its interest payments comfortably. Moreover, repayment of a big loan in a few years will put a cash strain on the company.

So what does the future hold for The College Shop? It depends. If the company returns to year-one levels of gross margin (when it made $0.45 on each $1.00 of sales), and if it can increase its sales volume, it might generate enough cash to reduce its long-term debt. But if the second-year decline in profitability continues, it will run into financial difficulty in the next few years. It could even be forced out of business when the bank demands payment on its long-term loan.

ABOUT NIKE   9.4

You used ratio analysis to see how The College Shop was doing over time and in comparison to its industry. You can also use ratio analysis to compare one company to another. Take a few minutes to see how Nike compares to its closest competitor.

Go to www.exploringbusinessonline.com

Challenges Facing the Accounting Profession

Had you visited St. Charles, Illinois (about 50 miles southwest of Chicago), back in 2001, you would have noticed an impressive training and conference center owned by Arthur Andersen (then one of the so-called "Big 5" public accounting firms). Had you gone in, you could have toured a room dedicated to the history of Arthur Andersen, a proud firm with 89 years of corporate history. You'd have learned how a company started by a young accounting professor from Chicago grew into one of the world's largest public accounting firms, with 28,000 employees and annual revenues of over $4 billion.

Had your travels taken you to Houston, Texas, you might have passed a glass-fronted high rise with a tilted *E* designating the home of one of the country's largest energy-trading companies—Enron. Although its history was short, its accomplishments were already impressive. In the mid 1980s, Enron had begun transforming itself from a relatively small natural-gas-pipeline company to a diversified energy business that was the darling of Wall Street. During the second half of the 1990s, it was constantly mentioned among the most innovative companies in the United States. By early 2001, it was the seventh-largest company in America, with revenues of over $100 billion. Under the management of founder and CEO Ken Lay, President Jeffrey Skilling, and CFO Andrew Fastow, Enron's stock price skyrocketed. Unfortunately, the company's performance on the stock market was due to management's practice of making it look financially better off than it was, primarily by overstating income and hiding liabilities.

In the summer of 2001, the financial practices of these two giant corporations—Enron and Arthur Andersen—would come together to bring about permanent changes to the accounting profession.[3] Volumes have been written about what went wrong, but it can be boiled down to this: Enron executives behaved unethically and Andersen auditors looked the other way. Instead of exercising its role as public watchdog, Andersen was watching its own pocketbook. The accounting firm protected its own revenues from lucrative consulting contracts with its client instead of protecting the client's stakeholders. Andersen not only shirked its fiduciary responsibilities as a public auditor but was willing to cover up evidence of its own inappropriate actions and those of its client.

What had taken years to build took only a few months to destroy. Within a relatively short period of time, Enron went from apparent prosperity to bankruptcy and Andersen from renowned accounting firm to butt of David Letterman jokes. Its 28,000 employees and partners, the vast majority of whom had no involvement in the Enron mess, lost their jobs. Moreover, the account-

interest coverage ratio
Financial ratio showing a company's ability to pay interest on its debts from its operating income.

ing profession lost the trust of the public, which perceived auditors as typically corrupt, incompetent, or both. An accounting firm's stamp of approval on financial statements (which should have provided assurance to investors and other stakeholders) was viewed skeptically.

From these problems and public embarrassments, however, came some corrections to the professional course—or at least a plan to make things better in the future. Most people, including accountants, were convinced that the profession was broken and needed to be fixed. Congress passed the Sarbanes-Oxley Act, which severely restricts the ability of accountants to serve the same clients as both auditors and consultants. The Public Company Accounting Oversight Board was set up to take over from its members the task of regulating the profession. To underscore management responsibility for a firm's financial statements and accounting records, new regulations require CEOs and CFOs to sign statements attesting to their accuracy. Finally, auditors have to be more vigorous in detecting and reporting fraudulent activities.

So, will things get better? The raft of scandals of which the Enron debacle was perhaps the most notorious was not solely the fault of the auditors. Granted, they were supposed to be looking for managerial fraud, and clearly they were performing this job with a good deal less than due diligence. Under new guidelines, auditors must perform the fraud-

detection responsibilities on which stakeholders and the public depend. But as a big part of the problem, management also has to be part of the solution. Needless to say, managers must display more integrity in reporting on the financial conditions of the companies for which they're responsible. Members of the accounting profession hope that as a broad range of new regulations and other guidelines are put into action, the profession (along with corporate America) will slowly regain some of the public trust that's been squandered in the last decade.

QUICK QUIZ 9.3

Before going on to the last section of this chapter, take a few minutes to test your understanding of the material covered so far.

Go to www.exploringbusinessonline.com

Careers in Accounting

You may know that Phil Knight is the founder Nike. But you may not know that he began his business career as an accountant. Another thing that you may not know is that accounting is a "people profession." A lot of people think that accountants spend the day sitting behind desks crunching numbers. This is a misconception. Accountants work with other people to solve business problems. They need strong analytical skills, and they must be able to analyze financial data, but they must also be able to work effectively with colleagues. They need good interpersonal skills, and because they must write and speak clearly and present complex financial data in terms that everyone can understand, they need excellent communication skills as well.

JOB PROSPECTS

Accounting graduates have always faced a favorable job market. According to a recent survey conducted by the National Association of Colleges and Employers, accounting firms headed the list of top employers in 2005.[4] Moreover, with starting salaries averaging $44,000, accounting graduates are among the highest-paid entrants into the workforce. If you choose to begin your career in accounting, you have two career options: work as a public accountant

Hundreds of Arthur Andersen employees make their way to a federal courthouse to show their support for their employer on March 20, 2002. The rally was in vain. The firm crumbled after it was convicted of obstruction of justice three months later, and all of these people lost their jobs.

(whether for a Big Four public accounting firm or for a smaller company) or work as a private accountant for a business, not-for-profit organization, or government agency.

Public accounting firms provide clients with accounting and tax services in return for fees. Most members of such firms are **certified public accountants (CPAs)** who have met education and work requirements set by the state and passed a rigorous exam. Although public accounting firms offer consulting and tax services, the hallmark of the profession is performing external **audits**: The public accountant examines a company's financial statements and submits an opinion on whether they have been prepared in accordance with GAAP. This "stamp of approval" provides the investing public with confidence that a firm's financial reports are accurate. Typically, public accountants are self-employed, work for small, sometimes regional firms, or are associated with one of the Big Four public accounting firms— Deloitte & Touche, Ernst & Young, KPMG, and PricewaterhouseCoopers.

Often called *management* or *corporate accountants*, **private accountants** work for a single company, a not-for-profit organization, or a government agency. A firm's chief accounting officer is called the *controller* and occupies a position at the vice-presidential level. The jobs of private accountants vary according to the company or industry in which they're employed. Most private accountants record and analyze financial information and provide support to other members of the organization in such diverse areas as marketing, strategic planning, new product development, operations, human resources, and finance. Private accountants also conduct *internal audits*. In this capacity, they ensure that accounting records are accurate, company policies adhered to, assets safeguarded, and operations efficiently conducted. Finally, they may also provide a variety of specialized services:

- Develop and prepare financial reports
- Prepare tax returns
- Perform cost accounting (determine the cost of goods or services)

Many people think public accounting is for individuals who like working with numbers. But those in public accounting spend most of their time working with people: fellow staff members, clients, bankers. Although you have to be able to analyze financial information, interpersonal and communication skills are what will bring you success in the profession.

- Prepare and supervise budgets
- Manage such functions as payroll, accounts payable, and receivables

Accountants who pass a special exam and meet other professional requirements in the field of management accounting are designated as *certified management accountants (CMAs)*. CMAs often have greater job responsibilities and receive higher compensation than other accountants.

Where We're Headed

This chapter introduced you to the role of accounting in business. You discovered the value of accounting information in helping managers and other stakeholders to make better business decisions. You learned how to prepare and interpret financial statements. You used ratio analysis to assess a company's performance and financial condition over time and to compare one company to similar companies or to an overall industry. The next chapter will build on this knowledge as you explore the world of finance and the securities markets.

---

certified public accountant (CPA)
Accountant who has met state-certified requirements for serving the general public rather than a single firm.

audit
Accountant's examination of and report on a company's financial statements.

private accountant
Accountant who works for a private organization or government agency.

Summary of Learning Objectives

1. Define *accounting* and identify the different uses of accounting information.

Accounting is a system for measuring and summarizing business activities, interpreting financial information, and communicating the results to management and other **stakeholders** to help them make better business decisions. Accounting can be divided into two major fields. **Management accounting** provides information and analyses to decision makers *inside* the organization (such as owners and managers) to help them operate the business. **Financial accounting** provides information to people *outside* the organization (such as investors, creditors, government agencies, suppliers, employees, and labor unions) as well as to internal managers to assist them in assessing the financial performance of the business.

2. Understand the functions of the three basic financial statements: income statement, balance sheet, and statement of cash flows.

The three **financial statements** prepared by accountants are the income statement, the balance sheet, and the statement of cash flows. In preparing financial statements, accountants adhere to a uniform set of rules called **generally accepted accounting principles (GAAP)**: principles for financial reporting that are established by an independent agency called the Financial Accounting Standards Board (FASB). The **income statement** shows what the firm's **revenues** and **expenses** are and whether it made a profit. The **balance sheet** indicates what **assets** and **liabilities** the business has and the amount that its owners have invested in it (**owner's equity**). The **statement of cash flows** shows how much cash the business has coming in and going out. It furnishes information about three categories of activities that either cause cash to come in or to go out: **operating activities**, **investing activities**, and **financing activities**.

3. Apply breakeven analysis to determine an appropriate sales level.

Breakeven analysis is a technique used to determine the level of sales needed to break even—to operate at a sales level at which you have no profit or loss. To break even, total sales revenue must exactly equal all your expenses (both **variable** and **fixed costs**). To calculate the **breakeven point in units** to be sold, you divide fixed costs by **contribution margin per unit** (selling price per unit – variable cost per unit). This technique can also be used to determine the level of sales needed to obtain a specified profit.

4. Understand the difference between cash-basis and accrual accounting.

Companies using cash-basis accounting recognize **revenue** as earned only when cash is received and recognize **expenses** as incurred only when cash is paid out. This method of accounting ignores **accounts receivables**, **accounts payables**, **inventories**, and **depreciation**. In contrast, companies using **accrual accounting** recognize revenues when they're earned (regardless of when the cash is received) and expenses when they're incurred (regardless of when the cash is paid out). Most companies use accrual accounting.

5. Evaluate a company's performance using financial statements and ratio analysis.

Two common techniques for evaluating a company's financial performance are **vertical percentage analysis** and **ratio analysis**. Vertical percentage analysis reveals the relationship of each item on the income statement to a specified base—generally sales—by expressing each item as a percentage of that base. The percentages help you to analyze changes in the income statement items over time. Ratios show the relationship of one number to another number—for example, **gross profit** to sales or **net profit** to total assets. Ratio analysis is used to assess a company's performance and financial condition over time and to compare one company to similar companies or to an overall industry.

Ratios can be divided into four categories. (1) **Profit margin ratios** show how much of each sales dollar is left after certain costs are covered. Two common profitability ratios are the *gross profit margin* (which shows how much of each sales dollar remains after paying for the goods sold) and *net profit margin* (which shows how much of each sales dollar remains after all costs are covered). (2) **Management efficiency ratios** tell you how efficiently your assets are being managed. One of the ratios in this category—**inventory turnover**—measures a firm's efficiency in selling its inventory by looking at the relationship between sales and inventory. (3) **Management effectiveness ratios** tell you how effective management is at running the business and measure overall company performance by comparing net profit to some measure of the amount of capital used in the business. The **return on assets ratio**, for instance, compares net profit to total assets to determine if the company generated a reasonable profit on the assets invested in it. (4) **Financial condition ratios** are used to assess a firm's financial strength. The **current ratio** (which compares **current assets** to **current liabilities**) provides a measure of a company's ability to meet current liabilities. The **debt-to-equity ratio** examines the riskiness of a company's **capital structure** by looking at the amount of debt that it has relative to total equity. Finally, the **interest coverage ratio** (which measures the number of times a firm's operating income can cover its interest expense) assesses a company's ability to make interest payments on outstanding debt.

6. **Discuss career opportunities in accounting and the future of the profession.**

Those beginning careers in accounting have two career options: work as a public accountant or work as a private accountant. Public accounting firms provide clients with external **audits** in which they examine a company's financial statements and submit an opinion on whether they have been prepared in accordance with GAAP. They also provide other accounting and tax services. Most members of such firms are **certified public accountants (CPAs)** who have met required education and work requirements. Private accountants, often called *management*

or *corporate accountants*, work for individual companies, not-for-profit organizations, or government agencies. Most private accountants record and analyze financial information and provide support to other members of the organization. Private accountants also conduct internal audits as well as a variety of specialized services. Those who pass a special exam and meet other professional requirements in the field of management accounting are designated as *certified management accountants* (*CMAs*).

Recently, the accounting profession has suffered through a number of public embarrassments. In response, Congress passed the Sarbanes-Oxley Act, which severely restricts the ability of accountants to serve the same clients as both auditors and consultants. The Public Accounting Oversight Board was set up to take over from its members the task of regulating the profession, and new regulations require CFOs and CEOs to sign statements attesting to the accuracy of their financial statements. Finally, auditors have to be more vigorous in detecting and reporting fraudulent activities. Members of the accounting profession hope that these measures will allow the profession (along with corporate America) to regain some of the public trust that has been lost in the last decade.

Questions and Problems

1. What is accounting and what purpose does it serve? What do accountants do? What career choices do they have? Which career choice seems most interesting to you? Why?

2. Who uses accounting information? What do they use it for, and why do they find it helpful? What problems would arise if they weren't provided with accounting information?

3. **AACSB ▶ Analysis**
Describe the information provided by each of these financial statements: income statement, balance sheet, statement of cash flows. Identify 10 business questions that can be answered using financial accounting information. For each of these questions, indicate which financial statement (or statements) would be most helpful in answering the question and why.

4. **AACSB ▶ Analysis**
You're the president of a student organization, and in order to raise funds for a local women's shelter, you want to sell single, long-stem red roses to students on Valentine's Day. Each prewrapped rose will cost $3. An ad for the college newspaper will cost $100, and supplies for posters will cost $60. If you sell the roses for $5, how many roses must you sell to break even? Because breaking even won't leave you any money to donate to the shelter, you also want to know how many roses

you'd have to sell to raise $500. Does this seem like a realistic goal? If the number of roses you need to sell in order to raise $500 is unrealistic, what could you do to reach this goal?

5. **AACSB ▶ Analysis**
To earn money to pay some college expenses, you ran a lawn-mowing business during the summer. Before heading to college at the end of August, you wanted to find out how much money you earned for the summer. Fortunately, you kept good accounting records. During the summer, you charged customers a total of $5,000 for cutting lawns (which includes $500 still owed to you by one of your biggest customers). You paid out $1,000 for gasoline, lawn mower repairs, and other expenses, including $100 for a lawn mower tune-up that you haven't paid for yet. You decided to prepare an income statement to see how you did. Because you couldn't decide whether you should prepare a cash-basis statement or an accrual statement, you prepared both. What was your income under each approach? Which method (cash-basis or accrual) more accurately reflects the income that you earned during the summer? Why?

6. Identify the categories used on a classified balance sheet to report assets and liabilities. How do you determine what goes into each category? Why would a banker considering a loan to your company want to know if an asset or liability is current or long-term?

7. **AACSB** ▸ **Analysis**

   You review a company's statement of cash flows and find that cash inflows from operations are $150,000, net outflows from investing are $80,000, and net inflows from financing are $60,000. Did the company's cash balance increase or decrease for the year? By what amount? What types of activities would you find under investing activities? Under financing activities? If you had access to the company's income statement and balance sheet, why would you be interested in reviewing its statement of cash flows? What additional information can you gather from the statement of cash flows?

8. **AACSB** ▸ **Analysis**

   The accountant for my company just ran into my office and told me that our gross profit margin increased while our net profit margin decreased. She also reported that while our debt-to-equity ratio increased, our interest coverage ratio decreased. She was puzzled by the apparent inconsistencies. Help her out by providing possible explanations for the behavior of these ratios.

9. Which company is more likely to have the higher inventory turnover ratio: a grocery store or an automobile manufacturer? Give an explanation for your answer.

10. **AACSB** ▸ **Analysis**

    What actions have been taken to help restore the trust that the public once had in the accounting profession? Do you believe these actions will help? Why or why not? What other suggestions do you have to help the accounting profession and corporate America regain the public trust?

Learning on the Web AACSB

Discounting Retailers

There was a time when Kmart was America's number-one discount retailer and Sears, Roebuck & Co. was the seventh largest corporation in the world. Things have changed since Wal-Mart came on the scene. In the 40 years since Sam Walton opened the first Wal-Mart store in Rogers, Arkansas, the company has propelled itself to the number-one spot in discount retailing, and (even more impressive) has higher sales than *any other company in the world*. Over this same 40-year period, Target emerged as a major player in the retail industry. The 40-year period was not kind to Kmart and Sears and both stores watched their dominance in the retail market slip away. In an effort to reverse the downward spiral of both retailers, in November 2004, Sears and Kmart merged into a new company called Sears Holdings. To learn more about how Wal-Mart, Target, and Sears Holdings are doing today, go to www.exploringbusinessonline.com to link to a report of the 2006 top 100 retailers. After reading the introduction and reviewing the list of top retailers, prepare a report comparing the three retailers on the following:

- Sales and percentage increase or decrease in sales
- Net income (or loss) and percentage increase or decrease in net income
- Number of stores and percentage increase or decrease in number of stores
- Net income as a percentage of sales

Based on your analysis and reading, answer the following questions:

1. Do you believe that Target will be able to compete against Wal-Mart in the future? If so, how?

2. What about Sears Holdings? Will the company survive?

3. Some people criticize Wal-Mart for forcing other retailers out of business and for lowering the average wage for retail workers. Is this a legitimate criticism? In your opinion, has Wal-Mart helped the American people or hurt them?

Career Opportunities

Is a Career in Accounting for You?

Do you want to learn what opportunities are available for people graduating with degrees in accounting? Go to www.exploringbusinessonline.com to link to the Web site of the American Institute of Certified Public Accountants and click on the "Today's CPA" icon. Watch the video clip featuring a CPA and read about other featured accountants. Select a job that interests you and answer each of the following questions:

- What is the job like?
- Why does the accountant enjoy the job?

- Why does the job seem interesting to you?

Explore career options in public accounting and business and industry. Learn about earning potential in these fields. Select the career path you find most appealing and answer these questions:

1. What opportunities would be available to you if you followed this career path?

2. How much should you expect to earn at the beginning of your career? After 5 years? After 15 years?

Ethics Angle AACSB

Counting Earnings Before They Hatch

You recently ran into one of your former high school teachers. You were surprised to learn that he'd left teaching, gone back to school, and, a little more than a year ago, started a business that creates Web sites for small companies. It so happens that he needs a loan to expand his business, and the bank wants financial statements. When he found out that you were studying accounting, he asked if you'd look over a set of statements that he'd just prepared for his first year in business. Because you're anxious to show off your accounting aptitude, you agreed.

First, he showed you his income statement. It looked fine: Revenues (from designing Web sites) were $94,000, expenses were $86,000, and net income was $8,000. When you observed how unusual it was that he'd earned a profit in his first year, he seemed a little uneasy.

"Well," he confessed, "I fudged a little when I prepared the statements. Otherwise, I'd never get the loan."

He admitted that $10,000 of the fees shown on the income statement was for work he'd just started doing for a client (who happened to be in big trouble with the IRS). "It isn't like I won't be earning the money," he explained. "I'm just counting it a little early. It was easy to do. I just added $10,000 to my revenues and recorded an accounts receivable for the same amount."

You quickly did the math: Without the $10,000 payment for the client in question, his profit of $8,000 would become a loss of $2,000 (revenues of $84,000 less expenses of $86,000).

As your former teacher turned to get his balance sheet, you realized that, as his accountant, you had to decide what you'd advise him to do. The decision is troublesome because you agree that if he changes the income statement to reflect the real situation, he won't get the bank loan.

1. What did you decide to do and why?

2. Assuming that he doesn't change the income statement, will his balance sheet be incorrect? How about his statement of cash flows? What will happen to next year's income: Will it be higher or lower than it should be?

3. What would happen to your former teacher if he gave the bank the fraudulent financial statements and the bank discovered the truth? How could the bank learn the truth?

Team-Building Skills AACSB

Taking Stock of Ratios

Your class has been told that each group of three students will receive a share of stock in one of three companies in the same industry. But there's a catch: Each group has to decide which of the companies it wants to own stock in. To reach this decision, your team will use ratio analysis to compare the three companies. Each team member will analyze one of the companies using the ratios presented in this chapter. Then, you'll get together, compare your results, and choose a company. Here are the details of the project:

1. The team selects a group of three companies in the same industry. Here are just a few examples:

   • Auto Manufacturers: Ford, General Motors, Daimler-Chrysler

   • Airlines: Southwest, Continental, American Airlines

   • Drug Companies: GlaxoSmithKline, Eli Lilly & Co., Bristol-Myers Squibb

   • Specialty Retailers: Bed Bath & Beyond, Linens 'n Things, Pier 1 Imports

   • Computers: Dell, Gateway, Apple Computer

2. Every team member gets a copy of one company's most recent annual report (which includes its financial statements) from the company's Web site (investor section).

3. Every member calculates the following ratios for the company for the last two years: gross profit margin, net profit margin, inventory turnover (if applicable), return on assets, current ratio, debt-to-equity, and interest coverage.

4. Get together as a group and compare your results. Decide as a group which company you want to own stock in.

5. Write a report indicating the company that your team selected and explain your choice. Attach the following items to your team report:

   a. a brief explanation of each ratio (how to calculate it and what it means)

   b. detailed calculations showing how each ratio was determined

   c. a chart comparing the ratios for the three companies.

The Global View AACSB

Why Aren't Shoes Made in the USA?

Having just paid $70 for a pair of athletic shoes that were made in China, you wonder why they had to be made in China. Why weren't they made in the United States, where lots of people need good-paying jobs? You also figure that the shoe company must be making a huge profit on each pair it sells. Fortunately, you were able to get a breakdown of the costs for making a pair of $70 athletic shoes:[5]

Production labor	$2.75
Materials	9.00
Rent, equipment	3.00
Supplier's operating profit	1.75
Duties	3.00
Shipping	0.50
Cost to the Manufacturer	**$20.00**
Research and development	0.25
Promotion and advertising	4.00
Sales, distribution, administration	5.00
Shoe company's operating profit	6.25
Cost to the Retailer	**$35.50**
Retailer's Rent	9.00
Personnel	9.50
Other	7.00
Retailer's operating profit	9.00
Cost to Consumer	**$70.00**

You're surprised at a few of these items. First, out of the $70, the profit made by the manufacturer was only $6.25. Second, at $2.75, labor accounted for only about 4 percent of the price you paid. The advertising cost ($4.00) was higher than the labor cost. If labor isn't a very big factor in the cost of the shoes, why are they made in China?

Deciding to look further into this puzzle, you discover that the $2.75 labor cost was for 2 hours of work. Moreover, that $2.75 includes not only the wages paid to the workers, but labor-related costs, such as food, housing, and medical care.

That's when you begin to wonder. How much would I have to pay for the same shoes if they were made in the United States? Or what if they were made in Mexico? How about Spain? To answer these questions, you need to know the hourly wage rates in these countries. Fortunately, you can get this information by going to www.

exploringbusinessonline.com and linking to the Foreign Labor section of the Bureau of Labor Statistics Web site. The table you want is "Hourly Compensation Costs in U.S. Dollars for Production Workers in Manufacturing." Use the most recent hourly compensation figures, which are listed on the last page of the table.

To investigate this issue further, you should do the following:

1. Recalculate the cost of producing the shoes in the United States and two other countries of your choice. Because operating profit for the supplier, the shoe company, and the retailer will change as the cost to make the shoe changes, you have decided to determine this profit using the following percentage rates:

   • Supplier's operating profit: 10 percent of its costs

   • Shoe company's operating profit: 20 percent of its costs (including the cost paid to the supplier to make the shoes)

   • Retailer's operating profit: 15 percent of its costs (including the cost paid to the shoe company)

2. Prepare a report which does the following:

   • Shows the selling price of the shoe for each manufacturing country (the United States and the other two countries you selected).

   • Lists any costs other than labor that might change if shoe production was moved to the United States.

   • Identifies other factors that should be considered when selecting a manufacturing country.

   • Indicates possible changes to production methods that would make production in the United States less costly.

3. Finally, draw some conclusions: Do you, as a U.S. citizen, benefit from shoe production in foreign countries? Does the United States benefit overall? Does the world benefit? Should shoe production return to the United States?

Business Plan Project

Group Report: *Estimating Sales*

REPORT

The team should submit a written report that answers these questions for *each* of the first *three years* of operations:

• How many different products (goods or services) will the company sell?

• How much will we charge for each product?

• How many units will we sell of each product?

• What will be our total sales in dollars?

Your report should also explain how the team arrived at its estimates. If you use competitors' financial statements to estimate sales, attach a copy of these statements to the report. Your report should be about two double-spaced typed pages. The name of your proposed business and the names of all team members should appear on the report.

For guidance on estimating sales, go to Appendix B, "Estimating Sales" (p. 310).

REASONABLE CONTRIBUTIONS

All members of the team who make a reasonable contribution to the report should sign it. (If any team member does not work on the report, his or her name should *not* appear on it.) If a student who has made a contribution is unable to sign the report (because of sickness or some other valid reason), the team can sign his or her name. To indicate that a name was signed by the team on a member's behalf, be sure to attach a note to the signature.

10

Managing Financial Resources

After studying this chapter, you will be able to:

1. Identify the functions of money and describe the three government measures of the money supply.

2. Distinguish among different types of financial institutions, discuss the services they provide, and explain their role in expanding the money supply.

3. Identify the goals of the Federal Reserve System and explain how it uses monetary policy to control the money supply and influence interest rates.

4. Explain the ways in which a new business gets start-up cash and the ways in which existing companies finance operations and growth.

5. Show how the securities market operates and how it's regulated.

6. Understand how market performance is measured and distinguish between equity and debt financing.

Henrik Sorensen/Photonica/Getty Images

HOW TO KEEP FROM GOING UNDER

How can you manage to combine a fantastic business idea, an efficient production system, a talented management team, and a creative marketing plan and still go under? It's not so hard if you don't understand finance. Everyone in business—not just finance specialists—needs to understand how the U.S. financial system operates and how financial decisions affect an organization. Businesspeople also need to know how securities markets work. In this chapter, we'll discuss these three interrelated topics. Let's start by taking a closer look at one of the key ingredients in any business enterprise—money.

The Functions of Money

Finance is about money. So our first question is: What is money? If you happen to have one on you, take a look at a $5 bill. What you'll see is a piece of paper with a picture of Abraham Lincoln on one side and the Lincoln Memorial on the other. Although this piece of paper—indeed, money itself—has no intrinsic value, it's certainly in demand. Why? Because money serves three basic functions. **Money** is:

1. A medium of exchange

2. A measure of value

3. A store of value

To get a better idea of the role of money in a modern economy, let's imagine a system in which there is no money. In this system, goods and services are *bartered*—traded directly for one another. Now, if you're living and trading under such a system, for each barter exchange that you make, you'll have to have something that another trader wants. For example, say you're a farmer who needs help clearing his fields. Because you have plenty of food, you might enter into a barter transaction with a laborer who has time to clear fields but not enough food: He'll clear your fields in return for three square meals a day.

This system will work as long as two people have exchangeable assets, but needless to say, it can be inefficient. If we identify the functions of money, we'll see how it improves the exchange for all the parties in our hypothetical set of transactions.

MEDIUM OF EXCHANGE

Money serves as a medium of exchange because people will accept it in exchange for goods and services. Because people can use money to buy the goods and services that they want, everyone's willing to trade something for money. The laborer will take money for clearing your fields because he can use it to buy food. You'll take money as payment for his food because you can use it not only to pay him, but to buy something else you need (perhaps seeds for planting crops).

For money to be used in this way, it must possess a few crucial properties:

1. It must be *divisible*—easily divided into usable quantities or fractions. A $5 bill, for example, is equal to five $1 bills. If something costs $3, you don't have to rip up a $5 bill; you can pay with three $1 bills.

2. It must be *portable*—easy to carry; it can't be too heavy or bulky.

3. It must be *durable*. It must be strong enough to resist tearing and the print can't wash off if it winds up in the washing machine.

4. It must be *difficult to counterfeit*; it won't have much value if people can make their own.

MEASURE OF VALUE

Money simplifies exchanges because it serves as a measure of value. We state the price of a good or service in monetary units so that potential exchange partners know exactly how much value we want in return for it. This practice is a lot better than bartering because it's much more precise than an ad hoc agreement that a day's work in the field has the same value as three meals.

STORE OF VALUE

Money serves as a store of value. Because people are confident that money keeps its value over time, they're willing to save it for future exchanges. Under a bartering arrangement, the laborer earned three meals a day in exchange for his work. But what if, on a given day, he skipped a meal? Could he "save" that meal for another day? Maybe, but if he were paid in money, he could decide whether to spend it on food each day or save some of it for the future. If he wanted to collect on his "unpaid" meal two or three days later, the farmer might not be able to "pay" it; unlike money, food could go bad.

money
Anything commonly accepted as a medium of exchange, measure of value, and store of value.

They may look like old Stone Age wheels, but they're actually coins. They're called *rai*, and they're used by the people of Yap, an island chain in the South Pacific, as a *medium of exchange*—money. They can be 12 feet in diameter and weigh several tons, and as *units of value*, they're measured not only by size but by mineral content. They're not very portable; usually, they're just left in one place while ownership is transferred from buyer to seller. Theft isn't much of a problem.

THE MONEY SUPPLY

Now that we know what money does, let's tackle another question: How much money is there? How would you go about "counting" all the money held by individuals, businesses, and government agencies in this country? You could start by counting the money that's held to pay for things on a daily basis. This category includes *cash* (paper bills and coins) and funds held in **demand deposits**—checking accounts, which pay given sums to "payees" when they demand them.

Then, you might count the money that's being "saved" for future use. This category includes *interest-bearing accounts, time*

deposits (such as *certificates of deposit*, which pay interest after a designated period of time), and **money market mutual funds**, which pay interest to investors who pool funds to make short-term loans to businesses and the government.

M-1 and M-2

Counting all this money would be a daunting task (in fact, it would be impossible). Fortunately, there's an easier way—namely, by examining two measures that the government compiles for the purpose of tracking the money supply: *M-1 and M-2*.

- The narrowest measure, **M-1**, includes the most *liquid* forms of money—the forms, such as cash and checking-accounts funds, that are spent immediately.

- **M-2** includes everything in M-1 plus *near-cash items* invested for the short term—savings accounts, time deposits below $100,000, and money market mutual funds.

So what's the bottom line? How much money *is* out there? To find the answer, you can go to the Federal Reserve Board Web site. The Federal Reserve reports that in April 2006, M-1 was about $1.4 trillion dollars and M-2 was $6.8 trillion. Figure 10.1 shows the increase in the two money-supply measures since 1980.

If you're thinking that these numbers are too big to make much sense, you're not alone. One way to bring them into perspective is to figure out how much money *you*'d get if all the money in the United States were redistributed equally. According to the U.S. Census Population Clock, there are 293,257,062 people in the United States. Your share of M-1, therefore, would be $4,774 and your share of M-2 would be $23,188.

What, Exactly, Is "Plastic Money"?

Are credit cards a form of money? If not, why do we call them "plastic money"? Actually, when you buy something with a credit card, you're not spending money. The principle of the credit card is buy-now-pay-later. In other words, when you use plastic, you're taking out a loan that you intend to pay off when you get your bill. And the loan itself is not money. Why not? Basically because the credit card company can't use the asset to buy anything. The loan is merely a promise of repayment. The asset doesn't become money until the bill is paid

Figure 10.1

The U.S. Money Supply, 1980–2005

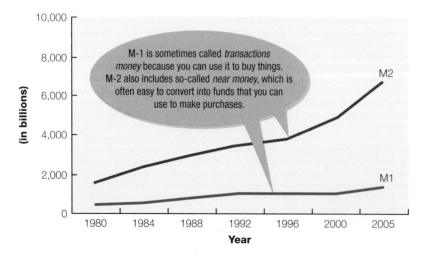

M-1 is sometimes called *transactions money* because you can use it to buy things. M-2 also includes so-called *near money*, which is often easy to convert into funds that you can use to make purchases.

(with interest). That's why credit cards aren't included in the calculation of M-1 and M-2.

Financial Institutions

For financial transactions to happen, money must change hands. How do such exchanges occur? At any given point in time, some individuals, businesses, and government agencies have more money than they need for current activities; some have less than they need. Thus, we need a mechanism to match up savers (those with surplus money that they're willing to loan out) with borrowers (those with deficits who want to borrow money). We could just let borrowers search out savers and negotiate loans, but the system would be both inefficient and risky. Even if you had a few extra dollars, would you loan money to a total stranger? If you needed money, would you want to walk around town looking for someone with a little to spare?

Wal-Mart is not a bank, but it would like to get permission to create banks. In the meantime, it provides several financial services: check cashing, money orders, and money transfers. It even issues a Wal-Mart credit card. More than 1,000 of its U.S. stores house a branch bank where customers can deposit or withdraw funds and obtain loans. Through a partnering arrangement with a national bank, the retailer has set up Wal-Mart Money Centers like the one in the picture. Because they're full-service banks, you can shop at Wal-Mart and then visit the money center to talk with someone about your investments.

DEPOSITORY AND NONDEPOSITORY INSTITUTIONS

Now you know why we have financial institutions: They act as intermediaries between savers and borrowers and direct the flow of funds between them. With funds deposited by savers in checking, savings, and money market accounts, they make loans to individual and commercial borrowers. In the next section, we'll discuss the most common types of depository institutions (banks that accept deposits), including *commercial banks, savings banks*, and *credit unions*. We'll also discuss several nondepository institutions (which provide financial services but don't accept deposits), including finance companies, insurance companies, brokerage firms, and pension funds.

Commercial Banks

Commercial banks are the most common financial institutions in the United States, with total assets of over $9.2 trillion—79 per-

cent of total bank assets.[1] They generate profit not only by charging borrowers higher interest rates than they pay to savers, but by providing such services as check processing, trust- and retirement-account management, and electronic banking. The country's 7,500 commercial banks range in size from very large (Citigroup, Bank of America, J.P. Morgan Chase & Company) to very small (local community banks). Because of mergers, the number of banks has declined significantly in recent years, but, by the same token, surviving banks have grown quite large. If you've been with one bank over the past 10 years or so, you've probably seen the name change at least once or twice.

Savings Banks

Savings banks (also called *thrift institutions* and *savings and loan associations*, or *S&Ls*) were originally set up to encourage personal saving and provide mortgages to local home buyers. Today, however, they provide a range of services similar to those offered by commercial banks. Though not as dominant as commercial banks, they're an important component of the industry, holding total assets of almost $1.8 trillion (about 15 percent of the total). The largest S&L, Washington Mutual, has 2,600 locations throughout the country. Savings banks can be owned by their depositors (mutual ownership) or by shareholders (stock ownership).

Credit Unions

To bank at a **credit union**, you must be linked to a particular group, such as employees of United Airlines, employees of the state of Nevada, teachers in Orange County, California, or current and former members of the U.S. Navy. Credit unions are owned by their members, who receive shares of their profits. They offer almost anything that a commercial bank or savings and loan does, including savings accounts, checking accounts, home and car loans, credit cards, and even some commercial loans.[2] Collectively, they hold about $685 billion in assets (around 6 percent of the total).

Figure 10.2 summarizes the distribution of assets among the nation's depository institutions.

Finance Companies

Finance companies are nondeposit institutions because they don't accept deposits from individuals or provide traditional banking services, such as checking accounts. They do, however, make loans to individuals and businesses, using funds acquired by selling securities or borrowed from commercial banks. They hold about $1.3 trillion in assets. Those that lend money to businesses are *commercial finance companies*, and those that make loans to individuals are *consumer finance companies*. Some, such as General Motors Acceptance Corporation, provide loans to both consumers (car buyers) and businesses (GM dealers).

Insurance Companies

Insurance companies sell protection against losses incurred by illness, disability, death, and property damage. To finance claims payments, they collect premiums from policyholders, which they invest in stocks, bonds, and other assets. They also use a portion of their funds to make loans to individuals, businesses, and government agencies.

Brokerage Firms

Companies like A.G. Edwards & Sons and T. Rowe Price, which buy and sell stocks, bonds, and other investments for clients, are **brokerage firms** (also called *securities investment dealers*). A **mutual fund** invests money from a pool of investors in stocks, bonds, and other securities. Investors become part owners of the fund. Mutual funds reduce risk by diversifying investment: Because assets are invested in dozens of companies in a variety of industries, poor performance by some firms is usually offset by good performance by others. Mutual funds may be stock funds, bond funds, and **money market funds**, which invest in safe, highly liquid securities. (Recall our definition of *liquidity* in Chapter 9 as the speed with which an asset can be converted into cash.)

Finally, **pension funds**, which manage contributions made by participating employees and employers and provide members with retirement income, are also nondeposit institutions.

FINANCIAL SERVICES

You can appreciate the diversity of the services offered by commercial banks, savings banks, and credit unions by visiting their Web sites. Wachovia for example, promotes services to four categories of customers: individuals, small businesses, corporate and institutional clients, and affluent clients seeking "wealth management." In addition to traditional checking and savings accounts, the bank offers automated teller machine (ATM) services, credit cards, and debit cards. It loans money for homes, cars, college, and other personal and business needs. It provides financial advice and sells securities

Figure 10.2

Where Our Money Is Deposited

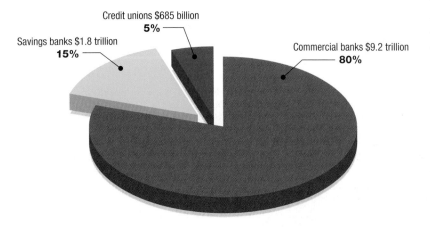

Credit unions $685 billion
5%

Savings banks $1.8 trillion
15%

Commercial banks $9.2 trillion
80%

and other financial products, including **individual retirement accounts (IRAs)**, by which investors can save money that's tax free until they retire. Wachovia even offers life, auto, disability, and homeowners insurance. It also provides electronic banking for customers who want to check balances, transfer funds, and pay bills online.[3]

BANK REGULATION

How would you react if you put your life savings in a bank and then, when you went to withdraw it, learned that the bank had failed—that your money no longer existed? This is exactly what happened to many people during the Depression. In response to the crisis, the federal government established the **Federal Depository Insurance Corporation (FDIC)** in 1933 to restore confidence in the banking system. The FDIC insures deposits in commercial banks and savings banks up to $100,000. So today if your bank failed, the government would give you back your money (up to $100,000). The money comes from fees charged member banks.

To decrease the likelihood of failure, various government agencies conduct periodic examinations to ensure that institutions are in compliance with regulations. Commercial banks are regulated by the FDIC, savings banks by the Office of Thrift Supervision, and credit unions by the National Credit Union Administration. As we'll see later in the chapter, the Federal Reserve System also has a strong influence on the banking industry.

HOW BANKS EXPAND THE MONEY SUPPLY

When you deposit money, your bank doesn't set aside a special pile of cash with your name on it. It merely records the fact that you made a deposit and increases the balance in your account. Depending on the type of account, you can withdraw your share whenever you want, but until then, it's added to all the other money held by the bank. Because the bank can be pretty sure that all of its depositors won't withdraw their money at the same time, it holds on to only a fraction of the money that it takes in—its *reserves*. It loans out the rest to individuals, businesses, and the government, earning interest income and expanding the money supply.

The Money Multiplier

Precisely, how do banks expand the money supply? To find out, let's pretend you win $10,000 at the blackjack tables of your local casino. You put your winnings into your savings account immediately. The bank will keep a fraction of your $10,000 in reserve; to keep matters simple, we'll use 10 percent. The bank's reserves, therefore, will increase by $1,000 ($10,000 × 0.10). It will then loan out the remaining $9,000. The borrowers (or the parties to whom they pay it out) will then deposit the $9,000 in their own banks. Like your bank, these banks will hold onto 10 percent of the money ($900) and loan out the remainder ($8,100). Now let's go through the process one more time. The borrowers of the $8,100 (or, again, the parties to whom they pay it out) will put this amount into their banks, which will hold onto $810 and loan out the remaining $7,290. As you can see in Figure 10.3 (page 258), total bank deposits would now be $27,100. Eventually, bank deposits would increase to $100,000, bank reserves to $10,000, and loans to $90,000. A shortcut for arriving at these numbers depends on the concept of the **money multiplier**, which is determined using the following formula:

Money multiplier = 1/Reserve requirement

---

credit union
Financial institution that provides services to only its members (who are associated with a particular organization).

finance company
Nondeposit financial institution that makes loans from funds acquired by selling securities or borrowing from commercial banks.

insurance company
Nondeposit institution that collects premiums from policyholders for protection against losses and invests these funds.

brokerage firm
Financial institution that buys and sells stocks, bonds, and other investments for clients.

mutual fund
Financial institution that invests in securities, using money pooled from investors (who become part owners of the fund).

money market fund
Fund invested in safe, highly liquid securities.

pension fund
Fund set up to collect contributions from participating companies for the purpose of providing its members with retirement income.

individual retirement account (IRA)
Personal retirement account set up by an individual to save money tax free until retirement.

Federal Depository Insurance Corporation (FDIC)
Government agency that regulates banks and insures deposits in its member banks up to $100,000.

money multiplier
The amount by which an initial bank deposit will expand the money supply.

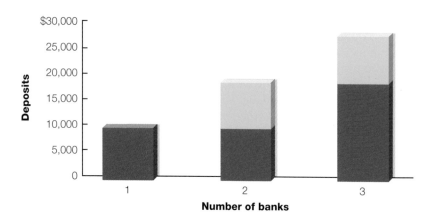

Figure 10.3

ACTIVE

The Effect of the Money Multiplier

In our example, the money multiplier is 1/0.10 = 10. So your initial deposit of $10,000 expands into total deposits of $100,000 ($10,000 × 10), additional loans of $90,000 ($9,000 × 10), and increased bank reserves of $10,000 ($1,000 × 10). In reality, the multiplier will actually be less than 10. Why? Because some of the money loaned out will be held as currency and won't make it back into the banks.

QUICK QUIZ   10.1

Before you read about the Federal Reserve System, take a quick quiz to test what you've learned about money and the institutions that handle it.

Go to www.exploringbusinessonline.com

The Federal Reserve System

Who decides how much banks should keep in reserve? The decision is made by the **Federal Reserve System** (popularly known as "the Fed"), a central banking system established in 1913. Most large banks belong to the Federal Reserve System, which divides the country into 12 districts, each with a member-owned Federal Reserve Bank. The 12 banks are coordinated by a board of governors.

THE TOOLS OF THE FED

The Fed has three major goals:

1. Price stability

2. Sustainable economic growth

3. Full employment.[4]

Recall our definition of *monetary policy* in Chapter 1 as the efforts of the Federal Reserve System to regulate the nation's money supply. We also defined *price stability* as conditions under which the prices for products remain fairly constant. Now, we can put the two concepts together: The Fed seeks to stabilize prices by regulating the money supply and interest rates. In turn, stable prices promote economic growth and full employment—at least in theory. To conduct monetary policy, the Fed relies on three tools: *reserve requirements*, the *discount rate*, and *open market operations*.

Reserve Requirements

Under what circumstances would the Fed want to change the reserve requirement for banks? The purpose of controlling the money supply is primarily to lessen the threat of *inflation* (a rise in the overall price level) or *recession* (an economic slowdown gauged by a decline in gross domestic product). Here's how it works (again, in theory). If the Fed *raises* the reserve requirement (for example, from 10 percent to 11 percent), banks must set aside more money. Consequently, they have *less to loan out* and so raise their interest rates. Under these conditions, it's harder and more expensive for people to borrow money, and if they can't borrow as much, they can't spend as much, and if people don't spend as much, prices don't go up. Thus, the Fed has lessened the likelihood of inflation.

Conversely, when the Fed *lowers* the reserve requirement (for example, from 10 percent to 9 percent), banks need to set aside less money. Because they have *more money to loan out*, they keep interest rates down. Borrowers find it easier and cheaper to get money for buying things, and the more consumers buy, the higher prices go. In this case, the Fed has reduced the likelihood of a recession.

A 1-percent change in the reserve requirement, whether up to 11 percent or down to 9 percent, may not seem like much, but remember our earlier discussion of the *money multiplier*: Because of the money-multiplier effect, a small change in the reserve requirement has a dramatic effect on the money supply. (For the same reason, the Fed changes reserve requirements only rarely.)

The Discount Rate

To understand how the Fed uses the discount rate to control the money supply, let's return to our earlier discussion of reserves. Recall that banks must keep a certain fraction of their deposits as reserves. The bank can hold these reserve funds or deposit them in a Federal Reserve Bank account. Recall, too, that the bank can loan out any funds that it doesn't have to put on reserve. What happens if a bank's reserves fall below the required level? The Fed steps in, permitting the bank to "borrow" reserve funds from the Federal Reserve Bank and add them to its reserve account at the Bank. There is a catch: The bank must pay interest on the borrowed money. The rate of interest that the Fed charges member banks is called the **discount rate**. By manipulating this rate, the Fed can make it appealing or unappealing to borrow funds. If the rate is high enough, banks will be reluctant to borrow. Because they don't want to drain their reserves, they cut back on lending. The money supply, therefore, decreases. On the other hand, when the discount rate is low, banks are more willing to borrow because they're less concerned about draining their reserves. Holding fewer excess reserves, they loan out a higher percentage of their funds, thereby increasing the money supply.

Even more important is the carryover effect of a change in the discount rate to the overall level of interest rates.[5] When the Fed adjusts the discount rate, it's telling the financial community where it thinks the economy is headed—up or down. Wall Street, for example, generally reacts unfavorably to an increase in the discount rate. Why? Because the increase means that interest rates will probably rise, making future borrowing more expensive.

Open Market Operations

The Fed's main tool for controlling the money supply and influencing interest rates is called **open market operations**: the sale and purchase of U.S. government bonds by the Fed in the open market. To understand how this process works, we first need to know a few facts:

- The Fed's assets include a substantial dollar amount of government bonds.

- The Fed can buy or sell these bonds on the open market (consisting primarily of commercial banks).

- Because member banks use cash to buy these bonds, they decrease their reserve balances when they buy them.

- Because member banks receive cash from the sale of the bonds, they increase their reserve balances when they sell them.

- Banks must maintain a specified balance in reserves; if they dip below this balance, they have to make up the difference by borrowing money.

If the Fed wants to decrease the money supply, it can *sell* bonds, thereby reducing the reserves of the member banks who buy them. Because these banks would then have less money to lend, the money supply would decrease. If the Fed wants to increase the money supply, it will *buy* bonds, increasing the reserves of the banks who sell them. The money supply would increase because these banks would then have more money to lend.

The Federal Funds Rate In conducting open market operations, the Fed is trying to do the same thing that it does in using its other tools—namely, to influence the money supply and, thereby, interest rates. But it also has something else in mind. In order to understand what that is, you need to know a couple more things about banking. When a bank's reserve falls below its required level, it may, as we've seen, borrow from the Fed (at the discount rate). But it can also borrow from other member banks that have excess reserves. The rate that banks pay when they borrow through this channel is called the **federal funds rate**.[6]

How does the federal funds rate affect the money supply? As we've seen, when the Fed sells bonds in the open market, the reserve balances of many member banks go down. To get their reserves back to the required level, they must borrow, whether from the Fed or from other member banks. When Bank 1 borrows from Bank 2, Bank 2's

---

Federal Reserve System (the Fed)
U.S. central banking system, which has three goals: price stability, sustainable economic growth, and full employment.

discount rate
Rate of interest the Fed charges member banks when they borrow reserve funds.

open market operations
The sale and purchase of U.S. government bonds by the Fed in the open market.

federal funds rate
The interest rate that a Federal Reserve member bank pays when it borrows from other member banks to meet reserve requirements.

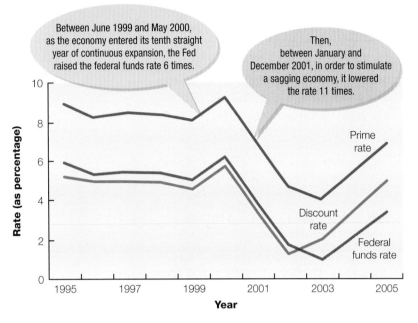

Between June 1999 and May 2000, as the economy entered its tenth straight year of continuous expansion, the Fed raised the federal funds rate 6 times.

Then, between January and December 2001, in order to stimulate a sagging economy, it lowered the rate 11 times.

Figure 10.4

Key Interest Rates, 1995–2005

supply of funds goes down; thus, it increases the interest rate that it charges. In short, the increased demand for funds drives up the federal funds rate.

All of this interbank borrowing affects you. When the federal funds rate goes up, banks must pay more for their money, and they'll pass the cost along to their customers: Banks all over the country will raise the interest rates charged on mortgages, car loans, and personal loans. Figure 10.4 charts 10-year fluctuations in the discount rate, federal funds rate, and **prime rate**—the rate that banks charge their best customers. Because all three rates tend to move in the same direction, borrowers—individuals as well as organizations—generally pay more to borrow money when banks have to pay more and less when banks have to pay less. Note, too, that the prime rate (which banks charge their customers) is higher than both the federal funds and discount rates (which banks must pay when they need to borrow). That's why banks make profits when they make loans.

THE BANKER'S BANK AND THE GOVERNMENT'S BANKER

The Fed performs another important function: It serves its member banks in much the same way as your bank serves you. When you get a check, you deposit it in your checking account, thereby increasing your balance. When you pay someone by check,

the dollar amount of the check is charged to your account, and your balance goes down. The Fed works in much the same way, except that its customers are member banks.

Just as your bank clears your check, the Fed clears the checks that pass through its member banks. The monumental task of clearing more than 15 billion checks a year is complicated by the fact that there are 12 district banks. If someone in one district—for example, Boston—writes a check to a payee in another district—for example, San Francisco—the check must be processed through both districts.[7]

In performing the following functions, the Fed is also the U.S. government's banker:

- Holding the U.S. Treasury's checking account
- Processing the paperwork involved in buying and selling government securities
- Collecting federal tax payments
- Loaning money to the government by purchasing government bonds from the Treasury

The Fed also prints, stores, and distributes currency and destroys it when it's damaged or worn out. Finally, the Fed, in conjunction with other governmental agencies, supervises and regulates financial institutions to ensure that they operate soundly and treat customers fairly and equitably.[8]

The Role of the Financial Manager

So far, we've focused our attention on the financial environment in which U.S. businesses operate. Now let's focus on the role finance plays within an organization. In Chapter 1, we defined *finance* as all of the activities involved in planning for, obtaining, and managing a company's funds. We also explained that a *financial manager* determines how much money the company needs, how and where it will get the necessary funds, and how and when it will repay the money that it's borrowed. The financial manager also decides what the company should do with its funds—what investments should be made in plant and equipment, how much should be spent on research and development, and how excess funds should be invested.

FINANCING A NEW COMPANY

Because new businesses usually need to borrow money in order to get off the ground, good financial management is particularly important to start-ups. Let's suppose that you're about to start up a company that you intend to run from your dorm. You thought of the idea while rummaging through a pile of previously worn clothes to find something that wasn't about to get up and walk to the laundry all by itself. "Wouldn't it be great," you thought to yourself, "if there was an on-campus laundry service that would come and pick up my dirty clothes and bring them back to me washed and folded." Because you were also in the habit of running out of cash at inopportune times, you were highly motivated to start some sort of money-making enterprise, and the laundry service seemed to fit the bill (even though washing and folding clothes wasn't among your favorite activities—or skills).

Developing a Financial Plan

Because you didn't want your business to be so small that it stayed under the radar of fellow students and potential customers, you knew that you'd need to raise funds to get started. So what are your cash needs? To answer this question, you need to draw up a **financial plan**—a document that performs two functions:

1. Calculating the amount of funds that a company needs for a specified period

2. Detailing a strategy for getting those funds

Estimating Sales Fortunately, you can draw on your newly acquired accounting skills to prepare the first section—the one in which you'll specify the amount of cash you need. You start by estimating your *sales* (or, in your case, revenue from laundering clothes) for your first year of operations. This is the most important estimate you'll make: Without a realistic sales estimate, you can't accurately calculate equipment needs and other costs. To predict sales, you'll need to estimate two figures:

1. The number of loads of laundry that you'll handle

2. The price that you'll charge per load

You calculate as follows: You estimate that 5 percent of the 10,000 students on campus will use the service. These 500 students will have one large load of laundry for each of the 35 weeks that they're on campus. Therefore, you will do 17,500 loads (500 × 35 = 17,500 loads). You decide to price each load at $10. At first, this seemed high, but when you consider that you'll have to pick up, wash, dry, fold, and return large loads, it seems reasonable.

Perhaps more importantly, when you projected your costs—including salaries (for some student workers), rent, utilities, depreciation on equipment and a truck, supplies, maintenance, insurance, and advertising—you found that each load would cost $8, leaving a profit of $2 per load and earning you $35,000 for your first year (which is worth your time though not enough to make you rich).

What things will you have to buy in order to get started? Using your estimate of sales, you've determined that you'd need the following:

- Five washers and five dryers

- A truck to pick up and deliver the clothes (a used truck will do for now)

- An inventory of laundry detergent and other supplies, such as laundry baskets

- Rental space in a nearby building (which will need some work to accommodate a laundry)

And, you'll need cash—cash to carry you over while the business gets going and cash with which to pay your bills. Finally, you'd better have some extra money for contingencies—things you don't expect, such as a machine overflowing and damaging the floor. You're mildly surprised to find that your cash needs total $33,000. Your next task is to find out where you can get $33,000. In the next section, we'll look at some options.

---

prime rate
Rate that banks charge their best customers.

financial plan
Planning document that shows the amount of funds a company needs and details a strategy for getting those funds.

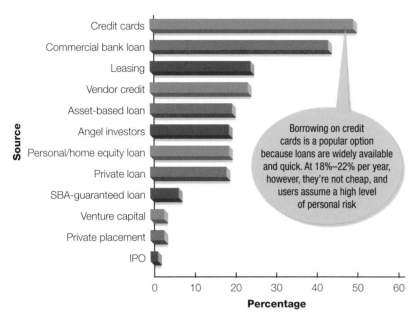

Borrowing on credit cards is a popular option because loans are widely available and quick. At 18%–22% per year, however, they're not cheap, and users assume a high level of personal risk

- Owners' personal assets
- Loans from families and friends
- Bank loans (including those guaranteed by the Small Business Development Center)

Remember that during its start-up period, a business needs a lot of cash: Not only will it incur substantial start-up costs, but it may suffer initial operational losses.

Personal Assets Its owners are the most important source of funds for any new business. Figuring that owners with substantial investments will work harder to make the enterprise succeed, lenders expect owners to put up a substantial amount of the start-up money. Where does this money come from? Usually through personal savings, credit cards, home mortgages, or the sale of personal assets.

Loans from Family and Friends For many entrepreneurs, the next stop is family and friends. If you have an idea with commercial potential, you might be able to get family members and friends to invest in it (as part owners) or to loan you some money. Remember that family and friends are like any other creditors: They expect to be repaid, and they expect to earn interest. Even when you're borrowing from family members or friends, you should draw up a formal loan agreement stating when the loan will be repaid and specifying the interest rate.

Getting the Money

Figure 10.5 summarizes the results of a survey in which owners of small and medium-sized businesses were asked where they typically acquired their financing. To simplify matters, we'll work on the principle that new businesses are generally financed with some combination of the following:

Bank Loans The financing package for a start-up company will probably include bank loans. Banks, however, will loan you some start-up money only if they're convinced that your idea is commercially feasible. They also prefer you to have some combination of talent and experience to run the company successfully. Bankers want to see a well-developed business plan, with detailed financial projections demonstrating your ability to repay loans. Financial institutions offer different types of loans with different payback periods. Most, however, have a few common characteristics.

How can you turn a $1,000 college loan into one of the most successful franchises in the world? Ask Fred DeLuca. At age 17, he needed money to go to college and asked a family friend, Peter Buck, for a loan. Buck wouldn't loan him money for college but advanced him $1,000 to open a submarine shop so DeLuca could earn money to put himself through college. As it turns out, the submarine shop, named Subway, did much more than that. Ten years later, DeLuca was franchising his business concept, and today, there are more than 26,000 Subway restaurants in 82 countries.

Maturity The period for which a bank loan is issued is called its **maturity**. A **short-term loan** is for less than a year, an **intermediate loan** for one to five years, and a **long-term loan** for five years or more. Banks can also issue **lines of credit** that allow you to borrow up to a specified amount as the need arises (it's a lot like the limit on your credit card).

In taking out a loan, you want to match its term with its purpose. If, for example, you're borrowing money to buy a truck that you plan to use for five years, you'd request a five-year loan. On the other hand, if you're financing a piece of equipment that you'll use for ten years, you'll want a ten-year loan. For short-term needs, like buying inventory, you may request a one-year loan.

With any loan, however, you must consider the ability of the business to repay it. If you expect to lose money for the first year, you obviously won't be able to repay a one-year loan on time. You'd be better off with intermediate or long-term financing. Finally, you need to consider **amortization**—the schedule by which you'll reduce the balance of your debt. Will you be making periodic payments on both principal and interest over the life of the loan (for example, monthly or quarterly), or will the entire amount (including interest) be due at the end of the loan period?

Security A bank won't loan you money unless it thinks that your business can generate sufficient funds to pay it back. Often, however, the bank takes an added precaution by asking you for **security**—business or personal assets, called **collateral**, that you pledge in order to guarantee repayment. You may have to secure the loan with company assets, such as inventory or accounts receivable, or even with personal assets. (Likewise, if you're an individual getting a car loan, the bank will accept the automobile as security.) In any case, the principle is pretty simple: If you don't pay the loan when it's due, the bank can take possession of the collateral, sell it, and keep the proceeds to cover the loan. If you don't have to put up collateral, you're getting an **unsecured loan**, but because of the inherent risk entailed by new business ventures, banks don't often make such loans.

Interest **Interest** is the cost of using someone else's money. The rate of interest charged on a loan varies with several factors—the general level of interest rates, the size of the loan, the quality of the collateral, and the debt-paying ability of the borrower. For smaller, riskier loans, it can be as much as 6 to 8 percentage points above the prime rate—the rate that banks charge their most creditworthy borrowers. It's currently around 4 percent per year.

Making the Financing Decision

Now that we've surveyed your options, let's go back to the task of financing your laundry business. You'd like to put up a substantial amount of the money you need, but you can only come up with a measly $1,000 (which you had to borrow on your credit card). You were, however, able to convince your parents to loan you $10,000, which you've promised to pay back, with interest, in three years. (They were wavering until you pointed out that Michael Dell started Dell from his dorm room.)

So you still need $22,000 ($33,000 minus the $11,000 from you and your parents). You talked with someone at the Small Business Development Center located on campus, but you're not optimistic about getting them to guarantee a loan. Instead, you put together a sound business plan, including projected financial statements, and set off to your local banker. To your surprise, she agreed to a five-year loan at a reasonable interest rate. Unfortunately, she wanted the entire loan secured. Because you're using some of the loan money to buy washers and dryers (for $15,000) and a truck (for $6,000), you can put up these as collateral. You have no accounts receivable or inventories, so you agreed to put up some personal assets—namely, the shares of Microsoft stock that you got as a high-school graduation present (now worth about $5,000).

---

maturity
Period of time for which a bank loan is issued.

short-term loan
Loan issued with a maturity date of less than one year.

intermediate loan
Loan issued with a maturity date of one to five years.

long-term loan
Loan issued with a maturity date of five years or more.

lines of credit
Commitment by a bank that allows a company to borrow up to a specified amount of money as the need arises.

amortization
Schedule by which you'll reduce the balance of your debt.

security
Collateral pledged to secure repayment of a loan.

collateral
Specific business or personal assets that a bank accepts as security for a loan.

unsecured loan
Loan given by a bank that doesn't require the borrower to put up collateral.

interest
Cost charged to use someone else's money.

ABOUT NIKE · 10.1

Now that you can identify a number of ways in which companies obtain funds, take a few moments to learn how Nike obtained the needed funds to start and expand its operations.

Go to www.exploringbusinessonline.com

FINANCING THE BUSINESS DURING THE GROWTH STAGE

Flash-forward two and a half years: Much to your delight, your laundry business took off. You had your projected 500 customers within six months, and over the next few years, you expanded to four other colleges in the geographical area. Now you're serving five colleges and 3,000 customers a week. Your management team has expanded, but you're still in charge of the company's finances. In the next sections, we'll review the tasks involved in managing the finances of a high-growth business.

Managing Cash

Cash-flow management means monitoring cash inflows and outflows to ensure that your company has sufficient—but not excessive—cash on hand to meet its obligations. When projected cash flows indicate a future shortage, you get additional funds from the bank. When projections show that there's going to be idle cash, you take action to invest it and earn a return for your company.

Managing Accounts Receivable

Because you bill your customers on a weekly basis, you generate sizeable *accounts receivable*—records of cash that you'll receive from customers to whom you've sold your service. You make substantial efforts to collect receivables on a timely basis and to keeping nonpayment to a minimum.

Managing Accounts Payable

Accounts payable are records of cash that you owe to the suppliers of products that you use. You generate them when you buy supplies with **trade credit**—credit given you by your suppliers. You're careful to pay your bills on time, but not ahead of time (because it's in your best interest to hold on to your cash as long as possible).

Budgeting

A **budget** is a preliminary financial plan for a given time period, generally a year. At the end of the stated period, you compare actual and projected results and investigate any significant discrepancies. You prepare several types of budgets: projected financial statements, a **cash budget** that projects cash flows, and a **capital budget** that shows anticipated expenditures for major equipment.

SEEKING OUT PRIVATE INVESTORS

So far, you've been able to finance your company's growth through internally generated funds—profits retained in the business—along with a few bank loans. Your success—especially your expansion to other campuses—has confirmed your original belief that you've come up with a great business concept. You're anxious to expand further, but to do that, you'll need a substantial infusion of new cash. You've poured most of your profits back into the company, and your parents can't loan you any more money. After giving the problem some thought, you realize that you have three options:

1. Ask the bank for more money.

2. Bring in additional owners who can invest in the company.

3. Seek funds from a private investor.

Angels and Venture Capitalists

Eventually, you decide on the third option. First, however, you must decide what type of private investor you want—an "angel" or a venture capitalist. **Angels** are usually wealthy individuals willing to invest in start-up ventures they believe will succeed. They bet that a business will ultimately be very profitable and that they can sell their interest at a large profit. **Venture capitalists** pool funds from private and institutional sources (such as pension funds and insurance companies) and invest them in businesses with strong growth potential. They're typically willing to invest larger sums but often want to "cash out" more quickly than angels.

There are drawbacks. Both types of private investors provide business expertise as well as financing and, in effect, become partners in the enterprises that they finance. They accept only the most promising opportunities, and if they do decide to invest in your business, they'll want something in return for their money—namely, a say in how you manage it.

When you approach private investors, you can be sure that your business plan will get a thorough going-over. Under your current business model, setting up a new laundry on another campus requires about $50,000. But you're a little more ambitious, intending to increase the number of colleges that you serve from 5 to 25. So you'll need a cash inflow of $1 million. Upon weighing your alternatives and considering the size of the loan you need, you decide to approach a venture capitalist. Fortunately, because you prepared an excellent business plan and made a great presentation, your application was accepted. Your expansion begins.

GOING PUBLIC

Fast-forward another five years. You've worked hard (and been lucky), and even finished your degree in finance. Moreover, your company has done amazingly well, with operations at more than 500 colleges in the Northeast. You've financed continued strong growth with a combination of venture-capital funds and internally generated funds (that is, reinvested earnings).

Up to this point, you've operated as a private corporation with limited stock ownership (you and your parents are the only shareholders). But because you expect your business to prosper even more and grow even bigger, you're thinking about the possibility of selling stock to the public for the first time. The advantages are attractive: Not only would you get a huge influx of cash, but because it would come from the sale of stock rather than from borrowing, it would be interest free and you wouldn't have to

repay it. Again there are some drawbacks. For one thing, going public is quite costly—often exceeding $300,000—and time-consuming. Second, from this point on, your financial results would be public information. Finally, you'd be responsible to shareholders who will want to see the kind of short-term performance results that boosts stock prices.

After weighing the pros and cons, you decide to go ahead. The first step in the process of becoming a public corporation is called an **initial public offering (IPO)**, and you'll need the help of an **investment banking firm**—a financial institution (such as Merrill Lynch, Goldman Sachs, or Morgan Stanley) that specializes in issuing securities. Your investment banker advises you that it is a good time to go public and determines the best price at which to sell your stock. Then, you'll need the approval of the SEC, the government agency that regulates securities markets.

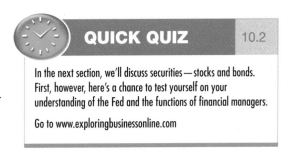

QUICK QUIZ   10.2

In the next section, we'll discuss securities—stocks and bonds. First, however, here's a chance to test yourself on your understanding of the Fed and the functions of financial managers.

Go to www.exploringbusinessonline.com

Understanding Securities Markets

So, before long, you're a public company. Fortunately, because your degree in finance comes with a better-than-average knowledge of financial markets, you're familiar with the ways in which investors will evaluate your company. Investors will look at the

cash-flow management
Process of monitoring cash inflows and outflows to ensure that the company has the right amount of funds on hand.

trade credit
Credit given to a company by its suppliers.

budget
Preliminary financial plan for a given time period, generally a year.

cash budget
Financial plan that projects cash inflows and outflows over a period of time.

capital budget
Budget that shows anticipated expenditures for major equipment.

angel
Wealthy individual willing to invest in start-up ventures.

venture capitalist
Individual who pools funds from private and institutional sources and invests them in businesses with strong growth potential.

initial public offering (IPO)
Process of taking a privately held company public by selling stock to the public for the first time.

investment banking firm
Financial institution that specializes in issuing securities.

overall quality of the company and ask some basic questions:

- How well is it managed?
- Is it in a growing industry? Is its market share increasing or decreasing?
- Does it have a good line of products? Is it coming out with innovative products?
- How is the company doing relative to its competitors?
- What is its future and the future of its industry?

Investors also analyze the company's performance over time and ask more specific questions:

- Are its sales growing?
- Is its income going up?
- Is its stock price rising or falling?
- Are earnings per share rising?

They'll assess the company's financial strength, asking another series of specific questions:

- Can it pay its bills on time?
- Does it have too much debt?
- Is it managing its productive assets (such as inventory) efficiently?

When Google went public in August 2004, it went through NAS-DAQ rather than the NYSE. Both exchanges wanted Google, which is not surprising, as they earn about 25 percent of their revenues from listing companies. Although the reasons for Google's choice were not disclosed, the decision was not surprising. NASDAQ is generally the exchange chosen by technology-based companies, such as Yahoo!, Microsoft, Amazon.com, and eBay.

PRIMARY AND SECONDARY MARKETS AND STOCK EXCHANGES

Security markets serve two functions:

1. They help companies to raise funds by making the initial sale of their stock to the public.
2. They provide a place where investors can trade already issued stock.

When you went through your IPO, shares were issued through a **primary market**—a market that deals in new financial assets. As we've seen, the sale was handled by an investment banking firm, which matched you, as a corporation with stock to sell, with investors who wanted to buy it.

Organized Exchanges After a certain period of time, investors began buying and selling your stock on a **secondary market**. The proceeds of sales on this market go to the investor who sells the stock, not to your company. The best-known of these markets is the **New York Stock Exchange (NYSE)**, where the stocks of the largest, most prestigious corporations in the world are traded. Other exchanges, including the **American Stock Exchange (AMEX)** and regional exchanges located in places like Chicago and Boston, trade the stock of smaller companies.

OTC Markets Note that a "market" doesn't have to be a physical location. In the **over-the-counter (OTC) market**, securities are traded among dealers over computer networks or by phone rather than on the floor of an organized exchange. Although there are exceptions, stocks traded in the OTC market are generally those of smaller (and often riskier) companies. The best known OTC electronic-exchange system is the **NASDAQ** (National Association of Securities Dealers Automated Quotation system). It's home to almost 5,000 corporations, many of them technology companies, that range from small start-ups to such giants as Microsoft and Intel.

REGULATING SECURITIES MARKETS: THE SEC

Because it's vital that investors have confidence in the securities markets, Congress created the **Securities and Exchange Commission (SEC)** in 1934. The SEC enforces securities laws designed to promote full public disclosure, protect investors against misconduct in the securities markets, and maintain the integrity of the securities markets.[9]

Before offering securities for sale, the issuer must register its intent to sell with the SEC. In addition, the issuer must provide prospective buyers with a **prospectus**—a written offer to sell securities that describes the business and operations of the issuer, lists its officers, provides financial information, discloses any pending litigation, and states the proposed use of funds from the sale.

The SEC also enforces laws against **insider trading**—the illegal buying or selling of its securities by a firm's officers and directors or anyone else taking advantage of valuable information about the company before it's made public. The intent of these laws is to prevent insiders from profiting at the expense of other investors.

MEASURING MARKET PERFORMANCE: MARKET INDEXES

Throughout the day, you can monitor the general drift of the stock market by watching any major news network and following the band at the bottom of your TV. News channels and broadcasts generally feature a "market recap" in the evening. Even music-oriented radio stations break for a minute of news every now and then, including a quick review of the stock market. Almost all of these reports refer to one or more of the **market indexes** with which investors can track trends in stock price. Let's look more closely at some of these indicators.

The Dow

By far the most widely reported market index is the **Dow Jones Industrial Average (DJIA)**, or "the Dow." The Dow is the total value of a "market basket" of 30 large companies headquartered in the United States. They aren't the 30 largest or best-performing companies, but rather a group selected by the senior staff members at the *Wall Street Journal* to represent a broad spectrum of the U.S. economy as well as a variety of industries. The 30 selected stocks change over time, but the list usually consists of household names, such as AT&T, Coca-Cola, Disney, IBM, General Electric, and Wal-Mart.

The graph in Figure 10.6 tracks the Dow for the ten-year period ended May 2006. The market measured by the Dow was on an upward swing from 1996 until 2000. At that point, it headed down until it reached its low point in 2002 and started its rebound. The path of the DOW during this ten-year period has been volatile (subject to up and down movements in response to unstable worldwide economic and political situations).

Figure 10.6

DJIA for Ten-Year Period Ended May 2006

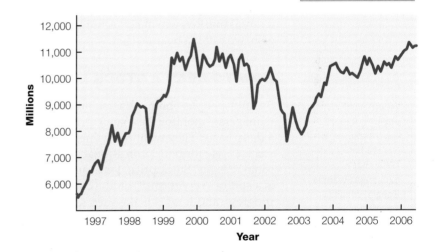

Year

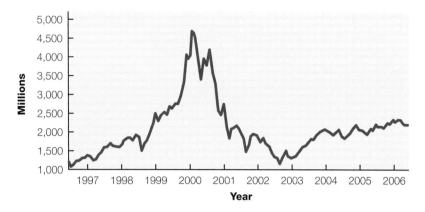

Figure 10.7

NASDAQ for Ten-Year
Period Ended May 2006

The NASDAQ Composite and the S&P 500

Also of interest is the performance of the **NASDAQ Composite Index**, which includes many technology companies. Note in Figure 10.7 that the NASDAQ peaked in early 2000 at an index of over 5000, but as investors began reevaluating the prospects of many technologies and technology companies, prices fell precipitously. Another broad measure of stock performance is **Standard & Poor's Composite Index (S&P 500)**, which lists the stocks of 500 large U.S. companies.

When the stock market is enjoying a period of large stock-price increases, we call it a **bull market**; when it's declining or sluggish, we call it a **bear market**.

HOW TO READ A STOCK LISTING

Businesspeople—both owners and managers—monitor their stock prices on a daily basis. They want the value of their stock to rise for both professional and personal reasons. Stock price, for example, is a sort of "report card" on the company's progress, and it reflects the success of its managers in running the company. Many managers have a great deal of personal wealth tied directly to the fortunes of the companies for which they work.

If you have any interest in investing, you'll want to know how to interpret stock market information. Step one is learning how to read a stock listing like those printed daily in the *Wall Street Journal* and other newspapers. Figure 10.8 reports the infor-

mation on Hershey Foods for June 1, 2006. Let's use the explanations in Table 10.1 to examine each item in greater detail.

What, exactly, does Hershey Food's stock listing tell us? Here are some of the highlights: The stock is doing about average for the past 12-month period. The closing stock price of $57.00 falls right in the middle of the annual high of $65.23 and the annual low of $48.20. The stock started high, fell, and is now rebounding. The company pays an annual dividend of $0.98 per share (which gives investors a cash return on their stock of 1.7 percent). At its current PE ratio, investors are willing to pay $28 for every $1 of Hershey's earnings per share.

ABOUT NIKE 10.2

After reviewing the factors to consider when buying a stock, take a few moments to decide whether you should invest in Nike.

Go to www.exploringbusinessonline.com

Financing the Going Concern

Let's assume that taking your company public was a good move: In posing questions like those that we've just listed, investors have decided that your business is a good buy. With the influx of investment capital, the little laundry business that you started in your dorm 10 years ago has grown into a very large operation with laundries at more than 700 colleges all across the country, and you're opening two or three laundries a week. But there's still a huge untapped market out there, and you've just left a meeting with your board of directors at which it was decided that you'll seek additional funding for further growth. Everyone agrees that you need about $8 million dollars for the proposed expansion, but there's a difference of opinion among your board members on how to go about getting it. You have two options:

1. **Equity financing**: raising the needed capital through the sale of stock

2. **Debt financing**: raising the needed capital by selling bonds

Let's review some of the basics underlying your options.

Figure 10.8

Stock Listing for
Hershey Foods

1		2	3	4	5	6	7	8
52-Week:		STOCK		YLD		Vol		NET
High:	Low:	(SYMBOL)	DIV:	%:	PE:	100s:	CLOSE:	CHG:
65.23	48.20	Hershey Foods HSY	0.98	1.7	28	9429	57.00	0.09

TABLE 10.1

Interpreting a Stock Quotation

52-WEEK HI	The highest price during the past year (June 1, 2005, to June 1, 2006) was $65.23.
52-WEEK LO	The lowest price during the past year was $48.20.
STOCK (SYMBOL)	The listing is for Hershey Foods, whose stock symbol is "HSY."
DIV	HSY pays an annual *dividend* of $0.98 on each share of stock.
YLD %	HSY's dividend provides each investor with a 1.7% return (or *dividend yield*), as based on the day's closing stock price ($0.98/$57.00 = 1.7%).
PE	The *price-earnings (PE) financial ratio* determines the amount that an investor would be willing to pay for every dollar of the company's earnings. This is a relative measure for comparing companies. For every $1 of HSY's *earnings per share* (the company's annual income divided by the number of shares of stock), investors are willing to pay $28 per share. High-growth firms usually have higher PE ratios, and vice versa.
VOL	A common unit size for trading stocks is 100 shares, called a *round lot*. On June 1, 2006, 9,429 round lots were traded; in other words, the *volume* of HSY shares traded was 942,900 shares (9429 × 100).
CLOSE	HSY is traded on the New York Stock Exchange, which opens at 9:30 A.M. and closes at 4:00 P.M. every business day. Throughout the day, the price of HSY stock fluctuates, and at the end of the day, it stood at $57.00.
NET CHG	The price of $57.00 is up by $0.09 from the previous trading day's close, which was $56.91.

STOCK

If you decide to sell stock to finance your expansion, the proceeds from the sale will increase your **stockholders' equity**—the amount invested in the business by its owners (which is the same thing that we called *owner's equity* in Chapter 9). In general, an increase in stockholders' equity is good. Your *assets*—specifically, your cash—will increase because you'll have more money with which to expand and operate your business (which is also good). But if you sell additional shares of stock, you'll have more stockholders—a situation which, as we'll see later, is not always good.

The Risk/Reward Tradeoff

To issue additional shares of stock, you'll need to find buyers interested in purchasing them. You need to ask yourself this question: Why would anyone want to buy stock in your company? Stockholders, as we know, are part owners of the company and, as such, share in the risks and rewards associated

---

NASDAQ Composite Index
Market index of all stocks listed on the NASDAQ Stock Exchange.

Standard & Poor's Composite Index (S&P 500)
Market index of the stocks of 500 large U.S. companies.

bull market
Period of large stock-price increases.

bear market
Period of declining or sluggish stock prices.

equity financing
Process of raising capital for a company through the sale of stock.

debt financing
Process of raising capital for a company through the sale of bonds.

stockholders' equity
Amount invested in a corporation by its shareholders.

with ownership. If your company does well, they may benefit through **dividends**—distributed earnings—appreciation in the value of their stock, or both. If your company does poorly, the value of their stock will probably decline. Because the risk/reward tradeoff varies according to the type of stock—*common* or *preferred*—we need to know a little more about the difference between the two.

Common Stock Holders of **common stock** bear the ultimate rewards and risks of ownership. Depending on the extent of their ownership, they could exercise some control over the corporation. They're generally entitled to vote on members of the board of directors and other important matters. If the company does well, they benefit more than holders of preferred stock; if it does poorly, they take a harder hit. If it goes out of business, they're the last to get any money from the sale of what's left and can in fact lose their investments entirely.

So who would buy common stock? It's a good option for individuals and institutions who are willing to take an investment roller-coaster ride: For a chance to share in the growth and profits of a company (the "ups"), they have to be willing to risk losing all or part of their investments (the "downs").

Preferred Stock **Preferred stock** is safer, but it doesn't have the upside potential. Unlike holders of common stock, whose return on investment depends on the company's performance, preferred shareholders get a fixed dividend every year. As usual, there are disadvantages and advantages. They don't usually have voting rights, and unless the company does extremely well, their dividends are limited to the fixed amount. On the other hand, they're *preferred* as to dividends: The company can pay no dividends to common shareholders until it's paid all preferred dividends. If the company goes under, preferred stockholders also get their money back before common shareholders get any of theirs. In many ways, they're more like creditors than investors in equity: Although they can usually count on a fixed, relatively safe income, they have little opportunity to share in a company's success.

Cumulative and Convertible Preferred Stock There are a couple of ways to make preferred stock more attractive. With **cumulative preferred stock**, if a company fails to make a dividend payment to preferred shareholders in a given year, it can pay no common dividends until preferred shareholders have been *paid in full for both current and missed dividends*. Anyone holding **convertible preferred stock** may exchange it for common stock. Thus, preferred shareholders can convert to common stock when and if the company's performance is strong—when its common stock is likely to go up in value.

BONDS

Now, let's look at the second option: debt financing—raising capital through the sale of bonds. As with the sale of stock, the sale of bonds will increase your assets (again, specifically your cash) because you'll receive an inflow of cash (which, as we said, is good). But as we'll see, your *liabilities*—your debt to outside parties—will also increase (which is bad). And just as you'll need to find buyers for your stock, you'll need to find buyers for your bonds. Again, we need to ask the question: Why would anyone want to buy your company's bonds?

Your financial projections show that you need $8 million to finance your expansion. If you decide to borrow this much money, you aren't likely to find one individual or institution who will loan it to you. But if you divided up the $8 million loan into 8,000 smaller loans of $1,000 each, you'd stand a better chance of getting the amount you need. That's the strategy behind issuing **bonds**: debt securities that obligate the issuer to make interest payments to bondholders (generally on a periodic basis) and to repay the principal when the bond matures. In other words, a bond is an IOU that pays interest. Like equity investors, bondholders can sell their securities on the financial market.

From the investor's standpoint, buying bonds is a way to earn a fairly good rate of return on money that he or she doesn't need for a while. The interest is better than what they'd get on a savings account or money market fund. But there is some risk. Investors who are interested in your bonds will assess the financial strength of your company: They want to feel confident that you'll be able to make your interest payments and pay back the principal when the time comes. They'll probably rely on data supplied by such bond-rating organizations as Moody's and Standard & Poor's, which rate bonds from *AAA* (highly unlikely to default) to *D* (in default).

Treasuries and Munis

Remember, too, that if you decide to issue bonds, you'll be competing with other borrowers, including state and local governments and the federal government. In fact, the U.S. government, which issues bonds through the Treasury Department, is the country's largest debtor. *Treasury bills*, for example, mature in one year, *Treasury notes* in one to ten years, and *Treasury bonds* in more than ten years. State and local governments issue bonds (often called *munis*) to support public services such as schools and roads or special projects. Both treasuries and munis are attractive because the income earned on them is generally tax free at the state and local levels.

CHOOSING YOUR FINANCING METHOD

Let's say that after mulling over your money-raising options—equity financing versus debt financing—you decide to recommend to the board that the company issue common stock to finance its expansion. How do you explain your decision? Issuing bonds is an attractive option because it won't dilute your ownership, but you don't like the idea of repaying interest-bearing loans: At this point, you're reluctant to take on any future financial obligation, and money obtained through the sale of stock doesn't have to be paid back. Granted, adding additional shareholders will force you to relinquish some ownership interest: New shareholders will vote on your board of directors and could have some influence over major decisions. On balance, you prefer the option of selling stock—specifically, common stock. Why not preferred stock? Because it has drawbacks similar to those of debt financ-

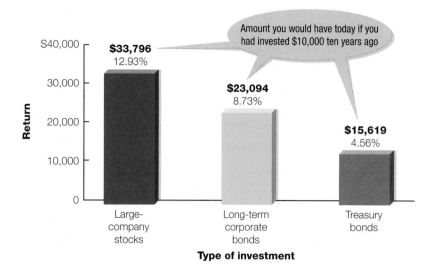

Figure 10.9

Ten-Year Investment Returns

ing: You'd have to make periodic dividend payments requiring an outflow of cash.

Besides, many investors prefer to buy common stocks and hold them as long-term investments. You can see why in Figure 10.9, which shows that, over a fairly recent 10-year period, common stocks (at least those of large companies) significantly outperformed other types of investments.

Once the matter has been settled, you take a well-deserved vacation. Unfortunately, you can't stop thinking about what you'll do the next time you want to expand. In particular, franchising seems to be a particularly attractive idea. It's something you'll need to research when you get a chance.

Careers in Finance

A financial career path offers some interesting entry-level jobs that can develop into significant senior-level positions. In addition to a strong finance education, you'll need to be familiar with both accounting and economics. Along with strong analytical skills and the ability to assess financial data, you'll need to work effectively with colleagues throughout an organization. So you'll need strong interpersonal and communication skills: You'll have to write and speak clearly and, in particular, you'll have to be able to

dividends
Earnings distributed to stockholders.

common stock
Stock whose owners bear the ultimate rewards and risks of ownership.

preferred stock
Stock that pays owners a fixed dividend annually.

cumulative preferred stock
Preferred stock that requires a corporation to pay all current and missed preferred dividends before it can pay common dividends.

convertible preferred stock
Preferred stock that gives its owner the option of exchanging it for common stock.

bonds
Debt securities that require annual interest payments to bondholders.

present complex financial data in terms that everyone can understand.

Generally, most positions in finance fall into one of three broad areas: *commercial banking, corporate finance*, and the *investment industry*.

POSITIONS IN COMMERCIAL BANKING

Commercial banks employ finance professionals as loan officers to work with clients requesting personal or business loans. It's the borrower's responsibility, of course, to present a clear and coherent application, and it's the loan officer who evaluates it—who decides whether the borrower will be able to meet the terms of the loan. Finance professionals also manage the deposits made at commercial banks, providing the bank with additional revenue by investing funds that don't go into loans.

POSITIONS IN CORPORATE FINANCE

Every organization needs financial expertise. Large companies need finance professionals to manage their cash, their debt requirements, and their pension investments. They're responsible for securing

capital (whether through debt or equity), and they may be called upon for any of the following tasks:

- Analyzing industry trends
- Evaluating corporate investment in new plants, equipment, or products
- Conducting financial planning
- Evaluating acquisitions (deciding, for example, whether to buy another company)
- Reviewing the financial needs of top management

In smaller firms, all of these same tasks may fall to a single finance professional. In addition, both large and small companies may occasionally use the services of financial consultants. They may be provided by investment bankers, specialized consulting firms, or by the financial-advisory departments of a major accounting firm.

From an entry-level position—usually called *analyst* or *junior analyst*—the finance professional will advance from *senior analyst* to a managerial position. With each step, you'll have greater exposure to senior management and face more important and more complex issues. Within 10–15 years, you may become a director or vice president. The rungs on the career ladder are pretty much the same in consulting and investment banking.

POSITIONS IN THE INVESTMENT INDUSTRY

In the investment industry, finance professionals can be stock brokers, investment analysts, or portfolio managers. Each of these positions requires an ability to assimilate great quantities of information not only about specific companies and their securities, but about entire industries and, indeed, the economy itself.

Some investment professionals work directly with individual clients. Others provide support to those who make sell or buy recommendations. Still others manage portfolios in the mutual fund industry. A mutual fund gathers money—ranging upwards from a few hundred dollars—from thousands or even millions of investors and invests it in large portfolios of stocks and other investment securities. Finance professionals review and recommend prospective investments to company managers.

Do you want to work at a fast-paced, exhilarating place? Consider working on the trading floor of the New York Stock Exchange. Perhaps the most exciting job is that of a trader—someone who buys and sells securities. The man with the earphones is a trader. He's busy receiving orders from a brokerage firm or client and placing those orders with specialists—individuals assigned to manage the buying and selling of a specific stock.

Because real estate (both commercial and personal) and insurance are investment fields, many financial professionals can be found working in these areas as well.

GRADUATE EDUCATION AND CERTIFICATION

After completing the undergraduate degree with a major or concentration in finance, accounting, or economics, a finance professional may start to think about graduate school. The typical path is an MBA with a finance track. Although some schools offer a Masters in Finance, programs are highly specialized, with rigorous math requirements that may not appeal to everyone with an interest in finance.

Certification is a means of achieving professional distinction in a finance career. The most popular certifications include:

- *CFA* or *Chartered Financial Analyst* (usually an investment-analyst designation)

- *CFM* or *Certified Financial Manager* (usually a corporate-finance designation)

- *CCM* or *Certified Cash Manager* (usually a corporate-treasury designation)

- *CFP* or *Certified Financial Planner* (usually an individual stockbroker designation)

The insurance and real estate industries have their own certifications. In addition, because the federal government requires anyone who sells securities to be licensed, there is an entire set of licensing procedures that must be followed.

QUICK QUIZ   10.3

Before wrapping up the chapter, take a few minutes to test your understanding of securities and securities markets.

Go to www.exploringbusinessonline.com

Where We're Headed

This chapter introduced you to the world of finance and securities markets. You learned about the role of money and banking in today's economy, and you found out how businesses obtain start-up capital, finance ongoing operations, and fund growth. You saw how securities markets operate and how market performance is measured. In the next chapter, we discuss the ways in which organizations use technology to collect and process information and apply it to business operations.

Summary of Learning Objectives

1. Identify the functions of money and describe the three government measures of the money supply.

Money serves three basic functions: (1) *Medium of exchange*: Because you can use it to buy the goods and services you want, everyone's willing to trade things for money. (2) *Measure of value*: It simplifies the exchange process because it's a means of indicating how much something costs. (3) *Store of value*: People are willing to hold onto it because they're confident that it will keep its value over time. The government uses two measures to track the money supply: **M-1** includes the most liquid forms of money, such as cash and checking-account funds. **M-2** includes everything in M-1 plus near-cash items, such as savings accounts and time deposits below $100,000.

2. Distinguish among different types of financial institutions, discuss the services they provide, and explain their role in expanding the money supply.

Financial institutions serve as financial intermediaries between savers and borrowers and direct the flow of funds between the two groups. Those that accept deposits from customers—depository institutions—include **commercial banks**, **savings banks**, and **credit unions**; those that don't—nondepository institutions—include **finance companies**, **insurance companies**, and **brokerage firms**. Financial institutions offer a wide range of services, including checking and savings accounts, ATM services, and credit and debit cards. They also sell securities and provide financial advice.

A bank holds onto only a fraction of the money that it takes in—an amount called its **reserves**—and loans the rest out to individuals, businesses, and governments. In turn, borrowers put some of these funds back into the banking system, where they become available to other borrowers. The **money multiplier** effect ensures that the cycle expands the money supply.

3. **Identify the goals of the Federal Reserve System and explain how it uses monetary policy to control the money supply and influence interest rates.**

Most large banks are members of the central banking system called the **Federal Reserve System** (commonly known as "the Fed"). The Fed's goals include price stability, sustainable economic growth, and full employment. It uses *monetary policy* to regulate the money supply and the level of interest rates. To achieve these goals, the Fed has three tools: (1) it can raise or lower reserve requirements—the percentage of its funds that banks must set aside and cannot loan out; (2) it can raise or lower the **discount rate**—the rate of interest that the Fed charges member banks to borrow "reserve" funds; (3) it can conduct **open market operations**—buying or selling government securities on the open market.

4. **Explain the ways in which a new business gets start-up cash and the ways in which existing companies finance operations and growth.**

If it hopes to get funding, a new business prepares a financial plan—a document that shows the amount of capital that it needs for a specified period, how and where it will get it, and how and when it will pay it back. Common sources of funding for new businesses include personal assets, loans from family and friends, and bank loans.

Financial institutions offer business loans with different **maturities**. A **short-term loan** matures in less than a year, an **intermediate loan** in one to five years, and a **long-term loan** after five years or more. Banks also issue **lines of credit** that allow companies to borrow up to a specified amount as the need arises. They generally require **security** in the form of **collateral**, such as company or personal assets. If the borrower fails to pay the loan when it's due, the bank can take possession of these assets.

Existing companies that want to expand often seek funding from private investors. **Angels** are wealthy individuals who are willing to invest in ventures that they believe will succeed. **Venture capitalists**, though willing to invest larger sums of money, often want to "cash out" more quickly than angels. Successful companies looking for additional capital might decide to go public, offering an initial sale of stock called an **initial public offering (IPO)**.

5. **Show how the securities market operates and how it's regulated.**

Securities markets provide two functions: (1) They help companies raise funds by making the initial sale of stock to the public, and (2) they provide a place where investors can trade previously issued stock. Stock sold through an IPO is issued through a **primary market** with the help of an **investment banking firm**. Previously issued securities are traded in a **secondary market**, where the proceeds from sales go to investors rather than to the issuing companies. The best known exchanges are the **New York Stock Exchange**, the **American Stock Exchange**, and the **NASDAQ**. They're all regulated by the **Securities and Exchange Commission (SEC)**, a government agency that enforces securities laws designed to protect the investing public.

6. **Understand how market performance is measured and distinguish between equity and debt financing.**

Stock market trends are measured by **market indexes**, such as the **Dow Jones Industrial Average (DJIA)**, the **NASDAQ Composite Index**, and **Standard & Poor's Composite Index (S&P 500)**. When the stock market is enjoying a period of large increases in prices, it's said to be in **bull market**. When prices are declining, it is often called a **bear market**.

Companies can raise funds through **equity financing**—selling stock—or through **debt financing**—issuing **bonds**. Each option has its advantages and disadvantages. Stock may be **common stock** or **preferred stock**. Preferred stock is safer than common stock but it doesn't have the upside potential—namely, the possibility shareholders will benefit greatly if a company performs very well. Unlike common stockholders, however, whose **dividends** vary according to a company's profitability, holders of preferred stock receive annual fixed dividends.

Questions and Problems

1. **AACSB ▸ Analysis**

Instead of coins jingling in your pocket, how would you like to have a pocketful of cowrie shells? These smooth, shiny snail shells, which are abundant in the Indian Ocean, have been used for currency for more than 4,000 years. At one point, they were the most widely used currency in the world. Search "cowrie shells" on Google and learn as much as you can about them. Then answer the following questions:

a. How effectively did they serve as a medium of exchange in ancient times?

b. What characteristics made them similar to today's currencies?

c. How effective would they be as a medium of exchange today?

2. AACSB ▸ Analysis

Does the phrase "The First National Bank of Wal-Mart" strike a positive or negative chord? Wal-Mart is not a bank, but it does provide some financial services: It offers a no-fee Wal-Mart Discovery credit card with a 1-percent cash-back feature, cashes checks and sells money orders through an alliance with MoneyGram International, and houses bank branches in more than 1,000 of its superstores. Through a partnering arrangement with SunTrust Banks, the retailer has also set up in-store bank operations at a number of outlets under the cobranded name of "Wal-Mart Money Center by SunTrust." A few years ago, Wal-Mart made a bold attempt to buy a couple of banks but dropped the idea when it encountered stiff opposition. Even so, some experts say that it's not a matter of *whether* Wal-Mart will become a bank, but a matter of *when*. What's your opinion? Should Wal-Mart be allowed to enter the financial-services industry and offer checking and savings accounts, mortgages, and personal and business loans? Who would benefit if Wal-Mart became a key player in the financial-services arena? Who would be harmed?

3. AACSB ▸ Analysis

Congratulations! You just won $10 million in the lottery. But instead of squandering your newfound wealth on luxury goods and a life of ease, you've decided to stay in town and be a financial friend to your neighbors, who are hardworking but never seem to have enough money to fix up their homes or buy decent cars. The best way, you decide, is to start a bank that will make home and car loans at attractive rates. On the day that you open your doors, the reserve requirement set by the Fed is 10 percent. What's the maximum amount of money you can loan to residents of the town? What if the Fed raises the reserve requirement to 12 percent? Then how much could you loan out? In changing the reserve requirement from 10 percent to 12 percent, what's the Fed trying to do—curb inflation or lessen the likelihood of a recession? Explain how the Fed's action will contribute to this goal.

4. AACSB ▸ Analysis

The most important number in most financial plans is projected revenue. Why? For one thing, without a realistic estimate of your revenue, you can't accurately calculate your costs. Say for example, that you just bought a condominium in Hawaii, which you plan to rent out to vacationers. Because you live in snowy New England, however, you plan to use it yourself from December 15 to January 15. You've also promised your sister that she can have it for the month of July. Now, in Hawaii, condo rents peak during the winter and summer seasons—December 15 to April 15 and June 15 to August 31. They also vary from island to island, according to age and quality, number of rooms, and location (on the beach or away from the beach). The good news is that your relatively new two-bedroom condo is on a glistening beach in Maui. The bad news is that no one is fortunate enough to keep a condo rented for the entire time that it's available. What information would you need in order to estimate your rental revenues for the year?

5. AACSB ▸ Analysis

Have you ever wondered what path your check (or an electronic facsimile) takes once you've used it to pay someone? To follow the life of a check, go to www.exploringbusinessonline.com to link to the Federal Reserve Education Web site. Diagram the steps in the check-clearing process that's described there, identifying each step by a number from one to seven.

Unfortunately, the process isn't always this simple. For one thing, the example on the Federal Reserve Web site assumes that your bank (Citizens Bank) and the store's bank (First National Bank) use the same Federal Reserve bank to clear checks. This assumption is valid only if both banks are in the same geographic area, and the country is divided into 12 Federal Reserve districts.

Say that, instead of paying by check at a local retail store, you're writing a check to pay your tuition, and you go to college in San Francisco but live in Boston. Your bank (the Bank of Boston) clears its checks through the Federal Reserve Bank of Boston. Your college's bank (Frisco Federated) clears its checks through the Federal Reserve Bank of San Francisco. Now go back and revise your diagram to reflect the changes entailed by this revised scenario. (*Hint:* The Federal Reserve Bank of San Francisco has to send the check to the Federal Reserve Bank of Boston for collection.)

6. AACSB ▸ Analysis

You're developing a financial plan for a retail business that you want to launch this summer. You've determined that you need $500,000, including $50,000 for a truck, $80,000 for furniture and equipment, and $100,000 for inventory. You'll use the rest to cover start-up and operating costs during your first six months of operation. After considering the possible sources of funds available to you, create a table that shows how you will obtain the $500,000 you need. It should include all of the following items:

• Sources of all funds

• Dollar amounts to be obtained through each source

• The maturity, annual interest rate, and security of any loan

The total of your sources must equal $500,000. Finally, write a brief report explaining the factors that you considered in arriving at your combination of sources.

7. AACSB ▶ Communication

For the past three years, you've operated a company that manufactures and sells customized surfboards. Sales are great, your employees work hard, and your customers are happy. In lots of ways, things couldn't be better. There is, however, one stubborn cloud hanging over this otherwise sunny picture: You're constantly short of cash. You've ruled out going to the bank because you'd probably be turned down, and you're not big enough to go public. Perhaps the solution is private investors. To see if this option makes sense, research the pros and cons of getting funding from an angel or venture capitalist. Write a brief report explaining why you have or haven't decided to seek private funding.

8. AACSB ▶ Analysis

The three most commonly used stock indices are the DJIA, the NASDAQ composite index, and the S&P 500. To create charts that compare these three indices, go to www.exploringbusinessonline.com to link to the BigCharts Web site and take the following steps (Note: These steps might change if the BigCharts Web site is changed):

- Click on "Interactive Charting" on the top bar.

- Type in the letters *DJIA* on the left sidebar.

- For "Time Frame," select "1 decade" and then "quarterly."

- For "Compare to," select "NASDAQ."

- Click on "Chart Style" and select "Mountain" and "blue and white."

- Return to the top of the sidebar and click on "Draw Chart."

- Print out the chart using the "Printer Friendly" format option.

Repeat this process to compare the DJIA with the S&P 500. Then, answer the following questions:

a. Which two indices tend to follow similar patterns—DJIA and NASDAQ or DJIA and S&P?

b. What accounts for this similarity? What types of companies does each index track? How many companies does each cover?

c. Which index had a large peak? What accounts for that peak?

d. Which index do you prefer for tracking the movement of the stock market? Why?

9. Below is a stock listing for P&G for February 16, 2005. This information appears daily in the *Wall Street Journal* and other newspapers. It's also available online on such Web sites as Yahoo! Finance.

YTD % CHG	52-WEEK HI	52-WEEK LO	STOCK (SYMBOL)	DIV	YLD %	PE	VOL 100s	CLOSE	NET CHG
1.5	57.40	50.53	Procter & Gamble PG	1.00	1.9	21	9686	53.48	0.78

To assess your ability to read and interpret this information, explain each item in the stock listing.

10. AACSB ▶ Communication

You've been out of college for 15 years that you're now the CFO for a large corporation. The CEO just showed you plans for a multimillion-dollar plant expansion and reminded you that it's your job to raise the money. You have three choices: sell bonds, issue common stock, or issue preferred stock. Write a brief report that explains the advantages and disadvantages of each option. Conclude by stating your opinion on the best choice in today's economic environment.

Learning on the Web AACSB

How Much Should You Reveal in *Playboy*?

What can you do if you're sitting around your dorm room with nothing else to do (or at least nothing else you want to do)? How about starting a business? It worked for Michael Dell, who found assembling and selling computers more rewarding than attending classes at the University of Texas. It also worked for two Stanford graduate students, Sergey Brin and Larry Page. They came up with a novel (though fairly simple) idea for a search engine that ranked Web sites according to number of hits and online linkages. Because their goal was to organize massive amounts of electronic data, they wanted a name that connoted seemingly infinite volumes of information. They liked the word *googol* (a child's coinage for a very big number—1 followed by 100 zeros), but, unfortunately, someone already owned the domain name "Googol." So Brin and Page did a little

letter juggling and settled (as we all know by now) for "Google."

By 2004, the company that they'd started in 1998 was the number-one search engine in the world. Their next step, like that of so many successful entrepreneurs before them, was to go public, and that's where our exercise starts. To learn more about this episode in the epic story of Google—and to find out what role *Playboy* magazine plays in it—go to www.exploringbusinessonline.com to link to these Web sites: CNN/Money, Thestreet and BusinessWeek. Check out the following articles posted on these sites:

- "Google Sets $2.7 Billion IPO"

- "Google's *Playboy* Issue"

- "Google Dodges a Bullet"

When you've finished reading the articles, answer the following questions:

1. What is an IPO? Why did Brin and Page take their company public? What disadvantages did they incur by going public? Are they likely to lose control of their company?

2. How does a *Playboy* interview enter into the Google story? What did Brin and Page do wrong? (By the way, the interview appeared in the August 2004 issue of *Playboy*; because Google incorporated the text into its revised IPO filing, it's now in the public domain and available online.)

3. Did the Google founders get off the hook? Was the punishment (or lack of it) appropriate?

Quitting school to run Google paid off big for Brin and Page. Their combined net worth as a result of the IPO suddenly skyrocketed to $8 billion. But how about you? Could you have gotten rich if you'd jumped on the Google bandwagon just as it started to roll? Could you at least have earned enough to pay another year's tuition? To respond to these questions, you need to know two things: (1) the IPO price of Google stock—$85—and (2) Google's current stock price. To find the current price, go to www.exploringbusinessonline.com to link to the finance.yahoo.com Web site. Enter Google's stock symbol—GOOG—and hit "Go." When you find the current stock price, answer the following questions:

1. If you'd bought Google stock on the IPO date and sold it today, how many shares of Google would you have had to buy in order to make enough to cover this year's tuition?

2. If you owned Google stock today, would you sell it or hold it? Explain your answer.

Career Opportunities

Financial Futures

One advantage of a finance major is that it prepares you for a wide range of careers. Some graduates head for Wall Street to make big bucks in investment banking. Others prefer the security of working in the corporate finance department of a large firm, while still others combine finance and selling in fields such as insurance or real estate. If you like working with other people's finances, you might end up in commercial banking or financial planning. To better acquaint yourself with the range of available finance careers, go to www.exploringbusinessonline.com to link to the Careers in Finance Web site. After reviewing the descriptions of each career option, select two areas that you find particularly interesting and two that you find unattractive. For each of your four selections, answer the following questions:

1. Why do you find a given area interesting (or unattractive)?

2. What experience and expertise are entailed by a career in a given area?

Ethics Angle AACSB

The Inside Story

You're the founder and CEO of a publicly traded biotech firm that recently came up with a promising cancer drug. Right now, life on Wall Street is good: Investors are high on your company, and your stock price is rising. On top of everything else, your personal wealth is burgeoning because you own a lot of stock in the company. You're simply waiting to hear from the FDA, which is expected to approve the product. But when the call comes, the news is bad: The FDA has decided to delay approval because of insufficient data on the drug's effectiveness. You know that when investors hear the news, the company's stock price will plummet. The family and friends that you encouraged to buy into your company will lose money, and you will take a major hit.

Quickly, you place an order to sell about $5 million worth of your own stock. Then you start making phone calls. You tell your daughter to dump her stock, and you advise your friends to do the same thing. When you tell your stockbroker the news, he gets on the phone and gives a heads-up to his other clients. Unfortunately, he can't reach one client (who happens to be a good friend of yours), so he instructs his assistant to contact her and tell her what's happened. As a result, the client places an order to sell 4,000 shares of stock at a market value of $225,000.

Let's pause at this point to answer a few questions:

1. Are you being a nice guy or doing something illegal?

2. Is your stockbroker doing something illegal?

3. Is the assistant doing something illegal or just following orders?

4. Is the stockbroker's client acting illegally?

Fast-forward a few months. Federal investigators are interested in the sale of your stock and the sale of your daughter's stock. Because all signs point to the truth as being an invitation to trouble, you lie. When they talked with your friend about her sale, say investigators, she explained a standing agreement that instructed her broker to sell the stock when the market price went below a specified level. It sounds like a good explanation, so you go along with it.

Now, answer this question.

5. What have you done wrong? What has your client friend done wrong?

THE REALITY VERSION OF THE STORY

At this point, let's stop protecting the not-so-innocent and name some names. The biotech company is ImClone, and its founder and CEO is Dr. Samuel Waksal. The Merrill Lynch broker is named Peter Bacanovic and his assistant Douglas Faneuil. The client friend who dumped her stock is Martha Stewart.

Let's focus on Stewart, who is the founder of Martha Stewart Living Omnimedia, a prosperous lifestyle empire. Her actions and their consequences are detailed in an article entitled "Martha's Fall," which you can access by going to www.exploringbusinessonline.com and linking to the MSNBC Web site. Read the article and then answer the following questions:

6. Do you believe Stewart's story that she sold the stock because of a pre-existing sell order and not because she learned that the cancer drug would not be approved? What did she do that was illegal? What was she actually *convicted* of doing?

7. Waksal got seven years for insider trading (and a few other illegal schemes). Bacanovic (Stewart's broker) got five months in jail and five months of home confinement for lying and obstructing the investigation into the sale of ImClone stock. In return for helping the prosecutors convict Stewart, Faneuil (the broker's assistant) got a federal "get-out-of-jail" card but was fined $2,000 for accepting a payoff (namely, an extra week of vacation and a bump in his commission) to stonewall investigators. Stewart went to jail for five months and spent another five under house arrest. Was her punishment too lenient? Too harsh? If you'd been the judge, what sentence would you have given her?

8. How could Stewart have avoided jail? Did her celebrity status or reputation help or hurt her? Did she, as some people claim, become a poster CEO for corporate wrongdoing?

9. Why are government agencies, such as the SEC, concerned about insider trading? Who's hurt by it? Who's helped by government enforcement of insider-trading laws?

Team-Building Skills AACSB

Looking for a High-Flying Stock

Congratulations! Your team has just been awarded $100,000 in hypothetical capital. There is, however, a catch: You have to spend the money on airline stocks. Rather than fly by the seat of your pants, you'll want to research a number of stocks. To get started, go to www.exploringbusinessonline.com to link to the airline-industry section of the Yahoo.com Web site. Scroll down to "Industry Profile" and click on "Airlines." Familiarize yourself with the airline industry by reading the posted information.

INDIVIDUAL REPORTS

Each team member is responsible for researching and writing a brief report on a different company. Don't duplicate your research. Be sure to include low-cost airlines as well as larger carriers. To cover the industry, pick airlines from the following list:

- AMR Corporation (American Airlines)
- Continental Airlines
- Delta Air Lines
- AirTran Holdings

- Jet Blue Airways
- Southwest Airlines

The first three airlines (AMR, Continental, and Delta) are considered major airlines. You access information on them by clicking on "Company Index." The other airlines (Delta, AirTran, Jet Blue and Southwest) are considered regional airlines. You access information on them by first clicking on "Regional Airlines" and then "Company Index."

Each member should prepare a report detailing the following information about his or her chosen company:

- A description of the airline
- The percentage change in revenue over the last fiscal year
- The percentage change in net income over the last fiscal year
- A chart comparing the movement in the company's stock price over the past year with the movement of the DJIA
- Current EPS
- Current PE ratio
- Current stock price

Here are some hints for finding this information on the Yahoo! page devoted to a given company:

- The company will be described in a "Company Profile" appearing toward the top of the page.

- You can get the remaining information by going to the bottom of the page and clicking on the following:

  - "Financials" for changes in revenues and net income

  - "Chart" for trends in stock prices

  - "Quote" for EPS, PE ratio, and current stock price

- When reviewing financial statements to calculate percentage changes in revenues and net income, be sure you click on "Annual Data" in order to get information for the entire year rather than for just the quarter.

TEAM REPORT

Once each member has researched one airline, the team should assemble and decide how to invest its $100,000.

Announce your decision in a final report that includes the following items:

1. An overall description and assessment of the airline industry, including a report on opportunities, threats, and future outlook.

2. A decision on how you'll invest your $100,000, including the names of the stock or stocks that you plan to purchase, current market prices, and numbers of shares.

3. An explanation of the team's investment decision.

4. Individual member reports on each researched company.

FOLLOW-UP

A few weeks later, you might want to check on the stock prices of your picks to see how you'd have done if you'd actually invested $100,000.

The Global View AACSB

Where's the Energy in the Chinese Stock Market?

Warren Buffett is the second-richest man in the world (behind Bill Gates) and its top investor. As CEO of Berkshire Hathaway, a holding company with large stakes in a broad portfolio of investments, Buffett spends a lot of his time looking for companies with promising futures. His time has been pretty well spent: The market price of a share in Berkshire Hathaway now tops $90,000—up from $16 a share in 1964.

Among other things, Berkshire Hathaway owns 2 million shares in PetroChina, an energy firm 90-percent owned by the Chinese government. Surprised? To evaluate Buffett's thinking in making such an investment, you'll need to do a little research. First, find out something about the company by going to www.exploringbusinessonline.com to link to the English version of the PetroChina Web site. Explore the sections "About PetroChina" and "Investor Relations." Look for answers to the following questions:

1. What does the company do? What products and services does it provide? How does it distribute its products?

2. On which stock exchanges are its shares sold?

Next, to learn about the company's financial performance, go to www.exploringbusinessonline.com to link to the Finance.Yahoo.com Web site. Enter the company's stock symbol—PTR—and review the information provided on the site. To see what analysts think of the stock, for example,

click on "Analyst Opinion." (While you're there, find out if Berkshire Hathaway still owns stock in PetroChina—Berkshire Hathaway's own stock isn't up from $16 to $90,000 because Buffett tends to sit on his laurels.)

Now, answer the following questions:

3. If Berkshire Hathaway still owns stock in PetroChina, how many shares does it hold and what is their value?

4. What do analysts think of the stock? If you were Buffett and were inclined to follow somebody else's recommendation, would you sell it, buy more of it, or hold onto what you have?

5. If you personally had $50,000 to invest, how likely is it that you'd buy stock in PetroChina? What factors would you consider in making your decision?

To learn more about the pros and cons of buying stock in Chinese companies, go to www.exploringbusinessonline.com to link to the MSNBC Web site and read the article, "Nice Place to Visit." Then answer these final questions:

6. What are the advantages of investing in the stock of Chinese companies? What are the disadvantages?

7. In your opinion, should the average investor put money in Chinese stock? Why or why not?

Business Plan Project

Group Report: *Accounting Reports*

REPORT

Your team should submit a team-written report which provides an assessment of your company's (preliminary) income or loss for the first three years of operations. You can prepare your projected financial statements by using a special Excel spreadsheet package that you can access at www.exploringbusinessonline.com. Attach a completed copy of the following sections of the business plan template:

- Business Type and Name
- Sales Plan
- Sales Plan Notes
- Human Resources Plan Notes
- Financial Assumptions
- Financial Assumptions Notes
- (Preliminary) Projected Income Statements

For guidance on completing these sections of the template, go to Appendix C (p. 314), "Preparing Financial Reports with Excel Template." The name of your proposed business and the names of all team members should appear on the report.

REASONABLE CONTRIBUTIONS

All members of the team who make **a reasonable contribution to the report** should sign it. (In other words, if any team member does not work on the report, his or her name should *not* appear on it.) If a student who has made a contribution is unable to sign the report (because of sickness or some other valid reason), the team can sign his or her name. To indicate that a name was signed by the team on a member's behalf, be sure to attach a note to the signature.

Group Report: *Financial Plan*

REPORT

Your team should submit a team-written report which provides a brief assessment of your company's income or loss for the first three years of operations, cash requirements to start your business, and sources of cash. You can prepare this report by using the Excel spreadsheet package that you can access at www.exploringbusinessonline.com. Attach a completed copy of all finalized sections of the business plan template:

- Business Type and Name
- Sales Plan
- Sales Plan Notes
- Human Resources Plan
- Human Resources Plan Notes
- Financial Assumptions
- Financial Assumption Notes
- Cash Requirements
- Cash Sources
- Cash Requirements and Sources Notes

For guidance on completing these sections of the template, go to Appendix C (p. 314), "Preparing Financial Reports with Excel template."

REASONABLE CONTRIBUTIONS

All members of the team who make **a reasonable contribution to the report** should sign it. (In other words, if any team member does not work on the report, his or her name should *not* appear on it.) If a student who has made a contribution is unable to sign the report (because of sickness or some other valid reason), the team can sign his or her name. To indicate that a name was signed by the team on a member's behalf, be sure to attach a note to the signature.

Managing Information and Technology

After studying this chapter, you will be able to:

1 Define *information system* (IS) and identify the tasks of the IS manager.

2 Explain how IS managers capture, store, and analyze data.

3 Discuss ways in which an IS can be designed to meet the needs of individuals at various organizational levels.

4 Describe the main systems for sharing information through networked computers.

5 Explain how four networking technologies—the Internet, the World Wide Web, intranets, and extranets—make data communication possible.

6 Identify and discuss challenges faced by companies engaged in e-commerce.

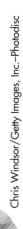

Chris Windsor/Getty Images, Inc.–Photodisc

A WINNING HAND FOR HARRAH'S

If you enjoy gambling and want to be pampered, the Las Vegas Strip is the place for you. The four-mile stretch is home to some of the world's most lavish hotels and casinos, each competing for its share of the 36 million visitors who pack the city each year.[1] The Strip is a smorgasbord of attractions. At the luxurious Mirage, you can witness the eruption of a 70-foot volcano every 15 minutes. The five-star Bellagio resort boasts a $300 million art collection (including Picassos and Van Goghs). There are star-studded shows, upscale retailers, and posh restaurants with award-winning chefs. You can relax at pools and spas or try your luck in the casinos.

So how does a gaming and entertainment company compete in this environment? If you've ever been to Las Vegas, you know that a lot of them erect mammoth neon-bathed brick-and-mortar casino-resorts. A few, however, do what Harrah's did in the late 1990s: They invest heavily in technology and compete through the effective use of information. What kind of information? Marketers at Harrah's collect information about the casino's customers and then use it to entice the same people to return. Does the strategy work? Harrah's is an industry leader.

Throughout this chapter, we'll discuss the information needs of Harrah's top executives, managers, and other employees. We'll examine the ways in which the company uses technology to collect data and process them into information that can be used at every level of the organization.

Harrah's Las Vegas Casino is not nearly as upscale as many of the other casinos on the strip, but Harrah's has been wildly successful in luring customers to its slot machines and gaming tables. Rather than differentiate based on elaborate facilities, Harrah's invests in information technology to fill its casinos and build customer loyalty.

Data Versus Information

By the time the company took the plunge and committed $100 million to marketing-related information technology (IT), Harrah's had been collecting and storing data about customers for almost 10 years. "While the company thought it important to collect customer information," recalls a senior marketing executive, "the problem was we had millions of customers to collect information on, but we had no systematic way of turning it into a marketing decision. We didn't know what to do with it." In other words, Harrah's was collecting a lot of *data* but not necessarily any *information*. So what's the difference?

As an example, suppose that you want to know how you're doing in a particular course. So far, you've taken two 20-question multiple-choice tests. On the first, you got questions 8, 11, and 14 wrong; on the second, you did worse, missing items 7, 15, 16, and 19. The items that you got wrong are merely **data**—unprocessed facts. What's important is your total score. You scored 85 on the first exam and 80 on the second. These two numbers constitute **information**—data that have been processed, or turned into some useful form. Knowing the questions that you missed simply supplied you with some data for calculating your scores.

Now let's fast-forward to the end of the semester. At this point, in addition to taking the two tests, you've written two papers and taken a final. You got a 90 and 95 on the papers and a 90 on the final. You now have more processed data, but you still want to organize them into more useful information. What you want to know is your average grade for the semester. To get the information you want, you need yet more data—

namely, the weight assigned to each graded item. Fortunately, you've known from day one that each test counts 20 percent, each paper 10 percent, and the final 40 percent. A little math reveals an average grade of 87.

Although this is the information in which you are interested, it may be mere data to your instructor, who may want different information: An instructor who intends to scale grades, for example, will want to know the average grade for the entire class. You are hoping that the class average is low enough to push your average of 87 up from a B+ to an A- (or maybe even an A—it doesn't hurt to hope for the best). The moral of the story is that what constitutes *information* at one stage can easily become *data* at another: Or, one person's information can be another person's data.

As a rule, you want information; data are good only for generating the information. So how do you convert data into information that's useful in helping you make decisions and solve problems? That's the question we'll explore in the next section.

INFORMATION SYSTEMS

To gather and process data into information and distribute it to people who need it, organizations develop an **information system (IS)**—the combination of technologies, procedures, and people who collect and distribute the information needed to make decisions and coordinate and control company-wide activities. In most large organizations, the IS is operated by a senior management team that includes a **chief information officer (CIO)** who oversees information and telecommunications systems. There may also be a **chief technology officer** who reports to the CIO and oversees IT planning and implementation. As for **information managers**, their tasks include the following:

- Determining the information needs of members of the organization
- Collecting the appropriate data

- Applying technology to convert data into information
- Directing the flow of information to the right people

Differences in Information Needs

The job is complicated by the fact that information needs vary according to different levels, operational units, and functional areas. Consider, for instance, the information needs of managers at different levels:

- *Top managers* need information for planning, setting objectives, and making major strategic decisions.
- *Middle managers* need information that helps them allocate resources and oversee the activities under their control.
- *First-line managers* require information that helps them supervise employees, oversee daily operations, and coordinate activities.

Figure 11.1 illustrates a hypothetical hierarchy of information needs at Harrah's. The president, for example, needs information to determine whether profitability is up or down or if the organization is facing any new competitive threats. At the vice-presidential

Figure 11.1

Information Needs and Flows

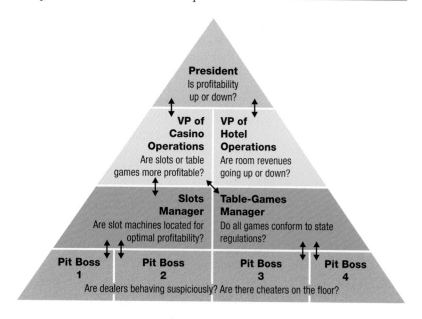

data
Unprocessed facts.

information
Data that have been processed or turned into some useful form.

information system (IS)
Computer system for gathering and processing data into information and distributing it to people who need it.

chief information officer (CIO)
Senior executive who oversees information and telecommunications systems.

chief technology officer
High-level executive who reports to the CIO and oversees information technology planning and implementation.

information manager
Manager with responsibility for determining the information needs of members of the organization and meeting those needs.

level, executives need information that will help them in controlling and planning for specific areas of operations. The VP of casino operations, for example, might need to know which operations are most profitable—slots, table games, or other gaming activities. The VP of hotel operations might want to know if room revenues are going up or down.

The information needs of middle-level and lower-level managers are different still. The slot-machine manager might want to know if the placement of machines on the casino floor affects profitability. The poker manager might want to know if all table games comply with state regulations. At a lower level, the pit manager (who's in charge of table games in a particular area) needs to know if there's a card-counter at his blackjack table or if a dealer's activities are suspicious.

Even at a given level, information needs can vary. A manager on the hotel side of the business, for instance, doesn't care much about profitability at the poker tables, while a pit manager doesn't have much use for hotel housekeeping reports. The reports that an accountant needs would hardly be the same as those needed by a human resources manager.

The Need to Share Information

Having stressed the differences in information needs, we should pause to remind ourselves that the managerial levels, operations, and functions of every organization are intertwined to a greater or lesser degree. If you'll glance again at Figure 11.1 (page 283), you'll be reminded that organizations need to share information, that information must flow, and that it must flow in both directions, bottom-up and top-down. At Harrah's, for instance, both casino and hotel managers are concerned about security, which is also of interest to managers in different functional areas. Information supplied by the security group is obviously vital to managers in the gaming areas, but HR managers also need it to screen potential employees. Marketing information is clearly important to both casino and hotel operations: To maximize overall profits, the company uses marketing data to fill hotel rooms with customers who spend big in the casinos.[2]

Harrah's information needs entail more than allowing individuals in a given casino to share information; information has to be shared among all of Harrah's 39 casinos. Thus, Harrah's relies on an *integrated IT system* that allows real-time communication among all of its properties. Installing the system (in the mid-1990s) was complicated, and not everyone in the organization liked the idea. Some managers felt that information sharing threatened their independence. Others, including some in the IT group, doubted that a large number of separate IT systems could be adequately integrated. To get everyone on board, John Bushy, Senior VP of Information Technology, pledged that he wouldn't cut his hair until the system was up and running. By the time it was operational in 1997, Bushy had hair down to his shoulders, but it was worth it: Harrah's ability to share real-time information across all of its properties has been a major factor in the company's success. Harrah's new system has cut costs by $20 million a year, increased brand recognition, and increased the number of customers playing at more than one Harrah property by 72 percent.[3]

Enterprise Systems Many large and mid-sized companies rely on a highly integrated system called an **enterprise resource planning (ERP) system** to channel information to multiple users. To understand what an ERP system does, forget about the *P* for *planning* (it really doesn't have much to do with planning) and the *R* for *resource* (it's an imprecise term). Focus on the *E* for *enterprise.*[4] An ERP system integrates the computer needs of all activities *across the enterprise* into a single system that serves all users. Such broad integration isn't a simple task, and you wouldn't be the first person to wonder if it wouldn't be easier to give each department its own computer system. Salespeople, for example, need a system that tracks sales and generates sales reports. Meanwhile, manufacturing personnel don't need to track sales but do need to track inventory. What's the problem with standalone computer systems? Quite simply, users in various departments can't share information or communicate with each other.

What If You Don't Have ERP? Imagine you're a sales manager for a fairly large manufacturing company that produces and sells treadmills. Like every other department in the organization, you have your own computer system. A local sporting-goods store orders 100 treadmills through a regional sales representative. It's your job to process the order. It wouldn't be much of a problem for you to go into your computer and place

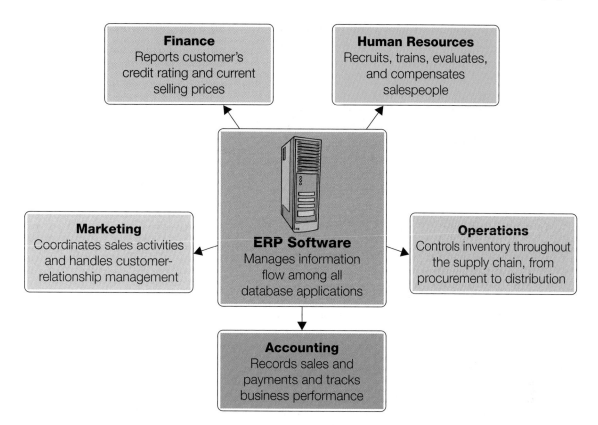

Finance
Reports customer's credit rating and current selling prices

Human Resources
Recruits, trains, evaluates, and compensates salespeople

ERP Software
Manages information flow among all database applications

Marketing
Coordinates sales activities and handles customer-relationship management

Operations
Controls inventory throughout the supply chain, from procurement to distribution

Accounting
Records sales and payments and tracks business performance

Figure 11.2

ERP System

the order. But how would you know if the treadmills were actually in stock and when they could be delivered? How would you know if the customer's credit was any good? You could call the warehouse and ask if the treadmills are in stock. If they are, you'd tell the warehouse manager that you're placing an order and hope that the treadmills are still in stock by the time your order gets there two days later. While you're at it, you'd better ask for an expected delivery date. As a final precaution, you should probably call the finance department and ask about your customer's credit rating. So now you've done your job, and it can hardly be your fault that because the cost of manufacturing treadmills has gone up, accounting has recommended an immediate price increase that hasn't shown up in your computer system yet.

What If You Do Have ERP? Wouldn't it be easier if you had an ERP system like the one illustrated in Figure 11.2—one that lets you access the same information as every other department? Then you could find out if there were 100 treadmills in stock, the ex-

pected delivery date, your customer's credit rating, and the current selling price without spending most of the day exchanging phone calls, e-mails, and faxes. You'd be in a better position to decide whether you can give your customer credit, and you could promise delivery (at a correct price) on a specified date. *Then*, you'd enter the order into the system. The information that you entered would be immediately available to everyone else. The warehouse would know what needs to be shipped, to whom, and when. The accounting department would know that a sale had been made, the dollar amount, and where to send the bill. In short, everyone would have up-to-date information, and no one would have to re-input any data.

Managing Data

Did you ever think about how much data you generate? Just remember what you went through to start college. First, you had to fill out application forms asking you about test scores, high school grades, extracurricular

enterprise resource planning (ERP) system
Integrated computer system used to channel information to multiple users.

activities, and finances, plus demographic data about yourself and your family. Once you'd picked a college, you had to supply data on your housing preferences, the curriculum you wanted to follow, and the party who'd be responsible for paying your tuition. When you registered for classes, you gave more data to the registrar's office. When you arrived on campus, you gave out still more data to have your ID picture taken, to get your computer and phone hooked up, to open a bookstore account, and to buy an on-campus food-charge card. Once you started classes, data generation continued on a daily basis: Your food card and bookstore account, for example, tracked your various purchases, and your ID tracked your coming and going all over campus. And, you generated grades.

And all of these data apply to just one aspect of your life. You also generated data every time you used your credit card and your cell phone. Who uses all of these data? How are they collected, stored, analyzed, and distributed in organizations that have various reasons for keeping track of you?

DATA AND DATABASES

To answer such questions, let's go back to our Harrah's example. As we've seen, Harrah's collects a vast amount of data. Its hotel system generates data when customers make reservations, check in, buy food and beverages, purchase stuff at shops, attend entertainment events, and even relax at the spa. In the casino, customers apply for rewards programs, convert cash to chips (and occasionally chips back to cash), try their luck at the tables and slots, and get complimentary drinks. Then, there are the data generated by the activities of the company itself: Employees, for instance, generate payroll and benefits data, and retail operations generate data every time they buy or sell something. Moreover, if we added up all of these data, we'd have only a fraction of the amount generated by the company's gaming operations.

How does Harrah's handle all of these data? First of all, it captures and stores them in several **databases**—electronic collections of related data that can be accessed by various members of the organization. Think of databases as filing cabinets that can hold massive amounts of organized information, such as revenues and costs from hotel activities, casino activities, and events reservations at each of Harrah's facilities.

Warehousing and Mining Data

What if Harrah's wants to target customers who generate a lot of revenue with a program designed to entice return visits? How would it identify and contact these people? Theoretically, it could search through the relevant databases—those that hold customer-contact information (such as name and address) and information about customer activity in the company's hotels, casinos, and entertainment venues. It would be a start, perhaps, but it wouldn't be very efficient. First of all, it would be time consuming. Plus, what if the same data were not stored in a similar fashion in each database? In that case, it would be quite hard to combine the data in a meaningful way. To address this problem, Harrah's managers will rely on a system like the one illustrated in Figure 11.3, which calls for moving all the relevant data into a **data warehouse**—a centralized database in which data from several databases are consolidated and organized so that they can be easily analyzed.

Data Mining With the data in one central location, management can find out everything it needs to about a particular group of customers. It can also use the data to address some pretty interesting questions. Why do people come to casinos? How can we keep customers coming back? How can we increase the number of visits per customer? How can we increase the amount they spend on each visit? What incentives (such as free dinners, hotel rooms, or show tickets) do customers like most? To come up with answers to these questions, they'll perform a technique called **data mining**—the process of searching and analyzing large amounts of data to reveal patterns and trends that can be used to predict future behavior.

Data Mining and Customer Behavior By data-mining its customer-based data warehouse, Harrah's management can discover previously unknown relationships between the general behavior of its customers and that of a certain group of customers (namely, the most profitable ones). Then, it can design incentives to appeal specifically to those people who will generate the most profit for the company.

To get a better idea of how data mining works, let's simplify a description of the process at Harrah's. First, we need to know how the casino gathered the data to conduct its preliminary analysis. Most customers who play the slots use a Harrah's player's card that offers incentives based on the amount of

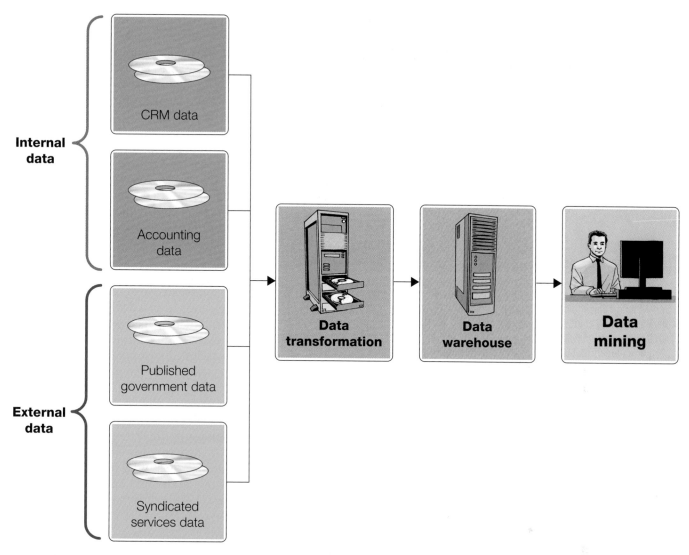

Internal data

CRM data

Accounting data

External data

Published government data

Syndicated services data

Data transformation

Data warehouse

Data mining

money that they wager on slot machines, video poker, and table games.[5] To get the card, a customer must supply some personal information, such as name, address, and phone number. From Harrah's standpoint, the card is extremely valuable because it can reveal a lot about the user's betting behavior: actual wins and losses, length of time played, preferred machines and coin denominations, average amount per bet, and—most importantly—the speed with which coins are deposited and buttons pushed.[6] As you can see from Figure 11.3, Harrah's primary data source was *internal*—generated by the company itself rather than provided by an outside source—and drew on a marketing database developed for *customer relationship management* (CRM).

What does the casino do with the data that it's mined? Harrah's was most interested in "first trippers"—first-time casino customers. In particular, it wanted to know which of these customers should be enticed to return. By analyzing the data collected from player's-card applications and from customer's actual play at the casino (even if for no more than an hour), Harrah could develop a profile of a profitable customer. Now, when a first-timer comes into any of its casinos and plays for a while, Harrah's can instantly tell if he or she fits the profitable-customer profile. To lure these people back for return visits, it makes generous offers of free or reduced-rate rooms, meals, entertainment, or free chips (the incentive of choice for Harrah's preferred

Figure 11.3

The Data Mining Process

database
Electronic collection of related data accessible to various users.

data warehouse
Centralized database that stores data from several databases so they can be easily analyzed.

data mining
Technique used to search and analyze data to reveal patterns and trends that can be used to predict future behavior.

Like business executives, basketball coaches supplement intuition with information when it comes to making strategic decisions. Studying previous games is an obvious starting point, but with teams averaging 200 possessions in each of about 1,200 games annually, there's a danger of data overload. That's why IBM and a partner called Virtual Gold developed data mining software for the National Basketball Association. The coaches of about 25 teams now use Advanced Scout to analyze an immense amount of in-game data and uncover meaningful patterns of information previously buried under a mountain of seemingly unrelated stats.

customers). These customers make up 26 percent of all Harrah's customers and generate 82 percent of its revenues. Surprisingly, they're not the wealthy high rollers to whom Harrah's had been catering for years. Most of them are regular working people or retirees with available time and income and a fondness for slots. They generally stop at the casino on the way home from work or on a weekend night and don't stay overnight. They enjoy the thrill of gambling, and you can recognize them because they're the ones who can't pump coins in fast enough.[7]

QUICK QUIZ   11.1

Before reading about types of information systems, give yourself a quick quiz on what you've learned about the principles of information systems and data mining.

Go to www.exploringbusinessonline.com

Types of Information Systems

As we saw earlier, different managers, operational units, and functional areas have different information needs. That's why organiza-

tions often tailor information systems to meet particular needs. Harrah's IT group, for example, developed the Player Contact System[8] to help its casino salespeople connect to top customers on a more personal basis. Working from a prioritized list of customer names displayed on a computer screen, the salesperson clicks on a name to view relevant information about the customer, such as background and preferred casino activities. There's even a printed script that can be used to guide the conversation. Such a system isn't very helpful, however, to middle or top-level managers, who need systems to help them carry out their oversight and planning responsibilities. To design marketing programs, for instance, marketing managers rely on summary information gleaned from a dedicated customer-relationship management system. Let's look at some of the widely available information systems designed to support people at the operational and upper-management levels.

OPERATIONS SUPPORT SYSTEMS

Operations support systems are generally used by managers at lower levels of the organization—those who run day-to-day business operations and make fairly routine decisions. They may be *transaction processing systems, process control systems,* or *design and production systems*.

Transaction Processing Systems

Most of its daily activities are recorded and processed by an organization's **transaction processing system (TPS)**, which receives input data and converts them into output—information—intended for various users. Input data are called **transactions**—events that affect a business. A *financial transaction* is an economic event: It affects the firm's assets, is reflected in its accounting statements, and is measured in monetary terms. Sales of goods to customers, purchases of inventory from suppliers, and salaries paid to employees are all financial transactions. Everything else is a *nonfinancial transaction*. The marketing department, for example, might add some demographic data to its customer database. The information would be processed by the firm's TPS, but it wouldn't be a financial transaction.

Figure 11.4 illustrates a TPS in which the transaction is a customer's electronic payment of a bill. As you can see, TPS output can consist not only of documents sent to outside

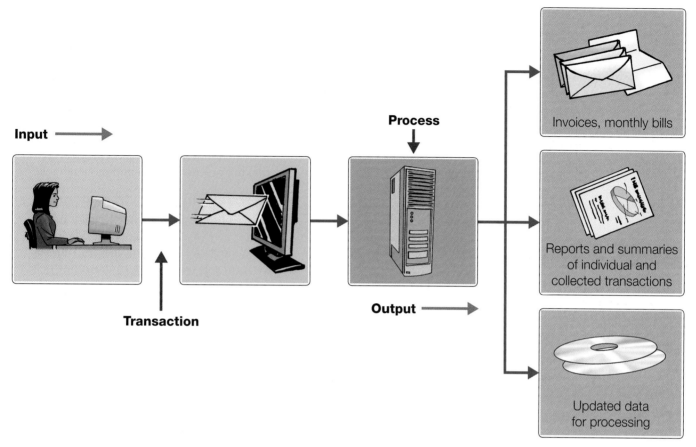

Input →

Process ↓

Transaction ↑

Output →

Invoices, monthly bills

Reports and summaries of individual and collected transactions

Updated data for processing

parties (in this case, notification of payment received), but information circulated internally (in the form of reports), and information entered into the database for updating.

Process Control Systems

Process control refers to the application of technology to monitor and control physical processes. It's useful, for example, in testing the temperature of food as it's being prepared or gauging the moisture content of paper as it's being manufactured. Typically, it depends on sensors to collect data on a periodic basis. The data are then analyzed by a computer programmed either to make adjustments or to signal an operator.

Harrah's uses process-control technology to keep customers happy. At any given point, some slot machines are down, whether because a machine broke or ran out of money

or somebody hit the jackpot. All of these contingencies require immediate attention by a service attendant. In the past, service personnel strolled around looking for machines in need of fixing. Now, however, a downed slot machine sends out an "I need attention" signal, which is instantly picked up by a monitoring and paging system called Messenger Plus and sent to a service attendant.

Design and Production Systems

As we saw in Chapter 6, modern companies rely heavily on technology to design and make products. **Computer-aided design (CAD)** software, for instance, enables designers to test computer models digitally before moving new products into the prototype stage. Many companies link CAD systems to the manufacturing process through **computer-aided manufacturing (CAM)** systems that not only

Figure 11.4

Transaction Processing System

determine the steps needed to produce components but also instruct machines to do the necessary work. A CAD/CAM system can be expanded by means of **computer-integrated manufacturing (CIM)**, which integrates various operations (from design through manufacturing) with functional activities ranging from order taking to final shipment. The CIM system may also control industrial robots—computer-run machines that can perform repetitive or dangerous tasks. A CIM system is a common element in a **flexible manufacturing system (FMS)**, which makes it possible to change equipment setups by reprogramming computer-controlled machines that can be adapted to produce a variety of goods. Such flexibility is particularly valuable to makers of customized products.

MANAGEMENT SUPPORT SYSTEMS

Mid- and upper-level managers rely on a variety of information systems to support decision-making activities, including *management information systems, decision support systems, executive support systems*, and *expert systems*.

Management Information Systems

A **management information system (MIS)** extracts data from a database to compile reports, such as sales analyses, inventory-level reports, and financial statements, to help managers make routine decisions. The type and form of the report depend on the information needs of a particular manager. At Harrah's, for example, several reports are available on a daily basis to a games manager (who's responsible for table-game operations and personnel): a customer-analysis report, a profitability report, and a labor-analysis report.[9]

Decision Support Systems

A **decision support system (DSS)** is an interactive system that collects, displays, and integrates data from multiple sources to help managers make nonroutine decisions. For example, suppose that a gaming company is considering a new casino in Pennsylvania (which has just legalized slot machines). To decide if it would be a wise business move, management could use a DSS like the one illustrated in Figure 11.5. The first step is to extract data from internal sources to decide whether the company has the financial

strength to expand its operations. From external sources (such as industry data and Pennsylvania demographics), managers might find the data needed to determine if there's sufficient demand for a casino in the state. The DSS will apply both types of data as variables in a quantitative *model* that managers can analyze and interpret. People must make the final decision, but in making sense of the relevant data, the DSS makes the decision-making process easier—and more reliable.[10]

Executive Information Systems

As we observed in Chapter 4, senior managers spend a good deal of their time planning and making major decisions. They set performance targets, determine if they're being met, and routinely scan the external environment for opportunities and threats. To accomplish these tasks, they need relevant, timely, easily understood information. Often, they can get it through an **executive information system (EIS)**, which provides ready access to strategic information that's customized to their needs and presented in a convenient format. Using an EIS, for example, a gaming-company executive might simply touch a screen to view key summary information that highlights in graphical form a critical area of corporate performance, such as revenue trends. After scanning this summary, our executive can "drill down" to retrieve more detailed information—for example, revenue trends by resort or revenue trends from various types of activities, such as gaming, hotel, retail, restaurant, or entertainment operations.

Artificial Intelligence

Artificial intelligence (AI) is the science of developing computer systems that can mimic human behavior. Ever since the term was coined in 1956, AI has always seemed on the verge of being "the next big thing." Unfortunately, optimistic predictions eventually collided with underwhelming results, and many experts began to doubt that it would ever have profitable applications.[11] In the last 10 years, however, there have been some significant advances in AI—albeit in the area of game playing, where activities are generally governed by small sets of well-defined rules. But even the game-playing environment is sometimes complex enough to promote interesting developments. In 1997, for example, IBM's Deep Blue—a specialized computer with an advanced chess-playing program—defeated the world's highest-ranked player.[12]

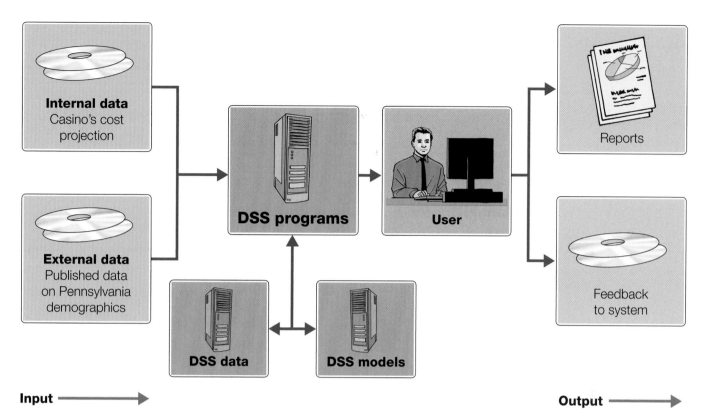

Input ⟶

More recently, several AI applications have been successfully put to commercial use. Let's take a brief look at two of these: *expert systems* and *face-recognition technology*.

Expert Systems Expert systems (ES) are programs that mimic the judgment of experts by following sets of rules that experts would follow. They're useful in such diverse areas as medical diagnosis, portfolio management, and credit assessment. For example, you've called the customer-service department of your credit-card company because you want to increase your credit line. Don't expect to talk to some financial expert who's authorized to say yes or no. You'll be talking to a service representative with no financial expertise whatsoever. He or she will, however, have access to an ES, which will give you an answer in a few seconds. How does it work? The ES will

prompt the representative to ask you certain questions about your salary and living expenses. It will also check internal corporate data to analyze your purchases and payment behavior, and based on the results, it will determine whether you get an increase and, if so, how much.

At Harrah's, an ES called the Revenue Management System helps to optimize the overall profitability of both hotel and casino operations. When a customer requests a room, the program accesses his or her profile in the database and consults certain "rules" for assessing the application.[13] One rule, for example, might be: "If the customer has wagered more than $100,000 in the past year, add 10 points." Eventually, the system decides whether your application will be accepted (and at what rate) by adding up points determined by the rules. While a tightwad may not get a room even when there are vacancies, a

Output ⟶

> **Figure 11.5**
>
> Decision Support System

---

computer-integrated manufacturing (CIM)
System in which the capabilities of a CAD/CAM system are integrated with other computer-based functions.

flexible manufacturing system (FMS)
System in which computer-controlled equiment is programmed to handle materials used in manufacturing.

management information system (MIS)
System used to extract data from a database and compile reports that help managers make routine decisions.

decision support system (DSS)
Interactive system that extracts, integrates, and displays data from multiple sources to help managers make non-routine decisions.

executive information system (EIS)
System that provides senior managers with strategic information customized to meet their needs and presented in a convenient format.

artificial intelligence (AI)
Science of developing computer systems that can mimic human behavior.

expert system (ES)
Program that mimics the judgment of experts.

high roller may get a good rate on a luxury suite even if the hotel is nearly full.

Face-Recognition Technology Harrah's uses another particularly interesting, and sophisticated, application of AI. In the hotel-casino business, it's crucial to identify and turn away undesirable visitors. One tool for this task is a digital camera-surveillance system that uses *face-recognition technology.* Using this technology, a program classifies a person's face according to the presence/absence or extent of certain unique features, such as dimpled chins, receding jaws, overbites, and long or short noses. If there's a match on, for example, 15 features between a person being scanned and someone in the company database, a staff member decides if the two people are the same. If a security manager then concludes that the face belongs to a skilled card-counter, the customer will be discouraged from playing blackjack; if it belongs to a known cheater, the individual will be escorted out of the casino. The system, however, does more than spot undesirables. It can also identify high rollers and send information about customers to managers on the floor. That's why a Harrah's manager can greet a preferred customer at the door with his favorite drink and a personalized greeting, such as "Hi Bill! How's Karen? Did you ever get that vintage Corvette? Have a gin rickey on the house."[14]

ABOUT NIKE 11.1

Now that you've seen how information systems can help organizations make better decisions, take a moment to examine the challenges encountered by Nike when it set out to install a complex information system.

Go to www.exploringbusinessonline.com

QUICK QUIZ 11.2

In the next sections, we'll discuss computer and data communication networks, e-commerce, and issues in electronic security. First, however, take an opportunity to give yourself a brief test on types of information systems.

Go to www.exploringbusinessonline.com

Casinos are not the only users of face recognition technology. It's of value at airports, banks, research labs, government buildings, or any other place where it's important to determine the identity of a person. Here, two employees demonstrate the use of a 3-D facial recognition system designed by their company, Siemens Corporate Tech AG (a German electronics and electrical engineering company). The system projects parallel colored lines onto this woman's face and a colored video camera takes a picture, which establishes the contour and characteristics of her face. The computer image is then analyzed using pattern-recognition methods.

Computer Networks

Once it's grown beyond just a handful of employees, an organization needs a way of sharing information. Imagine a flower shop with 20 employees. The person who takes phone orders needs access to the store's customer list, as do the delivery person and the bookkeeper. Now, the store may have one computer and everyone could share it. It's more likely, however, that there are a number of computers (several for salespeople, one for delivery, and one for bookkeeping). In this case, everyone needs to be sure that customer records have been updated on all computers every time that a change is required.

Likewise, many companies want their personal computers to run their own software and process data independently. But they also want people to share databases, files, and printers, and they want them to share **applications software** that performs particular tasks, including word processing, creating and managing spreadsheets, designing graphical presentations, and producing high-quality printed documents (*desktop publishing*).

The solution in both cases is *networking*—linking computers to one another. The two major types of networks are distinguished according to geographical coverage:

- A **local area network (LAN)** links computers that are in close proximity—in the same building or office complex. They can be connected by cables or by wireless technology. Your university might have a LAN system that gives you access to resources, such as registration information, software packages, and printers. Figure 11.6 illustrates a LAN that's connected to another network by means of a *gateway*—a processor that allows dissimilar networks to communicate with one another.

- Because a **wide area network (WAN)** covers a relatively large geographical area, computers are connected by telephone lines, wireless technology, or satellite. Computers at Harrah's properties are linked through a WAN.[15]

Like the one in Figure 11.6, some networks are **client-server systems**, which include a number of client machines (the ones used by employees for data input and retrieval) and a server (which stores the database and the programs used to process the data). Such a setup saves time and money and circulates more accurate information.

Data Communication Networks

In addition to using networks for information sharing within the organization, companies use networks to communicate and share information with those outside the

Figure 11.6

Local Area Network (LAN)

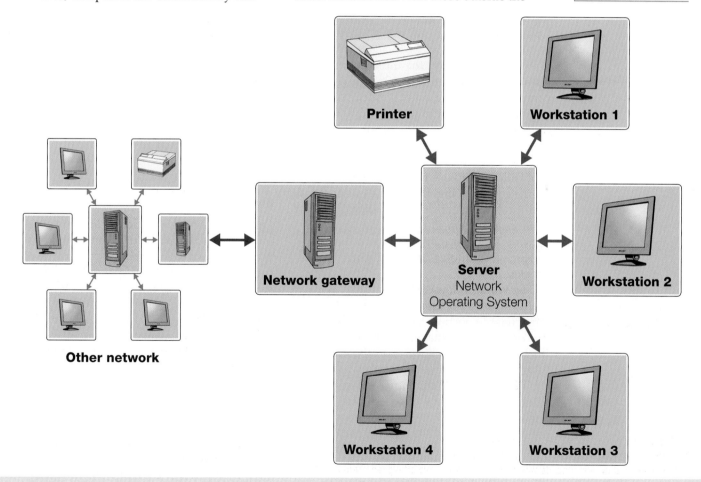

Printer **Workstation 1**

Network gateway **Server** Network Operating System **Workstation 2**

Other network **Workstation 4** **Workstation 3**

---

applications software
Software that performs a specific task, such as word processing or spreadsheet creation.

local area network (LAN)
Network that links computers that are in close proximity.

wide area network (WAN)
Network that links computers that are spread over a relatively large geographical area.

client-server system
System connecting client machines (which are used by employees for data input and retrieval) and a server (that stores shared databases and programs).

organization. All of this is made possible by **data communication networks**, which transmit digital data (numeric data, text, graphics, photos, video, and voice) from one computer to another using a variety of wired and wireless communication channels. Let's take a closer look at the networking technologies that make possible all of this electronic communication—in particular, the *Internet* (including the *World Wide Web*), *intranets*, and *extranets*.

THE INTERNET AND THE WORLD WIDE WEB

Although we often use the terms *Internet* and *World Wide Web* interchangeably, they're not the same thing.[16] The **Internet** is an immense global network comprised of smaller interconnected networks linking millions of computers around the world. Originally developed for the U.S. military and later adapted for use in academic and government research, the Internet experienced rapid growth in the 1990s, when companies called **Internet service providers (ISPs)** were allowed to link into the Internet infrastructure in order to connect paying subscribers. Today, ISPs, such as CompuServe, America Online, and MSN allow us to use the Internet for e-mail, online conferencing, instant messaging, and real-time communication (chatting). These services also connect us with third-party providers of information, including news stories, stock quotes, and magazine articles.

The **World Wide Web** (or simply "the Web") is just a portion of the Internet—albeit a large portion. The Web is a subsystem of computers that can be accessed on the Internet using a special protocol, or language, known as *hypertext transfer protocol* (*HTTP*). What's the difference between the Internet and the Web? According to Tim Berners-Lee (one of the small team of scientists who developed the concept for the Web in 1989), the Internet is a network of networks composed of cables and computers. You can use it to send "packets" of information from one computer to another, much like sending a postcard. If the address on the packet is accurate, it will arrive at the correct destination in much less than a second. Thus, the Internet is a packet-delivery *service* that delivers such items as e-mail messages all over the globe. The Web, on the other hand, is composed of *information*—documents, pictures, sounds, streaming videos, and so on. It's connected not through cables, but rather through *hypertext links* that allow users to navigate between resources on the Internet.[17]

Because it's driven by programs that communicate between computers connected to the Internet, the Web couldn't exist without the Internet. The Internet, on the other hand, could exist without the Web, but it wouldn't be nearly as useful. The Internet itself is enormous, but it's difficult to navigate, and it has no pictures, sounds, or streamed videos. They exist on computers connected to the Web, which also makes it much easier to retrieve information. The creation of Web **browsers**—software, such as Microsoft's Internet Explorer and Netscape Navigator, which locates and displays Web pages—opened up the Internet to a vast range of users. More than 60 percent of individuals in the United States age 18 and older use the Internet regularly.[18] So, who's in charge of the Web? No one owns it, but an organization called the World Wide Web Consortium (W3C) oversees the development and maintenance of standards governing the way information is stored, displayed, and retrieved.[19]

The Technology of the Web

Let's look a little more closely at some of the technologies that allow us to transmit and receive data over the Web. Documents on the Web are called *Web pages*, and they're stored on *Web sites*. Each site is maintained by a *Webmaster* and opens with a *home page*. Each Web page is accessed through a unique address called a *uniform resource locator* (*URL*). For example, if you want to find statistics on basketball star Shaquille O'Neal, you could type in the URL address http://www.nba.com/playerfile/shaquille_oneal. The prefix *http://* is the protocol name, *www.nba.com* the domain name, *playerfile* the subdirectory name, and *shaquille_oneal* the document name (or Web page). A computer that retrieves Web pages is called a **Web server**. A **search engine** is a software program that scans Web pages containing specified keywords and provides a list of documents containing them. The most popular search engine is Google; others include Yahoo!, Ask Jeeves, AllTheWeb, and Hotbot.

INTRANETS AND EXTRANETS

What's the difference among the Internet, an intranet, and an extranet? It depends on who can and can't access the information on the network. The Internet is a public network that anyone can use. A company's **intranet**, on the other hand, is a private network using Internet technologies that's available only to employees; access is controlled by a software program called a **firewall**. The information available on an intranet varies by company but may include internal job postings, written company policies, and proprietary information, such as price lists meant for internal use only.

An **extranet** is an intranet that's partially available to certain parties outside the organization. Say, for example, you've posted the following information on your intranet: company policies, payroll and benefit information, training programs, parts specifications and inventories, and production schedules. To allow suppliers to bid on contracts, you might give them access to sections of the site disclosing parts specifications, inventories, and production schedules. All other sections would be off-limits. You'd control access to employee-only and supplier-accessible sections by means of usernames and passwords. As you can see from Figure 11.7, which illustrates some of the connections made possible

Figure 11.7

How an Extranet Works

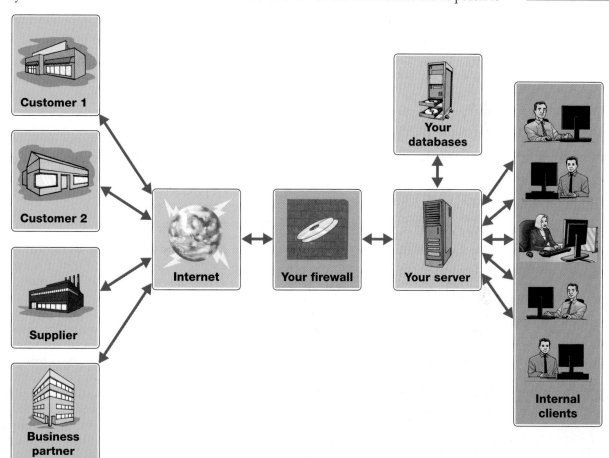

data communication network, Internet, Internet service provider (ISP), World Wide Web ("the Web"), browser, Web server, search engine, intranet, firewall, extranet

data communication network
Large network used to transmit digital data from one computer to another using a variety of wired and wireless communication channels.

Internet
Global network comprised of smaller interconnected networks linking millions of computers around the world.

Internet service provider (ISP)
Company, such as America Online, that links into the Internet infrastructure to connect paying subscribers.

World Wide Web ("the Web")
Subsystem of computers on the Internet that communicate with each other using a special language called HTTP.

browser
Software (such as Internet Explorer) that locates and displays Web pages.

Web server
Computer that retrieves Web pages.

search engine
Software program that scans Web pages for specified kewords and provides a list of documents containing them.

intranet
Private network using internet technologies that are available only to employees.

firewall
Software program that controls access to a company's intranet.

extranet
Intranet that's partially available to certain parties outside the organization.

by an extranet, access can be made available to customers and business partners as well.

E-COMMERCE

The level of **e-commerce**—conducting business over the Internet—varies by company. Some companies, such as Amazon.com, rely on the Internet for their existence. Others, especially smaller firms, have yet to incorporate the Internet into their business models, but these companies belong to a dwindling minority: More than 60 percent of small companies and 90 percent of large companies have Web sites, and a third of the companies that maintain Web sites sell products through them.[20] Larger companies now find that they must do business over the Internet, including selling and buying goods.

Why Business Uses the Internet

Businesses use the Internet for four purposes: *presenting information, selling products, distributing digital products*, and *acquiring goods and services*.

In only 10 years, eBay has changed the world of Internet commerce. The company was launched in 1995 by current chairman of the board Pierre Omidyar (shown here with eBay's president and CEO Meg Whitman). Although the rumor is that Omidyar started the company to help his girlfriend (now wife) trade her collection of Pez candy dispensers, this is only partly true. Here's the real story: While holding a full-time job, he started thinking that the Internet could be a great place to auction goods. He wrote some software and set up AuctionWeb, which later became eBay, and the rest is history. Oh, about the Pez collection: Shortly after he set up AuctionWeb, his girlfriend did start selling her Pez collection on the site.

Presenting Information By posting a Web site, a company can tell people about itself, its products, and its activities. Customers can also check the status of orders or account balances. Information should always be current, complete, and accurate. Customers should be able to find and navigate the site, which should be able to accommodate them during high-use periods.

Selling Products Selling over the Internet—whether to individuals or to other businesses—allows a business to enlarge its customer base by reaching buyers outside of its geographical area. A company selling over the Internet must attract customers to its site, make the buying process simple, assure customers that the site is secure, and provide helpful information.

Distributing Digital Products Some companies use the Internet to sell and deliver such digital products as subscriptions to online news services, software products and upgrades, and music and video products. In these businesses, the timely delivery of products is crucial. Sales of digital products over the Internet are expected to increase substantially in the future, particularly sales of digital music.[21]

Acquiring Goods and Services *E-purchasing* (which we introduced in Chapter 6) saves time, speeds up delivery, reduces administrative costs, and fosters better communications between a firm and its suppliers. Most importantly, it cuts the costs of purchased products because it's now feasible for buyers to request competitive bids and do comparative shopping. Many companies now use a technology called **electronic data interchange (EDI)** to process transactions and transmit purchasing documents directly from one IS to another. Figure 11.8 shows an EDI system at a company that subscribes to a *value-added network*—a private system supplied by a third-party firm—over which it conducts a variety of transactions.

The Virtual Company

Imagine a company that retails products for school teachers over the Internet—for example, books, software, and teaching supplies purchased from various manufacturers and distributors. It would need facilities to store inventories and personnel to handle inventories and fill customer orders. But what if this company decided to get out of the traditional retail business? What if it decided instead to team up with three trading partners—a book publisher, a software developer, and a manufacturer of office supplies? Our original company could recreate itself as a Web site for marketing the books, software, and supplies provided by its partners without taking physical possession of them. It would become a **virtual company**. Its partners would warehouse their own products and furnish product descriptions, prices, and delivery times. Meanwhile, the virtual company, besides promoting all three lines of products, would verify customer orders and forward them to its partners, who would ship their own products directly to customers. All four partners would be better off because they'd be competing in a business in which none of them could compete by itself. This business approach has allowed Spun.com, a CD Internet retailer, to avoid carrying the $8-million inventory that it would have needed to support its sales. Rather than hold its own inventory, Spun.com merely passes the orders on to Alliance Entertainment (a home entertainment products wholesale distributor), which ships them directly to customers.[22]

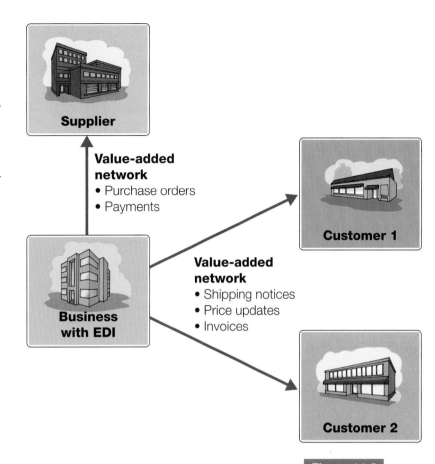

Figure 11.8

EDI and Value-Added Networks

ABOUT NIKE   11.2

Here's a chance to see how Nike uses the Internet to reach customers.

Go to www.exploringbusinessonline.com

Security Issues in Electronic Communication

E-commerce has presented businesses with opportunities undreamt of only a couple of decades ago. But it's also introduced some

unprecedented challenges. For one thing, companies must now earmark more than 5 percent of their annual IT budgets for protecting themselves against disrupted operations and theft due to computer crime and sabotage.[23] The costs resulting from electronic crimes are substantial and increasing at a significant rate. It's estimated, for example, that damage to personal computers and corporate networks from the so-called "Blaster worm" in August 2003 totaled $2 billion.[24] The battle against technology crime is near the top of the FBI's list of priorities, behind only the war against terrorism and espionage.[25] In addition to protecting their own operations from computer crime, companies engaged in e-commerce must clear another hurdle: They must convince consumers that it's safe to buy things over the Internet—that credit-card numbers, passwords, and other personal information are protected from theft or misuse. In this

---

e-commerce
Business conducted over the Internet.

electronic data interchange (EDI)
Computerized exchange of business transaction documents.

virtual company
Company without a significant physical presence that relies on third parties to produce, warehouse, price, and deliver the products it sells over the Internet.

section, we'll explore some of these challenges and describe some of the efforts being made to meet them.

DATA SECURITY

In some ways, life was simpler for businesspeople before computers. Records were produced by hand and stored on paper. As long as you were careful to limit access to your records (and remembered to keep especially valuable documents in a safe), you faced little risk of someone altering or destroying your records. In some ways, storing and transmitting data electronically is a little riskier. Let's look at two data-security risks associated with electronic communication: *malicious programs* and *spoofing*.

Malicious Programs

Some people get a kick out of wreaking havoc with computer systems by spreading a variety of destructive programs. Once they're discovered, they can be combated with antivirus programs that are installed on most computers and which can be updated. In the meantime, unfortunately, they can do a lot of damage, bringing down computers or entire networks by corrupting operating systems or databases.

Viruses, Worms, and Trojan Horses
The cyber vandal's repertory includes "viruses," "worms" and "Trojan horses." Viruses and worms are particularly dangerous because they can copy themselves over and over again, eventually using up all available memory and closing down the system. Trojan horses are viruses that enter your computer by posing as some type of application. Some sneak in by pretending to be virus-scanning programs designed to rid your computer of viruses. Once inside, they do just the opposite.

Spoofing

It's also possible for unauthorized parties to gain access to restricted company Web sites—usually for the purpose of doing something illegal. Using a technique called "spoofing," culprits disguise their identities by modifying the address of the computer from which the scheme has been launched. Typically, the point is to make it look as if an incoming message has originated from an authorized source. Then, once the site's been accessed, the perpetrator can commit fraud, spy, or destroy data. You could, for example, spoof a manufacturing firm with a false sales order that seems to have come from a legitimate customer. If the spoof goes undetected, the manufacturer will incur the costs of producing and delivering products that were never ordered (and will certainly never be paid for).

Every day, technically savvy thieves (and dishonest employees) steal large sums of money from companies by means of spoofing or some other computer scheme. It's difficult to estimate the dollar amount because many companies don't even know how much they've lost: The 2004 E-Crime Watch Survey found that only 50 percent of companies surveyed have a formal process in place to track computer crimes committed against them.[26]

REVENUE THEFT

In addition to the problems of data security faced by every company that stores and transmits information electronically, companies that sell goods or provide services online are also vulnerable to activities that threaten their revenue sources. Two of the most important forms of computer crime are *denial of service* and *piracy*.

Denial of Service

A denial-of-service attack does exactly what the term suggests: It prevents a Web server from servicing authorized users. Consider the following scenario. Dozens of computers are whirring away at an online bookmaker in the offshore gambling haven of Costa Rica. Suddenly a mass of blank incoming messages floods the company's computers, slowing operations to a trickle. No legitimate customers can get through to place their bets. A few hours later, the owner gets an e-mail that reads: "If you want your computers to stay up and running through the football season, wire $40,000 to each of 10 numbered bank accounts in Eastern Europe."

You're probably thinking that our choice of online gambling as an example of this scheme is a little odd, but we chose it because it's real: In the past year, the online-gambling industry suffered hundreds of such attacks.[27] Because most gambling operations opt to pay the ransom and get back to business as usual, denial of service to businesses in the industry has become a very lucrative enterprise.

Online gambling operations are good targets because they're illegal in the United States, where they can't get any help from law-enforcement authorities. But extortionists have been known to hit other targets, including Microsoft and the Recording Industry Association of America. The problem could become much more serious if they start going after e-commerce companies and others that depend on incoming orders to stay afloat.

Piracy

Technology makes it easier to create and sell intellectual property, but it also makes it easier to steal it. Because digital products can be downloaded and copied almost instantly over the Internet, it's a simple task to make perfect replicas of your favorite copyright-protected songs, movies, and computer software, whether for personal use or further distribution. When you steal such materials, you're cheating the countless musicians, technicians, actors, programmers, and others involved in creating and selling them. Theft cuts into sales and shrinks corporate profits, often by staggering amounts. Entertainment-industry analysts estimate that online thieves download more than 2.6 billion music files and 12 million movies every month.[28] The software industry estimates that the global market for pirated software reached $30 billion in 2004.[29]

So, what's being done to protect the victimized companies? Actually, quite a lot, even though it's a daunting task, both in the United States and abroad.[30] In 1998, Congress passed the Digital Millennium Copyright Act, which outlaws the copying of copyright-protected music (unless you're copying legally acquired music for your own use). The penalties are fairly stiff: up to three years in prison and $250,000 in fines.[31] To show that it means business, the music industry is also hauling offenders into court, but legal action is costly and prosecuting teenage music lovers doesn't accomplish much. Some observers believe that the best solution is for the industry to accelerate its own efforts to offer its prod-

ucts online.[32] Initial attempts seem to be working: People who are willing to obey copyright laws have downloaded more than 50 million songs from the iTunes site alone.[33]

Firewalls Builders install firewalls (or fireproof walls) in structures to keep a fire that starts in one part of a building from entering another part. Companies do something similar to protect their computer systems from outside intruders: They install firewalls—software and hardware systems that prevent unauthorized users from accessing their computer networks.

You can think of the firewall as a gatekeeper that stands at the entry point of the company's network and monitors incoming and outgoing traffic. The firewall system inspects and screens all incoming messages to prevent unwanted intruders from entering the system and causing damage. It also regulates outgoing traffic to prevent employees from inappropriately sending out confidential data that shouldn't leave the organization.

RISKS TO CUSTOMERS

Many people still regard the Internet as an unsafe place to do business. They worry about the security of credit-card information and passwords and the confidentiality of personal data. Are any of these concerns valid? Are you really running risks when you shop electronically? If so, what's being done to make the Internet a safer place to conduct transactions? Let's look a little more closely at the sort of things that tend to bother some Internet users (or, as the case may be, nonusers), as well as some of the steps that companies are taking to convince people that e-commerce is safe.

Credit-Card Theft

One of the most serious barriers to the growth of e-commerce is the perception of many people that credit card numbers can be stolen when they're given out over the Internet. Although virtually every company takes considerable precautions, they're not entirely wrong. Cyber criminals, unfortunately, seem to be tirelessly creative. One popular scheme involves setting up a fraudulent Internet business operation to collect credit-card information. The bogus company will take orders to deliver goods—say, Mother's Day flowers—but when the day arrives, it will have disappeared from cyberspace. No flowers will get delivered, but even worse, the perpetrator can sell or use all the collected credit-card information.

Password Theft

Many people also fear that Internet passwords—which can be valuable information to cyber criminals—are vulnerable to theft. Again, they're not altogether wrong. There are schemes dedicated entirely to stealing passwords. In one, the cyber thief sets up a Web site that you can access only if you register, provide an e-mail address, and select a password. The cyber criminal is betting that the site will attract a certain percentage of people who use the same password for just about everything—ATM accounts, e-mail, employer networks. Having finagled a password, the thief can try accessing other accounts belonging to the victim. So, one day you have a nice cushion in your checking account, and the next you're dead-broke.

When Tom Anderson, left, and Chris DeWolfe founded the social networking Internet site MySpace.com in July 2003, they had no idea their business would become an overnight success. But with this quick success came concerns about privacy. Parents, schools, and law enforcement agencies are worried that the site can make young people, who post personal information and pictures on the site, vulnerable to sexual predators. In response, MySpace.com appointed its first chief security officer, who will administer safety, education, and privacy programs for the company. In addition, MySpace.com started an advertising campaign to educate young people about Internet safety.

Invasion of Privacy

If you apply for a life-insurance policy online, you may be asked to supply information about your health. If you apply for a mortgage online, you may be asked questions about your personal finances. Some people shy away from Internet transactions because they're afraid that such personal information can be stolen or shared with unauthorized parties. Once again, they're right: It does happen.

How Do "Cookies" Work? In addition to data that you supply willingly, information about you can be gathered online without your knowledge or consent.[34] Your online activities, for example, can be captured by something called a *cookie*. The process is illustrated in Figure 11.9. When you access a certain Web site, it sends back a unique piece of information to your browser, which proceeds to save it on your hard drive. When you go back to the same site, your browser returns the information, telling the site who you are and confirming that you've been there before. The problem is not that the cookie can identify you in the same way as a name or an address. It is, however, linked to other information about you—such as the goods you've bought or the services you've ordered online. Before long, someone will have compiled a profile of your buying habits. The result? You'll soon be bombarded with advertisements targeted to your interests. For example, let's suppose you check out the Web site for an online diet program. You furnish some information but decide that the program is not for you. The next time you log on, you may be greeted by a pop-up pushing the latest miracle diet.

Cookies aren't the only form of online espionage. Your own computer, for example, monitors your Internet activities and keeps track of the URLs that you access.

SHORING UP SECURITY AND BUILDING TRUST

So what can companies do to ease concerns about the safety of Internet transactions? First, businesses must implement internal controls for ensuring adequate security and privacy. Then, they must reassure customers that they're competent to safeguard credit-card numbers, passwords, and other

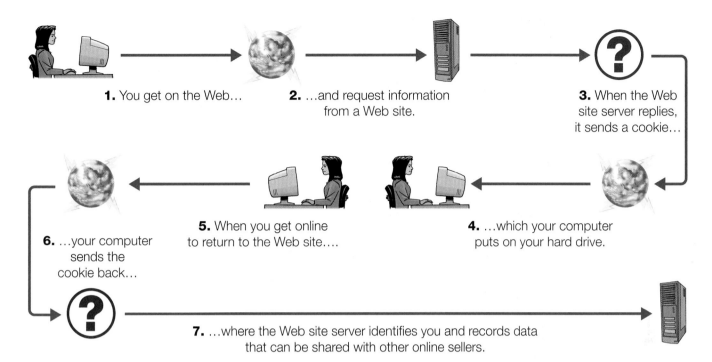

1. You get on the Web…

2. …and request information from a Web site.

3. When the Web site server replies, it sends a cookie…

6. …your computer sends the cookie back…

5. When you get online to return to the Web site….

4. …which your computer puts on your hard drive.

7. …where the Web site server identifies you and records data that can be shared with other online sellers.

personal information. Among the most common controls and assurance techniques, let's look at *encryption* and *seals of assurance*.

Encryption

The most effective method of ensuring that sensitive computer-stored information can't be accessed or altered by unauthorized parties is **encryption**—the process of encoding data so that only individuals (or computers) armed with a secret code (or key) can decode it. Here's a simplified example: You want to send a note to a friend on the other side of the classroom, but you don't want anyone else to know what it says. You and your friend could devise a code in which you substitute each letter in the message with the letter that's two places before it in the alphabet. So you write *A* as *C* and *B* as *D* and so on. Your friend can decode the message, but it'll look like nonsense to anyone else. This is an oversimplification of the process. In the real world, it's much more complicated: Data are scrambled using a complex code, the key for unlocking it is an algorithm, and you need certain computer hardware to perform the encryption/decryption process.

Certificate Authorities The most commonly used encryption system for transmitting data over the Internet is called *secure sockets layer (SSL)*. You can tell if a Web site uses SSL if its URL begins with *https* instead of *http*. SSL also provides another important security measure: When you connect to a site that uses SSL (for example, your bank's site), your browser will ask the site to authenticate itself—prove that it is who it says it is. You can be confident that the response is correct if it's verified by a **certificate authority**—a third-party (such as VeriSign) that verifies the identify of the responding computer and sends you a digital certificate of authenticity stating that it trusts the site.

Careers in Information Management

The number and variety of opportunities in the IS field have grown substantially as organizations have expanded their use of IT. In most large organizations, the senior management team includes a *chief information officer (CIO)* who oversees information and

Figure 11.9

How Cookies Work

---

encryption
Process of encoding data so only individuals or computers armed with a secret code (or key) can decode it.

certificate authority
Third-party (such as VeriSign) that verifies the identify of a computer site.

telecommunications systems. A large organization might also have a *chief technology officer* who reports to the CIO and oversees IT planning and implementation.

Most entry-level IS jobs require a business degree with a major in information systems. Many people supplement their IS majors with minors in computer science or some other business area, such as accounting, finance, marketing, or operations management.

If you're starting out with an IS degree, you may choose to follow either a management path or a technical path. At Kraft Foods, for example, IS professionals can focus on one of two areas: applications development (a management focus) and information technology (a technology focus). "Applications development," according to the company itself, "calls for an ability to analyze [Kraft's] clients' needs and translate them into systems applications. Information technology calls for the ability to convert business systems specifications

into technical specifications and to provide guidance and technical counsel to other Kraft professionals."[35] Despite the differences in focus, Kraft encourages IS specialists to develop expertise in both areas. After all, it's the ability to apply technical knowledge to business situations that make IS professionals particularly valuable to organizations. (By the way, if you want a career in casinos, you can major in casino management at a number of business schools.)

QUICK QUIZ   11.3

Before you finish the chapter, give yourself a quick quiz on the material covered in the preceding sections, including computer and data communication networks, e-commerce, and issues in electronic security.

Go to www.exploringbusinessonline.com

Summary of Learning Objectives

1. **Define *information system* (IS) and identify the tasks of the IS manager.**

   Data are unprocessed facts. **Information** is data that have been processed or turned into some useful form. To gather and process data into information and distribute it to people who need it, an organization develops an **information system (IS)**—the combination of technologies, procedures, and people who collect and distribute the information needed to make decisions and coordinate and control companywide activities. In most large organizations, the information system is operated by a senior management team that includes a **chief information officer (CIO)** who oversees information and telecommunications systems. There may also be a **chief technology officer** who reports to the CIO and oversees IT planning and implementation.

   The tasks of **information managers** include: (1) determining the information needs of people in the organization; (2) collecting the appropriate data; (3) applying technology to convert data into information; and (4) directing the flow of information to the right people. The job is complicated by the fact that information needs vary according to different lev-

   els, operational units, and functional areas. At the same time, information must be shared. To channel information to multiple users, large and mid-sized companies often rely on a highly integrated system called an **enterprise resource planning (ERP) system**. An ERP system integrates the computer needs of all business activities *across the enterprise* into a single computer system that serves all users.

2. **Explain how IS managers capture, store, and analyze data.**

   Organizations capture and store data in **databases**—electronic collections of related data that can be accessed by various people in the organization. To facilitate data analysis, IS managers may move data from various databases into a **data warehouse**—a centralized database in which data are consolidated and organized for efficient analysis. To come up with answers to a huge range of questions, managers perform a technique called **data mining**—the process of searching and analyzing large amounts of data to reveal patterns and trends that can be used to predict future behavior.

3. **Discuss ways in which an IS can be designed to meet the needs of individuals at various organizational levels.**

Information needs vary according to managerial level (top, middle, or first-line). An IS can be divided into two categories: (1) those that meet the needs of low-level managers and (2) those that meet the needs of middle- and upper-level managers. Low-level managers—those who run day-to-day operations and make routine decisions—use **operations support systems**, which usually fall into three categories. (1) Most daily activities are recorded and processed by a **transaction processing system**, which receives input data and converts them into output—information—intended for various users. (2) **Process control** refers to the application of technology to monitor and control physical processes, such as food preparation. The system depends on sensors to collect data for analysis by a computer programmed either to make adjustments or to signal an operator. (3) Technology can be used to design and make products. **Computer-aided design (CAD)** software, for instance, enables designers to test computer models digitally before moving new products into the prototype stage.

Mid- and upper-level managers may use one of four types of **management support system** to assist in decision-making activities. (1) A **management information system (MIS)** extracts data from a database to compile reports, such as sales analyses, needed for making routine decisions. (2) A **decision support system (DSS)** is an interactive system that collects and integrates data from multiple sources to assist in making nonroutine decisions. (3) To develop plans and make major decisions, managers may gather relevant, timely, easily understood information through an **executive information system (EIS)**; an EIS provides ready access to strategic information that's customized to their needs and presented in a convenient format. (4) An **expert system (ES)** mimics expert judgment by following sets of rules that experts would follow; it relies on **artificial intelligence (AI)**—the science of developing computer systems that can mimic human behavior.

4. **Describe the main systems for sharing information through networked computers.**

Once an organization has grown to more than a few employees, it needs to network individual computers to allow them to share information and technologies. A **client-server system** links a number of client machines (for data input and retrieval) with a server (for storing the database and the programs that process data).

Many companies want personal computers to run their own software and process data independently. But they also want individuals to share databases, files, printers, and **applications software** that performs particular types of work (word processing, creating and managing spreadsheets, and so forth). There are two systems that can satisfy both needs. A **local area network (LAN)** links computers in close proximity, connecting them by cables or by wireless technology. A **wide area network (WAN)** covers a relatively large geographical area and connects computers by telephone lines, wireless technology, or satellite.

5. **Explain how four networking technologies—the Internet, the World Wide Web, intranets, and extranets—make data communication possible.**

Data communication networks transmit digital data from one computer to another computer using a variety of wired and wireless communication channels. One such network, the **Internet**, is an immense global network of smaller interconnected networks linking millions of computers. By connecting paying subscribers into the Internet infrastructure, a company called an **internet service provider (ISP)** provides services, such as e-mail, online conferencing, and instant messaging.

A large portion of the Internet, the **World Wide Web** ("the Web"), is a subsystem of computers that can be accessed by means of a special protocol known as *hypertext transfer protocol (HTTP)*. Computers on the Web are connected with **hypertext links** that permit users to navigate among Internet resources. A Web **browser** is software that locates and displays Web pages. Although the Web couldn't exist without the Internet, it's the Web that provides such multimedia material as pictures, sounds, and streaming videos. Businesses use the Internet for four purposes: presenting information, selling products, acquiring goods and services, and distributing digital products.

Whereas the Internet is a public network that anyone can use, a company's **intranet** is a private network that's available only to its employees; access is controlled by a software program called a *firewall*. An **extranet** is an intranet that's partially available to certain outside parties, such as suppliers.

6. **Identify and discuss challenges faced by companies engaged in e-commerce.**

Though a source of vast opportunities, **e-commerce**—conducting business over the Internet—also presents some unprecedented challenges, particularly in the area of security. *Malicious programs*, such as viruses and worms, can wreak havoc with computer systems.

Unauthorized parties may gain access to restricted company Web sites in order to steal funds or goods. **Firewalls**—software and hardware systems that prevent unauthorized users from accessing computer networks—help to reduce the risks of doing business online.

Companies that do business online are also vulnerable to illegal activities. A *denial-of-service attack*, for example, prevents a Web server from servicing authorized users; the culprit demands a ransom to stop the attack. Companies that use the Internet to create and sell intellectual property (such as songs, movies, and software) face the problem of *piracy*. The theft of digital products, which can be downloaded and copied almost instantly over the Internet, not only cheats the individuals and organizations that create them,

but also reduces sales and shrinks corporate profits.

Finally, online businesses must convince consumers that it's safe to buy things over the Internet—that credit-card numbers, passwords, and other personal information are protected from theft. One effective method for protecting computer-stored information is **encryption**—the process of encoding data so that only individuals (or computers) armed with a secret code (or key) can decode it. A commonly used encryption scheme is a *secure sockets layer* (*SSL*), which directs the user's browser to ask a site to authenticate itself. Often, the user receives a digital certificate of authenticity, verifying that a third-party security provider called a **certificate authority** has identified a computer.

Questions and Problems

1. Using the college-application process as an example, explain the difference between *data* and *information*. Identify the categories of data that you supplied on your college application and the information generated from them by the admissions department.

2. **AACSB** ▸ **Analysis**
   Consider these three positions at Starbucks: retail store manager (in charge of the day-to-day operations at one store), district manager (responsible for the operations at multiple stores), and president of Starbucks North America (in charge of operations throughout the United States, Canada, and Mexico). Identify the information needs of managers at each level.

3. **AACSB** ▸ **Analysis**
   Harrah's uses data mining to identify its most profitable customers and predict their future behavior. It then designs incentives to appeal specifically to these customers. Do you see any ethical problems with this process? Is it ethical to encourage people to gamble? Explain your answer.

4. **AACSB** ▸ **Analysis**
   For each of the following situations, select the appropriate management support system (MSS) to aid the user: decision support system, executive support system, or expert system. In each case, describe the MSS that you recommend.

   • You're trying to identify a rash on your arm.

   • You own two golf courses in the Northeast, and you're thinking about building one in Florida. You need to gather and analyze information about your current operations in the Northeast as well as external information about the golf industry in Florida.

   • You own three McDonald's franchises. Every morning, you want to know the revenues and costs at each store. You're also interested in a breakdown of revenues by product and costs by category of expense (salaries, food and ingredients, maintenance, and so on).

5. What's the difference between a LAN and a WAN? Give an example of the use to which each type of system can be put. Does your college maintain either type of computer network?

6. If asked by your instructor, how would you explain the difference between the Internet and the World Wide Web?

7. **AACSB** ▸ **Analysis**
   Identify 10 specific ways in which your college uses the Internet.

8. **AACSB** ▸ **Analysis**
   In what ways could a large automobile dealership, with a service shop and body shop, benefit from an ERP system?

9. **AACSB** ▸ **Reflective Skills**
   Why is studying IT important to you as a student? How will competency in this area help you get and keep a job in the future?

10. **AACSB** ▸ **Reflective Skills**
    Are you, or someone you know, hesitant to buy things over the Internet? What risks concern you? What are companies doing to ease consumer's concerns about the safety of Internet transactions?

Learning on the Web

Taking Care of Your Cyber Health

It seems that some people have nothing better to do than wreak havoc by spreading computer viruses, and as a computer user, you should know how to protect yourself from malicious tampering. One place to start is by reading the article "How Computer Viruses Work," by Marshall Brain, which you can access by going to www.exploringbusinessonline.com and linking to the How Stuff Works Web site. After reading the article, answer the following questions:

1. Why do people create viruses?

2. What can you do to protect yourself against viruses?

Career Opportunities

Could You Manage a Job in IT or IS?

Do you have an aptitude for dealing with IT? Would you enjoy analyzing the information needs of an organization? Are you interested in directing a company's Internet operations or overseeing network security? If you answered yes to any of these questions, then a career in IT and IS might be for you. Go to www.exploringbusinessonline.com to link to the U.S. Department of Labor Web site and learn more about the nature of the work, qualifications, and job outlook in IT and IS management. Bearing in mind that many people who enter the IT field attain middle-management positions, look for answers to the following questions:

1. What kinds of jobs do IT managers perform?

2. What educational background, work experience, and skills are needed for positions in IT management?

3. What's the current job outlook for IS and IT managers? What factors drive employment opportunities?

4. What's the median annual income of a mid-level IT manager?

Ethics Angle AACSB

Campus Commando or Common Criminal?

Do you want to be popular (or at least more prominent) on campus? You could set up a Web site that lets fellow students share music files over the campus network. All you have to do is seed the site with some of your own downloaded music and let the swapping begin. That's exactly what Daniel Peng did when he was a sophomore at Princeton. It was a good idea, except for one small hitch: It was illegal and he got caught. Unimpressed with Peng's technological ingenuity, the Recording Industry Association of America (RIAA) sued him, and he was forced to settle for $15,000. Instead of delivering music, Peng's Web site now asks visitors to send money to help defray the $15,000 and another $8,000 in legal costs.

To learn more about the case, do some Internet research. Go to www.exploringbusinessonline.com to link to Peng's new Web site and check out the sources of information he provides. Then, conduct a Google search to find some information on your own. After researching the topic, answer the following questions:

1. The practice of sharing music files is illegal. Do you think that it's also unethical? Why or why not?

2. What steps to curb the practice are being taken by the music industry? By college administrators? By the government? Do you approve of these steps? Have they been effective?

3. What, ultimately, do you see as the solution to the problem?

Team-Building Skills AACSB

CampusCupid.com

It's no secret that college can be fun. For one thing, you get to hang around with a bunch of people your own age. Occasionally, you want to spend time with just one special someone, but finding that special person on a busy campus can take some of the fun out of matriculating. Fortunately, you're in the same love boat with a lot of other people, so one possible solution—one which meshes nicely with your desire to go into business—is to start an online dating service that caters to your school. Inasmuch as online dating is nothing new, you can do some preliminary research. For example, go to www.exploringbusinessonline.com to link to the Internetnews Web site and read the article "Online Personals: Big Profits, Intense Competition."

Next, you and several of your classmates should work as a team to create a business model for an online dating service at your school. After working out the details, submit a group report that covers the following issues:

1. **Services:** How will you earn revenues? What services will you offer? How will you price these services? What forms of payment will you accept? Will you sell ads? If so, what kinds?

2. **Appearance:** What will your site look like? Will it have graphics? Sound? Video? What will your domain name be? What information will you collect from customers? What information will you provide to visitors?

3. **Operations:** What criteria will you use to match customers? How will your customers interface with the Web site? How will they hook up with each other? Will you design your own software or buy or lease it from vendors, such as AE Webworks or EC Dating? Before you answer, go to www.prenhall.com/collins to link to the two Web sites and check out their dating software.

4. **Attracting Customers:** How will you attract customers to the site? How will you monitor and analyze site activity?

5. **Security:** How will you guarantee confidentiality? How will you ensure that your site is secure? How will you limit access to students at your school?

6. **Opportunities and Challenges:** What opportunities do e-businesses offer? What challenges do they create? How would your business model change if you decided to run it as a traditional business rather than as an e-business?

The Global View AACSB

"Hong Kong—Traditional Chinese"

Hewlett-Packard (HP) provides technology solutions to individuals, businesses, and institutions around the world. It generates annual revenues of $80 billion from the sale of IT products, including computers, printers, copiers, digital photography, and software. Anyone in the United States who wants to buy an HP product, get technical support, download software, learn about the company, or apply for a job can simply go to the HP Web site. But what if you live in Hong Kong? How would you get answers to your questions? You'd do the same thing as people in this country—go to HP's Web site.

Try to imagine, however, the complex process of developing and maintaining a Web site that serves the needs of customers in more than 70 countries. To get a better idea, go to www.exploringbusinessonline.com to link to the HP Web site. Start by looking at HP's line of notebooks and checking its

prices. Then, review the company information that's posted on the site, and, finally, look for a job (it's good practice).

Now pretend that you live in Hong Kong and repeat the process. If you can read Chinese, click on "Hong Kong—Traditional Chinese." Otherwise, click on "Hong Kong—English." Then, answer the following questions:

1. How easy was it to navigate the site and to switch back and forth between the U.S. and Hong Kong sections of the site?

2. Identify at least five differences between the two sections.

3. Does HP's Web site meet the needs of customers in both the United States and Hong Kong? Why or why not? How could it be improved?

Business Plan Project

Group Writing Assignment: *Final Plan*

REPORT

The team should submit a final version of its business plan. The "Introducing the Business Plan" document contained in Appendix A (page 307) provides details on the length of the plan, writing style, and section requirements.

REASONABLE CONTRIBUTIONS

All members of the team who make a reasonable contribution to the report should sign it. (If any team member does not work on the report, his or her name should *not* appear

on it.) If a student who has made a contribution is unable to sign the report (because of sickness or some other valid reason), the team can sign his or her name. To indicate that a name was signed by the team on a member's behalf, be sure to attach a note to the signature.

Appendix A

Introducing Your Business Plan

OVERVIEW

The purpose of the business plan project is to introduce you to the excitement and challenges of starting a business. We want you to be as fascinated with the prospect of running a business as Michael Dell was when he started Dell Computer from his college dorm. Or as enthusiastic as Phil Knight was when he thought of the company now called Nike in order to fulfill a graduate-school assignment.

We're going to give you the same opportunity that Knight seized when he was a student. Working with a team of classmates, you'll develop an idea for starting a company that competes in the same industry as the company that you're studying. Thus, if you're studying Nike, your proposed company will be part of the industry that sells athletic shoes, apparel, and equipment. Like Knight, you, too, will introduce and describe your future business in the form of a business plan.

The business plan project is a major component of the course and has been designed to guide you throughout the semester by helping you focus on the job of developing and preparing your business plan. The quality of the final product is up to you and your fellow team members. We hope that each team will not only provide a business plan that they're proud of but will enjoy the process of collaborating on the project.

CHOICES AND TASKS

As you progress with this project, you'll face a number of choices and tasks:

1. Type of Company

Your fictitious company can be any type of company as long as it's connected to the industry in which the company that you're studying competes. It doesn't have to do exactly the same thing that your sample company does. For example, it could be a component supplier to the industry, a competitor (making some innovative product), an industry publication, a company providing services to those in the industry, or a retailer.

The most important decision that your team will make is what your *great business idea* will be. Put a lot of thought into this task. A great business idea won't ensure a successful business plan, but you'll find it hard to construct a workable business plan if you don't build it around a good business idea.

2. Resources

Use multiple resources to develop your business plan. Resources include your text, other texts, the Internet, materials handed out in class or obtained from the class Web site, library research, newspapers (such as the *Wall Street Journal*, the *New York Times* and the *Financial Times*), business periodicals (such as *BusinessWeek* and *Fortune*), industry publications, materials received directly from companies in the industry, discussions with business leaders, and consultations with your course instructor.

To produce an excellent business plan, you should also take advantage of the constructive feedback that you'll get throughout the course from your classmates, your instructor, and others.

3. Format for the Written Business Plan

A **business plan** is a written description of a business. It provides the reader with an interesting story of what the proposed business will be like. It's also an indispensable tool for attracting investors and/or obtaining bank loans for a new business. The standard business plan format section of this document lays out the format to follow in creating your business plan.

4. Group Writing Assignments (Subsections of the Business Plan)

During the course, your team will complete 10 group writing assignments, in addition to the final version of your business plan. Each of these group writing assignments pertains to a subsection of the business plan. These subsections are described in the "Section Descriptions" section of this document. The group writing assignments are designed to ensure that teams make steady progress on their business plan projects. You'll receive feedback from your instructor on these group writing assignments, and you'll be expected to respond to these suggestions and incorporate your responses into the writing of your final business plan.

Although your final business plan will build on the subsections submitted throughout the semester, the final version should be more than just a cut-and-paste version of previously submitted sections. Producing a final version of the business plan requires additional research and substantial rewriting of the sections that you've produced during the course. In addition, your final version will include sections that haven't been assigned earlier.

STANDARD BUSINESS PLAN FORMAT: INSTRUCTIONS

Length

The team-prepared business plan should be no more than 15 single-spaced pages (not including the title page and table-of-contents page), with a maximum of 10 pages of appendixes. Double space after headings and between paragraphs and use 12-point type.

Writing Style

Spelling errors are inexcusable (there's a spelling-check on your computer), and grammatical errors are frowned upon. Although it will be a team effort, you want your business plan to read as if one person wrote it, not as if individually written sections had been glued together at the last minute. With these stipulations in mind, each group should assign someone to ensure that the individual sections fit together into a coherent presentation.

Minimum Requirements

Your team-prepared business plan should address all the issues raised in this document. Each team is encouraged to supplement required information with additional relevant material. For example, if social responsibility issues are particularly relevant to your company, you can add a section even though the topic is not required.

Deviations from Standard Format

Because the structure and content of a business plan can vary according to the type of business proposed, your team may need to alter some details in the sample format in order to describe your proposed company. You should let your instructor know of any significant changes in format.

Section Descriptions

1. Title Page

The title page must contain the following:

- Name of the proposed business
- Name of each team member

2. Table of Contents

Self-explanatory.

3. Executive Summary

The **executive summary** is a synopsis that should give the reader a preview of what's contained in the business plan. It's what the reader looks at first and should capture the reader's attention. An effective approach in writing the executive summary is to paraphrase important sentences from each section of the business plan. This process will ensure that the essential information of each section is included in the executive summary. The executive summary should be one to three pages long and should be written *after the entire business plan is completed*. This section is very important. Spend time on it.

4. Description of Proposed Business

Here, you present a *brief* description of your proposed company. The purpose of this section is to tell the reader why you're starting your business, what benefits it provides, and why it will be successful. Some of questions to answer in this section include:

- Why are you starting your company? What market need will you meet?
- What is the basic activity of the business?
- Will the company focus on manufacturing, retail, or service?
- What goods or services will the business provide?
- Who will be your primary customers?
- Where will your company be located?
- Why will your company be successful?

Because later parts of the plan will provide detailed answers to many of these questions, this section should provide only an overview.

5. Industry Analysis

In developing this section of your business plan, the team's first challenge will be to identify the industry in which its company will compete. Next, you'll need to learn as much as possible about that industry. The industry analysis section of your plan should provide an overall assessment of the industry. It should answer such questions as:

- How large is the industry? What are total sales for the industry in volume and dollars?
- Is the industry mature or are new companies successfully entering it?
- What opportunities exist in the industry? What threats?
- What factors will influence future expansion or contraction of the industry?
- What is the overall outlook for the industry?
- Who are your major competitors in the industry?
- How does your product differ from those of your competitors?

6. Mission Statement and Core Values

The **mission statement** describes the purpose or mission of your organization—the reason for its existence. It tells the reader what the organization is committed to doing.

Core values are fundamental beliefs about what is and is not appropriate and what is important in conducting company activities. Core values are not about profits, but rather about ideals. Their function is to help guide the behavior of individuals in the organization.

7. Management Plan

Management makes the key decisions for the business, such as its legal form and organizational structure. This section of the business plan should outline these decisions and provide information about the qualifications of the key management personnel.

A. **Legal Form of the Organization.** Report the legal form of business ownership chosen by your company, along with the rationale for your choice.

B. **Qualifications of Management Team and Compensation Package.** (*Note: In describing management qualifications, pretend that all team members graduated from college 10 years ago.*) Provide information about the qualifications of the management team members (education, experience, expertise, etc.). Also indicate the estimated annual salary to be paid to each member of the management team.

C. **Organizational Structure.** Describe the relationships among individuals within the company, listing the major responsibilities of each member of your management team. Present these relationships graphically by including an organization chart (either in the body of the document or as an appendix).

8. Goods or Services and (If Applicable) Production Process

This section provides a detailed description of all goods and services to be provided to the marketplace. You should identify the characteristics of your goods or services, such as appearance, features, quality, reliability, durability, usability, and ease of maintenance. Explain why your proposed goods or services have advantages over those offered by your competitors. In other words, be sure to answer the question: What competitive advantage will your company have over similar goods or services now on the market?

This section should also indicate how the company intends to obtain or produce the products that it will sell. Your write-up will depend on whether your company is a service company, a retailer, or a manufacturer.

A. **Service Companies.** For each service offered, indicate how the service will be provided. Also furnish information about the number and qualifications of people that the company will employ.

B. **Retail Companies.** Explain where the company will purchase the products that it will resell. Who will be your key suppliers?

C. **Manufacturers.** Furnish information about product design and production process. Be sure to address the following questions: How will products be designed? What technology will be needed to design and manufacture products? Will the company run its own production facilities, or will products be manufactured by subcontractors? Where will production facilities be located? What type of equipment will be used? What are the design and layout of the facilities? How will the company ensure that its products are of high quality?

9. Marketing

This section should focus on your target market and customer needs as well as product characteristics, pricing, distribution, and promotion. Each of these items is briefly described below:

A. **Target Market.** Provide a profile of your intended customers (age, gender, income, interests, etc.). If your company plans to sell to other companies, profile the typical business customer who will purchase your products.

B. **Customer Needs and Product Characteristics.** Identify your customers' needs or wants and link them to the characteristics (appearance, features, quality, reliability, durability, usability, ease of maintenance) you described in your "Goods or Services and Production Process" section.

C. **Pricing.** Describe your proposed pricing strategy for each product and indicate why you selected that particular pricing option. Compare your pricing strategy to that of your competitors.

D. **Distribution.** Describe the means by which your goods or services will be distributed to customers. Will you sell to customers directly, over the Internet, or through retailers or wholesalers? How will you get your products from your suppliers, subcontractors, or manufacturing facilities to your customers? Will you have your own warehouse?

E. **Promotion.** Outline a promotion strategy for your company. How will you tell people about your product and persuade potential customers to buy it? What types of advertising will you use? How will you maintain positive relationships with your customers?

F. **E-Business.** If you intend to use the Internet to promote or sell your products, also provide answers to these questions:

- Will your company have a Web site? Who will visit the site?
- What will it look like? What information will it supply?
- Will you sell products over the Internet?
- How will you attract customers to your site and entice them to buy from your company?

10. Global Issues (If Applicable)

Will your company be involved in international markets, whether by buying, manufacturing, or selling in other countries? If so, what obstacles will you face because you're operating in a global environment? How will you overcome these obstacles? If you don't plan to operate internationally when you first start up, what strategies, if any, will you use to move into international markets at a later time?

11. Financial Plan

This section will provide projected sales forecasts and income statements for a three-year period. It will also indicate the funding you need for start-up and initial operations as well as proposed sources of funding. We provide details on how to estimate sales in Appendix B. We'll tell you what you'll need for your financial plan and how to prepare your financial reports in Appendix C.

12. Appendixes

You may want to provide certain information in an appendix rather than in the body of the document. For example, you might want to include the detailed financial reports in the appendix (although you should still include a summary discussion of financing in the body of the document). Other possible attachments you could include in the appendix: organization chart, résumés of your management team, drawings or pictures of your product, sketches or pictures of your facilities, floor plans of manufacturing facilities, results of any marketing surveys, or documents used to apply for a patent.

13. References

Be sure to cite any outside sources that you use in preparing your business plan.

Appendix B

Estimating Sales

You're about to start one of the most interesting activities in the whole business plan project—figuring out the money. At this point, you must determine three things:

1. How much money you'll need to start your business
2. Where you'll get the money
3. Whether you'll operate at a profit (or incur a loss) for your first three years of operations

The most important aspect of this exercise—and the first thing you need to do—is *to estimate sales in both units and total dollars*. Why are these estimates so important? Because your proposed level of sales will determine the size and scope of your business: how many employees you'll have, how much equipment you'll need to buy, how much money you'll spend on advertising, how much money you'll need to borrow to get started, and so on. Moreover, spending time right now to estimate a reasonable level of sales will give you a head start on a much bigger job—completing the financial section of your business plan. Before you get started, remember that your sales estimates will probably change as you make headway with the financial planning process, but that's okay.

APPROACHES TO ESTIMATING SALES

There are several different ways to estimate sales, but we'll restrict ourselves to four of the most manageable:

1. Calculating percentage of the total U.S. market
2. Calculating percentage of a geographical market
3. Using competitors' financial reports
4. Backing into an estimate.

In illustrating these four approaches, we'll assume that your company plans to sell athletic shoes. To keep things simple, we'll also assume that you'll be offering just one model of athletic shoe and that you'll be selling shoes only in the United States.

Calculating Percentage of the Total U.S. Market

First you need to find information on the total number of pairs of athletic shoes sold each year in the United States. Then, you'll multiply that total by *the percentage of the market that you expect to capture.* Remember: As a newcomer, you'll be getting a *very* small slice of the market; thus, the percentage of the total that you allot yourself should be *very* small (we can hardly overemphasize how *very* small we're talking about). Once you've come up with an estimate of the number of shoes that you expect to sell—that is, *units*—you can determine total sales *dollars* by multiplying the number of units by the price that you intend to charge for each unit.

But watch out here: In determining the amount of money that you'll get for each pair of shoes, you're interested in determining *how much your company gets for each pair of shoes*, not *how much the customer pays for each pair.* Say, for example, that a customer buys a pair of your shoes for $70. You—that is, your company—won't get the whole $70; you'll get only

about half of it. Why? As a manufacturer, you don't sell shoes directly to customers; you sell them to retailers who, in turn, sell them to customers. It's the retailer, not the manufacturer, who's charging $70 per pair; the retailer probably paid about $35 per pair and has marked up the price to $70 in order to turn a profit. As the maker of the product, you should figure on getting about 50 percent of the price that the customer ultimately pays to the retailer.

Calculating Percentage of a Geographical Market

If you plan to sell shoes in only one geographical area (a particular state or even a particular city), you can obtain useful demographic information—say, the number of people within a certain age range—for estimating the number of athletic shoes that are sold in your designated area. If you plan to limit your sales to a particular city, you could talk with local shoe retailers and ask them how many pairs of athletic shoes they sell in a year. Armed with the pertinent information, you can then estimate your percentage of this market by following the same procedures that we described previously.

Using Competitors' Financial Reports

Competitor's financial statements can be a big help as you work on the financial section of your business plan. In this document, we'll discuss the ways in which competitors' financial statements can help you estimate sales. In subsequent documents, we'll highlight other ways in which competitors' statements can be useful.

Earlier, you analyzed the industry in which you planned to sell your goods or offer your services. Now that your product idea is more clearly defined, you might want to revisit your analysis and revise your list of competitors. There are several ways to identify competitors—conducting Internet searches, talking with people in the industry, reviewing industry publications, and so forth.

After an initial search, you may conclude that your product is unique and that you don't have any direct competitors. That's a mistake: Most of you should be able to identify a few competitors. Identifying competitors is a big advantage in estimating sales and in completing the financial section of your business plan.

Identifying Competitors and Finding Income Statements There are many ways to identify competitors and find copies of their income statements, and your faculty adviser will probably be able to give you some suggestions. The method we cover here includes an Internet search and begins with a five-step process: (Note: These instructions might need to be altered slightly if Yahoo! changes the format of its Web site.)

1. Go to Yahoo! (at <www.yahoo.com>).
2. In the list of topics on the left side, click on "Finance."
3. Scroll down until you find the box labeled "Investing" and click on "Industries."

4. Scroll down until you find the box labeled "Tools" and click on "Industry Index."

5. Following the instructions and examples that we give in the next section, identify your industry from the list that appears.

Our sample industry is athletic shoes. To continue with this example of an online search for financial information, follow the steps (beginning at Step 6) delineated below:

6. Toward the top of the screen, just under the heading "Industry Index," find the heading "View: By Sector/ Alphabetical." If the page is set on "Alphabetical" rather than "By Sector," click on "By Sector."

7. Scroll down the sector list to "Consumer Goods."

8. Scroll down and click on "Textile—Apparel Footwear & Accessories."

9. Under the heading "More on This Industry," click on "Company Index."

The main part of the screen will now give you an alphabetized list of companies.

10. Select Nike (or the company you are looking for).

11. At the bottom of the page, under the heading "More on NIKE, Inc.," click on "Financials."

12. If you're not looking at the company's "Income Statement," scroll down to the heading "Financials" at the bottom of the lower left-hand side of the screen and click on "Income Statement."

13. To get annual (as opposed to quarterly) financial information, click on "Annual Data."

14. Print out the annual income statement, which you will use to estimate your own sales (and to learn other relevant information about your competitor).

15. While you're on the Web site, explore some of the other information that the company has posted.

Here are a few more sample companies that you can explore by substituting the appropriate categories in Steps 7 through 10:

Product = Athletic Apparel

Sector = Consumer Goods
Click on "Textile—Apparel Clothing"
Click on "Company Index"
Click on "Quiksilver"

Product = Golf Clubs

Sector = Consumer Goods
Click on "Sporting Goods"
Click on "Company Index"
Click on "Callaway Golf Company"

Product = Sports Theme Parks

Sector = Services
Click on "Sporting Activities"
Click on "Company Index"
Click on "All-American SportPark, Inc."

Product = Nutrition Bars

Sector = Consumer Goods
Click on "Food Major Diversified"
Click on "Company Index"
Click on "PowerBar"

If you check out the last company on the list, you'll find that something interesting happens. Your next step would normally be to click on "Financials," but no such section is available for PowerBar. Now, if you go to the bottom-right corner of the PowerBar page, you'll find a promising listing headed "Top Competitors." Pick one of these—for example, Slim-Fast Foods Company—and click on it. Again, there are no financials available. What's the problem? Neither company releases separate financial statements because both are wholly owned subsidiaries of larger companies—PowerBar of the Swiss conglomerate Nestlé and Slim-Fast of Unilever, an international maker of packaged consumer goods.

How can you overcome such obstacles if you're determined to compete in the market for nutrition bars? Go back to the top of the "Company Index" and click on "Public." You'll now get a list of about 30 companies that are *publicly traded* and are required to make their financial information available to the public. If you click on each of these companies, you can find out if any of them is in the nutrition-bar business. As it turns out, none of them is, and although that might be good news for your projected business, you still don't have any more specific financial information than you had to start with. All you know (and this might be bad news) is that two goliaths of the food industry—Nestlé and Unilever—carry nutrition bars in their product mixes.

There are certain situations that make it difficult to obtain the kind of information you need. You might, for example, have a product that's so new or unique that it really has no competitors. There are alternative ways to get the information you need, but your best option is to search for another competitor. If you run into trouble, talk with your faculty advisor about different ways to estimate first-year sales.

Using Competitors' Financial Reports   Now that you have a good idea about how to find information about your competitors, you need to know how to use this information to estimate your own projected sales. As an example, we'll use K-Swiss, which makes white leather athletic shoes, and we'll provide a shortcut by giving you a Web site from which you can get started: <http://finance.yahoo.com/q/is?s=KSWS&annual>. Here, you'll find K-Swiss' income statement, which lists annual revenues for the year ended December 31. For 2005, the income given is $508,574. (Note that because this figure is *in thousands*, be sure to add three zeros—K-Swiss' sales for the year are actually $508,574,000).

Next, you need to know how many pairs of shoes K-Swiss sold. To keep things simple, we're going to assume that all K-Swiss' sales involve shoes. Finally, we need to determine how much each pair of K-Swiss shoes would sell for.

Let's estimate the average price paid by a buyer of K-Swiss shoes at $70 per pair. K-Swiss itself doesn't get $70 a pair because it sells the shoes to stores that mark them up in order to make a profit. Because K-Swiss sells shoes to stores for about half of what a customer pays for them, the manufacturer gets $35 for each pair of shoes it sells.

You're now in a position to estimate the number of shoes sold by K-Swiss for the year ending December 31, 2005:

$$\frac{\$508,574,000}{\$35} = 14,530,686$$

Let's pause for a moment to review what we've learned so far:

1. K-Swiss has annual sales of about $509 million.
2. K-Swiss sells about 15 million pairs of shoes a year (at a price to the retailer of $35).

Now, what are we going to do with this information? Recall that your team's task is to estimate sales for your company's first year in terms of both *number of units* and *dollars*. So let's start by using the K-Swiss information to estimate the number of units that you're going to sell.

First, you need to decide *what percentage of the market you can expect to capture*. To a certain extent, this task is a guessing game. Although you'd be extremely lucky if your first-year sales were even 1 percent of K-Swiss' sales, let's use 1 percent as an estimate. You can now calculate your first-year sales for pairs of shoes:

$$15,000,000 \times .01 = 150,000$$

Now, to get your final number—*sales in dollars for the first year*—you have to multiply the estimated number of pairs of shoes by the estimated price that you'll get from the retailer for each pair of shoes. For example, you expect to sell your shoes to the retailer for $50. (The retailer would sell them to the customer at double this amount—$100 a pair.) You can now determine your first-year sales in dollars:

$$150,000 \times \$50 = \$7,500,000$$

More than $7 million in sales—not bad for a first year. Unfortunately, it's not very realistic, either. You should probably reduce your expected sales (relative to those of K-Swiss) to 1/4 (or even 1/8) of a percent.

If you settle for the more realistic estimate of 1/4 of a percent of K-Swiss' sales, your first-year sales in dollars would be:

$$(15,000,000 \times .0025) = 37,500 \times \$50 = \$1,875,000$$

A little under $2 million is a much more rational number. You could probably afford an even more modest estimate. The key to your estimate (and to the likely success of your business) is the fact that the business must be large enough to support your executives (the members of your team) but not so large that the company is unmanageable. In general, revenues that range from $1 million to about $3 million work well (depending on the product).

Backing Into Your Sales Figure   Let's assume that you're going to sell something other than athletic shoes. What if, instead, you're going to produce a product that's so unique that there's no history of prior sales or past users? You've searched high and low for competitors but haven't been able to find a single company making a product even remotely similar to yours. In this case, you might have to "back into" your sales figure. Here's how the process works.

Your goal is to determine *the dollar amount of gross profit* (sales – cost of goods sold) that you'd need to accomplish the following:

- Cover salaries for the management team
- Generate enough cash to pay for advertising
- Allow your company to invest in R&D
- Pay salaries of other employees
- Pay other non-itemized expenses

Instead of estimating *sales*, therefore, you need to estimate these *costs*. When you add up your projected costs, you'll know the *estimated dollar amount that you'll need to turn a gross profit*. Then, applying the percentage figure called *gross profit as a percentage of sales*, you can project sales dollars. Finally, by dividing this dollar sales estimate by the selling price of your product (to the retailer), you can estimate the quantity of sales that you'll need.

Business Plan Project

The Facts   The following is a simple example. Let's start with a few facts:

- Each of the four members of your management team wants an annual salary of $60,000.

- You want to spend about $150,000 on advertising.

- R&D costs will about $100,000.

- Each of your five non-executive employees will earns $40,000 a year.

- Other (non-itemized expenses) will total approximately $110,000.

- You expect your cost of goods sold (CGS) to be 60 percent of sales; gross profit (sales minus CGS) will be 40 percent of sales.

- The projected selling price of your product (to the retailer) is $50.

The Process   Now, let's follow a four-step process designed to make use of these facts.

Step 1.   Add up your costs:

Executive salaries	$240,000 (4 × $60,000)
Advertising	150,000
R&D	100,000
Other salaries	200,000 (5 × $40,000)
Other expenses	110,000
Total	$800,000

In order to *break even* (have sales equal to expenses), your gross profit must be about $800,000.

Step 2. Determine sales by dividing $800,000 by .40 (which will give you gross profit as a percent of sales)

$$\frac{\$800,000}{.40} = \$2,000,000$$

Step 3. Check the accuracy of your sales figure by creating an *income statement*:

Sales	$2,000,000
CGS ($2M × .60)	1,200,000
Gross profit ($2M × .40)	800,000
Executive salaries	240,000
Advertising	150,000
R&D	100,000
Other salaries	200,000
Other expenses	110,000
Net income	$ 0

Congratulations! Your net income is $0, but your calculations are correct: If your sales total $2 million, your company breaks even. If you want to make a profit, you have to increase sales; if sales are under $2 million, you'll be operating at a loss.

Step 4. To determine the quantity of product that you must sell in order to break even, divide total sales dollars by the selling price of the product (to the retailer):

$$\frac{\$2,000,000}{\$50} = 40,000 \ units$$

This approach has certain flaws, but it does give you ball-park figures for sales in both dollars and units. You can then use this sales figure (and quantity sold) as a starting point in preparing your financial statements. As you complete these statements, you can revise your numbers. For years two and three, you'll want to increase both the quantity of items sold and the selling price per unit.

A FEW WORDS ABOUT FIRST-YEAR SALES

Be very conservative in estimating your first year's sales. They'll probably be much lower than sales for years two and three. Why? Because your business is new and people don't know your product. It will take time to build up demand. In addition, if you're making a product (or subcontracting the manufacture of a product), you'll need up to six months to get the product designed, produced, and distributed to store shelves, leaving you with only a six-month selling period in the first year.

Appendix C

Preparing Financial Reports with the Excel Template

HOW TO USE THE TEMPLATE

We have created an Excel template to help you prepare financial reports for your proposed business. You don't need experience in Excel to use this template, but there are a few things that you should know:

- A **yellow block** means that you fill in a number or words.
- The numbers in the **white blocks** are filled in by the template.
- You navigate through the template by clicking on the **worksheet tabs** located at the bottom of your screen.
- Because some tabs will be covered, you must access them by using the **arrows in the bottom right-hand corner** of the worksheet.
- You can use the **"Notes" pages** to provide explanations of various items contained in your financial reports.
- **Graphs** are created automatically as you fill in numbers.
- You can **copy graphs** into other documents, such as your business plan or PowerPoint slides.
- Remember to **save your template** after each use.

As you fill in the yellow blocks, the template automatically creates the following:

- A three-year projected income statement using a format that's appropriate for your type of business
- A graph comparing annual sales and income figures
- A statement showing the cash required to start your business
- A pie chart displaying the breakdown of cash requirements for your business
- A statement showing the cash sources that you'll use to fund your business
- A pie chart displaying the breakdown of your cash sources

The template also keeps track of the difference between cash required and sources of cash and lets you know if you have too much or too little cash.

Working Your Way Through the Template

You should complete the template in the following order:

Required for Accounting Reports group assignment:

- Business Type and Name
- Sales Plan
- Notes for Sales Plan
- Human Resources Plan
- Notes for Human Resources Plan
- Financial Assumptions
- Notes for Financial Assumptions

Required for Financial Plan group assignment:

- Cash Requirements
- Cash Sources
- Notes for Cash Requirements and Cash Sources

The process of creating the financial reports for your business plan is iterative. You'll change many of the numbers several times until you achieve the desired results—*realistic financial reports that support your business concept.*

Justification of Numbers

It would be nice if you could simply run through the template and put down any numbers you feel like, but you can't do that. First, your projected income statements (which are generated by the numbers that you input into the spreadsheet) will look unrealistic. Second, your instructor will require you to justify many of your numbers (thereby preventing you from just making them up).

Let's focus for a moment on the requirement that you *justify* your numbers. (We'll address the realism issue in a later section.) *At a minimum*, you must justify certain numbers for each of the three years covered by your income statement. Using the appropriate "notes" sections of the worksheet, you must explain how you came up with all the following numbers:

Sales Plan

- Unit price
- Unit sales

Human Resources Plan

- Percentage chosen to calculate benefits
- Position salaries
- Number of people

Financial Assumptions

- Cost-of-goods-sold percentage (if applicable)
- Commissions, bonuses, and other incentives
- Advertising expenses
- Research and development expenses
- Shipping expenses
- Building space (in square feet)
- Rent per square foot
- Unique and miscellaneous expenses (if significant)

Cash Requirements

- Building (including a discussion of the lease-versus-buy decision)
- Vehicles
- Research and manufacturing equipment
- Months of inventory

- Months of cash expenses
- Other cash needs

Cash Sources

- Interest rates (for all loans)
- Repayment periods (for all loans)
- Security

COMPLETING EACH SECTION

We'll now provide some guidance on completing each section of the spreadsheet. We'll cover each section in its recommended order of completion.

Business Type and Name

Begin working with your template by clicking on the worksheet tab labeled "Business Type and Name." First, put an "X" in the appropriate box to indicate whether your company is **goods based** or **service based**. In making this distinction, ask yourself this question: Am I supplying a *tangible (physical) good*? If you are, then you should classify your company as a goods-based company. Otherwise, you should classify yourself as a service-based company. Goods-based companies include retailers, manufacturers, and restaurants. Gyms, hotels, golf courses, advertising agencies, and sports consultants are service-based companies—they provide personal services or expertise rather than tangible goods. If your company provides both goods and services, put an "X" in both boxes.

Next, type in the name of your company so that it will be displayed in all your financial statements.

Sales Plan

To work on your sales plan, click the "Sales Plan" worksheet tab. The information that you recently gathered to complete your **estimating sales group report** will come in handy here. Recall that you were asked to decide on all the following: (a) the goods or services that your company will offer, (b) the amount that you'll charge for each product, (c) the number of units that you'll sell of each product, and (d) your total sales in dollars. Get in the habit of reviewing your estimates regularly and revising them as needed.

To complete the Sales Plan section of the template, you'll do something similar: indicate what goods or services you'll provide, what price you'll charge per item, and the quantity you expect to sell. You'll provide this information for each of the first three years of operations. Note that your price per unit will probably increase each year by at least the rate of inflation (unless you're following a *skimming pricing strategy* in which you start out with high prices and then drop them). You identified your *pricing strategy* in the **marketing group report** that you completed earlier, and that information will help you here.

Remember that the price that you'll put on your product is the *amount that you'll get from your customer*—the person or company to whom *you* sell. Thus, if you produce a product that's sold through a retailer, your price is the amount that you charge the retailer. Here's an example:

- A customer buys a shoe from a retailer for $100.
- The retailer probably bought the shoe from the producer (your company) for half of this amount—$50—and marked it up in order to make a profit.
- The price of your product, therefore, is $50, not $100.

Also, remember to be very conservative in estimating first-year sales. They will probably be much lower than sales for years two and three. Why? Because it takes time to get your goods or services known to consumers, sales are often slow when you first start out. Finally, note that if you're starting a company that produces a good or subcontracts the manufacture of a good, it can take up to six months to get a product designed, produced, and distributed to store shelves; if your company falls into one of these categories, you may have only a six-month selling period in your first year.

Justification Before you finish with the Sales Plan section of your financial reports, click on the "Sales Plan Notes" tab and explain how you arrived at the following numbers:

- Unit price
- Quantity of units to be sold

HR Plan

To work on the HR portion of the template, click the worksheet tab labeled "HR Plan." This section asks you to identify the categories of workers that you'll employ and to stipulate their compensation (including benefits). Begin by filling in the yellow block marked "Cost of benefits as a percentage of salary." If you're not sure what benefits you should offer, return to Chapter 5 of the text ("Recruiting, Motivating, and Keeping Quality Employees") and review this topic.

Next, list the types of positions that your company will have in each functional area (accounting, finance, marketing, operations, and management). Then, indicate the number of people who will hold the stated positions and the *average salary* for each functional group. You'll find the group report that you completed on **management qualifications and compensation** helpful in setting salaries for your management team. The organization chart that you drew up for your **management plan group report** might help you in estimating the total number of employees and the areas in which they're needed. In estimating total number of employees, consider the size of your company as measured by sales. It's highly unlikely, for example, that your company can manage $2 million in sales with only five people on the payroll.

In identifying the people who work for you, do *not* include those who make your product(s). The cost of their salaries fall into the category of *Cost of goods sold* (which we'll discuss later). Finally, don't forget to give everybody a yearly raise: Everyone deserves some type of annual increase.

Justification Before you complete this section, go to the "Human Resources Notes" section and explain how you arrived at the following numbers:

- Percentage used to calculate benefits
- Salaries
- Number of employees in each functional category

Financial Assumptions

Click on the worksheet tab labeled "Financial Assumptions." Your team will make a series of financial assumptions that the spreadsheet uses to create projected income statements for the first three years of your company's operations. In completing this section of the worksheet, you're following a "business-decision" approach: Instead of creating your income statements directly, you'll be making a series of key business decisions, which, in turn, will create your income statements. You'll work with other members of your team to answer such questions as "What percentage is cost of goods sold relative to sales?" "How much should we spend on advertising?" "How much office space do we need, and how much will we pay per square foot?" These are all debatable items, and all members of the team should contribute to the decisions made about them.

Let's take a closer look at the format of the "Financial Assumptions" section. You'll notice that some of the white blocks are already filled in. These figures have been carried over from your Sales Plan and your Human Resources Plan. The spreadsheet reports *Planned sales* because this is an important figure in determining associated costs, such as advertising. Having it listed on this sheet saves you the task of going back to the sales plan to look for it. Another interesting figure calculated by the template is *Sales growth*. It should be fairly large for year two because, as we previously indicated, year-two sales will probably be substantially higher than year-one sales. Some HR information (number of people, cost of salaries, and cost of benefits) is also carried forward to the Financial Assumptions sheet. This information will be useful in estimating such people-related costs as commissions/bonuses and travel.

The white blocks next to *Buildings, equipment, and vehicles* and *Average life of assets* are blank. The program will fill these in later, as you're working on the Cash Requirements section of the worksheet. At this point, we'll focus on the numbers that *you* need to supply.

Cost of Goods Sold [*Note: ignore this section if you have a service business that does not produce a good.*] The most important business-plan estimate that you'll make is for *Sales. Cost of goods sold (CGS)* is number two. *CGS* represents the cost of making or buying your product for resale. If you're in the business of buying products for resale (or of outsourcing the production of your products), your CGS is the *amount you paid for the products that you sold during the year.* If your company manufactures its own products, your CGS includes the *cost of the materials used to make your products as well as the cost of labor and overhead utilized in the production of those products,* such as utilities and supplies. (We tend to discourage the self-manufacture of products: It's a lot easier to outsource manufacturing.)

CGS as Percentage of Sales Price The easiest way to predict CGS is by basing your estimate on a percentage of your sales price. Nike's CGS, for instance, is about 60 percent of sales. When Nike sells something to a retailer for $50, it has spent, on average, $30 to make the product. A good way to get a percentage figure for your CGS is to look at competitors' financial statements. If you didn't collect competitors' financial statements when you were creating your **estimating sales group report**, you might want to do it now. How can you determine the percentage figure for CGS from a competitor's financial statement? By using the following formula:

$$\frac{\text{Cost of goods sold}}{\text{Sales}}$$

Thus, if sales are $10,000 and CGS is $6,500, then

$$\frac{\$6,500}{\$10,000} = 65\%$$

CGS and Volume Note that CGS is sensitive to volume: As volume goes up, CGS—as a percentage of sales—goes down. Don't be surprised, then, if your percentage of CGS goes down a little (for example, a percent or two) as sales volume rises each year.

Commissions, Bonuses, and Other Incentives In addition to regular paychecks, some workers receive financial rewards based on performance. Salespeople, for example, might receive commissions on every product they sell; managers might receive year-end bonuses (or maybe prizes, like a trip to Hawaii). To calculate dollar amounts for incentives, you need to determine two things:

1. The criteria on which a reward is based (volume of sales, dollar amount of sales, performance on the job)
2. The number of employees who are included in the incentive program

Advertising Expenses Generally, advertising expenses are a fairly large number relative to sales. Nike, for example, spends about $.10 of each $1 of sales on advertising. You must estimate a total dollar amount for each year, and because businesses naturally try to attract customers and then spend less on advertising as a percentage of sales each year, you might want to start out high in year one. On the other hand, if you're coming out with a new product in year three, you might increase advertising dollars in year two to promote your forthcoming new product. Some forms of advertising are more expensive than others, and to estimate your cost, you'll need some understanding of the *type* of advertising that you'll be using. Your **marketing group report** should spell out the forms of advertising you plan to use.

Research and Development Expenses If you're designing a product, you'll probably incur research-and-development (R&D) costs—costs that can be significant in the early years. If you're a high-tech company or you're periodically improving your product or coming out with new products, your R&D costs might remain high for all three years. Your **products and production group report** should indicate how you intend to design and produce your product. In estimating R&D costs, do *not* include:[1]

- Costs for salaried R&D employees listed in your HR plan
- Costs of R&D *equipment*, which will be included in your cash requirements schedule

Costs that you *should* consider include:

- Materials consumed in R&D efforts
- Contract services performed by nonemployees
- Software development
- Engineering associated with product design
- Prototype development
- Testing

Shipping Expenses These costs apply to companies that ship goods from one location to another (for example, from a factory in Arizona to a warehouse in China). Depending on the distance and the volume of goods, shipping costs can be significant. Nike, for example, spends $.50 to ship a $35 shoe to a retailer—about 1.5 percent of each $1 of sales. The easiest approach to estimating shipping expenses is to assume that you'll use commercial shippers (such as FedEx or UPS) and to calculate costs as a percentage of sales dollars (naturally, total shipping costs will go up as sales dollars increase). You can get cost estimates for shipping by conducting an Internet search or by calling a commercial shipper.

Building Space and Rent The type of building and amount of building space that you'll need will depend on your business model. Here's a list of likely space needs by type of business:

- **Manufacturers who make their own products:** factory, warehouse (possibly), office space
- **Companies who outsource production:** warehouse (possibly), office space
- **Retailers:** retail space, office space
- **Specialized businesses, such as restaurants, fitness centers, hotels:** specialized space, office space
- **Consulting companies, such as advertising agencies:** office space

To Buy or to Rent? That's Not Really the Question Should you run out and buy a factory, office building, or warehouse? No. Most small businesses *rent* factory, warehouse, and office space, especially when the business is new. Even specialized businesses, such as restaurants and fitness centers, generally rent space rather than buy it. This practice makes sense for two reasons: First, as a start-up, you don't have the money to buy a new building; second, because it's hard to predict future needs, you're better off seeing how things work out before you commit money to real estate.

Researching Rental Costs How much does renting cost? Let's begin with office space. You can determine office-space costs by performing a two-step Internet-search process:

1. Search for an "office space calculator" that will help you determine the square footage that you'll need for the kind of office that you intend to set up.
2. Search for a price per square foot (per year) for office space in the geographic location where you intend to locate your office.

Now, enter the numbers that you find in the template, which will use them to calculate your rent or lease expense.

You might decide that your square-footage needs are the same for all three years, or you might decide that you'll eventually need more space. For our purposes, you can assume either that you have a three-year lease and that costs will stay the same for three years or that costs will rise over the course of three years. In either case, fill in the numbers for all three years. [*Hint:* Be sure that you get an *annual* cost-per-square-foot figure, not a monthly figure.]

How about leasing a warehouse? This is something that you'll have to consider if you're going to manufacture a good. If you arrange with a contract manufacturer to ship your products directly to your customers (retailers), you won't need a warehouse. Whether or not this approach is feasible depends on the number of retailers to whom you plan to sell.

If you decide to lease a warehouse, you can research the costs on the Internet. If you decide to lease a factory, you'll have to work with commercial real estate people to find out how much factory space costs in your chosen geographic area.

Utilities This is the stuff that makes your space workable—electricity, water, and the telephone. Make an estimate for *each year*, bearing in mind that costs go up every year.

Insurance This can be a big expense in some lines of business. If, for instance, you operate a gym—where people can and will get hurt—your insurance will probably be costly. Take the time to find out *how* costly (either by going online or by calling insurers). In addition, be sure to increase the cost of insurance *each year*. The extent of the increases will depend on the type of insurance. Insurance for company assets (office equipment, nonleased vehicles, research labs, and so on) will creep up by at least the rate of inflation. Insurance based on product liability (the prospect of someone getting hurt or becoming sick because of your product) will go up at the same rate as sales increases.

Repairs and Maintenance These expenses include repairs to equipment and building space (vehicles are covered in another category, appropriately called *Vehicle expense*). Because most of the assets in question will be new, this cost won't be very high in the beginning years; it will, however, go up over time.

Office Expenses These expenses cover such things as paper, postage, copying—all the costs associated with running an office. (It's not a big expense, so don't take much time estimating it.)

Travel Expenses Business trips cost money, and if you have to run around the country to promote your product, you might have some hefty travel costs. The more people you have running around the country (and the more lavishly they entertain themselves), the higher the cost.

Vehicle Expenses   You could buy some cars (or trucks) and show them on the list of items that you're buying to start your business (*Cash requirements*). In that case, these items would be *depreciated* (a concept that we'll discuss later). On the other hand, you could save your cash for other purposes by leasing any vehicles that your company will need. If you lease, this is the category in which you'd show the expense. It's also the place where you'd show the costs of gasoline and vehicle maintenance.

Unique and Miscellaneous Expenses   This category is for showing any expenses that are unique to your company. For example, if you're opening a golf course and you've hired Tiger Woods to promote it, his (huge) fee would go here. In addition, you might want to set aside some amount for miscellaneous expenses. Then, when your instructor asks you about a particular expense that you forgot about, you could say that you put it under *Miscellaneous expenses*.

Justification   As you work your way through this section, go to the "Financial Assumptions Notes" section (by clicking on the tab) and explain how you arrived at the following numbers:

- CSG percentage (if applicable)
- Commissions, bonuses, and other incentives
- Advertising expenses
- R&D expenses
- Shipping expenses
- Expenses for building space (in square feet)
- Building rent per square foot
- Unique and miscellaneous expenses (if significant)

The explanations of your financial assumptions are extremely important: They reflect the logic that underlies your key business decisions.

REVIEW YOUR INCOME STATEMENTS

At this point, you've completed everything required for your **accounting reports group assignment**. In addition to giving your instructor copies of the three sections of the template that you just completed (Sales Plan, Human Resources Plan, and Financial Assumptions), you'll turn in the notes to these sections so that your instructor can see how you arrived at your figures. You'll also turn in the preliminary income statements generated by the template. Before you submit these documents, however, you should review them carefully and do a quick check to see if they make sense. To access your income statements, click the worksheet tab labeled "Income Statement."

Some Tips on Reviewing Income Statements

- The template uses a format called *vertical percentage analysis*, which shows both dollar amounts and percentages. Each item on the income statement is expressed as a percentage of sales. If, for example, sales are $100,000

and CGS is $60,000, the percentage next to *CGS* would be 60 percent ($60,000/$100,000).

- Two expense items will be blank: *Depreciation expense* and *Interest expense*. The template won't calculate these numbers until you've completed the remaining sections of the template: *Cash Requirements* and *Cash Sources*. You'll notice that once these items have been entered into your income statement, your income will be reduced.

- If your company has generated an income at this early stage, your *Net income* amount won't have parentheses around it; if you have a loss, it will. Thus, a figure of *$10,000* means that you've generated a positive net income and a figure of (*$10,000*) means that you've sustained a loss.

Income (Loss) Ranges

Remember that when they're ultimately entered into your statement, the two missing expense items—depreciation and interest—will reduce your income. With that fact in mind, we'll suggest some acceptable preliminary income (loss) ranges:

- **First year:** 30 percent loss to 5 percent income
- **Second year:** 15 percent loss to 15 percent income
- **Third year:** 5 percent income to 20 percent income

Generally, new businesses operate at a loss in the first year (because sales are low and expenses are high). Thus, a net income above 5 percent might be high for year one. However, you don't want to post a huge loss, which will hamper your ability to get financing; any expected loss greater than 30 percent, therefore, might be problematic. By the second year, when your company should have started to turn things around, your loss shouldn't be greater than 15 percent. Because you're still a relatively new company, your income probably won't top 15 percent. By year three, you should show a profit of at least 5 percent but nothing that's unreasonable (for example, above 20 percent of sales).

Making Changes   If you fall out of these ranges, you might want to revisit some of your estimates and ask yourself certain questions, such as the following:

- Are Sales under- or overestimated?
- Is the percentage figure for CGS reasonable?
- Are executive salaries too high or too low?
- Are R&D estimates too high or too low?
- Are advertising expenses reasonable?
- Are any other expenses out of line relative to sales?

After addressing such issues, your team may change some of its estimates (and the justifications for them). *Don't worry if you have to make changes: Make them and see what happens.* Again, because the process of producing the financial reports for your business plan is iterative, the template allows you to see instantly how your changes will affect your bottom line.

PREPARING YOUR FINANCIAL PLAN GROUP REPORT

Now, let's discuss the remaining two sections of the template: *Cash requirements* and *Cash sources*. You must complete these two sections in order to prepare your **financial plan group report**.

Cash Requirements

Starting a business requires a tremendous outlay of cash. You need to buy equipment and perhaps a building or vehicles. If you sell products to customers, you need cash to build up an inventory. And, of course, you need cash to pay for expenses, such as salaries, advertising, and rent. This section of the template, which you can access by clicking on the "Cash Requirements" tab, allows you to calculate the amount of cash that you'll need to start your business. To simplify things, we require that you buy everything you need to get started at the outset. (In the real world, it's possible to postpone some purchases for a year or two.)

As you work your way through each category of cash requirements, note that the running tab at the top of the worksheet keeps an ongoing tally of your total cash requirements. In addition, the graph entitled "Breakdown of Cash Requirements" changes to reflect the relationships among the three major categories of cash requirements: *Building, vehicles, equipment, and other*; *Inventory*; and *Cash for expenses*.

Depreciation of Property   When you start filling in numbers for the sections devoted to *Building, vehicles, and equipment*, you'll notice that you're asked to indicate the life of each asset in terms of years. Why? You need to decide how long you will use a particular asset so that you can calculate a figure for *depreciation* (which we mention in Chapter 9 of the text, "The Role of Accounting in Business"). Let's review the concept in a little more detail.

When you buy something big that you plan to use in your business for several years (for example, a fancy desk for yourself), you include the cost of the asset on your cash requirements schedule. Each year that you use the asset, you need to list a portion of its cost as a *Depreciation expense* on your income statement (actually, the template does it for you automatically). How do you calculate depreciation expense? Divide the cost of the item by its *asset life*—the number of years that you'll be using it in your business. In other words, you have to forecast the number of years that you plan to use the stuff that you buy. You might decide, for instance, that your office equipment has a life of 10 years. (Note, by the way, that computers have an asset life of only 4 years—not because they wear out, but because they become obsolete.)

Building   As we've already indicated, start-up companies typically lease space rather than buy buildings. While it's relatively easy to find office and warehouse space, finding factories or specialized buildings (for restaurants, fitness centers, and so on) is more difficult, though not impossible. If you do decide to buy a building, you'd list its cost here. To determine this cost, you'll have to do some research. You might want to talk to a commercial realtor in the geographic area in which you plan to operate.

Vehicles   As with buildings, you have to decide whether to buy or lease vehicles, which fall into two categories—trucks and cars. If you use commercial shipping, you can probably avoid buying trucks. If you lease cars, you don't have to commit the cash needed to buy them at the outset. It's your choice, but if you decide to buy vehicles, list all of the following on the schedule:

- Cost
- Quantity
- Expected useful lives

The template will calculate depreciation and put the annual *Depreciation expense* on your income statements.

Research and Manufacturing Equipment   Few retailers or personal-service businesses need either research or manufacturing equipment. Any company that designs a product, however, needs research equipment, and any company that does its own manufacturing (rather than using contract manufacturers) needs manufacturing equipment. If you're designing complex, high-tech products, research equipment can be very costly: You'll need not only labs for your engineers but equipment for designing and testing your products. Because determining the actual costs entailed by such equipment is extremely difficult, rough (but reasonable) estimates are acceptable.

Office Equipment   Every company needs stuff for its offices—desks, chairs, computers, copy machines, and so on. Thus, you'll need to go online and find out how much such equipment and furniture costs. Bear in mind that this is no time to be cheap: Because you plan to be in business for a long time, whatever you buy needs to last. Don't go to Wal-Mart; Staples is okay, but head for the high-end stuff. List all the following on the schedule:

- Items purchased
- Cost per unit
- Quantity
- Asset life

Incidentally, in shopping for office equipment, you need to know how many employees you have; you don't want to buy four desks and chairs for eight employees (or vice versa).

Inventory   If you sell products, you must have an inventory of goods on hand. Retailers certainly don't want customers asking for something they don't have in stock. Restaurants don't want to run out of steaks and wine. Likewise, companies that produce their own goods want to have enough on hand to fill orders from wholesalers or retailers. Unfortunately, while recognizing that you need an inventory of goods is easy, figuring out *how much* you need is much tougher. The template requires that you indicate the number of *months* of inventory that you want to keep on hand—a period that will probably range from one to six months, depending on your product. A restaurant, for example, would be fine with a one-month inventory of frozen foods; an athletic-shoe store would want about two months of inventory (much more would leave the store with too many out-of-style shoes), and a manufacturer of golf carts might want a four-month supply on hand.

Once you've entered the number of months of inventory that you need, the template will use the CGS information that you supplied earlier to calculate your inventory costs.

Cash for Expenses A reality that all start-up companies must face is the fact that, in the first months of operations, a lot of cash is going out while little is coming in. If you're a brand-new business, you haven't started selling goods or providing services, but you still have to pay people, turn on the lights, advertise, and so on. To ensure that you don't run out of money and go out of business, the prudent thing to do is borrow money before you start your business to carry you over until your cash flow improves. This cash provides you with positive *working capital*—enough cash to pay your bills when they're due.

The template asks you to indicate how many months' worth of expenses you need to cover by borrowing. That number will depend on your type of business: While a service-based company (such as a gym), which might expect to bring in customers quickly, may need to cover only three months of expenses, a company producing a complex product—say treadmills—might need to cover at least six months. To understand why the treadmill maker needs so much cash to cover expenses, consider what has to happen *before the company brings in its first sales dollar*: It needs to design the treadmills, have them manufactured and shipped to the company warehouse, sell and ship them to retailers, and then wait for retailers to pay for them. This process can take a long time; meanwhile, the manufacturer is churning out checks to pay its expenses.

How does the template calculate total cash needed for expenses? By multiplying the number of months that have to be covered by your average monthly cash expenses (as listed on your income statement).

Other Cash Needs If you have any other cash needs, you can list them next. If, for example, you have to pay LeBron James an up-front fee of $10 million to use his name on your product, you'd list that cost here.

Justification Before wrapping up this section, go to the "Cash Requirements and Sources Notes" section and provide details and justifications for the following items:

- Building (be sure to discuss your lease-versus-buy decision)
- Vehicles
- Research-and-manufacturing equipment
- Months of inventory
- Months of cash expenses
- Other cash needs

THE FINAL TALLY: TOTAL CASH REQUIREMENTS

While you've been shopping and recording your cash needs, your template has been busy calculating your **total cash requirements**—the amount that you need to start your business. This is an important number because it dictates *how much cash you must bring in through owners' contributions*

and loans. With this fact in mind, we proceed to the next section of the template, which raises the all-important question: *Where will you get the cash?*

Cash Sources

Your cash requirements sheet shows you how much cash you need. The next step is figuring out how to get it. All of the decisions that you make in solving this problem will be recorded in the cash sources section of the template (which you can access by clicking on the "Cash Sources" tab). As you'll see, you have three choices in cash sources: *Owners' investments, Family and friends,* and *Bank loans.* Before we cover these three options, however, let's discuss some general issues involving sources of cash.

Cash Requirements Must Equal Cash from Sources As you identify sources of funding, the template will keep a running tab on *Total cash from sources.* It will compare this figure with the *Cash requirements* figure. Your job is to continue identifying sources of funds until you reach the point where *Cash requirements* comes out exactly equal to *Total cash from sources.* When you attain this point of balance, you won't have any excess cash, but you will have enough to cover your needs. When a gap develops between *Cash requirements* and *Total cash from sources,* the template will send you a message alerting you to this fact.

A few examples might help. Let's say that, with cash requirements of $100,000, you decide to raise $40,000 from owners, $10,000 from family and friends, and $50,000 from bank loans. *Total sources of cash* ($100,000) equals *Cash requirements* ($100,000) and you're in balance. But let's change things a little. You still have cash requirements of $100,000, owners' contributions of $40,000, and loans from family and friends of $10,000. But you plan to borrow only $30,000 from the bank. *Total Sources of cash* ($80,000) is less than *Cash requirements* ($100,000), and your template will alert you that you're not in balance by stating "You do not have enough cash to meet requirements." To bring the two numbers into balance, you'll have to identify additional cash sources of $20,000 (or reduce your cash requirements by $20,000). Be sure you don't go in the opposite direction either: You don't want your *Total sources of cash* to exceed *Cash requirements*; there's no sense having extra cash lying around. If this happens, your template will state: "You have more cash than required."

The Problem of Interlocking Financial Sheets Here's the tough part. Your three input sheets—*Cash requirements, Cash sources,* and *Financial assumptions*—are interlocking: A change in one affects a change in the others. If, for example, you increase a *Cash expense* on your *Financial assumptions* sheet, the amount of cash that you need to borrow in order to cover monthly expenses will increase—which, in turn, increases your total *Cash requirements.* Likewise, if you change the interest rate for one of your loans (on your *Cash sources* sheet), you'll also change both your expenses and your *Cash requirements.*

How do you deal with this problem? As you get close to the end of the project, get your income-statement figures set. Then, identify any gap between *Cash requirements* and

Cash sources. Close that gap by increasing or decreasing amounts in any of the following categories:

- Building
- Vehicles
- Equipment
- Other cash needs
- Owners' investments

Interest Rates Should Be Realistic The interest rate that you'd be charged for a loan will vary according to a number of factors: prevailing interest rates at the time of the loan, the amount you borrow, the collateral you supply, the repayment period, and the bankers' perception of the loan's riskiness. *Don't simply make up interest rates.* Research rates on the Internet or call a bank and speak with a commercial-loan officer. A good place to start is by finding the current *prime interest rate*—the rate that banks charge their best customers. What good is knowing "the prime"? Although you won't be considered one of the bank's best customers, at least you'll know the figure that your rate will exceed.

You Won't Pay Off Your Loans in the First Three Years
To make life simpler, assume that, although you'll be paying interest during the period, you won't be repaying the principal on your loans in the first three years. If for some reason you take out a loan with a repayment period of less than three years, you should assume that it will be renewed at the same interest rate. The template will automatically calculate annual interest cost for all loans and enter this amount on your income statement as *Interest expense.*

Loans Must Be Secured In addition to not being a bank's best customer, you're also not a good credit risk. Any loan that you get will have to be a *secured* loan—one that's backed by *collateral*, such as inventory, equipment, or even the owners' personal assets. If the borrower fails to repay the loan, the lender gets to keep the items securing it. This is why borrowing money for a business by securing your personal assets (savings, investments, even a personal home) is risky. (A bit of advice: Putting up your home to start a business is probably a big mistake.) In reality, however, you will in all likelihood have to secure at least some of your loans with personal assets. The good news (at least for our purposes) is that *you can pretend that you have assets*, such as stock in other companies, a savings account, a vacation home, or some rental property.

Terms of a Loan Should Match Its Purpose In general, when you take out a loan, you want to match its repayment terms with its purpose. For example, if you're buying a car that you plan to use for 5 years, you'd request a 5-year loan; if you're financing a building that you'll use for 20 years, you'd want a 20-year loan. Short-term needs, such as buying inventory, call for short-term loans.

An Exception to the Rule Even if you have a fantastic business idea, and even if you prove extremely competent in implementing it, you aren't likely to show a profit in year

one (or possibly in year two). Consequently, you should avoid *short-term loans*, which—by definition—come with repayment terms of one year. (In any case, you probably couldn't convince a banker to give you a short-term loan. Would you loan money to a friend who had no way of paying you back?)

Now that we've gotten this overview out of the way, let's get on to the task of deciding where you're going to get your money. As you work your way through the categories of *Cash sources*, remember that the running tab at the top of the worksheet keeps a tally of your *Total cash sources.* In addition, the graph entitled "Breakdown of Cash Sources" changes to reflect the relationships among the three major categories of *Cash sources: Owners' contributions, Family and friends*, and *Bank loans.*

Owners' Investments The most important source of funds for any new business is its owners. Bankers expect owners to put up a substantial amount of the money that they need to start a business: They tend to operate on the assumption that, with their own money invested in the business, owners will fight harder to make it succeed. As the owners of your company, your management team should expect to contribute at least 20 percent of the funds needed by the business. Unless the members of the management team are extremely wealthy (or the business requires only a small amount of cash), total contributions from owners probably won't exceed 40 percent.

Partners' Capital and Corporate Stock If your company is a *partnership*, the money put into the business by its owners is called *partners' capital.* Typically, each partner invests an equal sum. For example, if the business needs a total of $100,000 in cash and the partnership, consisting of five individuals, is funding 25 percent of this total ($25,000), each partner would contribute $5,000.

If your company is a corporation, the owners will invest in the company by buying *stock* (shares in the company). Generally, each owner buys an equal dollar amount of stock.

Note that the template doesn't differentiate between a partnership and stock contribution; it calls both *Owner's contribution.* Thus, if you're setting up either a partnership or a corporation, simply enter the names of all team members and the amount that each will contribute. Note, too, that the template doesn't ask you to stipulate an interest rate or repayment period for *Owner's contributions.* Why not? Because owners don't receive interest on their investments and there's no scheduled repayment: Owners are *equity investors*, not creditors.

Family and Friends Family and friends are viable sources of funding for your business. In the real world, you should draw up a formal loan agreement stating the interest rate and the period over which the loan will be repaid. In other words, treat your family and friends like any other creditor: They expect to be repaid, and they expect to earn interest. As generous as some family and friends are, their contributions will probably account for only 5 percent to 10 percent of the funds that you need. For each loan in this category, indicate all the following:

- Source of the loan
- Amount borrowed
- Annual interest rate

Also state the repayment period in years (that is, the number of years before you repay the loan).

Short-Term Bank Loans A short-term loan is made for *one year* and should be used for short-term purposes, such as buying inventory. As noted earlier, you should try to avoid this type of loan, especially if you expect to incur a loss in your first year of operation.

Notes and Lines of Credit If you meet the criteria for a short-term loan, you can borrow funds in one of two ways: (1) by signing a *note* (which falls due in one year) or (2) by taking out a *line of credit*. A line of credit works like a credit card: The company arranges with the bank to make available a specified sum that the company can borrow if the need arises. Like credit cards, lines of credit must be paid off periodically. For each short-term loan that you take out, indicate all the following:

- Amount of the loan
- Interest rate
- Repayment period
- Security for the loan

Intermediate-Term Bank Loans Intermediate-term debt is for needs that last *between one and five years*—such as buying equipment or funding an expansion. You can secure intermediate-term loans with such items as equipment, vehicles, or (if needed) owners' personal assets. For each loan that falls into this category, indicate all the following:

- Amount of the loan
- Interest rate
- Repayment period
- Description of posted security

Long-Term Financing Long-term financing covers needs of *five years or more* and is used to fund asset purchases that you intend to pay off over a long period of time, such as buildings. You can secure long-term loans with the asset that you're buying or with owners' personal assets. If you take out a long-term loan, be sure to list all the following:

- Purpose of the loan
- Amount borrowed
- Annual interest rate
- Repayment period
- Description of security posted

Justification Before completing this section, click on the "Cash Requirements and Sources Notes" tab and provide justification for all the following items *for all loans*:

- Interest rates
- Repayment periods
- Security

MAKING SENSE OF FINANCIAL REPORTS

As you've completed the template, you've made dozens of decisions about your business: How many products will you sell and at what price? What expenses will you incur? How much cash do you need to get started? Where will this cash come from? These aren't easy decisions to make, and in answering such questions, you've come a long way toward entering the world of business ownership. Unfortunately, you're not quite done.

As you've been inputting the results of your decisions, the template has been using your input to create three reports (and accompanying graphs):

- Three-Year Projected Income Statement
- Statement of Cash Requirements
- Statement of Sources of Cash

The next step is analyzing these financial statements and deciding if they're reasonable. If they're not reasonable, you'll need to revisit some of your decisions.

What is and isn't *reasonable*? Most businesses show losses the first year. If, therefore, you're showing a profit in the first year, you need to ask yourself if your forecast makes sense. Have you overestimated sales? Have you underestimated CGS percentage or expenses?

Likewise, because most businesses should start to break even (or generate a small income) in the second year, you should be a little skeptical if you've projected a fantastic second year. Say, for instance, that you've projected second-year *Net income* (after income taxes, which are automatically calculated) at 35 percent of your sales. That number is too high: It's more profit than even such high-performance companies as Nike generate. Your instructor will probably endorse your calculations if your reports forecast earnings of $.10 on every $1 of sales (or less) but will question $.35 (unless you're selling illegal drugs—a product which, by the way, is not acceptable for this project).

What about the third year? What if you forecast a loss in year three as well as in years one and two? Would you loan money to a company that expects to lose money for three years? Probably not and neither would a bank. Your calculations should project an income by at least year three.

What if you project a superlative year-three income—for example, $.30 for every $1 of sales? Your instructor might be suspicious: 15 percent is believable, but not 30 percent. You've probably overstated sales or understated expenses.

What if your business idea will work only if you get the word out about your product to large numbers of people but you show advertising expense of only 3 percent of sales? What if you're a high-tech company with R&D expenses of only $500? What if you're a gym with total insurance costs of $400 a year?

The Teamwork Touchstone

Here's the point: To do well on this project, you need to do more than just fill in a bunch of numbers. You need to work as a team to make good business decisions, and you need to *understand* the financial statements that you generate. You must be able to *justify* your financial assumptions and the output generated by them. Moreover, *everyone on your team* must fulfill these requirements. This project can't be a one-person show; you can't, for example, delegate all the number crunching to a designated financial whiz. Everyone must be involved in arriving at the team's financial assumptions. Everyone must understand and be able to explain the financial reports generated from these assumptions.

It's not an easy process, but we hope that it's a rewarding one. Done well, it will allow you to see how all the pieces of your business plan come together and interact. We're confident that you can meet the challenge.

Glossary

A

absolute advantage Condition whereby a country is the only source of a product or is able to make more of a product using the same or fewer resources than other countries. [199]

accountant Financial advisor responsible for measuring, summarizing, and communicating financial and managerial information. [3]

accounting System for measuring and summarizing business activities, interpreting financial information, and communicating the results to management and other decision makers. [225]

accounting equation Accounting tool showing the resources of a business (assets) and the claims on those resources (liabilities and owner's equity). [231]

account payable Record of cash owed to sellers from whom a business has purchased products on credit. [233]

account receivable Record of cash that will be received from a customer to whom a business has sold products on credit. [233]

accrual accounting Accounting system that records transactions when they occur, regardless of when cash is paid or received. [233]

advertising Paid, nonpersonal communication designed to create an awareness of a product or company. [179]

advertising agency Marketing consulting firm that develops and executes promotional campaigns for clients. [189]

American Stock Exchange (AMEX) Stock market where shares of smaller companies are traded. [267]

amortization Schedule by which you'll reduce the balance of your debt. [263]

angel Wealthy individual willing to invest in start-up ventures. [265]

application Document completed by a job applicant that provides factual information on the person's education and work background. [107]

applications software Software that performs a specific task, such as word processing or spreadsheet creation. [293]

arbitration Process of resolving a labor-contract dispute by having a third party study the situation and arrive at a *binding* agreement. [125]

artificial intelligence (AI) Science of developing computer systems that can mimic human behavior. [291]

asset Resource from which a business expects to gain some future benefit. [231]

audit Accountant's examination of and report on a company's financial statements. [245]

autocratic leadership style Management style identified with managers who tend to make decisions without soliciting input from subordinates. [85]

B

balance of payments Difference between the total flow of money coming into a country and the total flow of money going out. [201]

balance of trade Difference between the value of a nation's imports and its exports during a specified period of time. [199]

balance sheet Report on a company's assets, liabilities, and owner's equity at a specific point in time. [231]

bear market Period of declining or sluggish stock prices. [269]

behavioral segmentation Process of dividing consumers by behavioral variables, such as attitude toward the product, user status, or usage rate. [167]

benchmarking Practice of comparing a company's own performance with that of a company that excels in the same activity. [157]

benefits Compensation other than salaries, hourly wages, or financial incentives. [121]

board of directors Group of people who are legally responsible for governing a corporation. [93]

bonds Debt securities that require annual interest payments to bondholders. [271]

bonuses Annual income given to employees (in addition to salary) based on companywide performance. [121]

boycotting Method used by union members to voice displeasure with certain organizations by refusing to buy the company's products and encouraging others to follow suit. [125]

brand Word, letter, sound, or symbol that differentiates a product from similar products on the market. [171]

brand equity Value of a brand generated by a favorable consumer experience with a product. [171]

brand loyalty Consumer preference for a particular brand that develops over time based on satisfaction with a company's products. [171]

breakeven analysis Method of determining the level of sales at which the company will break even (have no profit or loss). [229]

breakeven point in units Number of sales units at which net income is zero. [231]

brokerage firm Financial institution that buys and sells stocks, bonds, and other investments for clients. [257]

browser Software (such as Internet Explorer) that locates and displays Web pages. [295]

budget Preliminary financial plan for a given time period, generally a year. [265]

bull market Period of large stock-price increases. [269]

business Activity that provides goods or services to consumers for the purpose of making a profit. [3]

business cycle Pattern of expansion and contraction in an economy. [13]

business ethics Application of ethical behavior in a business context. [47]

business plan Formal document describing a proposed business concept, management team, goods or services, competition, product-development, production methods, and marketing model, and stating financial projections. [29]

C

capacity Maximum number of products that a facility can produce over a given period of time under normal working conditions. [145]

capital budget Budget that shows anticipated expenditures for major equipment. [265]

capitalism Economic system featuring the lowest level of government control over allocation and distribution. [7]

capital structure Relationship between a company's debt (funds acquired from creditors) and its equity (funds invested by owners). [241]

cash budget Financial plan that projects cash inflows and outflows over a period of time. [265]

cash-flow management Process of monitoring cash inflows and outflows to ensure that the company has the right amount of funds on hand. [265]

cellular layout Layout in which teams of workers perform all the tasks involved in building a component, group of related components, or finished product. [145]

centralization Decision-making process in which most decision making is concentrated at the top. [81]

certificate authority Third-party (such as VeriSign) that verifies the identify of a computer site. [301]

certified public accountant (CPA) Accountant who has met state-certified requirements for serving the general public rather than a single firm. [245]

chain of command Authority relationships among people working at different levels of an organization. [83]

chief information officer (CIO) Senior executive who oversees information and telecommunications systems. [283]

chief technology officer High-level executive who reports to the CIO and oversees information technology planning and implementation. [283]

classified balance sheet Balance sheet that totals assets and liabilities in separate categories. [233]

client-server system System connecting client machines (used by employees for data input and retrieval) and a server (that stores shared databases and programs). [293]

code of conduct Statement that defines the principles and guidelines employees must follow in the course of all job-related activities. [55]

collateral Specific business or personal assets that a bank accepts as security for a loan. [263]

collective bargaining Process by which management and union-represented workers settle differences. [123]

commercial bank Financial institution that generates profits by loaning funds and providing customers with services, such as check processing. [255]

commission Compensation paid to employees based on the dollar amount of sales. [121]

common stock Stock whose owners bear the ultimate rewards and risks of ownership. [271]

communism Economic system featuring the highest level of government control over allocation and distribution. [7]

comparative advantage Condition whereby one nation is able to produce a product at a lower opportunity cost compared to another nation. [199]

comparative income statement Financial statement showing income from more than one year. [199]

computer-aided design (CAD) System using computer technology to create models representing the design of a product. [151]

computer-aided manufacturing (CAM) System using computer technology to control production processes and equipment. [151]

computer-integrated manufacturing (CIM) System in which the capabilities of a CAD/CAM system are integrated with other computer-based functions. [151]

conceptual skills Skills used to reason abstractly and analyze complex situations. [89]

conflict of interest Situation in which an individual must choose between the promotion of personal interests and the interests of others. [51]

consumer behavior Decision process that individuals go through when purchasing or using products. [187]

consumer confidence index Measure of optimism that consumers express about the economy as they go about their everyday lives. [15]

consumer market Buyers who want a product for personal use. [167]

consumer price index (CPI) Index that measures inflation by measuring the prices of goods purchased by a typical consumer. [13]

contingency planning Process of identifying courses of action to be taken in the event a business is adversely affected by a change. [77]

contingent worker Temporary or part-time worker hired to supplement a company's permanent workforce. [107]

continuous improvement Company's commitment to making constant improvements in the design, production, and delivery of its products. [155]

contribution margin per unit Excess of revenue per unit over variable cost per unit. [229]

controlling Management process of comparing actual to planned performance and taking corrective actions when necessary. [87]

convertible preferred stock Preferred stock that gives its owner the option of exchanging it for common stock. [271]

core values Statement of fundamental beliefs describing what is appropriate and important in conducting organizational activities and providing a guide for the behavior of organization members. [33]

corporate social responsibility Approach that an organization takes in balancing its responsibilities toward different stakeholders when making legal, economic, ethical, and social decisions. [47]

corporation Legal entity that is entirely separate from the parties who own it and is responsible for its own debts. [93]

cost-based pricing Pricing strategy that bases the selling price of a product on its cost plus a reasonable profit. [173]

cost of goods sold Cost of the products that a business sells to customers. [229]

credit union Financial institution that provides services to only its members (who are associated with a particular organization). [257]

crisis management Action plans that outline steps to be taken by a company in case of a crisis. [77]

culture System of shared beliefs, values, customs, and behaviors that govern the interactions of members of a society. [205]

cumulative preferred stock Preferred stock that requires a corporation to pay all current and missed preferred dividends before it can pay common dividends. [271]

current asset Asset that a business intends to convert into cash within a year. [233]

current liability Liability that a business intends to pay off within a year. [233]

current ratio Financial ratio showing the relationship between a company's current assets and current liabilities. [241]

customer division Organizational structure that groups employees into customer-based business segments. [81]

customer-relationship management Strategy for retaining customers by gathering information about them, understanding them, and treating them well. [181]

customer value triad Three factors that customers consider in determining the value of a product: quality, service, and price. [179]

D

data Unprocessed facts. [283]

database Electronic collection of related data accessible to various users. [287]

data communication network Large network used to transmit digital data from one computer to another using a variety of wired and wireless communication channels. [295]

data mining Technique used to search and analyze data to reveal patterns and trends that can be used to predict future behavior. [287]

data warehouse Centralized database that stores data from several databases so they can be easily analyzed. [287]

debt financing Process of raising capital for a company through the sale of bonds. [269]

debt-to-equity ratio (or debt ratio) Financial ratio showing the relationship between debt (funds acquired from creditors) and equity (funds invested by owners). [241]

decentralization Decision-making process in which most decision making is spread throughout the organization. [85]

decision-making skills Skills used in defining a problem, analyzing possible solutions, and selecting the best outcome. [89]

decision support system (DSS) Interactive system that extracts, integrates, and displays data from multiple sources to help managers make nonroutine decisions. [291]

deflation Decrease in overall price level. [13]

delegation Process of entrusting work to subordinates. [83]

demand Quantity of a product that buyers are willing to purchase at various prices. [9]

demand-based pricing Practice strategy that bases the price of a product on how much people are willing to pay for it. [173]

demand curve Graph showing the quantity of a product that will be bought at certain prices. [9]

demand deposits Checking accounts that pay given sums to "payees" when they demand them. [255]

democratic leadership style Management style used by managers who generally seek input from subordinates while retaining the authority to make the final decision. [85]

demographic segmentation Process of dividing the market into groups based on such demographic variables as age and income. [167]

departmentalization Process of grouping specialized jobs into meaningful units. [79]

depreciation expense Costs of a long-term or fixed asset spread over its useful life. [233]

depression Severe, long-lasting recession. [13]

directing Management process that provides focus and direction to others and motivates them to achieve organizational goals. [85]

discount rate Rate of interest the Fed charges member banks when they borrow reserve funds. [259]

discrimination Practice of treating a person unfairly on the basis of a characteristic unrelated to ability. [105]

distribution All activities involved in getting the right quantity of a product to the right customer at the right time and at a reasonable cost. [173]

distribution center Location where products are received from multiple suppliers, stored temporarily, and then shipped to their final destinations. [175]

dividends Earnings distributed to stockholders. [271]

divisional organization Form of organization that groups people into several smaller, self-contained units, or divisions, which are accountable for their own performance. [81]

Dow Jones Industrial Average (DJIA) Market index that reflects the total value of a "market basket" of 30 large U.S. companies. [267]

downsizing Practice of eliminating jobs to cut costs. [119]

dumping Practice of selling exported goods below the price that producers would normally charge in their home markets. [213]

E

e-commerce Business conducted over the Internet. [297]

economic indicator Statistic that provides information about trends in the economy. [15]

economics Study of how scarce resources are used to produce outputs—goods and services—that are distributed among people. [5]

economic system Means by which a society makes decisions about allocating resources to produce and distribute products. [7]

electronic data interchange (EDI) Computerized exchange of business transaction documents. [147]

embargo Extreme form of quota which bans the import or export of certain goods to a country for economic or political reasons. [213]

employment-at-will Legal doctrine that allows an employer to fire an employee at will. [119]

encryption Process of encoding data so only individuals or computers armed with a secret code (or key) can decode it. [301]

enterprise resource planning (ERP) system Integrated computer system used to channel information to multiple users. [285]

entrepreneur Individual who identifies a business opportunity and assumes the risk of creating and running a business to take advantage of it. [23]

Equal Employment Opportunity Commission (EEOC) Federal agency in charge of enforcing federal laws on employment discrimination. [105]

equilibrium price Price at which buyers are willing to buy exactly the amount that sellers are willing to sell. [9]

equity financing Process of raising capital for a company through the sale of stock. [269]

equity theory Theory of motivation which focuses on our perceptions of how fairly we're treated relative to others. [113]

ethical decision Decision in which there is a right (ethical) choice and a wrong (unethical or illegal) choice. [49]

ethical dilemma Morally problematic situation. [49]

ethical lapse Situation in which an individual makes a decision that's unmistakably unethical or illegal. [49]

ethics Ability and willingness to distinguish right from wrong and when you're practicing one or the other. [47]

European Union Association of European countries that joined together to eliminate trade barriers among themselves. [215]

exchange rate Value of one currency relative to another. [209]

executive information system (EIS) System that provides senior managers with strategic information customized to meet their needs and presented in a convenient format. [291]

executive summary Overview emphasizing the key points of a business plan in order to get the reader excited about the prospects of the business. [33]

expectancy theory Theory of motivation which proposes that employees will work hard to earn rewards they value and consider obtainable. [111]

expenses Costs incurred by selling products to customers. [229]

expert system (ES) Program that mimics the judgment of experts. [291]

exporting Practice of selling domestic products to foreign customers. [201]

external marketing environment Factors external to the firm that present threats and opportunities and require shifts in marketing plans. [185]

extranet Intranet that's partially available to certain parties outside the organization. [295]

F

factors of production Resources consisting of land, labor, capital (money, buildings, equipment), and entrepreneurial skills combined to produce goods and services. [5]

Federal Depository Insurance Corporation (FDIC) Government agency that regulates banks and insures deposits in its member banks up to $100,000. [257]

federal funds rate The interest rate that a Federal Reserve member bank pays when it borrows from other member banks to meet reserve requirements. [259]

Federal Reserve System (the Fed) U.S. central banking system, which has three goals: price stability, sustainable economic growth, and full employment. [259]

fiduciary responsibility Duty of management to safeguard a company's assets and handle its funds in a trustworthy manner. [57]

finance Activities involved in planning for, obtaining, and managing a company's funds. [3]

finance company Nondeposit financial institution that makes loans from funds acquired by selling securities or borrowing from commercial banks. [257]

financial accounting Branch of accounting that furnishes information to individuals and groups both inside and outside the organization to help them assess the firm's financial performance. [225]

financial condition ratio Financial ratio that helps to assess a firm's financial strength. [239]

financial plan Planning document that shows the amount of funds a company needs and details a strategy for getting those funds. [261]

financial statements Financial reports—including the income statement, the balance sheet, and the statement of cash flows—that summarize a company's past performance and evaluate its financial health. [227]

financing activity Activity that creates cash inflows or outflows through the obtaining or repaying of borrowed or invested funds. [237]

firewall Software program that controls access to a company's intranet. [295]

first-line managers Those at the bottom of the management hierarchy who supervise employees and coordinate their activities. [79]

fiscal policy Governmental use of taxation and spending to influence economic conditions. [15]

fiscal year Company's designated business year. [231]

fixed costs Costs that don't change when the amount of goods sold changes. [229]

fixed-position layout Layout in which workers are moved to the product, which stays in one place. [145]

flexible manufacturing system (FMS) System in which computer-controlled equipment is programmed to handle materials used in manufacturing. [151]

flextime Alternative work arrangement that allows employees to designate starting and quitting times. [115]

focus group Group of individuals brought together for the purpose of asking them questions about a product or marketing strategy. [169]

foreign direct investment (FDI) Formal establishment of business operations (such as the building of factories or sales offices) on foreign soil. [203]

foreign subsidiary Independent company owned by a foreign firm (called its parent). [203]

franchise Form of business ownership in which a *franchiser* (a seller) grants a *franchisee* (a buyer) the right to use a brand name and to sell its products or services. [31]

free market system Economic system in which most businesses are owned and operated by individuals. [7]

full employment Condition under which about 95% of those who want to work are employed. [13]

functional organization Form of business organization that groups together people who have comparable skills and perform similar tasks. [79]

G

Gantt chart Graphical tool for determining the status of projects. [149]

General Agreement on Tariffs and Trade (GATT) International trade agreement which encourages free trade by regulating and reducing tariffs and provides a forum for resolving trade disputes. [213]

generally accepted accounting principles (GAAP) Uniform set of rules for financial reporting established by an independent agency called the Financial Accounting Standards Board (FASB). [227]

generic branding Product with no branding information attached to it except a description of its contents. [171]

geographical division Organizational structure that groups people into divisions based on location. [81]

geographic segmentation Process of dividing a market according to such variables as climate, region, and population density. [167]

goals Major accomplishments that a company wants to achieve over a long period of time. [75]

goods-producing sector All businesses whose primary purpose is to produce tangible goods. [27]

grievances Union worker complaints on contract-related matters. [125]

gross domestic product (GDP) Measure of the market value of all goods and services produced by a nation's economy in a given year. [13]

gross national income (GNI) per capita Estimate of each citizen's share of national income. [209]

gross profit (or gross margin) Positive difference between revenues and cost of goods sold. [229]

H

hierarchy-of-needs theory Theory of motivation which holds that people are motivated by a hierarchical series of unmet needs. [109]

high-context cultures Cultures in which personal and family connections have an effect on most interactions, including those in business. [207]

human resource management (HRM) All actions that an organization takes to attract, develop, and retain quality employees. [103]

I

importing Practice of buying products overseas and reselling them in one's own country. [201]

incentive program Program designed to financially reward employees for good performance. [121]

income statement Financial statement summarizing a business's revenues, expenses, and net income. [229]

individual retirement account (IRA) Personal retirement account set up by an individual to save money tax free until retirement. [257]

industrial market Buyers who want a product for use in making other products. [167]

industrial robot Computer-controlled machine used to perform repetitive tasks that may also be hard or dangerous for human workers. [151]

industry Group of businesses that compete with one another to market products that are the same or similar. [135]

inflation Rise in the overall price level. [13]

information Data that have been processed or turned into some useful form. [283]

information manager Manager with responsibility for determining the information needs of members of the organization and meeting those needs. [283]

information system (IS) Computer system for gathering and processing data into information and distributing it to people who need it. [283]

initial public offering (IPO) Process of taking a privately held company public by selling stock to the public for the first time. [265]

insider trading Practice of buying or selling of securities using important information about the company before it's made public. [51]

insurance company Nondeposit institution that collects premiums from policyholders for protection against losses and invests these funds. [257]

interest Cost charged to use someone else's money. [263]

interest coverage ratio Financial ratio showing a company's ability to pay interest on its debts from its operating income. [243]

intermediary Wholesaler or retailer who helps move products from their original source to the end user. [175]

intermediate loan Loan issued with a maturity date of one to five years. [263]

international contract manufacturing (or outsourcing) Practice by which a company produces goods through an independent contractor in a foreign country. [201]

international franchise Agreement in which a domestic company (franchiser) gives a foreign company (franchisee) the right to use its brand and sell its products. [201]

international licensing agreement Agreement that allows a foreign company to sell a domestic company's products or use its intellectual property in exchange for royalty fees. [201]

International Monetary Fund (IMF) International organization set up to loan money to countries with troubled economies. [215]

Internet Global network comprised of smaller interconnected networks linking millions of computers around the world. [295]

Internet service provider (ISP) Company, such as America Online, that links into the Internet infrastructure to connect paying subscribers. [295]

interpersonal skills Skills used to get along with and motivate other people. [87]

interview Formal meeting during which the employer learns more about an applicant and the applicant learns more about the prospective employer. [107]

intranet Private network using internet technologies that are available only to employees. [295]

inventory Goods that a business has made or bought and expects to sell in the process of normal operations. [233]

inventory control Management of inventory to ensure that a company has enough inventory to keep operations flowing smoothly but not so much that money is being wasted in holding it. [147]

inventory turnover ratio Financial ratio that shows how efficiently a company turns over its inventory. [241]

investing activity Activity that creates cash inflows or outflows through the selling or buying of long-term assets. [237]

investment banking firm Financial institution that specializes in issuing securities. [265]

ISO 9000 Set of international quality standards established by the International Organization for Standardization. [157]

ISO 14000 Set of international standards for environmental management established by the International Organization for Standardization. [157]

J

job analysis Identification of the tasks, responsibilities, and skills of a job, as well as the knowledge and abilities needed to perform it. [105]

job description Outline of the duties and responsibilities of a position. [105]

job enlargement Job redesign strategy in which management enhances a job by adding tasks at similar skill levels. [113]

job enrichment Job redesign strategy in which management enriches a job by adding tasks that increase both responsibility and opportunity for growth. [113]

job redesign Management strategy used to increase job satisfaction by making jobs more interesting and challenging. [113]

job rotation Job redesign strategy which allows employees to rotate from one job to another on a systematic basis. [113]

job sharing Work arrangement in which two people share one full-time position. [115]

job specification Detailed list of the qualifications needed to perform a job, including required skills, knowledge, and abilities. [105]

joint ventures Alliances in which the partners fund a separate entity (partnership or corporation) to manage their joint operations. [203]

just-in-time production System for reducing inventories and costs by requiring suppliers to deliver materials *just in time* to go into the production process. [147]

L

labeling Information on the package of a product that identifies the product and provides details of the package contents. [171]

labor union Organized group of workers that bargains with employers to improve its members' pay, job security, and working conditions. [123]

lagging economic indicator Statistical data that measure economic trends after the overall economy has changed. [15]

laissez-faire leadership style Management style used by those who follow a "hands-off" approach and provide relatively little direction to subordinates. [85]

layout Arrangement in a facility of equipment, machinery, and people to make a production process as efficient as possible. [145]

leadership style Particular approach used by a manager to interact with and influence others. [85]

leading economic indicator Statistical data that predict the status of the economy three to twelve months in the future. [15]

legal monopoly Monopoly in which one seller supplies a product or technology to which it holds a patent. [11]

liability Debt owed by a business to an outside individual or organization. [231]

limited liability Legal condition under which an owner or investor cannot lose more than the amount invested. [93]

limited partnership Partnership made up of a single general partner (who runs the business and is responsible for its liabilities) and any number of limited partners. [93]

lines of credit Commitment by a bank that allows a company to borrow up to a specified amount of money as the need arises. [263]

liquidity Speed with which an asset can be converted into cash. [233]

local area network (LAN) Network that links computers that are in close proximity. [293]

lockout Management tactic of closing the workplace to union workers. [125]

long-term asset (or fixed asset) Asset that a business intends to hold for more than a year before converting it to cash. [233]

long-term liability Liability that a business need not pay off within the following year. [233]

long-term loan Loan issued with a maturity date of five years or more. [263]

low-context cultures Cultures in which personal and work relationships are compartmentalized. [207]

M

M-1 Measure of the money supply that includes only the most liquid forms of money, such as cash and checking-account funds. [255]

M-2 Measure of the money supply that includes everything in M-1 plus near-cash. [255]

make-to-order strategy Production method in which products are made to customer specification. [143]

management Process of planning for, organizing, directing, and controlling a company's resources so that it can achieve its goals. [3]

management accounting Branch of accounting that provides information and analysis to decision makers inside the organization in order to help them operate the business. [225]

management effectiveness ratio Financial ratio showing how effectively a firm is being run and measuring its overall performance. [239]

management efficiency ratio Financial ratio showing how efficiently a company's assets are being used. [239]

management information system (MIS) System used to extract data from a database and compile reports that help managers make routine decisions. [291]

manager Individual in an organization who is responsible for making a group of people more effective and efficient. [73]

manufacturer branding Branding strategy in which a manufacturer sells one or more products under its own brand names. [171]

manufacturing resource planning (MRP II) System for coordinating a firm's material requirements planning activities with the activities of its other functional areas. [149]

market Group of buyers or potential buyers who share a common need that can be met by a certain product. [135]

market index Measure for tracking stock prices. [267]

marketing All of the organizational activities involved in identifying customers' needs and in designing, pricing, promoting and delivering products to meet those needs. [3]

marketing concept Basic philosophy of satisfying customer needs while meeting organizational goals. [165]

marketing mix Combination of product, price, place, and promotion (often called the four Ps) used to market products. [169]

marketing research Process of collecting and analyzing data that's relevant to a specific marketing situation. [169]

marketing strategy Plan for selecting a target market and creating, pricing, promoting, and distributing products that satisfy customers. [165]

market segment Group of potential customers with common characteristics that influence their buying decisions. [135]

market share Company's portion of the market that it has targeted. [137]

mass customization Production method in which fairly high volumes of customized products are made at fairly low prices. [143]

mass production (or make-to-stock strategy) Production method in which high volumes of products are made at low cost and held in inventory in anticipation of future demand. [143]

master production schedule (MPS) Timetable that specifies which and how many products will be produced and when. [149]

material requirements planning (MRP) Technique of using a computerized program to calculate the quantity of materials needed for production and to reschedule inventory ordering. [147]

materials handling Process of physically moving or carrying goods during production, warehousing, and distribution. [175]

materials management All decisions pertaining to the purchase of inputs, the inventory of components and finished products, and the scheduling of production processes. [147]

matrix structure Structure in which employees from various functional areas form teams to combine their skills in working on a specific project. [83]

maturity Period of time for which a bank loan is issued. [263]

mediation Approach used to resolve a labor-contract dispute by following the recommendation of an impartial third party. [125]

middle managers Those in the "middle" of the management hierarchy who report to top management and oversee the activities of first-line managers. [79]

mission statement Statement describing an organization's purpose or *mission*—its reason for existence—and telling stakeholders what the organization is committed to doing. [33]

mixed market economy Economic system that relies on both markets and government to allocate resources. [7]

monetary policy Efforts exerted by the Federal Reserve System ("the Fed") to regulate the nation's money supply. [15]

money Anything commonly accepted as a medium of exchange, measure of value, and store of value. [253]

money market fund Fund invested in safe, highly liquid securities. [257]

money market mutual funds Accounts that pay interest to investors who pool funds to make short-term loans to businesses and the government. [255]

money multiplier The amount by which an initial bank deposit will expand the money supply. [257]

monopolistic competition Market in which many sellers supply differentiated products. [9]

monopoly Market in which there is only one seller supplying products at regulated prices. [11]

motivation Internally generated drive to achieve a goal or follow a particular course of action. [109]

multinational corporation (MNC) Large corporation that operates in many countries. [203]

mutual fund Financial institution that invests in securities, using money pooled from investors (who become part owners of the fund). [257]

N

NASDAQ Best known over-the-counter, electronic exchange system. [267]

NASDAQ Composite Index Market index of all stocks listed on the NASDAQ Stock Exchange. [269]

national debt Total amount of money owed by the federal government. [17]

natural monopoly Monopoly in which, because of the industry's importance to society, one seller is permitted to supply products without competition. [11]

net income (or net profit) Positive difference between gross profit and total expenses. [229]

New York Stock Exchange (NYSE) Best-known stock market where stocks of the largest, most prestigious corporations are traded. [267]

niche Narrowly defined group of potential customers with a fairly specific set of needs. [135]

North American Free Trade Association (NAFTA) Agreement among the governments of the U.S., Canada, and Mexico to open their borders to unrestricted trade. [215]

not-for-profit (or nonprofit) organization Organization that has a purpose other than returning profits to owners. [3]

O

objectives Intermediate-term performance targets that direct the activities of an organization toward the attainment of a goal. [75]

odd-even pricing Practice of pricing products a few cents (or dollars) under an even number. [173]

off-the-job training Formal employee training that occurs in a location away from the office. [109]

oligopoly Market in which a few sellers supply a large portion of all the products sold in the marketplace. [11]

on-the-job training Employee training (often informal) that occurs while the employee is on the job. [109]

open market operations The sale and purchase of U.S. government bonds by the Fed in the open market. [259]

operating activity Activity that creates cash inflows or outflows through day-to-day operations. [239]

operating expenses Costs of selling products to customers, not including costs of goods sold. [229]

operational plans Detailed action steps to be taken by individuals or groups to implement tactical plans. [77]

operations management (OM) Management of the process that transforms resources into products. [137]

operations manager Person who designs and oversees the process that converts resources into goods or services. [3]

operations support system Information system used by lower-level managers to assist them in running day-to-day operations and making routine decisions. [289]

organizational structure An arrangement of jobs in an organization that's most appropriate for the company at a specific point in time. [79]

organization chart Diagram representing the interrelationships of positions within an organization. [81]

organizing Management process of allocating resources to achieve a company's plans. [77]

orientation Activities involved in introducing new employees to the organization and their jobs. [109]

outsourcing Practice of using outside vendors to manufacture all or part of a company's actual products. [157]

over-the-counter (OTC) market Market in which securities are traded over computer networks and phones rather than on the trading floor of an exchange. [267]

owner's equity Amount which is invested in a business by its owners and which owners can claim from its assets. [231]

P

packaging Container that holds a product and can influence a consumer's decision to buy or pass it up. [171]

partnership (or general partnership) Business owned jointly by two or more people. [91]

patent Grant of the exclusive right to produce or sell a product, process, or invention. [141]

penetration pricing Pricing strategy in which the seller charges a low price on a new product to discourage competition and gain market share. [173]

pension fund Fund set up to collect contributions from participating companies for the purpose of providing its members with retirement income. [257]

perfect competition Market in which many consumers buy standardized products from numerous small businesses. [7]

performance appraisals Formal process in which a manager evaluates an employee's work performance. [117]

personal selling One-on-one communication with customers or potential customers. [181]

PERT chart Tool for diagramming the activities required to produce a product, specifying the time required to perform each activity in the process, and organizing activities in the most efficient sequence. [149]

physical distribution Activities needed to get a product from where it was manufactured to the customer. [175]

picketing Union tactic of parading with signs outside a factory or other facility to publicize a strike. [125]

piecework Compensation paid to workers according to the quantity of a product that they produce or sell. [121]

planning Process of setting goals and determining the best way to achieve them. [73]

preferred stock Stock that pays owners a fixed dividend annually. [271]

prestige pricing Practice of setting a price artificially high to foster the impression that it is a product of high-quality. [173]

price stability Conditions under which the prices for products remain fairly constant. [13]

primary data Newly collected marketing information that addresses specific questions about the target market. [169]

primary market Market that deals in the sale of newly issued securities. [267]

prime rate Rate that banks charge their best customers. [261]

private accountant Accountant who works for a private organization or government agency. [245]

private branding Product made by a manufacturer and sold to a retailer who in turn resells it under its own name. [171]

private (or closely held) corporation Corporation that restricts the transfer-ability of its stock. [95]

privatization Process of converting government-owned businesses to private ownership. [7]

process control Application of technology to monitor and control physical processes. [289]

process division Organizational structure that groups people into operating units based on various stages in the production process. [81]

process layout Layout that groups together workers or departments who perform similar tasks. [145]

product Something that can be marketed to customers because it provides a benefit and satisfies a need. [133]

product concept Description of what a new product will look like and how it will work. [139]

product development process Series of activities by which a product idea is transformed into a final product. [139]

product division Organizational structure made up of divisions based on product lines. [81]

product layout Layout in which products are produced by people, equipment, or departments arranged as an assembly line. [145]

product life cycle Four stages that a product goes through over its life: introduction, growth, maturity, and decline. [183]

profit Difference between the revenue that a company brings in from selling goods and services and the costs of generating this revenue. [3]

profit margin Amount that a company earns on each unit sold. [175]

profit margin ratio Financial ratio showing how much of each sales dollar is left after certain costs are covered. [239]

profit-sharing plan Incentive program that uses a predetermined formula to distribute a share of company profits to eligible employees. [121]

project team Individuals from different functional areas assigned to work together throughout the product development process. [139]

promotion mix Various ways to communicate with customers, including advertising, personal selling, sales promotion, and publicity. [179]

prospectus Written offer to sell securities that provides useful information to prospective buyers. [267]

protectionism Use of trade controls to reduce foreign competition in order to protect domestic industries. [213]

prototype Physical model of a new product. [141]

psychographic segmentation Process of classifying consumers on the basis of individual lifestyles as reflected in people's interests, activities, attitudes, and values. [167]

public corporation Corporation whose stock is available to the general public. [95]

publicity Form of promotion that focuses on getting a company or product mentioned in a newspaper, on TV, or in some other news media. [181]

public relations Communication activities undertaken by companies to garner favorable publicity for themselves and their products. [181]

purchasing Process of acquiring materials and services to be used in production. [147]

Q

quality Ability of a product to satisfy customer needs. [155]

quality circle Employees who perform similar jobs and work as teams to identify quality, efficiency, and other work-related problems, to propose solutions, and to work with management in implementing their recommendations. [155]

quota Government imposed restrictions on the quantity of a good that can be imported over a period of time. [213]

R

ramp-up stage Stage in the product development process during which employees are trained in necessary production processes and new products are tested. [141]

ratio analysis Technique for financial analysis that shows the relationship between two numbers. [239]

recession Economic slowdown measured by a decline in gross domestic productivity. [13]

recruiting Process of identifying suitable candidates and encouraging them to apply for openings in the organization. [105]

reporting relationships Patterns of formal communication among members of an organization. [81]

resources Inputs used to produce outputs. [5]

restructuring Process of altering an existing organizational structure to become more competitive under changing conditions. [79]

retailers Intermediaries who buy goods from producers and sell them to consumers. [175]

revenues Amount of money earned by selling products to customers. [229]

S

salary Compensation paid for fulfilling the responsibilities of a position regardless of the number of hours required to do it. [119]

sales promotion Sales approach in which a company provides an incentive for potential customers to buy something. [181]

savings bank Financial institution originally set up to provide mortgages and encourage saving, which now offers services similar to those of commercial banks. [225]

search engine Software program that scans Web pages for specified keywords and provides a list of documents containing them. [295]

secondary data Information used in marketing decisions that has already been collected for other purposes. [169]

secondary market Market in which investors buy previously issued securities from other investors. [267]

Securities and Exchange Commission (SEC) Government agency that enforces securities laws. [267]

security Collateral pledged to secure repayment of a loan. [263]

selection Process of gathering information on candidates, evaluating their qualifications, and choosing the right one. [107]

Service Corps of Retired Executives (SCORE) SBA program in which a businessperson needing advice is matched with a team of retired executives working on a volunteer basis. [37]

service-producing sector All businesses whose primary purpose is to provide a service rather than make tangible goods. [27]

shareholders Owners of a corporation. [93]

short-term loan Loan issued with a maturity date of less than one year. [263]

skimming pricing Pricing strategy in which a seller generates early profits by starting off charging the highest price that customers will pay. [173]

small business According to the SBA, a business that is independently operated, exerts little influence in its industry, and employs fewer than 500 people. [25]

Small Business Administration (SBA) Government agency that helps prospective owners set up small businesses, obtain financing, and manage ongoing operations. [23]

Small Business Development Center (SBDC) SBA program in which centers housed at colleges and other locations provide free training and technical information to current and prospective small business owners. [37]

socialism Economic system falling between communism and capitalism in terms of government control over allocation and distribution. [7]

sole proprietorship Business owned by only one person. [91]

span of control Number of people reporting to a particular manager. [83]

specialization Process of organizing activities into clusters of related tasks that can be handled by specific individuals or groups. [79]

stakeholders Parties who are interested in the activities of a business because they're affected by them. [47]

Standard & Poor's Composite Index (S&P 500) Market index of the stocks of 500 large U.S. companies. [269]

statement of cash flows Financial statement reporting on cash inflows and outflows resulting from operating, investing, and financing activities. [237]

statistical process control (SPC) Technique for monitoring production quality by testing sample outputs to ensure that they meet specifications. [151]

stock Share of ownership in a corporation. [93]

stockholders' equity Amount invested in a corporation by its shareholders. [269]

stock-option plans Incentive program that allows eligible employees to buy a specific number of shares of company stock at a set price on a specified date. [121]

storage warehouse Building used for the temporary storage of goods. [175]

strategic alliance Agreement between two companies (or a company and a nation) to pool resources in order to achieve business goals that benefit both partners. [201]

strategic human resource planning Process of developing a plan for satisfying an organization's human resource needs. [103]

strategic planning Process of establishing an overall plan or course of action for an organization. [73]

strike Union tactic by which workers walk away from their jobs and refuse to return until a labor-management dispute has been resolved. [125]

strikebreakers Nonunion workers who are willing to cross picket lines to replace strikers. [125]

subsidies Government payments given to certain industries to help offset some of their costs of production. [213]

supply Quantity of a product that sellers are willing to sell at various prices. [9]

supply chain Flow that begins with the purchase of raw materials and ends in the sale of a finished product to an end user. [177]

supply chain management (SCM) Process of integrating all the activities in the supply chain. [177]

supply curve Graph showing the quantity of a product that will be offered for sale at certain prices. [9]

SWOT analysis Approach used to assess a company's fit with its environment by analyzing its strengths, weaknesses, opportunities, and threats. [75]

T

tactical plans Short-term plans that specify the activities and resources needed to implement a company's strategic plan. [77]

target costing Practice strategy that determines how much to invest in a product by figuring out how much customers will pay and subtracting an amount for profit. [173]

target market Specific group of customers who should be interested in your product, have access to it, and have the means to buy it. [167]

tariffs Government taxes on imports that raise the price of foreign goods and make them less competitive with domestic goods. [213]

technical skills Skills needed to perform specific tasks. [87]

telecommuting Work arrangement in which the employee works from home on a regular basis. [115]

time-management skills Skills used to manage time effectively. [89]

top managers Those at the top of the management hierarchy who are responsible for the health and performance of the organization. [79]

total quality management (TQM) (or quality assurance) All the steps taken by a company to ensure that its products satisfy customer needs. [155]

trade controls Government policies that restrict free trade. [213]

trade credit Credit given to a company by its suppliers. [265]

trade deficit Condition whereby a country buys more products than it sells, resulting in an unfavorable trade balance. [199]

trademark Word, symbol, or other mark used to identify and legally protect a product from being copied. [171]

trade surplus Condition whereby a country sells more products than it buys, resulting in a favorable trade balance. [199]

trading blocs Groups of countries which have joined together to allow goods and services to flow without restrictions across their mutual borders. [215]

transactional leaders Managers who exercise authority based on their rank in the organization and focus their attention on identifying mistakes. [85]

transaction processing system (TPS) Information system used to record and process an organization's daily activities or transactions. [289]

transactions Financial and nonfinancial events that affect a business. [289]

transformational leaders Managers who mentor and develop subordinates and stimulate them to look beyond personal interests to those of the group. [85]

turnover Permanent separation of an employee from a company. [117]

two-factor theory Theory which holds that motivation involves both motivation factors (which contribute to job satisfaction) and hygiene factors (which help to prevent job dissatisfaction). [111]

U

unemployment rate Percentage of the total labor force that's currently unemployed and actively seeking work. [13]

unlimited liability Legal condition under which an owner or investor is personally liable for all debts of a business. [91]

unsecured loan Loan given by a bank that doesn't require the borrower to put up collateral. [263]

V

value chain Entire range of activities involved in delivering value to customers. [179]

variable costs Costs that vary, in total, as the quantity of goods sold changes but stay constant on a per unit basis. [229]

venture capitalist Individual who pools funds from private and institutional sources and invests them in businesses with strong growth potential. [265]

vertical percentage analysis Analysis of an income statement treating the relationship of each item as a percentage of a base (usually sales). [237]

virtual company Company without a significant physical presence that relies on third parties to produce, warehouse, price, and deliver the products it sells over the Internet. [297]

W

wages Compensation paid to employees based on the number of hours worked. [119]

Web server Computer that retrieves Web pages. [295]

whistle-blower Individual who exposes illegal or unethical behavior in an organization. [53]

wholesalers (distributors) Intermediaries who buy goods from suppliers and sell them to businesses who will either resell or use them. [175]

wide area network (WAN) Network that links computers that are spread over a relatively large geographical area. [293]

World Bank International financial institution that provides economic assistance to poor and developing countries. [215]

World Trade Organization (WTO) International organization that monitors trade policies and whose members work together to enforce rules of trade and resolve trade disputes. [213]

World Wide Web ("the Web") Subsystem of computers on the Internet that communicate with each other using a special language called HTTP. [295]

Endnotes, Sources, and Credits

■ ENDNOTES

CHAPTER 1

1. David Baron, "Facing-Off in Public," *Stanford Business* (April 15, 2006), at http://www.gsb.stanford.edu/news/bmag/sbsm0308/feature_face_off.shtml.
2. According to many scholars, *The Wealth of Nations* is not only the most influential book on free-market capitalism but remains relevant today.
3. United States Patent and Trademark Office, *General Information Concerning Patents* (April 15, 2006) at http://www.uspto.gov/web/offices/pac/doc/general/index.html#laws.
4. Mary Bellis, "Inventors—Edwin Land—Polaroid Photography—Instant Photography/Patents (April 15, 2006), at http://inventors.about.com/library/inventors/blpolaroid.htm.

CHAPTER 2

1. U.S. Small Business Administration, "State Winner! BTIO Educational Products, Inc." (April 21, 2006), at http://app1.sba.gov/sbsuccess/2002/.
2. U.S. Small Business Administration, "First Steps: How to Start a Small Business" (April 21, 2006), at www.sba.gov/starting/indexsteps.html.
3. Kathleen Allen, *Getting Started in Entrepreneurship: Entrepreneurship for Dummies* (Oakland, CA: IDG Books Worldwide, 2001), 14.
4. U.S. Small Business Administration, "What Is a Small Business?" (April 21, 2006), at www.sba.gov/starting/indexwhatis.html.
5. Office of Advocacy, U.S. Small Business Administration, "2005—The Small Business Economy: A Report to the President," (April 22, 2006), at http://www.sba.gov/advo/research/sb_econ2005.pdf.
6. Office of Advocacy—U.S. Small Business Administration (1998), "The New American Evolution: The Role and Impact of Small Firms" (April 21, 2006), at www.sba.gov/advo/stats.
7. U.S. Small Business Administration, "Small Business Statistics," (April 21, 2006), at http://www.sba.gov/aboutsba/sbastats.html.
8. Office of Advocacy—U.S. Small Business Administration (2000), "Contribution of Small High Tech Firms to the New Economy" (April 21, 2006), at www.sba.gov/advo_apptback.pdf.
9. Office of Advocacy—U.S. Small Business Administration, "Contribution of Small High Tech Firms."
10. Office of Advocacy—U.S. Small Business Administration (2000), "A New View of Government" (April 21, 2006), at www.sba.gov/advo/laws/test99_0804.pdf.
11. Office of Advocacy—U.S. Small Business Administration (2000), "Contribution of Small High Tech Firms."
12. Office of Advocacy—U.S. Small Business Administration (2000), "Contribution of Small High Tech Firms."
13. John Case, "What Businesses Are Small Companies Really In—And Where Are They Scarce," *Inc.com* (April 21, 2006), at www.inc.com/magazine/20010515/22612.html.
14. Laura Baughman, "Why Congress Should Fund Better Services Data" (April 20, 2006), at www.sitrends.org/ideas/expert.asp?EXPERT_ID=49.
15. Reveal Games (April 21, 2006), at www.revealgames.com.
16. Nach Maravilla, "How Do You Know If Your Product Will Sell Online?" (April 21, 2006), at www.powerhomebiz.com/vol48/know.htm.
17. Isabel Isidro, "What Works on the Web: 12 Lessons from Successful Home-Based Online Entrepreneurs," (April 21, 2006), at www.powerhomebiz.com/vol63/whatworks.htm.
18. Isabel Isidro, "Geese Police: A Unique Business Concept" (April 21, 2006), at www.powerhomebiz.com/OnlineSuccess/geesepolice.htm.
19. Small Business Development Center, "Pros and Cons of Owning a Business" (April 21, 2006), at http://72.14.203.104/u/siu?q=cache:DFSPVtmg7j0J:www.siu.edu/sbdc/buscheck.htm+pros+and+cons+of+owning+a+business&hl=en&gl=us&ct=clnk&cd=1&ie=UTF-8.
20. Cicco and Associates, Inc., "Type E Personality—Happy Days—Entrepreneurs Top Satisfaction Survey," *Entrepreneur.com* (April 21, 2006), at http://entrepreneur-online.com/mag/article/0,1539,226838--3-,00.html.
21. From Kathleen Allen, *Getting Started in Entrepreneurship*, 46.
22. Scott Thurm and Joann S. Lublin, "Peter Drucker's Legacy Includes Simple Advice: It's All about the People," *The Wall Street Journal*, November 14, 2005, B1, (April 21, 2006), at http://online.wsj.com/public/article/SB113192826302796041.html?mod=2_1194_3.
23. Peter Krass, "Sam Walton: 10 Rules for Building a Successful Business" (April 21, 2006), at www.powerhomebiz.com/vol76/walton.htm.
24. Howard Schultz and Dori Jones Yang, *Pour Your Heart into It* (New York, NY: Hyperion, 1997), 24-109.

25. Norman M. Scarborough and Thomas W. Zimmerer, *Effective Small Business Management: An Entrepreneurial Approach*, 8th ed. (Upper Saddle River, NJ: Pearson Education, 2006), 99.

26. "Franchise 500," *Entrepreneur.com—Franchise* (April 21, 2006), at www.entrepreneur.com/franzone/franzone/listings/fran500/0,5831,,00.html.

27. Michael Seid and Kay Marie Ainsley, "Franchise Fee—Made Simple," *Entrepreneur.com* (April 21, 2006), at www.entrepreneur.com/article/0,4621,299085,00.html.

28. "D&B—The Challenges of Managing a Small Business" (September 2, 2002), at www.dnb.com/communities/smbiz/resource_center/challenges_managing_smbiz.

29. U.S. Small Business Administration, "SBA Profile: Who We Are and What We Do" (April 21, 2006), at www.sba.gov/aboutsba.

30. See Scarborough and Zimmerer, *Effective Small Business Management*, 485–87; U.S. Small Business Administration, "Basic 7(a) Loan Program" (April 21, 2006), at www.sba.gov/financing/sbaloan/7a.html.

31. Office of Small Business Development Centers, "Mission" (April 21, 2006), at www.sba.gov/sbdc.

32. Service Corps of Retired Executives, "SCORE—Counselors to America's Small Businesses" (April 21, 2006), at www.score.org.

33. Amy E. Knaup, "Survival and Longevity in the Business Employment Dynamics Data," *Monthly Labor Review*, 128:5 (May 2005), 50-6, (April 21, 2006), at www.bls.gov/opub/mlr/2005/05/ressum.pdf.

CHAPTER 3

1. This case is based on Susan Pullman, "How Following Orders Can Harm Your Career," *Wall Street Journal*, June 23, 2003, *CareerJournal.com* (April 24, 2006), at www.careerjournal.com/myc/killers/20030630-pulliam.html.

2. Quoted by Pullman, "How Following Orders Can Harm Your Career," 4.

3. Amanda Ripley, "The Night Detective," *Time*, December 22, 2002 (April 24, 2006), at www.time.com/time/personoftheyear/2002.

4. Jeff Clabaugh, "WorldCom's Betty Vinson Gets 5 Months in Jail," *Washington Business Journal*, August 5, 2005, *Albuquerque Bizjournals.com* (April 24, 2006), at http://albuquerque.bizjournals.com/washington/stories/2005/08/01/daily51.html *Washington Business Journal*—August 5, 2005.

5. Scott Reeves, "Lies, Damned Lies and Scott Sullivan, Forbes.com, February 17, 2005 (April 24, 2006), at www.forbes.com/business/2005/02/17/cx_sr_0217ebbers.html/; and David A. Andelman, "Scott Sullivan Gets Slap on the Wrist—WorldCom Rate Race," *Forbes.com*, August 12, 2005 (April 24, 2006), at www.mindfully.org/Industry/2005/Sullivan-WorldCom-Rat12aug05.htm

6. Pullman, "How Following Orders Can Harm Your Career," 4.

7. "World-Class Scandal at WorldCom," *CBSNews.com*, June 26, 2002 (April 24, 2006), at www.cbsnews.com/stories/2002/06/26/national/main513473.shtml.

8. Daniel Kadlec, "Enron: Who's Accountable?" *Time*, January 21, 2002, 31.

9. David Lieberman, "Prosecutors Wrap Up $3.2B Adelphia Case," *USA Today*, June 25, 2004 (April 24, 2006), at www.usatoday.com/money/industries/telecom/2004-06-25-adelphia_x.htm.

10. "Tyco Wants Its Money Back," *CNNMoney*, September 17, 2002 (April 24, 2006), at money.cnn.com/2002/09/17/news/companies/tyco/index.htm.

11. Nancy Gibbs et al., "Summer of Mistrust," *Time*, July 22, 2002, 20.

12. Alan Axelrod, *My First Book of Business Ethics* (Philadelphia: Quirk Books, 2004), 7.

13. "100 Best Corporate Citizens for 2004," *Business Ethics: Corporate Social Responsibility Report* 18:1 (Spring 2004) 8-12.

14. Axelrod, *My First Book of Business Ethics*, 7.

15. Quoted by Adrian Gostick and Dana Telford, *The Integrity Advantage* (Salt Lake City: Gibbs Smith, 2003), 3–4.

16. John C. Maxwell, *There's No Such Thing as "Business Ethics": There's Only One Rule for Making Decisions* (New York: Warner Books, 2003), 19–21.

17. See Tamara Kaplan, "The Tylenol Crisis: How Effective Public Relations Saved Johnson & Johnson" (April 24, 2006), at www.personal.psu.edu/users/w/x/wxk116/tylenol/crisis.html.

18. Yaakov Weber, "CEO Saves Company's Reputation, Products," *New Sunday Times*, June 13, 1999 (April 24, 2006), at http://adtimes.nstp.com.my/jobstory/jun13.htm.

19. Online Ethics Center for Engineering and Science, "Advice from the Texas Instruments Ethics Office: What Do You Do When the Light Turns Yellow?" *Onlineethics.org* (April 24, 2006), at http://onlineethics.org/corp/help.html#yellow.

20. J.C. Penney Co., "Statement of Business Ethics for Associates and Officers: The 'Spirit' of This Statement" (April 24, 2006), at http://ir.jcpenney.com/phoenix.zhtml?c=70528&p=irol-govconduct/.

21. Quoted by Gostick and Telford, *The Integrity Advantage*, 103.

22. Adapted from Gostick and Telford, *The Integrity Advantage*, 16.

23. See Gostick and Telford, *The Integrity Advantage*, 13.

24. National Whistleblower Center, "Labor Day Report: The National Status of Whistleblower Protection on Labor Day, 2002" (April 24, 2006), at www.whistleblowers.org/labordayreport.htm.

25. Paula Dwyer et al, "Year of the Whistleblower," *BusinessWeek Online*, December 16, 2002 (April 24, 2006), at www.businessweek.com/magazine/content/02_50/b3812094.htm.

26. Scott Waller, "Whistleblower Tells Students to Have Personal Integrity," *The* (Jackson, MS) *Clarion-Ledger*, November 18, 2003, (April 24, 2006), at www.clarionledger.com/news/0311/18/b01.html.

27. Gostick and Telford, *The Integrity Advantage*, 98–99.

28. Saul W. Gellerman, "Why 'Good' Managers Make Bad Ethical Choices," *Harvard Business Review on Corporate Ethics* (Boston: Harvard Business School Press, 2003) 59.

29. Gostick and Telford, *The Integrity Advantage*, 12.

30. See especially Tom Fowler, "The Pride and the Fall of Enron," *Houston Chronicle*, October 20, 2002 (April 24, 2006), at www.chron.com/cs/CDA/story.hts/special/enron/1624822.

31. Episode recounted by Norm Augustine, "Business Ethics in the 21st Century," speech given to the Ethics Resource Center, Ethics Resource Center (April 24, 2006), at www.ethics.org/resources/speech_detail.cfm?ID=848.

32. Augustine, "Business Ethics in the 21st Century."

33. William McCall, "CEO Will Get Salary, Bonus in Prison," *CorpWatch* (April 24, 2006), at www.corpwatch.org/print_article.php?&id=11476.

34. Hershey Foods, "Code of Ethical Business Conduct" (April 24, 2006), at www.thehersheycompany.com/about/conduct.asp.

35. See David P. Baron, *Business and Its Environment*, 4th ed. (Upper Saddle River, NJ: Prentice Hall, 2003), 650–52.

36. Gellerman, "Why 'Good' Managers Make Bad Ethical Choices," 49–66.

37. Gellerman, "Why 'Good' Managers Make Bad Ethical Choices," 53.

38. Procter & Gamble, *2003 Sustainability Report* (April 24, 2006), at www.pg.com/content/pdf/01_about_pg/corporate_citizenship/sustainability/reports/sustainability_report_2003.pdf.

39. U.S. Equal Employment Opportunity Commission, "Facts about Sexual Harassment" (April 24, 2006), at www.eeoc.gov/facts/fs-sex.html.

40. Joanna Grossman, "Sexual Harassment in the Workplace: Do Employers' Efforts Truly Prevent Harassment, or Just Prevent Liability," *Find Laws Legal Commentary, Writ* (April 24, 2006), at writ.news.findlaw.com/grossman/20020507.html.

41. Grossman, "Sexual Harassment in the Workplace."

42. Procter & Gamble, "Respect in the Workplace," *Our Values and Policies* (April 24, 2006), at www.pg.com/content/pdf/01_about_pg/01_about_pg_homepage/about_pg_toolbar/download_report/values_and_policies.pdf.

43. U.S. Department of Labor, "Minimum Wage Laws in the States" (April 24, 2006), at www.dol.gov/esa/minwage/america.htm#.

44. Henry A. Waxman, House of Representatives, "Remarks on Proposed Consumer Bill of Rights Day, Extension of Remarks," March 15, 1993, 1–2 (April 24, 2006), at http://thomas.loc.gov/cgi-bin/query/z?r103:E15MR30-90.

45. Target Brands Inc., "Target Gives Back over $2 Million a Week to Education, the Arts and Social Services" (April 24, 2006), at http://target.com/target_group/community_giving/index.jhtml.

46. Jennifer Barrett, "A Secret Recipe for Success: Paul Newman and A. E. Hotchner Dish Up Management Tips from Newman's Own," *Newsweek*, November 3, 2003, (April 24, 2006), at http://msnbc.msn.com/id/3339645/.

47. Fannie Mae, "Social Responsibility" (April 24, 2006), at www.fanniemae.com/aboutfm/responsibility/index.jhtml?p=About+Fannie+Mae&s=Social+Responsibility.

48. Dan Ackman, "Bill Gates Is a Genius and You're Not," *Forbes.com*, July 21, 2004 (April 24, 2006), at www.forbes.com/2004/07/21/cx_da_0721topnews.html.

49. Philip Kotler and Nancy Lee, "Best of Breed," *Stanford Social Innovation Review*, Spring 2004, 21.

50. Patagonia, "Environmental Action" (April 24, 2006), at www.patagonia.com/enviro/main_enviro_action.shtml.

51. John Carey, "Global Warming," *Business Week*, August 16, 2004, 64.

52. Carey, "Global Warming," 60.

53. Carey, "Global Warming," 64.

54. David Krantz and Brad Kifferstein, "Water Pollution and Society," University of Michigan (April 24, 2006), at www.umich.edu/~gs265/society/waterpollution.htm.

55. Kotler and Lee, "Best of Breed," 20.

56. Simon Zadek, "The Path to Corporate Responsibility," *Harvard Business Review*, December 2004, 1–9.

57. Chris Burritt, "McDonald's Shrugs Off Obesity Case,"

Sina.com, January 27, 2005 (April 30, 2006) at http://english.sina.com/business/1/2005/0127/19504.html.

58. Bruce Horovitz, "By Year's End, Regular Size Will Have to Do," *USA Today*, March 4, 2004 (April 30, 2006) at www.usatoday.com/money/industries/food/2004-03-02-mcdonalds-supersize_x.htm.

59. Eric Herman, "McDonald's Giant Drinks Return," *Chicago Sun-Times*, June 17, 2005 (April 30, 2006) at www.freerepublic.com/focus/f-news/1424786/posts.

CHAPTER 4

1. Lee Scott, "Three Basic Beliefs," *About Wal-Mart* (May 3, 2006), at www.walmartstores.com/GlobalWMStoresWeb/navigate.do?catg=252.

2. Volvo Cars of North America, "Why Volvo" (May 3, 2006), at http://new.volvocars.com/whyvolvo.

3. The Coca-Cola Company, "Code of Business Conduct" (May 3, 2006), at www2.coca-cola.com/ourcompany/business_conduct.html.

4. American Management Association, "Ethics and Integrity Are Listed as Core Values by 76% of Companies," June 26, 2002 (May 3, 2006), at www.amanet.org/press/amanews/corporate_values.htm.

5. Scott Safranski and Ik-Whan Kwon, "Strategic Planning for the Growing Business" (1991), U.S. Small Business Administration (May 3, 2006), at www.sba.gov/library/pubs/eb-6.doc.

6. McDonald's Corp., "McDonald's Announces Plans to Revitalize Its Worldwide Business and Sets New Financial Targets," *McDonald's Financial Press*, April 7, 2003 (May 3, 2006), at www.mcdonalds.com/corp/news/fnpr/2003/fpr04072003.html.

7. Brian Perkins, "Defining Crisis Management," *Wharton Alumni Magazine*, Summer 2000 (May 3, 2006), at www.wharton.upenn.edu/alum_mag/issues/summer2000/feature_3b.html.

8. Stewart Elliott, "Wendy's Gets a Break, but Still Has Work Ahead of It," *The New York Times*, April 29, 2005, *NYTimes.com* (May 4, 2006), at www.nytimes.com/2005/04/29/business/media/29adco.html?ei=5088&en=bb0e017145269f5e&.

9. Sara Lee Corp., "Our Company" (May 3, 2006), at www.saralee.com/ourcompany/profile.aspx.

10. Johnson & Johnson Services, "Business Segments" (May 3, 2006), at www.jnj.com/careers/segments.html.

11. Northwest Forest Industry, Pulp and Paper Manufacturing, "From the Forest to the Office and Home: Bowater—A Case Study in Newsprint and Kraft Pulp Production," *Borealforest.org* (May 3, 2006), at www.borealforest.org/paper/index.htm.

12. McDonald's Corp., "Organizational Structure" (September 28, 2004), at www.mcdonalds.com/corp/career/busfunction.html.

13. F. John Reh, "Management 101," *About Management* (May 3, 2006), at http://management.about.com/cs/generalmanagement/a/Management101.htm.

14. See Karen Collins, *Accountants' Management Styles and Effectiveness* (American Woman's Society of Certified Public Accountants, 1997).

15. Brian Perkins, "Defining Crisis Management," *Wharton Alumni Magazine*, Summer 2000 (May 3, 2006), at www.wharton.upenn.edu/alum_mag/issues/summer2000/feature_3b.html.

16. Brian L. Davis et al., *Successful Manager's Handbook: Development Suggestions for Today's Managers* (Minneapolis: Personnel Decisions Inc., 1992), 189.

17. Davis et al., *Successful Manager's Handbook*, p. 189.

18. Shari Caudron, "Six Steps in Creative Problem Solving," *Controller Magazine*, April 1998, 38. Caudron describes a systematic approach developed by Roger L. Firestien, president of Innovation Systems Group, Williamsville, NY.

19. U.S. Census Bureau, "Legal Form of Organization" (May 3, 2006), at www.census.gov/prod/2000pubs/cc92-s-1.pdf.

CHAPTER 5

1. Introductory material on Howard Schultz and Starbucks comes from Howard Schultz and Dori Jones Yang, *Pour Your Heart into It: How Starbucks Built a Company One Cup at a Time* (New York: Hyperion, 1997), 3–8.

2. Schultz and Yang, *Pour Your Heart into It*, 138.

3. Schultz and Yang, *Pour Your Heart into It*, 6–7.

4. "Starbucks Mission Statement," *Starbucks.com* (May 6, 2006), at www.starbucks.com/aboutus/environment.asp.

5. Schultz and Yang, *Pour Your Heart into It*, 125.

6. "Starbucks Mission Statement," *Starbucks.com*.

7. "Job Center," *Starbucks.com* (May 6, 2006), at www.starbucks.com/aboutus/jobcenter.asp.

8. "How Disney Puts the Magic in Recruiting," *Vault* (May 6, 2006), at www.vault.com/nr/newsmain.jsp?nr_page=3&ch_id=400&article_id=51875&cat_id=1083.

9. "Overview of Careers on Cruise Ships," *Career Prospects in Virginia* (May 6, 2006) at http://www3.ccps.virginia.edu/career_prospects/briefs/PS/SummaryCruise.shtml.

10. The U.S. Equal Employment Opportunity Commission, "Discriminatory Practices"

(May 6, 2006), at www.eeoc. gov/abouteeo/overview_ practices.html.

11. The U.S. Equal Employment Opportunity Commission, "Federal Equal Employment Opportunity (EEO) Laws" (May 6, 2006), at www.eeoc. gov/abouteeo/overview_ laws.html.

12. Bob Nelson and Peter Economy, *Managing for Dummies*, 2nd ed. (New York: Wiley, 2003), 60.

13. "Target Your Recruitment Market," *InFocus: Recruiter News* (May 6, 2006), at http://www.net-temps.com/ recruiters/infocus/article. htm?op=view&id=662.

14. David Lee, "Becoming a Talent Magnet: Your First Task as a Recruiter: Recruit Senior Management onto Your Team" (May 6, 2006), at www.humannatureatwork.com/ Recruiting-Employees.htm.

15. The information in this section comes from two sources: Federal Bureau of Investigation, "Jobs: Special Agents" (May 6, 2006), at https://www.fbijobs.com/ JobDesc.asp?scr=001& requisitionid=368; *Special Agent Selection Process: Applicant Information Booklet*, rev. September, 1997 (May 6, 2006), at www.fbi.gov/employment/ booklet/SAapplinfobooklet.pdf.

16. "Induction: Orienting the New Employee," *HRM Guide Network* (May 6, 2006), at www.bestbooks.biz/learning/ induction.html.

17. Susan Heathfield, "Top Ten Ways to Turn Off a New Employee," *About, Inc.* (May 6, 2006), at http:// humanresources.about.com/ library/weekly/aa022601a.htm.

18. "Top 100: Top Five Profile and Rank," *Training Magazine*, March 2004, 42.

19. Tammy Galvin, "The 2003 Training Top 100," *Training Magazine*, March 2003, 2.

20. Brooke Locascio, "Working at Starbucks: More Than Just Pouring Coffee," *Tea and Coffee*, January/February 2004 (May 6, 2006), at www. teaandcoffee.net/0104/ coffee.htm.

21. Schultz and Yang, *Pour Your Heart into It*, 250–51.

22. "What Makes a Great Place to Work?" Great Place to Work Institute (May 6, 2006), at www.greatplacetowork.com/ great/index.php.

23. "What do Employees Say?" Great Place to Work Institute (May 6, 2006), at www. greatplacetowork.com/great/ employees.php.

24. Sandra Kerka, "The Changing Role of Support Staff" (May 6, 2006), at http://calpro-online. com/eric/docgen.asp?tbl= archive&ID=A019.

25. Jeffrey Greenhaus, Karen Collins, and Jason Shaw, "The Relationship between Work-Family Balance and Quality of Life," *Journal of Vocational Behavior* 63, 2003, 510–31.

26. For information on KPMG's programs and benefits, see "KPMGCareers.com" (May 6, 2006), at http://www.us.kpmg. com/careers/index.asp.

27. Reported in "Study Finds No Downside to Telework," *Work & Family Newsbrief*, February 2004, (May 6, 2006), at www. findarticles.com/p/articles/ mi_m0IJN/is_2004_Feb/ai_ 113315775.

28. Leslie Truex "Work-at-Home Success" (May 6, 2006), at http://workathomesuccess. com/wahsnews.htm.

29. Bonnie Harris, "Child Care Comes to Work," *Los Angeles Times*, November 19, 2000 (June 24, 2004), at www. childrennow.org/newsroom/ news-00/ra-11-19-00.htm.

30. "New List of Best Companies for Mom," *CNNMoney*, September 23, 2003 (May 6, 2006), at http://money.cnn. com/2003/09/23/news/ companies/working_mother/ ?cnn= yes.

31. See Karen Collins and Elizabeth Hoover, "Addressing the Needs of the Single Person in Public Accounting," *Pennsylvania CPA Journal*, June 1995, 16.

32. Data was obtained from 1988 and 1991 studies of stress in public accounting by Karen Collins and from a 1995 study on quality of life in the accounting profession by Collins and Jeffrey Greenhaus. Analysis of the data on single individuals was not separately published.

33. Susan Heathfield, "Performance Appraisals Don't Work," *About* (May 6, 2006), at http://human resources.about.com/cs/ perfmeasurement/l/ aa061100a.htm.

34. Nelson and Economy, *Managing for Dummies*, 140.

35. Archer North & Associates, "Reward Issues," *Performance Appraisal* (May 6, 2006), at www.performance-appraisal. com/rewards.htm.

36. Michele M. Melendez, "Business Can Gain When Worker Gets to Evaluate Boss," *Newhouse News Service*, June 6, 2004 (May 6, 2006), at www. mindbridge.com/news/boss. htm.

37. Gregory P. Smith, "How to Attract, Keep and Motivate Your Workforce," *Business Know-How* (May 6, 2006) at http://www. businessknowhow.com/ manage/attractworkforce.htm.

38. "Companies Are Finding It Really Pays to Be Nice to Employees," *Wall Street Journal*, July 22, 1998, B1 (May 6, 2006), at www.octanner.com/news/ July1998.html.

39. Great Place to Work Institute, "Innovation Awards: SAS" (May 6, 2006), at http://www. greatplacetowork.com/ education/innovate/ honoree-2003-sas.php; Morley Safer, CBS 60 Minutes, Interview with Jim Goodnight, President and Founder of SAS Institute, April 20, 2003 (May 6,

2006), at http://www.cbsnews.com/stories/2003/04/18/60minutes/main550102.shtml; and "SAS Makes Fortune's '100 Best Companies to Work For'" (May 6, 2006), at http://www.sas.com/news/feature/12jan06/fortune.html. For a description of the company's work/life initiatives, visit its Web site at http://www.sas.com/corporate/worklife/index.html.

40. Robert McGarvey, "A Tidal Wave of Turnover," *American Way*, December 15, 2004, 32–36.

41. The Container Store, "Careers" (May 6, 2006), at http://www.containerstore.com/careers/index.jhtml;jsessionid=0C2Q2LP3RTG0XQFIAIMCM44AVABBMJVC.

42. Freda Turner, "An Effective Employee Suggestion Program Has a Multiplier Effect," *The CEO Refresher* (May 6, 2006), at www.refresher.com/!ftmultiplier.html.

43. Gregory P. Smith, "Top Ten Reasons Why People Quit Their Jobs," *The CEO Refresher* (May 6, 2006), at www.refresher.com/!gpsquit.html.

44. Charles J. Muhl, "The Employment-at-Will Doctrine: Three Major Exceptions," *Monthly Labor Review*, January 2001, 1–11 (May 6, 2006), at http://www.bls.gov/opub/mlr/2001/01/art1full.pdf.

45. Robert Levering and Milton Moskowitz, "Special Report: The 100 Best Companies to Work For," *Fortune*, January 12, 2004, 56–62+.

46. See "Crab Pickers," *Crisfield Off the Beaten Path* (May 6, 2006), at www.crisfield.com/sidestreet/ickers.html; and Neil Learner, "Ashore, A Way of Life Built around the Crab," *Christian Science Monitor*, June 26, 2000 (May 6, 2006), at http://csmonitor.com/cgi-bin/durableRedirect.pl?/durable/2000/06/26/fp15s1-csm.shtml.

47. The Hartford, "Career Opportunities" (May 6, 2006), at http://thehartford.hire.com/joblist.html.

48. Texas Instruments, "Benefits" (May 6, 2006), at www.ti.com/recruit/docs/benefits.shtml.

49. Jeff D. Opdyke, "Getting a Bonus Instead of a Raise," *Wall Street Journal*, December 29, 2004 (December 29, 2004), at www.azcentral.com/business/articles/1229wsj-bonuses29-ON.html.

50. Lee Ann Obringer, "How Employee Compensation Works—Stock Options/Profit Sharing," *HowStuffWorks* (May 6, 2006), at http://money.howstuffworks.com/benefits.htm.

51. Texas Instruments, "Benefits" (May 6, 2006), at www.ti.com/recruit/docs/profit.shtml.

52. Ibid.

53. U.S. Chamber of Commerce, "Chamber Survey Shows Worker Benefits Continue Growth," January 2004 (May 6, 2006), at http://www.uschamber.com/press/releases/2004/january/04-07.htm.

54. *National Compensation Survey: Employee Benefits in Private Industry, 2003,* U.S. Department of Labor, Bureau of Labor Statistics, March 2003, 2 (May 6, 2006), at www.bls.gov/ncs/ebs/home.htm.

55. Judith Lindenberger and Marian Stoltz-Loike, "Diversity in the Workplace," The Economics and Policy Resource Center (May 6, 2006), at http://www.advertisingknowhow.com/article-archives/Business/Diversity-In-The-Workplace.html.

56. U.S. Equal Employment Opportunity Commission, "Occupational Employment in Private Industry by Race/Ethnic Group/Sex, and by Industry, United States, 2002" (May 6, 2006), at www.eeoc.gov/stats/jobpat/2002/us.html.

57. U.S. Equal Employment Opportunity Commission, "Federal Laws Prohibiting Job Discrimination: Questions and Answers," Federal Equal Employment Opportunity (EEO) Laws (May 6, 2006), at www.eeoc.gov/facts/qanda.html.

58. U.S. Equal Employment Opportunity Commission, "EEOC Agrees to Landmark Resolution of Discrimination Case Against Abercrombie & Fitch" (May 6, 2006) at http://www.eeoc.gov/press/11-18-04.html.

59. See Michael R. Carrell and Christina Heavrin, *Labor Relations and Collective Bargaining: Cases, Practice, and Law,* 7th ed. (Upper Saddle River, NJ: Pearson Education, 2004), 52–54.

60. U.S. Department of Labor, Bureau of Labor Statistics, "Union Members in 2003" January 2004, (December 30, 2004), at www.bls.gov/cps and U.S. Department of Labor, Bureau of Labor Statistics, Union Members Summary, January 20, 2006 (May 6, 2006), at http://www.bls.gov/news.release/union2.nr0.htm.

61. "Hawaii Professors End Strike," *USA Today*, June 19, 2001 (May 6, 2006), at www.usatoday.com/news/nation/2001-04-18-hawaii.htm.

62. Union Label and Service Department, AFL/CIO, "AFL-CIO National Boycott List," November–December 2004 (May 6, 2006) at http://www.unionlabel.org/boycott.jsp.

63. National Hockey League Labor Dispute (2004), *Wikipedia* (May 6, 2006), at http://en.wikipedia.org/wiki/National_Hockey_League_labor_dispute_(2004).

64. AFL-CIO, "How & Why People Join Unions," *Unions 101* (May 6, 2006), at http://www.aflcio.org/joinaunion/union101.cfm.

CHAPTER 6

1. Seth Godin, *Purple Cow: Transform Your Business by Being Remarkable* (New York: Penguin Group, 2003).

2. See "Discover the Segway HT Revolution," *Segway* (May 11, 2006), at www.segway.com/segway/; and "Segway HT," *The Great Idea Finder* (May 11, 2006), at www.ideafinder.com/history/inventions/story089.htm.

3. See "The JD Batball," *The Great Idea Finder* (May 11, 2006), at www.ideafinder.com/history/inventions/jdbatball.htm; and "Molds Designer Uses SolidWorks Software to Make 8-Year-Old's Dream a Reality," *SolidWorks Express* (May 11, 2006), at www.solidworks.com/swexpress/jan/200201_feature_04.html.

4. "Awards and Media," *PowerSki Jetboards* (May 11, 2006), at www.powerski.com.

5. See *Eureka!Ranch* at www.eurekaranch.com.

6. "Success Calls for Creativity," *CNN Money*, February 4, 1997 (May 11, 2006), at http://money.cnn.com/1997/02/04/busunu/intv_hall/.

7. "Why Eureka," *Eureka!Ranch* (May 11, 2006), at www.eurekaranch.com/eureka/default2.asp/.

8. This approach is adapted from Kathleen Allen, *Entrepreneurship for Dummies* (Foster, CA: IDG Books, 2001), 73–77.

9. See Allen, *Entrepreneurship for Dummies*, 67.

10. Karl Ulrich and Steven Eppinger, *Product Design and Development*, 2nd ed. (New York: Irwin McGraw-Hill, 2000), 66; and Allen, *Entrepreneurship for Dummies*, 79.

11. "Long Distance Running: State of the Sport," *USA Track & Field* (May 11, 2006), at www.usatf.org/news/special Reports/2003LDRStateOfThe Sport.asp.

12. National Sporting Goods Association (May 11, 2006), at http://nsga.org.

13. "Trends in U.S. Physical Fitness Behavior (1987–Present)" (May 11, 2006), at www.americansportsdata.com/phys_fitness_trends1.asp.

14. Alan Scher Zagier, "Eyeing Competition, Florida Increases Efforts to Lure Retirees," *Boston Globe*, December 26, 2003 (May 11, 2006), at www.boston.com/news/nation/articles/2003/12/26/eyeing_competition_florida_increases_efforts_to_lure_retirees/.

15. Ulrich and Eppinger, *Product Design and Development*, 3.

16. Tony Ulwick and John A. Eisenhauer, "Predicting the Success or Failure of a New Product Concept," *The Management Roundtable* (May 11, 2006), at www.roundtable.com/Event_Center/I@WS/I@WS_paper3.html.

17. Steve Hannaford, "Slotting Fees and Oligopolies" (May 11, 2006), www.oligopolywatch.com/2003/05/08.html.

18. U.S. Patent and Trademark Office (May 11, 2006) www.uspto.gov/web/patents/howtopat.htm.

19. "International Property and Licensing" IBM (May 11, 2006), at www.ibm.com/ibm/licensing/.

20. "Facts and Figures from the World of Patents," European Patent Office (May 11, 2006), at www.european-patent-office.org/epo/facts_figures/facts2000/e/5_e.htm.

21. U.S. Patent and Trademark Office (May 11, 2006) at www.uspto.gov/web/offices/com/iip/index.htm.

22. Jonathan Krim, "Web site Providers Say Patent System Stalls Technology," *Boston.com* (May 11, 2006), at www.boston.com/business/technology/articles/2003/12/21/website_providers_say_patent_system_stalls_technology.

23. Wayne Chaneski, "Cellular Manufacturing Can Help You," *Modern Machine Shop Magazine*, August 1998 (May 11, 2006), at www.mmsonline.com/articles/0898ci.html; and "Better Production—Manufacturing Cell Boosts Profits and Flexibility," *Modern Machine Shop Magazine*, May 2001 (May 11, 2006), at www.mmsonline.com/articles/0501bp2.html.

24. U.S. Department of Labor, Bureau of Labor Statistics, *Industry at a Glance: Employment in Manufacturing, 1993–2002* (May 11, 2006), at www.bls.gov/iag/manufacturing.htm.

25. Laura Baughman, "Why Congress Should Fund Better Services Data" (May 11, 2006), at www.sitrends.org/ideas/expert.asp?EXPERT_ID=49.

26. Information on Burger King was obtained from an interview with David Sell, former vice president of Central, Eastern, and Northern Europe and president of Burger King France and Germany.

27. Charles J. Nuese, *Building the Right Things Right* (New York: Quality Resources, 1995), 102.

28. " ISO 9000–The Whole Story," International Organization for Standardization (May 11, 2006), at www.iso.org/iso/en/commcentre/pressreleases/archives/2003/Ref865.html.

CHAPTER 7

1. Wow Wee Toys, "Robosapien: A Fusion of Technology and Personality" (May 21, 2006), at www.wowwee.com/robosapien/robo1/robomain.html.

2. American Marketing Association, "Marketing Glossary Dictionary" (May 21, 2006), at www.marketingpower.com/mg-dictionary.php?

3. Michael Arndt, "High Tech—and Handcrafted," *BusinessWeek Online*, July 5, 2004 (May 21, 2006), at www.businessweek.com/magazine/

content/04_27/b3890113_
mz018.htm.

4. Hyundai Motor America,
"Special Programs: College
Graduate Program" (May 21,
2006), at www.hyundaiusa.
com/financing/specialoffers/
collegegraduate.aspx.

5. "McDonald's Test Markets
Spam," *Pacific Business News*,
June 11, 2002 (May 21, 2006), at
www.bizjournals.com/pacific/
stories/2002/06/10/daily22.
html.

6. "The Super McDonalds,"
Halfbakery (May 21, 2006), at
www.halfbakery.com/idea/
The_20Super_20McDonalds.

7. "Coolest Inventions 2003:
Parking-Space Invader," *Time*
(Online Edition) (May 21, 2006),
at www.time.com/time/2003/
inventions/invprius.html.

8. Rob Rubin and William
Bluestein, "Applying
Technographics," Forrester
Research (May 21, 2006),
at www.forester.com/ER/
Marketing/0,1503,84,FF.html.

9. Information in this section was
obtained through an interview
with the director of marketing
at Wow Wee Toys Ltd. con-
ducted on July 15, 2004.

10. Brendan Light, "Kellogg's Goes
Online for Consumer Research,"
Packaging Digest, July 2004, 40.

11. "2002 Global Brands
Scoreboard," *BusinessWeek
Online*, August 5, 2002
(May 21, 2006), at http://
bwnt.businessweek.com/
brand/2002/index.asp.

12. Diane Brady et al., "Cult
Brands," *Business Week*,
August 2, 2004, 65–71.

13. "Nabisco Introduces 100
Calorie Packs as a Way to
Count Calories When Reaching
for a Snack," *Packaging Digest*,
July 12, 2004 (May 21, 2006), at
www.packagingdigest.com.

14. Cliff Edwards, "Ready to Buy a
Home Robot?" *Business Week*,
July 19, 2004, 84–90.

15. Andres Lillo, "Wal-Mart Gains
Strength from Distribution

Chain," *Home Textiles Today*,
March 24, 2003 (May 21, 2006),
at http://print.google.com/
print/doc?articleid=gwh63Dh
HmV5.

16. BMW Manufacturing Co.,
"Virtual Plant Tour" (May 21,
2006), at http://bmwusfactory.
com/build/default.asp.

17. "BMW Oxford Plant: The MINI
Plant," *Automotive Intelligence*,
July 10, 2001 (May 21, 2006), at
www.autointell.com/european_
companies/BMW/mini/
oxford-plant/bmw-oxford-
plant-01.htm.

18. U.S. Department of
Transportation, Bureau of
Transportation Statistics,
*Commercial Freight Activities in
the U.S. by Mode of Transportation
(1993, 1997, and 2002)* (May 21,
2006), at www.bls.gov/oco/cg/
cgs021.htm#nature.

19. U.S. Department of Labor,
Bureau of Labor Statistics, *Truck,
Transportation and Warehousing*
(May 21, 2006), at www.bls.gov/
oco/cg/cgs021.htm.

20. Lawrence D. Fredendall and
Ed Hill, *Basics of Supply Chain
Management* (Boca Raton, FL:
St. Lucie Press, 2001), 8.

21. Simone Kaplan, "Easter in
November, Christmas in July,"
CIO Magazine, November 1,
2001 (May 21, 2006), at
www.cio.com/archive/110101/
easter.html.

22. Domino's Pizza LLC, "About
Domino's Pizza" (May 21,
2006), at www.dominos.com.

23. Philip Kotler, *Marketing
Management*, 11th ed. (Upper
Saddle River, NJ: Prentice Hall,
2003), 11.

24. The concept of the value chain
was first analyzed by Michael
Porter in *Competitive Advantage:
Creating and Sustaining Superior
Performance* (New York: The
Free Press, 1985).

25. Seth Godin, *Permission
Marketing: Turning Strangers
into Friends, and Friends into
Customers* (New York: Simon &
Schuster, 1999), 29.

26. Godin, *Permission Marketing*, 31.

27. Nantucket Allserve, Inc.,
"Nantucket Nectars from the
Beginning" (May 21, 2006), at
www.juiceguys.com.

28. Kevin J. Clancy, "Sleuthing for
New Products, Not Slashing
for Growth," *Across the Board*,
September–October 2001
(May 21, 2006), at www.
copernicusmarketing.com/
about/docs/new_products.
htm.

29. "2004 to Bring Loads of
'Free' Net Music," *CNN.com*,
December 22, 2003 (May 21,
2006), at www.cnn.com/2003/
TECH/biztech/12/22/
digital.music.reut/index.

30. "Tickle Me Elmo: Using the
Media to Create a Marketing
Sensation," *Media Awareness
Network* (May 21, 2006), at
www.media-awareness.ca/
english/resources/educational/
handouts/advertising_
marketing/tickle_me_elmo.cfm.

31. PricewaterhouseCoopers,
"2003 World's Most Respected
Companies Survey" (May 21,
2006), at www.pwc.com/
Extweb/ncsurvres.nsf/docid/
D2345E01A80AC14885256CB00
033DC8F.

32. Randall B. Bean, "We're Not
There Yet," *Direct Marketing
Business Intelligence*, September
30, 1999 (May 21, 2006), at
http://directmag.com/mag/
marketing_not_yet/index.html.

33. Stephane Fitch, "Stacking the
Deck: Harrah's Wants Your
Money," *Forbes.com*, July 5, 2004
(May 21, 2006), at www.
forbes.com/business/forbes/
2004/0705/132.html.

34. Godin, *Permission Marketing*,
40–52.

35. Anthony Bianco, "The
Vanishing Mass Market,"
Business Week, July 12, 2004,
61–68.

36. LEGO Group, *Annual Report
2003* (May 21, 2006), at
www.lego.com/eng/info/
default.asp?page=
annualreport.

37. See "Lego Attempts to Woo Back Preschoolers by Relaunching Duplo Series," *KeepMedia*, February 2, 2004 (May 21, 2006), at www.keepmedia.com/pubs/AFP/2004/02/02/364595; "Is There a Future for Lego in Kids' High-Tech Game World?" *KeepMedia*, January 10, 2004 (May 21, 2006), at www.keepmedia.com/ShowItemDetails.do?item_id=348949; Charles Fishman, "Why Can't Lego Click," *Fast Company*, September 1, 2001 (May 21, 2006), at www.fastcompany.com/online/50/lego.html.

38. LEGO Group, *Annual Report 2003*.

39. Sandra Tsing Loh, "Nannyhood and Apple Pie," *The Atlantic*, October 1, 2003, 122–23.

40. Jessica R. Sincavage, "The Labor Force and Unemployment: Three Generations of Change," *Monthly Labor Review*, June 2004, 34.

41. John Leo, "The Good-News Generation," *U.S. News & World Report*, November 3, 2003 (May 21, 2006) at www.keepmedia.com/pubs/USNewsWorldReport/2003/11/03/293076?extID=10026.

42. Ellen Neuborne and Kathleen Kerwin, "Generation Y," *BusinessWeek Online*, February 15, 1999 (May 21, 2006), at www.businessweek.com/1999/99_07/b3616001.htm.

43. Ibid.

44. Ibid.

45. Ibid.

46. Ibid.; Kari Richardson, "Zell Conference Reveals Next Marketing Wave," *Kellogg World* (Kellogg School of Management, Northwestern University, Winter 2002) (May 21, 2006), at www.kellogg.northwestern.edu/kwo/win02/inbrief/zell.htm; Michele Fernandez-Cruz, "Advertising Agencies Target Generation Y," *youngmoney.com* (May 21, 2006), at www.youngmoney.com/lifestyles/campus_life/031202_01.

47. Bruce Tulgan and Carolyn A. Martin, "Book Excerpt: *Managing Generation Y—Part I*," *BusinessWeek Online*, September 28, 2001 (May 21, 2006), at www.businessweek.com/smallbiz/content/sep2001/sb20010928_113.htm.

48. Gerry Kobe, "Automakers Push Image for Generation-Y Customers," *Automotive Industries*, December 2001 (May 21, 2006), at www.findarticles.com/p/articles/mi_m3012/is_12_181/ai_84377750.

49. Bianco, "The Vanishing Mass Market," 61–68.

50. Stephen Baker, "Channeling the Future," *BusinessWeek Online*, July 12, 2004 (May 21, 2006), at www.businessweek.com/magazine/content/04_28/b3891013_mz001.htm.

CHAPTER 8

1. World Trade Organization, "World Trade Developments in 2004 and Prospects for 2005" (May 25, 2006), at www.wto.org/english/res_e/statis_e/its2005_e/its05_general_overview_e.pdf.

2. Warren E. Buffet, "Why I'm Not Buying the U.S. Dollar," *Wall Street Week with Fortune* (May 25, 2006), at www.pbs.org/wsw/news/fortunearticle_20031026_03.html.

3. "Why Are Prices in Japan So Damn High?" *The Japan FAQ* (May 25, 2006), at www.geocities.com/japanfaq/FAQ-Prices.html.

4. Buffet, "Why I'm Not Buying the U.S. Dollar."

5. Fine Waters Media, "Bottled Water of France" (May 25, 2006), at www.finewaters.com/Bottled_Water/France/Evian.asp.

6. H. Frederick Gale, "China's Growing Affluence: How Food Markets Are Responding" (U.S. Department of Agriculture, June 2003) (May 25, 2006), at www.ers.usda.gov/Amberwaves/June03/Features/ChinasGrowingAffluence.htm.

7. Viacom International, "Viacom Announces a Strategic Alliance for Chinese Content Production with Beijing Television (BTV)" (October 16, 2004), at www.viacom.com/press.tin?ixPress Release= 80454169.

8. Liz Borod, "DA! To the Good Life," *Folio*, September 1, 2004 (May 25, 2006), at www.keepmedia.com/pubs/Folio/2004/09/01/574543?ba=m&bi=1&bp=7; Jill Garbi, "Cosmo Girl Goes to Israel," *Folio*, November 1, 2003 (May 25, 2006), at www.keepmedia.com/pubs/Folio/2003/11/01/293597?ba=m&bi=0&bp=7; Borod, "A Passage to India," *Folio*, August 1, 2004 (May 25, 2006), at www.keepmedia.com/pubs/Forbes/2000/10/30/1017010?ba=a&bi=1&bp=7; Jill Garbi, "A Sleeping Media Giant?" *Folio*, January 1, 2004 (May 25, 2006), at www.keepmedia.com/pubs/Folio/2004/01/01/340826?ba=m&bi=0&bp=7.

9. Daniel Gross, "The 2005 Global 500," *Fortune*, July 25, 2005 (May 27, 2006), at money.cnn.com/magazines/fortune/global500/

10. James C. Morgan and J. Jeffrey Morgan, *Cracking the Japanese Market* (New York: The Free Press, 1991), 102.

11. McDonald's India, "Respect for Local Culture" (May 25, 2006), at www.mcdonaldsindia.com/loccul.htm.

12. McDonald's Corp., "A Taste of McDonald's Around the World," *media.mcdonalds.com* (May 25, 2006), at www.media.mcdonalds.com/secured/ products/international.

13. Morgan and Morgan, *Cracking the Japanese Market*, 117.

14. Anne O. Krueger, "Supporting Globalization" (Remarks at the 2002 Eisenhower National Security Conference on "National Security for the 21st Century: Anticipating Challenges, Seizing Opportunities, Building Capabilities," September 26, 2002) (May 25, 2006), at www.imf.org/external/np/speeches/2002/092602a.htm.

15. The World Bank Group, "Country Classification," *Data and Statistics* (May 25, 2006), at www.worldbank.org/data/countryclass/countryclass.html.

16. David Ricks, *Blunders in International Business* (Malden, MA: Blackwell, 1999), 137.

17. Dustin Smith, "The Truth About Industrial Country Tariffs," *Finance & Development*, September 2002 (May 25, 2006), at www.imf.org/external/pubs./ft/fandd/2002/09/smith.htm.

18. See William F. Buckley, "W.T.O. at Bat," *Uexpress* (May 25, 2006), at www.townhall.com/opinion/columns/wfbuckley/2003/12/06/160423.html.

19. See George Will, "Sugar Quotas Produce Sour Results," *Detroit News*, February 13, 2004 (October 17, 2004), at www.detnews.com/2004/editorial/0402/15/all-62634.htm.

20. See Buckley, "W.T.O. at Bat"; and Matthew Benjamin, "Steeling for a Trade Battle," *U.S. News & World Report*, November 24, 2003 (May 25, 2006), at www.usnews.com/usnews/biztech/articles/031124/24trade.htm.

21. Bernard Sanders, "The International Monetary Fund Is Hurting You," *Z Magazine*, July–August 1998 (May 25, 2006), at www.thirdworldtraveler.com/IMF_WB/IMF_Sanders.html.

22. See "The Euro: The Basis for an Undeniable Competitive Advantage" (May 25, 2006), at www.investinwallonia.be/an/marche_euro01.htm

CHAPTER 9

1. John Price, "The Return of the Buffetteers," *Investor Journal*, August, 1998 (May 29, 2006), at www.sherlockinvesting.com/articles/buffetteers.htm.

2. Interview with Warren Buffet. "Warren Buffet: What Does He Have That You Don't?" *Cool Avenues* (May 26, 2006) at www.coolavenues.com/know/fin/.

3. Much of the discussion in this section is adapted from Mike Brewster, *Unaccountable: How the Accounting Profession Forfeited a Public Trust* (Hoboken, NJ: John Wiley & Sons, 2003).

4. Jeanne Sahadi, "Average Starting Salaries for Class of '05 Higher—in Some Cases Notably—Than last Year," *CNNMoney.com*, April 19, 2005 (May 26, 2006) at http://money.cnn.com/2005/04/15/pf/college.

5. From Tom Vanderbilt, *The Sneaker Book: Anatomy of an Industry and an Icon* (New York: The New Press, 1998), 111.

CHAPTER 10

1. Insurance Information Institute, *Financial Services Fact Book 2006*, Banking: Commercial Banks (May 30, 2006), at http://financialservicesfacts.org/financial/

2. Pennsylvania Association of Community Bankers, "What's the Difference?" (May 30, 2006), at www.pacb.org/banks_and_banking/difference.html.

3. See Wachovia Bank, NA, "Wachovia" (May 30, 2006), at www.wachovia.com.

4. Federal Reserve System, "Monetary Policy FAQs," *FED101* (May 30, 2006), at www.federalreserveeducation.org/fed101_html/policy/basics_print.htm.

5. Robert Heilbroner and Lester Thurow, *Economics Explained* (New York: Simon & Schuster, 1998), 134.

6. Federal Reserve System, "Monetary Policy FAQs," *FED101* (May 30, 2006), at www.federalreserveeducation.org/fed101_html/policy/basics_print.htm.

7. Federal Reserve System, "Financial Services," *FED101* (May 30, 2006), at www.federal-reserveeducation.org/FED101_HTML/services/index.cfm; Federal Reserve System, "Banking Supervision," *FED101* (May 30, 2006), at www.federalreserveeducation.org/FED101%5FHTML/supervision/.

8. U.S. Securities and Exchange Commission (May 30, 2006), at www.sec.gov.

CHAPTER 11

1. Robert L. Shook, *Jackpot! Harrah's Winning Secrets for Customer Loyalty* (Hoboken, NJ: John Wiley & Sons, 2003), xi.

2. Jim Kilby, Jim Fox, and Anthony F. Lucas, *Casino Operations and Management*, 2nd ed. (Hoboken, NJ: John Wiley & Sons, 2005), 183–84.

3. Meridith Levinson, "Jackpot! Harrah's Big Payoff Came from Using IT to Manage Customer Information," *CIO Magazine*, February 1, 2001 (June 2, 2006), at www.cio.com/archive/020101/harrah.html.

4. Christopher Koch, "The ABCs of ERP," *CIO.com* (June 2, 2006), at www.cio.com/research/erp/edit/erpbasics.html.

5. Harrah's, "Total Rewards" (June 2, 2006), at www.harrahs.com/total_rewards/overview/overview.jsp.

6. Shook, *Jackpot!*, 228–229.

7. Gary Loveman, "Diamonds in the Data Mine," *Harvard Business Review*, May 2003, 3.

8. Darrell Dunn, "Client-Tracking System Helps Harrah's Tailor Sales Efforts for Frequent Visitors," *Information Week*, November 4, 2003 (June 2, 2006),

at www.informationweek.
com/story/showArticle.jhtml?
articleID=16000115.

9. Shook, *Jackpot!*, 248–252.

10. "Decision Support System,"
Webopedia (June 2, 2006), at
www.webopedia.com/TERM/
D/decision_support_system.
html.

11. "Artificial Intelligence,"
Webopedia (June 2, 2006), at
www.webopedia.com/TERM/
artificial_intelligence.

12. "Artificial Intelligence,"
Webopedia.

13. John Goff, "Head Games:
Businesses Deploying Analytical
Software to Get a Better Fix on
Customer Behavior," *CFO
Magazine for Senior Financial
Executives* 20:9, July 1, 2004
(June 2, 2006), at www.cfo.com/
article.cfm/3014815.

14. See Daintry Duffy,
"Technology's Winning Hand,"
CSO.online, October 1, 2003
(June 2, 2006), at www.
csoonline.com/read/100103/
kind_sidebar_1787.html; Larry
Barrett Gallagher and Sean
Gallagher, "NORA and ANNA:
Non-Obvious Relationship
Awareness," *Baseline*, April 4,
2004 (June 2, 2006), at
www.baselinemag.com/
article2/0,1397,1615733,00.asp.

15. Levinson, "Jackpot!"

16. See "The Difference Between
the Internet and the World
Wide Web," *Webopedia* (June 2,
2006), at www.webopedia.com/
DidYouKnow/Internet/2002/
Web_vs_Internet.asp.

17. Richard T. Griffiths, "Chapter
Two: The World Wide Web
(WWW)," *The History of the
Internet* (June 2, 2006), at
www.let.leidenuniv.nl/history/
ivh/chap2.htm.

18. Rob McGann, "People Aged 55
and Up Drive U.S. Web
Growth," *ClickZ Network* (June
2, 2006), at www.clickz.com/
stats/sectors/traffic_patterns/
article.php/3446641.

19. "World Wide Web," *Wikipedia*
(June 2, 2006), at http://

en.wikipedia.org/wiki/
World_Wide_Web.

20. Don Jones, Mark Scott, and
Rick Villars, *E-Commerce for
Dummies* (New York: Wiley,
2001), xxvi.

21. Matt Phillips, "Digital Music
Services Hit First Major
Milestone as Downloads
Outsell Physical Formats
for the First Time," *British
Phonographic Industry*,
September 2, 2004 (June 2,
2006), at www.bpi.co.uk/
index.asp?Page=news/stats/
news_content_file_743.shtml.

22. "Can E-Tailers Find Fulfillment
with Drop Shipping?" *Research
at Penn* (June 2, 2006), at
www.upenn.edu/research
atpenn/article.php?21&bus.

23. Steve Alexander, "Feds Take
Up Arms as Computer Crime
Becomes Multibillion-Dollar
Problem," *Minneapolis Star
Tribune*, Computer Crime
Research Center (June 2, 2006),
at www.crime-research.org/
news/2003/10/Mess0601.html.

24. "2004 E-Crime Watch Survey
Shows Significant Increase in
Electronic Crimes," Carnegie
Mellon, Software Engineering
Institute, May 25, 2004 (June 2,
2006), at www.sei.cmu.edu/
about/press/e-crime-release.
html.

25. Alexander, "Feds Take Up
Arms."

26. "2004 E-Crime Watch Survey."

27. Stephen Baker and Brian Grow,
"Gambling Sites, This Is a
Holdup," *BusinessWeek Online*,
August 9, 2004 (June 2, 2006),
at www.businessweek.com/
magazine/content/04_32/
b3895106_mz063.hl.,mktm.

28. Lorraine Woellert, "Why the
Grokster Case Matters,"
BusinessWeek Online, December
27, 2004 (June 2, 2006), at
www.businessweek.com/
magazine/content/04_52/
b3914038_mz011.htm .

29. "Pirates' Share," *Foreign Policy*,
January/February 2005 (June 2,
2006), at http://foreignpolicy.

com/story/cms.php?story_
id=2766.

30. Office of Intellectual Property
Rights, *Strategy Targeting
Organized Piracy* (June 2, 2006),
at www.stopfakes.gov/.

31. Vangie Aurora Beal, "When Is
Downloading Music on the
Internet Illegal?" *Webopedia*,
December 22, 2004 (June 2,
2006), at www.Webopedia.
com/DidYouKnow/Internet/
2004/music_downloading.asp.

32. Heather Green, "Digital Media:
Don't Clamp Down Too Hard,"
BusinessWeek Online, October
14, 2002 (June 2, 2006), at
www.businessweek.com/
magazine/content/02_41/
b3803121.htm; Melissa Lynn,
"Piracy and Economic National
Security," *BusinessWeek Online*,
August 2, 2004 (June 2, 2006), at
http://www.businessweek.com/
bwdaily/dnflash/aug2004/
nf2004082_1497.htm?campaign_
id=search.

33. International Federation of
the Phonographic Industry,
"Recording Industry World
Sales, 2003" (June 2, 2006), at
www.ifpi.org/site-content/
statistics/worldsales.html.

34. The Office of the Federal Privacy
Commissioner, "Protecting Your
Privacy on the Internet" (June 2,
2006), at www.privacy.gov.au/
internet/internet_privacy.

35. "Careers at Kraft: Information
Systems" (June 2, 2006), at
www.kraftfoods.com/careers/
careers/systems.htm.

APPENDIX C

1. Here's why these two categories are excluded: If you list
salary costs for R&D employees
in both the HR and R&D sections, you're counting salary
costs for these employees twice.
When you buy R&D equip-
ment, you're purchasing a
long-term asset. This asset is
included on the list of items
you're buying to start your
business (on your **cash requirements schedule**). The template

will calculate the cost associated with the use of this asset (called *Depreciation expense*) and automatically add this cost to your other expenses.

■ SOURCES

CHAPTER 1

Figure 1.2 Adapted from Karl E. Case and Ray C. Fair, *Principles of Economics*, 7th ed. (Upper Saddle River, NJ: Prentice Hall, 2004), 102; **Figure 1.3** Adapted from Ronald M. Ayers and Robert A. Collinge, *Economics: Explore and Apply* (Upper Saddle River, NJ: Pearson Education, 2005), 6; **Figure 1.7** Data from Bureau of Labor Statistics, "Civilian Unemployment Rate" (U.S. Dept. of Labor, June 4, 2006), at http://research.stlouisfed.org/fred2/series/UNRATE; **Figure 1.8** Data from "Annual Inflation," *InflationData.com* (June 6, 2006), at http://inflationdata.com/Inflation/Inflation_Rate/CurrentInflation.asp; **Table 1.1** Data from "Historical CPI," *InflationData.com* (June 6, 2006), at http://inflationdata.com/inflation/consumer_price_index/HistoricalCPI.aspx; **Figure 1.9** Data from U.S. Department of Labor, Bureau of Labor Statistics; see "Economic Time Series Page," *Economagic.com* (March 16, 2005), at http://economic-charts.com/em-cgi/data.exe/blsin/inu0021us0.

CHAPTER 2

Figure 2.1 Data from "Small Business Answer Card" (U.S. Small Business Administration: Office of Advocacy, April 1999) (April 6, 2005), at www.sba.gov/advo/stats/ec_anscd.html; **Figure 2.2** Data from "Women-Owned Firms, 2002," (U.S. Census Bureau, 2002 Economic Census, February 2006) (August 3, 2006), at http://www.census.gov/csd/sbo/women2002.htm; "Hispanic-Owned Firms: 2002," (U.S. Census Bureau, 2002 Economic Census, March 2006) (August 3, 2006), at http://www.census.gov/csd/sbo/hispanic2002.htm; "Black-Owned Firms: 2002," (U.S. Census Bureau, 2002 Economic Census, April 2006) (August 3, 2006), at http://www.census.gov/csd/sbo/black2002.htm;

Figure 2.3 Adapted from Norman M. Scarborough and Thomas W. Zimmerer, *Effective Small Business Management: An Entrepreneurial Approach*, 8th ed. (Upper Saddle River, NJ: Pearson Education, 2006), 26; data from U.S. Small Business Administration; **Figure 2.4** Thomas W. Zimmerer and Norman M. Scarborough, *Essentials of Entrepreneurship and Small Business Management*, 3rd ed. (Upper Saddle River, NJ: Pearson Education, 2002), 11; data from Ernst & Young LLP; **Figure 2.5** Adapted from Norman M. Scarborough and Thomas W. Zimmerer, *Effective Small Business Management: An Entrepreneurial Approach*, 8th ed. (Upper Saddle River, NJ: Pearson Education, 2006), 99; data from "The Big Bang," *Entrepreneur.com*, January 2004 (March 14, 2005), at www.entrepreneur.com/article/0,4621,312275-3,00; reprinted with permission from Entrepreneur Media, Inc.; **Figure 2.6** Adapted from Norman M. Scarborough and Thomas W. Zimmerer, *Effective Small Business Management: An Entrepreneurial Approach*, 8th ed. (Upper Saddle River, NJ: Pearson Education, 2006), 486; data from U.S. Small Business Administration.

CHAPTER 3

Figure 3.4 Adapted from David P. Baron, *Business and Its Environment*, 4th ed. (Upper Saddle River, NJ: Pearson Education, 2003), 650–52; **Figure 3.5** Data from Bureau of Labor Statistics, "Table 1. Fatal Occupational Injuries by Event or Exposure, 1998–2002," *News* (U.S. Dept. of Labor, September 22, 2004), at www.bls.gov/news/release/cfoi.t01.htm; Bureau of Labor Statistics, "Table 2. Fatal Occupational Injuries by Industry and Selected Event Exposure, 2003," *News* (U.S. Dept. of Labor, September 22, 2004), at www.bls.gov/news/release/cfoi.t02.htm; **Figure 3.6** Data from "2003 Median Annual Earnings by Race and Sex," *Infoplease* (2000–2004), at www.infoplease.com/ipa/A0197814.html; Daniel E. Hecker, "Earnings of College Graduates," *Monthly Labor Review*, March 1998, 62–71, Table 1 (at http://stats.bls.gov/opub/mlr/

1998/03/art5exc.htm); **Figure 3.7** Adapted from Simon Zadek, "The Path to Corporate Responsibility," *Harvard Business Review*, December 2004, 1–9.

CHAPTER 4

Figure 4.1 Adapted from Stephen P. Robbins and Mary Coulter, *Management*, 8th ed. (Upper Saddle River, NJ: Pearson Education, 2005), 8; **Figure 4.2** Adapted in part from Samuel C. Certo and C. Trevis Certo, *Modern Management*, 10th ed. (Upper Saddle River, NJ: Pearson Education, 2006), 135; **Figure 4.9** Adapted from Henry R. Cheeseman, *Business Law: Legal, E-Commerce, Ethical, and International Environments*, 5th ed. (Upper Saddle River, NJ: Pearson Education, 2004), 609; **Figure 4.10** Adapted from Henry R. Cheeseman, *Business Law: Legal, E-Commerce, Ethical, and International Environments*, 5th ed. (Upper Saddle River, NJ: Pearson Education, 2004), 615; **Figure 4.11** Data from Internal Revenue Service, *SOI Bulletin—Winter 2004–2005* (Department of the Treasury, 2005), at www.irs.gov/taxstats/bustaxstats/article/0,,id=137167,00.html.

CHAPTER 5

Figure 5.2 Adapted from Abraham Maslow, *Motivation and Personality*, 2nd ed. (Upper Saddle River, NJ: Prentice Hall, 1970); **Figure 5.3** Jerald Greenberg and Robert A. Baron, *Behavior in Organizations: Understanding and Managing the Human Side of Work*, 8th ed. (Upper Saddle River, NJ: Pearson Education, 2003), 153; **Figure 5.4** Adapted from Jennifer M. George and Gareth R. Jones, *Understanding and Managing Organizational Behavior*, 4th ed. (Upper Saddle River, NJ: Pearson Education, 2005), 187; **Figure 5.5** Adapted from Jerald Greenberg and Robert A. Baron, *Behavior in Organizations: Understanding and Managing the Human Side of Work*, 8th ed. (Upper Saddle River, NJ: Pearson Education, 2003), 216; **Table 5.1** U.S. Equal Employment Opportunity Commission, "Occupational Employment in Private Industry by Race/Ethnic Group/Sex, and by

Industry, United States, 2002"
(December 16, 2004) at www.eeoc.gov/
stats/ jobpat/2002/us.html; **Figure 5.7**
Michael R. Carrell and Christina
Heavrin, *Labor Relations and Collective
Bargaining: Cases, Practice, and Law*, 7th
ed. (Upper Saddle River, NJ: Pearson
Education, 2004), 53; data from Bureau
of the Census and Bureau of Labor
Statistics. Data for 2005 from Bureau
of Labor Statistics, "Union Members
in 2005," January 20, 2006, (August 3,
2006), at www.bls.gov/news.release/
union2.nr0.htm.

CHAPTER 6

Figure 6.1 Jay Heizer and Barry
Render, *Operations Management*,
7th ed. (Upper Saddle River, NJ:
Pearson Education, 2004), 160; **Figure
6.4** Adapted from Roberta S. Russell
and Bernard W. Taylor III, *Operations
Management*, 4th ed. (Upper Saddle
River, NJ: Pearson Education, 2003), 3;
Figure 6.5 Adapted in part from Jay
Heizer and Barry Render, *Operations
Management*, 7th ed. (Upper Saddle
River, NJ: Pearson Education, 2004),
161; **Figure 6.8** Adapted in part from
Jay Heizer and Barry Render,
Operations Management, 7th ed. (Upper
Saddle River, NJ: Pearson Education,
2004), 340.

CHAPTER 7

Figure 7.5 Adapted in part from Anne
T. Coughlan et al., *Marketing Channels*,
6th ed. (Upper Saddle River, NJ:
Prentice Hall, 2001), 8; **Figure 7.6**
Adapted in part from Ronald H.
Ballou, *Business Logistics/Supply Chain
Management: Planning, Organizing, and
Controlling the Supply Chain*, 5th ed.
(Upper Saddle River, NJ: Pearson
Education, 2004), 8.

CHAPTER 8

Figure 8.2 Data from U.S. Census
Bureau, "U.S. Total Trade Balance
in Goods and Services" at
www.census.gov/foreign-trade/
statistics/historical/goods.txt; and
"U.S. Trade in Goods and Services—
Balance of Payments" (June 6, 2006),
at www.census.gov/foreign-trade/
statistics/historical/gands.txt; **Table
8.1** Adapted from Kathleen Maclay,
"UC Berkeley Study Assesses 'Second
Wave' of Outsourcing U.S. Jobs,"
UC Berkeley News, October 29, 2003

(March 25, 2005), at www.berkeley.
edu/news/media/releases/2003/
10/29_outsource.shtml; **Figure 8.3**
Adapted from Karl P. Sauvant,
"Recent FDI Trends, Implications for
Developing Countries and Policy
Changes," *New Horizons and Policy
Changes for Foreign Direct Investment
in the 21st Century* (OECD Global
Forum on International Investment,
November 2001) (April 11, 2005), at
www.oecd.org/dataoecd/24/62/
2421851.pdf; **Figure 8.4** Data from
"Fortune Global 500," *Fortune*, July 25,
2005, (August 3, 2006) at http://
money.cnn.com/magazines/fortune/
global500/snapshots/88.html.; The
World Bank Group, "Total GDP 2003,"
Data and Statistics, 2005 (April 11,
2005), at www.worldbank.org/
data/databytopic/GDP.pdf; "The
Forbes Global 2000," *Forbes*, April 18,
2005, 66–67; **Table 8.2** David A. Ricks,
Blunders in International Business,
3rd ed. (Malden, MA: Blackwell
Publishing, 1999); **Figure 8.5** Ricky W.
Griffin and Michael W. Pustay,
*International Business: A Managerial
Perspective*, 4th ed. (Upper Saddle
River, NJ: Pearson Education, 2005),
24; data from The World Bank, *World
Development Report 2003* (Washington,
DC: World Bank Publications, 2002),
238–39. Data for 2004 from *World
Development Indicators* database,
World Bank, (June 6, 2006) at http://
siteresources.worldbank.org/
DATASTATISTICS/Resources/
GDP.pdf; **Table 8.3** Transparency
International, *Corruptions Perceptions
Index 2004* (Berlin, October 2004).

CHAPTER 10

Figure 10.1 Data from Federal Reserve
Bank of St. Louis, "M1 Money Stock,"
and "M2 Money Stock," *Economic
Research*, June 4, 2006 (June 6, 2006), at
http://research.stlouisfed.org/fred2/
series/M1SL/downloaddata and
http://research.stlouisfed.org/fred2/
series/M2SL/downloaddata; **Figure
10.2** Data from *Financial Services Fact
Book* (Financial Services Industry,
Assets of Financial Service Sector by
Industry, 2006), (May 31, 2006), at
http://financialservicesfacts.org/
financial/; **Figure 10.3** Adapted in
part from Arthur O'Sullivan and
Steven M. Sheffrin, *Economics:*

Principles and Tools, 4th ed. (Upper
Saddle River, NJ: Pearson Education,
2006), 630–32; **Figure 10.4** Data from
Federal Reserve Board, Select Interest
Rates), June 4, 2006 (June 6, 2006), at
www.federalreserve.gov/datadown
load/Choose.aspx?rel=H.15; adapted
in part from Arthur J. Keown et al.,
*Financial Management: Principles and
Applications*, 10th ed. (Upper Saddle
River, NJ: Pearson Education, 2005),
469–72; **Figure 10.5** Data from Arthur
Andersen and National Small
Business United, *Trends for 2000*
(1998); adapted from Thomas W.
Zimmerer and Norman M.
Scarborough and, *Essentials of
Entrepreneurship and Small Business
Management*, 3rd ed. (Upper Saddle
River, NJ: Pearson Education, 2002),
407; **Figure 10.6** Big Charts
(Interactive Charting), a service of
Market Watch, (June 1, 2006) at
http://bigcharts.marketwatch.com/;
Figure 10.7 Big Charts (Interactive
Charting), a service of Market Watch,
(June 1, 2006) at http://bigcharts.
marketwatch.com/; **Figure 10.8 and
Table 10.1** Data from "Hershey Food
Corp (HSY)," *Yahoo!Finance*, June 1,
2006 (June 1, 2006), at http://
finance.yahoo.com/q?s=HSY; Figure
10.9 Arthur J. Keown, *Personal Finance:
Turning Money into Wealth*, 3rd ed.
(updated) (Upper Saddle River, NJ:
Pearson Education, 2004), 439.

CHAPTER 11

Figure 11.2 Adapted from James A.
Senn, *Information Technology:
Principles, Practices, Opportunities*, 3rd
ed. (Upper Saddle River, NJ: Pearson
Education, 2004), 556; **Figure 11.3**
Adapted from Ross A. Malaga,
Information Systems Technology (Upper
Saddle River, NJ: Pearson Education,
2005), 108; **Figure 11.4** Adapted in part
from James A Senn, *Information
Technology: Principles, Practices,
Opportunities*, 3rd ed. (Upper Saddle
River, NJ: Pearson Education, 2004),
537; Leonard Jessup and Joseph
Valacich, *Information Systems Today*
(Upper Saddle River, NJ: Pearson
Education, 2003), 173; **Figure 11.5**
Adapted in part from James A Senn,
*Information Technology: Principles,
Practices, Opportunities*, 3rd ed. (Upper
Saddle River, NJ: Pearson Education,

2004), 213; Leonard Jessup and Joseph Valacich, *Information Systems Today* (Upper Saddle River, NJ: Pearson Education, 2003), 184; **Figure 11.6** Adapted from Kenneth C. Laudon and Jane P. Laudon, *Management Information Systems: Managing the Digital Firm*, 8th ed. (Upper Saddle River, NJ: Pearson Education, 2004), 259; **Figure 11.7** Adapted from Kenneth C. Laudon and Jane P. Laudon, *Management Information Systems: Managing the Digital Firm*, 8th ed. (Upper Saddle River, NJ: Pearson Education, 2004), 292; **Figure 11.8** Adapted from Leonard Jessup and Joseph Valacich, *Information Systems Today* (Upper Saddle River, NJ: Pearson Education, 2003), 137; Kenneth C. Laudon and Jane P. Laudon, *Management Information Systems: Managing the Digital Firm*, 8th ed. (Upper Saddle River, NJ: Pearson Education, 2004), 268; **Figure 11.9** Adapted from Kenneth C. Laudon and Jane P. Laudon, *Management Information Systems: Managing the Digital Firm*, 8th ed. (Upper Saddle River, NJ: Pearson Education, 2004), 155.

▪ CREDITS

CHAPTER 1

2, James A. Finley/AP Wide World Photos; 6, AP Wide World Photos; 10, Copes Van Hasselt Johan/Corbis/Sygma; 10, Porsche AG/AP Wide World Photos; 11, Paul Sakuma/AP Wide World Photos; 15, Andy Sacks/Getty Images Inc.—Stone Allstock

CHAPTER 2

24, Kim Kulish/Corbis/Bettmann; 26, Bob Riha, Jr.; 27, John Hayes/AP Wide World Photos; 30, Timothy Fadek/Polaris Images; 37, STEVE SMITH/Getty Images, Inc.—Taxi

CHAPTER 3

45, Louis Lanzano/AP Wide World Photos; 53, Gergory Heisler/Getty Images/Time Life Pictures; 60, Gregory Heisler/Getty Images; 61, Patagonia, Inc.

CHAPTER 4

73, © Scott Adams/Dist. by United Feature Syndicate, Inc.; 80, © Scott Adams/Dist. by United Feature Syndicate, Inc.; 85, © Scott Adams/Dist. by United Feature Syndicate, Inc.; 86, © Scott Adams/Dist. by United Feature Syndicate, Inc.

CHAPTER 5

106, © Scott Adams/Dist. by United Feature Syndicate, Inc.; 108, © Marc Asnin/CORBIS All Rights Reserved; 113, SAS Institute Inc.; 116, © Scott Adams/Dist. by United Feature Syndicate, Inc.121, Adam Berry/Bloomberg News/Landov LLC

CHAPTER 6

132, Powerski International; 140, © Scott Adams/Dist. by United Feature Syndicate, Inc.; 143, Courtesy of Dell Inc.; 156, Powerski International; 152, Bill Aron/PhotoEdit Inc.

CHAPTER 7

164, © 2004 Wowwee Ltd.; 167, John Coletti; 171, Robert Brenner/PhotoEdit Inc.; 183, Michael Newman/PhotoEdit Inc.; 187, Bill Aron/PhotoEdit Inc.

CHAPTER 8

197, Fujifotos/The Image Works; 202, MTV photograph used with permission by MTV: MUSIC TELEVISION. © 2004 MTV Networks. All Rights Reserved. MTV: Music Television, all related titles, characters and logos are trademarks owned by MTV Networks, a division of Viacom International Inc.; 207, Manfred Rutz/Photonica/Getty Images; 214, Keith Dannemiller/Corbis/SABA Press Photos, Inc.; 217, Bill Brooks/Masterfile Corporation

CHAPTER 9

225, Nati Harnik/AP Wide World Photos; 230, DaimlerChrysler Corporation; 233, Alan King/Alamy Images; 244, AP Wide World Photos; 245, SuperStock, Inc.

CHAPTER 10

254, Ed Robinson/Tom Stack & Associates, Inc.; 255, John Bazemore/AP Wide World Photos; 262, Subway Restaurants/DAI; 266, REUTERS/Peter Morgan/Landov LLC; 272, AP Wide World Photos

CHAPTER 11

282, Isaac Brekken/AP Wide World Photos; 288, Copyright 2005 NBAE (Photo by Glenn James/NBAE via Getty Images); 292, Thomas Langer/Bloomberg News/Landov LLC; 296, James D. Wilson/Woodfin Camp & Associates; 300, Damian Dovarganes/AP Wide World Photos

Index